PRAISE FOR *FIRE EXIT*

"*Fire Exit*, Morgan Talty's debut novel, is utterly consuming. With this book, Talty more than fulfills the promise of his glorious short story collection, *Night of the Living Rez*. The storytelling is both spellbinding and quietly devastating. The novel is ultimately about family and belonging, about the stories we need to know even when they threaten to burn our lives down. A father desperately wants to let his daughter know about her body's secret history, even while his mother forgets her son altogether. This book is filled with humor, and humanity's strange wonder at its own desperation and depravity, as only Talty can do, with his subtle charm and crystalline prose, his sober reckoning with what love can and cannot do, what healing is and is not possible in our families. The novel absolutely smolders." **—TOMMY ORANGE**

"*Fire Exit* is gorgeous. A genuinely original examination of the costs we pay to tell ourselves certain stories about who we are and where we come from. Talty is a revelation on matters of the heart, particularly the tenderness and warfare of contemporary manhood. This is that rare thing: a frankly honest novel about hard things written without a trace of bitterness. I loved it." **—BRANDON TAYLOR**

"Talty's writing feels to me like a gift of many lifetimes. Forgiveness, Morgan shows us, is also the work of a lifetime. The people to whom we feel closest can somehow be right beside us in the kitchen and simultaneously on some unreachable, distant planet. People rotate away from each other for days or seasons at a time, and it's miraculous when they return to find each other again, turning towards each other instead of away. It's a treacherous thing, to love another person in this world that mixes so much beauty with so much sorrow. Thank you for reminding us, Morgan, that it is the necessary thing." **—KAREN RUSSELL**

PRAISE FOR MORGAN TALTY

"Morgan Talty is a master of the way dependency and pain transition from one body to another; the way both separating and refusing to separate become modes of saving ourselves; and the way, for all of our failures, we never stop doing what we can to provide each other hope." **—JIM SHEPARD**

"Talty is a powerful new voice in Native American fiction." **—BRANDON HOBSON**

"I am a fan for life. Mahsi cho, Morgan!" **—RICHARD VAN CAMP**

"Morgan Talty is a thrilling talent." **—LAURA VAN DEN BERG**

"I am not predicting literary success for Morgan Talty, I am guaranteeing it. He is a fascinating and powerful and singular writer." **—RICK BASS**

FIRE EXIT

ALSO BY MORGAN TALTY

Night of the Living Rez

FIRE EXIT

A NOVEL

MORGAN TALTY

TIN HOUSE / PORTLAND, OREGON

First US Edition 2024
Printed in the United States of America

Manufacturing by Lake Book Manufacturing
Interior design by Beth Steidle

Library of Congress Cataloging-in-Publication Data

Names: Talty, Morgan, 1991– author.
Title: Fire exit : a novel / Morgan Talty.
Description: Portland, Oregon : Tin House, 2024.
Identifiers: LCCN 2024000288 | ISBN 9781959030553 (hardcover) |
ISBN 9781959030638 (e-book)
Subjects: LCGFT: Novels.
Classification: LCC PS3620.A586 F57 2024 |
DDC 813/.6—dc23/eng/20240109
LC record available at https://lccn.loc.gov/2024000288

Tin House
2617 NW Thurman Street, Portland, OR 97210
www.tinhouse.com

DISTRIBUTED BY W. W. NORTON & COMPANY

1 2 3 4 5 6 7 8 9 0

For our children
And their children, and their children, and their children

FIRE EXIT

I

I WANTED THE GIRL TO KNOW THE TRUTH. I WANTED her to know who I was—who I really was—instead of a white man who had lived across from her all her life and watched her grow up from this side of the river.

It was late spring. I sat outside drinking coffee and not smoking because my lighter had run out of gas. Fog rolled off the water that divided the Penobscot Nation from the rest of the state of Maine. I was waiting, as I usually did. Soon, across the river and on the reservation, my girl—a woman by that point—came out of the house and got in her car to go to work. I didn't know how many times I'd been through this same routine, but that morning, something took hold of me. Something was different this time.

She started her car and backed out of the driveway, and then, as usual, she was out of sight. I got up and drank the rest of my coffee and thought about calling Louise, my mother, but decided she was probably sleeping, so I went inside to make breakfast, not because I was hungry but because I needed something to do so I could think about what had come over me. Maybe the change had come about because I'd stopped working in the woods so much and had more time to think, but the fact was that I'd gone along for too long with Mary's plan to lie and say that the girl was another man's, an enrolled Native man's, so that she, our daughter, could be on the census—Mary's Penobscot blood plus Roger's—giving Elizabeth exactly what she needed to be enrolled. But that morning I wanted our daughter to know the truth. I was tired of holding that secret.

I was going to make eggs and some seasoned hash and think about all this, but when I cut up the washed potato, I nicked the tip of my thumb real good with the knife and got blood all over my hand and said forget it. I went to the couch and sat down, and I wrapped a paper towel around my thumb and watched the blood seep through and then there was no denying what I wanted. I did want the truth to be known. The blood that came out of me was blood that ran through her veins. It's strange: all blood looks the same, yet it's different, we're told, in so many various ways and for so many various reasons. But one thing is for certain, I thought: you are who you are, even if you don't know it.

. . .

I didn't know much about her, except what her mother used to tell me—which was years ago now, maybe twenty-three or twenty-four—when she'd come to check up on me, to give me a little news about her and to see if I was drinking. I was, but told her I wasn't, that it had been four days, eight days, twelve days. But I'll get to that, the lying—mine and hers.

. . .

Her name is Elizabeth Eunice Francis, and her maternal grand-parents were Eunice and Philip. She was born in January 1991. I'm afraid to say I don't know the exact date, but I think it was the fifteenth, sixteenth, or seventeenth. Those were the days her house was empty and I waited anxiously across the river for her to be brought home.

. . .

She knew my house. She'd seen it, both from over there at Roger and Mary's—her parents—and once, when she was young, on my road with her mother. But she'd never been inside, and there was no reason to believe her mother had told her what it looked like. My father, Fredrick, and I built the house in 1983 (thirty-five years goes by fast, faster than the Penobscot River in spring with all that water and ice). I don't know if I can call it a house—it's only five hundred square feet—but this place, while small on the outside, feels big on the inside: there's the living room and kitchen, which are connected and form one room, and then there's a small hallway, just wide enough an entry to turn around in and go into the bathroom or bedroom. The doors to those rooms open inward, but if you open the door to the hallway closet too wide it will catch the lightbulb hanging above that space. Over the years it filled with boxes whose contents I'd forgotten and the gun—a pump .22 Fredrick gave me when I was a boy.

Fredrick and I built the small house three years after the Maine Indian Claims Settlement Act was passed. Fredrick was strongly against the act and spent a great deal of time with the tribal council trying to persuade them to go after a better deal as well as a great amount of time laying out his frustrations for my mother and me during dinner. The act, when passed by

Congress, had restored to the tribe its inherent sovereignty, so they could make and pass laws. While the white folks who had owned land prior to the act could remain, as well as those who had married in, one of the first laws the tribe passed concerned non-Natives: anyone who wasn't Native at all had no right to live on the reservation. And since Fredrick was my stepfather, I wasn't Native, and so I couldn't remain on the reservation when I came of age. My mother, a non-Native, could stay, of course, since she had married in.

Around that time Fredrick's father, Joseph, was dying, and the bills were adding up—and what little money I was making working in the woods wouldn't be enough for me to buy a place of my own off the reservation. When the time came to pay for his father's funeral—Joseph died, not peacefully, in the summer of 1982—Fredrick sold his father's camp and land, which got a lot of money. The place was densely forested and far from any town, and bear trappers stay out there now and take people out to hunt. Fredrick still owned his land, which was not very far from his father's, and after settling the medical bills he used the rest of the money to pay for my land and the building supplies. Since the settlement gave the tribe some land outside the reservation or the option to buy some at a low cost, Fredrick was able to buy from the tribe a lot cheaper than the state would have sold it. It was purely coincidental that the land we bought was across the river from Roger's house. I had no idea how important that place would be to me, or the role it would play in my being able to see her.

Fredrick and I spent all summer building the house. And it was a hot summer. My boss at the woodyard let me borrow the buncher—and so we were able to clear the land very quickly, just enough for a road and a yard. We laid the cement and put up all the walls with a good-quality chipboard, and we stuffed the walls with insulation, which we stapled, and we laid all the floors with a cheap linoleum, except in the bedroom, which is carpeted.

It took over four months to build the place. We measured and cut and swore and sweated and got dust and flakes of wood in our eyes, and we built each day after work and even more so on the weekends until it was finished. Louise, my mother, kept us fed during that time, when she was well enough, which was not most of the time. She suffered terrible bouts of depression, which she always would. It was three and a half decades since we'd built the house and I had yet to put trim up or even hang a picture. Who did I have to frame? I'd stopped saying I'd get to it.

As soon as it was built, Fredrick signed the land over to me, and for a number of years until he died, I gave him as much money as I could spare to help pay for what he'd put into this place, what he had given me. I insisted each and every time, but he always tried not to take the money, always said this is what fathers are supposed to do.

. . .

We met once when she was three. For a few years after she was born, her mother used to visit me. It was always the same routine: park way down the dirt road and walk through the woods to the back of my house and crawl in through the window. She used to give me news about our child, the only one Mary would ever have, but sometimes she just showed up and gave me nothing but her company for an hour or so. Once she was inside, she would visit like a neighbor would, and we'd have coffee at my kitchen table. We'd smoke a few cigarettes and she'd ask after my mother and after my work and after my drinking and would tell me I should do something to the place, like get some decorations. "At least get a painting or something," she'd say.

It was during a late spring Saturday when Mary asked, "Do you think it would be a good idea if you met her?" She drank her coffee and smoked, lounging, taking her time because Roger was not home; he had taken Elizabeth ice fishing. I don't know who it was Mary felt bad for: Elizabeth or me. Maybe both of us?

"Of course I want to meet her," I said.

"But is it a good idea?" She held her hands together on the table.

"I don't know," I said.

"Neither do I. Get me a coin. A quarter, dime, whatever."

I got her a penny.

"Heads you meet her, tails we forget I asked."

The coin landed on tails.

"Two out of three?" I said.

The next one landed on heads. And so too did the next one.

And that was it. Mary left through the window and every so often a branch would snap and echo in the woods. A car door slammed shut and the engine revved and faded until everything but my breathing quieted.

. . .

The week after Mary's visit, I went to the grocery store. I bought two Lunchables. I didn't know which she liked, or even if she liked them at all or if Mary ever bought them for her. I got one with crackers and squares of ham and cheese and another with chips made for tiny fingers and nacho cheese and salsa. I bought a two-liter of Sprite and a big bottle of apple juice and a small tub of red powdered Kool-Aid. As I went to check out, I remembered Mary. I went back to the deli and got slices of ham and roast beef and turkey and American cheese and a loaf of white bread. In the produce section, on my way back to the checkout, I grabbed a tomato and a head of lettuce that looked like it was dying.

I left the grocery store and drove up to the strip mall across the way from the on-ramp to I-95. I smoked a cigarette before I went into the dollar store. They had two aisles of toys, and a lot of stuff was for the summer, plastic buckets and shovels for sand and crinkly bags stocked with water balloons and mesh bags bulging with colored blocks for building. The bottom shelves were filled with stuffed animals, and I crouched down and pawed through them, holding and turning them over in my hands, petting them for their softness, squeezing them to see if any made noise. Buried deep in one metal bin was an elephant, upside down. I squeezed its soft center and out came the most realistic elephant trumpet I'd heard, and I started laughing, this slow, low laugh that took me over, and I kept squeezing and squeezing the elephant and laughing and laughing and shaking until my face was wet, until the noise coming out of me was so unclear that a worker, a man in a green vest whose name was written in unreadable cursive on the sewed-on name tag, stood over me and asked if I was all right.

. . .

On the day Mary decided she'd bring our child by, I waited all morning outside, sipping coffee and smoking. I watched their house across the river. Roger had left about seven, and Mary's car remained. It must have been about eleven or twelve when I saw them come out of the house. Mary helped her into the car. Then she got in, started it, and backed out.

About halfway down my dirt road, I waited. But Mary didn't show up. I went back to the house and saw across the river that Mary had returned, her car parked and nobody in it. I sat again, waiting and waiting and waiting. Finally, she came out of the house again with our child. It was about two in the afternoon. Again her car started, backed up, and disappeared from view.

I went back to that same spot on the dirt road. Cars drove by at the end, and each vroom made me more and more nervous. Then came a car that slowed, a green Elantra that eventually became Elizabeth's, and it turned toward me. I started walking back to the house a bit. I had this feeling I had to move. But then I turned and watched Mary park her car where she always did.

Did she remember this day? Did she remember it at all? Or was she too young, as Mary hoped, to remember? Did she know this history—this story—her body held secret from her?

She was here, on this road.

Mary took her from the back seat, and her feet touched the dirt. Mary said something and pointed down the road. She started to run-wobble in my direction, but Mary chased after and held her by the hand. She pulled her back, told her to wait. Mary was getting something from the back seat. Elizabeth waited, holding back an eagerness in herself to get to me, to get to the end of this road.

And when Mary started for me, not through the woods and through my window but directly for me, she followed. But then she saw something and stopped moving. She grabbed her mother's leg. No amount of ushering her along could get her to move from that spot. I realized, right then, that she hadn't seen me, but now she had, and once she did, the sight of this man down the dirt road frightened her.

Mary picked her up and carried her down the road, with her face buried in Mary's hair and neck, and right as she got close she started to scream, started to yell so loud it echoed, the noise carrying every which way. Mary walked her back to the car, stopped, put her down, and waved me over.

She didn't look at me and held Mary's leg. I couldn't get over how full her face was, her cheeks more precious than air.

"She's just shy," Mary said. We leaned on the hood of the car and watched.

"Is she hungry? I bought her lunch. And you too, if you want."

"We're fine," Mary said. "What did you buy?"

I told her.

"She doesn't like the ham. She likes the cheese and crackers, but that's it. She's never tried any of the others."

We were quiet. Some birds chirped and bounced from branches. Elizabeth kicked at the hard dirt and waved a long piece of grass. Then she smelled it.

"Keep that away from your mouth," Mary said. "Come over here and say hello."

I thought it was funny that she didn't listen, that she stayed right where she was, sniffing that piece of grass.

"Hey," Mary said. "Doosis. I'm talking to you."

I turned to face her by the brush. "You want to see something?" I asked.

She didn't look at me and kept on swinging the grass.

"I'll be right back," I said to Mary, and I walked down the dirt road to the house and inside I got the elephant. I held it behind my back as I returned.

"You want to see something?" I repeated.

She looked at her mother, who looked at what I held behind my back.

"You didn't need to," Mary whispered.

"Well I did," I said.

Mary looked at her. "Wait until you see this," she said. "You'll like it."

The long piece of grass fell to the ground. She lifted her little hand and extended her even littler finger. She pointed, and her nails—on that one hand, anyway—were painted pink. The gesture, the first time recognizing me, how could I forget it? And to have it followed by her voice, the first intelligible words I heard her speak, so near, the only time I've regretted the wind, wished it away, that slight breeze that carried her breath away from me.

How terribly did I want to know her.

"What is it?" she said. She spat out her hair that was in her mouth. She reached for it, the animal I'd forgotten I held behind my back. I held it out for her.

"What do you say?" Mary said.

"Wikawɑt." Please.

Together, we held the elephant between us. She didn't try to take it. She simply touched its gray soft ears and long trunk, squeezed its legs, and patted its head.

She called it a cow.

"It's an elephant," I said. She did not repeat my words, and she wouldn't take the stuffed animal from my hands. She kept touching it, feeling it, inspecting it for something unknown to everybody but herself.

"Here," I said. "You can have it."

She took the elephant and held it.

"Let me show you," I said.

My hands held her hands as she held the elephant.

I don't know if I should have prepared her for what was to come, should have said something else, like "Ready?" or "Listen to this!" but I didn't say anything besides "Let me show you." I gave her hands holding the elephant a squeeze, and out from the elephant came that loud, realistic trumpet. Her eyes widened and she let go.

"No, cow! No!" she said, and she started to cry and ran to Mary, who was laughing.

"No more," Mary said, either to me or to her, I don't know. She picked her up and put her in the back seat of the car.

"You're leaving?" I said, holding the elephant to my side.

"She's tired."

She was still crying, calling for her mother. Mary went to her, calmed her a little bit, but she started again the moment Mary left and came back to me.

From outside the car I waved to her, a hello and a goodbye. She kept on crying.

"I take it she won't want this," I said about the elephant.

"I have to go," Mary said.

"Should you bring her back here?" I said. "Another day?"

"Charles," Mary said.

"I'm just asking," I said.

There was nothing but her screaming.

Mary went to the car and dug around in the center console. She got out of the car but leaned back in.

"Heads another day, tails no more."

It landed on tails.

"Two out of three?" I asked, again.

But Mary said no, and it took me some time to realize that that would be the last time for a long, long while that we'd all be so close.

. . .

Now, more than twenty years later, I knew something Elizabeth didn't know, or something she didn't remember.

2

IT WAS 1996 WHEN I STARTED AA, AND I MADE IT A point to reconnect with my mother. Maybe I felt enough years had gone by for us to move past what had happened.

I knew where she lived off reservation because I had helped her move in years before, not long after Fredrick died, but when I arrived, I found out from the landlord that she hadn't lived there for more than three years. I felt something like betrayal, but not quite so, that my mother would move without letting me know. She called every so often and would leave these long voicemails telling me about her day or week, and so I wondered why she hadn't told me she was moving or had moved.

The place my mother now rented was, as the landlord said, three streets over and at the bottom of a steep hill. I'll never forget it: I drove to the top of that high hill, and as I started descending, I saw something at the very bottom, right where the road leveled out. It looked like a hole—not a pothole—that stretched the width of the street, and it looked portal-like, and endless. The closer I got to it, the more frightened I became. But before it could swallow me and the truck, I splashed through it: a puddle.

I buzzed the buzzer that went to my mother's apartment, but my mother was not home. Her neighbor—a tall, skinny guy I learned Louise called "shovel man" because he was always outside shoveling snow or, when there wasn't snow, dirt, which he used to keep his dirt driveway flat—was outside, sitting on the bottom step, smoking and inspecting a worn nightstand, its wood chipped and flaking. He seemed to have a lot of garbage in his driveway, right at the end near his house. I felt him watching as I kept buzzing the buzzer to my mother's apartment next door, and when nobody answered I started for my truck, but thought maybe it was worth asking him about her.

And so I did, and he said to me, "I ain't selling anything right now."

"No, no," I said, looking at the nightstand and other junk he had there. "Louise. The lady that lives here. Do you know her?"

He set the nightstand aside and stood up. "Who are you looking for?" he said.

Again, I told him who. I still stood by my truck.

"Your mother?" he said. "What's your name?"

I told him that too.

He laughed. "I thought she was making you up," he said.

"What do you mean?"

He waved me over. "My throat's sore and I'm not going to yell."

He told me Louise had told him to tell me that she was going away, that she'd be back in a few days, and that I shouldn't worry. "She's been telling me to tell you that for years, every time she left. I thought she was crazy. But you are real."

I asked him if he knew where she'd gone, and he said he didn't know. "I told you all she told me."

"Do you have a phone I could use?"

"I don't," he said. "You got a cigarette?"

I gave him one, and he lit it.

"Hey what's that in your truck there?" he said, blowing smoke and pointing. "You throwing it out?"

He was talking about my fuel tank for work. And I told him as much.

"Fuel tank, huh?" he said.

I didn't find Louise that day and when she finally called I wasn't at home—I was at work up north clearing land—and I called her back in the evening. This was a few days after I'd gone looking for her. We talked for a bit. She sounded tired, like she wasn't up for talking, and so I didn't tell her anything about having gone to her old house and then to her new apartment. I just said I'd come by on Sunday, and it was then that she told me she'd moved and it was my turn to act surprised by it.

When that Sunday came, I almost didn't go. Elizabeth was outside, in her backyard, with her father. She was playing ring toss. I didn't know how big or small five-year-olds were, but she was so little and couldn't throw the rings very far. What she did was toss one, then take a step forward, reaching, and toss another, and so on until she was right over the pole, and she'd drop the last ring from her hand, and it wobbled in place.

I stayed watching until Roger looked at me, and then I walked to my truck.

Louise was outside when I showed up. I don't know what I expected when we saw each other. It had been at least three years since I'd seen her, but she acted as if she had just seen me the other day, as if I had just seen her. The only time she got close to acknowledging how long it had been since we'd seen each other came when she said, "You look good." That was it. My mother didn't care very much for discussing things in the past. I don't think she liked talking about the future, either, and she always, when I was young, changed the subject when Fredrick talked about the what-ifs of the Settlement Act, particularly my having to leave the reservation when I turned eighteen.

From that day I saw her on as many Sundays as possible, which was typically once a month. She gave me a key to her place—both the house door and her apartment door—and when I asked about the dead bolt, she said it didn't work so I didn't need to worry. She stopped telling shovel man to tell me she was leaving, and instead would call me and say, "I'll be out and about on Sunday, so don't come by." Out and about. I learned where she went eventually when I saw the medical bills on her kitchen sideboard. She went to the wellness center, where they gave her a bed and fed her and monitored her for a few days. She never told me though, and I don't know if she knew I knew. But when I heard her say "out and about," I came to know where she was.

. . .

When I began to visit her more often, I only ever asked her a few questions about her past. One was about my father, what his name was.

"His name?" Louise repeated. "Brian. Isn't that a boring fucking name? Brian." She stopped talking for a bit, and then said, "I wonder where he is."

She never said what happened to him, but I took it he left. You'd think men would come up with a better story, or a different one.

I came to realize, through my visits with her, that I didn't really know my mother. I started to think that Fredrick had understood her in a way nobody else could. It explained how well they worked together. But what exactly made them so close I never found out. I guess the simple answer is: Just because. That's how it happened.

They fit together. Louise's mother, my grandmother, who Louise and I lived with when my birth father left, eventually disowned my mother for seeing Fredrick. And apparently she tried—and was successful, only for a bit—to get me taken away by telling the state that Fredrick beat me. I was almost four, but not old enough to remember.

"And when they saw you had no bruises," Louise said, "no swelling, nothing at all, they let us take you back. We were all in court, even my mother, who thought she was going to leave that day with my child. That's the last I saw or heard from her."

For days after hearing that story, I felt strange. There was this history I was a part of, a history my body had experienced and moved through, but I never knew it. It made me wonder how much I didn't know. We had that in common, Elizabeth and I. And I felt she should know her body was special, and she should know its history, especially the one it would not tell her and the one she could not see. And I decided to tell what I knew, because she deserved to know it.

. . .

For the first time in nearly two and a half decades, I spoke with Elizabeth's mother. I wasn't seeking her out—I just wanted to know about burial rights. After seeing my mother age, I'd started to think a great deal about how, like all mothers everywhere, mine would one day die, and I hadn't given any thought to what would become of her body. She had never said what she wanted done at the end. Maybe she didn't care, or maybe she was like me: afraid to talk about it. My guess was that she would like to be buried with Fredrick on the reservation and that was my business: to see if that was possible, since my mother was not Penobscot.

I didn't know who to speak with and so I went to the chief's office at the community building next to the school. I looked for Elizabeth's car, the green Elantra, the one Roger had kept alive over the years until Mary had passed it down, but didn't see it. Nobody was at the community building. Nobody at all. And all the lights were off. It was when I was leaving that I saw the printed pink sign on the door that said all offices had been moved across the street to the building behind the health center. I wasn't surprised the tribe was tearing down the community center; it had been there for so long that it must have needed to be taken down before it decided to do so on its own.

I walked across the street and took the small path behind the health center to the building where the pink sign said everyone was. Every room in that building was occupied, some doors open, some shut, but each with a sign: "Finance," "Department of Natural Resources," "Tribal Clerk," and so on, and I checked almost all the doors until I found the chief's office. The door was partly open, and so I pushed it open to find not the chief but instead Elizabeth's mother. Mary sat behind a large brown desk, a computer in front of her. She never wore glasses when I'd known her. At first, I did not recognize her. But when I did, I forgot what I wanted to know—about burying my mother—and I asked what she was doing there, and for a moment she stared at me, or maybe she wasn't staring but thinking about things shared and hidden, a thing that, no matter what, connected us.

"I work here," she said, and whatever wall had come down between us for those brief seconds was back up. "Can I help you?"

I asked her what I wanted to know—if my mother could be buried with Fredrick on the reservation—and if someone had asked me such a question about a person I had known and liked but hadn't seen or heard of for many, many years, and especially with no other context, I too would have reacted how she did. She stood up from the desk.

"Louise?" she said, that wall coming down again. "She passed away?"

"No, no, no," I said. "She hasn't died. But she's ill."

"With what?" She sat back down.

"Old age and what comes with it," I said.

She said she was sorry to hear it. She asked again what it was I wanted to know. She thought my mother could be buried with Fredrick, but she needed to call the funeral director of the church on the reservation to make sure. She called, and I don't know who she talked to, but it wasn't the director.

"He's going to call in a minute," Mary said, hanging up. "He's away for the moment."

She said I could have a seat. There were two chairs, one on each side of a small end table with a lamp that was turned on. I sat. Neither of us spoke while her keyboard clacked.

I could have said or asked a number of things in those moments while we waited for the call: "Louise asks about you," or "How's your family?" or "I've been sober for twenty-two years," or "How could you have done this?" or "I understand why you did this," or "What is she like?" or "Are you as lonely as I am?"—or, or, or. So many things I could have said, but I said nothing, asked nothing, and it was sadder than anything I could have said or asked. Here we were, Mary and I, in the same room, both at the same end of our lives' biggest secret.

The phone rang and Mary answered.

"Calling about what?" she said, and she took off her glasses as if that helped her understand whatever the person on the phone was saying to her, as if the voice needed to be seen to be understood.

"I did?" she said, and it must have been me in that room who reminded her why the person was returning her call, and it must have been me too in that room who had made her forget. "That's right, sorry, busy day."

When she got the answer, she hung up.

"Since they were married at the time of his death," Mary said, "Louise has the right to be buried next to him."

I said OK, and Mary coughed.

"But you have to buy the plot beside his," she said.

Dying isn't cheap and I didn't ask how much the plot was.

Before I left, I found the courage to ask, in a whisper, how Elizabeth was doing.

"She could be better, but she'll be OK," is what she said. It hurt me deeply to know that she was not well, and it hurt just as deeply not to know what was wrong, and it hurt more than both those things to know I couldn't do a damn thing to fix it. I couldn't help but feel that I had abandoned my daughter, and I was afraid to know if what I was feeling was the truth.

I hoped it would get better, whatever was going on with her. For the next several days, I speculated on why she could be unwell, and each time I arrived at the reason I most feared: that she was suffering in the same way my mother had all her life.

. . .

At home I was thinking about what Fredrick had told me when I was young, that the reservation used to be a burial ground. I must have been about ten or eleven when he told me the story. For a long while after I didn't dare walk in any of the woods, and I think that's what Fredrick wanted: this was about the time Roger's parents both drowned in the river and his cousin and her boyfriend moved in to take care of him. For years the tribe held donation gatherings on Sundays in the Kateri Center for those in need, and the people who could chipped in money and food and other necessities. Fredrick always donated some of the meat he'd gotten from hunts with Joseph, usually deer but sometimes moose and even rabbit.

Fredrick told me the story to keep me away from the woods and the river, since all the woods on that island, that reservation, lead to it.

I don't remember where we were when Fredrick told me the story. It wasn't even a story as much as it was a detail. Before his ancestors—and Elizabeth's—had given up much of the land, and had much, if not more of it, taken, they used the island as a place to bury the dead. "That's why there are large boulders everywhere," Fredrick said, "on all the paths, that stick out in awkward places and look to have been put there." I'd never noticed them before, never noticed all the rocks, some the size of basketballs, others the size of garden sheds. "They mark the dead," Fredrick said.

I wish I could say Fredrick told me more intimate details about the burials. How were they performed? Who attended them? I was eight when the last "traditional" burial occurred on the reservation, but for reasons I didn't know then I wasn't allowed to attend. When it was over, I sneaked out to where everyone had gathered, and I looked at the carved pole that's still out there today but has since toppled over. It was down by Joe Pease, that rocky-water part of the river by Rolling Thunder Drive. When I was a boy it looked as tall as any tree, and now it's as long as any fallen one.

Maybe Fredrick made the whole story up—maybe the whole reservation wasn't a burial ground. While he wasn't my real father, I always thought of him as such. I was two when he and my mother met, and I was three when I moved into that house with him. It was 1967. So I felt I belonged to Fredrick, and to his family: his father, Joseph, and his mother, Maxine. It didn't take time to grow into that feeling of being welcome. I was so young when we joined their family. My mother and I were not Penobscot, but I spent all my early years on the reservation and was taught at the school, the Kateri Center, which used to be right near the church, before they built the new school where Elizabeth went and where I figured out over the years she taught now. I was around the tribe day and night, and I felt it was where I belonged, who I was. Gizos, a boy my age and my only real friend on the reservation, certainly made it easier to feel this way.

Growing up, I should have asked Gizos about the boulders, but I never did. He might have had a different version, or maybe it would have been the same. For all the stories that Gizos told, only one dealt with the topic of death, but it equally told of creation.

He told a story about Gluskabe's attempt to create the first people. Rock people. I can't remember which attempt Gluskabe was on, or how many attempts he would make before he got it right, but during one try he made people out of stone. Gizos said that Gluskabe tried to teach them, these tall rock pillars, but they were unteachable. They could not hear, they could not talk, and they could not see. They were brash, and they moved about the earth with their heavy bodies and stripped trees of their bark and crushed the animals. When they collided, they would fight and smash each other until all that remained of one was a pile of pebbles and sharp, pointed fragments and rock dust.

They were violent. Gluskabe thought he'd let them destroy one another until only one remained, and then Gluskabe would shatter it and start over. But, Gizos said, before they could finish one another off, something happened. Their joints of quartzite sparked and created fire that caught the grass and spread to the oak ferns and then to the shagbark hickory and birch bark and oaks until half the world was burning. Having thought that the stone people could not reason, Gluskabe was shocked to see one stone man point into the sky—to the sun—and point back at the earth, as if predicting that the earth, too, would become a ball of flames. Right then, Gluskabe set out to destroy all of them. But Gluskabe wouldn't get them all, Gizos said. While he destroyed many, some escaped to the mountains.

"They have no hearts," Gizos said, and then he said that maybe his father was part stone person. "They like to come down once in a while."

Even if Gizos's story were true, Fredrick's wouldn't be entirely wrong: the boulders are markers of the dead, of beings fallen and smashed before our time. And at the end of both these stories—Gizos's and my father's—the reservation is covered with bodies. While Gizos's story seems far from the truth, and my father's closer to it, the reality is that today four Catholic cemeteries dot the small reservation, and so in any case many people have been buried under the earth there. The reservation is a burial ground all right, just as the rest of the world is. Land is land, and one day, I knew, Louise would return to it.

3

I GREW UP JUST DOWN THE ROAD FROM ROGER'S house. Ours was the big one on the corner, right by that stop sign that everybody rolls past. Fredrick had left the house to my mother, but she couldn't stand to live there anymore, especially since I stopped visiting her after he died, and so she sold the house, and the man who bought it from my mother planned to turn it into a little museum. Henry David Thoreau had stayed there with my father's great-grandfather for a day or two until Thoreau found someone in the tribe who would guide him through the woods. The buyer thought the house had enough history to warrant a museum, but it never came to fruition. I heard later that he ended up selling the house to the tribe, who planned to burn it for firefighter training. When I first heard about that, for weeks I kept watch from outside, looking for smoke, but I never saw any and the house kept standing.

The house was smaller indoors than it appeared on the outside. From the street you'd think there were many rooms upstairs given the several windows and thin curtains, but in fact there were no rooms—it was just an attic filled with junk. Louise had a curtain addiction, and many of the boxes were filled with curtains, which she kept clean and neatly folded in case she had to hang them up, which was never. The downstairs had a kitchen and a living room, and down the hallway were three rooms: mine, Fredrick and my mother's, and a spare where Fredrick's father, Joseph, lived until his death. Before its roof caved in, the garage was filled with a heavy ash-pounding machine, which I had never seen run at all during my time living there. The garage was also the place where Fredrick and his father used to store what they'd hunted at camp, usually deer and the occasional moose, and they had a freezer out there too, filled with meat. That place always smelled of the cold and sawdust and guts.

. . .

Going to AA makes you think a lot about the past and how it shapes you. And thinking about AA now makes me think of the future and the past all at once and about how I met Bobby. Bobby—a friend from way back—wanted to go away, and he asked if I'd go with him. He said Florida, but I wasn't sold on it. I didn't tell him that—I told him I needed to think about it. There was still time though. He was waiting to retire, though I was pretty sure he could have done it already. He'd owned his own plumbing and heating company for a number of years, of which he was the sole employee. He'd made good money doing it, or so he said. But I couldn't leave until Elizabeth knew the truth. That was all I wanted.

. . .

I met Bobby in AA in the spring of '96. Back then, Bobby had few people in his life, which is still the case today, I guess. He'd been divorced three times—no children—and he was going through that third divorce when we met. AA was held in the Elks Club on Main Street. Bobby had been attending for almost a year. I can't say he'd been clean for almost a year, because I came to learn he was still drinking some nights a week. When meetings were over, a lot of folks stuck around and smoked outdoors if the weather was fine enough. I had gone to four meetings so far and when that fourth one ended, I didn't want to go home. I felt a certain strength the more I was around the building and those people. And I don't mean a strength put toward not drinking but rather a general, spirited strength. Maybe to live, I guess.

We were all outside after the meeting and we stood in a circle under an orange streetlight, some of us smoking. Some were waiting for rides, some were waiting for those who were waiting for rides to leave, and some, like me, didn't know what they were waiting for. In time, everyone went go home, one after the other, until it was just Bobby and me and this guy whose name, I think, was Melvin or Kelvin. He wasn't there too long before his ride showed up. The quiet was sharp when he left. He'd been the one talking to us, keeping the conversation going.

Bobby, this non-Native, asked if I was waiting for a ride, and I told him no.

"I have a truck," I told him, and he said he did too, that his wife had dropped him off in it, and so he was waiting for her to pick him up.

"But she probably ain't coming," he said.

I had no idea then that he was on his third marriage, and I had no idea then either that that third marriage was unstable, like something stacked too high. I guess I should have known something wasn't right when she didn't show up. I ended up bringing him home, which was the beginning of me always bringing him home and picking him up for meetings.

He didn't live too far from the Elks Club. That night, however, he made me believe he did. For most of the drive he kept saying, "I appreciate this, I do," and "I can't thank you enough, really, I can't."

No problem, no problem, no problem, I told him over and over again, until finally I just said to him, "You don't got to thank me anymore. I don't mind."

He told me his house was three miles down a dark road with very few streetlights. It was out near the border of Overtown. "Just keep going straight," he told me. "I'll tell you when we're almost there."

"Take a left," he said. "Take a right." Bobby seemed nervous; he kept tapping his fingernails on the window.

"Take this left," he said. "I'll tell you when to turn again."

He tapped on that window.

He asked me three times if I had a cigarette he could bum. The first time I told him I was out. I said the same thing again when he asked the second time. I thought maybe he hadn't heard me. But when he asked that third time, I said to him, "What's the matter with you?"

He stopped tapping on the glass and he shook his head. "I'm fucked," he said, and he said it as quietly as somebody would say it who truly was fucked.

I stopped the truck on the side of the road. We'd been driving for twenty minutes.

I pointed up ahead at a stop sign. "It doesn't matter which way we turn," I said to him. "Both ways bring us to the same road we were just on. Where is your house?"

"We passed it," he said.

"We passed it?"

"Look, I'm sorry," he said.

I started to think that Bobby was a liar. I wondered about all sorts of things: Did he have a house? Did he have a wife? Had she dropped him off in his truck? Did he have a truck? Was he even an alcoholic?

"I can't go home," he told me.

"Then why are you making me drive you somewhere you can't go?"

"I'm sorry," he said again. "All right, it's up there. Just drop me at the curb. I can go there, really, I can."

He told me not to pull into the driveway but to park on the street. I did. He got out of the truck, and he didn't say anything to me. I watched him walk across the front lawn, the grass up to his shins. He was halfway to the front porch when he turned around and looked at me. He waved me off.

The front door of the house opened, and a woman—who was his wife, he'd tell me after, while on the way back to my place—screamed at him. I rolled down my window to listen, but I couldn't understand a word she was saying, not anything Bobby was saying when he spoke over her. It was all in French. But when I recognized what she threw at him—thick glass bottles. I didn't need to know what they were saying to know what was going on.

Bobby ducked and dodged as she threw the bottles, and he looked to be returning to my truck. But he wasn't. He searched the dark grass for a bottle, and when he found one, he pelted it in her direction on the front porch. It shattered against the house right above the porch, and glass sprinkled down on her. Only then did he run back to my truck, because she ran after him.

"Go, go, go!" he yelled, hitting the dashboard.

I could have decided not to be a part of his mess, especially after his wife hit my truck with a bottle. I could have decided to drop him back off at the Elks Club, could have told him to sort it all out himself, to leave me out of it. But I didn't. I told him he could stay the night at my place, and he said no, he couldn't do that. And then he asked if I could bring him to work in the morning, and I told him I could, but that he might get there earlier than he'd like, since I had to be out and on the road by 4:00 AM.

I didn't sleep at all that night. When we got home, Bobby used my landline to call her. But he didn't speak to her for very long before he handed the phone to me. "She wants to talk to you," he said.

Her name was Heather or Gael. I can't remember which. I didn't have to talk to her—I could have hung up—but Bobby kept saying, "Tell her, just tell her," and I wasn't sure at first what he wanted me to say. But when she accused me of drinking with her husband, I knew what he wanted me to tell her.

"It's not like that," I told her. "If your husband's drinking, it ain't with me."

"He is drinking," she said.

"Well it ain't with me."

I don't know at what point she believed me, that I was telling her the truth—or if she didn't believe me but just got tired of asking—but eventually she stopped talking, stopped arguing, and I thought she hung up.

"Hello?" I said.

"What do I do?" she said. "What do I do?"

Right then, I realized I knew very little about Bobby, about this man who was sitting on my couch in my house. I saw him holding Elizabeth's stuffed elephant, the one I bought and tried to give her when she visited with her mother that one and only time as a young child, and Bobby mouthed, "You have kids?"

"He won't stop," she said. "Why can't he stop?"

"Are you asking me?" I said.

"How did you stop? What made you stop?"

I wanted to say what had made me stop was myself. But that wasn't true, and I didn't know what had made me stop. Maybe it was fear; maybe it was what I wanted. Or maybe it was just time to stop, something unexplainable working below the surface of my being. Or maybe it was the guilt I felt about my father Fredrick's death, wanting to get clarity enough so I could finally tell my mother the truth about what had happened.

"Can you help him?" she said.

I told her I'd try, told her I'd see what I could do, which turned out to be very little. She asked to talk to Bobby again, and I was expecting those two to be on the phone for a long while. But they said barely anything. "I won't, won't," Bobby said quietly, and then they hung up.

I sat with him for a bit on the couch, and when he looked to be sleeping, sitting up, I started to leave.

"How do you do it?" he asked. "How do you not drink?"

"I just don't," I told him.

"You don't ever just want to?"

"Sure," I told him. It's been so long since then that I can't remember if that was true. We hear all the time that to quit something is to battle with the desire not to quit, but to be honest I don't think that's how it was with me. I wanted to drink once or twice, but that was it. Today, it would be just about impossible to convince me to drink.

"Look," Bobby said. He rubbed his eyes, and then he took out some cigarettes he'd found in his jacket. He held the pack up, and I told him he could smoke on the couch. I brought him a cup of water for an ashtray. He blew smoke and sat forward. "I just don't want to quit. I don't want to be sober."

And he didn't want to be. He tried, for whatever reason he tried—whether for her or for some small part of himself that wasn't sure what he wanted—and he stopped drinking only long enough to remember that he did not want sobriety. He didn't drink at work, but he oftentimes went in buzzed from the night before. That was when he drank the most, at night, even on the weekends. He avoided it all day until it got dark or close to dark. But he tried to quit; for three weeks while he stayed with me he didn't drink anything, or if he did, I knew nothing about it. When he finally went home, he stayed sober for a while, and then he was right back where he started, on my couch again while I talked to his wife, but she didn't ask for help. She said he could go back home when she left in a week. She was going to her parents' in Quebec. It's interesting: I never, not once, met her. I saw her silhouette that one time as she stood on the porch in the dark, chucking bottles at Bobby. But besides that one time I knew her only by the conversations we had on the phone, her body the shape of a voice on the other end of the line.

4

IN THE DAYS AFTER I SAW ELIZABETH, WHEN I learned her mother would never again bring her to my road, I got to thinking about the word "dirt." Maybe it was the memory of her little feet touching the ground that brought the word to my attention. This is embarrassing, or maybe the better word is dramatic. I was upset. And drunk. I took that elephant and set it sitting upright on a blue plastic chair on my front lawn, and I put the .22 to its head, the .22 that Fredrick had given me. I didn't shoot the elephant. I held the gun to its head, and before I pulled the trigger I lowered the rifle and the bullet flew and shattered the leg of the blue plastic chair, and pieces went flying all over the earth's dirt. "Dirt," Middle English: "excrement, dung, feces, any foul or filthy substance." If you look the word up, there's also a line about it meaning "mud" or "loose earth." I guess I just don't understand this, this one word for two different things. Like Gizos: his name meant sun and moon. Is it indecisiveness? Is it neatness we're after, tidiness? Is it a desire to make sense of a thing on the basis of another? Maybe all we are is creation's translators, putting things like granite or oak or elephant or corn in a language they want to be put in, to give them bodies made of sound so they're measurable. "Measurable" sounds like "miserable" when I pronounce it.

There's a story I want to tell, and it has to do with Gizos and his father, Lenno. To get it right, I thought I had to ask Bobby. We were at the bar, but I wasn't drinking. The story happened in the mid-'70s. Bobby grew up right off the reservation on French Island, and so he might have heard it, I thought. And when I asked him, he snapped his fingers and pointed at me.

"I know what you're talking about," he said, and he began.

. . .

According to Bobby, there were two guns and two men.

"I had an aunt. My dad's sister. She was living with this Lebritton on the reservation. She saw it happen. The two men are drunk. One is standing on his steps, looking down the barrel of his rifle at the other man, who is at the end of the driveway, right near the road, looking down the barrel of his own rifle at the man on the steps. She said they both were swearing and stumbling, telling the other to shoot. The men yelled it over and over again—'Go on, shoot! Come on!'—and they each walked closer and closer to the other."

Bobby took a drink of his fourth beer of the night and said, "I guess one of them—I think the guy who was standing on the steps, that's what my aunt said—was sleeping with the other's wife. If that were me, I would've already shot the bastard."

But neither man pulls the trigger, according to Bobby. They both yell and swear, slurring their words. The rifles are pointed at the other. The street is full of neighbors, all Indian except Bobby's aunt, all watching. Some are trying to approach, trying to take the guns, to defuse the situation. But the two men want nothing but the rifles between them, and so they point the guns at those trying to help until there's nobody left in their line of view but the other with a weapon.

"They got close enough that each of their guns was in the other's face," Bobby said. "'Do it! Do it!' they kept saying. 'You don't think I will!'"

Bobby was laughing. "When my aunt told me this—well, she was telling my father, who'd come down too, he needed to fix something in her house—anyway when she told us this, I didn't think neither one would do it."

There are two men and two guns, as Bobby said, each pointed at the other's head, and as they each tell the other to do it—two voices screaming—they each pull the trigger. For the briefest of time, an amount hard to measure, two bullets are between them. But then it's over, and the bullets are no longer between them but in each man's head.

"They died right then and there," Bobby said.

I laughed in his face. "Your aunt told you this story?"

"Yeah," he said.

"Well, she got that one way wrong."

"What do you mean?"

"They didn't die," I said. "I was there. I saw it. One of those men was Fredrick, my father."

Bobby asked the bartender for another drink.

"Remember you're driving," I told him.

"Yeah, yeah," he said. When the drink came, he took a tiny sip and set the glass down with a thud. "So then why did you ask me if I knew the story?"

"I just wanted to know what you knew about it, that's all."

"Well, there you go," he said.

I asked him if he wanted to hear the real version.

"Does one of them die?" he asked.

"No," I told him.

"Then I don't want to hear it."

But I told him anyway.

. . .

Bobby got some parts of the story right. There were two men, and there were people watching. There weren't two guns, though, just the one, that .22 I now owned and kept in my closet. Fredrick held it, aimed it at the other man, Gizos's father, Lenno, as he stood on his steps. Neither was drunk—well, maybe Lenno was, since he did drink a great deal, but Fredrick didn't drink.

But there were things Bobby couldn't have known. It was winter 1976, and I was thirteen. The day was bright and sunny, the sky blue, the white snow on the ground hard but melting. Fredrick and I had spent the better part of the day up at camp clearing Joseph's roof of snow while he made us lunch, and inside under a lantern at a wobbly table we ate it and then played a game of cribbage. When we came back home we did the same to the house, pushed the snow off the roof and then cleared the giant piles away from the foundation, and when the roof was clear and we were back inside, Fredrick made dinner. Louise had not felt well for the last few weeks. "I'm sorry," she would say to my father as he brought her food. "I need to sleep. I don't feel well today. Maybe I'll be better tomorrow." Fredrick cooked the blanched and frozen fiddleheads he'd collected in the fall, and we ate them with salted pork for most of our meals.

Whenever Louise was ill, Fredrick seemed to talk and talk. But that day I didn't listen to a word he said. My mind was elsewhere. I had this terrible feeling that something bad had happened to Gizos. For over a week he hadn't been in school, which for many of the kids wasn't abnormal. I sometimes missed that much. But for Gizos it was. And whenever I went to his house, nobody answered the door. He was home too: through the window, I'd seen his shoes neatly tucked on the floor against the wall.

When I finished eating what little I could that day, I told Fredrick I was going out to meet Gizos, and Fredrick asked why Gizos hadn't been by. "Did his father finally convince him that we're Goog'ooks?" he said, meaning evil spirits. Gizos was usually the one to come and get me. I told Fredrick I didn't know why he hadn't been around, that we'd simply decided to meet by the river.

We'd gotten so much snow that the roads on the reservation were as narrow as wooded paths, and all the trees, heavy and bending with wet snow, leaned in as if listening. All the way to Gizos's I felt I was being watched.

Gizos's house was up on a small hill, where the road rose and then dipped back down. It was the highest point on the reservation, which wasn't spectacular because it wasn't that high a hill. The house, whose red siding was faded, had an upstairs, and above that an attic too, but what was up there, if anything, was a mystery to me. Lenno had grown up right there. It wasn't the same house though—before Gizos was born, Lenno, according to Fredrick, had ripped down the old home and had built in its place this red one. That was when his wife still lived there, before she left them. Gizos very rarely talked about her, his mother, not because he had some painful memories but because he didn't remember her.

The sun was setting, and with it what little warmth it offered. At the bottom of the hill to his house, a giant rock split the road in two, one branch going all the way through the reservation, past the lumberyard and continuing to the bridge to Overtown, and the other just a dead end, a cul-de-sac with a dense thicket of pines through which the river flowed. Lenno's gray truck was parked in the driveway, and so I waited at the rock, watching and hoping he'd leave. But the sun set more and more, and with each inch of its sinking the cold grew deeper and deeper. I waited for as long as I could, and then I walked up that hill and down the driveway to the door. I took my glove off and knocked on the window in the door, the glass frigid on my knuckles.

Footsteps. They got louder and louder until the noise stopped right behind the door. The white curtains that hung over the glass parted, and Lenno looked at me. He gestured with his hand—leave—and the curtains fell back in place.

I went back to the rock and waited. But for what I didn't know. It was almost dark, the sky purple and pink on one horizon and the other, opposite, almost black, the sky a huge fruit starting to rot.

I sneaked around the house to Gizos's window. It was hard to keep quiet. The snow creaked, and every so often it collapsed under me and made a loud thump. There was no way to approach without making any sound, and so the best I could hope for was that Lenno wouldn't hear me. As I got to the back of the house, which was almost pitch-black because of the thick pines blocking what was left of the sun, a light from indoors shone through the window, Gizos's window. I went to it as quietly as I could and crouched down right below it. I stood up and looked inside.

It's hard to remember what, exactly, Gizos was doing. He was on the bed, I know that, sitting against the wall. He may have been reading, I don't know. Even saying this seems impossible given his situation. When I looked, all my attention was drawn to his face: his forehead was swollen and protruded out, and his eyes, equally swollen, were small slits. He had dark skin, and so it was difficult to tell if his face was bruised, but his face was so deformed—so changed by violence—that he didn't even look like Gizos but instead like some alien, some extraterrestrial, that was waiting, wounded, for the mother ship.

A glass bottle shattered next to me. I looked up, and Lenno, hanging out the second-floor window, aimed another, and it would have hit me if I hadn't fallen backward. To a boy, he was a terrifying man. He had wide shoulders, and he just looked large. But up there he looked smaller. And so it must have been that that made me feel safe. I picked up half a broken glass bottle and hurled it in his direction. He ducked back inside as the bottle shattered near the top of the window and glass fell down on me. I picked up another, waiting and waiting for his head to pop out again, but it didn't. And in not very much time at all the front door opened and banged shut, and I heard the snow crunching loudly under his feet as he came around the corner. I felt that something depended on my staying right there, but whatever it was, it left the moment I saw he held an iron fireplace poker, the end curled like a finger. I ran as fast as I could, climbing over fallen trees until I got back to the road, and when I was on that road, I looked back to see him still behind me, coming out of the woods. I slowed, thinking those lines of trees were as far as he'd go, that he'd quit. But he ran for me, and I ran with all I had down the road, and I kept going, turning on one narrow road after the other until my legs were as heavy as the snow around me and I collapsed, breathing deep and long, a hunted animal. I looked back, and I was alone.

I don't remember the walk home, and before I knew it, I was inside. I was sweating, and I felt the sweat run cold when I took my jacket off and hung it by the woodstove. The lights were bright, and I had to squint, and I didn't see Fredrick.

"What happened to your hand?" he said.

I didn't know what he meant. "I lost it," I said, talking about my glove. "I'll find it tomorrow when there's light."

"No," he said. I could see him now. He was coming from down the hallway. He stood in the kitchen, facing me. He pointed. "Your hand," he said.

I looked at my hand. The blood was dried like mud.

"What happened to you?" he said. "You have no color in your face."

Maybe I was still afraid he'd get me, but I just blurted it out. "He tried to kill me," I said, and I told Fredrick what had happened, all of it, starting with how long it had been since I'd seen Gizos. He came to me and brought me to the sink and scrubbed the blood off my hand and was inspecting the cut, and as he turned my hand over in the light, I saw there were multiple cuts, none of them deep. My hand felt swollen and the water and soap stung.

He didn't ask if I was sure. He didn't press me, didn't act as if what I was telling him was untrue. In fact, the only thing he said to me was, "Get in the truck."

I've had a long time to think about this incident, particularly Fredrick's wrath, his anger, that brought him to Lenno. If Gizos's father hadn't been the chief, if he hadn't been pushing the tribe so hard to accept what little the Settlement Act would give them—which was less than what Fredrick felt the tribe was owed and was a constant point of contention between the two—I wonder whether Fredrick would have done what he did. I've questioned the source of his desire to act, to stand up to something that was wrong: Was it what Lenno had done to Gizos? Was it what Lenno had done to me? Or was it what he planned to do to the tribe, to sell his people out for less than their suffering was worth? Maybe it was all three things working together that filled Fredrick with a rage I never saw again. He's been gone now for more than a quarter century, and regardless of how much thinking I've done on the matter—about where his anger came from that day—I remind myself and I will continue to remind myself that it's easy, too easy, even natural, to doubt the character of someone who is gone. Fredrick was a good person.

As he drove the narrow roads that night, Fredrick made me load the gun, the .22. It was hard to do so in the truck. I had to roll down my window so there'd be enough room to pull out the loading rod, and my hands were shaking when I loaded it and slid it back in place. I tried to hand the gun to him.

"Keep holding it," he said.

I didn't want to hold the gun. The more I held it, the more responsible I felt, and if there was one thing I didn't want, it was to feel responsible.

"Can I set it down?" I asked. "Lean it against the seat?"

He answered with a grunt, and I wasn't sure what it meant. I kept holding it, and the steel grew warm in my hands.

We arrived at the house, and Fredrick parked in the driveway. He kept the truck running, and he put the high beams on. Fredrick grabbed the gun from me, but I didn't let go.

He pulled again, and again I didn't let go.

"What are you going to do?" I said. It was the first time Fredrick saw my fear. I was scared, frightened at how wrong this could go.

"I'm going to fix this," he said. "Now let go."

I didn't plan to, but when I heard Lenno's voice, heard and felt a bottle shatter over the windshield, I let go of the gun.

How fast Fredrick lifted the gun has never left me—it was one quick movement, the butt of the rifle to his shoulder, his eye peering down the scope.

"Where's your boy?" Fredrick said to Lenno, who came outside.

"You should be pointing that gun at your son for what he did," Lenno said.

"Your boy," Fredrick said. "Where is he?"

"He's a little faggot," he said, pointing to me. He spat and, ignoring the gun, took a step. "Go on," he said, yelling to me in the truck. "Tell your stepfather. Tell him what you did to my son when he wouldn't do what you wanted."

I felt Fredrick look at me, but only briefly.

Fredrick then yelled Gizos's name. "Come out here."

Lenno looked over his shoulder. "You stay in the fucking house," he said. He looked at Fredrick. "What do you want?"

"I want to know the boy is safe."

"'Safe,' says the man coming to my house and holding a rifle. Get out of here and take that gay son of yours with you."

Fredrick shot and cracked the ice sealing the concrete steps.

"Aim better," Lenno said.

Fredrick aimed the gun at him as he took a step toward him. I sat watching, as frozen as the world that held us. I had no idea what Lenno was talking about. Fredrick's gay son?

I don't remember how long this standoff lasted. Both Fredrick and Lenno grew more and more annoyed at the other, yet each did nothing. They were yelling, screaming, and I hoped somebody, anybody who was outside now, watching the two in each other's faces, would call the police. But I had to remind myself that nobody besides Native people cared about Native men going at it, however violent they were. I didn't know what to do, how I could end this. I was about to get out of the truck when Gizos appeared on the steps. His face, obviously, looked the same as it had. Both Fredrick and Lenno quieted.

"Did he do this to you?" Fredrick asked Gizos. Lenno said nothing. His people, his tribe, many of them gathered at the end of the driveway, were watching. I thought I heard Lenno tell Gizos to get back in the house, but his sentence was cut off by Gizos finally speaking up. Whatever emotion Gizos had, it did not show through his deformed face. He looked at his father, and then he looked at me. He nodded his head toward me: an accusation.

"He did it," Lenno said, and he raised his voice to be heard by everyone there, watching. It was as if he had rehearsed it: he said I had beaten Gizos, beaten him so badly when he refused what I wanted. I was out of the truck now, standing behind the open door, calling him a liar, saying he had done it. Fredrick looked at me, listening to Lenno. Gizos was no longer in the doorway. I would, of course, in my life, encounter deeper loneliness than this—much, much deeper, more pronounced—but right then I felt that that was the loneliest I could be.

"Liar!" I yelled, but Lenno spoke louder than me.

"That's the truth," he said, not addressing Fredrick or me but speaking to those who had gathered to watch, those who mattered to him: the ones who kept him in power.

Fredrick told me to get in the truck. As we backed out, Lenno walked in the headlights with us, almost pushing the truck. Those who were in the driveway parted for us, and they banged on the truck as we pulled away. Fredrick said nothing the entire drive home, and the gun lay in his lap, almost pointing at me.

. . .

Bobby set his mug down.

"Well, did you?" he asked.

And I said, "Did I what?"

"Beat him up when he wouldn't give you a blow job?"

A very old guy with no teeth sat not far from us, and he laughed with Bobby.

"I don't know whose version I liked better," Bobby said, "yours or my aunt's."

I wasn't really done telling him the story, but he was done listening, wanting to go home and drink some more. He paid, said he'd see me later as he laughed his way toward the door.

But there was more to the story.

We got home that night and Fredrick didn't get out of the truck. He sat there, hands on the wheel, gun across his lap, the barrel still pointed in my direction. When he made no move to leave, to shut off the truck or the lights, or even to speak, I said, "Are you going inside?"

I think he nodded, but maybe that's not right. He said nothing, I know that.

"It's not true," I told him. "What he said. What either of them said."

If I had felt betrayed by Gizos, I don't remember. Right then, I was too disoriented to feel anything but unsafe. I don't mean that in terms of being physically safe. I guess what I mean is that my situation on the reservation was already precarious, and this—this story—could snap what little thin line had held me in this place. Finally, Fredrick made a move. He opened his door and turned the gun around. He removed the loading rod and emptied the bullets into his lap. He dropped one and had to fish around for it on the floor of the truck. Then, when he'd given up looking for it, he pocketed the bullets and handed the gun to me.

"Keep this," he said.

I told him I didn't need it. What was I going to do with a gun?

"Exactly," Fredrick said. "It's safer with you."

He turned the truck off, and I followed him into the house.

Maybe I should have said nothing, should have let Gizos heal, let everything go back to normal. I drank three glasses of water at the sink. Fredrick was in his bedroom, and then he was in the bathroom, and then he was back in the bedroom. I didn't expect to see him again that night. He'd gotten ready for bed.

But as I was drinking another glass of water, I heard him come down the hall.

"You should know I don't believe him," he said. "Not one bit of it."

I felt relieved for only a moment that he didn't believe the story. It wasn't the accusations, wasn't the story and its particulars that bothered me. I was more upset with the lie than what the lie said.

All relief I felt disappeared when he spoke again. "But it doesn't matter what I believe," he said. "It's what they will believe. And they will believe his story, believe the display in front of his house."

My mother coughed, and Fredrick looked down the hallway. If she was there, out of bed, I didn't know. I don't think she was—I didn't hear a door open or close. She must have still been in bed. In any other world, my mother would have come out, would have risen in this time to help in any way she could. But she didn't; she was sick.

"Good night," Fredrick said.

I said it back to him.

In the morning, Fredrick acted as if nothing had happened. He went on living. And this is important, because it's when, I think, I learned to carry on through an untrue story that pushes back, and this was the moment I thought of the most when I felt hopeless about Elizabeth and her mother, how I'd never see my child so close again.

. . .

After that incident, all the work Fredrick had put in with the tribal council was gone. People, he said, stopped listening to him, stopped caring. He used to stay late at council meetings, leaving

Louise and me home alone to eat dinner together (or leaving me to eat by myself, when she didn't leave her room). He started coming home halfway through the meetings, and then he stopped going altogether. He spent time away, at camp, with Joseph, who was getting weaker and more careless, skipping meals and carrying too much wood as if he were still young.

It might be too easy to assume that Fredrick began to think about things that mattered more, like his family—Louise, me, his father—although maybe that's true. We can complicate things, offer explanations that are as grand as sculpted marble, but sometimes simplicity is best and truest. In its simplest, I think Fredrick was just plain tired, tired of fighting against something that so many wanted. And whether or not he was right—right to seek more for everyone, on the basis that he thought there was more to take—didn't matter: Who wouldn't want that, who wouldn't want more, not for the sake of having more but because it was owed?

With people believing the story Lenno let loose on the reservation—that Gizos's wounds were from me—he was able to go back to school. No questions were asked. It was known or believed I'd done it. But no students said a thing to me about it, maybe out of fear I'd do it to them, I don't know. Three days after—when a deep loneliness had taken hold of me—Gizos spoke to me. He didn't offer an apology, nothing like that. His face had started to look normal again, had started to reverse itself from how the violence had shaped it. It was during lunchtime, and he came by the table I was sitting at, and he said to meet him down by the river, the same place and time we usually met: 4:00 PM.

After school, I went home. Louise seemed to feel better and was moving around the house. She no longer lay in bed but sat in the living room, on the couch, reading and drinking tea, while

Fredrick worked or was outside doing who knows what—he was always either chipping ice or trying to fix the ash-pounding machine. Louise didn't look up from her book as she asked how school was, and I didn't turn from the sink where I was washing a cup when I said it was fine. I usually ate something when I got home, but I wasn't hungry.

In my room, on the bed, I waited for four. Each second felt longer than the last, and with that I had more time to think. When it was time to leave and meet him, I took that .22 Fredrick had given me without the bullets. I was halfway down the driveway with it when I remembered that, that it wasn't loaded, and I felt weaker with that empty gun than I would have unarmed. And then it came to me: that one bullet Fredrick had dropped in the truck. In the daylight—or whatever of it remained—I found the small bullet the size of a carpenter ant, and I loaded it into the rod and snapped the rod back in place.

I was on the path, in the woods, heading for the bank of the river where we usually met, where Gizos told his stories. The gun grew cold in one of my hands, the other gloved, and so I took to holding the gun in that gloved hand. I turned the bend in the path and saw him down there, standing and looking my way, hands in his jacket pockets, and when I got to him, he said nothing about the gun. He looked at it once and only once.

"Here," he said, and from his pocket he took out my glove. It was an awkward exchange: I wouldn't let go of the gun, wouldn't set it down. When he saw I wouldn't let the gun go, he took the glove back and grabbed my cold hand and put the glove on for me. And then he wouldn't let go of my hand. Even when I pulled away, he held on, kept looking at the hand he'd just gloved, and I looked too, started to think he saw something there, on me, something of such great importance, and right when I accepted that there must have been something miraculous we were looking at, Gizos began to cry. Not a little, a lot. Since that day I've never seen a boy, or a man, cry that hard. Now I know such a thing could do the world good, not the crying, not simply the body and spirit's self-recognition of pain, but the publicness of it, the body and spirit's communicating to another's body and spirit in one and only one language—that of deep, deep emotion—between the flesh of two free bodies. I say "free" here because it's true—what is freer than that, freer than one body welcoming and receiving another's in a state or condition so unchanged since the very beginning of bodies, a state or condition that has continually been jailed time and time again since that very beginning?

If you had asked me at that age what I'd done while he cried, I would have said I'd watched him, watched him cry and cry and cry along the frozen river and below the bending branches covered in hard snow. But the truth is that I cried just as hard as he did until we both saw how ridiculous we each looked. And then we laughed, that type of heavy laughter that comes after an escape from some sort of danger.

Of course our moment had to end. When it did, we were both quiet, still, listening to the crackling of the ice and its echo upriver. Finally, he spoke.

"You want to hear a story?" he asked.

But the strange thing was this: I felt as if I had just heard one, and I told him that and said I didn't need another one.

"Not all stories are spoken," he said. "But your loss. It would have been a good one too."

I still wonder what it was he would have told me, and I regret not hearing it.

"Give me that gun," Gizos said, and I handed it to him. "We can't go home not having done nothing out here but cry like wimps. Is it loaded?"

"With one bullet."

He looked at me. "Psycho," he said. He took aim out over the river.

"What are you aiming at?" I asked him. It was almost dark, and the sky was that dim fading blue.

"I don't know," he said, but he looked to be aiming at something; he followed it with the barrel, whatever he saw out there. And then he pulled the trigger. A small pop.

"Got him," he said, and he handed me back the gun. He said we'd see each other the next day, which we did. On the way home that night, I wondered who, or what, Gizos had seen out there, at the end of that barrel. All I had seen was a cold dark over the ice. But what he'd seen could have been anything, anyone, including me.

5

WHEN MY MOTHER AND I CAME BACK TOGETHER
in 1996—years after Fredrick had died and when I joined AA—
Louise was who she always had been: my mother who suffered
from severe depression. But as the years went on, she began to
change. Her memory started to fail her. At first, she mixed up
details in a story or lost the words for things, words as simple as
"chair" or "phone" or "cup," and would say, "You know what I
mean." I thought it was just old age getting at her, but then it got
worse, and by the fall of 2017 I knew it wasn't old age.

I went to visit her. It was Sunday, as usual, and I hadn't been
by for about a month, as usual. And as usual her neighbor was
outside, the snow melted mostly, and he spread dirt and leveled
the soft ground near the junk he collected—a mangled metal bed
frame was new. She must have heard me coming up the steps
because when I went to unlock the door, Louise opened it and
asked what I was doing there.

"Did something happen?" she asked. "What's the matter?"

I told her no, that I was there to visit for the afternoon.

"Why?" she said. "You were just here yesterday."

I asked her what she was talking about, but before she could answer me, something righted itself in her brain.

"Never mind, never mind," she said. "Just come in."

I shut the door behind me. I asked again what she was talking about, and that time she yelled at me.

"I said never mind! If you want to stay, stay; if you don't, leave."

I dropped it, but I paid close attention to how she behaved. Whatever version of her I saw at the door—the one that thought I was there the day before—did not show itself again while I was there that day. But it did show itself again the next time I visited, the following week.

She began to call me Fredrick.

Sometimes she owned the slip—"I mean Charles," she'd say. "Ha! Not Fredrick." Other times she would not—"Stop that!" she'd say when I corrected her. "You listen to me."

One Sunday I made the mistake of suggesting that we go to the doctor, and she kicked me—well, Fredrick—out of the house. If she hadn't rolled her ankle on a bunched-up rug by her bedroom door the next Sunday, I don't know how I would have convinced her to go to the doctor. Before I brought her in, I made it a point to tell the doctor that, yes, the visit was about her ankle, but it needed to be about her memory too. I had him all caught up.

Louise and I were in a room in the back of a local clinic, and the doctor tapped on the door and came in. "Let's see that ankle," he said, and if Louise suspected that the tests he was completing on her had nothing to do with the ankle, she said nothing about it. But he did not lie to her. He began to ask about her memory, and she caught on then.

"What is this?" she said. "What are you on about?" He was straightforward, but he knew not to aggravate her.

Everything but her memory of people and her occasional loss of words was fine. She wasn't forgetting how to care for herself, wasn't forgetting how to live—she could clean and cook, never forgetting to turn off a burner and always remembering not to put soap on the cast-iron skillet. She didn't forget to lock her door at night, and she didn't forget to turn off her candle wax burner.

"It will get worse," the doctor said when we were alone in the hallway. "It could happen quickly or slowly over a long period of time. Just pay attention to her."

And so I did. I paid close attention.

The doctor gave her Seroquel, and it helped her sleep and helped with her irritation and her depression. It alleviated the anxiety she didn't talk about but that I knew was there, especially when she thought I was Fredrick. It wasn't that often she called me by his name, but when she did, she became very fearful, not of me (or him) but of something else, something that was clear only to her. Maybe she remembered, or could sense, the memory: that for so long she and I had not faced the truth of what happened about his death.

Now when she got in these moods, when she thought I was Fredrick, I pretended I was. No revelations came, no hidden knowledge between Louise and Fredrick was ever revealed. She only talked about simple things: "How much wood do we have? Is it all chopped? I can help stack this afternoon. Don't forget to clean the chimney. Do you want me to check on Joseph this weekend? He should come home for a bit and have a real dinner instead of canned chili."

I told her we were all set with wood, that it was all chopped and stacked, and that I'd cleaned the chimney before I went and checked on my father, who was fine.

"But he needs a real meal," she said.

I told her I'd bring him something.

When I left her house that random day, she sent me home with meatloaf and mashed potatoes and green beans. It wasn't the first time she had done this, wasn't the first time she'd sent me off with food for a man who had not eaten on this earth for many, many years.

I never had the stomach to eat it.

Until very recently, I had thought her condition was worsening at a slow pace, if worsening at all. But earlier that spring, as we were watching TV—a show about a medical examiner, Dr. Something or other who solves crimes by looking at the body, the vessel, with a standard Y incision, as the narrator calls it—I felt her looking at me.

I had been Charles, her son, all day. I said her name. When she didn't respond, I sat forward to get closer, and I said her name again.

"What are you doing here?" she said. "How are you here?"

She was terrified. She gripped her blankets and held them up to her neck, as if she were trying to hide.

"Mom," I said. "It's me, your son."

I rarely called her Mom; we had a mutual understanding that that was what we were: mother and son. All those years of silence after Fredrick died, that distance and separation we created between us because neither of us knew how to approach it.

I was no stranger to the great sadness I was filled with. Elizabeth comes to mind—knowing that your own blood doesn't know who you are, that you exist. But in Louise's bedroom that day as she became frightened, all I could feel was fear that she was passing a point we'd never come back to, that any chance of fixing ourselves, our relationship, was gone.

"Am I dead?" she asked me. "Where is he?"

"You're not dead," I said.

She got up from the bed.

"My ankle is sore," she said, limping out of the room.

I stood up, and when I tried to explain and follow her, she told me to sit, to stay away from her.

"Don't come near me," she said, and she began to walk around her apartment.

Doors opened and shut, and cabinets creaked and banged closed. When she came back to the bedroom, she held a rolling pin.

"Where is he?" she said again. "They took him, didn't they?"

I didn't move. I felt that any movement might make her worse or more fearful. I asked her who she was talking about.

"You know who," she said. "My son. Did Mother take him again?"

It's sharp, like cold air—that feeling of remembering your body knows something—that feeling of remembering that your body knows something about your past that you don't.

"Louise," I said. "He's at school."

"Don't you lie to me, Fredrick, don't you lie!"

"He's at school, I promise."

"I want to see him," she said. "Get him."

"I can't take him from school."

"Call there," she said. "I want to talk to him."

. . .

The first time Bobby met my mother, it was over the phone. I called him, and I told him what I could while Louise kept telling me to give her the phone ("the secretary is going to get him right now, you need to wait"). When Bobby understood what I was asking him to do, he laughed.

"Are you serious?" he said. "You're serious. All right, put my mother on the phone then."

I handed the phone to Louise.

"Charles," she said, her hand on her chest. "Are you all right?"

They weren't on the phone for very long, and I couldn't hear what Bobby said to her. I met him that night at the bar, and he told me that all he'd said was he was fine, that he was in class. He asked her if she was all right, which helped make sense of her constantly saying, when they'd hung up, "I think I worried him."

. . .

Louise saw a lot of Bobby that spring and summer, and aside from their phone introduction, she had yet to think that he was anybody but Bobby. I never asked Bobby to watch her, but he offered to do it when I couldn't, if I had a job somewhere, clear-cutting. And it wasn't like she didn't know him. A few days after the phone incident, I'd taken her out to lunch to meet Bobby. She was doing fine, was her old self as much as she could be. She didn't recognize Bobby's voice at all as the voice of the person on the phone and she rather liked him.

"You remind me of my cousin's ex-husband," she said, pointing at him with her fork.

"Maybe I am," he said.

That afternoon when I dropped Louise off at home, Bobby and I helped her upstairs. As I've said, her body was fine, and she could have gotten indoors with no help, but we went up anyway. We didn't stay long, and we didn't drink any of the coffee she offered. As I was driving Bobby to his car, which was back at the restaurant, he asked how fast my mother's condition would worsen.

"She doesn't seem that bad," he said.

I told him I didn't know, that the illness came and went as it pleased.

He asked if I was up there every day. I told him no, that I couldn't go every day, but that I called her every night. And that was when he asked if I needed any help, and he said he didn't mind going to check on her or even visiting with her when I couldn't.

I didn't know if Bobby thought my mother's illness might affect whether I would go to Florida with him, if he thought at all about it and if he believed at all that I would go with him, which I was still unsure about. I had nothing keeping me there, except Elizabeth, of course. Every so often Bobby would bring up leaving, and he had started to look up apartments and small houses in other states. Florida, California, North Carolina, all these places that were on the coast and had a beach. He'd never struck me as a beach person, but he'd even started to tell Louise about it, that he would be moving soon. "Sometime next year," he would say, which was what he'd been saying for a while.

6

SUMMER WAS TURNING TO FALL. BOBBY PLANNED
to visit states and look for property for "our move," as he called it.

And so he left for about two weeks. He wanted me to go, but
he knew my mother was unwell. Part of me wanted to go, wanted
to get away with him and out of the normal rhythm of what life
I lived, but another part of me knew I had to stay for Louise. Up
until he left, Bobby had been requesting information on small
houses and condos from all over the country, and the day after
we last saw each other, he was heading to North Carolina to see
about a place.

"I'll take some pictures and show you," he said.

I don't know why he wanted me to go with him so badly. I
shouldn't say badly—it didn't come across that way. But how can
someone's big plan that includes you not seem like that person
wants it that way so badly?

He took the bus as close as it would get him, and then rented
a car. I got a call from him a couple of days later, when he was

supposed to arrive, but he was a day behind because he'd stopped off at the casino in Connecticut.

"Christ," he said. "Why can't our Indians up there have a casino like this?"

It was the first time I'd felt animosity toward him. I didn't say anything though. In fact, all I said was, "Hey, there's the Bingo Palace," but Bobby said, "Fuck the Bingo Palace. They need cards."

At first it was the "our" part of his sentence that bothered me, the way he laid claim. After we hung up and I had more time to think about it, I started to wonder about the possibility that I was just upset that he didn't say, "Why can't you Indians up there have a casino like this one?"

There's nothing strange about a white person wishing to be Indian. It's comical, if anything. And white people saying they're Indian happens all the time, and it's laughed at by Native people. "Oh yeah, your great-great-grandmother was an Indian princess? Boy, here's your per capita then." And I get it. I do. I'm not skeejin—not Native—and I can't say with any pride that I'm "Panawahpskewi" because I contain no blood connecting me to ancestors long gone. But I feel that I am, or that I have a stake in their experience. I don't feel this way because I grew up on a reservation. To think that the reservation is what makes an Indian an Indian is to massacre all over again the Natives who do not populate it. I could have grown up with my mother and Fredrick in a city, or in a country town, or, hell, in a dirty wet sewer, and I'd still feel this way. No place makes a Native a Native. It strengthens it, I'll say that, but it's not the deciding factor.

It was Fredrick's love that made me feel Native. He loved me so much that I was, and still am, convinced that I was from him, part of him, part of what he was part of. That was how I felt about Elizabeth—in truth, she was a descendant only from her mother's side, and if that were to come out and she were taken off the census, would she feel any less Native? I didn't think so. Blood matters only enough to keep us alive. She was Roger's daughter in the same way I was Fredrick's son, and I knew deep down he was as good to her as Fredrick had been to me.

And it seemed here, at least in my thinking, that to say blood doesn't matter was to let her go, to tell her that she was not mine, that we had no connection. And while all of that might have been true, it was all untrue, because I saw her as mine, as part of me. I guessed the only true thing I could be certain about—and this was really what had upset me about what Bobby had said—was that blood is messy, and it stains in ways that are hard to clean, especially if that stain can't be seen but we know it is there, a trail of red or dark red leading back to a time we cannot go to remove it. Or that red or dark red trail is our timeline, and if we could clean it away, then it would be some type of self-erasure, no different from the ways I've seen Native people erase their own kind. Mary has a story like that.

. . .

When the cattails swelled and bloomed like marshmallows, Mary and I used to snap them below the brown fuzz and together we'd slam them against the concrete to watch them explode. The cattails were the ones by the pond. Not on the side where the water flows under that small bridge out to the river but the other side by the light yellow service garage whose remnants are still there. We were teenagers then. Fourteen, fifteen. She was always coming to find me, and I think if she hadn't, I would have been the one looking for her. She had a walk about her—like the world could be falling down around her and she'd keep on going. It was such a different way of being from what I was used to at home, always seeing Louise fall away into that dark abyss of her mind. Mary was the joy that would get me leveled, that would set me right. I spent a great deal of time with her. If I wasn't with Gizos, and if I wasn't home or with Fredrick or Joseph or my mother, then I was with Mary. Like I said, I don't think I ever once sought her out to do something; it was always her coming up to my house and asking me outside.

Elizabeth is evidence enough of our bond, of where our relationship went, but that came later and was always secondary to our friendship.

One spring we were outside together, slowly making that side of the pond bald by plucking the cattails, the road littered with brown and white fluff. I don't remember the day, but it was near the weekend. The tribe was having a social at the community center. Two other drum groups were coming, one from the Point and the other from someplace else, some tribe I'd never heard of. There are so many of them.

We plucked most of the cattails. So few remained that we had to stand back and really try to find them among the tall spring-water grass. We were sharing a cigarette, searching, when Mary said, "I'm going to drum this weekend."

I've seen women drum since then. I watched Elizabeth drum when Roger taught her all the songs as a small girl. He set her up out back of their house on numerous occasions, and I always wished I could hear her. However in the late '70s, women weren't drummers. It wasn't "traditional." But Mary wanted to drum.

I asked her if she knew how. I didn't know how. I knew the songs and the footwork, and Mary and I danced once in a while. She said, "Of course I know how." After a pause, she laughed and said, "I asked Roger if I was doing it right."

"And?" I said to her.

"And what?"

I wanted to know more, since Roger had a thing for Mary. But I stayed the course. "Were you doing it right?"

"Duh," she said. "Want to see?"

Mary found another cattail, and she snapped it a foot below the top. With it in hand, she told me to follow her. We crossed the street and passed the service garage and went into the woods, where it was mostly swamp. River water flooded the area from the spring melt, and as we walked, we hugged the hillside. I didn't know where she was taking me, what she was looking for, and I didn't think she knew either until she said, "There's one."

It was a giant mushroom with a purple cap growing on the wet hill.

"This is the drum," she said. "Now sit and watch."

I sat right next to her, my shoulder almost touching hers, and she drummed and sang through a few songs: the welcome song, the honor song, and the snake dance. Whether she drummed them right, I'm not sure, because the cattail on the mushroom made little noise, just a small thump. But I'm thinking now that it isn't about the noise—it's part of it, sure—but rather it's the performance of it, the act of engaging with it, respecting it the way you respect anything that gives you life.

There in the woods with Mary, I listened, everything smelling of the spring dirt and wet leaves and cold, melted ice, until she finished singing. In my mind she'd sung and drummed perfectly, and when I went to tell her so, she said, "I fucked up like ten times." And then she crushed the mushroom with her boot and flung the cattail into the swamp.

"I'll get it right this weekend," she said. "You'll be there, right?"

Of course, I told her, even though I hadn't planned on going. I'd stopped attending them after Gizos's father had done what he did to Gizos and to me. Lenno was always at the socials. He organized them. But I knew I would go. I had to.

· · ·

The location of the socials always changed and depended on the weather. If the ground wasn't wet and soggy, and if it wouldn't rain, they were usually held outside on the school's football field. We'd had such a wet spring—but not as wet as it would be eight years later in '86 when the spring melt and ice ripped the flat one-way bridge and took it away forever—and so the social was held indoors at the community building. This was before they got the basketball court and wood floors. It was smooth concrete back then—so many children cracked their teeth on that floor. I wonder, when they rebuild it across the street, if they'll have a good basketball court.

The building was full of people, everyone under the bright yellow lights high above. People mingled, paper plates of food in their hands. The whole place smelled like beef stew. The three drum groups were set up, and when one played, the other two listened. It was during those times that others—always boys, of course—would go over to the waiting drum group and ask if they could be part of the next song, and always some older Native would hand them his drumstick and move for them. Gizos drummed once in a while at other socials, but he wasn't there that day. He always said the older Natives teased him. Not just him, no, they teased all the young boys who drummed. Not in a way, Gizos said, where you felt embarrassed, but in a way that made you laugh too: "Jesum, gwus, last time you were here you had two whiskers, now it's three," and "I saw you with Alberta last week. You know she's your cousin, right?" But it wasn't always like that, the teasing, I mean. After Gizos's father had done what he did to him, I guess Ronnie, who was a distant cousin of Fredrick's and was as big as Gizos's father, told Gizos that he could always come to him if anything like that with his father happened again. Gizos liked to say that to be around the drum was to be ready for both the teasing and the seriousness, but that each was a source of strength in its own way.

I waited in the community building for Mary. I was near the stage, behind some tables where a few elder women sat over empty plates of food, talking to one another once in a while but for the most part sitting turned and watching the drummers and the children dance or run through with Hula-Hoops or basketballs until someone took them away. I thought Mary would find me, thought she'd come up to me and talk for a bit, and when our tribe's drum group was paused, their drumsticks resting on the drum in the shape of a snowflake, all of them waiting, turned in their seats, listening to another tribe's group, she would say, "Here I go," and she'd walk over to the group, tap on someone's shoulder, and he'd rise and give her his seat, and she'd drum the next song, and then the next.

But that's not how it happened, and I stopped looking for her. Lenno watched me closely, and I watched him talk to tribal member after tribal member as he kept on staring in my direction.

The drum group from the Point played an honor song. Lenno stared and stared and stared, and then his eyes caught something and he started to move toward it. He shouted. Or maybe somebody else shouted. A lot of people were shouting. I looked, and a wave of men—some from around our tribe's drum—were hurrying in one direction, not fast enough to suggest something terrible was happening and not slow enough not to catch the eye. The Point group didn't stop drumming, and they didn't stop singing. They were too focused, I think, to realize that anything else was happening.

Some of the men gave up on whatever they were pursuing, but others kept going through the double doors and outside. The older women sitting near me were really laughing at something, and as I went to ask them what had happened, a hand squeezed my shoulder.

"Where did she go?" Lenno said. I said nothing. I was too frightened. He put his other hand on my other shoulder and shook me. If people weren't watching, I wonder what he would have done. But he saw all their eyes on him. Then he let go and was gone. Maybe he saw the truth: that I had no idea what Mary planned to do.

The men eventually came back through those double doors and the social went on, and I left to find Mary. She was where we'd sat a few days before, right on the hillside deep in the swamp, near the large mushroom now crumbled and smooshed. In her hand she held several drumsticks, all ripped apart: the hide on each one torn open, all the beads and leather strips strewn on the wet ground, and the ones with feathers plucked, frayed, and bent.

"You're lucky," she said, looking at what she'd broken on the wet earth. "So lucky."

"I think if they had to choose between us, they'd let you drum over me."

She stuck a stripped drumstick into the ground. "That's not what I mean," she said.

"Then what?" I asked, but somebody was coming through the woods.

Mary and I looked back toward the noise, and when we both saw people, we ran. If Mary hadn't, I would have stayed, so I wasn't running away but following. My shoes and feet were soaked, and I tripped once over a hard root sticking out of the earth and got my knees wet. I kept following her through the woods and out of the woods on the road and then back into the woods until we were way away from that place and down by a fallen tree, sitting on it and breathing heavy.

"Fucking Native men," Mary said. "Fuck them."

"What happened?"

"They said no."

"I know that, but what happened?"

"You were there," she said. "You saw. I don't need to tell it."

"I didn't see," I said, and I told her how Gizos's father kept my attention, and I went on for too long, talking about how he grabbed me and shook me.

"I went up to the drum when they weren't playing," Mary said. "All of them were watching the Point group. I asked one person if I could have his seat, and he started to get up and was going to let me. But when he saw it was me—not even just me, but a girl—he sat right back down and told me to go. To go!"

"Who was it?" I said. "Henry?"

"So I asked the person next to him, and he said no too. It wasn't even that that made me mad. The first person I asked stood up and was saying, 'Go on, go on, you can't, go on, go on, it's bad medicine,' all the while flapping his hand at me like a dog."

"Who was it?"

"It doesn't matter who it was, they're all the same. But it was Henry."

"So you took the drumsticks because of that?"

"Let me finish. Henry sat back down, and he made eye contact with someone else drumming, and he pointed his thumb at me, and people laughed. That's what pissed me off. Their laughing."

She peeled piece after piece of bark off the log we sat on and flicked one after another.

"Bad medicine," she said. "Yeah, they got bad medicine all right. They all had their drumsticks resting on the drum, and I reached in and grabbed them and ran. The next thing I knew, you were here with me in the woods. How'd you find me?"

I didn't know how I'd found her.

"It doesn't matter," she said.

As we sat that day on that log, and before she went home, I told her about the women, the elders, how they'd laughed when Mary had done what she did.

"They're probably sick of it too," Mary said. She looked at me. "Were they all laughing?"

I didn't know, but I said they all were.

"Good," she said. "That's good."

I don't know if Mary's actions had anything to do with why women are now able to drum. And it's not like the next social or the one after featured an all-women's drum group. I guess what happened—how it worked out—was that she grew up, and so did the other women, and they made room for themselves at their own drums.

. . .

My mother thought what Mary had done was funny. I told her while we were eating dinner. Breakfast for dinner and the eggs ran thick and clung to toasted bread. While Louise thought it was spectacular, Fredrick was appalled.

"She shouldn't have done that," he said. "That's not right." He didn't mean that she shouldn't drum, no, he meant that she shouldn't have destroyed the drumsticks.

Louise had highs and lows, and she was at a high then. She laughed and laughed and laughed at how upset Fredrick was.

"It's not funny," he said. "Drumsticks should be revered."

"Revered!" Louise said, and she laughed and laughed.

It was always heartening to see my mother in such a mood, where she laughed at anything and everything. And while it was nice, it was also a reminder that just around the corner was that darkness, that deep, deep low that would put her to bed for weeks.

"Go ahead, laugh," Fredrick said. He looked at me, and I was laughing too. If he was upset about what Mary had done—and upset that we were both laughing about it—he didn't show it. He laughed too, and he shook his head. I think Fredrick knew how rare this moment was—Louise's laughter—and he'd give up anything, even all the reverence he held, to be part of it. Because what's more sacred than laughter at the dinner table?

7

WHEN THE DOCTOR TOLD ME MY MOTHER'S MEMORY would get worse, I started to sleep less and less. I would sleep for about three or four hours a night. This would have been a problem if I were tired and simply could not sleep, but I wasn't tired. I wasn't sleeping much because it seemed I constantly had something to think about: Mary's cryptic answer to my question about how Elizabeth was doing, my mother's health, Bobby's plans, and the guilt I carried about Fredrick's death. It was like everything was piling on at once.

Maybe if my house were cleaner—or even decorated in a way that made it feel like a home—I would have slept better. My place wasn't dirty, but I hadn't been taking much care of it. The kitchen chairs around the table jutted out and away, and the rug under that table was bunched up. The sink was filled with dishes and glasses and mugs. The garbage wasn't full, but the plastic tub needed a wash. Coffee grounds littered the bottom. It used to smell only like cigarettes in here, but not since I'd started smoking outdoors. Now the place had a smell to it. Not foul-smelling, but there was a smell, and I won't be so delusional as to say it was a good one. The other rooms in the house weren't in too bad a shape. The bathroom smelled like toilet bowl cleaner. The tidiest thing in my house was my bed. Fredrick always said a made bed cleared the mind and helped with sleep. Maybe that's true, but I barely slept and when I did, it was on the couch.

And so I was awake the night of the fire. I saw from over here—and then from over there—what happened on the reservation. The news said it was arson and would later say it was that kid who'd done it, the young man who had robbed the tribal museum those years back.

It was a little past midnight. I sat on the couch with the TV on. I wasn't really watching it. I wasn't tired yet. I went outside to have a smoke and I sat facing the river. The good thing about having so few lights in the house is that when you go outside it does not take long for your eyes to adjust to the darkness. But maybe it wasn't that dark: the stars were out, and so too the moon. It was a dark blue night. A quiet one. I could faintly see the outline of Mary and Roger's house across the gurgling river. (I did miss seeing Elizabeth every day—she had moved at the end of that summer into a house she'd bought on the other side of the reservation.) Some people wouldn't consider silence a sound, but it is, and at night there's a certain silence emitted during the dark of night. Between the river's flow and the summer breeze rippling hard-to-see leaves and the sound my scraping shoe made on the porch, I heard night silence. I heard the workings of my inner body, the pump of my heart and the expanding of my lungs.

I smoked. When I finished, I smoked another. Something in me did not want to go back inside. But immediately as I sparked a third, I smelled something else burning. It was not my cigarette. I put it out and walked toward the river. I smelled fire smoke, and part of the sky above the trees across the river was graying like a storm cloud. At first that's what I thought it was: a storm, and that the fire smoke was just a coincidence, that somebody somewhere was awake around a flame. But when yellow light filled the gray clouds, I knew something wild was burning.

By the river I watched the sky grow brighter: a reddish-orange hue not quite unlike the soft chest of an eastern bluebird. Sirens wailed for a brief moment and then quieted, but that silence of night, the sound of myself, had been compromised: people, across the river somewhere, shouted.

Watching burn whatever burned, I wondered, What could it be over there on the island? The church, and mainly just houses. And then I thought of my old house, the one that the tribe had bought and planned to burn for training.

I should have known that they wouldn't have burned the old, crooked house that late at night, but I had watched day after day, night after night for smoke and fire. I'd never wondered about how I would feel when it was destroyed, whittled down to its bones and ash. I'd only felt the waiting for knowing how I would feel. And so that night, when I saw the fire and thought of the old home, the waiting was over. I drove my truck over to the reservation. I was prepared to be stopped, prepared to be told I could not go that way, that the way was blocked, and while stopped I was prepared to see the house burning, flames flicking the smoke up.

But the house was not on fire. I kept on driving down that road, and I turned toward the pond. I was on the side where the pond water flows out into the Penobscot River. While I was the only person there in a vehicle, I wasn't alone. A few tribal members stood along the bent traffic barrier, watching across the pond as both the tribal fire department and Overtown's tried to subdue the flames, which grew higher and higher. I got out of my truck and watched with them.

I asked what was burning. Not to anybody in particular, but to the group of us there.

"I think it's the community garden," somebody said.

"No, can't be," somebody else said. "I think it's the garage."

"I can see the garage just fine," said somebody. "It ain't on fire."

"Well I can't see it."

"It's right there." A person pointed.

"I can't see it."

It was just the two of them talking.

"Well I can," said one, "and it's the garden that's on fire."

"Who would light the garden on fire?"

"Any one of those kids using drugs, that's who. Get your cousin to straighten this place out."

"He's trying."

"I didn't vote for him to try."

"Go to council then."

"They don't do nothing."

Someone asked me for a cigarette. In my hurry I hadn't brought them, and so I didn't have any to give.

"I got one," somebody said.

"Damn it's cold out."

We all kept watching the fire. I stepped back and then forward, and I could feel the fire's heat from across the pond. More people began to arrive.

People talked.

"I just texted my uncle," someone said. "He'll know what's burning."

"It's the garden," another said.

"I told him I think it's the garage."

"I just came from that way, it's the garden."

"You didn't come from that way. You live back over there. You didn't see anything."

I wanted to say I had thought it was my old house—and I was about to, when someone said, "Maybe they finally burned down Fredrick's old place."

"They ain't burning that down," somebody else said.

"Why not?" I said.

People looked at me. Even in the dark they knew who was who. That's how it is over here.

"Who are you?" somebody said.

"Who is this guy?"

Someone got in my face and then backed up. "I don't recognize him," she said, and she disappeared among the people.

"Charles," I said. "Fredrick's boy."

Those who remembered remembered, and those who didn't didn't care. I was recognized and placed.

"Jesum, gwus," someone said, laughing. "I heard you died. Your mom still around?"

I had no idea who was asking. I told her she was.

"That's good," she said. Then I saw how she was standing: bent over a bit and leaning on a cane. Her voice didn't sound old, but the sight of her showed she was.

Somebody asked if it was the garage on fire, and before anybody could say no—or yes—something across the way in the fire boomed and the flames curled and bloomed black into the sky.

"Christ, what kind of tomatoes they growing over there?"

Everyone laughed. A warmness from the blast rolled over me.

Soon the fire was under control, but not before it had spread to the garage.

"But it wasn't on fire before is what I'm saying," someone said as both fires were shrinking. "You thought it was on fire, not the garden, but the garden was on fire, and now the garage is."

"You think you know everything," somebody said.

I walked to my truck, feeling forgotten enough to leave.

8

WE WERE ON OUR WAY BACK FROM HOME DEPOT,
Bobby and me, having just bought an elbow pipe to fix my
mother's sink—Bobby said he'd do it, "it's my trade"—when I
called him on his bullshit. He'd been back from North Carolina
for almost a week and he hadn't talked much at all about his trip.

"It wasn't good," he'd say, or "It's too humid there; I couldn't
breathe by the end," or, a new one, "The piping was a mess."
Every time I asked to see pictures of the place, he said, "Why
do you want to see a place that's no good?" But that's Bobby: he
almost never discusses things that aren't or weren't good. Maybe
that's why I know so little about his childhood, his parents, his
three marriages, his life before we met in AA.

But this time, I really wanted to know. It had nothing to do
with my wanting or not wanting to go—I was just so damn curious. Bobby had been excited about the place. While he was there
he had called and left voicemails, telling me what he was up to,
the price of the place.

"If I sell my house and you sell yours," he'd said, "we can buy the place outright, including a strip of beach." It sounded good, truly it did, and his trip and what he'd told me through voicemail was in its own small way one of the reasons I'd been sleeping so little over the past few weeks. I won't lie: when he came back and kept deflecting, I felt a bit let down. When I did sleep, I had started to dream of a house that would never be mine, this small shack on a strip of beach under a dark blue sky. But that feeling lasted only so long as it could. Louise's illness reminded me why I could not leave. My mind still wasn't made up about going with him; some days I wanted to, some days I didn't. Who wouldn't want, at times, to get away from a life that seemed so empty? But one thing was certain: I wanted to know what had happened to him there in North Carolina.

And so we had just left Home Depot when I finally asked: "What really happened on your trip?"

He tried at first to say again what he'd been saying to me: too humid, the people weren't nice, it was overcast all the time.

"Really, though," I said, "what happened? I know you liked that place. I worried you wouldn't come home."

He took a corner too sharp and I was pushed into the passenger door. He braked hard at a red light. "I fucked it all up. That's what."

"How could you fuck it up?"

"I found the perfect place—" He waved his hands in the air like that described it. "Small gray cottage on the beach, two bed-rooms, two baths, porch with a white wooden enclosure. The living room walls were painted light blue, and it was like you were in the ocean. It was just perfect. Perfect! Two neighbors, one on each side of the house, dry beach grass separating us from them."

"The light's green," I said.

"I know, I know," he said. He drove on. "And we could have afforded it, the both of us. Just down the beach—not even half a mile—was an outdoor bar. Indoors, too, but you could sit outside and drink and watch the ocean."

"So what happened?"

"I slept with the neighbor, that's what."

I really didn't see the big deal in it.

"Trust me," he said. "It's a big deal. She's married."

We were at another red light. Bobby inspected the elbow pipe. "Goddammit," he said. "Motherfucker. This is the wrong one. They need to organize those boxes better. I know I got this from the right box, but it was the wrong piece."

Instead of going back to Home Depot, Bobby drove us to Lowe's. I went in with him, and he went and found the right elbow pipe.

"She's married," I said. "So what? Just pretend it didn't happen, that's all."

We were headed to checkout, but he went to the service desk instead.

"I'm going to swap this," he said.

"You didn't buy that here," I said.

"They don't know that."

We were back in the truck with the right pipe and on our way to Louise's.

"Did you hear me in there?" I asked. "Just pretend it didn't happen."

"I can't pretend it didn't happen. Her husband knows."

"How?"

"I told him," Bobby said. "Or maybe he already knew. I don't know, Charles. But that's how."

I was laughing. "You're making this up, aren't you? Why would you tell him?"

"I didn't know he was her fucking husband. We were at that little bar, and we were talking, you know, just shooting the shit.

He's asking me why I'm here, and I'm telling him, and he's asking me what I do for work, and I tell him, and I ask him and he says he's a retired cop but does some freelance security shit. Anyway, we have some more drinks and he starts talking about how in the summer all these young women come down to the beach, and he whistles and goes, 'Damn nice sight.' And then I say I like the older ones, and he goes, 'Oh, yeah?' and I say, 'Yeah. Listen.' And I lean in close and say, 'Saw this lady the other night, right down the way,' and I'm describing her to him and he's getting all quiet and not looking at me. Finally he asks, 'What's her name?' and I tell him, and then the next thing I know he's got me round the neck and he's squeezing and the bartender's yelling at him to stop, and when he does stop, he goes, 'I didn't like you when you first opened your mouth. Come down this way again and I'll kill you.'"

"Get out of here," I said. "Why are you lying?"

"I ain't lying about this. That's the truth."

"So you're not going to tell me what really happened?" I said.

"That's what happened!"

"All right," I said, and I let it go.

"There's other places," he said. "There's always other places."

We were quiet for a bit. And as I had called him on his bullshit, Bobby called me on mine.

"So do you really want to go with me?" he said.

I didn't know what he meant at first, and so I said, "Go where?"

"Anywhere, away from this place."

I told him maybe, that I wasn't sure. That for as many reasons as I had to stay, there were an equal number of reasons to leave.

"I know you're busy with your mother," he said. "Christ, I am too, and she ain't even my mother. But what about when she dies? Sorry to say it, but it'll happen. There ain't going to be much else for you here. Especially if I'm gone."

I told him there was my daughter, and I told him that I had a feeling she wasn't doing good.

"How do you know?" he said.

I told him about seeing Mary, when I'd gone to ask her about burial rights a few months ago and found the courage to ask after Elizabeth and how she'd said she could be doing better but that she'd be OK.

"She could have meant something else," he said.

"If it wasn't bad," I said, "then why would Mary tell me? Why would she say anything at all that made it seem like Elizabeth wasn't doing well?"

"You think she wants you to worry just to worry?"

I did, but I couldn't see why.

"I don't know, Charles."

We were off the highway and driving Route 3, that long stretch of cracked, uneven road, back to Louise's.

While we'd gone to get the pipe, Louise had done what Bobby told her not to do: run the faucet. Water was all over the slanted floor, flowing into the thin space where the floor met the wall. Where it went, I don't know. It wasn't a lot of water, but enough of a mess to need six towels to clean it. It was an accident, her turning it on. Louise simply just forgot. But she didn't look at it that way. She sat in bed, crying.

"It's just a little water," I said. "It's all cleaned."

She looked at me. In a whisper she said, "Are you alone? Is he in the other room?"

Bobby was in the kitchen, on his back with half his body under the sink. I sat on the bed near Louise.

"Are you?" she said.

"Yes."

"How are you going to tell him?" she asked.

"Tell who what?"

She pointed at the wall, behind which lay Bobby. "Him."

"How am I going to tell him what?"

"That you're dead."

Even though she made no sense, the seriousness she said this with chilled me.

"I'm not dead," I said to her.

She yell-whispered, pointing at me. "You are! How are you going to tell him? Or am I going to have to tell him?"

"I'll tell him," I said. "I'll tell him."

She lay back in the bed and shut her eyes. I went to Bobby in the kitchen and watched him take apart the bottom of the sink. A flashlight was in the crook of his neck, and his hands were oily and wet. He made a scrunched-up face, squinting.

"If she asks if I told you," I said to him, "say I did."

"All right," he said, not even questioning it.

I went outside for a smoke. Louise's neighbor, shovel man, was out there smoking too, looking at his small, muddy lawn.

He hollered to me: "How's your mom?"

"Fine," I said.

"I hate to ask," he said, "but you got three bucks?"

I didn't have three bucks on me. Just change. I'd never noticed before, but he had a really thin and narrow head, and his cheekbones were sharp, like he never ate.

I gave him the change, and I told him that that was all I had.

"It helps," he said, sucking on his cigarette. "I need to catch the bus and get down to my appointment. I was late for the last one, and they were all upset about it there, and they were trying to kick me out."

I didn't know what he was talking about. "Sorry," I said.

"It's fine, it's fine," he said, counting the change in his palm. "Thanks for this."

He went inside, and I walked back inside and climbed the stairs to Louise's. Bobby was working on the sink. I asked him how it was going, but he must not have heard me.

"I told her you told me," he said. He tightened something. "This is done. Turn the water on."

I turned the sink on.

"Dammit, I'm good," Bobby said.

While Bobby cleaned up, I went in Louise's room. She was in bed with the blankets pulled over her head. She couldn't have been sleeping, I thought, and so I shook her gently.

"We're leaving," I said.

She looked at me. And it was her eyes that spoke: they skimmed over my face and the room as if everything was unfamiliar.

"Do you need anything?" I said.

She waved me away and rolled over. I could still see her looking about the room.

It was a flutter. That's the only way I can explain her state of mind. One minute she was over there, and then the next she was over here. But sometimes I didn't know where she was, where her thinking was at. And when I didn't know, I had to ask.

"Louise," I said. "Do you know where you are?"

She looked at me again. "Where I am?" she repeated.

"Yes," I said. "Do you know where you are?"

Never before had I heard such certainty in a voice. "I'm in my bones," she said, and she rolled back onto her side.

. . .

I stayed with her that night. Bobby and I had come in his truck, and he told me he could come and get me the next morning or late afternoon—not near midday, though, he had somewhere to be—and I said the morning was fine. Back upstairs, I shut her front door and locked it and went down the hall to Louise's bedroom.

She slept in the deep way she always had during those months of darkness when I was young. She stayed on her side, the blanket pulled up to her forehead. She made no noise, except occasionally when the comforter would crinkle. I kept the TV on as the only source of light, and I kept it turned down low. I could barely hear the voices, news anchors. Talking, updating.

The room was darker when I woke, and footsteps fell in the hallway. Not careful steps, but somebody hurrying.

Before I could say "Bobby?"—because I thought it was him, that he'd forgotten something and had come back to get whatever it was he'd left behind—a single hand came into the bedroom and reached for the light switch. The room lit bright and I squinted and stood up.

It was that man from next door. And when he saw me he turned the light off, yelled, "Sorry, sorry, I'm sorry," and hurried back down the hallway and out the front door, and maybe he meant to shut the front door but I'll never know because I was right behind him, after him, chasing, outside in the dark, watching him spring down the driveway and run down the street, and I lost him somewhere three roads down, near a gas station.

When I got back to Louise's, she was sitting up in bed.

"I shouldn't have been sleeping," she said. "Now he's gone."

I was out of breath. "Are you OK?" I said. "Did you see him?"

"Why would you do that?" she said.

"Do what?"

"He was coming for me," she said. "I told him I'd give him some."

"What are you talking about? Give him what?"

But she wouldn't say. I wasn't sure what was going on at the time, but the more I thought about it, the more I began to think she was giving him money. Why, I didn't know.

I called the police that night. Two officers came over, and I told them what happened. And I made the mistake of saying "I think" when saying it was the neighbor.

"You think?" they said, each of them. "You need to be certain."

"I'm certain," I told them, but the doubt was already there.

They said they would find him and talk to him, would take it from there. One of the officers said he was on this road a lot, and that he'd watch the house when he was on duty. It made me feel better, sure, but what if that man got away, was able to convince them it wasn't him?

The police found him, and he said he didn't know what they were talking about. They could not get him to confess—"I wasn't up there," he said, "so he didn't see anything."

If the officers were convinced, so be it. But I wasn't. After that night, I tried four times to find Louise's neighbor. He was never home, or if he was, he wouldn't answer the door. The last time— that fourth time—I didn't knock but stood on his steps and listened for any noise. But there was none except for the pigeons that whirred as soft as their feathers, up near the attic window.

9

ON THE DAY LOUISE BROUGHT UP FREDRICK'S DEATH, she wasn't agitated or upset. I went into her room, where she was watching TV in her recliner. "Hello, hi," she said, which was what she said when she wasn't sure who the person was. When she knew it was me, she would say, "It's not Sunday," except for when it was Sunday; then she would say, "What do you want for lunch?"

I asked if I could get her anything, and she pondered it. "No, nothing, thank you."

From the edge of the bed, I watched TV with her. It was the same show that always seemed to be on, that Dr. Something who solves crimes by cutting the body open and looking at the innards.

No wonder she thought about death so much. It was all she watched.

As the show played, I didn't listen. I was thinking about that man next door. I asked her again about him, asked if she gave him money. "Money?" she said. "What money? I don't have any money, if that's what you want."

She was quiet for a while. And then she said, "When do I need to be ready?"

I asked her what she meant.

"For dinner."

"Are you hungry?" I said.

"Is it dinnertime?"

It was a little past noon.

"So not for a few hours," she said. "I see. Have you called them for reservations?"

"Who?" I said.

"The Chocolate Moose," she said, a restaurant long gone now.

"You want to go out to eat?"

"If I do," she said. Except for the time I took her out to lunch and to meet Bobby, I never brought her anywhere.

It wasn't close to dinnertime, but I knew how she got in the evening hours. If I was going to take her out, I thought, better now than later.

"Our reservation is in an hour," I said, playing into her story. "You have to get ready soon."

She thought that was funny, and she pointed to the clothes she wore. "This is as good as it gets," she said. "I just want to do something before I leave."

For a bit, she tidied up the apartment. She washed dishes and set them to dry; she swept the kitchen and hallway floors, and bathroom. She vacuumed the living room, and she picked up bits of torn paper and junk receipts from the table and threw them away. With a small wastebasket in her hands, she checked each room twice for garbage.

"I didn't take too long, did I?" she said.

"You're fine," I said. "There's plenty of time."

"Not really," she said, and before she could leave me to think about that, I followed her.

She put on her shoes and asked if she needed a jacket. I told her no, that it was warm out, perhaps too warm out for October. As we went outside and I brought her to the passenger door of my truck, I watched for movement from the neighbor's house. Nothing.

"This is nice," Louise said as I backed out of the driveway. "It's nice to get out."

I felt it too, what she felt.

"You know," she said, "my son never brings me out. Can you believe it? I just moved here last week—last week—and he doesn't even know it. I wonder how long it will take him to find out."

Too long.

"And he drinks an awful lot," she said. "At least he works. At least he has that."

I wish I knew who it was she thought she was talking to. Part of me thought to ask, "Do you know my name?" but that, I thought, would work her brain in a way it should not work.

"He hasn't been right for a while," Louise said. "Not for a while. Not since his father died. Maybe you can talk to him."

We were at a red light. A dump truck was in front of us, and I could smell the garbage.

"I can try," I said.

I felt Louise staring at me. "What will you say?"

"What should I say?"

"Maybe you're not the right person then," she said. "You need to know what to say."

. . .

We got off the highway and drove toward the dam and the main street that ran along it. The dam was not running, and at the bottom, jagged, dry rocks rose from the shallow bed like crooked, crowded teeth.

"My son lives near here," Louise said. "Just down that way. Let's go see him."

I turned the way she pointed.

"He might be at work," she said.

We drove on.

"Take this right, right here."

It wasn't my road, but I turned anyway.

"It's the next one," she said.

It was not. And I realized I was not alone here. We shared a mutual distance.

She took me down seven dirt roads, and on that seventh road she said never mind. If only she'd gone one road more, we would have made it. But instead we were going back, back the way we'd come.

"I don't feel well," Louise said. "I want to go home."

"You don't want to eat?"

She said nothing.

I drove past the bridge to the reservation.

"I want to go home," she said. "Take me home."

"I am," I said.

"Where are you bringing me?"

And then I slipped, called her Mom, telling her I was bringing her home.

"You're not my son," she said. "Pull over, stop, let me out!"

She opened the truck door as we were driving, and if she hadn't been wearing her seat belt, she would have completed the jump onto the passing pavement.

I stopped the truck and she struggled to get out. She did not know how to work the seat belt that I'd strapped on for her before we left. She yanked on it and bit it and kicked and screamed. The glove compartment popped open, and with her body weight she pressed down on it and it cracked and fell between her feet. She screamed, and then she quit. Her chest heaved. She didn't look at me. I touched her arm, and she started back up.

"Don't touch me," she said, and she swung her hand at me, at my face. "Who are you? You son of a fucking bitch, who are you?"

The whites of her eyes were red.

Cars passed by and did not stop.

I could not answer her question; I did not know.

. . .

I parked in her driveway and got out of the truck. I did not unbuckle her; I left her there. I did not know what to do but wait. So that's what I did. I waited and smoked and waited and smoked. I listened to those pigeons next door whir near the attic window, and I watched cars whiz by, kicking up dirt that floated and settled like a dirty, thin mesh net. I waited until she fell asleep, and I let her stay that way for almost an hour.

The truck ding-ding-dinged as I unbuckled her.

"You're home," I said.

She was calmer, but still on edge.

"I can do it," she said, getting out of the car.

I walked her to her apartment and brought her to her room. She sat down in her recliner.

"Has he told you?" she said.

"Who?" I said.

"My son. Has he told you why he didn't go with him that day?"

"Go with who?" I said, even though I knew who.

"His father," she said. "My husband. Why didn't he go hunting with his father that day? Has he said?"

"He has not," I told her.

"Can you ask him for me?" she said. "I'd really like to know."

"I will," I said. "I'll ask him."

She said nothing more. I was afraid to leave her, yet I was afraid to stay too. I made her some dinner. A plate of corn and brown rice and a slice of haddock, and I covered it with Saran Wrap and placed it in the fridge. When I went back to her, she had crawled into bed. I don't know if she was sleeping or not. A better son would have checked, or a better son would have stayed.

I do wonder who she thought she was talking to. Bobby? That's the only person I can think of. But then again, part of me thinks she didn't know who she was talking to. I don't know. I won't linger too long on this, because what does it matter who she was talking to?

I want to tell the full story, the full history of the family Elizabeth belongs to yet does not know exists, and to do that I have to explain Fredrick's death.

10

AM I AT FAULT FOR FREDRICK'S DEATH? IS A QUESTION I've asked over and over again. I could have saved him. But does that make it my fault? I was convinced Louise thought so, and part of me felt that way too. Would I feel at fault when my mother died?

. . .

The reason I didn't go hunting with Fredrick is simple: my daughter was being born, and I was waiting, watching from my place across the river, for her to be brought home.

January 1991, either the fifteenth, sixteenth, or seventeenth. In the same way I do not know Elizabeth's exact date of birth—her exact arrival to this world—I do not know the exact date of Fredrick's death, his exact departure from this world. I do not know what I believe in when it comes to the afterlife, or the before life, but I've had this strange vision—when I was drunk, sadly—of the both of them passing by each other, one on the way in, one on the way out, their bodiless heads turned, bodiless eyes locked, knowing. A hello and a goodbye.

. . .

Fredrick asked if I wanted to hunt with him. I was outside my house, the one we'd built, in the cold, bundled up in a jacket, my body warm from drinking. A new snow had fallen the night before, about four or five inches. As I sat outside, I smoked, watching both the frozen river and Elizabeth's parents' house, waiting. Fredrick got out of his truck, and when he knocked on my door, I had to say, "Over here," and he made his surprised noise, "Ho, there you are," and he grabbed a cold metal foldout chair leaning against the side of the house and it opened with a loud creak and he pressed the chair's legs down into the snow next to me and sat in it, crookedly.

I knew why he'd come: the only way Louise would let him hunt was if I, or somebody else, was with him. It wasn't that Fredrick didn't want me to go—he'd be happy to have me along with him—but he knew I didn't like hunting. Fredrick wasn't old—in his late fifties—but Louise was worrying more and more about his health, about his ability to be out there in the cold and trudge through the snow, his ability to grapple with the immense weight of a dead deer or moose.

Fredrick was in fine condition. He was in better shape than me. But Louise wanted him safe. When she was in one of those dark places, she used to worry about anything and everything. A loose nail, a strange passing car, a heavy rain, a heavy snow, or no rain, no snow.

He sat with me, and I asked him if he had anybody else to go with him.

"Everybody's busy," he said. "I want to get out there now with the fresh snow."

"And she won't let you go alone?" I said.

"She probably would," he said, "but I don't want to worry her when I can avoid it."

I was quiet and so was he.

"I don't want to twist your arm into coming," he said. "It's fine if you don't want to go."

My eyes were set on Mary's house.

Fredrick laughed. "What if I tell her you're going with me? That would make her feel better."

"But what if something happens?"

"Nothing's going to happen, gwus," he said. "I'm going out tomorrow for the day, that's it. And I probably won't even get anything."

"You say that all the time, yet you always get something."

"It's best to expect nothing," he said. "That way you don't get your hopes up."

Across the river out back of Elizabeth's parents' house, snow loosened and rolled down to the river ice and spread like powder over glass.

Fredrick stood up and refolded the chair with a creak. "She'll call and ask you," he said.

"And I'll tell her."

. . .

I have this memory, and I don't know if it's true, where I felt he had something more to tell me, something more to say. It's a look on his face, but instead of saying what he wants, he says something else, that he'll see me when he gets back. And then he left. I think he wanted to say something more, and even all these years later I still feel that way.

. . .

Louise called that night and asked if I was going.

"Yes," I told her, and she asked if I wanted to sleep over there with them, so that way Fredrick wouldn't have to come and get me in the early morning. But before I could say anything I heard Fredrick's voice in the background, like it was far, far away, already departing our station. "I don't mind getting him," he said. "We have to go out that way anyway."

That voice, so distant. It was the last time I heard it.

. . .

He was only to spend the day out there at camp. He was supposed to stop by on his way back to "drop me off." And when he did not show up that night, I should have gone out there to find him. But I remained home and drank and watched the empty house across the river stay empty, going inside every so often to warm up and to get more to drink. I had taken the days off from work, and so I barely slept. One, two hours a night. I drank the rest of the time, and in the late hours I moved in and out of anger and sadness and worry as if they were rooms in a house I was pacing about.

Into the next day, into the next afternoon and evening, Fredrick did not return. It wasn't unusual. He oftentimes would stay longer than he had intended, longer than he had said he would.

And then in the morning on that third day—the seventeenth of January—tires rolled and cracked the snow in my driveway. I rose and turned to the coming noise. Of course it was not Fredrick. It was a taxi.

"Oh, thank goodness," Louise said. "I must have just missed him."

I stood from the chair but fell over into the snow, dizzy, and before I could try to get up Louise was in my face, looking at me, and so too was the taxi driver, a man whose gray hair stuck out from under his winter hat. They both lifted me up and propped me in the metal foldout chair. I don't remember what I said to her. It could have been any number of things, like, "I didn't go with him," or "I don't know where he is," or "He said nothing would happen." Whatever I said put Louise in a place I had never seen. She grabbed me by the jacket and was yelling, shaking me and shaking me. The taxi driver tried to pull her from me, and he could have if he'd wanted to, but I think all he wanted was anything but this. He stood back and watched as Louise shook me and screamed until she fell back onto the snow and sat blank-faced, her cheeks red, snow stuck to her eyebrows and hair.

She stood. "Get up," she said. "Start your truck."

"I can't drive," I said. I could barely look straight.

And so she drove the truck. On the ride she said nothing to me, and I said nothing to her. The drive would have been in silence if the radio hadn't been turned on to the lowest volume, but as it was there were voices with us, unintelligible mumblings with soft static. My window was not up all the way, and it made a slight whistle. We drove for over an hour with these noises.

Fredrick's truck was parked where it should have been: in a small clearing he had cut to make room for vehicles. The camp was a half-mile walk, and both Louise and I walked in the boot prints Fredrick had made. The shoes I wore were hiking shoes. Snow packed down around my ankles and every so often I would stop and stick a finger in my shoe and scoop out the watery snow, and each time I did so I had to hurry to catch up to Louise, who stopped for nothing.

The closer we got, the more I envisioned the scene: Smoke rises from the chimney. By the small shed an animal carcass rests, gutted and stiff. Louise and I both stand by the door, breathing. "Thank goodness," she says, and she opens the door to the camp and there he is—Fredrick. Sitting at the table, oiling his rifle. He looks up, and even if he is confused by our arrival, he says, "Ho, come in, come in," and like smoke he rises. He stands and walks to us. "Bang your boots good," he says, and he asks if we are hungry, and we say no but he starts frying something up anyway—salted pork or whatever meat he carved from the bones of the animal's sacrifice outside. And we unknowingly eat our way toward another, different future.

But no smoke rose from the chimney. No animals rested against the small shed. No voice greeted us when we opened the door into the camp. Everything was still. There was no smell except for the cold.

My head pounded. "Maybe he's still out," I said.

Louise brushed past me, and when I asked where she was going, she gave no answer, but I followed behind her. She found his boot prints, and they marched north into the woods. His boot prints pointed only away from camp; none pointed back.

We walked in his prints. Louise in front, me in back. I don't know how long we were out there, how long we walked, following where he had gone, but it was long enough to sober me up, and I got sick, sick, sick. I threw up time and time again as we walked and turned this way and that through sparse trees until all that came out of me was a groan. It was endless, where he seemed to go. It was like he was walking to walk; or he had been following something.

Daylight was disappearing. It was not dark, but I knew that if we did not turn around, there was a chance we'd lose ourselves and the prints and not make it back. Louise was way in front of me, and I had lost sight of her. I quickened my pace, and I caught up to her, but only because she had stopped walking.

Fredrick had shot something that did not die. Blood soaked the snow in patches, and every hundred feet we found the blood and his footsteps alongside it, and sometimes we found the large, bloody balls of shit—moose shit—and the outline in the snow of a monstrous body tired and wounded but that had risen to live.

I would have followed her all night, but she turned around and started back to the camp. Night beat us there, but we weren't too far behind it. I can't recall if any stars were out.

I still don't understand how she was able to summon the strength to pull herself together. Inside, she lit a small kerosene lantern and got the fire going. And then she went straight to the small cot pressed against the wall. She lay down and covered herself with a thin gray blanket. She faced away from the room. She had been so adamant about finding him, but when we got back to that cabin she fell into a deep sleep. One moment she was aflame; the next she was out.

I did not sleep that night. I don't know if Louise heard me tell her that I'd be back, but I spoke that into her ear. Before I left, I made sure the fire burned strong, and I made sure the door was shut tight.

I got back to the truck through the footprints we all had made. I still felt sick, and I was sweating. I drove all the way back to Overtown with my window rolled down, and I rolled it up only when I crossed over the bridge to the reservation. The wind whooshed hard over the ice. When I made it to the tribal police department—not the old one, the one as small as my house—I realized I had forgotten my jacket at camp and was wearing only a T-shirt.

Fat Rob worked dispatch that night. His fourth heart attack finally killed him seven or eight years later. He sat behind a coarse wooden desk with a small lamp turned on that lit the hideous dispatch console, acquired when the tribe had been restored its sovereignty and began operating its own law enforcement. I don't know much about radios or dispatch consoles, but this one was old and outdated, which I realized when Fat Rob gave it little kicks every time the machine didn't cooperate.

Soon he was able to contact the officer on duty, Darren, who, before returning to the station, stopped off at the game warden's house on Rolling Thunder and woke up Shay. Darren arrived first, and I told him how Fredrick had gone missing, and then when Shay made it, I told him the story too. I drove between their two vehicles, pinched between silent spiraling red and blue lights, and we drove together out to the camp and parked in the clearing and Shay offered me a jacket and I told him I had one back at camp, but he made me take it anyway and he offered me a cigarette, which I took too, and then we all crunched the snow in single file through the path, both Darren and Shay lighting the way with flashlights while I hurried behind with the red tip of my cigarette and breath frosted, smelling the smell of smoke coming from camp.

At the camp I walked up the steps to the door, and before I could open it, it opened and Louise was in my face holding up a lantern, and she squinted her eyes like she had just woken up and the night was too bright for her. And then she said, "Did you find him?" and she looked past me at Darren and Shay with their flash-lights pointed to the snow that looked like the fur of a white rabbit.

We were all inside. Darren and Shay asked questions, and Louise answered. When you got here, was the camp completely shut up? No fire? Nothing? Which way did he walk? How far? Were the tracks fresh? Did you find anything of his out there? Did you see any smoke or smell any? A moose? There was blood? So he was chasing something?

"We'll go," Darren said.

I showed them to the footprints, and I walked with them to the place where Louise had found the first blood of the moose, and then I could not walk anymore. I was shaking, and I felt dizzy. I was hot, overheated, and I crouched down in the snow and pinched the bridge of my nose.

"Are you all right?" Shay asked.

"I'm sick," I said.

"Go wait back at the camp," he said, and I tried to walk but I found it extremely difficult, like I was not in control of my legs.

Shay spoke to Darren. "I'll take him back," he said. "I'll catch up." And like an echo, I heard, "Radio me."

. . .

Halfway back, Shay had to help me walk. His flashlight shone every which way as I leaned on him, and he struggled to light the snowy path. We got back, and I didn't even know it. I could barely keep my eyes open, and I tripped on the first step indoors. The door opened, and for the second time that night Louise looked upon those on the camp steps hoping that one was Fredrick. She was no longer in the doorway when I went inside, and when I turned to shut the door, Shay had hurried away and gone back into the woods.

For the longest time I sat in the kitchen table's small wooden wraparound bench. Time passed by. I may have slept or dozed— I'm not sure. But I do know I wanted desperately—or needed—a drink. A beer or two. Liquor. Mouthwash. Sterno. Anything.

The next day arrived and Fredrick still had not been found. The sun was rising, but the inside of the camp was still dark. Louise was awake and she finally spoke to me.

"You look like shit," she said. My eyes were shut in the dark behind my eyelids, so there is only sound in my memory. Louise's knees popped as she knelt down and rummaged through the cabinets, the doors slamming shut. A can or two banged on the sideboard. A drawer opened and fingers sifted through clanking metal, the drawer shut, and then there was the short one-two-three-four-five-six grind of a can opener. The click-click-click-fwoo of the stove and the searing of something in a cast-iron skillet. A crinkle of thin plastic, and then the smell of toast burning—"Dammit"—on the woodstove.

"Go get me water," she said.

The house was full of light now. Bright, white light. The sun behind me through the windows washed the back of my neck in warmth like heated water. I didn't want to move from it, but I did.

Part of a stream was not far from camp. Fredrick's father's camp used to rest right along it. There was nothing there then, not even the guide business. The walk there and back was only twenty minutes. I brought a blue bucket with a white handle, and when I got there I kicked a hole through the ice, below which the river still worked and flowed away. I got water and returned.

Louise did not eat any of the corned beef hash she had cooked. She ate only half a piece of toast and drank just a little bit of water. I ate a small pile of the hash no larger than a fist and a piece of toast plus the other half Louise did not eat.

Louise left the kitchen and the sideboard a mess, and I didn't clean it either. We were sitting in the quiet of the camp—listening to the crackle and pop of the woodstove—when she spoke to me, not asking for anything, her voice calm, as if the torment were over. But it wasn't over.

"I don't blame you," she said.

I didn't believe her, and that was not what I wanted to hear. For a while I didn't say anything. For her to say that, that she didn't blame me, meant she had reached a conclusion, an end, even though we did not know for certain if that was where we were: the end.

"Did you hear me?" she said.

"It was his idea to lie to you," I said.

. . .

All these years later I saw how each of us told the truth, yet we couldn't believe each other. And that we didn't believe each other made each of us reconsider our own truth, our resentment, until it turned us against each other and in our minds we settled upon what was not true.

I blame you.

It was my idea to lie to you.

This was the friction in our lives. This was the moment we separated and had to try to love each other. Sometimes I would visit her in our old home, Fredrick's home that had become ours, but the weight of his absence was too much. She was better at keeping in touch than I was: always calling me every week or so, checking in and seeing how I was getting on. But I never answered her calls, never knew she moved from the house I'd helped her move into until years had gone by. And now, even as I was trying to bridge those years of silence, she was slipping away, both forgetting and remembering, remembering and forgetting into nothingness.

. . .

It was past noon when Darren and Shay returned. Only Darren stayed. Shay went out to the road to radio for help. They had found Fredrick stiff as iron and partly buried under the snow.

. . .

After Fredrick's body was removed from the woods, I tried to stop drinking. I don't know how long I made it, but I began to hallucinate. I started to see Fredrick in my house. I saw him outside. And when I did not see him, I felt him, his presence.

In a dream I saw him, which sounds comforting, but it was not: the dream was of his death. The gun had been fired: out in the distance the moose was hit and it ran and Fredrick chased after it for a long while and when he lost sight, he followed the blood and shit and he saw the wide brown fur of it out there lying down, and as he lifted the rifle again, the moose rose like a baby learning to walk and staggered through sparse trees, leaving behind a trail of odorous frost breath. Fredrick cursed and followed until again the moose rested, but Fredrick could not get a clear shot, and when the moose saw him again, it rose a time more and there in the woods the both of them were after life itself, which was somewhere in the distance, and neither reached it. The moose was breathing heavy, and Fredrick was a foot away. He was praying, speaking in a language that was not mine, and in the revered moment between the hunter and the hunted, the ascendancy of life itself spread its bright black wings over the horizon and over them both and the moose rose and charged Fredrick, who could not fire soon enough, and the moose rammed into him and collapsed on him, and the bone fragments from Fredrick's rib cage punctured his internal organs and he was dying, dying, dying, and the moose was dying, dying, dying. The dream ended before I could see who moved on first.

Now, I had to decide: Should I tell my mother the simple truth: that I did not go because I was waiting for my daughter to be brought home? Or should I reaffirm the other truth, the one she knew but wouldn't believe: that it wasn't my idea to lie? I didn't think either one of those would do any good. In a perfect world, Fredrick wouldn't have gone hunting—he would have been at the hospital with me, with Louise, with Mary's parents, Philip and Eunice, as Mary brought our child into this world for us all.

II

AT OUR LAST DOCTOR'S VISIT, THE DOCTOR HAD
mentioned the possibility of putting her in a home. But I didn't
think it was necessary. Louise recognized me most of the time,
though I knew that some days she didn't know who I was and
that she was just pretending. But she still had not lost the ability to take care of herself. And then the doctor recommended
a doll, but I didn't have one and so I gave Louise that stuffed
elephant. The one I wanted to give to Elizabeth all those years
ago. Her doctor had mentioned how some people with her illness responded well to having to take care of something. Did
they really think it was real? I could see a small doll dressed as
a baby in pajamas or in a jean outfit being convincing enough,
but a stuffed elephant? But the elephant seemed to work for
her. When she loved it, she set it on her lap as she watched TV,
and every so often when I was there I would see her bouncing
her leg so the elephant went up and down. But that was only
sometimes.

That fall, she was sleeping a lot. She wasn't eating. She rarely talked, not saying goodbye when I left, and she said my name only so often when I visited. It saddened me, because she was never like this when she couldn't remember—that is, when she saw me but did not know who I was, when she lost touch with reality and took care of that stuffed elephant as if it were her child. When she went back to that dark place was when she knew who she was.

When I wasn't worrying about my mother, I worried about Elizabeth. Since the day I'd seen Mary to ask about burial rights and she said our daughter could be better, I'd started to arrive at all sorts of crazy conclusions. How could I not when her blood was Louise's blood? How could I not when the night after Louise's doctor appointment, after I gave her that elephant, two tribal police cruisers showed up in Elizabeth's parents' driveway, and all ideas pointed to the worst? I wouldn't find out anytime soon what had happened, but when I did, I learned my suspicions of blood and what it carries were not so crazy.

· · ·

In mid-October I brought Louise back to her doctor, and I ended up getting a small checkup too. I had an accident while we were there, but nothing big. It was going on noon when I showed up to get her. Her appointment was at one. I still hadn't seen her neighbor, but I knew he'd been home. At the end of his dirt driveway he'd piled more garbage. Bicycles that were missing tires and chains; dressers with drawers off the tracks; sheet metal, one sheet black with paint; cardboard boxes, lots and lots of boxes, most damp from the rain we'd had; and a white couch with no cushions. There was other stuff, but I can't remember it all. I don't know why it was all there, and I don't even know where it came from. His house? Dumpsters?

When I went inside Louise's, she was asleep under the blankets in bed. I shook her arm, and it startled her.

"What time is it?" she said.

I told her.

"What time do we have to leave?"

I told her that too.

She was herself, or as much so as she could be. She knew my name and called me by it when she asked me to turn the coffee maker on. And she said my name again when she told me to turn it off and that she'd have a cup of tea instead.

I heated the water in her microwave until it was steaming and then dunked in a bag of this peppermint tea she likes, and when it was ready I set it on her nightstand and I had to wake her up again.

"I don't know if I can go today," she said. "I don't feel well."

"Then maybe that's reason enough to go," I told her.

She made a grunting noise.

"Sit up," I said, and I helped her with the pillows. "It'll help you wake up."

She reached for her tea, yawning.

"It's hot," I said. "Be careful."

I sat down in her recliner.

She picked up the mug and blew ripples across the top. Between blows she asked, "Is it raining?"

"No," I said.

"They said it's supposed to rain."

"Who?" I said.

She sipped her tea and made a pained face. "Jesus," she said.

"What?"

Louise sipped her tea again and then swore. "How long did you heat this for?"

"I said it was hot. Jesus said it's supposed to rain?"

She set down the tea. "Yeah," she said.

"You're talking about Jesus?"

Her tone was flat. "I'm messing with you. The weather people said it."

I laughed only because that's what I was supposed to do; and she did too. But I think both of us found it difficult to find things funny lately. It was hard to tell how much she really knew about her condition. I think she had an idea of what was going on but could not name it, like when you know the answer to something but you're pressured by time.

Louise yawned again and with her arms she slowly spun her body so her feet hung from the bed. Her face was scrunched up as she rubbed her ankle.

"Something hurt?" I said.

"Everything," she said, and she stood. She leaned on the back of the recliner for a moment and then took steps like her joints were rusted. As she passed by me, I could smell her. She did not smell terrible, but she smelled like she hadn't been showering.

It took her a while to get ready. She was in the bathroom for a long time. The sink sprayed and the fan hummed. Something fell and clanked on the linoleum. She left the sink on when she came out, and I expected her to be dressed in something other than her pajamas. She was not. She passed by me and her bed and went to her dresser and pulled out clothes from different drawers. Jeans, shirt, socks, all of it, and with a pile of neatly folded clothes in her hands she went back to the bathroom, but then came right out into the bedroom again and was looking for something.

"What are you trying to find?" I said.

"Um . . ." She looked on the top of her dresser and then in her nightstand drawers on both sides of her bed. "I don't know," she finally said. "Maybe it's in the bathroom."

The next time I saw her she was dressed and was in the kitchen.

I asked her if she was ready, and she said she felt she should bring something to eat.

"Are you hungry?" I said.

"Not really."

"We won't be gone long," I told her.

I helped her put on her shoes.

"Is it raining out?" she said.

I told her it was not.

Outside, she said it looked like it was going to rain and asked me to go get her jacket from inside. I did, and when I came out she was sitting in my truck and from behind the windshield she pointed at something and I turned around to look. It was the pile of garbage.

I got in the truck and started it.

"He sells that stuff," Louise said. "Goes around and digs in dumpsters to find it. Can you believe it?"

That was the first I'd heard of that.

"How do you know?" I said.

"He's tried to sell me stuff before."

"When?"

"I don't know," she said.

"Recently?" I said.

"Why do you care?" she said.

"I'm just curious. Was it recently?"

"A couple days ago," she said. "Can you turn the heat on? I'm cold."

I turned the knob to red and the fan to four.

"He came to your house?" I said.

"Who?"

"Your neighbor."

She mumbled two things. One I could not hear, and the second was "I don't know."

Rain droplets hit the windshield.

"Good thing I said to get my jacket," Louise said. "It's going to pour."

The rain stopped and then started again, but it was never more than a few drops here and there. Halfway to her doctor I turned the heat off, but she asked me to put it back on. I closed the vents on my side because I was sweating, like something in me was trying to get out, trying to surface.

Louise was quiet for the rest of the drive. There was an accident at a light a mile up, and we had to go a different way. Right as traffic was turning around and going back through a detour that had been set up, I caught a glimpse of a car and a truck, the front of the truck smooshed in and the back of the car crunched up. That's all I know; if anybody was injured, I did not see it. And Louise did not see it. For the rest of the drive she kept her head back and her eyes shut like it was something she had to try to do.

Louise said nothing when we got to the doctor. She struggled but succeeded in unbuckling herself. She got out of the truck and started for the doors that parted open. A cold breeze. Or maybe a wall AC. She took a seat while I went and told the man behind the sliding glass window that she was here for her appointment, and he handed me a clipboard with a form and a see-through pen with red ink.

"I don't know why I have to keep filling these out," Louise said, and since I didn't know I said nothing.

A few minutes passed.

"Here," she said, and I brought the clipboard and the form written in red ink back to the window. It was no longer a man on the other side but a young woman in giant spectacles who took the clipboard and started inputting Louise's answers into a database on a computer screen I could not see.

While I sat and waited with Louise, I saw the man come back to the window and sit down, and I was relieved to see him, to know he was real. I felt strange, like something was wrong or off; like seeing a glass of water too close to the edge of a table. I was anticipating something.

We waited close to thirty minutes. They said the doctor was backed up with appointments, which was hard to believe since we were the only ones in the waiting room and nobody had come out through the heavy wooden door leading to the back rooms. But then it seemed like all at once, patient after patient came out through that door, and a large line grew in front of the glass window and both the man and the young woman were busy scheduling next appointments and answering questions about when and where so-and-so's prescription would be. One man, an older man, got angry when the young woman told him he had no refills on file, and he told her that the doctor had just written him a script for them, that he'd just seen him, and the woman had to say that it wasn't in the system yet, and she had to get the doctor, Louise's doctor, to tell him that it would be ready later that day, and only then did the man leave and only then did the doctor come to the heavy wooden door, and he opened it with a clank and he said, "Louise?"

He said sorry for the long wait, and we followed the doctor through the door and down a white hallway with a few rooms until we got to one at the very end, and we each went in except for the doctor, who said, before shutting the door, "I'll be in shortly," and I don't know why but I felt as if it were me he was addressing, as if this appointment were mine, and I could not shake the feeling, again, that something was wrong with me.

A nurse came in and took Louise's vitals. When she finished, she knocked over a small jar holding long wooden sticks with swabs on the ends, and after she cleaned them up, she was gone.

She was not very talkative, the nurse. She said nothing, not an "oops" or anything when she knocked over the jar, which was fine, because I had nothing to say and neither did Louise.

Red, yellow, and blue colored blocks were stacked in a thick wicker basket on the floor by my chair. I took a few out and stuck them together, and as Louise told me to leave that stuff alone, the door swung open and a doctor who had never seen Louise came in and I dropped the blocks to the floor and picked them up. I had no sense of embarrassment until the doctor said with a smile that closed up his eyes, "What are you building?" and he said it like I was a child, and so I said, "Nothing, just killing time," and when I'd put the blocks back in the basket I stood up for some reason— maybe to shake the doctor's hand—and then everything dimmed slowly to black and I expected to come out of it but I did not. The next thing I knew I was on the ground looking up at the doctor, who was looking into my eyes and talking and talking to me.

"Can you sit up?" he said.

I did.

"What's the matter with him?" a voice I did not recognize said.

"I'm fine," I spoke, and I stood up and walked to the chair I had been sitting in before. I sat.

The doctor knelt in front of me, the ends of his white coat draping the floor around him, and he questioned me.

Are you still dizzy? Have you eaten today? Do you have a history of this? We can take some blood work if you'd like. No, don't try to stand. Catch your breath. Breathe, breathe, breathe. In through your nose, out through your mouth. Good.

Some minutes passed.

"How do you feel?" he asked.

"I'm fine," I said, and I told him I thought I'd just stood up too quickly.

"Yeah," that same voice said. "I'm still here."

"Do you want to do some blood work?" the doctor said again.

"No," I said. "I'm fine."

"Do you ever feel anxious?" he said. "Do you get panicky?"

"Good Lord," the voice said, "he's fine."

"No," I said, which was partly true. Never before had that happened. From drinking and lack of food, sure, but not when I'd been sober and full. I could pinpoint the doubt I felt only because the doctor had brought up being anxious or panicky, and since we'd gotten to the doctor that day, I'd had a strange feeling like there was something in me that was slowly vibrating and numbing me. And every time there was a noise—the slam of a door, the squeak of a shoe on the floor, a cough, the sound of that sliding glass window behind which was a man and then a young woman and then both—my body was sensitive to it, and that sensitivity frightened me in a hard-to-describe way, like I'd known somehow I was going to be frightened by it even though it had yet to happen, and so that knowing what was to come only increased the fright or the fear. The only comparison I can really make is to playing hide-and-seek. It was like that—I knew somebody was hiding, and I knew to expect they'd pop out from somewhere, and so that knowing made it worse when they did, when the future came.

After I told the doctor no—that I never felt anxious or panicky—I knew he was going to say OK.

"OK," he said, but I had not known that while he turned his attention to my mother, the doctor would continue to pay close attention to me, glancing at me to make sure I was all right.

Her appointment should not have been very long. And maybe it wasn't, but it seemed that way. Louise was having trouble staying focused and answering the doctor's questions. She was forgetting. He asked her about the medication he'd prescribed for her, and she said, "What medication?" and he had to look at me and I had to say, "Yes, she's finished them," and then the doctor scribbled something on a sheet of paper and Louise looked at me and then at the doctor and she laughed hard and said, "I remember, yes, yes, I've finished them," but I don't know if she really remembered or if she just knew that was what she should say. And this went on and on until the end, which was after the nurse had come back and taken some blood from Louise and brought it to get checked and the doctor had come back with the news that things were looking good, and when he prescribed another set of medications and set out to say how they should be taken and when they should be taken, Louise looked at me and then at the doctor and again she laughed. "You're talking to me," she said. "I thought you were talking to him." And I told the doctor I'd run through it again with her and make sure she took the pills correctly, but then he went through the directions again because he had her attention.

My body had that feeling again, like we were done, or like we were going to be done. I stood up to leave with Louise but then I remembered I had things to tell the doctor. I wasn't sure if I should say them in front of Louise.

I asked him if we could talk, and he stayed seated in his little round swivel chair with his white coat hanging down, and he said, "Sure."

I don't know what he saw in my face. I know I tried to say something, but it did not come out, and he saw my eyes flick toward Louise. Whatever clues my face showed, he picked up on them. He turned to Louise, who stood with her purse over her shoulder as she studied the poster on the wall of the anatomy of a man, and he said to her, "You can bring this prescription up to the front if you'd like," and he handed her a sheet of paper he'd printed out and then signed. She took it and was glad to be out of that room.

I asked him if he was aware of her depression or her moods.

"All I know is what you tell me or what she says," he said. "Her medical history isn't very long."

I explained that that was because if she had gone to the doctor, it had been on the reservation, and that they would have her medical history, or more of it. She wasn't one to go. Only when Fredrick made her.

"She's suffered all her life from severe depression," I said. "My father—not my real father, my stepfather, the man my mother married when I was young—my father used to take care of her when she got in her moods."

The door opened and Louise came back in. "Is it this way?" she said, and the doctor went to the door and pointed down the hall, but then he told me to wait and he took her down the hall and back to the lobby.

He was not gone long. He came back and sat down. The door stayed open.

"What were her moods like?"

I told him that for days or even weeks she would lie in bed, that she barely ate and whatever talking she did was usually one- or two-word sentences, or else she spoke by not saying a word, that it was her silences that spoke for her.

"It would last for a few days or weeks?" he asked.

"Sometimes more, sometimes less."

He wrote down nothing of what I said.

"She still gets like this," I said. "But only when she remembers."

"What do you mean?"

"When she remembers things," I said. "When she knows it's me she's talking to, when she knows what year it is and where she is and where she's supposed to be and when she remembers fully who she is. When she's like that, when she's herself, is when she's most likely to slip into whatever dark place it is she goes to. She's been quite aware today of everything, and when I found her this morning, she did not want to get up and go to her appointment."

"Is this often?"

"I don't know how to quantify it," I said.

"Depression is normal," he said, "but would you say she's depressed more than she's happy?"

I told him yes.

"Do you think she will harm herself?"

I told him no. "As far as I know, she's just always waited it out."

"Waited what out?"

I will be honest—I was getting a bit annoyed with him.

"The depression," I said.

He stared at me, thinking. Or maybe he wasn't staring but was just thinking with his eyes facing me.

"What bothers me," I said, "is that when she doesn't remember anything, she is never depressed. I can't say for certain that that's true, but all the times she's been unable to remember me or the year or where she is or what she has to do, she hasn't been depressed, or hasn't acted depressed. She's never in bed but is awake and talkative. Of course, I'm not with her all the time, but the times I am, this is what I see."

Again, he stared at me or in my direction, thinking. He stayed like that for so long that when his lips moved, I expected more than the "OK" he let out.

"OK," he said.

"OK what?" I asked.

"Her appointment is when her ten days of medication are up, so when she comes in, I'll talk to her about this. There are some options that might help both her depression and her memory, such as medication or even electroconvulsive therapy."

I said that last thing back to him.

"ECTs," he said.

"You mean the things that fried Jack Nicholson's brain in that movie with the big Indian guy?"

Fredrick used to call him FBI for Fucking Big Indian because that's what he was. Fredrick also hated that movie, maybe because of the Indian.

"The treatment is nothing like that," he said. "It's been improved over the years and is still very effective in the short term."

"Louise isn't too old?" I said.

"No, but that's something I have to consider. We can talk more next time you're both here. And to see if this is something Louise would like to pursue as an option."

He stood up, and I stood up even though I felt I had more to say, and I think he saw that because he looked to be waiting for me to say something more, something on my mind, but all I said was, "Ten days, got it," and he let me pass first through the door and then he followed, and when we had not yet gone our separate ways but were already some feet apart, he asked me if I was feeling bitter. "I haven't been bitter in years," I told him, and I would not realize until after I'd left and was driving Louise home that he'd asked if I was feeling better.

· . . .

Louise was waiting for me in the parking lot, looking up at the sky, which was no longer gray but a cloudless bright blue, and the sun at its zenith rayed down a sharp warmth, which would fade in the coming months as the sun distanced itself from us, when everything would whiten and gray and the life of the earth in these parts, except the pines, would wither and die, waiting to be brought back for the millionth or plus time.

12

BOBBY SEEMED TO CARE A LOT FOR LOUISE. HE stopped calling me to check on her and called her directly, and he was always curt with me when I asked how long they spoke for, as if he were embarrassed by the time spent on the phone with her. And this connection made me wonder why he didn't care that much about his own parents, who he—reluctantly—went to visit one weekend for a few days during the fall when none of his three brothers or one sister could make it. Around the time of his visit, his father's lungs were filled with fluid, and he was hospitalized. I was a bit relieved when Bobby left—I'd told him about the neighbor and what he'd done, and it got him riled in a way I had never seen.

The night before he left, we were sitting at the bar. He must have known that his father was ill, but all he talked about that night was the Celtics and how he thought they'd do this season, and when he had nothing more to say about them, when he'd run out of talk, he switched back to North Carolina and how he wished that woman's husband wasn't a cop.

"What are the fucking odds?" he said. When he had no more to say about it, but I could tell it was still on his mind, I started talking to him about Louise's neighbor—"He's a wacko," Bobby said—and I told him about the garbage or junk at the end of his driveway—"I hear there's good money in dumpster diving"—and I said he liked to shovel and shovel and shovel the snow and even the mud when there was no snow—"Like I said, a wacko"—and he only got serious when I told him about the night he'd broken into Louise's house.

"What do you mean?" he said.

It was a mistake to tell Bobby.

"He broke in?" he said. "You were there?"

I told him the story, how I thought it was the neighbor but how I had a sliver of doubt because I'd been half-asleep.

"Don't doubt this," he said. "It was him. Who else would it have been?"

Maybe somebody else, I wanted to say, but he was right.

Finally, he said: "I'm going to see him. I'm going to knock on his door."

I told him not to, that it was over, even though I had plans to say something to the neighbor when I saw him. But Bobby wouldn't drop it. He was appalled I planned to do nothing.

"He broke into your mother's house," he said. "And you want to drop it? Let it go?"

He finished his beer and the bartender brought him another, and Bobby asked him for a quarter, and the guy didn't understand what for. I didn't either. And so he said he couldn't give him a quarter. "Check the register for one, I'll give it right back," and the guy said he couldn't open the register unless there was a transaction, so Bobby said never fucking mind and he asked me for a quarter. He pulled out a twenty-dollar scratch-off ticket.

"I don't like him," Bobby said, quarter scraping away the ticket dust.

I think he meant the bartender, but he could have meant Louise's neighbor.

"I'm going to talk to him," he said. "That's fucked up."

He scrutinized the ticket, which was all scratched off.

"Don't do anything stupid," I told him, and that was the end of it for the night. The next day he was gone, and I hoped that when he got back, he would have forgotten about it.

. . .

With Bobby gone to his parents, my mother sometimes here and sometimes not, and my helplessness when it came to my daughter, I thought of Gizos. He'd come to visit me once, and he'd planned to bring his son, who ended up not coming.

I can't say for certain which year he visited—I think it was in 1998. I guess I could check the library's newspaper archive, because it was also the year Lenno got out of jail. All I know was it was the first time I'd seen Gizos since he'd left the reservation. It was spring or early summer, the season when, some years, I worked the least. The ground was too soft and wet, so when I did work it was in the garage fixing equipment, and I could take time off with no loss of progress in the woods. When he did show up, I was able to see a lot of him.

Because it had been twenty years since that visit, how he was back then was still how I knew him. He had married a Lakota man—Dave, who hated to be called David—who he'd met in California at an Indian center in the city. Gizos was out there working for a company as a technical writer. I'd always thought that his reason for moving so far away had to do with his father. Maybe it did have a small part, but the truth was that he still maintained a relationship with Lenno.

What his father thought of his son's marriage to a man and their adoption of a boy is beyond me. I like to think he fixed himself, or pretended to be fixed, but I doubt it. Part of me believes he continued to hurt Gizos in certain ways. Not violently, since Gizos was no longer a boy, but mentally. Verbally. I guess that's still violence.

A few years before Fredrick died in '91, Lenno had been sentenced to prison for involuntary manslaughter. He was driving 110 miles per hour drunk on I-95 northbound when he rammed into the back of a car and the driver, a white guy, spun down into the median and smashed headfirst into the trees and was dead on impact. He had a wife and son. It was all over the papers and in everybody's mouths and ears on the reservation, but only until the surviving wife's cousins—these two men from up north—came down and tried to light Lenno's house on fire. Except it wasn't his house but Bethany Francis's place right next to the elder apartments, and then everybody talked only about that. And so they forgot about Lenno, or they stopped talking about him, and a new chief was elected. Fredrick said Lenno would have lost that year even if he hadn't killed somebody. Lenno ended up serving only nine or ten of the fifteen years he was given, and that's why Gizos had come up: his father had been released.

Gizos and his husband were not poor. Where they lived, they weren't rich, but up this way they had money. Lenno knew that about his son, and maybe that's why he held him as close as his sick spirit would let him. While he was in prison, he ended up selling his house to the tribe so he could pay the restitution the court had ordered. When he was released, he had nowhere to go.

For some weeks before he could visit, Gizos put his father up in a motel. Gizos told me this when we spoke on the phone, and he told me again when he finally came up. Because I'd told him, Gizos knew that my mother had sold Fredrick's house, and he told his father, who wanted to buy it. But the person who had bought the house from my mother planned to turn it into a museum, thinking that Thoreau's stay merited such a thing, which is what he told Lenno, who told Gizos, who then told me, and of course that guy's plan never worked out and the tribe bought it. So Lenno, Gizos said, was looking off reservation. I really don't think Lenno had money. I mean, where would he have gotten money from? His son was paying his motel bills. Even though he said his father was the one paying, this is what I think: Gizos was the one who was buying the property and was going to give it to his father.

Lenno ended up finding a place about an hour south, and that's where he moved to after he—or Gizos—closed on the house. It had been so many years since then, and I still wondered sometimes what had happened to Lenno, if he was still living in that place or if he was dead.

The last time Gizos and I had spoken before he made the trip up here, he said he was bringing his son, and I was relieved he didn't bring him. I don't want to say I was jealous. But something in me felt off every time I thought of Gizos's boy. Maybe it was jealousy—his child knew him, where mine did not know me. But he didn't bring the boy. If he had, I wonder how Lenno would have thought of him, how he would have treated him. I like to think he would have loved him.

Gizos stayed for a little over a week, and for the first few days he slept at the motel with his father. And then one day when he stopped by I noticed he had all his luggage in the back of his rental car, this ugly orange hatchback Subaru with mud caked all up over the chassis and doors. He was the type of driver that always backed into a place, so I saw all his stuff through the window when he parked.

The front of my house was a giant mud puddle, and I had set down square pieces of chipboard and set foldout chairs on top of those, and that was where I was sitting when he arrived. He came over from his car, and I can still remember that sharp sigh—a real one—that he let out as he sat. And then he asked if he could stay with me for the rest of the time he was here.

When I said yes, he offered to pay me.

I told him no.

. . .

We went hiking one day up to Katahdin and we went to the coast and he bought some craft beer from Bar Harbor Brewing, which was a type he liked, but he didn't drink when he was with me, maybe because I was in AA. We went to the movies one day and watched *The Truman Show*, and when we left, we kept saying to each other, "You'd tell me, right, if I were in a TV show but didn't know it?" and every so often one of us would pretend to talk into some invisible radio and mumble that the other was on to us.

. . .

Gizos told me he wanted to find his mother, but that he didn't know where she would be. We were sitting in the chairs on the wet chipboard covering the soggy and muddy ground.

"Did you ask your father if he knows?" I said.

"He won't tell me," Gizos said.

Maybe this was why he'd had all his luggage with him that day. Maybe they'd gotten into a fight.

"Your birth certificate?" I said. "Her name must be on that."

"It is," he said. "Willow Wintle." He puffed air from his mouth. "Isn't that a nice name? Willow Wintle. Willow Wintle."

He kept saying the name but grew quiet.

"Have you thought to look for your father?" he asked. "I mean your biological father?"

"No," I said. And that was the truth. I still don't know where he is or if he's alive.

"Why not?" he asked.

"I always felt I had a father," I said.

I was kind of like Elizabeth. And based on what I knew, how I felt about my own father, I expected nothing to come from this story I wanted to give her. But I didn't know if anybody else had lived within such a strange set of circumstances as I had, as she had, as we had.

"Always?" he said.

"Sure," I said. "I grew up with Fredrick, and since my earliest memories he's been there."

"But you must think about your birth father? Or have wondered about him?"

"I have, yes," I said. "But I've never wanted to find him."

I could see why Gizos thought I might be like him: we were both without a blood parent. But there was a difference between us: I had somebody to fill that space, while he did not.

"I sometimes worry that our son—Dave's and mine—will wonder about his birth parents too much, and that wonder will pull him toward them, to find them, kind of like how I want to find my mother. Did I tell you I know his birth parents? I don't *know them* know them, but I know enough. They're not together. I know more about his mother than I do about his father. They were both bad off. Very bad off. Well, I think the mother more so than the father. The boy was addicted to drugs when he was born. His mother is Coeur d'Alene and his father's Tukudeka or Shoshone—I forget which, but I think it's Tukudeka—but he's not on the census.

"Dave and I had a long talk before we adopted the boy. I get that it's best to put Native children with Native families, I do, but we worried about his culture, what he, this Coeur d'Alene and Tukudeka boy, was losing by growing up with a Lakota and Penobscot. What would his culture be? Would he take Dave's? Mine? Some mix of both?" Gizos laughed. "This is such an Indian thing to worry about."

It was, and still is. There are too many unnecessary things to think about when it comes to existing as a skeejin.

"But the boy had nowhere to go," Gizos said. "I mean nowhere. His mother didn't want him, his father didn't want him. The boy's grandmother on his mother's side was dead, and the grandfather was too sickly. I worry he'll wonder about them and only find out that his place with them was never real or could not work out, that his culture may have been, since the beginning, inaccessible to him. But here's the thing: he's Coeur d'Alene and Tukudeka. He can't be Lakota or Penobscot. He can only be what he is, and he'll always be there. I just hope he grows up to know that, to understand it. That's his blood.

"He is cute though," Gizos added. "Damn cute. Funny what wins in the end."

For one of the only times in my life, I felt like an outsider around Gizos. This was something I had no claim to talk about—as in I had no Native blood—yet I knew and still know what it was like to both not belong and belong, what it was like to feel invisible inside the great, great dream of being. We're all alike, even when we're not.

. . .

When Gizos went back to California, I stopped going to AA for about two weeks, and of all the people to get on my back about it and to worry, it was Bobby. I started to have these strange existential thoughts, like I wasn't really real. It's hard to explain exactly, because I knew I was real, but I didn't feel it. It was like my spirit did not match my body, as if my body were where it should be but my invisible innards were not. I could not for the life of me reconcile my existence.

And I did fear these strange feelings would take Elizabeth should she learn of her blood, learn that she had a secret part in her and that, in this world, that part might erase another. But she needed to know that her blood was her blood. Nothing could take that away, and nothing could even come close to capturing it, especially not percentages on pieces of paper. Because we're more than that. Or at least she was—she'd got it in her, that connection to a past time and people, no matter what anybody said.

It's not always funny what wins in the end.

13

WHILE HE WAS VISITING HIS PARENTS, BOBBY CALLED twice from a number I didn't recognize, and since I didn't recognize it, I didn't answer. But when the phone stopped ringing and then not fifteen seconds later again started its brrring, I picked up. He sounded sober, which I found interesting because it was past ten in the evening and he was usually drunk by then.

He didn't have much to say, really, and he didn't know when he'd be back. He didn't even fill me in—he spoke as if I were up to speed with where he'd gone and why he'd gone there, and I thought about pretending I had no idea what he was talking about. But he sounded down, so I thought better of it.

The only specific thing I can really remember that he said was, "He's going soon, so I'll be here till he's left," and whether or not his siblings would be joining him he did not say.

· · ·

Sometimes Louise got overwhelmed by the elephant, her baby, and she got snippy and sharp with me. The first time this happened was a few days after I gave it to her. She was sitting in her recliner with the elephant in her arms. I was sitting on the bed, and I thought we both were watching TV, but she was not. She was trying to put the elephant to sleep, or so I suppose, because she said, "He won't get any rest, and you're not helping."

At first it took most everything in me not to laugh, and if her face had not been so serious, I would have.

"You never help me," she said. "Never."

I asked her what she wanted help with, and she said I should know.

"It's not rocket science," she said. "It's a baby. And I need help."

"Do you want me to take him?" I said.

"No," she said, and she put her head back and shut her eyes.

I laughed about this that night, and even Bobby thought it was funny when I told him on the phone. He said she never acted that way when he was around, and he said that maybe I was shit with kids and she was just pointing that out. The next time I saw the elephant in her arms, I laughed to myself about the seriousness with which she took caring for that stuffed animal and again her jab at me for not helping.

She wasn't always like this, wasn't always scrutinizing me. It was rare, that behavior, and when it happened, it never lasted very long. Around the fifth or sixth time it did happen, though, it became unfunny. Bobby was still gone, and so I had been with Louise for quite some time. Louise was in her recliner, and she had set the elephant in the bed, right behind me, had it tucked between two pillows. The TV was on—that same show that always seemed to be playing, the one about the mortician. I don't know how long I'd been there, but I was getting uncomfortable on the bed, so without thinking I took one of the pillows holding the elephant in place and I used it to prop myself up on my elbow.

Louise said, "You're unbelievable."

I put the pillow right back, but it was too late.

"Unbelievable," she said again, and she rose and went to the bed and took the elephant.

How do you correct such a mistake as this?

"You're lucky you didn't wake him," she said.

I could only play along. "Sorry," I said, holding back that laugh.

She was shaking her head, looking down at the elephant or at something past it, some idea in her lap, and then said what sounded like, "No wonder I'll leave you."

At first it made no sense, just gibberish. But that night at home I couldn't stop thinking about it, couldn't stop trying to make sense of it. It came to me the next day as I was out in the woods on a small job, working the skidder. Did she mean my father? My real father, the one she had left? Had she seen him sitting on the bed, taking his son's pillow? Had she thought that child, that elephant, was me as an infant? That seemed to fit, seemed to make sense, and if that was the truth of this situation, it was such a strange feeling to be both so loved and so hated at the same time.

I didn't know what type of hatred my mother felt for my blood father. While nobody can fix what's been done—nobody can erase the memory—I thought I could at least try to be better, in her eyes, than my father, even if it was just for a stuffed elephant, even if it was for a daughter who didn't know her blood father.

. . .

Bobby came back and wanted to meet me at the bar, and I left him hanging. I intended to go, to meet him, but when I stepped outside, I saw Roger coming back home, and with him, in the bed of his truck, was a bed, a mattress. Maybe full-size. It was wrapped in plastic, because I'm sure Roger smelled what I smelled: rain.

He carried the mattress by himself across the yard and up the stairs to the house, where Mary held the screen door open for him, and when she tried to help him carry it, he set the mattress down on the steps so it was slanted, and she tried to pull it but it was too heavy. He carried it all the way in by himself, and he went back to the truck and grabbed the bed frame, long metal boards that had been disassembled and taped together into a bunch. As he carried them up the steps, Mary was not at the door, and he struggled to get inside but he managed.

He then left in his truck, and he was back again before too long. This time he unloaded boxes. Many boxes, twenty or more. And baskets. One was a nice utility basket, filled with blankets, and another, worn, had pots and pans sticking out. Mary helped with this load, carrying a box indoors and going to get another. Roger carried two boxes at a time. None fell from his grip, even though he moved with haste, the way an animal might when it has fallen behind in building a nest, a home.

Again, the truck emptied. Again, gone and back in little time. This time, he had brought back a large object, and only when he stood up in the bed of the truck and removed the blanket that covered it did I see that it was a dresser with what I think were many stickers stuck to one side (it can be hard to see from so far away). Roger needed help carrying the dresser. I don't know who helped him load it in the back to begin with. Maybe he'd done it himself, had exerted the last of his energy. He needed Mary's hands, her strength. But before they carried it indoors, she brought him water in a cup, which he drank in one tilt.

My phone rang and I ignored it. Roger and Mary unloaded the dresser, and Roger walked backward up the steps and through the door propped open with a cinder block. When it was inside, Mary came back out and with her foot she pushed the cinder block off the steps and shut the door. Neither of them came back out for close to thirty minutes, and in the meantime I stayed outside, sitting, and I went indoors only once to get a jacket.

During that silence, I thought I heard yelling from inside their house. But the shouts could have been from somewhere else, carried downriver by the wind. When they came out, Mary stayed on the steps and Roger got in his truck. If they said anything to each other, they did so quietly. That was my curse, my distance.

Gone and back, and it was the last trip. In the back of the truck were two nightstands, each a different type of wood. One a two-drawer mahogany, the other taller and built of light wood the color of sand. Besides those two items was an assortment of things like a tall lamp and a mirror and a wardrobe box filled with what, I don't know.

And then there was Elizabeth, up front. I noticed she was there only when she got out of the truck and Mary shut the door for her and walked behind her up the steps.

And then she was gone, and I thought I wouldn't see her again that night. Roger carried each item in. Mary did not help. When he finished unloading the nightstands, he walked to his truck but turned around and spoke with somebody—Mary or Elizabeth— about something. Whatever it was, he said he'd get it.

After he'd gone, Elizabeth came outside. She had on a sweatshirt with her hood up as she sat on the steps, cigarette between her fingers. When did she start smoking? Could she hear me from there? I wondered if I was that far away.

When she was done, she was gone again, and in her long absence, with no distractions, I felt it, the wondering, the speculation, the why, until I settled on my worst fears. How can I possibly describe what I felt? How is the spirit's rapid descent accurately captured? What I felt was not unlike the rumble of the ground to an ant crossing a freeway.

Roger came back, and with him a man I could not recognize. The sun was going down and night was coming.

Out back of the house they made a fire, a small one that crackled and sprayed flamed ash. They fed it logs, kept it burning, until all was dark except that side of the river. Their bodies were just bodies, their features disfigured by shadow and occasionally by the fire smoke as it swirled this way and that, a screen of gases and water vapor. The smell was calming.

For what I had thought—the why of it all—I felt this was ceremonial. Fredrick had done something similar for Louise countless times, and I kept thinking this even when Elizabeth and Mary joined Roger and the man out back around the fire.

My side of the river was pure dark. No lights were on in my house, and I sat where I had all afternoon, in the same chair. But I was there, felt present at that fire, the one I so stupidly thought was ceremonial. It turned out it wasn't. It was just a fire, the life around it, and they all cooked with the flame. Two of them held long sticks and handed around a bag, their shadowed heads rising as Elizabeth blew out the flaming tip of the stick before eating.

This is ceremony too, I suppose.

The fire did not go out for hours. Elizabeth left first, then Mary, and then Roger and that man but not until late in the night. It was two in the morning when he and Roger drove off together, and when they came back, they were in separate vehicles. One was Elizabeth's car. They left once more, but only Roger returned. Only after all this did the fire die. But still: it glowed red until the sun rose—the fire burned all night in the cold of fall.

So that is what I saw: Elizabeth coming home. And I didn't think it was a good thing.

14

ONCE ELIZABETH ARRIVED BACK HOME, I RARELY went anywhere. I went to check on Louise once—wanting to make sure she was locking her door—but that was it. I stayed outside, every day, watching, acting like I had things to do in case anyone spotted me from across the river. And after a while, the strangest thing began to happen. Late at night, somebody kept ringing me. If I didn't pick up, whoever it was didn't leave a message. If I answered, they hung up. It went on for eight days total.

At first, I thought it was Bobby, calling drunk about something and then hanging up when I answered. He could get weird, fifteen, twenty beers in. But I asked him, and when he said it wasn't him, he seemed sincere about it.

So somebody else was calling me, and I started to think it was Mary. The calls came after midnight, around one in the morning. For a few nights I took my house phone outdoors with me and waited in the cold, cold fall for the call. As I waited, I watched across the river for any life, light, any movement from within

Elizabeth's parents' house. But I saw none. And of course the call came. I sat on the steps, holding the ringing phone. Across the river the house was quiet, stilled, no light or movement from within. When I answered, the caller hung up. If it was Mary, I thought, she was calling quietly, discreetly, from somewhere in the dark of that house.

I thought it was her, trying to build up the courage to tell me what was wrong with Elizabeth, especially since Elizabeth wasn't going to work; she was home all day except sometimes when she left with Mary.

I went out and bought a new phone at Best Buy that could display the digits of incoming calls. I was excited to see what number would come up, and when the call came—same time, one in the morning—I was ready, pen in hand, to write down the number that lit up on the small rectangular screen on the phone. But no number showed.

I had no goddamn clue I had to add that caller ID to my phone from the phone company. So that's what I did the next day. Right when they opened at eight. It turned out the calls weren't coming from Mary. The call that came in that night was from a motel in Sterling, Colorado. When I called the number back, nobody answered. I thought to try it again, but I held off until late morning, and when I did call back, somebody answered, a woman, and she said she hadn't used the phone, that she had just checked into the room. I asked her where she was, and she said none of my business, and so I said, No, no, what state are you in, where is this call coming from, and she said Super 8 in Sterling, Colorado.

The next night the call came again, this time from a number I couldn't trace, so I had to call the operator and pay an extra fee for the information. The operator had a nice voice, like he was meant to do what he was doing, and he said the call came from

South Yankton, Nebraska, and he said the phone wasn't registered with any business, or it was a pay phone.

The next night, the call came once more. This time from Iowa City. They were getting closer and closer and closer to me. What next? I thought. Illinois? Indiana? Massachusetts? Portland? Overtown? Maybe all of this was coincidental, I thought, but there was something too neat about it. I won't lie: I was a bit worried. It was like somebody was stalking me, coming for me.

. . .

My obsessive worrying about why Elizabeth was home and the mysterious callers made me forget about Bobby for a while, and I wish it hadn't, because maybe I could have prevented him from beating up Louise's neighbor and getting arrested. But instead, I spent my days outside, tending to a yard that needed no tending, tinkering with my truck that needed no tinkering, tidying the riverbank where garbage had floated downriver and gotten stuck, and the whole time I made it look like I was doing these things, but I was really watching for my daughter across the river. And at night it was much of the same, except I'd sit out on the porch with that phone in my hand and my sights set on something I thought was coming. It got to the point where I wasn't eating anything, and it reminded me of the days I used to drink, which sort of snapped me out of whatever I was in and got me to leave for a while.

Bobby didn't tell me right away about what he'd done. We were at Louise's, watching her after her first ECT treatment, and he was telling me about his father's passing. We were in the kitchen, and he didn't seem sad. In fact, I was the one who brought up the funeral.

"Was it a nice service?" I asked him.

"I don't know," he said. "It was a service. My sister organized it. She organized it before he even died. It was like she saw his death, had everything planned, right down to the meals at the funeral parlor."

"Were your brothers there too?" I asked.

"No," he said, and that was as far as he let me in on the matter.

Bobby got a glass of water, drank some of it, and started to tell the story.

It had happened after Bobby left the bar that night—the night I was supposed to meet him, the night Elizabeth moved back home.

"I got him to admit it," Bobby said, and he finished the water.

I didn't know what he was talking about at first, so I asked, "Who?"

"What do you mean, who? The neighbor. You should have seen the look on his face."

I was stunned. Bobby leaned on the sideboard and I stood in the center of the kitchen, listening to him.

"I came up here after the bar the night you didn't show up," he said, "and parked along the road and waited, just shut my truck off and was in the dark. I really didn't think I'd see anybody. Christ, it was going on midnight when he came out. That little fucker. I didn't know where he was heading, but he shut the screen door all soft and walked down the steps and started digging around in that pile of shit he's got. That sheet metal was loud too. I heard it through my closed windows. I'm surprised it didn't wake up the whole street.

"Right, so he's digging and digging and tossing shit, making all this noise"—Bobby was waving his arms—"and so I get out of my truck and let the door shut quiet and start walking toward him. 'You,' I say to him. I'm right at the beginning of his mud driveway. He turns around and goes—this is what he says—'Me?'

Me! That's what he says. 'Yeah, you,' I say back. Who the fuck else would I be talking to?"

"You said that to him?" I asked.

"No, I'm telling you that. Listen. 'What do you want?' he says, and I say, 'What do you got there?' And he says, 'I already sold what I want to sell. The rest is mine.' The rest is his? I couldn't see that well, but I imagine everything there—all of it—was crap. I step closer to him and just start talking like meeting, at this hour, is normal. I ask him where he goes to find stuff, and he has loads to say about that: on Tuesdays he's up at Burlington Coat Factory, that's the day they dump merchandise, and then on Wednesdays he's over at Old Navy—the one by the on-ramp to 95 south, not the one near the mall—out in the back, but he goes there at night because workers can see the dumpster during the day and they phone the police, and then Thursdays and Fridays he goes around all the other stores because he doesn't know the day they dump out stuff. Can you imagine doing that? Something's got to be wrong with you."

"Did he ask what you were doing?" I said.

"Yeah, he asked, after he ran out of shit to say about the art of dumpster diving."

Bobby leaned forward and looked out the kitchen window at the neighbor's house. He leaned back again on the sideboard.

"And I tell him I'm there to see him," Bobby said, "which he again says he isn't selling anything else. I tell him he misunderstands me. I'm there to see him about something that happened. 'What happened?' he asks, and I say, 'You know what happened,' and I point up at Louise's window. He knows right then what I'm talking about, and he bolts for his house. But I grab him by the shirt and yank him back. 'What were you doing up there?' I ask him, still pointing, and he says, 'I don't know what you're talking about, I wasn't anywhere.' Bullshit, I say to him. There's something about seeing a frightened face at night that's scary, the way his porch light reached and lit his face so the bags under his eyes looked sunken and dark."

Bobby laughed. "Poor kid," he said.

"So what happened?" I said. "You beat him up?"

"I didn't beat him up," he said. "I just slapped him around is all. I didn't even punch him. I open-handed him a few times, and then he started screaming real loud and kicking me and digging his fingernails into my face, so I held him in a way he couldn't dig at me, had to put him on the ground and put my knees over his arms. I was about to punch him until he says, 'I'm sorry!' Just like that: 'I'm sorry!'"

"You know there's something obviously wrong with him, right?" I said. "He's not all there."

He waved off what I had said. "He is now," Bobby said. "I'm sorry—who does that, breaks into an old lady's house?"

I asked if he'd found out why the neighbor had done it.

"He didn't say," Bobby said. "I asked him why, but by that point in time he was spitting at me and trying to squirm away. I started to get up—I felt I'd scared him enough—and as I did, I heard an engine, tires on the road, coming down our way. That skinny-headed fuck flagged them down before I could get in my truck. And as luck would have it, it was the police—'We watch this place closely,' one of them said—and when they had me in cuffs, two more showed up and even an ambulance to check out the neighbor, whose name is either Brett or Rhett, and Brett or Rhett started to act real hurt and was taken up to Saint Joe's while I was taken to the station. All they had there was one little tiny cell, and they didn't even put me in it. They let me sit in a chair in one of the back offices. Christ, I could have escaped if I wanted to."

Bobby continued to tell me how they'd treated him well. The two officers who had shown up and arrested Bobby were the two

I'd spoken with when the neighbor had broken in, so they knew the case. They also knew about the neighbor, Brett or Rhett—he had all sorts of strange charges in his past; he'd once stormed a store butt-naked, or so Bobby said—and so they didn't see Bobby as a vicious criminal but more of an idiot who could not behave under intense circumstances. So maybe that was why they didn't put him in a cell or cuff him when they brought him to the station. Or maybe it was because he was white.

Bobby had no remorse for attacking the neighbor, but he was upset about being caught. He was facing criminal charges and would have to go to court, and until his hearing in December he was unable to leave the state, which got him angry, and while he was cursing, getting another glass of water, I asked who had bailed him out.

"Someone you don't know," he said, but I knew Bobby had no one besides me, and so Louise was the only person I could think of.

15

I WAS AT LOUISE'S, SITTING ON THE BED, WHEN SHE started talking to me about Bobby's father. I wasn't supposed to leave her alone after a treatment (you have to sign a paper saying you won't), but I didn't want to be at her place, because I couldn't stop worrying about Elizabeth. All Elizabeth did was go in and out of her house, taking smoke breaks, always wearing her hoodie and a pair of basketball shorts. She'd never been like that before—it was a strange sight. She was dressing differently. I was so used to seeing her leave in a blue dress or jeans with a red blouse that seeing her in the same outfit every day had me worried. It reminded me of my mother, the days she would stay in the same clothes. I wanted to be home, wanted to be able to watch and see if Elizabeth or Mary or Roger would come home and give something away by saying something loud enough to hear, but Louise's ECT treatments took up a lot of time. At first it was one every so often, a gradual upward climb, and then she was up to three a week: Monday, Wednesday, Friday.

Bobby had brought her to one once because I'd had to work, and I thought he'd take her again if need be, but he had found the experience to be a bit worrisome, especially the part when the nurses or whatever they were brought her out and she walked slowly, sloppily, to the wheelchair, and her eyes were glazed and jellied as she handled the stuffed elephant.

There was something peaceful in her face when her treatments were over. When she sat in that wheelchair after a treatment, her face was the most restful I had seen it, like the electricity had put up a wall blocking the terribleness that can be human feeling. I wonder what, exactly, she felt.

While I was visiting with her that day, she was having difficulty remembering, was sitting in her recliner with the stuffed elephant, and then she said, "That poor boy, that poor boy."

When I asked who, she couldn't give a name.

"You know," she said, but I didn't know. And I don't think she did either. I don't think she even knew who I was that day.

"Remember?" she said. "That boy. The one whose father just died."

"Bobby?" I said.

"No, no, that's not it."

Who else would she be talking about? It's only now I have this strange thought that she could have been speaking for all boys everywhere.

"I saw him," she said. She held the elephant in the dip of her arm and scratched its head. "He was very upset about it."

"About what?"

"His father," she said. "Poor, poor thing. I couldn't console him. Not one bit."

"When was this?"

"I don't know. Does it matter? The boy was upset. Was crying so hard he could barely breathe. I said to him, 'You must have loved him so much. He was lucky to have you as a son.' And at that he cried even harder. I cooked him a meal. I asked him what he wanted, and he tried to say he didn't need anything, but I said, 'No, no, you need to eat.' I made him eggs and a can of corned beef hash I've had since, jesum, I don't even remember when, and I made him some grilled bread. Did I mention my toaster's broken? I had to make it in a frying pan with some butter. He stopped crying by the time he went back home."

I never really knew what the two of them did or talked about when they were alone. Honestly, I never thought much about it until it was clear Louise knew things I didn't, and I imagine Bobby too knew things I didn't. I used to think they just watched TV like us, her and me. I never thought differently of Bobby after that. Maybe I did, but in a good way. He became more human, more knowable.

I asked Louise if, as he ate, he stopped talking about the death of his father.

"Oh, no, Lord no. That's all he talked about that day." She paused. "Do I smoke?"

"Do you smoke?" I said.

"I want a cigarette."

Louise had never smoked.

"Maybe that boy left one of his."

She got up from the chair and carried the elephant in her arms. She puttered around the bedroom, looking on top of her dresser and in drawers. When she found none, she sat back down.

"Does he give you cigarettes?" I said.

"Who?"

"Bobby—I mean that boy."

"Just forget I said anything."

If the elephant were a child, its leg would be broken; Louise was sitting on it in a way that it had bent backward.

That doctor was on the TV, and the narrator was talking about the standard Y incision.

"I do hope he's feeling better," Louise said.

And from what she said then, Bobby's father—or the boy's father—worked all day, every day, his entire life to support his family. He worked at a lumberyard that no longer existed, doing work similar to mine, and he was up every morning at three and didn't get home until six in the evening. He worked most Saturdays, and on Sundays he spent most of his time tending to everything else, from fixing the house to repairing their car, an old four-door Buick that I guess he still had, or did until he died. When nothing else needed to be done—or what could be done was put aside—Bobby's father, Andrew was his name, worked on projects in most seasons besides winter. He built his children a tree house, and he built his wife a garden shed—"about the size of a small cabin," Louise said. And one summer, when he had no projects, after he'd helped his wife landscape the yard, he borrowed an excavator and dug a hole out back of the house and made a pond where frogs croaked in the tall, tall grasses, and where two ducks returned each summer and had their babies; and when time was kind and opened up to him an empty space in an afternoon in which his biggest wants and dreams could flourish, he tinkered with the truck he'd hoped to drive one day but knew he never would: a red tarnished Chevrolet from the late '40s.

What a life, I think now, one I would have given anything to have.

"The boy was upset most about that," Louise said. "That his father never got to finish the truck. I think he said he had to sell it. Not the boy, his father."

"Why?"

"He didn't say."

"And you didn't ask?"

"Why would I pry?" Louise said. "He was upset enough as it was."

I don't know why I said this next bit to her, but I did: "Did it occur to you that maybe he wanted you to ask about it?"

"What do you know?" she spat. "You're just a boy."

. . .

Before I went home that night I left a single cigarette on her dresser, and as I was leaving through the front door, I looked back down the hall and watched her shadow rise to the dresser and then fall back down and disappear.

. . .

Mary used to sleepwalk. Before I bought the phone with the caller ID, I thought maybe she was calling me in her sleep.

She didn't sleepwalk all the time, just some of the time. The way she slept, it was like she was always fighting something: she twitched and closed her eyes tightly. She never complained about getting poor sleep, but to me it looked very unrestful. Occasionally, I woke to find her sitting up in bed, talking. Nothing coherent. It was always mumbles or one or two clear words here and there. Once, I woke to her pulling my hair, and she leaned in close to my face and said, "Stay out of my way."

. . .

In the late spring—almost summer—of 1990, I found Mary in the kitchen in the middle of the night, messing with the wall clock. (This was when she began to stay with me the most, when she had three dresser drawers full of clothes and makeup in my bathroom.) I really didn't like that clock; the numbers were roman numerals and always confused me. She had taken the clock off the small nail and was twisting the dial in the back. I don't know what she was trying to do, what her brain was telling her, but she kept twisting and twisting the knob in the back until both the big and little hands were where she wanted them—some specific time in the past.

In the morning, we were drinking coffee at the table, which was what we always did before work. She asked why the clock was off the wall and why it was set to the wrong time. I usually told her what she did in the night, but for some reason I lied and said that in the night I had woken and the ticking of the clock had disturbed me, so I'd gone and taken it off the wall and removed the battery, which I'd since put back in, but I had yet to reset the time.

She righted the time and put the clock on the wall.

This was the day she would tell me she was pregnant.

. . .

When I got back from work that day—the day after Mary took down the clock—I found her on the porch steps, in shorts and a long-sleeve black shirt. Her hair was pulled back, as it always was when she was home, or when she was comfortable. Usually I found her like this: on those steps, holding a lit cigarette. But on that day, she held nothing.

She told me to sit down and she scooted over and between us set my overlarge lunch pail streaked with motor oil, and she said without looking, "I'm pregnant, Charles," and to that I said, "No shit," not knowing—and still not knowing—if that was appropriate, but my intent was and still is that of joyful surprise.

"Yes shit," Mary said. "Yes shit."

I said we could build on my place, if she wanted, that I could put in a new bedroom, and I even recall saying I'd get things done, things I'd intended to do but had not, like fix the leaky sink and get at the mold that was spreading on the wall beside the refrigerator. But Mary looked at me with red and watery eyes, her cheeks the light pink color you'd get if you rubbed a pink flower across a piece of white paper. And she said, "The baby can't be yours."

I asked her what she meant. How could I not? But Mary wouldn't tell me. She stopped talking. I got angry. Why wouldn't I? I was yelling and yelling and yelling, but then I began to beg her. "Would you please talk?" I said. "Say something, anything."

She said it had to be this way.

"Why?" I said. "What do you mean?"

But then she rose and went inside and was back out no more than five minutes later, and in her hands she had black garbage bags filled with her clothes. I stayed on the steps as she brought the bags to her car. She came back to me, and I didn't know that that was the last time I'd see the Mary I had loved, the one I had grown up with and thought I'd spend the rest of my life with.

She did not say goodbye to me that day, and she did not give me a hug or anything of the sort. All she said was, "This is for the baby, you have to understand that."

I never knew what her plan was. I pieced it together from over here as I watched my world unfold in someone else's hands. And when I knew, I knew, too, the why. Then I understood immediately: she wanted Elizabeth to be "Native." There was a time I did think that Roger really was her father, that Mary had something going on with him, but then it did not make sense why over the years she would come back when she did, to see me, and even that one day when she brought her, my child.

No matter what she did, no matter how big the lie was, Mary loves Elizabeth. It was for her she did this. It was for those who would come after her. It was for a chance at something greater. It goes deeper than blood.

I was a mess after, and all these years later I still was. After she left that day, having told me she was pregnant, I had so much hope she would come back, that we would be a family, that I'd build that extension, our child's bedroom, that I'd fix the sink and the mold. And over the years I'd watch Elizabeth grow before my eyes and I'd teach her what I could—maybe not a lot, since I'm not the greatest of men, the greatest of fathers—and then down the road she would have a brother, or a sister, just some small body that the child would look at and see and admire as the soul's responsibility to love, and the two of them would grow up together and fight and laugh and fight and cry for the other until they were both old enough and began to go separate ways but were forever held together by the invisible rope of having experienced each other, and they both would watch us, their mother and father, get closer to the Silence until we entered it, and the rest would go on, and on, and on.

16

THE BUILDING WHERE LOUISE GOT HER ECTS ADMIN-
istered reminded me of a spider. I was telling Gizos that as we
walked inside with Louise. I'd been surprised when he showed
up, but also not surprised. He'd been on my mind. He was back
for reasons that seem all too familiar to this story, for reasons
concerning death: his father's liver was going.

As we walked, I told Gizos that if you had an aerial view
of the layout of the building, if you could look down from way
above as if you were a cloud, it would be exactly like a spider.
The very core, the body of the building, was the main entrance:
a security guard was the first person you saw when you entered.
He was a tiny, tiny man with pale skin and a shirt and pants too
big for him, was always making sure we carried nothing sharp
that a patient could get hold of. Past him was a lady behind
a desk, who knew us now, and let us—Louise and me—go by
without name tags (they made Gizos wear one, though). Louise usually sat in a wheelchair, which I pushed, even though

she could walk. Eight hallways branched out from the spider's body, and they each ended in a dead end. I had walked them all, waiting for Louise, so I knew that at least all but one ended with double doors that read "Exit," the signs lit with plastic red flames. The one hall I wasn't sure about was inaccessible unless you were visiting somebody who was under watch or somebody who was severely depressed. When you made it to that door you had to ring a buzzer, and the overhead camera would turn with a vrrrr and if you were permitted to pass, the door would bing and the locks would release. It was a place my mother would have gone, could have gone, and, I thought, still could go.

It's hard to believe that Elizabeth knows this place.

. . .

I should have known. I shouldn't have been surprised. The moment I wheeled Louise down that spider's leg and into the ECT waiting room, the moment I saw Mary sitting there on the little green bench, a magazine spread open and hiding half her face like a scarf, the moment Louise, not quite herself but partway so, said to her, to Mary, "Were you here last time? I remember you," and the moment Mary and I looked, horrified, into each other's eyes like we had been here before, not quite in this place but in this feeling of dread and warning and rupture, that was when I realized whose appointment was before Louise's, who I would see wheeled out through that door.

. . .

Elizabeth did not come out for some time. It was in this waiting that I began to understand how long these treatments could last. Louise, once, was back there for an hour and a half.

At some point after the first few moments when Louise and I were settling down in the chairs, waiting, I remembered that he, Gizos, was with us, off using the bathroom. It's so hard to remember and make two monumental moments coexist, but it's true: on the day I learned the truth about her, Gizos was with me. And now, looking back on that time in the waiting room, I wish he had not been there, hadn't been with us, hadn't shown up after all these years, unchanged except that his skin was growing a bit paler and coarse. I wish he hadn't had car trouble that morning, hadn't said he would come, that he could do nothing else without a car, that he'd love to see Louise. If he hadn't been there, Mary and I could have ignored each other, but when he walked through that door and he saw her, Mary, he could not help himself. He had to talk to her. He called her doos and got so close that Mary had no other option but to give in and set her magazine down and rise up from the cushioned bench she sat on.

"I heard about your dad," Mary said. Two people from the same place, the same people. They did not embrace, but Gizos had his hand on her shoulder. While Mary went to the bathroom, Gizos said he felt a sort of discordance between him and her, and I told him it was probably because I was there.

"Why's that?" he asked.

"I'll tell you later."

My wait for Elizabeth to come out, even though it must have been a little less than an hour, was the longest wait of my life, and that's saying something when I consider the wait for her to come home from the hospital, and then the wait to find Fredrick, to learn what had happened to him. The blood she did not know about that ran through her body was tainted, flawed. This was why it was so important she know all of this, who I was and who her grandmother was. This was why her body's secret history was important to know.

I did not want to look at her when she came out through the door, wheeled in the wheelchair.

"So young," Louise said. "That poor girl. So young."

I shushed her, which made her speak more. "I'm just saying that it's a shame. That's all I'm saying. That's all."

Gizos began to talk to her, to distract her.

Elizabeth was gone so fast from that room. And she spoke only once, and it was when she was down the hall and almost out of earshot. Mary whooshed her away.

Louise almost did not have her appointment that day. Something in her became irate and uncooperative. As the nurse came to get her, Louise asked Gizos if he was ready. She did not remember him, and she kept referring to him as Gus, like she was afraid to mispronounce his name, and she was convinced he needed to go back there with her.

"I don't trust that man," she said. I think she was referring to the doctor. "Gus needs to be with me. He needs to."

Maybe I would have handled this situation better if, you know, what happened hadn't happened. I'm not proud of it, but I screamed at Louise, crouched right down to her level and yelled inches from her face: "You're going back there and that's that! Got it?"

"Sir"—that's what the nurse said, Sir—"don't you yell at her like that."

"Fine," Louise said. "It'll be your fault then. Like everything else is."

Nothing happened except for regret.

. . .

I heard her. I heard Elizabeth as Mary wheeled her out the door.

"Who were they?" she asked.

"Nobody," Mary said.

Is there a word that means something is both true and false? I've looked, and I've yet to find one. I can come up with statements that are the example. "I am your father" is one that comes to mind.

. . .

Back at Louise's, I told Gizos. I told him the secret Mary and I shared, that that girl, that young, wonderful girl Mary had had with her, was our daughter. And for the first time ever, I said out loud what I wanted to do, what I planned to do: tell her the truth.

"What?" was all he said, but I didn't say anything because Louise cut us off and asked Gus to make her tea, which I made but told him to bring to her when it was ready. We waited in the kitchen while the microwave warmed water for tea; I was sitting on the windowsill, blowing smoke into that sharp fall cold. Gizos stood in the center of the room.

Gizos knew about our past, Mary and me, but I didn't think he wanted to believe what I said, that Elizabeth was my daughter and that I wanted her to know the truth. And there's no real point here in going back through it all. He just didn't want to believe it, and when he asked why she would do that—why Mary would lie—I told him why, and he said that was ridiculous, and I said that was the truth, and he said something else was going on here, and I told him there was nothing going on there, that if there were something else I would have figured it out over these past twenty-some-odd years, and he said I could have missed something, that she—Mary—wasn't like that, and I said to him,

So it was me, then? No, that's not what I'm saying, he said, and I said, It sure sounds like it, and he said, Well maybe, and I said, Well maybe what? and he said, Nothing, nothing at all.

"Forget it," he said, but he didn't stop there. "You can't tell her."

"It's none of your business," I said.

"Sure," he said. "Just my thoughts."

"Just your thoughts."

Louise yelled from the bedroom, asking about her tea.

Before he brought Louise the tea, which he spilled a little of on the floor, he said it one more time. "Don't."

I wanted to say, "You don't want me to tell her the truth? You don't want me to give her the part of her she doesn't know belongs to her? You would have me deny her her full story?" but instead I pointed to the floor and said, "Clean that up after."

17

I KEPT TAKING LOUISE TO HER APPOINTMENTS. I DID think about asking Bobby to help. But even if I had wanted to, I don't think he would have let me ask the question. After I told him what had happened, he was too busy saying "Jesus Christ" over and over again as I drove him to the bar. "Jesus. She was there?"

I was driving Bobby to the bar, and he had no other words. Nothing sympathetic, I mean, but that's him. What he jumped on and stayed focused on was that I said I was going to tell her the truth.

"Charles," he said. "You can't tell her the truth. Look at her. You've seen her."

She reminded me of my mother, except younger and not my mother but my own child.

Bobby continued, "It'll put her over the edge. She's gone all her life knowing one thing to be true. Why would you fuck that up?"

147

He had some other words to say, but what stuck with me the most after we talked was this: "What do you expect to get out of this?"

Elizabeth was Mary and Roger's daughter. Nothing could change that. And so I expected nothing to come from telling her except that she would know there was more to her story than she had thought. I didn't hope she'd love me. I didn't hope to be brought together. All I wanted was that she know the history that was hers, that this history wasn't lost or wasted because of the illusion we'd tried to live in so neatly, that there was a life she could have lived and been a part of, and that she know she was as much a part of me as she was not. That's the truth, the absolute truth.

When I dropped Bobby off at the bar, he thought I was going with him. "You coming?" he said, and I told him I had to be back home to see if Gizos had got on all right with the car troubles. Bobby really wanted to meet Gizos because he lived in California ("I've always thought about moving there, that might be a nice spot, Charles"). Before I left him at the bar and before he shut the truck door, I told him that I would stop back by later and take him home—but when I did, he would not be there; the waiter would tell me that he had left in a cab.

Gizos was not at my place when I went home. Why would he have waited for me? His father was dying. On my kitchen table he'd left a phone number that went direct to the hospital room where his father was laid up. I called him, and he answered in a very low and quiet voice.

He couldn't talk long, he said, because the doctor—his father's doctor—was going to be on shift soon and would stop by the room to talk. His father was sleeping, and Gizos said he was unsure if the doctor would wake him, Lenno, but that he hoped he would just let him sleep.

"He probably will," I said about the doctor, yet I had no clue. I just thought I had to say that.

Before we hung up, Gizos asked if I was going to visit. I didn't want to, but he'd come to me to visit, and he had come to see Louise, even though that coming had more to do with his car crapping out and less to do with the fact that he hadn't seen her in many years, but I do think—no, I know it—that he would have seen her or made time to see her regardless.

. . .

On the drive out to the hospital the next evening, I found a sense of calm. That Elizabeth was getting help made me feel better, slightly. And so while I drove, I thought about her briefly between my thinking of Gizos. He hadn't come clean about it, but I had a feeling all those mysterious calls were from him. He had mentioned driving cross-country to get here, that he could have flown but that he wanted to see the land between here and there. It made sense that the calls had come from everywhere— he'd been moving in a straight shot across the country, but with stops each night between places.

It was only when I got to the hospital that I questioned if I was supposed to bring this dying man something. What do you get a man you hate? What do you get a man who has done so much wrong?

I settled on nothing.

Lenno's stomach was swollen so much that he looked pregnant. He was unconscious while I was there, and he had a tube shoved down his throat and white tape all around his mouth. In that room with Lenno, I felt compelled to act in some peaceful manner, and so I stood beside his bed with my hands on the bed rails, and in my head I said a prayer for him, said some words about a death with no suffering, but he looked like he had been suffering for some time. Maybe what I meant was that I hoped he stopped suffering. I could see the veins lining his skin, not just on his swollen belly but all along his arms and bruised hands, and I could not—and I still cannot—help but feel sorry for him, even though I disliked him the most out of anybody I had met in my life.

Seeing somebody so helpless and close to the Silence puts things in perspective.

Gizos and I did not stay in that room for very long. We went down to the cafeteria. I expected a flavorless meal, but the chicken thighs and mashed potatoes tasted fine. I ate while Gizos didn't. It might have appeared he was drinking coffee, but he'd been holding that same Styrofoam cup when I showed up, and then, at that table, he only stirred it with a red stirrer.

He told me he hadn't meant to tell me what I should do. About Elizabeth. He was talking about that, looking into his cold coffee and stirring it.

"It's all right," I said, which was what I'd said when we talked on the phone the night before. When he apologized.

"It's not any of my business," he said, "but does Roger know?"

"I don't know," I told him. I really didn't know what Roger knew, what he didn't know, but I thought it would be stupid of me to say he did not, that he was unaware, and so I wanted to say to Gizos, "I think he knows," but then I knew Gizos would ask me why I thought that, and I didn't want to get into it.

I asked Gizos how long his father had.

"I'm leaving in two weeks," he said, "and so I expect sometime between now and then."

I asked him if his father had been conscious at all while he'd been here visiting, and he said he had been a little bit at first, but that he'd grown quiet even when he seemed to be awake and aware.

I asked Gizos why he cared so much about his father. "Like you said, it's not any of my business, but I just want to know."

He shrugged and said, "I just do."

We're not so different, Gizos and I, when it comes to why we love who we love.

We left the table thinking we'd come back, but we wouldn't. We went out front of the hospital, across the street near the bus that would head into Overtown to pick folk up, and when I lit a cigarette this guy walked by with a big hiking backpack that wasn't too full and he asked for a smoke, and he took the one I gave him and lit it and kept on going down the road without a thanks or nothing.

"Where do you think he's going?" I asked Gizos. I felt like we were kids again.

"How should I know?"

"But where do you think?"

He paused so long I didn't think he'd answer. Then he said, "He's got a date. A good one by the looks of it."

"Then why the backpack?"

"West's a long way away. And it's going to go so well she'll ask him to stay."

"And will he?"

"Oh, no," he said. "He'll chicken out, and he'll go back home to his wife."

"He's married?"

"Of course. A few years back."

"And what happened?"

"They both got tired," Gizos said.

"From what?" I asked, and the feeling of being a child once more disappeared. We were grown right then.

He paused, thinking. And then he said, "They don't know."

The outside gray darkened the sky, and we walked down the cracked sidewalk around the corner to the parking lot and found my truck, whose window I had left open.

"I want to ask you something," he said.

"What is it?" I said.

"Do you remember when we stopped talking?"

I told him yes.

"Why?" he asked.

"I felt it was just easier that way," I said.

"Easier than what way?"

"Than going on as we were."

"And how was it that we were going on?" he asked.

"Whatever it is you want," I told him, "I don't have it."

"But you do," he said, and I had nothing to say.

It took some moments for me to realize what he wanted. Love never dies, and he wanted me to love him in a way I could not. But even if I could, I thought, what about his husband? What about their son? It would be impossible—I had already destroyed so much. Any more would have destroyed me. I loved him—I did—but not how he wanted. And he loved me so much he wasn't able to accept it.

Before he left me there by my truck, walking away through the lines of parked vehicles and then around the corner and out of sight, back to his father, he said, "I'm sorry," and he wrapped his arms around me.

"For what?" I asked, but he did not say.

The sides of our faces pressed together in equal weight, and we held on for one, two, three, four, five, six, and then he let go. Maybe we looked at each other before he turned away. Maybe we didn't.

· · ·

I met up with Bobby at the bar. Under the hanging lights he asked me where that guy was. I think he was embarrassed to try to pronounce Gizos, because he messed it up once and then started referring to him as "that guy." I told him he left.

"Left?" Bobby said. "What do you mean, he left? I told you I wanted to talk to him about California."

For a long while we sat in silence.

"Why are you so quiet tonight?" he said.

"Just tired," I told him.

"You don't have to sit here with me," he said. "I can get home fine. I might stick around and see what these dance parties are like."

"It's Tuesday," the bartender said. I want to say he was standing there cleaning a glass, but the truth is that he was leaning back on the counter, almost right between us, like we were his friends. "They only have them on Thursday and Friday."

"Since when?" Bobby asked.

"It's always been that way," I said.

"Maybe so," he said, "but I'll get home fine. Go. And when you talk to that guy, would you ask him what he thinks about California?"

"Sure thing," I said.

18

WHEN I PICKED LOUISE UP EARLY FOR HER NEXT ECT treatment, she asked where her baby was. "I need to bring him," she said, and so I said I'd get him while she got in the car.

"Thank you," she said. "I do really need a break."

Usually, on the days she brought the elephant, she would tuck it by her waist, right next to the seat belt. But today she looked panicked, and when I put the truck in reverse she said, "No. Not without a car seat."

"He'll be fine," I said.

"You *would* think that. You're not taking us anywhere until the conditions of this vehicle are safe enough to do so."

I tried to suggest that maybe he could stay home. "He looks like he's sleeping, anyway."

She laughed at that. "That is neglect, and I'm a better mother than that."

I had no idea where to get a car seat. She wouldn't even allow me to drive the truck anywhere, so I could not go and get one at the store.

"I'll be right back," I said to Louise, and she told me to start the truck and put the heat on.

I went straight to the neighbor's door. The screen door had no springs, no mechanics, and so when I opened it, it flung back and banged the side of the house and slowly crept back to me. I knocked once, and then once more. Nobody answered, but I thought I heard noises. Again, I knocked, but nobody came.

The pile of garbage or junk that he kept on the ground was soaked, especially the couch and pillows, and all the boxes sagged. I had only just begun to dig when the neighbor's door ripped open and he said, "What the fuck are you doing?"

Was this all I had to do to get him outside?

Louise spoke from the truck. "Rhett, honey, hi."

Rhett waved to her and then came down the stairs to me, right by the pile of garbage. He said the words slow, each syllable a jab in the chest.

"What—the—fuck—are—you—doing?"

I had no reasonable explanation for what I was doing. It was his stuff, and I had no right to go through it, even though it was just garbage.

So I just said it. "Please tell me you have a car seat? I'll give you anything you want for it."

"Why would I keep a car seat in this pile where it rains?"

I thought of the couch, but said nothing.

"How much money do you have?" he said.

I didn't know, so I took out my wallet and checked. I had no cash on me.

"Look," I said to him, and I explained why I needed it. "It sounds ridiculous, I know, but I promise I'll pay you when I come back."

He turned away and went back up the stairs and inside the house. I thought he was not coming back, that his leaving was the end of the conversation. But as he got indoors, he yelled to someone.

"Do we still have Corinne's car seat?"

A woman's voice spoke, but I could not hear what she said.

"Huh?" Rhett said.

Again, I could not hear what she said.

"The car seat! Do we still have it?"

"Why?" I heard her say that.

"Someone needs it," he said. "Do we or don't we?"

I think she said "No."

"You don't know what you're talking about," Rhett said. "We do too."

He disappeared from the doorway, and both the screen door and interior door were wide open. He was not gone long, and when he came out and down the steps, he held in one hand a car seat.

"Sorry about the crumbs," he said. As he handed me the car seat he said, "How old's the baby?"

I don't think he understood at all what I had explained to him, so I tried again, but he just looked at me and shook his head. He turned away.

"Thanks for this," I said. I don't know why I said what I said next, but I did. "You won't need this soon, will you?"

He laughed. "The state took our kid. Just leave it on the steps when you're done with it."

I looked at the crumbs in the car seat—there was even most of a deformed cracker lodged between the armrest and seat cushion—and I wondered where, in this world, the mouth was that had chewed this food.

For all the trouble Louise had put me through in wanting a car seat, she didn't even buckle the elephant in. She set it in the car seat and then set the car seat on the ground between her feet, and she had the heat cranking through the bottom vents.

. . .

I never would have guessed Elizabeth went by the name Ellie.

I imagine the last thing she wanted was to be bothered as she waited for her appointment; the last thing she imagined was that an old, senile woman would wheel herself over to her and say, "Hello, what is your name?"

"Ellie," Elizabeth said.

She was kind.

"And yours?" Louise said.

Mary, too, was kind.

"Mary," she said. "I'm her mother."

"Mary was also Jesus's mother," Louise said.

"That's true," Mary said.

"Is your husband's name Joseph?" Louise asked.

"It's Roger," Mary said. "He'd be here, but he's working."

"That's your father?" Louise asked.

"No, that's my husband," Mary said. "He's Ellie's father."

"And he's working?" Louise asked.

"Yes," Mary said.

"Men do need to work." Over her shoulder, she glared at me.

I went to the window to get the clipboard with paperwork from the woman behind the glass, and as I sat and filled it out for Louise, she grew quiet. Mary asked after her stuffed elephant, and I wondered if she recognized it. Then Louise asked if she, Elizabeth, wanted to hold it.

"Sure," she said. "What's her name?"

"It's a him," Louise said.

"What's his name?" she asked, but Louise didn't answer.

Elizabeth held him for only a moment, no longer, before Louise wanted him back.

"He's tired," Louise said. "I'm sorry."

"That's all right," Mary said.

"He needs to be put down for a nap," Louise said. "Don't you, darling?"

Louise wheeled herself over to me.

"Where is his car seat?" she asked me.

"In the truck," I told her.

"Why didn't you bring it in?"

"I'll go get it," I said.

I returned the clipboard and paperwork to the woman behind the window, and I walked back down the narrow hallway to the entrance, and I went outside to the truck but remembered my keys were in the locker—they didn't allow some items in the building, yet I never understood keys—so I had to go back and get them, and then go to the truck. Having gotten the car seat and put my keys back into the locker, I made it back to the waiting room to find Elizabeth not there.

I set the car seat at Louise's feet, and she put the stuffed elephant in it.

I asked Louise if she wanted a magazine, but she didn't answer me. I got her one anyway, a *National Geographic*, an issue about the cosmos, and I didn't think she was going to look at it. She had it on her lap with her hands folded over it. But then she started to look at it, began to flip through the pages, pausing only to look at the photos, and the bigger the picture, the more time she spent inspecting.

There was noise—there's always noise—but even so the room was quiet. The loudest sound came from Louise as she turned, rather roughly, the pages of the magazine. Mary still sat where she had, right across from us on that bench with green cushions, and she looked to be reading a magazine, but her eyes did not move. They looked down at the magazine and stayed straight. I looked back to Louise, who wasn't reading and instead was looking at a photo. Without taking her eyes from the page, Louise asked, "Have we been to space?"

Mary answered her. "We have," she said. "A few times, I think."

"For what?" Louise asked. "To find out we can't get away?"

"What do you mean?" Mary said.

"Never mind," Louise said. "Pass me another."

I got up and grabbed a different issue, which I gave to her. This one had a photo of a young woman in a safari shirt standing in a forest and holding a camera. The caption said "Becoming Jane," or something like that.

Again, Louise just stared at the cover for some time before she began to flip through the pages. But then she went back to the cover and held the image in front of her face.

"Do I look like her?" she asked.

"A little bit," I said. "Do you think you do?"

She didn't answer me. At least not in a way that responded to my question. She set the magazine down and looked right at me.

"Does my mother know I'm here?" Louise said. "Where is she? Can I see her?"

I was glad Elizabeth was missing this.

"Do you want to go for a ride?" I asked Louise. "In the wheelchair?" I did not want to answer her question.

"I want to see my mother," she said. "Where is she?"

"She's not here," I said.

"Is she home?"

I went to the window and told the woman I was taking Louise for a stroll, that I'd still be in the building, that if I wasn't back by her appointment, to come looking.

"Of course," she said.

I turned Louise around and pushed her toward the door. "I can't steal this," she said about the magazine, so I took it and tossed it onto the table.

"Do you want your baby?" I said about the elephant.

"I have a baby?" Louise said.

"He was talking to me," Mary said, trying, for some reason, just a human one, to ease Louise's spirit.

And Louise said to me, "She should want her baby."

We were away from the room and going down the hall when Louise asked where we were going. I said for a short walk.

"Is my mother walking too?"

"Maybe," was all I said.

"She's here," Louise said. "She is."

Fredrick used to call them Goog'ooks—spirits. It's like you're not alone, like something is just over your shoulder, peering.

That's what I felt. And maybe that's what Louise felt too. But it was only my body's remembering something I did not—this woman, Louise's mother, from a time that I had no memory of. And I wonder, looking back at Louise wanting her mother, how strange it is to want something you did not like, or something that seemed a bad part of your life. But maybe, like most things, it wasn't all bad.

. . .

On our way back through the hallway to the waiting room, we passed Mary pushing Elizabeth out in the wheelchair. I did not look at her. I kept my eyes down at the floor, and I looked only to make sure we would pass by them with no accident.

As we passed by, Louise said, "I remember you."

19

THAT NIGHT, AFTER LOUISE'S MOST RECENT ECT
treatment, I was dreaming of Fredrick—we were driving to some
unknown place in the middle of a snowstorm—when Mary woke
me.

"Get up" is how she said it.

I really don't know if her unannounced visit frightened me.
Maybe I thought I was still dreaming, which might explain my
saying, "Is that you?" when I walked out into the kitchen, which
was too warm. I'd left the heat cranked. The light above the sink
was on, and she was by my cupboard, crouched down.

"Do you not keep your coffee here anymore?" she said.

"I do, but I'm out. The last of it's in the maker. Turn it on."

We sat in silence while the coffee brewed.

I somehow knew she would come.

I wanted to smoke—needed to smoke—even though I didn't
do that in the house anymore, but I felt something momentous

was about to occur, and so I asked her if she minded if I smoked a cigarette, like it was her house.

"Yes," she said. "I do. I don't want to go home smelling like one."

The coffee finished brewing, and Mary went to get some. There was only a cup's worth.

"Drink it," I told her. She got a cup from the red drying rack and poured the coffee. She put two sugars in, no cream.

"Dairy rips me up inside," she said, sitting. Thin steam rose from the cup, and she blew it away in a swirl. She seemed to take a sip, but I didn't see her swallow. Maybe it was still too hot and so she only touched her lip to the coffee, checking. She set the cup down.

"How'd you get here?" I asked her. "Did you park down the dirt road?"

This time she did drink the coffee, but I could tell it burned her tongue.

"No," she said. "I paddled over. It was quicker."

I stood up to look out the window.

"Roger didn't hear you leave?" I asked.

"Maybe," she said. "But he knows I'm here."

"He knows?"

Mary laughed. "He's always known."

I wanted to ask Mary why, if Roger knew, she hid the canoe, but then I realized why: for Elizabeth.

I sat back down.

The obvious question to ask was why she was here, especially if Roger knew. And I would have asked it if she hadn't started talking.

"She's sick, Charles," was how Mary began. "She's been sick her whole life. When she moved out, when she'd been teaching third grade for a few years and had bought her house—which she's thinking of selling—before all that, I thought she had been cured, that what she'd suffered from had gone. But it hadn't gone.

I guess I was just hopeful. Since she was a little girl, she's been ill. Not physically, I don't mean, but in her spirit." She paused a moment. "No, that's not true—she was sick physically for a few years when she was eight or nine. She suffered seizures, but the medication helped with that."

Mary started laughing, and I asked her why that was funny.

"It's not, it's not," she said, but she kept laughing. Maybe she needed to laugh.

"Listen," she said. "Before we knew she had epilepsy, we— Roger and I, I mean—Roger and I used to think she was just a bad kid, one of those children who would grow up to be criminals, like that boy who set the community garden on fire—did you hear he did it because he was bored? Anyway, Ellie's epilepsy's gone, if you're wondering. I once had Marissa over— do you remember Marissa? It doesn't matter—Marissa was over once on a Saturday, and this is when she was studying to be a manicurist, which she never finished, and she was doing my nails at the kitchen table. She was gluing on acrylics. Ellie had been watching TV in the living room, and she came into the kitchen and stood right between Marissa and me. She had this blank look on her face, and she looked me in the eyes. I asked if she was all right, if she was going to be sick. That's what she looked like. Her face was pale and her cheeks were sunken. 'What's the matter?' Marissa said to her, but Ellie kept on staring at me. I scooted in my seat so I was right in her face, and as I went to speak to her, Ellie slapped me. And I don't mean gently. She smacked me hard, right across the cheek.

"I grabbed her by the arm and brought her straight to her room. I think it was the only time I yelled at her—I mean really yelled— and she started to cry. Of course I thought she did it on purpose. Who wouldn't think that? Marissa—she's always been nosy, she gets it from her mother, but then again so is everybody on the reservation—Marissa stuck her head in the room. 'Is everything all right?' she said, and I took her back out to the kitchen, where we sat back down at the table and I asked her to finish my nails. One of the fake nails she'd glued on me had come off.

"'What was that all about?' Marissa asked me, and I really didn't know, which is what I said. 'Does she do that often?' she asked. I told her no."

Mary went to the microwave and heated her coffee. As it heated, she kept talking.

"Later, when I went to her room, I asked her if she was sorry. 'For what?' Ellie said. 'For hitting me,' I told her. 'I didn't hit,' she said. 'I didn't!' We went back and forth until she started to cry again."

She stopped the microwave before it beeped at zero. She came and sat back down.

"She never hit me again, and it took a few more weeks to find out something was wrong. She was not remembering things she did, and then finally she had a seizure at school during lunch. After a sleep test, the doctors were able to explain what was wrong with her, which included her not remembering moments, things she'd done."

Mary laughed again. "That slap though. I'll never be able to take it seriously, since I know she couldn't help it. It was a hell of a smack. My face was bright red for at least an hour. I was, and still am, glad she got better over the next few years. She was eventually able to come off the seizure medication, and she's not had a seizure since then. Well, she has, because of her treatments now, as you more than well know, but those are controlled. How long has Louise been sick?"

"A year or more," I told her.

"No," Mary said. "I mean with her depression. I take it that's why she's getting treatments."

I explained what I could to her, that she'd been sick all my life—"Sounds like Ellie," Mary said, not knowing the weight of those words—and that she was confined to bed for weeks while Fredrick tended to her.

"She rolled her ankle," I said, "and on one of our visits to the doctor I mentioned her depression to him. He recommended the treatments, for her memory and for her mental health."

"And are they working?" Mary asked.

I shrugged. "It's not like her memory can be improved. I think this treatment was more for her depression. Maybe they're working. But her memory has been the same. Sometimes she remembers me, sometimes she does not."

And for the first time, I felt frightened about losing Louise. Gizos was gone forever, and besides Bobby, she was the only other person I had in my life who knew I existed, however rare it was for her to recognize me, to know I was her son. Although I couldn't recall the last time she'd looked upon me with the knowledge of who I was. I hoped she knew it was an accident. That it wasn't my fault.

I cleared my throat. "Other than her memory issues," I said, "and the bouts of her not feeling well mentally, she is doing all right. She's still strong in her body."

"I want you to know I was sorry to hear about your mother," Mary said. "That day you came by to ask about the burial. I've always liked Louise, and I've thought about her from time to time. She was always kind."

It was my turn to laugh. "She was, and still is. I don't know who it is she thinks I am, but she has a big issue with me."

"So I saw," Mary said. I don't think she meant what she said next to be malicious, because she does not know the story about Fredrick, but it did set me to wonder darkly. "You think she knows who you are but still treats you like that?"

Fredrick was a dream now, but he was still very much alive between my mother and me. Had I missed my opportunity to tell Louise the truth once again? To report back to her about what her son had said, why he hadn't gone with his father that day?

I want to say I told Mary I had thought about that, that maybe Louise knew who I was but still treated me badly. But all I said was, "Maybe."

"I remember the first time I brought Ellie to the doctor's," Mary said, "when she wasn't feeling well. This was in high school. She was up all night and sleeping all day. That's a bit dramatic. It wasn't always like that, but for the most part she couldn't sleep at night. Only during the day. The doctor asked if there was anybody else in our family that suffered from depression. I felt like saying, 'We're Indians, of course it runs in our family,' but I didn't say that. I told him yes, which made Ellie look at me. She asked who, and I told her Roger's mother, which was not true, but she was not alive to say otherwise. After, Ellie asked her father about it, and he told her that that was the truth. I don't know why she had difficulty believing that, but she did."

"So what did the doctor do for her?" I said.

"Gave her medication. She tried a few over the course of a year and some months, and then she settled on one that she kept taking through the end of college. But they stopped working, and she stopped taking them. She's since gone back on them while also going through the treatment, which is helping. She'd gone back to that pattern of staying up all night and sleeping most days, but now she's starting to sleep through the night again. She'd sit outside and smoke—I don't know where she picked that up—and play on her phone or just sit. I watched her once from the kitchen. She stayed outside for hours."

"I've seen her out there before," I said.

"I figured you had," Mary said. "She thought once she heard a Goog'ook outdoors, late at night, heard this jingle"—she waved her hand and wiggled her fingers—"echo across the water. She told us the next day, sometime in the afternoon. She thought Roger should smudge."

I thought of the phone calls and said as much to Mary.

"I thought it was you she heard. Roger smudged though, to make her feel better."

We were quiet a moment, and then I said, "So they're working," but Mary took that as a question.

"Yes," she said. "As I said, she sleeps through the night, and she's up early. She's even started talking about going back to work."

"I thought you said she lost her job?"

"I didn't say that," Mary said. "She took this year off, and they didn't hire somebody new but instead got a long-term substitute, or something like that."

"Is she going to go back next year?" I said.

"She hasn't said just yet."

We were quiet. My chair creaked. Again that rush of wondering why she was here, and Mary seemed to hear my inner thoughts: she answered the question I never posed.

"Gizos told me," Mary said. "He called me last night. That's why I'm here."

"Told you what?" I asked, but I knew.

Mary got up and heated her coffee for six seconds. There was barely any in her cup, and so when it was done warming, she drank it all.

"Do you have any tea?" she said.

"Check in the cupboard."

Mary crouched and dug around in the cupboard for the tea I knew was not there. Her knees popped as she shifted cans and bags of flour and sugar and containers of salt and pepper all around, looking for tea. When she found none, she poured a glass of water.

"Your water's gritty," Mary said.

"What is it you want?" I asked.

"You need to keep the story to yourself."

But it was already let loose.

"Who else knows about this?" she asked. "Who else have you told?"

"Gizos knows, and he only found out recently, and somebody you don't know knows. He's non-Native and doesn't care about anything except drinking and leaving here. Just them. And now you."

"And Roger."

"Then why isn't he here? Why is it only you?"

She said nothing.

"I'm going to tell the story," I said.

"You can't," Mary said.

"Why? Tell me why. Tell me one good reason."

"What good does it do for her to know?" she asked.

"She has a right to know."

"And so the past twenty-seven years of her life won't be true?" Mary said.

"Of course they will," I said. "And that's what I want to say. I want to make it clear that knowing her history will only make her more real, more true. She has a right to know."

"Charles," she said, "it's sometimes best not to know. Take Roger. He knew from the very start what I was doing as well as why. Sure, he was an exceptional father to Ellie, but there were days I was afraid he would back out of this. I was afraid he would leave us."

"But he didn't," I said.

"Let me finish—" she said.

"And that's why he's her father," I said. "That's why he will always be her father. That's why she will always see him as so. All I will be to her is a man who told her a story and who is her biological father. All I will be is a history she had no part in but nonetheless belongs to. What damage can that do?"

"Let me finish," she said. "How different would it have been if Roger hadn't known, if he had thought she was his?"

"What kind of question is that?" I said. "We can't know. All we can know is that would have been the cruelest trick to have been played, even more so than what you did to me. I wondered whether or not he knew about where she came from. I felt sorry for him, when I thought that way. What am I saying—this is not about Roger. This is about Elizabeth."

"Ellie," Mary corrected.

"This is about her," I said. "All about her. Maybe that's why she's sick—maybe she needs to know her full story. Have you thought about that? Maybe her body and mind know something is missing."

"I don't know what you're talking about," Mary said. "But please, consider what I'm saying, what Gizos has said. You can't let this story get out. She can't know. It has the potential to ruin everything I've worked toward giving her as well as everything you've sacrificed for her to be where she is and who she is."

"I never agreed to sacrifice anything," I said. "And percentages on paper don't mean shit."

"In a way they don't, but those percentages, those numbers, also do. And you need to understand that. By giving her this story, you're creating a situation where she's learning more about herself, yes, but she's also questioning who she is—or at least I would, if I were her. And her learning all this on top of managing her well-being? It could break her, Charles. This could break her. Your daughter. Let her keep living knowing what she knows."

Maybe I was blinded by my experience, by my own suffering, by my deepest desire—that she know I exist, that she know we were part of a story or a history that very much mattered, not in some grand scheme of things but in a simple way concerning our spirit.

"I can't do it," I said.

Mary threw the water from her cup in my face, and then she left through the front door. She did not close it, and the cold rushed in across the floor and brushed my ankles. I went to the door but did not close it. It was dark out, but in the glimmers of light shining from behind me and lighting the steps and the air around me, snow was falling, gently in large flakes. Mary yanked the canoe from around the house and guided it into the water. She got in, and with the paddle she pushed herself away from the riverbank. I closed the door before I saw her make it to the other side, but as I sat back down at the table I thought I should watch her leave, and so I went back to the door and looked through the glass window. The river is not so wide, and so she made it back home. I could not see her, so I turned off my lights and went back to watch. No lights shone from across the way, but I could make out the movement. In the dark, I watched her as she shimmied the canoe up the small incline and over the dying grass, and she flipped the canoe over against the house.

I locked my door and could not go back to sleep.

20

A FEW DAYS AFTER MARY VISITED ME, LOUISE GOT sick and was unable to go to her ECT treatment. She had a high fever, and I brought her to the doctor. I don't know how long we waited, but it was a while. And the whole time I kept thinking about Mary and what she had said. I still stood by what I'd said to her, still planned to do what I'd said I would do. It had to be done. It was our daughter's, all of it.

The doctor did not sit for too long with Louise, and it probably would have been faster if she had talked some. I don't know what was the matter with her that day. She said no words at all, though she was conscious and able to hear and move about. And so for all the questions the doctor asked, I answered them.

He thought it was just a cold, and he gave her some cough medicine. She wasn't coughing terribly, I said, but he said just in case it should get worse.

I asked him if it was OK if she missed her appointments, which he didn't answer right away and instead asked if they were working.

"I don't know," I told him. "Maybe. But is it all right?"

"It's fine, yes. Call them and tell them what happened. Say you'd like to reschedule."

I stayed with Louise until late afternoon, watching TV on low and listening every so often to her breathing as she slept. Before I left to go pick Bobby up from the bar—he'd called and asked for a ride—I checked her fever, which was gone. I told her I was going home and that I'd be back in the morning. As I was on my way out, her phone rang and it was Bobby again, asking where I was.

"I'm coming," I said.

I had every intention of telling him what had happened with Mary, but I never got the chance. When I picked him up he was loaded, had sixteen beers in him, or so the bartender told me when Bobby wobbled off to piss, which was also the only time he was quiet. He talked and talked and talked about how angry he was at the neighbor, at the court date, how it was "fucking up" his plans.

"I'll kill him," he told me. "That's why you, Charles, you, you, you have to talk to him. Tell him to drop the charges. I'll kill him."

I didn't disbelieve him, so I suppose that's why I decided to try and find him first—Rhett, that is—when I went back to Louise's. Maybe he would drop the charges.

It was only a little past six when I brought Bobby home. He was falling asleep at the bar, and the bartender helped me carry him out and put him in my truck, at which point he was miraculously awake, like the five or ten minutes he had dozed off had somehow been enough to strengthen him.

"How's our girl, anyway?" he said as I drove him home.

"She's good," I said, and I was about to tell him about Mary.

"Does she remember us?"

He meant my mother.

"Maybe," I said.

"I've got to go see her," he said. "It's been a bit. Pull over."

I stopped on the side of the road and he got out and puked. He wiped his mouth.

"Better out there than in here," he said. He shut the door. "I've been thinking," he said. "You should get your land appraised so when we move you can sell your lot and that shitty little house of yours."

"You thought that?"

"Fuck you," he said, laughing. "But really. It'll give us some more money."

"I'll think about it."

"You do that," he said.

Bobby coughed and spat out the window.

"I'm gonna call Louise when I get home," Bobby said. "Do you think she's up?"

"Don't bother her," I said, and I meant it. "She's sleeping. She's got a cold."

"You said she was good. What do you mean, a cold? She go to the doctor's?"

"Yes, he said it was a cold."

"She got a fever?"

"She did."

"And you left her? Jeez Louise," he said, and then he laughed until he was coughing. "I said that to her once. The jeez Louise. Couldn't get her to laugh all day, but she thought that was pretty funny. You got a cigarette?"

He asked that as he was taking one from my pack sticking out of the console.

"I should call her," he said, blowing smoke out the open window.

"Don't call her," I said again. "She's sleeping."

He was quiet, and after a time of silence he said, looking out the window, "You shouldn't have left her."

He could have meant anybody right then.

. . .

When I got home, I could hear singing and drumming—an honor song—and I looked around for the source of the noise, but it was nowhere to be found. It was a ways away. And then I saw something else, across the river by their house. The tribal police were just leaving it. It was just one cruiser, and all I could see was them driving away, and behind them followed an ambulance. No lights were on. It was one of those quick flashes of a moment, the tail end of something, and so both cruiser and ambulance could have been coming from down the street and just so happened to pass as I was looking about for the drumming and singing.

The singing and the drumming grew louder when the wind quit blowing. If she was home, she probably heard it. I sat outside and listened for a while, wondering, and then it came to me. Lenno. It's not that I wanted to be right about that; I felt I had to be right about it. I hopped in my truck and drove over to the reservation, and I watched them from the parking lot of the football field, right next to the school. I don't know for how many days they'd had the sacred fire burning, but it was still going, and not even fifty feet away was the drum, seven men—one of them must have been Gizos, but I could not tell—around it, and around them a dozen or so people, all singing.

I did not stay very long, but long enough to feel part of it. Because I suppose I was. And how strange that after all these years I still remember the words to that song, and I drove off singing them:

kchee-da-mee-d'haa-da-moo-neh dun elee
    ul'naa-buy-ol'dee-yagw
nijee ul'naa-bettook maa-weeh-laa-neh
kchee-da-mee-d'haa-da-moo-neh dun wedaa-beksol-dee-yagw
nijee ul'naa-bettook we-jooh-kem-dol-dee-neh
we-jooh-kem-dol-dee-neh dun gizeeh-ol-lugw
elee boon'lugw eeyo wskit-ka-migk
wey-yo-hey-hi-ya-ya-wey-oh-hey-ho-hey-hi-ya-awey-yo-hey-hi-
    ya-ya-wey-yo-hey

21

I WENT TO LOUISE'S THE NEXT DAY, ON A SATUR-day. Her door was locked, and I unlocked it with the key. I found her in the living room, a garbage bag opened and partly filled by her feet. She was going through all the junk mail she'd had piled up for who knows how long, tossing pieces. But what caught my attention was a cream-colored cord hanging out of the black bag.

"Hi, yes, come in," she said, as if I had knocked on her front door. She did not take her eyes from the mail as she tossed envelopes in the garbage. Two or three pieces lay flat on the floor around it.

Louise coughed once, and then once more.

I grabbed hold of the cream-colored cord and pulled it.

"Leave it," Louise said. "I won't have it anymore."

"What?" I kept pulling until from below the many envelopes her phone emerged.

"All night," Louise said, "that machine would not stop making noise. I had to rip it out of the wall."

"You can't throw away your phone," I said.

"I don't use it," she said.

"What about when I call?"

She tossed an envelope into the garbage.

I hooked the phone back up in the kitchen, and I hung it on the wall where it had been, that part of the wall whiter than the rest of the kitchen. I expected it to ring, but it did not.

In the living room, I put my hand to Louise's forehead, and it was warm.

"Help me," she said.

"You need some Tylenol?"

"With the mail," she said.

Most of the day was spent going through her junk mail in the living room—taking a break only so I could cook her an early lunch of canned green beans, microwavable mashed potatoes, and this ham from a can I fried in her skillet. I wrapped half of it up for her dinner and gave her the other half, which she picked at as she watched TV. I made sure she took the Tylenol I set beside her plate. For the entire time we worked together, gutting envelope after envelope, she said nothing, and every time I asked her a question about herself, she responded with short answers, mostly, "I don't know, sir."

The quiet bothered me intensely, like the sun beating down on my neck. And I couldn't take it anymore, feeling so alone, so I asked: "Do you have any children?"

I felt like a stranger.

For a moment she thought on it. "If I do . . ." she said. A brief wait, a second, and then she asked: "Do I?"

Before I could answer she cut me off with a wave and looked back at her envelopes, many of which were upside down, so I don't think she was reading what they were.

"I don't know," she said.

She was dozing when I left her that day, and I thought it might be time for her to go into a home. Not that she couldn't take care of herself—she could do that. But I was concerned that she was forgetting too much.

. . .

I called Bobby when I got home.

"What the fuck did I tell you?" I said.

"Goddammit I thought I dreamt it," he said.

"She threw her phone out because of you."

I was nowhere near him obviously, but I imagined him rubbing his eyes.

"I'm sorry, Charles."

"She's too sick for this shit," I said.

"Then maybe she shouldn't be on her own," he said. "She can live with me. I'll watch her."

"And get drunk and bother her all night? What happens when you move away? What then?"

He knew what he'd said was ridiculous, and that it would never happen, but even so he still argued with me because that's what he does.

"The neighbor isn't dropping the charges anytime soon," he said. "So it looks like I'm here for quite a while."

I had seen him, Rhett, when I was leaving Louise's apartment. I was trying to pay him for the car seat, but he seemed to have forgotten and wanted only one thing. "Stay away from me," he said. "You're friends with that lunatic, aren't you? He's getting sued for all he's worth."

"I ain't worth much," Bobby said when I told him how the neighbor had put it.

. . .

The next week, Louise did not look well. She was pale, and her skin was very warm. And she was coughing more. But she would not stay home and in bed. She kept saying she was fine, and so I listened to her and said we'd still go to her appointment. "I have to be there," she said, and when I asked her where, she did not answer me. I thought, however, it was better to take her. The doctor there might see her sickness and help convince her that she was unwell.

I really expected to see Elizabeth there. We sat in the waiting room, and I kept wondering: Had her appointment been changed? She did not show up in the hour we were waiting for Louise's treatment. Louise rested in her wheelchair, and at her side slept her elephant in a car seat I'd bought for her. She kept taking it out and rubbing its face, and she'd take its trunk and massage it between her bony fingers.

The door to the treatment room opened, and the nurse said Louise's name.

"Here," Louise said. "I'm here." She tried to rise from her wheelchair, but she collapsed back into it.

"I'll wheel you over," I said, "and the nurse will take you the rest of the way."

She tried to rise again, but again she failed.

The nurse came over.

"I'll push you," she said.

"I'm hot," Louise said. "I need to breathe."

"Stay seated," the nurse said.

She felt Louise's head, put her hand against her cheek.

"Is she sick?" the nurse asked me.

I told her about her cold.

"Let's bring you back so the doctor can see you." And then to me she said, "You can come with us."

Louise's fever had returned, and it was the highest it had been—102.9. I told the doctor what I could—that she had been sick, that she'd seen her normal doctor, that he had prescribed her cough medicine that she had not yet taken because her fever had gone away and the cough wasn't as bad as it had been. As I spoke, the doctor listened to Louise's lungs, checked her mouth and throat. Both of us listened to her cough, which spoke more to him than to me.

"Take her home," he said. "Call and reschedule when she's better. And monitor her closely. If she gets any worse at all, take her to the emergency room."

He looked at his watch, and he never glanced back at us.

When I wheeled her out of the treatment room and down the hall to the waiting room, I expected to see Elizabeth sitting out there with Mary. Where are you? I thought. Where she normally sat, on the green cushioned bench, were two women, and a young girl, about five or six, red all around her mouth, was sitting on the floor beside the elephant in the car seat, looking at it. I'm sure she had touched it.

"Get," Louise spat at her, and the girl scooted back, quickly, to the women she was with.

I carried the car seat and the elephant as I pushed Louise back to the truck.

. . .

When the first snowstorm of the season hit, and all the pine branches bent under the weight of snow, I fantasized about—prepared for—Louise's death. It's always a cold that gets the elderly, or so we hear, but still it catches us off guard. We act surprised by something that is not quite surprising—it's expected. It's more unexpected for them to survive the cold, to get better, to live on.

But Louise recovered. I checked her temperature with the thermometer. It had gone down 0.4 degrees, and then the next time it was down more, and then again, more, until it was normal. She still coughed a little bit here and there, and she still was picky with her food, but at least she started to eat.

Before the storm hit, Bobby stayed with Louise while I went up north for a job. I came back Tuesday night to find him sleeping in the recliner, Louise sleeping in the bed. The TV was on very loud, and the first thing I did was turn it down.

I shook Bobby awake. "You can go if you want," I said to him.

"Storm's coming," Bobby said.

"Wake up," I said.

"I am awake. Shit. A storm's coming."

It was not until the eleven o'clock news that I saw what he meant. A nor'easter would hit Thursday evening and would go out to sea at some point, the soonest, according to their models, late Friday evening or early Saturday morning.

Before the storm, I left Louise to go back to my place and make sure the windows were shut and locked and to get my shovel and a flashlight and a small kerosene stove that used to be Fredrick's. Before I went back to her, I went to the store for batteries and kerosene and canned food and three packs of cigarettes and cold cuts and bread, which was almost sold out, and I bought a cribbage set that came with a deck of red cards in case Louise wanted to play.

When I got to Louise's, she said the phone wouldn't stop ringing, and it rang right before she could finish the sentence. It was Bobby saying he wanted to come and stay with us, but he never showed up. I told him I didn't want him there if he was going to drink.

"I won't," he said. "I swear to God I won't have a drink while I'm there." I pressed him about it. "I won't," he said. "Christ sakes. I won't." And so I said fine, come on over. But he never showed, and he didn't answer when I called his house, so I figured he couldn't stay sober for a day or more. I thought it was good of him. Why have two sick people when one is enough? He had said he was cutting back on his drinking—how much, I didn't know—because he wanted to be ready for his court date, which would be here soon. He was convinced he was going to get his case dismissed, especially with my testimony, which would be what, I didn't know.

The news was right about the storm starting Thursday evening. The flakes fell few and far between around six. I was outside Louise's place, smoking, watching past my smoke-and-cold breath as the white drifted like fuzz to the ground. For dinner that night, I made Louise canned soup. It was mainly broth, which she had some of but not all, and I made two sandwiches with cold turkey. I drank water, and then I made tea for Louise and me but she took only one sip of hers to swallow a Tylenol, and then her tea got cold and stayed cold all night on her nightstand.

All Louise did was sleep, which was something I still could not do. I think I did get some sleep around four in the morning for about an hour, but for the rest of the night I was awake. At two, I went outside for a smoke and I went to my truck and got my shovel, and I smoked three cigarettes while I cleared from the driveway and front steps what snow had already fallen, about four inches. Shoveling got me thinking about Fredrick. He hated to shovel after all the snow had fallen. He liked to break it up. He'd go out and shovel in thirds. As a boy, I was always with him for some part of it. And since then, I'd done the work the same way he did it: in parts. He'd always said it was easier on the body that way, and I agreed.

. . .

All day Friday it snowed, snowed, snowed, and I'd go out in it and shovel, but could not keep up with the snowfall. By late afternoon, I'd shoveled and cleared away the snow. For a time, I leaned on the shovel and watched some children in oversize coats build a fort, a tiny dugout in which they crawled until their mother told them to get out, and then they turned their attention to a green sled, which they used to slide over and over again down into a ditch. By the time I looked back at my work, the ground was covered again.

When inside, I started to worry about Louise. She was in a deep sleep, her fever burning, and she kept shivering. Once I thought she'd stopped breathing, but she was just barely breathing. If she did have to go to the hospital, then it was best I keep the driveway as clear as possible, even though the roads were barely plowed. They were drivable, but dangerous. I worked to keep the driveway clear, going out every forty-five minutes.

When the wind came, the lights would flicker once, maybe twice, and the house would shift and creak. I could never tell if it was my blinking that caused the lights to flicker or if it was actually the lights. But they did blink once, I know that. I was inside, getting ready to head back out, when they dulled and came back on, and I was surprised to find them still lit when I finished shoveling the snow and went back indoors.

Before Louise got better, I sat near her in the recliner, waiting to go back out and shovel more, and I thought very much about her getting worse. I was sitting there, my eyes on the TV but not taking it in, and I imagined myself rising from the chair, standing over her as she slept. I nudged her shoulder, trying to wake her. But she did not wake. I said her name: "Louise, Louise, Mom, wake up," but she did not. She was sweating, the saltwater drops sliding down her temples. Her pillow was soaked, her hair damp. In that vision, I checked her temperature, and it was too high, too high, so high that I saw myself run down the hall and put on my boots and not tie them, and I went two steps at a time to the outside, where I started my truck and cleaned off the snow just enough to see, and back upstairs I tracked snow on the floors as I raced to her bed. I threw the blankets off her and sat her up, but she could not hold herself steady, so I set her back down and went, hurriedly, to get her jacket. Again I sat her up and wrapped the jacket around her, over her light pink pajamas, and I stood her up and guided her down the hall until I realized she was light—so light, like dust, or like how I imagine the weight of a star to be, just the dot of it in the dark sky, in the middle of your palm—and I picked her up and carried her out the door and to the truck, and I almost dropped her in the snow but I didn't because the fierceness with which we love gave me enough strength.

This is where a winter storm brings you.

Like Fredrick's shoveling, like my shoveling, this vision was broken up into parts. I did not think at all about it while I was shoveling. I was thinking only about getting back to her, and when I did, I would pick back up where I had left off, except I did not envision too long a drive, only a quick bumpy and snowy road that I skidded over once and we were there, in the emergency room, waiting to be seen. There, the noise of snow falling was all I heard, that muffled quiet. We were there, I envisioned, for days, and I'm wondering only now if I thought about the storm, if I wondered about its ending while I stayed in the apartment with Louise, while the children played with their green sled. In that moment—in that fantasy—I don't know, but I do know in this imagination she did not make it. She was gone.

And I let the sadness take me, and it gripped me so tightly around the throat I could not breathe. The vision and its effect were over with a blow of my nose in a tissue, the weight of possibility, the weight of expectation, released, no longer pushing down on the top of my head. I felt like I had gotten over something, some sadness, had come to some exaltation. At the same time, I felt like something was yet to come, something big, something so big that if I hadn't made room for it I would not have made it, that the grief and sadness and fear yet to arrive would have been too much to carry.

. . .

When her temperature finally went down, she was not all better, of course. There was no miracle during this storm, or maybe there was, but she was well enough to sit up with her eyes open and stare at the TV. I made her breakfast: a fried egg and toast, the yolk broken, runny—"Can I have some water, please?"—and she pecked at the yellow, sticky pool with the corner of her toast, which she ate completely. She left the white of the egg. After, she went back to sleep, and I woke her only to take her temperature again, which was normal.

When she woke next, it was Saturday afternoon. I had slept most of the morning, and my lower back hurt, either from sleeping in the recliner or from shoveling. Maybe from both. But when I woke, she was not in bed but coming back into the room.

"I thought I was going to pee myself," she said, sitting. "I see it snowed."

"It did," I said. "How do you feel?"

"Tired," she said. "I had terrible dreams." She rubbed the space between her eyes.

I did not want to know what she'd dreamed.

Louise yawned, looked at me, and said my name. "Charles." She said it again. "I heard you crying."

I told her I wasn't crying, but she only looked at me and then looked to the floor, the space between us. She went to speak but did not. Do I tell her? I thought. Do I bring it up or let it go? I let it go. If that was one of the final times she spent knowing herself, knowing me, did I want to ruin it by pushing her into some dark depth about some truth that did not even matter? What difference did it make in the end? He had died. And she already knew why her son had not gone with him. She just wouldn't believe it.

Louise lay back in bed and asked for some tea, which I brought her, and I asked if she would be OK for a few hours. I wanted to go home and check on the place, see a neighbor the road over from me to ask to use his plow.

"You don't need my permission to leave," she said.

I was out the door and in the hallway when she asked what tomorrow was.

"Sunday," I said, and I asked why.

She was quiet.

Again, I asked why.

"I don't know," she said. "I feel like I have something to do."

. . .

The sun was out, and the miles and miles of snow shone bright white. The roads were not that great, and they were narrow from the banks of dirty snow. I took the highway, and everybody except for a select few in large trucks drove forty-five.

I drove straight to my neighbor's. He was not home, but his driveway was plowed and at the end, pressed into a pile of snow, was his plow. I didn't think he'd mind if I took it, which is what I did. I hooked it up to my truck, the metal of it cold on my hands, and I went back down the driveway and hung a left and drove down some ways. I slowed, tried to lower the plow, but it would not, so I had to get out and see what was the matter. I'd missed a plug.

It did not take me too long to plow. When I finished, I returned the plow.

The power was out, and my place was chilled. It was times like those I wished I had a woodstove. I did not plan to stay, but I ended up falling asleep on my couch for some hours under a blanket. It was not a restful sleep. The sun shone so hard on the white snow outside that the brightness woke me every so often, and when I was sleeping good, was in a real deep sleep where dreams would come, my stove beeped and my fridge banged and hummed. The power returned, and so did I to the world.

. . .

Louise was sleeping again when I returned to her place. She stayed sleeping while I took a shower and while I boiled pasta and twist-popped open some ready-made sauce that I poured on it. I made her a plate too, which I set aside on the kitchen sideboard. She woke sometime after I'd eaten, and I checked her temperature again. It was still normal.

I stayed with her again that night. She rarely spoke. In fact, I remember her speaking to me only two times the entire time I was there. The first was when she asked me if we were getting another nor'easter, and when I told her no, she waved me away and said she'd heard we were going to get one, that I didn't know what I was talking about, so I agreed, "We're bound to get another one," to which she said nothing and didn't look at me.

The second thing she said was also a question. She asked for her baby, which was right beside her in her bed. After that, she did not speak, but she did laugh quite a bit at the television.

We were watching the Justice Channel, and the show featured reenactments of 911 calls. The one she laughed at the most was about a woman who was in her own apartment when a man broke in. The woman hid in the closet with her son and was on the phone with 911. She had a gun, but the dispatcher kept telling her to put it down, officers are on the way, put it down on the floor. As soon as she did, you could hear the man crash through the closet door and the woman screaming, and the 911 dispatcher saying, "Ma'am? Ma'am?" and more screaming and yelling, and all of the fight was made louder by Louise laughing hysterically at this story of violence, laughing so hard she had to wipe tears from her face.

. . .

I wasn't sure Louise knew who I was anymore, but I was quite certain I was nobody. And as I sat there I felt myself slipping away to damp depths of sadness as I had done the night before, and I was thinking and thinking and thinking about how, in just the past year, I had just started to know her, but then I began to unknow her, getting farther and farther away like watching a boat drift from the shore and head out not to some other land but to an open water that never, ever ends. And she did not even know this, that she was on the boat.

22

WHEN LOUISE WAS BETTER, I BROUGHT HER TO her next ECT treatment. Again, Elizabeth was not there. I thought about going to Mary's work to ask about her, to see if she was OK and ask why she was not at her treatments. Instead, I went to the lady behind the glass and asked after her.

"I can't discuss patients," she said to me.

I asked her again.

"Sir," she said.

And then I said it. "But I'm her father."

"Name?" She typed something and looked at her computer screen.

"Charles Lamosway."

"That's not the name we have here. You said you were her father?"

"Never mind," I said, and I sat down.

The longer I waited for Louise, the larger my worry grew, and the less rational my thinking became. It's hard to say exactly how I felt, but however it was pushed me to think that I had to go to Mary's work. My bones could not withstand the pressure of having to wait at Louise's apartment with her until it was obvious the treatment would not cause any problems, until I could leave her and go.

Back in the truck, Louise lifted up the seat cushion and set in the empty space the car seat with the stuffed elephant, and the farther away we got from the spider-legged treatment center, the more I forgot she was there. Every now and then she massaged the stuffed elephant's gray hair, and her movement in my periphery, the reminder that she was there, frightened me.

I should have brought her home first, and I should have waited there with her until I knew I could leave. But I didn't.

We drove over the bridge to the reservation, and as we passed by our old home, I watched Louise stare at the house covered in snow.

I remembered the offices had been moved, and so I went to the correct place this time. I parked in back of the tribal offices, in the spots against the small decline that leads to the river.

"Can you wait here?" I asked Louise. "I'll only be a second."

She looked out at the river, and I got out of the truck.

"Are you bringing me home?" she asked.

"Soon," I said. "Very soon. Wait here, and don't get out of the truck."

I reached in and turned off the engine, and I locked the doors.

Behind her desk, Mary was typing. Her eyes flitted to me and then back to the computer's screen.

I shut the door behind me.

"Leave that open," Mary said.

"No," I said.

She stopped typing and set her elbows on the desk.

"What do you want?" she asked.

"What happened to her?" I said.

"Please leave."

I said it again.

"She is fine," Mary said. "Now leave."

"Where is she?"

"I won't say any more than that. She's fine. Now go."

"I haven't seen her at the treatments and I haven't seen her outside the house, so I find it hard to believe that she's fine."

"She's fine. She's not home with us, but she's fine."

"So she moved back home?"

"She's fine," Mary said. "Now leave."

"I want to know."

Mary stood up and walked around her desk to the chief's door, which was closed. She knocked.

"You'll leave," she said. "Now."

"Fuck you," I said, and I left.

. . .

I drove to Elizabeth's house. The one she was thinking she might sell. I knew it was hers because all the houses on this road were plowed and tended. Hers wasn't. The driveway was buried in a snow that was cold and hard. No smoke climbed out of her chimney, and no lights were on. When I honked my truck's horn, nobody came to the door, to the window. I did not enter her home, but I walked around the house in the snow and looked through the windows, the ones with the blinds open. It was nearly empty; none of the furniture I'd seen brought back to her parents' house was in the home.

Mary hadn't been lying, but from what I could see, Elizabeth was nowhere.

"Whose house is that?" Louise asked me when I got back in the truck.

"A friend," I said.

"When did they build that house?"

I backed out of the driveway.

"I don't know," I said.

"It's too new for this street," she said.

We drove, hearing only the hum of the heater. It was a bright blue sky day, but the air was frigid. As I headed to the bridge, once again we drove by our old home.

"Where are you going?" she asked, her head turned back, her eyes on our old house.

"I'm bringing you to your house," I said.

"It's all your fault." She said it so flatly, so matter-of-factly.

I knew what she meant, so I didn't say anything; and she also knew what she meant, exactly what she meant, and by my silence she knew I had understood her.

Maybe she was right; maybe I'd gotten it all wrong. Maybe it was all my fault.

. . .

Bobby's court hearing was later that week. I picked him up from his house in the morning. He was dressed nicer than I'd ever seen. A blue checkered button-up and brown slacks and brown sneakers. He told me not to smoke as we were driving, but then he said, "Leave the windows open. It'll be fine." I keep a roll of blue paper towels in the back seat for when I check my oil or poke around under the hood of the truck, and Bobby took the roll and ripped a few pieces for the sweat pouring down his face. I didn't think it was nerves—I could smell the old alcohol on him, squeezing through his skin and emerging to the air of the world.

We got to the courthouse early. It was in downtown Over-town. Most of the roads were one-way, and the concrete sparkled with the cold of the morning. I parked in back of the courthouse, this old stone building with copper or brass signs with dates and words. They're moving this place somewhere else now, somewhere newer and closer to the jail.

We were early, but people were outside, some smoking in nice suits and some rubbing their hands in old loose clothes. Bobby said nothing while we waited. He wiped his face with another blue paper towel.

The truck was warm, and so when I got out, the cold bit hard, so hard that for the rest of the day I would be unable to shake that chill from my body. I walked beside Bobby toward the door, and by the door he turned and leaned against the wall and lit a cigarette. He rubbed his eyes with the hand that held his long 100. He smoked it so fast his ash grew long and orange like a traffic cone.

We waited and waited. For what, I didn't know. I was waiting for Bobby, sure, but what was he waiting for?

He looked at the sky and I said, "We should go inside."

"How's my hair?" Bobby asked.

I don't know why, but I laughed at him. Maybe it was the stubble on his cheek that he missed.

"What's so fucking funny?" he said.

"It's fine," I said. "Looks fine."

Under the stubble on his cheek, his jaw clenched and released, as quick as a pulse.

. . .

I never gave any testimony. The court didn't allow it. I sat and sat and sat and listened and listened and listened to all the cases. A woman who stole a chicken and vodka and Legos from Walmart. A man on bail who got caught with cocaine. A young woman who crashed her car into a store, not by accident. And Bobby, who slapped my mother's neighbor around. Only a few people that day were sentenced to time—the woman who stole the chicken and vodka got three months; she had prior theft convictions—and the rest were hit with fines or probation or both. Bobby got a fine of $300 and six months' probation with one month served.

"He didn't even want your testimony," Bobby said when I drove him home, but I wasn't there fully. My mind was on the courtroom, the murmurs of voices, some with power, some without. I sat in two places: in the truck, turning left with Bobby yapping in my ear, and in the courtroom, situating myself on the polished oak bench, thinking about how much the judge reminded me of a man I never knew: my father, the blood one. I saw no resemblance in him, nothing, and I still can't quite figure out why I thought this, why I think this. Maybe it was because he was over there, across the way in a high seat, hunched over, looking, looking, untouchable at that distance but untouchable regardless. Always untouchable, but there, hovering. And he knew this, that man up there. Like all fathers, he knew this.

. . .

I dropped Bobby off at his house, and he said, "You were a real fucking help today, you know that?" and I thought that was the end, but before he shut the door in my face, he told me he'd need a ride home from the bar later. It didn't end, but continued.

I left him and took Louise to her treatment. Elizabeth, again, was not there—of course she was not there. The waiting room was colder than it had been in the past.

"A technician is working on the heat," the woman behind the glass said as I handed her the forms Louise had filled out.

The TV was on in the waiting room. The Weather Channel. Louise had a hold of the stuffed elephant, and she watched the TV.

"Look," she said, pointing. "A storm's coming."

The report was about Montana, and I told her so.

"But it'll come for us," she said.

This was the last week of her treatments.

"What did she say?" Louise asked. She was looking at me. I think she meant the weather lady.

I told her I didn't know.

"You never listen," she said. "Never."

. . .

I took her home, stayed the required number of hours, and told her I'd see her tomorrow.

"Don't forget the list," she said. "I need things from the store. It's on the table."

There was no list, but I pretended to take it.

23

AFTER ALMOST TWO MONTHS, ELIZABETH REAPPEARED. It was the middle of winter, the new year, and her birthday had passed. I first saw her when I came home from Louise's—she was outside shoveling snow at her parents'. I watched her from inside my house. When she finished, she went to the shed and came out with a foldout chair, which she opened and set right in the middle of the hole she had dug. I didn't know what she was doing, but from where I stood, I could see her from her chest up as she sat. And she was facing this way, looking across the river at my house. For the next few days, off and on, she sat there, smoking, rarely taking her eyes away.

· · ·

If the news hadn't made the storm out to be the worst one Maine would see in years, I wouldn't have come—I would have stayed at home and tried to see, through the falling snow, my daughter.

"I knew it would come," Louise said to me about this second nor'easter. The wind shook the house, and the air whipped through the window screen and whistled.

"Don't whistle back," Louise told me sharply, which was something Fredrick used to say. It had been some time since she'd made any mention of Fredrick, even by use of phrases. But that day she began to act removed from where the ECTs had put her, or where I had thought they had put her—in a better place— and instead seemed to be embodying some time now long past, a time we all hoped to forget.

I was staying with her through the storm. That was the plan, anyway.

"It started in Montana," Louise was saying. She was sitting up in bed, explaining to me how she had told someone it would make its way to us, this storm. She was confusing me with me, and this storm with the one we'd seen the month before on the Weather Channel in the ECT waiting room.

"He thought I was a liar," Louise said.

I said, "He sounds like a jerk."

The snow started at about three in the afternoon. I made Louise dinner, and she ate it—all of it, which led me to believe that she was well—and she finished it before the six o'clock news was over. In each of my hands I held a plate—mine, hers—and I walked them to the kitchen and rinsed them and washed them with soapy bubbles, and I put the pots and pans I'd used in the sink and soaked them with hot water. I was away from Louise for some fifteen minutes, spraying and wiping the counters and scrubbing the pots and pans I had soaked for not very long so it was still hard to scrub them clean. When I got them clean, I set them with the other dishes to dry on a red hand towel and cleaned the sink and the sideboard around it. Drops of water had dripped from the tips of my fingers, dotting the floor, so the floor was wet and I cleaned it, and on the floor below the trim of the baseboard I saw dirt and dirt and crud and more dirt, and so I swept. I was in mid-sweep, the pile of dirt and crumbs and a loose lentil and a grain of rice or two and a tangle of thin hair at my feet, when I heard what sounded to be Louise on the phone.

It was. Behind me the cream-colored cord ran around the corner to her bedroom. I stepped over the pile and ducked under the cord as I went to her.

"You don't advise it?" she was saying.

"Who are you talking to?" I asked.

With a wave of her hand, she told me to be quiet.

"OK, well thank you for your time," Louise said. "Goodbye."

She held the phone out to me. "Hang this up," she said.

I did, and then I asked again who she was talking to.

"None of your business," she said.

I finished in the kitchen, went outside for a smoke, and then found myself back in Louise's room and sitting in the recliner. Louise was no longer sitting up but was lying back with her arm over her forehead. For the longest time I thought she was sleeping, and it was only after I watched two and a half episodes of that doctor show that I heard her crying.

"What's the matter?" I said.

She said it three times, each louder than the last: "Shut up, shut up, shut up! My head."

"Do you want ibuprofen?"

Through her crying, she said, "I want you to shut up. Do not talk to me. This is your fault." Here, she sat up. "All of it is your fault! You, you, you . . ."

She plucked a tissue from her nightstand, lay back with it, and rolled over onto her side, facing away from me.

At around ten, I went outside to shovel, and across the way next door the neighbor sat out on his porch, smoking, drawing with his finger in the freshly fallen snow. I paid him no attention; I just simply shoveled away what snow had fallen so far, but at some point, a woman yelled, which startled me, and the neighbor, Rhett, flicked his cigarette and got up and went inside, the red ember fading out in the snow.

I made myself coffee when I went back indoors. I didn't want the coffee, just the warm mug in my cupped hands.

I did not watch the news, but at a quarter to eleven a preview showed for the next hour's news. Louise's room was dark except for the glow of the television, and I sat in the recliner, mug in hand, watching right as the news anchor said, "The search continues for a missing Indian Island woman. More at eleven."

Louise was sleeping, snoring in little bursts, the tissue held tight in her hand. I shook her gently.

"Louise," I said. "What did you see on the news?"

She grunted and would not look at me.

"Louise," I said again, nudging her. "What did you see?"

She looked at me with her eyes barely open. "It's your fault," she said. "All your fault."

I tried to wait for the news to come on. I waited for ten minutes, and when it did come on, they did not talk about the missing woman but kept saying they would, soon.

. . .

I suppose it was panic that pushed me toward the door and into my boots and coat and outside to my truck, and as I turned the key and the engine flared on and the headlights flashed and the snow fell in their light I realized I was leaving her.

I went to the neighbor's and knocked.

He pulled the door open and then pushed the screen door so it nudged me back. "What do you want?" he asked, and I told him, too quickly, what I needed. He looked at me. "Sure, I can do that," he said. "Lois is a nice lady. Just give me a second." He was gone down the hall to his girlfriend or wife or whoever the voice belonged to, I don't know. He came back and followed me outside. He stopped walking.

"What do you think of this?" he said, lifting something from the pile of garbage. The snow fell off the object like an animal was shaking it loose. But I was rushed, and I don't know what he was trying to show me.

"Later," I told him. "I really have to go."

He dropped whatever it was back into the snow.

"I'll be back soon," I said. "Or as soon as I know what's going on." I tried to give him some advice, some guidance on how to talk to Louise—who he kept calling Lois—and I could not, and still cannot, believe what he said.

"I know how Lois is," he said. "I used to take her for walks to the store." He pointed down the road. "She walks fast for an old lady, and I told her that. I like her, and so does my lady. Listen," he said, but I had no time, although I'm very curious now to know what he wanted to say. That's my life, though—not knowing, but wishing.

I thanked him too many times on my way to my truck. He passed through the headlights and falling snow to the stairs to Louise's, and he banged his boots on each step as he climbed. I was gone before I saw him enter the house. When you're in need, even the person you hate or distrust the most is someone you can rely on, especially when they, the hated, know they are needed for something important.

. . .

The first turn I took, the truck skidded, and so after that I drove more careful, but not careful enough. On straight roads I drove too fast, and every once in a while the snow fell too hard and I lost sight of the road. But I thought nothing of the condition of the road then, just the weight of my foot on the pedal and brake and what that news anchor had said. *The search continues, the search continues, the search continues, the search continues. More at eleven. More at eleven. More at eleven.*

I took I-95 instead of the back roads. Every few miles, signs flashed yellow to drive forty-five. I did not. I don't know how fast I drove, but it was probably closer to sixty, and I even passed two plows.

I stopped at a red light. There were no cars, just me in my truck and the snow falling slanted through the streetlights. I went to light a smoke, but I realized I had forgotten them. So I did nothing but focus on driving, on my two hands gripping the wheel. When the red turned green, my tires lost traction and the truck's back end swung left, right, left, then steadied when the wheels found something to grip.

Nobody would have known people were out searching for a missing person. The streets were empty, both in Overtown and on the reservation. After I crossed the bridge to the reservation, I parked in the church parking lot and rolled my window down. There was the sound of falling snow, the noise outside not unlike pressure in the ear, but without the discomfort. I thought I heard a plow approaching, the metal scraping the road, but no vehicle passed by.

I waited in the church parking lot for I don't know how long, and I didn't quite know what I was waiting for. A sign, something more to push me to Mary's house. The feeling to act had disappeared, reason had come back to me. My plan had been to go to Mary's, but now that I was so close, I was second-guessing. This is silly, that's what I thought. It was silly to think what I had thought, to hurry as I had and ask the neighbor to watch my mother while I chased after something I thought was falling apart. But that had been my life: a pursuit of only remains.

. . .

I drove home. Not to Louise's but to my house. The dirt road wasn't that covered—much of the snow had landed on the pines—and I could see turned-up dirt frozen hard, my old tire tracks. I drove through the soft falling white down to my house, and I could see a light on inside—the kitchen light above the stove. I turned it off when I went indoors and left the house in darkness. For a time, I stood on the porch with no light.

I watched. Across the river, all was quiet. The yellow of a kitchen light lit the window of her parents' house. The porch light was off, and so I could not see the driveway too well. Maybe both of the cars were there, I thought. What was I doing? What was my plan? I had wanted to go to her parents' house to make sure it was all in my head, that it wasn't her, but then, cowardly, or wisely, I had decided not to. It could have been anybody they were look-ing for. And so I had come to my house? For what? To see what? The same thing I always saw across the river: an untouchable past, present, future.

I kept watching across the river. Waiting. Ten, fifteen minutes. The cold was that real cold, the Maine cold. And then the lights came. Headlights. No cars had been parked in the driveway, as I had thought. Across the river and through the trees, the two lights swung and shone all the way from over there to here, and the vehicle parked in their driveway, pulled right up to the end, where the little hill down to the river began. The headlights shone, and in the light the snow dropped faster and faster and faster, my eyelashes wet with snow and so too my shoulders, and in the one or two seconds that the snow slowed I saw the footprints—not mine—leading from the end of my porch down to the river and across the frozen ice, where they disappeared up the bank on the other side.

The footprints, smaller than my own, were not fresh. Snow had filled them in partway. And so I walked in them—or I should say I walked over them, step by step, across the river. The person was moving from the car and up the porch steps. I hurried, and somewhere the ice split just enough for the sound to crack like a bone into the night.

Through the falling snow I looked, and the person stood still on the steps. I breathed heavy, hard, and maybe it was that noise that stopped the person too; they heard the sound of this human. But then the figure was gone, only for a moment, a glance, and then the porch light flicked on. I climbed up the bank, fell on my knees into the snow, and then rose.

"Where have you been?" It was Mary. She was on the porch, holding the screen door open with her leg, the wind whipping the snow indoors.

My chest was heaving. The snow, even in the footprints I had walked in, was deep across the river to this side.

"I've been trying to find you," she said. "I've been driving all over the place in this shit weather to find you. Come inside."

"Should I take my boots off?" I said to her.

She didn't answer me, so I left them on.

The lights were bright. Mary disappeared down the hallway and into a back room, and while she was gone the warmth of the indoors revealed how heavy my clothes were, how soaked with melted snow, with water.

Puddles and streaks of dirty water and salt covered the kitchen floor from boot tracks. Mary came back down the hall, and she stood in the middle of the kitchen.

I asked her. "So it's her?" I said. "It's her?"

She didn't answer my question.

"Sit," she said.

"But is it her?"

"Just sit," she said. "Please just sit." And at this she began to cry. Not quiet crying but crying with tears and heaves so loud it rocked the flesh of the fleshless, my spirit.

"What is it?" I said. "Is it her?"

We were both on our knees amid the dirty water covering the linoleum and the tiny, tiny rocks that pressed into my kneecaps and later left bruises, and the closer I moved toward her, the more she shook, and when I was near to her, just inches, she began to swing at me with her closed fist, back and forth at my arms again and again and again, screaming the incomprehensible into my ear, which she pulled at once or twice, tried to rip it off my head. If she didn't stop, if she didn't slow, I would have let her take me piece by piece by piece, if that was what it took to know.

"We didn't know it would go like this," she said. She was shaking. Her face was wet, her nose running, and she wiped at it with her sleeve. "We didn't know. We told her. We had to."

"Told her what?"

Here she stood up and looked down at me. "What do you think?" she said. She went to the kitchen sink. She wet her hands and wiped her face. I stood up.

"Roger will be back soon," she said. She wiped her nose on her sleeve. "And maybe the game warden. You can go with him.

They're upriver right now, looking along those banks. They've checked all the others."

"When did this happen?"

"Earlier," she said. "Before the snow started to fall, before we got home from work."

"That's when you told her?"

"We told her weeks ago, Charles, because what if you told her—what would she think of us?" Mary said. She didn't look at me. Over the sink, she held a glass of water, but she did not drink from the glass.

"And what happened?" I said.

"Exactly what I told you would happen."

It was around here that I wondered if I was dreaming. Mary said something. Was I dreaming?

She repeated only part of what she had said. "Are you?"

I was awake. "Am I what?" I said. It was like bugs had burrowed under my skin.

She dumped the water and let the glass roll from her palm into the sink.

"Am I what?" I asked again.

"Thirsty."

I told her no.

She sat at the table, but I did not.

"She was on watch," Mary said. "When you came to my work that day."

"What do you mean?"

"She was on watch," she said again, "up where she was getting her treatments. They have that ward. That's why you did not see her. That's where she was. Behind those locked doors in the west part of the facility. You know the ones. You've seen the doors. They'd take her in the morning for her treatments, before any appointments."

"How long was she there?" I asked.

"Long," Mary said.

"Why were they watching her?"

"You know," she said.

"I'll have some water."

Mary never told me how it happened, how she chose to try it. I never want to know. Or do I?

I got a cup and filled it. I sipped the water slow until a single drop remained at the bottom. I refilled it and went back to the kitchen table, where we sat in silence for a long, long time.

. . .

We both rose at the sound of a car approaching the front of the house, and we both sat back down when the plow passed by, kicking up snow and leaving behind brown, brown dirt. We did the same again when the plow passed by once, twice, three times more.

Again, nothing to say, but everything to think about until, for me, the thinking was too loud to keep in.

"You asked where I was?" I said.

"What do you mean?"

"When I came over," I said. "You asked where I had been. You said you were looking for me."

"I was," she said.

"And you came to my house?" I asked.

She said yes.

I was quiet. Then I told her she left my stove light on.

"You must have left it on," she said. "I didn't go inside. I drove down your dirt road, and when I didn't see your truck, I backed up and went to meet Roger near the river, the place near the dam. After the dam. I should call him and see where he is."

Mary stood.

"Wait a minute," I said.

"It's been almost two hours," Mary said. "I'm calling."

"Just wait a minute. Or don't. Call him. Fine." I went out the door and down the porch steps. Mary yelled after me, the noise muffled by the snow falling. I crawled down the snowy bank to the river and I found the way I had come. I stood up and I crossed back over the river, following my prints, under which the smaller ones were buried.

They belonged to her.

I followed the prints to my house and up the porch and inside, Mary still yelling to me from across the river all the while, a faint calling. Maybe the melted snow in the kitchen was from me, but I knew the wet linoleum down the small hallway and the wet carpet in my bedroom was from her. On my knees, I pushed my palms into it and felt the damp and dirt. She was here, had been here, in this house.

24

AFTER THAT, IT DID NOT TAKE VERY LONG FOR Roger and the game warden to show up, as well as two tribal police who had been out there searching with them. We were inside Mary's, all of us. Roger, Mary, Mel the game warden—the nephew of Shay, the man who helped search for Fredrick—and two officers whose names I did not know. One was white, I'm pretty sure, and the other tribal. We all stood over the table upon which lay a wet map of this side of the land, the page ending at some unknown boundary. Someone said something about following the tracks for as long as we could, and something about dogs, dogs, they might pick up the scent. For a time, standing there at the table, I was drunk on embarrassment: I could not help but feel like some drunken uncle who had caused so great a problem that others had to clean it up. What if, all those years ago, I had just never let Mary do what she did? What if I had said no, that I wouldn't allow it? What if I had said fuck blood quantum? But that was not how it went.

Roger stood there, sweating, the wet tips of his hair sticking out from under his blue hat. He said nothing to me while we stood in the kitchen. No—I did not expect him to say anything to me. The mess that Mary and I had made had put Roger in such a place. He reminded me of Fredrick.

. . .

I crossed the river alone. The ice cracked once, twice. The others drove on the roads. Afraid I would ruin any of her marks, I waited on my porch for them to show up. The police lights shone through the bare trees on the road, and they grew brighter and brighter as the cars came to my house and parked. There was only one cruiser. The other officer had gone to get a dog, as if they just had them in storage. The police lights were so bright I could not see behind the cruiser to Roger and Mary and the game warden as they parked.

I showed the footprints to Mel. The snow fell hard and fast, and he wiped his face as he walked, shining the flashlight at the white ground. Around the house, he knelt in the snow and dug his gloved finger into the fresh powder.

"They go this way," he said.

I've been here before, I thought. And there was something more to think about, right then, something I knew that would have been powerful if it had come to me, but her father spoke to me for the first time and stole my attention.

"We'll find her," he said.

. . .

We kept going and going and going out into the cold dark of the earth that we disturbed with all our hollering.

My hands were numb, and I walked with them in my pockets. Snow filled in the tops of my boots, and my ankles too were not warm. I was losing feeling in my body; it was as if I were separating into two things, each not unlike the other but not whole. And the snow fell harder and faster and harder—it was said that overnight the storm would be at its worst, an inch or more an hour—and it kept coming slanted and harder and faster until not even our flashlights could penetrate the wall of falling snow.

"This isn't safe," Mel said. But he did not mean for him. He was talking to Mary, to Roger, to me. Our group of six had stopped walking, had our backs to the snow falling so dense around us, the cold as deep as it had been this winter, and we had to holler to one another. The tracks, the prints, stopped there, and the dog had no sense of where to go, had got turned around and tried to go back the way we'd come. Mel said he'd radio another county for help, that they'd meet him out this way, and that they'd press on.

The four of us—the white officer brought the dog back—followed our tracks back to my house, where we had set out from. It did not seem to take us very long to return, and that was because my mind was preoccupied with what Mary and Roger were going to do—would they come in? Would they stay? Or would they go back to their home?—or because the falling snow was deafening in its own quiet way, a thing to be focused on intently, like a room furnished with only the spinning of a fan.

"Can we wait here?" Roger asked. In the porch light, his wet face sheened. And Mary's, too, was wet like that, and inside I would see she'd been crying. It was those tears that reminded me of Louise, and I wondered how she was.

I made coffee. We each held a mug, but nobody drank. I had hung our wet clothes, our jackets, hats, their gloves, above the floorboard heater all along the wall, and I had given a quick call to Louise, who had answered and given no indication that the neighbor was there. I suppose I should have expected that he'd leave. Before she hung up, she said I had woken her and not to call again.

Roger and I sat at the kitchen table across from each other while Mary stood by the front door, looking out into the storm. It was close to three in the morning, and our coffees grew cold. Nobody heated their mug in the microwave. I had never turned off the coffeepot, so I could smell the coffee burning, but I let it burn.

Every so often Mary would speak. It was always a mumble or simply words to herself, but each time Roger would say, "Huh?" She never said anything back. She was speaking just to speak, like that act was the only thing keeping her going, keeping her awake.

"I can't sit here anymore," Roger said.

"There's nothing we can do," Mary said. She did not take her eyes from the window.

"It's slowing down out," he said.

It was not slowing down. It was easy to trick ourselves into thinking that.

"They've been gone a long time," he said.

It was now around four in the morning.

"When it's light," Roger said, "I'm going out."

"You're not," Mary said.

"I am," he said.

She said nothing more.

Roger asked where the bathroom was. I told him, but then he said he'd go outdoors, and while he was gone, for the first time since we'd been there, Mary said something to me.

"Do you think they'll find her?" she asked.

"Of course," I said.

"Of course," she repeated.

While Roger was outside the power finally cut out. It would not return for three days.

"I have a lantern," I said, and I went to the closet in the hall. I crouched with a lighter, looking through a box. I found it, but it would not turn on. The batteries in it were dead. I knew I had no more, but I searched like I did, and as I searched the front door banged shut and Roger coughed and Mary told him I was looking for a lantern. I went through as many boxes as I could until the metal of the lighter was too hot and burned my fingers. In the dark I leaned against the wall. Then light—Roger had set his flashlight upright on the kitchen table. But I felt I needed batteries, felt I needed this lantern, so I kept on looking until what I found was the absence of something.

"Hand me your flashlight," I said to Roger. I needed to know with certainty. He brought it over.

I shined the light in the closet.

"You find the lantern?" Mary said.

"No," I said.

My gun was gone.

It was like a click, an alignment.

"Where are you going?" Mary said. "Those are my gloves."

I dropped the gloves to the floor.

"She took my gun," I said, and I did not wait for them to follow.

· · ·

Dawn had not yet come. I could not see anything but the falling snow and the trees before I bumped into them. My hat kept slipping down over my eyes. Three, four times I tripped, trying to walk in the deep snow, and, stupidly, I had forgotten a flashlight.

I didn't even know if I was going the right way or if I was going toward the tracks. I was near them, or so I thought, running horizontal to them.

Was that Mary yelling? Roger?

I yelled her name. I crossed a neighbor's driveway, right up near the beginning of it, and so I knew I was off track, and I cut back into the woods a bit, managing to find our old prints, almost filled with new snow. I followed them, going off in this new direction, and before I knew it I had gone too far right and found myself along the riverbank, and I stepped on thin ice, below which was hollow. I dropped down to my knee, my shin scraping against the thickening ice, an injury that would later require stitches, but that would be the least of my problems. It was a struggle to get back up, but when I did, I went more inland again until, once more, I came to the road.

I zigzagged in this way: to the road, to the river, to the road, until I knew how to stay centered. They called after me, and only now do I wonder why it was me they were looking for, not her— did they think I would lead them to her, take them to her? I kept on through the dark and rising trees and cold falling snow until the sky grew a little bit brighter, just a smear of light, straight ahead to the east, that lit the sky as if far away a fire blazed.

But it was only the sun.

Here, the shivers began. I ran for so long, the cold getting colder, that I forgot what I was chasing. Her? Fredrick? Louise? Myself? I began to talk to nobody. Out here in the cold lay only trees and snow and snow and more snow up to my knees, my thighs. It went deep, as do most things if you look hard enough. My running turned to walking, then limping. The sky grew a brighter and brighter gray with each step, but there was no sun to be seen—it was behind the dense clouds. I remember think-ing my hat was down over my eyes, but it was not: I could not lift my head. My fingers had no feeling. Neither did my ankles, my feet. Time passed the way it does when you don't pay it any attention: fast.

More light.

My pant leg was frozen to the blood that seeped from my shin wound, and it hurt when I tore it, when I peeled the fabric from the skin. The wound must have bled again, because it got warm. But then again, everything got warm: my head, my neck, my torso and arms and fingers, my waist, my thighs, my knees, my calves and my ankles and my toes. My chest.

I shed my clothes, piece by piece, as I stumbled along, until I felt I could no longer go on. I fell backward into the fresh powder, and when I lifted my head, I saw the hidden sun, and when I rested my head back, upside down and looking not east but west, I saw a sun too, blazing, it seemed, like it had crashed into the earth and was setting the world on fire.

She wasn't out here. We had it all wrong. We were all going in the wrong direction—or we had failed to notice when she turned around.

I smelled the smoke.

I don't remember how long it took me to get there, I don't remember how many clothes I was wearing, but I do remember thinking, So what, I didn't rescue him then and I wasn't going to rescue him now. But her. I could rescue her. And she was this way, not toward the east but toward the west, the future.

Fredrick's house was on fire. Fire trucks and ambulances and police cruisers and their red and white and blue lights lit the air as I made my way back to my house and called for Mary and Roger. I ignored their questions about what was happening as I crossed the frozen river, the both of them behind me. The bright lights lit the snow that fell like ash.

"Why aren't you putting it out?" Mary asked the firemen.

"Our lines are frozen," a firefighter said. "We're waiting for Overtown to come—" He looked at me. "Are you OK?"

I wasn't. I barely had any clothes on, my leg was bleeding, and my head hurt like it had been cracked by a rock. Before I could even tell him no, two EMTs brought over a blanket and wrapped it around me as they guided me toward the ambulance. They were preparing to settle me in the back when Mary screamed so loud and hard I knew a part of the world was about to die. I turned and looked and one officer dragged Mary from where she stood, and then three took hold of Roger.

"Get in the ambulance, please," an EMT said to me.

I looked at Mary, who yelled with what she had left. "She's in the house, Charles! Right there! I see her! She's in the house!"

Part of it, the left side, crumbled, and smoke and flame billowed. I felt the heat, and I pushed the two EMTs from me, took the blanket and wrapped it around the face of a man who tried to grab me and yanked him to the ground. I passed the fire truck and lifted a steel axe from two hooks, and I ran for the house. The firefighter closest to the home went to grab me but I raised the axe, and he took several steps back as I limped for the house, the house that would be gone in the morning.

The main door was a wall of fire, and so I went into the small garage with the old ash-pounding machine, went right to the far wall. On the other side of that wall, I knew, was the living room. I put my hand to it and it was warm, so warm, and if I had been here under any other circumstance I could have easily just fallen asleep against that wall and fallen with the rest of the house. But I lifted the axe and swung and swung and swung, the way Fredrick and I would cut wood, and I eventually split the wall enough that I could fit through.

She was in sight: she was across the empty room, leaning against the other wall, two wooden boards across her lap as she awaited the approaching flames.

"Elizabeth!" I told her to hold on. What little clothes remained of my pants were on fire, literally, my skin burning. I patted the flames out as best I could with the wet blanket the EMTs had thrown over my shoulders, and when I took one step there was a small yet distinct pop and then a searing pain in my side. I looked up, and Elizabeth had my gun, Fredrick's gun, Joseph's gun—her gun. She kept it aimed at me.

I was on my knees, crawling in the fire toward her, hands burning. "Don't," I said. She pumped the .22, but before she could fire another shot at the only real target—my head—two things happened: the front of the house collapsed, and then jets of water sliced through the snow and cold and ash and fire and blinded us both like light that burned hotter than fire, than the sun, and before I could say one more word to her, a burnt two-by-four dropped from the ceiling and put me to sleep.

25

I WOKE TWO DAYS LATER. THE ROOM WAS LIT ONLY by the hospital's hall light. I thought I was alone. Machines beeped when I pulled wires from my gauze-wrapped arms, and then a hand was on me.

"Jesus Christ," Bobby said. "Don't go nowhere."

"Where is she?" I asked, but he was gone.

I felt I had somewhere to be, except I did not have the strength to bring myself there. I wondered how Bobby had found me here. And I asked him later, in the morning, after I had slept again and dreamed of fire and water.

He sipped coffee from a white Styrofoam cup. "Your mother told me," he said.

And I wondered how she knew. And before Bobby explained, in those brief moments, it was as if she loved me more than anything, as if some miracle had occurred, some vision, maybe sent by Fredrick himself, had spoken to her, told her what had happened to me.

But no. Bobby had called Louise after the storm to see if I was there, and she said, "Who? Stop calling. Don't you know she's missing?"

"Then I saw it on the news," Bobby said. "That she'd been found and that someone else was brought to the hospital. I don't know why, but I just felt like I had to call around and ask for you. Sure as shit you were here. They didn't tell me a goddamn thing. I had to tell them you were my brother, and only then would the fucking bitch tell me you were alive."

I suppose this was the miracle: the part where I woke up and Bobby was there.

I was in the hospital for nine days, and before I was discharged, I called Mary. I don't think she wanted to ask how I was feeling, but she did. And when I told her I'd be fine, she said, "That's good," and we were both silent until I asked her about Elizabeth. "Her thighs are burned bad," she said. "They did two skin grafts."

"Is she here?" I asked. I coughed, and the bullet wound made me wince.

"She was," she said. "But they moved her back to the building where she gets her ECTs. She refuses to see any of us. We can't get in to see her. She only has one name on her visitors list, and it's not Roger or me."

"Maybe it's me," I said.

She hung up.

26

I WENT UP TO THE FACILITY TO SEE HER. IT WAS half past four on a Wednesday, and I parked in the same lot I parked in when I took Louise to her ECT appointments. I got out of the truck, my leg hurting and my neck a bit sore. My body was broken still from the search, from the fire. It was almost dark when I limped to the front doors; a last sight of blue cut across the horizon, right above those tall pines. The security guard—not the tiny, tiny man with pale skin; I don't know what happened to him, maybe he had moved on somewhere else—stood up from behind his desk. Before he could speak, I said, "Just car keys, I'll get a locker," and he sat back down and looked past me to the outdoors, as if that was what he wanted. Or maybe a smoke.

I told the woman behind the desk I was there to visit some-body. I said that. "Somebody," like Elizabeth was still a secret. And the woman said I'd missed visiting hours, that they were from two to four Monday through Friday and ten to six on Sat-urday. When I left, not a sliver of blue remained up above: just the black licorice of the night sky. And no stars shone, but they were there, and I'd see them on the highway as I drove home on that last stretch of 95, where the lights are few and far between, crumbs to an ant.

On the drive home I was relieved, and maybe it was that relief that had blinded me to the fact that I had not even checked to see if I was on the visitors list. So all that night I barely slept, thinking about how dumb I was for not having asked. Even when I did fall asleep, I could never stay asleep for more than five minutes, one reason being I kept thinking about Elizabeth and the other being the pain in my leg. This went on until four in the morning, when I decided to just get up and watch the sun rise, and it rose, but the day was a cloudy one, and all I saw was the change from dark to light gray, hazy, clouded in the way wax sometimes gets.

I had to wait until two, and that waiting reminded me of the day Mary planned to bring Elizabeth to see me. I stuck around home for some time, but by ten I had begun to feel restless, and so I drove up to Louise's. When I got to her, she was in the living room, the elephant in her lap as she sat at the table and played games in a book filled with crosswords and word search puzzles and sudoku.

Louise looked up from her book but said nothing.

I asked her if she wanted coffee or tea, and with the pencil she held she tapped the mug in front of her.

"Do you want it heated?" I asked.

"No," she said.

I asked how she was feeling.

"Are you a nurse?" she asked. I didn't know if it was an honest question or if it was a taunt.

I went to ask if she knew my name, but she cut me off.

"I shit myself this morning," she said, writing something in the margins of the sudoku she played. "That's how I'm feeling."

I asked stupidly, "Where?"

"Where do you think?" she said. "In my pants."

I told her I'd be right back, and I went to her room. A few months ago, she would have cleaned the mess. But now she had not. I stripped her bed of the soiled sheets and carefully brought them to the house's basement. A sink was down there, and under the water I washed out what I could before loading the sheets into the washer. Back upstairs, Louise continued to work away at her game.

"Did you change your clothes?" I asked her.

"I'm not an animal," she said.

I could smell it.

"I'm not saying you are," I said. "I'm just asking."

"You're the animal," she said. Now she looked at me. "A dog. Nothing but somebody's dog."

I could see it now, all of it. It ran down her leg and up her back and down the chair legs.

I called her Mom, and she said, "I'm not your mother."

"Louise," I said. "You have to wash and change. Come on."

"I already did," she said, setting the elephant upright on the table. It fell forward on its face.

"You did not," I said to her. She needed to see. I felt this was the only way: I ran my hand along her back and showed her.

That face. Like all things she knew to be true were turned upside down. Like all things right were now not right.

She said, "But I did. I know I did. I know I did. I did." Her hands were covered as she stood up and looked at it all. And here she said, looking me in the eyes, trying to touch my face with her shit hands, "Charles, you, Charles, I did. I did." She walked toward her room, and in there she pointed to a pile of soiled clothes in the corner I had not seen before.

So she had. "But it happened again," I said.

I led her to the bathroom, and I turned on the shower.

"Wash off," I said, "and I'll bring you clothes."

While she sat in one of those white shower chairs under the water, I cleaned the living room chair and its legs and the floor below it all. And then I brought her clothes down to the laundry room and set them to the side until the sheets were done. Back upstairs, I brought her fresh clothes and draped them over the towel rack and let her know they were there.

I was sitting in the living room when she came out. The clothes she had on—just pajama bottoms and a long-sleeve shirt—were wet, like she had not dried off before putting them on.

"I'm going to lie down," she said to me.

I checked the time, and then I followed her.

"Your sheets aren't clean yet," I said.

"My sheets?"

"I put them in the wash," I told her. "To clean them."

"But I cleaned them," she said. "Go get them."

"They'll be wet," I said. "Do you have other sheets?"

She didn't answer me. She got in the sheetless bed and pulled the blankets up to her neck.

"Are you cold?" I asked.

"Am I?"

"I'm asking. Are you?"

"No," she said.

"I can put the heat on if you are."

"I'm not," she said, and she rolled onto her side.

I put the heat up just a bit.

"I'll be back," I said to her. "I have to be somewhere. And when I'm back, I'll dry your sheets and cook you something to eat."

"You have to see another patient?" she asked.

"Another patient?"

"You're my doctor, right?"

"I'm not your doctor," I said.

She paused a moment, rolled over, and looked at me.

"The nurse," she said. "Wait. No, no, that's not right. You're not the nurse."

"You're right," I said. "Do you know who I am?"

She looked at me like you look at a puzzle. "I do," she said with what seemed to be a smile but could have easily been a frown, and she rolled back onto her side.

. . .

It was half past two when I parked in the lot of that spider building. I sat in my truck for I don't know how long. Ten, fifteen minutes. I smoked two cigarettes and dumped out the truck's ashtray in a small bag I kept in the back for garbage. And then I smoked another.

I could not bring myself to go inside. It wasn't because I didn't want to—I did—but I felt unprepared. Like I was coming with nothing, which wasn't far from the truth. But I needed to bring her something, didn't I? I started the truck and went down to that Rite Aid near downtown, and I bought two bars of Hershey's and a *People* magazine and spearmint gum. And after I checked out, I started to worry I smelled bad, like shit, and so I went back in and bought some body spray, which was too strong, but I used it anyway. I drove back with the windows down, trying to blow that smell away, and I grew cold with the air cutting across my knuckles. When I made it back, I had to park in a different spot because somebody had taken mine.

It was three fifteen.

"It's for somebody who I'm visiting," I said to the security guard as he looked in the bag. He told me to give it to the woman behind the desk, that she'd make sure the patient got it.

"I can bring it up," I said to him.

"You can't," he said. "They need to search it."

"But you just did," I said.

The woman behind the desk spoke. "Bring it over here."

"It's food and a magazine," the guard said.

I brought the bag over.

"We have to take the staples out," she said about the magazine. "Who is it for?"

"It's for somebody who I'm visiting."

"Does the somebody have a name?" the woman said. A Styrofoam tray of rice and curry the color of wet sand lay on the desk in front of her. Her white plastic fork was stained brown.

"Elizabeth. Elizabeth Francis."

She typed something on her computer. "Your name?"

I told her.

"Hold on one second," she said. She picked up the phone and made a call.

"If I'm not on the list, that's OK," I said.

"It's not that—"

She was not on the phone for too long. "There's no last name here," she said. "Can you check with her?"

A minute or two of silence. Then she put her hand over the receiver. "This will just take a second," she said to me.

Of course Elizabeth wouldn't know my last name. Or maybe she'd forgotten. Or maybe she didn't care to remember.

"So it's right," the woman said. "OK, thank you."

The woman wrote my name on a tag, which I pressed to my shirt. She said that once they—I don't know who—had gone through what I'd brought, they'd give it to Elizabeth. And then she told me where to go. Left down that hall and to the door with the buzzer. When the door buzzes and unlocks, go straight. On the left is the elevator. Take it to the third floor.

Then there's another set of doors. Ring the buzzer. "They'll bring you to her," she said.

They did not bring me to her, because as I passed through those last doors, she was right there, waiting, the staff and patients and other visitors going about their business while a man with a yellow over-the-head radio earmuff walked up and down and up and down the hall, talking to nobody. She was right there and I didn't even know it, among them all, near the main desk, and I walked past her, right past her to the desk, and asked this tall man with glasses where I could find Elizabeth Francis.

"I'll go get her," the man said, but then he asked another to get her, and it was the other—a very old man with a gray beard—who said, "Sure." And when he rose, he said, "Oh, she's right there behind you," and all of them—the tall man with glasses, the old man, and a young woman who was standing beside them—they all laughed.

She was wearing blue hospital pants and a gray hoodie that said "Penobscot" across it.

"I got you some—"

"Come with me," she said, and I followed her. The hallway was long and warm.

We reached the end of that hall, and against the wall were two blue plastic chairs. She sat down in one, each of the corners rounded.

"This floor is for retarded people," she said. "See that guy down there?" She pointed down that long hallway to the man with the yellow radio earmuffs, who was running in circles. "He thinks he's a German spy. He keeps telling me they're keeping him here against his will, that they caught him trying to transmit sensitive government information. At least once a day he tells me he has a secret, a secret so big it could change the course of human history. Are you going to sit?"

I sat down.

"The floor below us is for people on watch. People who aren't like him are down there. There were no beds, so they put me on this floor. What I'm saying is that I'm not like them. Or maybe I am."

"You're not," I said.

"I'm joking—I know I'm not."

We were quiet for some time. Elizabeth lifted her legs up and tucked them under her.

"Did she tell you to come?" she said.

"Who?" I asked.

"My mother."

"No," I said. "She said you were here. I thought to come up."

Elizabeth put her hands in her sleeves. "My mother kept saying that it was the right thing to do. Telling me the truth. Why did she tell me?"

"Because she felt it was the right thing to do?" I asked.

"Why? Why was it the right thing to do? Why, all of a fucking sudden, did she tell me? Look, I'm not in this place because of what she said. I'm not. So don't sit there and look sorry. I'd be here no matter what. I just want to know why."

"Why she told you?" I said.

"Are you listening to me?"

I told her why. And she listened to me, in that chair with her hands in her sleeves. I told her that my plan was to tell her the truth, that I felt she should know it, that she deserved to know the history that was hers. We are made of stories, and if we don't know them—the ones that make us—how can we ever be fully realized? How can we ever be who we really are?

"So what are you saying?" she asked. "You think my life would have been different if my mother married you and you raised me?"

"I'm not saying that," I said.

"Well, what are you saying?"

"I'm saying there's more history that belongs to you than you know."

Elizabeth stood up and went into a room—a woman in there yelled at her to get out—and she came back and sat down. "You have ten minutes before visiting time is over," she said. "Can you tell me that history in ten minutes?"

"No," I said.

"You better try," she said. "There was a reason why I tried to shoot you. This is the only time you have with me."

I got what I could out. I was lucky in that they let me stay a bit longer. But there was so much more to say and not enough time to say it. I wanted to say it all: wanted to give her all the history that is hers. This past. This family. I wanted her to know, wanted her to understand what it meant that she was being stretched beyond the walls of her parents' house, that she was of that house, certainly, but also of others—the one across the river, and the one down the road that almost became a museum but didn't because Elizabeth burned it to the ground so that all that remained was the charred, burnt wood of the story that is hers.

At the end of the hallway, before I turned the corner to leave through the locked doors, I glanced back at her. She still sat with her legs tucked under her, her hoodie up, and then she raised her arm and gave me a wave, a goodbye, a see ya never.

27

IT WASN'T UNTIL THE NEXT DAY—ALMOST 5:00 AM—
that I remembered I'd completely forgotten about Louise and her
clothes and bedding I'd put in the wash for her. After I left the
treatment center, I went to the bar and talked with Bobby, told
him how it went—"Jesus," he had said, "she tried to kill you? She
must really hate your guts"—and after I brought him home, I
drove home and had a strong urge for apple pie. I drove out to
Jim's Corner and the whole way I had my high beams on and when
I got there all he had were packaged Hostess Fruit Pies, which I
still bought, and at home I ate them outside on the cold steps and
drank coffee and smoked until I couldn't take the chill anymore. I
went to bed, meaning I lay there restless on the couch until morning, until I remembered what I'd forgotten about: my mother.

The sun was bright off the white hard snow when I left my
house to go to Louise's. I wanted to stop and get her a coffee and
toast and eggs, but I'd left her for far too long to stop off and
figured I'd make her some when I got to her house. I didn't have

much gas left, but it was enough to get me there and I figured I'd go fill up after.

The neighbor was outside when I pulled in and parked my truck. He was jabbing an ice chopper into the ice that covered his driveway. I said, "How you doing?" and he stopped and in the bright sunlight looked up and squinted and said, "Fine," and went back to cracking the ice. With a limp, I walked up the steps to Louise's and the neighbor yelled to me.

"You still owe me money," he said. "For the car seat."

I was halfway up the stairs and said back to him, "I know. I'll get it for you the next time. Is that OK?"

He said he could use it today, and so I said I'd get it today.

"Let me see Louise for a bit and then I'll go to the bank," I told him.

He didn't say anything and went back to chipping the ice.

I went inside, and before climbing the steps up to Louise's apartment, I went downstairs to the washer and dryer in the basement that smelled like oil. They were both empty. I thought maybe someone had taken her sheets out and put them somewhere so they could use the washer, but I couldn't find anything. I left and went up the steps to the first floor and then climbed the stairs to Louise's apartment. The doorknob turned, but the door didn't move. She had the dead bolt turned, the dead bolt she'd said so very long ago was broken, and so I knocked a few times. Nothing, and so then a few times more.

"Louise?" I said loudly. "You sleeping?"

Nothing.

"Louise?" I said again. I could hear her TV on, could hear that show with Dr. Something.

"Louise!" I knocked again, harder and louder. "You gotta undo the dead bolt!"

But she didn't answer.

I thought maybe I could get her attention by going outside and yelling at her through the window high above, even though it was closed. I yelled her name a few times before I started picking up chunks of hard snow and throwing them at her window, hitting the glass.

"Louise!" I said, and then I paused, trying to think who I should say I was. The doctor? The nurse? Fredrick? Her son? I decided against them all.

"It's me!" I yelled. "It's me! Go open the door!"

The window opened and the woman who lived next to Louise stuck her head out.

"What the fuck do you want?" she said, and I realized I was at the wrong window.

I apologized and told her what I was doing.

"Well, her window's over there," she said. I went to that one and started again, throwing the chunks of hard snow and ice at the window. I would have kept going but from behind me, the neighbor spoke.

"What's the matter?" he said.

"Louise locked the damn dead bolt," I said.

"I got a key for it," he said.

"Why do you have a key for my mother's door?"

"She gave it to me," he said. "A long time ago."

I waited outside with my hands on my hips, looking up at the window and my cold breath rising. A cloud had passed by and the sun sneaked out and blinded me, so I looked down and blinked a few times and walked to the front of the building where the neighbor was with the key.

"Here," he said. "Just give it back when you're done."

"You're not getting the fucking key back," I said, "and you're not getting any fucking money for that fucking car seat neither. Now fucking get."

I climbed the narrow steps to the top floor. At her door, I slid the dead-bolt key into the keyhole and turned. The door swung open, and then I shut it behind me. I banged my shoes on the mat and then took them off.

The TV was blaring, the narrator of Dr. Something's show talking about that standard Y incision.

"Louise," I said, walking to her bedroom. "Why the hell did you give that neighbor a key to—"

With the sheets I forgot to dry, Louise's bed was made so neatly, the corners and sides tucked in tightly, and in the middle of the bed lay my mother, her hands gripping the blanket and holding it up to her neck, and right beside her was that elephant, equally tucked in and equally still.

"Louise?" I said.

She didn't move.

". . . and this finding confirms that the attack on Matthew's face was not by . . ."

I turned the TV off, and in the quiet I walked to the side of her bed.

"Mumma?" I said, and I put my finger on her stiff neck.

I sat in the recliner I always sat in and smoked a cigarette. Louise's phone rang in the kitchen, and then it stopped. I turned the TV back on but put the volume down to three. Before I sat down again, I took the elephant away from her body, and I held it, rolled it over in my hands and rubbed its fur. And then I set it next to me in the recliner, closed my eyes, and took a deep breath, and when I opened them, she was still the way she had been, lifeless, and so I just started talking, told her body the truth of every story I had ever been part of, beginning with who that elephant belonged to.

28

I CREMATED HER. THE GROUND WAS TOO HARD for any burials, and so I held on to her ashes until the earth softened. There was a part of me that didn't want to put her all in the ground, and so I bought one large urn and then two small ones. I kept one and I gave the other to Bobby, who was so torn up about Louise. He stopped drinking at the bar and started drinking at my house, almost every single night, from late January to May, when we could finally put my mother to rest next to Fredrick. I don't know how many drunken toasts Bobby gave my mother during those months. "To the best woman this earth has seen," "To the mom I wish I had," "She didn't give a fuck about nothin'," and "Why'd she have to go like this?" When he was particularly drunk, he would open the tiny urn and speak French: "Vous nous manquerez et on se souviendra d'eux," "Une vie trop tranquille est une mer morte," and "Après la pluie, le beau temps."

And after the rain, the good weather did come.

. . .

The only other person besides Bobby—and Gizos—to know my mother died was Mary, because I went through her to buy the plot next to my father. And so it had to have been Mary who told the others on the reservation that Fredrick's wife had passed away, because who else would have said something?

On the day we buried Louise—on the day I got down on my knees, my leg and body still hurting, and lowered her large urn into a square hole in front of a headstone that read "Loving Mother & Loving Wife"—a small group of people gathered to watch. I recognized a few of them, but mostly they were random people stopping by to give their condolences. I didn't know why, but I expected Gizos to show up. He didn't, although he did send flowers and make a donation in her name to that treatment center that looked like a spider. I stayed longer than I wanted to—Bobby was inconsolable and drunk—but I suppose it was good because Mary showed up, and she wasn't alone. Elizabeth was with her, as was Roger, and all three came over to me.

The first thing Mary said to me wasn't about my mother but instead was about Bobby. "Who is that?" she asked. "He's freaking people out."

I didn't know it until Mary said it, but Bobby was going around showing people Louise's ashes, and so I went up to him and told him to quit it or get in the fucking car, that Mary and my daughter had shown up, that Louise's granddaughter was here, and he looked so, so very sorry and went and sat down against the chain-link fence of the cemetery.

"He's done," I said to Mary. "Thanks for coming."

"I am sorry she's gone," Mary said.

A moment later she said, "I always liked her," and then she grabbed Roger gently by the arm and pulled him away so it was only me and Elizabeth standing there.

"You would have gotten a kick out of your grandmother," I said to her. "She was a lot like you in so many ways."

"I thought she was funny when we used to wait together for our ECTs," Elizabeth said.

"You look good, by the way," I said. She did. She had on a flower-patterned dress, and her hair was braided. "How are you feeling?"

"You should stop worrying about me and start worrying about yourself," she said.

She was probably right. I looked terrible. I hadn't been taking care of myself. My nails were dirty, and if you lifted my pant leg, you'd see my wound had gotten infected again. I imagine both of my eyes looked like they'd been punched.

It got too quiet, and Elizabeth went to speak, but I cut her off.

"I have something for you," I said. "If you want it."

I said I'd be right back. A few people stopped me and said they were sorry. Bobby was asleep against the fence.

In the back seat of my truck, I grabbed the elephant, and in the front seat I dug around for the small urn I'd meant to keep. I took them with me and went back to Louise's grave, where Elizabeth stood waiting.

"Here," I said, and I handed her the elephant and the urn.

"Isn't that your mom's baby?"

"It is," I said. "And if Louise knew everything, she would have wanted you to have it. The elephant is actually yours, anyway."

"Mine?" Elizabeth asked.

"Yours," I said. "I can tell you about it, if you want. I can tell you about her." I got down on my knees one more time, and with my hands I pulled the pile of moist dirt next to the headstone and dragged it and dumped it into the hole, covering my mother in her urn. The wind blew and rippled the trees, their pale green underbellies showing. I thought I was alone then, just me and my mother, but before I could pull the last bit of dirt that was there, Louise's granddaughter told me to move, and she got on her hands and knees and with her arm she pushed the rest of the earth, our sweet, sweet earth, over our shared blood that was now turned to ash.

ACKNOWLEDGMENTS

MY DEEPEST THANKS TO THE WONDERFUL PEOPLE at Tin House: Win McCormack, Masie Cochran, Becky Kraemer, Nanci McCloskey, Craig Popelars, Beth Steidle, Alyssa Ogi, Elizabeth DeMeo, Anne Horowitz, Allison Dubinsky, Jae Nichelle, and Jacqui Reiko Teruya. In my last acknowledgments page for *Night of the Living Rez*, I wrote, "You all feel like family."

Things have changed since then: You are family.

Infinite thanks to Masie Cochran, my wonderful editor, whose indelible genius helped guide me in making this novel what it is today. Without her brilliant editorial eye, her kind heart, and wise advice, my reworking and revising of *Fire Exit* might have been a book you would set Fire to and then Exit.

Fire Exit would also not be the book it is today without the help from so many people. Shout out to Aaron Hamburger for being an early, early reader of this book. The draft he read was so bad it could have spontaneously combusted. My many thanks must also go to the writers I do not know personally but whose work I read or revisited while working on *Fire Exit*: Louise Erdrich, Ocean Vuong, Marilynne Robinson, Leslie Marmon Silko, Colson Whitehead, and James Welch.

To my older "sister" Cara Hoffman: with so much love and respect, I thank you for everything—being there for me whenever I need help; having intellectually irreverent conversations about art, literature, writing, and South Park; and always telling me what I need to hear. Again, this is all with so much love and respect. Where would I be without you? Especially since you helped me find my other older "sister".

Rebecca Friedman. Thank you for being the best agent—no—the best "sister" who just so happens to be an agent. You care so deeply about my work, but you care even deeper about me as a person. With love, thank you.

I will always give thanks to the people in my early life who encouraged me to write, and I extend my many thanks to Carol Lewandowski and John Goldfine. You were the best teachers a student could ask for.

And, of course, my many thanks to all the booksellers and librarians I met and have yet to meet. You all have dedicated your lives to a work, a passion, that sustains the life of the literary community. Lastly, many thanks yous are owed to my readers and followers. Thank you for supporting me and my work.

As always, I am indebted to the Penobscot Nation—and to all my ancestors who came before me, who endured and persisted for us to be here—for its immense support. Tribal resources allowed me to pursue my dreams in higher education, which undoubtedly helped get me to where I am. Thanks must also go to the Penobscot community at large: you all have cheered me on and have always encouraged me. I hope this second book makes you as proud as my first.

To my mother, Carol Morgan: I miss you and I love you. You were always proud of my achievements and bragged about them to anyone, and so I hope this book makes you proud wherever it is we go when that time comes. To my father, John Talty, I miss you and I love you. We're both sorry, I know that, and we both have forgiven each other—or so my strange dreams have told me. Thank you to my Grammy; thank you to my real sister, Jessica Moores, for always being supportive and reading everything I write—I love you, Jess. Many thanks to my aunts and uncles: Aunt Linda and Uncle Mike; Aunt Susie and Uncle Tom; Aunt Dot Dot and Uncle Albert; and Aunt Barbara and Uncle Conrad. Thank you to my cousins Stephanie, Mike, Jade, Julie, and Lily. A special sweet thanks to my nieces and nephews: Joao, Josie, and Lizzy.

And lastly, thank you to my mother- and father-in-law—Linda and Kevin—for all you do and continue to do. To my brother- and sister-in-law and my nephew—Keven, Melanie, and Cole—I thank all three of you once again mainly because you live right next to me and if I didn't that might cause some tension. You still need to remove the tree that fell from your property onto ours, by the way. But in all seriousness, you know I love you all very, very much, and I couldn't be happier to have you all in my life. And a special, special thank you to Robin, who, in writing *Fire Exit*, walked across my keyboard countless times, her paws typing and adding letters to the book that made no sense. We will do *head bonks* one day again.

To nəčičis (my baby): Charlie. There is nothing more beautiful and sacred than you. While I wish you would stop screaming like a pterodactyl so I can write this, you have taught me more about love than anything. And one day I will teach you it's not nice to slap your father in the face for the entire duration of your bottle-feeding time. I love you, gwusis. I love you so, so much, as does you-know-who…

Your mumma, Jorden! To my best friend, wife, and the mother of our child: Thank you. Thank you, thank you, thank you, thank you, thank you, thank you, thank you, thank you. Nothing would be as it is today if we had never met. Charlie, my man—you and I lucked out. Big time. Listen, gwusis: your mom? I've never seen her love anything more than you. Jord, love has no measurement, but if it did, my love for you would be immeasurable.

MORGAN TALTY is a citizen of the Penobscot Indian Nation. His debut short story collection, *Night of the Living Rez*, won the PEN/Robert W. Bingham Prize, the American Academy of Arts and Letters Sue Kaufman Prize, the National Book Critics Circle John Leonard Prize, the New England Book Award, the National Book Foundation's 5 Under 35 Honor, and was a finalist for the Barnes & Noble Discover Great New Writers Award, the Andrew Carnegie Medal for Excellence in Fiction, the Mark Twain American Voice in Literature Award, and The Story Prize. His writing has appeared in *The Georgia Review*, *Granta*, *Shenandoah*, *TriQuarterly*, *Narrative*, Lit Hub, and elsewhere. Talty is an assistant professor of English in Creative Writing and Native American and Contemporary Literature at the University of Maine, Orono, and he is on the faculty at the Stonecoast MFA in Creative Writing as well as the Institute of American Indian Arts. He lives in Levant, Maine.

The People's Pharmacy

A Guide to Prescription Drugs, Home Remedies and Over-the-Counter Medications

The People's Pharmacy

A Guide to Prescription
Drugs, Home Remedies and
Over-the-Counter Medications

Joe Graedon

St. Martin's Press
New York

Library of Congress Cataloging in Publication Data

Graedon, Joe.
The people's pharmacy.

Bibliography: p.
Includes index.
1. Drugs. 2. Drugs—Side effects.
3. Medicines, Patent, proprietary, etc.
4. Medicine, Popular. I. Title. [DNLM:
1. Pharmacy—Popular works. 2. Drugs—Popular
works. 3. Pharmacology—Popular works. QV704
G734p]
RM122.5.G7   615'.1   75-40788

This book is dedicated to:

Terry Snail

*Without whose advice, assistance, constant support, and
love this book could never have been completed*

Mom and Dad

*Who were always there offering encouragement and love,
especially when the going got rough*

People Everywhere

*Who care about their health and who want to learn more
about the drugs their doctors prescribe*

Acknowledgments:

During the past eight years many people contributed in one way or another to making this book possible. Although it would be impossible to mention everyone, special thanks go to the following:

John Barth, who helped me ask the question and who started me writing
Katy Kimura, who started the ball rolling
Joseph Gardocki, who opened the first door
Carl Pfeiffer, who made pharmacology come alive
Leonide Goldstein, a magnificent teacher, who taught me how to think "scientifically"

Maurice Seevers, who took a chance on a long shot
Edward Domino, who supported and encouraged me when times got tough
C. B. Smith, who made life miserable
Henry Swain, who planted the original idea
Fernando Galindo, a beautiful person, who gave me a great opportunity

The following friends all contributed directly or indirectly to the development of my thinking and as a result to the development of this work:

Abel Arango; Leo Ars; Jorge Ayala; Helen Brand; Mary Bye; Alice and Chuck Cambron; Peter Clark; Mark Cohen; Belita Cowan; Rusty Davenport; Marvin and Carolyn Davidson; Denny Dietz; Tom Dunne; Henrietta Eolis; Trudy Esch; Chris Fitch; Joseph Frany; Christine Gailey; Francis Goldstein; Dick and Karen Gorini; Julie Graham; Jim Greenberg; Kathe Gregory-Silvera; Karen Grote; Wanda Grove; Jonathon Harris; Jennifer, Marcia, and Ricardo Hofer; John Howe; Betty Jenny; Devva Kasnitz; Emil and Marguerite Marty; Lee and Kaye Miller; David and Peggy Mohrman; Lorna and Bill Moore; Caty and Fernando Mora; Dee and Paul Mundschenk; Mike Naimark; Pat Niemeyer; Judi, Bernard, and Barney Nietschmann; Wayne and Jan Ohlsson; Nancy Peace; John Pfeiffer; Skip Rappaport; Anita Rosas; Ed and Mary Scheier; Carol Schmer; Richard Schulman; Robert and Phyllis Schultz; Henry Selby; Steve and Martha-Julia Sellers; Benjamin Sidon; Tom and Barbara Smigel; Arthur Soll; Vicki Swain; Hector Tenorio; Brian Weiss; Robert White; Anne Wilson

TABLE OF CONTENTS

additives. * What is a Dose-Effect-Relationship? Does **ANACIN** really have extra strength? * Suggestibility and the Placebo cure. Bio-Feedback for the future.

Drug induced illness. Side effects and adverse reactions; who is at risk? * The doctor's responsibility to communicate. * Medications that affect sexual performance and desire. * What you should know about the dangers of three common drugs: **INDOCIN, AMPICILLIN,** and **LASIX.** * How to protect yourself from your drugs and your doctor. * The pharmacist's responsibility to inform. How to take care of your medicines. What to do about **TETRACYCLINE** and **NITROGLYCERIN.** * Spray cans and your health: the consumer's responsibility. * Over-used and dangerous drugs: oral diabetes medicine: **ORINASE, DBI, TOLINASE.** * An American horror story: **STILBESTROL (DES)** and cancer. Drugs and pregnancy: How to avoid birth defects. **RESERPINE, *PREMARIN** and **ATROMID-S,** are the benefits worth the risk?

Bee stings and insect bites: Hooray for meat tenderizer. * Hot water for itching. The dangers of popular topical sprays. * Insect repellants that really work. Vitamin B₁ and mosquitoes. * **PREPARATION H** and hemorrhoids: What's in it; why it won't work. How to really treat hemorrhoids. * How to cure hiccups quickly and painlessly with sugar. * Cooper's Droop. * Burns and how to treat them correctly. * Frigid headache: Hope for ice-cream lovers. * Colds: The junk versus Vitamin C. Is Vitamin C. dangerous to your health? Is Vitamin C a contraceptive? Why should women on the "Pill" take larger doses of Vitamin C? Is Vitamin C good for the heart? * Can plain Aspirin help prevent heart attacks? * Heavy coffee drinking: The great heart attack controversy.

Are we suckers for advertising? How Americans throw away $3,000,000,000 every year on non-prescription junk. * Over-The-Counter (OTC) drugs may be hazardous to your health. How can the consumer protect himself from dangerous reactions? * **ALKA-SELTZER:** Does this product do the job? Indigestion and antacids: What products work and what do not? * Deodorant soaps: It may be dangerous to "smell clean". * Feminine Hygiene Sprays: We're All Bozos On This Bus! * Menstrual cramps: How to pick the right medicine. * Bad breath: Do mouthwashes help? Why **LISTERINE** may be bad for a sore throat. * Body odor: How to pick a deodorant or anti-perspirant. * Warts: Love em' and leave em'. * Dandruff: How to pick shampoo. * Athlete's foot: How to beat it without **DE-SENEX**. * Insomnia: a $30 million scandal. * Bringing it all back home.

What are the dangers of taking more than one drug at the same time? The hazards of hospitalization. Multiple prescribing by ignorant physicians. **TETRACYCLINE** and milk. * How can the patient protect himself or herself from an adverse drug interaction? * Drugs which are especially dangerous when taken with something else: **ANTICOAGU-**

LANTS, ANTIDEPRESSANTS, CHLOROMYCETIN, CORTISONE-TYPE DRUGS, DIABETES MEDICINE, DIGITALIS, SALICYLATES, and SEDATIVES. * A handy guide to drug interactions. * How to use your pharmacist.

LIST OF TABLES

1.

Introduction

This is a book for people. It is an attempt to dispel the secrecy which surrounds medical treatment today. People are fed up with being treated as objects by doctors who often do not care about, or can't discuss in easy-to-understand language, the medicines which they prescribe. Instead of encouraging their patients to actively participate in their treatment, many doctors prefer to keep their patients in ignorance. "Take as directed" is often the most information patients receive about the chemicals they are expected to put in their bodies.

There is no such thing as a safe drug. Each medication is a double-edged sword, with a good side and a bad side. Successful treatment is a careful balance between the beneficial and **1** harmful effects, hopefully weighted in favor of the beneficial. Unfortunately, just the opposite is often the case. The original disease may be less of a problem than the reaction to treatment, and the old dictum "The cure was worse than the disease" has frequently been all too true. With any controversial topic, it is possible to find groups of scientists or "experts" who can quote studies and statistics on both sides of the issue, and such is the case with the volatile subject of adverse drug reactions. In the respected *New England Journal of Medicine*, Dr. Louis Sherwood and Dr. Edith Parris state that 18–30 percent of all hospitalized patients end up with drug reactions which often double their stays in the hospital.[1] In Sherwood and Parris's study, a "drug reaction" was defined as "all unwanted consequences of drug administration including administration of the wrong drug to the wrong patient, in the wrong dosage, at the wrong time, for the wrong disease." And believe me, all these "wrongs" happen much more commonly than you may think. Other medical investigators have reported anywhere from a low of 15 percent to a high of 40 percent for serious drug reactions in hospitalized patients.[2] To quote Dr. Hershel Jick, who represents one of the most comprehensive drug-monitoring organizations in the world, the Boston Collaborative Drug Surveillance Program: "We have reported that in about 30 per cent of hospitalized medical patients at least one adverse drug reaction develops during hospitalization, and using the estimate that about one third of the approximately 30 million people admitted to the United States general hospitals per year are admitted to general medical services, we may estimate that about 3,000,000 hospital patients suffer an adverse drug reaction in medical units each year."[3] According to Dr. K. L. Melmon, "economic consequences [of drug reactions] are staggering: one seventh of all hospital days is devoted to the care of drug toxicity, at an estimated yearly cost of $3,000,000,000."[4]

Of the 3 million Americans who experience a severe drug reaction, it has been calculated (depending upon which ax you are grinding) that between 6,000 and 140,000 die each year.[5] Although there is scant data on the number of drug reactions which actually lead directly to hospitalization, reliable evidence suggests that about 4 percent of hospital admissions result from drug-induced illness (300,000 patients).[6,7,8] Incredible as it sounds, some U.S. hospitals have even reported that as many as 20 percent of their patients were admitted because of drug-provoked disease.[9] If that doesn't scare you, it should. The real crime in this whole tragic situation is that the great majority of these reactions should not have taken place. According to Dr. Sherwood, 70–80 percent of all adverse drug reactions can be predicted, which means possibly prevented.

Too many drugs are prescribed in our pill-popping society. The evidence that we are overmedicated is voluminous. It is clear from the distribution of particular kinds of medicines that the quantity which are sold far outnumber "the known incidence of disease in which such drugs are of known value. The evidence for overmedication also includes the proportion of total prescribing made up of drugs for which the practitioner has only a probable, possible, or placebo [inactive sugar pill] expectation of success."[10] Americans spend about $11 billion on prescribed medications each year, and that does not include the $2.6 billion we shell out for nonprescription, over-the-counter (OTC) pharmaceuticals (many of which can mess you up almost as fast as the heavy-duty, prescription products).[11,12] That is an awful lot of cabbage. According to a study carried out in twenty-four Boston hospitals in 1972, more than 75 million Americans consume a drug at least once a week and usually every day.[13] Is it any wonder that drugs are killing us faster than automobile accidents or certain major diseases?

Although modern medical science has developed highly sophisticated methods of diagnosis and surgery, the average physician still relies almost exclusively on drug therapy in his treatment of illness. The typical doctor gives at least one drug prescription to 75 percent of his patients.[14] In fact, we have reached a point where a patient feels cheated if he is not given a prescription for something when he leaves a doctor's office. What distinguishes our modern-day practitioners from their medical ancestors is not so much the great quantity of new agents at their disposal (though that in itself is a gigantic difference), but rather their almost total reliance upon this form of treatment. Today's overworked doctor, in fact, has little choice but to turn to quick, impersonal remedies. By *3* analyzing statistics on medical practice supplied by the American Medical Association, it is possible to come up with the following figures: the average doctor sees about ninety patients a week for roughly seventeen minutes per patient.[15] And millions of patients are not lucky enough to get that much attention. A prescription is a quick way to satisfy patients, get them out of the office, and allow doctors to feel that they have really done something "beneficial." It should not surprise you that the most-prescribed drugs today are tranquilizers (**Valium** and **Librium** head the list); the pain-killer **Darvon** is Number 3 on the hit parade. Incidentally, **Darvon** is no better than aspirin when it comes to alleviating pain; it only costs more.[16]

This book is meant not to replace a trip to the doctor, but rather to explain in understandable, everyday English just what those pills your doctor prescribes really do. The medical profession has too long ignored people's curiosity and concern about their illnesses and the drugs which they are supposed to take. Unfortunately, people have too readily assumed that they were incapable of understanding "medical language." It is time medicine was demystified. One need not be familiar with the gigantic words doctors so commonly employ to describe the best treatment for pyrosis (heartburn) or cephalalgia (headache). Nor is it necessary to know the chemical structure or correct pronunciation of phenylpropanolamine hydrochloride (a decongestant frequently found in hay fever medications) to understand how it works.

One tantalizing piece of evidence which demonstrates the lack of communication between doctor and patient is presented by Dr. George J. Caranasos et al. in the *Journal of the American Medical Association (JAMA):* "Patients also cannot identify correctly 60% of their medicines. Forty percent of patients receive drugs prescribed by two or more physicians, increasing the possibility of drug interactions. Twelve percent of patients take drugs prescribed for someone else, and 60% of patients consider their drugs completely safe."[17] What utter fools we are to have allowed ourselves to become so complacent.

The intent of the following chapters is to reduce the modern pharmacological basis of therapy to practical, readable language. In addition to a discussion of simple mechanisms of action and common side effects, this book will try to alert

4

people to important facts about standard drugs which physicians rarely mention. In this connection, major emphasis will be placed upon the phenomena of drug interactions or incompatibilities: the unexpected (and usually undesirable) effects resulting from the combination of more than one drug. A case in point would be the greatly increased level of intestinal bleeding caused by aspirin when it is preceded by alcohol. I wonder how many of us, after having one drink too many, pop two aspirin tablets, or an **Alka-Seltzer** as protection against a future hangover. This could be a serious drug interaction. Drug-to-drug reactivity is an especially acute problem when you are receiving prescriptions from two or more doctors simultaneously (a common situation). This information could in some instances be life-saving when two or more drugs "don't mix."

Perhaps one of the most useful sections of this book is the chapter on wild home remedies, which includes fantastic, practical cures for hiccups, bee stings, mosquitoes, "frigid" headaches, and itches, to mention just a few of the goodies. And they really work. This is definitely not some kind of hokey put-on. All this material is in solid medical literature. In fact, there is a good possibility that your doctor knows all about it, though he may prefer not to mention it. In any case, this book should prove useful for problems ranging from hemorrhoids to athlete's foot.

Finally, for those of you who have headed back to the land, or who for one reason or another are just out of touch, this book may provide you with a really honest and useful way to take care of yourself when a physician can't be reached. If you have access to a sympathetic doctor, it is possible that you may be able to put together your own "little black bag" for common medical problems.

The true goal of this book, then, is to provide people with basic information regarding the potential hazards of simple drugs as well as of those medications physicians prescribe most often. My hope is to enable people to understand how the medicines they take work in their bodies and how to approach simple medical problems before, during, and after professional medical intervention. It may help save you some money, but more important, it may help save your life.

REFERENCES

1. Melmon, K. L. "Preventable Drug Reactions—Causes and Cures," *New Engl. J. Med.* 284:1361–1368, 1971.
2. Gotti, E. W. "Adverse Drug Reaction and the Autopsy." *Arch. Pathol.* 97:201–204, 1974.
3. Jick, Hershel. "Drugs—Remarkably Nontoxic." *New Engl. J. Med.* 291:824–829, 1974.
4. Melmon, K. L. op cit.
5. Koch-Weser, J. "Fatal Reactions to Drug Therapy." *New Engl. J. Med.* 291:302–303, 1974.
6. Hurwitz, N. "Admissions to Hospitals Due to Drugs." *Br. Med. J.* 1:539–540, 1969.
7. Jick, Hershel, op. cit.
8. Miller, R. R. "Hospital Admission Due to Adverse Drug Reactions." *Arch. Intern Med.* 134:219–223, 1974.
9. Miller, L. C. "How Good Are Our Drugs? Distinguished Lecture delivered Dec. 30, 1969, before the American Association for the Advancement of Science, Boston, Mass." *Am. J. Hosp. Pharm.* 27:367–374, 1970.
10. Muller, Charlotte "The Overmedicated Society: Forces in the Marketplace for Medical Care." *Science* 176:488–492, 1972.
11. Ibid.
12. Rucker, Donald T. "Drug Use Data, Sources, and Limitations." *JAMA* 230:888–890, 1971.
13. Jick, op cit.
14. Moertel, C. G., et al. "A Comparative Evaluation of Marketed Analgesic Drugs." *New Engl. J. Med.* 286:813–815, 1972.
14. Sherwood and Parris, op cit.
15. Muller, op cit.
16. Moertel, C. G., et al. "A Comparative Evaluation of Marketed Analgesic Drugs." *New Engl. J. Med.* 286:813–815, 1972.
17. Caranasos, George J., et al. "Drug-Induced Illness Leading to Hospitalization." *JAMA* 228:713–717, 1974.

2.

What Is a Drug?

With so much misinformation, emotion, and plain ignorance surrounding the whole field of "drugs" today, it is no wonder that people are confused and apprehensive. Our so-called drug culture is a never-ending source of editorials, commercials, and apprehension. Yet drugs are nothing new to our generation. Probably the oldest "medication," fermented beer, dates back six thousand years. Wine-making was well established in the early Stone Age. The ancient Egyptians were masters of drug therapy, and one medical papyrus lists over nine hundred prescriptions. In fact, it is very likely that as far back as 2000 B.C., Egyptian physicians were treating wounds and infections with a chemical derived from a fungus which 7 probably was a near relative to penicillin. There is even a suggestion in some ancient manuscripts that the Egyptians might have had a birth control pill. Almost every culture has taken advantage of the chemicals nature has provided in the form of leaves, roots, and bark in order to fashion remedies and cures. Such staples of modern therapeutics as aspirin, digitalis, and quinine (first used for fevers, then for malaria) are derived from natural plants. From a bird's-eye view, it is only fairly recently that we have learned how to isolate the active ingredients in plants and synthesize our own by-products chemically.

So what is a drug? Well, in reality it is just a word which exists in people's minds. When the potato first arrived in Europe, it was considered something very special, selling not as a food but rather—at a high price—as a "medicine" for its aphrodisiac qualities. In its broadest sense, most people would consider any prescriptive agent a drug and, as a result of the current furor over abuse, any agent which is used illicitly for its psychological effects. Either naïvely or unconsciously, people generally fail to realize that many of the chemicals they casually consume are themselves drugs. As defined by a standard pharmacological textbook, a drug is "any chemical agent that affects living matter."[1]

Are vitamins drugs? Most people would say No without thinking twice. However, when **Vitamin C** is ingested in very large amounts—for example, as Dr. Linus Pauling's cold remedy—it is no longer the simple vitamin you find in your orange juice. Nor does the eighteen-year-old girl who was taking really huge amounts of **Vitamin A** daily for her acne typify a simple case of the ingestion of a natural product found in carrots. She wound up in a hospital with severe headache, blurred vision, sleep disturbances, signs of mental illness, and an initial diagnosis of a brain tumor. All this was due to excessive amounts of **Vitamin A**.[2]

No one in his right mind would ever classify cigarettes, martinis, aspirin, food additives, or air as drugs. Yet nicotine, alcohol, aspirin, nitrates, and yes, even air—or more specifically oxygen—each has a distinct pharmacology with special effects upon your body. (Premature babies given large doses of oxygen may suffer from irreversible blindness.) Perhaps I overstate the case; yet we have been lulled into complacency about what we put into our bodies, both by the industries that manufacture and advertise their products and by the doctors who prescribe them. Remember, one study reported that 60 percent of patients consider their drugs completely safe.

I don't want to be an alarmist, since there already is an overabundance of people proclaiming disaster around every corner, but I do intend to make people aware of the properties of some of the things we consume so casually. I am definitely not a food freak or on a puritan trip suggesting that you stop smoking or drinking or living. However, I want you to be aware of what to expect when you do take this stuff or, more precisely, what to expect when your doctor gives you something to take.

Because people today, as well as their doctors, are so cavalier about consuming many different agents simultaneously without the awareness that they are in fact consuming "drugs," it is important to talk about interactions between these agents. By now everyone is probably aware of the potentially lethal interaction of alcohol and barbiturates or tranquilizers. In this case the simultaneous consumption of a "couple" of drinks and a few tranquilizers can together produce an additive effect greater than either one alone. The result can be an unintentional suicide. But interactions do not necessarily occur just between two drugs. They can just as easily happen between something in the diet or in the environment. An interesting case is the "photosensitivity reaction" which can occur between some common household soaps and the sun. It has been widely reported that certain antiseptic soaps, such as **Irish Spring**, **Lifebuoy**, **Phase III**, **Dial**, **Safeguard**, or **Zest**, can induce this kind of reaction after the skin has been exposed to direct sunlight.[3,4,5] The reaction may appear as an exaggerated sunburn or a local rash (contact dermatitis). The same kind of response takes place with certain perfumes, or foods such as figs, celery, or carrots. (A skin reaction of this type is best treated with cool water compresses and not with creams or ointments.)

Another example of a highly reactive substance is aspirin. Aspirin can interact with over forty other drugs, including **Vitamin C**. In this kind of interaction, aspirin can decrease the **9** effect of **Vitamin C** by increasing its urinary elimination from the body, while **Vitamin C**, on the other hand, can increase or potentiate the effect of the aspirin by slowing its elimination from the body.[6] How many of us take a batch of **Vitamin C** tablets with a couple of aspirin when we feel a cold coming on?

This whole fascinating area of drug interactions will be tackled in much greater detail in Chapter 6. My immediate goal is to demonstrate how tricky and difficult drug awareness can be. The examples mentioned above are fairly simple reactions and not particularly dangerous. However, there are many interactions which can be severe and at times life-threatening. Your doctor may not be aware of the various medications you are taking simultaneously, so you will have to guard against potentially dangerous combinations very carefully.

There is a growing movement in this country to reject all forms of drug therapy. The cry "I never take anything," usually proclaimed in a tone of moral superiority, is increasingly familiar. Even though this is rather admirable in our pill-popping age, those who carry this to irrational extremes are risking their health and sometimes their lives. There is nothing wrong or immoral about taking a necessary drug so long as it is really necessary and so long as it is the appropriate treatment for one's ailment.

Another large movement today involves "organic" and "natural foods". We are bombarded with shampoos, toothpastes, foods and vitamins which are regularly labeled "organic." Marketing experts understand that people often assume that a product which is or contains a chemical or a drug must be bad, while one which is natural or organic has to be good for you. This distinction is artificial, since in essence everything "organic" *is* chemical. Vitamin C, for example, is a chemical, whether it is consumed in a glass of orange juice or a manufactured tablet of ascorbic acid. The chemical structure is identical. It is true that organic vitamins contain bioflavinoids and other elements, which some researchers believe enhance the effect of the vitamin. Still, if one wants straight vitamin C, spending additional money for the organic variety is not advantageous. To quote Dr. Linus Pauling: "So-called synthetic ascorbic acid is natural ascorbic acid, identical with vitamin C in oranges and other foods. There is no advantage whatever to buying 'all natural Vitamin C,' 'Wild Rose Hip Super Vitamin C,' 'Acerola Berries Vitamin C,' or similar preparations."[7] There are distinct advantages to organically grown foods, but there are also some potential disadvantages. Food which does not contain pesticides, fumigants, preservatives, artificial flavors, coloring agents, emulsifiers, and so forth are clearly better than those which do. Though people sometimes panic over unfounded or incomplete reports of the dangers of a given pesticide or preservative, it is still a good idea to avoid foods with these additives as much as possible. One way is simply to read the label of every canned or frozen food you buy. Another way is to purchase organically grown fresh fruits and vegetables. Such products are usually much more expensive than the usual supermarket product. And there is little evidence that organic foods are more nutritious per se than the typical product. Still, even if three out of four supposed poisons are proved harmless, the fourth one can hurt you, and if you are willing to spend the money, it can't hurt to buy (or better, grow) organic foods. But this brings us to a major problem.

Because many people are willing to pay significantly more for fruits, vegetables and meat raised without chemical additives and fertilizers, a number of charlatans have moved into this business. The health food market is now a billion dollar a year industry, and it is sad to say that many people are being cheated. Various consumer agencies have pointed out that as much as 50% of the food labeled "organic" is identical in every respect to average supermarket food, including the amount of pesticide residue. The rip-off health food stores simply buy the same product and sell it to the unwary consumer for 80%-120% more.[8] Certainly the flavor of organic food is superior to the average supermarket product, and when the product is *really what it claims to be*, the lack of pesticides and artificial ingredients is an advantage. If the consumer is willing to pay the higher price for these products it is essential that he be sure that his dealer is honest; otherwise he is simply paying a great deal more for the magic label "organic."

Let's get back to the question of how drugs work. The principle of dose-effect relationships has helped generate much 11 controversy in recent years regarding the safety of various drugs and chemicals. If a particular drug produces a toxic side effect in an experimental animal at a really high dose, will it be safe in humans at a much smaller dose? This question is hard to answer, especially when it relates to diseases, like cancer, which are all-or-none phenomena: you either have cancer or you do not. Scientists prefer to deal with more easily observable problems, like indigestion. Two aspirin tablets probably do not affect the stomach lining very much, but five will irritate it and ten could be quite toxic. Thus, as the dose increases so does the effect. The whole question of whether a small dose of cyclamates could be dangerous is still controversial, and much of the battle going on over carcinogenic chemicals in our water and food hangs on this issue of dose. The whole discussion of the response to marijuana is intertwined in this subject. Charges have been made that this weed can produce all kinds of terrible consequences. Unfortunately, scientists and laymen alike tend to ignore dose when discussing this issue. In the amount usually purchased in the United States, marijuana has few dangerous or psychic effects except the well-publicized euphoria (and even that is sometimes more fancy than fact). However, in high doses, such as in the pure chemical extract or in special varieties purchased in Morocco or Mexico, it is possible the top of your head will come off. Hallucinations are not uncommon at this dose, and a whole range of pharmacological responses can be noted.

The real significance of dose-effect relationships becomes apparent when evaluating advertisers' claims. Comparisons of different drugs often state that Drug X is more potent than Drug Y and therefore, it is assumed, more effective. In itself this kind of statement is meaningless and misleading. The claims which are made for pain remedies demonstrate this point. When I hear the **Anacin** commercial with its assertion of extra strength, I see red. The statement that **Anacin** has more pain-reliever than any of the other leading brands is one of the most inaccurate advertisements floating around. Unfortunately, it is technically pretty much true. The way it works is this. Never once does **Anacin** tell you what the magical pain reliever found in their product really is. They are not being very forthright with their high, higher, highest level of medication—because their superfantastic pain-reliever is nothing but plain old **aspirin**. Yup, you heard right, nothing but **aspirin**. Their product contains 400 milligrams of **aspirin**, while **Alka-Seltzer**, **Bayer**, **Bufferin**, and **Fizrin** only contain 324 milligrams. Stuff like **Empirin Compound**, **Excedrin**, or **Vanquish** all contain less than that amount. So in point of fact they are not lying when they say **Anacin** has more pain-reliever than any of the other leading brands and is thus more "potent." It has 76 more milligrams of plain old **aspirin**, but that does not make it better, and obviously, if you wanted or needed "more pain-reliever," all you would have to do is buy yourself a bottle of cheap **aspirin** at your nearest discount drug store and take an extra half tablet. Now it happens to be true that **aspirin** really is the most effective pain-reliever available short of a narcotic, but it is a crime to fork over ten times the price for a fancy brand name. In a study conducted by C. G. Moertel of the Mayo Clinic, various prescription and nonprescription pain-relievers were analyzed.[9] It was found that when a typical dose of regular **aspirin** (two five-grain tablets, equal to 650 milligrams) was compared to these other products, "each of these agents was significantly inferior to aspirin in analgesic effect." And this study was really heavy-duty. The patients who were tested suffered from inoperable cancer. Neither the doctors nor the patients were told what kind of pain-reliever the patients were receiving, so that bias would not be introduced beforehand. Other common pain-relievers evaluated were **Codeine**, **Darvon**, and **Talwin**, as well as **Acetaminophen** and **Phenacetin**. If these last two goodies are not familiar to you, they would be if you knew which brand names contained them as ingredients: **A.P.C.**, **Empirin Compound**, **Excedrin**, **Febrinol**, **Nebs**, **Percogesic**, **Tempra**, and **Tylenol**, to name just a few. According to these investigators at the Mayo Clinic, "In this study, simple aspirin at a dosage of 650 mg was the superior agent for relief of cancer pain among the tested marketed analgesics. Indeed, among all analgesics and narcotics available for oral use, none have been demonstrated to show a consistent advantage over aspirin for the relief of any type of pain." Now that is dynamite. They go on to say, "These advantages, coupled with minimum price (usually less than $1 for 100 doses of 650 mg), *13* should make the aspirin the drug of preference for any pain problem requiring an oral analgesic." What is even more incredible is that their probe demonstrated that **aspirin** ranked higher in terms of therapeutic pain-relief than the ingredients found in **Nebs, Talwin, Tempra**, and **Tylenol**, as well as **Empirin Compound** and **Excedrin** (though these two both contain **Aspirin** as an additional ingredient). Even better than that, **Darvon** was "significantly inferior to aspirin" and—now get this—did not even show a significant advantage over a sugar pill (placebo). And that makes the eighth study in which **Darvon** was proved to be no better than an inactive sugar pill.[10]

Now guess which pain-relievers are prescribed most often by doctors? You got it: **Darvon, Empirin Compound, Talwin**, and **Tylenol**. Now figure out the difference in price for these less-effective rip-offs. Right again: **Darvon** costs almost ten times what an equivalent dosage of simple **aspirin** would run you. Infuriating, isn't it? We get charged outrageous prices because our doctors prescribe expensive pain-relievers which are touted for their "potency" yet turn out to be less effective than aspirin. (If bleeding may be a problem—ulcers, hemophilia, etc., aspirin is contraindicated). And all this information is readily available to physicians, since it has been published in outstanding medical journals, including the *Journal of the American Medical Association*. But, you exclaim in indignation, you take **Excedrin**, or **Empirin**, or **Darvon**, or **Talwin**, or **Tylenol**, and they do too work better than plain old aspirin. Well, I am not going to argue, but consider: Your doctor prescribes a pain-killer which he emphasizes is "potent." You pay an exorbitant price to have the prescription filled. Don't you think that the positive results you obtain might in part have to do with suggestibility? The study at the Mayo Clinic was presumably done with no ax to grind and in such a manner as to prevent anyone, patient or doctor, from being influenced by preconceptions.

The fascinating issue of anticipation and suggestibility raises another question about medical treatment. The active chemical ingredient in most nonprescription sleeping pills can cause drowsiness and conceivably promote sleep in high doses. Investigators now doubt however, that in the doses available in popular brands—**Nite Rest, Nytol, San-Man, Sleep-Eze, Sominex,** and **Sure-Sleep**—this agent is in any way superior to placebos. And yet people continue to buy and find relief from their insomnia with these apparently useless drugs. People also continue to pay outrageous prices for pain-relievers such as **Darvon** when their efficacy is doubtful. How can this apparent paradox be explained?

The ability of a drug to affect a cure or relieve a symptom is often a mystical process. Part of the process is a direct scientific cause-and-effect relationship, but much of medicine relies on your own body to do the job. Antibiotics, for example, often only slow down the invading bugs, allowing the body's own defense mechanism to take over and get a better hold on the little devils. In many cases, drugs can only provide symptomatic relief rather than actually produce a cure: they can decrease the intensity of diarrhea, peptic ulcers, or angina pectoris without actually curing the underlying problem. Thus your own body, and especially your psychological state, can profoundly modify the manner in which a drug exerts its curative powers. If a person wants to believe that the medicine she buys will help her go to sleep, it will. If someone thinks he is taking a powerful pain remedy, it will help alleviate his suffering. And if he has to pay through the nose for the medication, the chances are that it will "work" that much better.

Although we have been taught to scorn anything "mental," it is important to recognize that the role our heads play in our attitudes to and recovery from disease is probably tremendous. There are countless examples of recovery from disabling infirmities under the guidance of a friendly radio preacher, or at various miracle-cure locations. Even though modern medicine refutes such cures, it is often unable to determine the role of the placebo effect in its own practices. A visit to your white-coated doctor provides significant psychological support for any cure.

In carefully controlled clinical experiments, investigators who took the time to look for placebo effects discovered startling results. Anyone who has ever had a bad case of poison ivy can testify to the fact that it is terribly uncomfortable. It is clearly not an imagined or "psychological" reaction. However, A. M. Kligman did an extremely interesting experiment. He **15** took individuals who were sensitive to poison ivy and "treated" them with a purely bogus placebo medication. The patients did not know that this completely inactive "therapy" was not the real thing. Afterward, these patients were exposed once again to poison ivy. Incredibly, some were immune to the distressing effects of this itchy weed.[11] It has also been long known that colds are extraordinarily responsive to the sugar pill treatment.[12]

Peritendonitis, a painful inflammatory disorder, commonly attacks the shoulder, hip, and Achilles tendon. It has been reported that when patients with this disease are treated with ultrasonic therapy (a deep-heat type of treatment), they often show improvement. But H. J. Flax discovered that when the plug was pulled out of this impressive piece of equipment, comparable results were obtained. That is, the patients still thought that they were receiving deep-heat treatment, despite the fact that the machine was turned off. Yet these patients had a definite decrease in the amount of calcification and pain after this bogus procedure. Placebos can provide relief for some cases of rheumatoid arthritis, hayfever, headache, peptic ulcer, cough, and high blood pressure. It is understandable why we can be "cured" with grapefruit juice, copper bracelets, and vitamins—not because they have any intrinsic curative powers, but because we believe in them and they allow our bodies to cure themselves with a little help from our minds.

Although placebo treatment is often unreliable and delegated to the realm of pseudo medicine, it is quite possible that when "modern medicine" better understands the relationship of mind to body, drug therapy may be less necessary. Already exciting experiments are being conducted with biofeedback and conditioning to replace drug treatment in such diverse areas as heart disease, epilepsy, asthma, and mental wellbeing. Dr. Barbara B. Brown's book, *New Mind, New Body Bio-Feedback: New Directions for the Mind* is a magnificent description of this brand new field.[13] Perhaps in the advance of scientific knowledge, doctors will discover what any witch doctor worth his salt always knew: that the body is incredibly susceptible to manipulation and control by the brain. Quite possibly the future of medicine lies more within our minds rather than in drug therapy. However, until that day arrives, we

must learn how drugs work and how we can protect ourselves
from their potential dangers.

References

1. Goodman, Louis, and Gilman, Alfred. *The Pharmacological Basis of Therapeutics*, 4th ed. New York: Macmillan, 1970, P. 1.
2. Restak, R. M. "Pseudotumor Cerebri, Psychosis, and Hypervitaminosis A." *J. Nerv. Ment. Dis.* 155:72–75, 1972.
3. Harber, L. C., et al. "Contact Photosensitivity Patterns to Halogenated Salicylamides." *Arch. Derm.* 96:646–656, 1967.
4. Epstein, John H., et al. "Photocontact Dermatitis to Halogenated Salicylamides and Related Compounds." *Arch. Derm.* 97:236–244, 1968.
5. "Photosensitivity to Systemic and Topical Drugs." *Medical Letter* 10:32, 1968.
6. Martin, Eric W. *Hazards of Medication*, Philadelphia: Lippincott, 1969.
7. Pauling, Linus *Vitamin C and the Common Cold*. New York: Bantam Books, 1971. P. 88.
8 .Jukes, Thomas H. "The Organic Food Myth." *JAMA* 230:276–277, 1974.
9. Moertel, C. G., et al. "A Comparative Evaluation of Marketed Analgesic Drugs." *New Engl. J. Med.* 286:813–815, 1972.
10. Miller, R. R., Feingold, A., and Paxinos, J. "Propoxyphene Hydrochloride: A Critical Review." *JAMA* 213:996–1006, 1970.
11. Kligman, A. M. "Hyposensitization Against Rhus Dermatitis." *Arch. Derm.* 78:47, 1958.
12. Diehl, H. S., et al. "Cold Vaccines A Further Evaluation." *JAMA* 115:593, 1940.
13. Brown, Barbara B. *New Mind, New Body Bio-Feedback: New Directions for the Mind*. New York: Harper & Row, 1974.

3.

Drug Safety and Effective-ness or
The Double Edged Sword

The whole question of drug safety is a sticky wicket. How safe is safe? What is a reasonable risk? There is no such thing as a 100 percent harmless drug, but obviously some drugs are safer than others. If your doctor says that a drug he prescribes for you has absolutely no side effects, he is straining credulity. He may choose to ignore some of the uncommon, but nevertheless conceivable, adverse reactions in order not to scare you unnecessarily. A given dose of a certain medication may not cause any reaction in one individual, while someone else may experience a very severe response. An adverse drug reaction may be caused by the drug or by the special charac-teristics of the patient. It is therefore damn difficult to predict

18

with assurance how a person is going to react to a particular drug. As a result of this unpredictability, it becomes your responsibility to watch carefully for any possible side effects, no matter what drug has been administered.

Doctors who feel that they cannot bring themselves to warn their patients of a medication's potential side effects and dangers are taking an unnecessary risk that could lead to disaster. Of course, just as every medical student tends to "come down" with almost every disease that he studies, so, too, many patients will "experience" the potential side effects the doctor has cautioned about, even if they are more imaginary than real. Let's face it, we are all extremely susceptible to suggestion. Nevertheless, if it is possible to prevent one serious reaction for every ten false alarms, it is worth the extra trouble. And remember, you can die from a drug-induced illness. According to Robert Talley, "We can conjecture the range of 60,000 to 140,000 ADR (Adverse Drug Reaction) deaths to be probably extremely conservative since we have no data measuring drug-induced deaths in ambulatory and extended care populations."[1] Of course the Pharmaceutical Manufacturers Association and many doctors resist these figures and claim that the problem is much less serious. Since there are too few doctors who take the time to adequately educate their patients about possible dangerous or "untoward" effects, it falls to the patient to protect himself. Each of us must make a real effort to observe any unusual reactions or different feelings and report them immediately to his doctor.

One of the most important responsibilities of any doctor is to evaluate his patient's characteristics before prescribing a specific dose of a given medication. Nowadays, the local pharmacist essentially transfers pills from big bottles into little ones and does very little actual preparation herself. While drug companies may make some drugs in different dosage forms, all too often there is little flexibility and the doctor is forced to prescribe the drug in the only dose supplied by the manufacturer. But people *are* very flexible and everything from age, sex and weight to personality, genes, and type of illness can modify a person's reaction to a drug. Thin people often need less medication than large. Older people and young children also tend to require a reduced dosage 19 schedule. Babies may not be able to tolerate some drugs at all because their developing systems cannot metabolize or eliminate the foreign chemicals. Alcoholics often need increased doses of certain medications because the booze stimulates their livers to metabolize drugs extra-fast. Anesthesiologists have learned the hard way that it is sometimes extremely difficult to put an alcoholic under sedation. Since elderly patients are often more susceptible to a "normal" dose of common tranquilizers like **Valium** or **Librium**, these drugs should be prescribed with caution. Women appear to be more sensitive to side effects and drug reactions in general and may require a reduced dose of most drugs. It is the responsibility of your doctor to take all of these factors into account when prescribing any medication and adjust the dose accordingly. And his responsibility does not end once you have left his office and paid his bill. He should monitor your response to the drug (or drugs) in order to be certain that you are responding favorably and not experiencing adverse effects.

Doctor–Patient Communication

It is the responsibility of your doctor to COMMUNICATE with you about the medicines he has prescribed. A 1970 *JAMA* editorial stated, "When a physician prescribes a drug, he has an obligation to warn the patient about the drug's potential for causing adverse reactions, especially the more serious ones. For example, the possibility of drowsiness resulting from an antihistamine can be serious for an automobile driver ..."[2] It is absolutely essential that you as the patient and consumer understand the nature of your illness and the consequences of treatment. Dr. Barry Blackwell writing in the *New England Journal of Medicine* (1973) says it eloquently. "Prescriptions written in illegible Latin abbreviations may serve as a secret shared with the pharmacist but are a poor start to communication with the patient. As has been pointed out,[3] they often do neither and tend instead to cause confusion or inaccuracies. It is better to write the prescription in plain English and to explain what it means, encouraging the patient to ask questions and make comments on whether the regimen matches his daily activities."[4]

It sounds great, but what do you do when your doctor refuses to provide the information even after you ask for it? Well, in the first place, do not let him get away with treating you like an ignoramus. A physician is providing a service, for which you pay handsomely. He or she is no different than a hairdresser, TV repairman, plumber, or any other person with an expensive skill. You do not tolerate a condescending attitude from your hairdresser, so why should you accept it from your doctor, especially since your doctor is a helluva lot more likely to kill you than your hairdresser. Unfortunately, our culture has loaded the physician with the impression that he belongs to a "prestige profession," and he bought it along with his gullible patients, hook, line, and sinker. It is time to STOP this practice. Your doctor is not divine. He makes mistakes and sometimes some real stupid bloopers. The medical literature is filled with horror stories about doctors who have prescribed the wrong drug in the wrong dose to the wrong patient. You do not want that to happen to you, so ask— demand if necessary—what your doctor has prescribed, and make sure that he has informed you about the effects of the drug as well. If necessary, make a copy of the American Medical Association Journal's editorial ("Inform the Patient". *JAMA* 211:654, Jan 26, 1970) and show it to him. It amazes me when I think of George Caranasos' study which demonstrated that patients did not know 60 percent of the drugs they were receiving.[5] Quote to your doctor the statement made by a past commissioner of the Food and Drug Association: "The public has a right to know about the side effects as well as the benefits of the drugs they are taking."[6] If, after all this, he still treats you with less than total confidence and candor, then maybe it is time for a change, even if he is the "greatest" doctor in the vicinity.

Drugs and your Sex Life

Doctors are afraid to talk about sex. They have hangups just **21** like the rest of us, but their problem should not interfere with their practice of medicine. A number of drugs reduce sexual performance and desire. Very few doctors have the guts to mention this important side effect to their patients for fear the patient would be reluctant to take the medication. But people are not dummies. Many folks can figure out that their sexual problems are related to the medication they are taking. It is hardly surprising that they often discontinue the prescribed regimen. If the doctor leveled in the first place and had some sympathetic words to offer, the patient would understand the situation and be more likely to follow through, especially if he understood the importance of the treatment.

One of the drugs with the worst reputation for affecting sexual performance is *Guanethidine*. It is prescribed under the brand names **Esimil** or **Ismelin** and is very effective for reducing high blood pressure. People who suffer from hypertension must keep their blood pressure under control and must take an effective medication. Unfortunately, when many men find out that their pill prevents ejaculation they stop taking it. This could produce potentially disastrous long-term results. A physician should determine whether or not his patient will tolerate such a side effect or whether it would be more practical to switch to some other blood pressure lowering drug. Other anti-hypertensive medications that could possibly interfere with sexual desire or performance in some people are **Aldomet**, **Eutonyl**, and **Eutron**.

Drugs which affect the nervous system can occasionally mess up sexual function. Although **Mellaril** (a major tranquilizer) is often blamed for preventing ejaculation, other anti-psychotic drugs may also produce this effect. Two drugs used to treat psychological depression, **Nardil** and **Parnate** have been reported to induce impotence. A depressed patient is not likely to respond favorably to a drug that hinders sexuality. Even common minor tranquilizers, **Librium** and **Valium** can affect sexual desire in some people.

Doctors have a moral obligation to inform their patients about sexual side effects of drugs. Nothing could be more devastating for a man than the guilt and self doubt that impotence produces. A high-level business executive would obviously be relieved to learn that the drug **Pro-Banthine**, that he takes for his ulcer, was causing his impotence, rather than some complicated psychological neurosis. Although there is a terrible lack of knowledge about this whole area, the medical profession has a responsibility to communicate what little we do know.

The Dangers of Indocin

Every drug has the potential for doing some harm. Most times it is minimal, but sometimes it can be quite serious. Let us take a peek behind the cloak of secrecy and find out what doctors should be telling us. We are going to look at some commonly prescribed drugs and their potential for mucking up our bodies. A good drug to begin with is **Indocin** (generic name: **Indomethacin**). This medication is prescribed in enormous quantities in order to relieve the pain and inflammation associated with rheumatoid arthritis. Now I am going to let the drug company (Merck Sharp & Dohme) which makes **Indocin** speak for itself. The following statements have been obtained from advertisements published in the *Journal of the American Medical Association*: [These advertisements are placed in medical journals in order to induce physicians to increase their prescribing of a particular product.] "**Indocin** *cannot be considered a simple analgesic and should not be used in conditions other than those recommended* [essentially, rheumatoid arthritis] *and only after an adequate trial of aspirin and sufficient rest.*" They also emphasize that "**Indocin** frequently affords relief of symptoms. However, it does not alter the progressive course of the underlying disease." They are saying that **Indocin** cannot cure or even reverse the damage of arthritis, just provide symptomatic relief. Their ad goes on to state, "Because of the high potency of the drug and the variability of its potential to cause adverse reactions, the following are strongly recommended: 1) the lowest possible effective dose for the individual patient should be prescribed...; 2) careful instructions to, and observations of, the individual patient are essential to the prevention of serious and irreversible, including fatal, adverse reactions, especially in the aging patient."

23

Okay, now that is just the introduction. Let us see what special warnings, precautions and adverse reactions are listed in the drug company's advertisement:

Should Not Be Given To:
Children 14 years of age and under; pregnant women and nursing mothers; Patients with active gastrointestinal lesions or history of recurrent gastrointestinal lesions [ulcers]; allergy to aspirin or **Indocin.**

Potential Adverse Reactions:Stomach Reactions: Single or multiple ulcerations of the esophagus, stomach, duodenum, or small intestine, including perforation and hemorrhage, with fatalities in some instances; gastrointestinal bleeding without obvious ulcer formation; gastritis, which may persist after the cessation of the drug; nausea, vomiting, anorexia [loss of appetite], . . . abdominal pain, and diarrhea.

Eye Reactions: Corneal deposits and retinal disturbances . . . have been observed on prolonged therapy; blurring of vision.

Blood Reactions: Since some patients manifest anemia secondary to obvious or occult gastrointestinal bleeding, appropriate blood determinations are recommended.

Allergic Reactions: Acute respiratory distress, including dyspnea [difficulty in breathing] and asthma; . . . pruritis (itching); . . . skin rashes. . . .

Central Nervous System Reactions: Psychic disturbances including psychotic episodes, depersonalization, depression, and mental confusion; coma; convulsions; . . . drowsiness; lightheadedness; dizziness; headache.

Precautions:
Blurred vision may be a significant symptom that warrants a thorough ophthalmological examination. Patients should be cautioned about engaging in activities requiring mental alertness and motor coordination, as driving a car [while taking **Indocin**]. Headache which persists despite dosage reduction requires complete cessation of the drug. [**Indocin**] may mask the usual signs and symptoms of infection; therefore, the physician must be continually on the alert for this and should use the drug with extra care in the presence of existing controlled infection. After the acute phase of the disease is under control, an attempt to reduce the daily dose should be made repeatedly until the patient is off entirely.[7]

Whoa! That, fellow Americans, was the drug company speaking, and not some Ralph Nader–type health organization. And believe it or not, the side effects listed do not include all possible serious outcomes of **Indocin** treatment. While it is true that most people will not experience all or even many of these adverse reactions, a great many individuals do find some discomfort unavoidable. According to a major pharmacological textbook, "On usual therapeutic doses, approximately 35 to 50% of patients experience untoward [adverse] symptoms and about 20% must discontinue its use. . . . The most frequent Central Nervous System effect is severe frontal headache occurring in 25 to 50% of patients who take the drug chronically."[8] If you take **Indocin**, did your doctor warn you to stop taking it immediately if a headache persists? Did he emphasize that it *must* be taken with food or immediately after meals in order to diminish the terrible stomach upset so often encountered? Did he suggest that the first day you begin taking **Indocin** you should start with half a pill, or at most one, and then slowly increase that dose each successive day until you reach the recommended level? Did your doctor recommend occasional blood tests to make sure you do not develop anemia? Did he stress that you should not drive a car while on **Indocin** because mental alertness and motor coordination may not be up to par? And did he tell you to try and get off the drug completely as soon as the immediate flare-up of your arthritis is under control? If he did not communicate many or most of the above warnings and side effects, then your doctor is not following the guidelines set down by the *Journal of the American Medical Association* or the FDA.

The Dangers of Ampicillin

Well, how about antibiotics? Doctors are prescribing antimicrobial agents in ever-increasing numbers. The potential for abuse and overprescribing is one of the real tragedies of antibiotic therapy. For one thing, any doctor who prescribes an antibiotic (especially penicillin) for a cold or sore throat is out of his mind. Before *any* antibiotic is administered, the physician should determine by laboratory testing whether the infection is viral or bacterial in origin. If it is a virus, no antibiotic will make your cold or sore throat better. If a bac- 25 terium is responsible, it is extremely important for the doctor to know which specific bug is causing the trouble so that he can treat it with the right drug. Using a "broad spectrum" antibiotic is a cop-out. It is the lazy way to do medicine, since it allows the doctor to cut out the time necessary to do a proper laboratory work-up and diagnosis. Of course there are times when this shotgun approach is necessary—for example, during a medical emergency before the laboratory results are in or if nothing else will work.

A three-year study of hospitalized patients in the Shands Teaching Hospital of the University of Florida determined that of 2,877 patients receiving antibiotics, 157 (5.4 percent) "developed one or more reactions to an antimicrobial drug."[9] Of these, 58 percent suffered moderate to life-threatening reactions and "forty-five percent of the reactions to antimicrobials contributed to an increase in the duration of hospitalization by one or more days." It is clear, therefore, that antibiotics are quite capable of ruining us. Is your doctor telling you everything you should know about the antibiotics he prescribes so often?

One of your doctor's favorites is a high-priced, broad-spectrum antibiotic called **Ampicillin**. This drug is sold generically as **Ampicillin** in various dosages and in various forms (capsules and oral suspension). It is also prescribed and sold under the following brand names: **Amcill, Omnipen, Pen A/N, Polycillin, Penbritin, Principen**, and **QID Amp**. Although **Ampicillin** is a broad-spectrum antibiotic, it is considered a member of the **Penicillin** family. Therefore, your doctor *must* ask if you have any history of **Penicillin** allergy before prescribing, because **Ampicillin** is absolutely forbidden for people with a sensitivity to **Penicillin**. It should be administered only after thorough laboratory testing. Pregnant women should avoid such a drug if possible since its safety in respect to the fetus has not been adequately demonstrated. Side effects of **Ampicillin** therapy are the following:

Stomach Reactions: Nausea, diarrhea, vomiting, and scuzzy tongue (inflammation of the mouth).
Allergic Reactions: Any difficulty in breathing requires immediate emergency treatment. Skin rashes are quite common especially in patients taking **Zyloprim** at the same time. (**Zyloprim** is a

drug for gout.) Any skin problem is an indication that treatment should be discontinued unless removal of **Ampicillin** would be life-threatening.

Blood Reactions: **Ampicillin** may affect the blood in many ways. Anemia is not uncommon. A blood disease called serum sickness does occur and may manifest itself as hives, joint pain and fever. Discontinue the drug with approval.

Superinfection Reactions: One of the real disadvantages of broad-spectrum antibiotic therapy is that it results in the death of many useful bacteria. Thus the change in normal flora and fauna creates an ideal environment for the growth of other bad bugs. Consequently, other infections, particularly Candida, may take over.

Although **Ampicillin** is a relatively safe drug, your doctor should not prescribe it casually, especially without laboratory analysis. A textbook on medical pharmacology states unequivocally, "**Ampicillin** has no advantages over **Penicillin G** in most infections and is much more costly."[10] Since it is expensive, your medic should prescribe it generically as **Ampicillin** rather than as **Amcill, Omnipen, Polycillin**, or **Principen**. He should also try to inform you about potential adverse reactions. Finally, your doctor should avoid prescribing this potent antibiotic to your young children. According to Jacques Caldwell, "Certain practices, such as the administration of ... **Ampicillin** to children less than 10 years of age is particularly hazardous, and their use for prophylaxis or for any situation lacking a clear indication is to be condemned."[9]

The Dangers of Lasix

Another drug on your doctor's hit parade of all-time favorites is **Lasix** (known generically as **Furosemide**). This little honey is a very potent water pill, or diuretic. That means it helps eliminate excess fluids from the body by sending you to the john at frequent intervals. People with heart trouble, cirrhosis of the liver, and kidney disease often retain fluids. **Lasix** is often given to help remove this excess accumulation, especially when the liquid ends up in the lungs (pulmonary edema). It has also been prescribed for people with high 27 blood pressure, though this use is less common and of questionable value. Clearly, this is a very useful drug which is an important component in your doctor's arsenal of therapeutic agents. Nevertheless, it does have some side effects which your doctor should warn you about. Because it is such a potent diuretic, **Lasix** can cause a very rapid depletion of fluids from the body, which could lead to a serious dehydration. According to a Hoechst Pharmaceutical's advertisement in the *Journal of the American Medical Association*, "careful medical supervision is required, and dose and dose schedule have to be adjusted to the individual patient's needs." This means that your doctor cannot just send you out of his office with a prescription written for a particular dose without carefully explaining how to modify that dose if the anticipated results are not obtained. **Lasix** should *never* be prescribed for pregnant women; in fact, no woman who is of child-bearing age should ever receive it. Laboratory evidence suggests that birth defects (remember **Thalidomide**) are a distinct possibility if **Lasix** is taken during pregnancy.

The greatest danger associated with **Lasix** therapy is that too great a water loss over too short a period of time could lead to collapse of the circulatory system. The patient could go into shock and life-threatening blood clots might form. This is particularly dangerous in elderly patients, who are more susceptible to this reaction. The other serious complication of fluid elimination is the change in blood chemistry which results. A significant loss of potassium almost always accompanies administration of **Lasix** and requires supplementation with either a special diet high in potassium or a specially prescribed potassium formulation. Fruit, especially dried apricots, is high in potassium. Frequent blood tests must be made during the early weeks and months of **Lasix** therapy in order to keep careful track of blood changes. Symptoms of excessive potassium loss are: marked muscle weakness and leg cramping, weakness, dizziness, loss of appetite, and mental confusion. For a patient who must take a **Digitalis** drug (**Acylanid, Digitaline, Digoxin, Digitoxin, Gitaligin,** or **Lanoxin**) at the same time as a potent water pill like **Lasix**, the level of potassium in his blood is a matter of life or death. If it gets too low, fatal heart rhythms are a distinct possibility.

Other less serious problems encountered after **Lasix** treatment might include diverse skin reactions (rashes and itching), diarrhea, nausea, and blurring of vision. Diabetics may have trouble controlling their blood sugar level, for which frequent tests should be made. For patients on high blood pressure medication, **Lasix** poses a special problem. When therapy with a potent diuretic is initiated, care must be taken that blood pressure does not drop too rapidly. It would probably be a good idea to lessen the dose of your blood pressure medication by half until your body adjusts to **Lasix**.

Whew! What a bunch of bull! That is an awful lot of information for a doctor to lay on his patients. Some of it obviously can be left out (like the bit about diabetes or high blood pressure) if it does not apply to an individual patient. But the other stuff could be absolutely critical.

So what's it all mean? We have looked at three drugs, **Indocin**, **Ampicillin**, and **Lasix**, an arthritis medicine, an antibiotic, and a water pill. They are prescribed in almost unbelievable quantities to millions and millions of Americans. Although only examples, they should help give you an idea what kind of information your doctor must provide you about these and all other drugs he prescribes. **Aldomet**, **Antivert**, **Butazolidin**, **Gantrisin**, **Inderal**, **Ornade**, and **Premarin**, to name a few of the most popular drugs on your doctor's list, all have warnings, precautions, and adverse reactions which should be communicated to you, the patient.

Buying and Storing Drugs Wisely

Let's give the doctor a break for a little while and turn our attention to another health professional. Your druggist also has a certain accountability when it comes to filling your prescriptions. Typing out a label with a prescription number is not adequate. He should put the name of the drug and the dose on the container when he sells it to you. There is absolutely no good reason in the world why you should not know the name of the medicine you are expected to take. In fact, **29** there is every reason for you *to* know it. Just as important as the name, is the date on which the pharmacist sells the drug and the expiration date of the medication. When your pharmacist receives a shipment of drugs, it always has an expiration or termination date stamped on it. This is because of a Food and Drug Administration ruling. According to Peter J. Weiss of the FDA's National Center for Antibiotic Analysis, "There is even more reason to be concerned with the stability of pharmaceuticals since the issuance of the latest revision of the Good Manufacturing Practices in the *Federal Register* January 15, 1971. According to this document, specifically Section 133.13, the manufacturer must be assured of the stability of the finished drug product. It further states that to assure that drug products *liable to deterioration* meet appropriate standards . . . at the time of use, the label of all *such* drugs shall have suitable expiration dates which relate to stability tests performed on the product."[11] Additionally, Jonas L. Bassen, past director of FDA's Division of Industry Liaison, has quoted the preamble of the Current Good Manufacturing Practice Regulations: "The commissioner of Food and Drugs concludes that the interests of consumers must be served by the establishment of valid expiration dates for all drug products. No drug container-closure system is indefinitely stable and the manufacturer or packer of a drug product is responsible for determining the stability characteristic for each of his products."[12] Unfortunately, your pharmacist almost never places the expiration date on your drug container, which means that you have absolutely no idea when the medicine loses its effect or changes chemical composition. Many drugs should be discarded after a certain length of time, but you will never be aware of that fact unless your pharmacist types the date on the label.

Once you have your little bottle of expensive drugs clutched in your hot sweaty palm, you cannot just truck it on home and store it in your medicine cabinet and forget about it. The careful storage and maintenance of medicine is absolutely essential to its safe and effective utilization. How many times have we read the little note that says "store in a cool dry place" and just ignored it completely? Many of today's powerful and complex new drug preparations are not very stable chemically. Rapid changes in environmental conditions, such as temperature and humidity, may affect them adversely. In fact, on the way home from the drugstore, the chances are pretty good that you might leave the medicine on the seat of the car or in the glove compartment while you head off to take care of other errands. The amount of time the medicine sits in a hot car in the summer or in a freezing car in the winter can seriously affect the active ingredients. By the way, if possible, avoid having the pharmacy deliver your drugs, since you have no idea how long your medicine has been sitting in the delivery vehicle while the delivery person makes his rounds.

If the storage conditions are not maintained within certain narrow limits, then not only may you be receiving a less than therapeutic dose, but the breakdown products may produce unexpected and hazardous side effects. For example, improperly stored **Tetracycline (Achromycin-V, Sumycin,** etc.) may deteriorate to a toxic by-product and produce an anemia-like reaction in some patients. Do you leave your medicine on a heater near your bed in the winter, or perhaps on a kitchen table where the sun could rapidly destroy the contents? Light is detrimental to many drugs, especially vitamins, some major tranquilizers (**Thorazine, Mellaril,** etc.), various antibiotics, and certain blood pressure medications (**Hydropres, Rauside, Reserpine, Salutensin, Ser-ap-es,** or **Serpasil**).[13] The color of a drug's container, as well as how well it is stoppered, may also contribute to the preservation of a medicine.

An illustration of the gravity of this whole storage problem has been reported in the *New England Journal of Medicine* by Ralph Shangraw.[14] People with serious heart problems must carry their **Nitroglycerin (Nitro-Bid, Nitroglyn, Nitrong, Nitrospan, Nitrostat**) tablets with them at all times to treat the sudden onset of an attack of angina pectoris. **Nitroglycerin,** one of the most common medications for this type of illness, is often taken by letting it dissolve slowly under the tongue. Now it has long been noted that patients can have very variable therapeutic responses to their medications. This variability may be from one batch of medicine to another and from one patient to another. The point of Shangraw's study at the University of Maryland School of Pharmacy was to determine the *31* factors responsible for this unequal therapeutic effect. He rapidly determined that packaging and storage were the most important factors in the uneven medical response to **Nitroglycerin**. One three-month-old package had lost 84 percent of the original potency. The label, which had been placed *inside* the drug container (how many of us routinely receive our drugs in this fashion?), had absorbed a significant amount of the active ingredients of the tablets. Would you believe that there were ten tablets' worth of drug in the paper alone? It was also established that the plastic vial in which the pills were stored had absorbed some of the drug. To top this off, it was demonstrated that the cotton which serves as a filler in so many drug bottles had sucked up the phenomenal amount of 33 percent of the total packaged drug in only one week of storage time. If a **Nitroglycerin** tablet is left open to the air long enough, all of the active drug will evaporate into the atmosphere. Come an emergency, there is no drug left. Another potential problem lies in wait for those who store their medicine in a pill box. Never place your medicine (particularly **Nitroglycerin**) inside a container which is not perfectly airtight, or with other drugs. It could interact with them and lose its strength. Aspirin, for one, is capable of absorbing **Nitroglycerin**. So heart patients beware—the only place to store your drug is in a glass bottle that has a tight screw cap. Do not allow your pharmacist to place the label on the inside of the vial (tape it to the outside), and by all means, remove any cotton filler which may have been placed inside.

It is true that **Nitroglycerin** is not typical of your usual drugs, since it is highly volatile. Nevertheless, many medications can be influenced by the type of bottle and the tightness of the cap. Humidity is an absolute disaster for most drugs, since pills tend to absorb water vapor and will then deteriorate much faster than in a dry environment. It is darn hard to "store in a cool, dry place" during the summer when the temperature is 95° and the humidity is out of sight. Ask your pharmacist about the best conditions for storage if you have any doubts. And while you are at it, make sure he packages your drugs in child-proof containers. Sure it's a chore to get one of those bottles open; but over three million children under the age of five suffer from accidental drug poisoning every year. Aspirin alone probably accounts for over one million of those cases.

Did Your Doctor Tell You . . .

Okay folks, you have carried your medicine home and stored it in a reasonably safe place. Now you are supposed to take it. But when? Before meals, after meals, with water, without milk? This is almost *the* most important part of the whole chain of events. But directions for drug ingestion are often sorely lacking. Too many doctors are careless or lazy about the instructions they give their patients regarding the medications they must take. Some medicines must not be taken at meals, while others are ineffective or dangerous unless they are. A classic example is **Tetracycline**. This broad-spectrum antibiotic is one of the most commonly prescribed drugs in this country. It is almost handed out like candy. Everyone should be familiar with names such as **Achromycin V, Mysteclin-F, Sumycin, Terramycin,** and **Tetrex**. These are but a few of the many **Tetracycline** preparations available. For the millions of you who have received this drug, I ask you, how many times has your doctor *emphasized, stressed,* or in effect *screamed* that you *cannot* take **Tetracycline** at the same time as **milk**? And that means milk, cheese, yogurt, ice cream, cream in your coffee, or any other product that could remotely be made up of the white stuff from a cow. The calcium in milk grabs on to **Tetracycline** and renders it useless. So the high-priced antibiotic which you hope will be doing you some good is just getting eliminated before it even gets into your bloodstream. Your doctor should warn you that **Tetracycline** should not be taken anywhere near a mealtime—and that means anywhere from one hour prior to eating up to two hours after eating. But that's not all. Drugs that contain calcium, aluminum, and magnesium also impair the actions and absorption of **Tetracycline**. Has your doctor ever told you that antacids (they almost invariably contain calcium, aluminum, or magnesium) are absolutely out when you are taking any type of **Tetracycline**? And let me tell you, there will be great temptation to **33** take one of the old favorites like **Tums, Rolaids,** or **Gelusil,** because these broad-spectrum antibiotics can really give you a sad tummy. There you are caught in the middle, but if you want the drug to work, you have to suffer.

The **Tetracycline** story does not end there, however. This useful antibiotic *definitely cannot* be prescribed to young children. And yet doctors all too often ignore this fundamental law of prescribing. Because **Tetracycline** has a great affinity for calcium, it can cause permanent mottling, or brown discoloration, of the teeth in children. (This unsightly deposit has been characterized as a "cosmetic deformity," since it will remain for a lifetime.) Every physician in this country has learned in medical school that, short of a life-and-death situation, **Tetracycline** should not be administered to kids. And the risk is just as great in babies who have not yet developed their teeth. Even pregnant women (nursing mothers too) should not receive **Tetracycline,** since the unborn child can also absorb this antibiotic and develop the discoloration later in life.

Despite the fact that this information has been available to doctors for years (both in textbooks and in journal articles), they continue to prescribe these drugs for young children. A study published in 1973 noted that of 505 children who had their molar teeth extracted, 70 percent had received **Tetracycline** within the first three years of their lives at least twice.[15] This was a 12 percent increase in exposure over the preceding five years. Absolutely incredible!

There are many drugs like **Tetracycline** which require special instructions. It is your doctor's responsibility to make sure the proper information is relayed to you and that you understand his directions perfectly. Some medications can be deadly if taken in the wrong manner. There are all kinds of horror stories about people who have swallowed medicine their doctor meant for them to wash with. Nurses have injected drugs into the veins of patients when they were supposed to stick them in the butt instead, all because a physician's instructions were not clear. If your medic does not provide clear and detailed directions about the medicine he prescribes voluntarily, then you bug him until he does. And make sure that you

know the name (both generic name and brand name) of any

drug the good doctor prescribes *before* you leave the office. If you have to visit another physician for some other problem, you must be prepared to answer her or his question about what other drugs you are taking. And you should be able to do it in an intelligent manner rather than by trying to describe the size, shape, and color of your pills.

Consumer Responsibility: Spray Cans and your Health

The doctor and the pharmacist are not the only ones responsible for drug safety and effectiveness. We must be just as vigilant. Too many people think that they can medicate themselves without fear of unwanted reactions. If Aunt Martha says that she has just the thing for diarrhea, gallstones, bladder infections, or heartburn, stay away. Her prescription is not meant for you! She is not a doctor, and what works for her could be extremely dangerous in your body. And that goes for many nonprescription drugs. As I have already mentioned, we are often exposed to many chemicals which can affect our systems in an adverse way but which we tend to take for granted.

A classic example of a dangerous substance which is found in every home is the common aerosol spray can. This apparently innocuous household item contains many active and "inactive" ingredients which are often absorbed directly into the body after inhalation. Stop and think a moment. When you use your aerosol cans, how much of the junk do you end up breathing? If you can smell the stuff, you are inhaling it. A 1974 article disclosed that hairsprays could alter the normal functioning of the lungs in healthy individuals.[16] A twenty-second direct exposure produced chest tightness and difficulty in breathing lasting up to ten minutes after exposure. Some individuals noticed effects for as long as sixty minutes. Subjective symptoms of "respiratory distress" were confirmed by physiological tests of breathing capacity. And remember, twenty seconds' exposure is peanuts when compared to the length of time some of us may breathe in this crap. The au- *35* thors of this report state, "It is a matter of concern . . . that a commonly used consumer product should have a systematic effect on the airways of healthy persons. It is possible that repeated exposure to aerosolized products such as hair spray are causal factors in some cases of asthma or bronchitis." A beautician who receives massive contact with these chemicals on a daily basis could be at quite some risk. Many beauty parlor workers concede that there are plenty of rumors and stories of serious illness associated with the profession, and many people try to get out of this direct contact work as soon as possible. Until the summer of 1974, various aerosol products—most notably insecticides and cosmetic sprays—contained a polyvinyl chloride gas as a propellant. This chemical has caused fatal liver cancer in men who worked with it.

Have you ever stopped to think how much of the junk in your underarm deodorant you inhale each morning when you point the can in the general direction of your armpit and push the button? Besides the active chemicals (often aluminum hydroxychloride), you are getting a direct hit of solvent and the gas which propels the active stuff out of the can. There is probably some perfume thrown in as well. These "inactive" ingredients have been proven deleterious to the heart and nervous system. If you insist that you must use **Right Guard** or **Arrid Extra Dry** in aerosol form, the very least you should do is to try to hold your breath during application and then get out of the room fast. People with allergies and asthma should switch to roll-on or stick deodorants. As a matter of fact, people with any respiratory-tract problem should stay far away from aerosol cans of any sort. That also holds for people who wear hearing aids or use contact lenses. There have been reports that hair sprays can muck up these devices. So why don't we all just ditch all the spray cans we have? They mess up the environment, and clearly they do a nasty job directly on our bods. They sure as hell aren't worth the convenience if they do permanent damage. Although you might hope that your physician would warn you about the dangers of nonprescription drugs and things like spray cans, they either do not know about such things, refuse to commit themselves, or just plain do not have the time or inclination to mention it.

Drugs of Dubious Value

There is, however, another aspect of drug safety and effectiveness which is your doctor's direct responsibility. We automatically assume that our doctors would not prescribe a medicine which is useless or unnecessarily dangerous. Sadly, all too many doctors fail to keep up with the medical literature. They continue to prescribe a certain drug long after it has been found to be worthless. Sometimes, after a drug has been available for a long time, it is found to be extremely dangerous. Yet it continues to be prescribed for an incredibly long time after the news is published. One frightening example of this practice has been the use of drugs to treat something called late-onset diabetes. For those individuals who began developing signs of high blood sugar after the age of forty, it used to be the practice to place them on drug therapy right off the bat. In 1970, a long-term study carried out on more than eight hundred diabetics at twelve university medical centers shook the medical profession to its foundation. Two of the most common drugs to treat this kind of diabetes were tested. One was **Orinase (Tolbutamide)** and the other was **DBI** or **Meltrol (Phenformin)**. During the study, which lasted from three to eight years, it was determined that the patients receiving these two drugs seemed to be more prone to heart attacks and related heart problems than those patients who were being treated by diet alone or by insulin. In fact, because this study, sponsored by the National Institute of Health, discovered that the patients on **Orinase** were twice as prone to develop heart trouble as the nondrug controls, the investigation had to be terminated before completion. More recent studies have suggested that as many as half of the patients taken off the drugs (also including **Tolinase** and **Dymelor**) did not require this kind of medication at all. Yet years after the investigation published its conclusions, 1.5 million Americans are probably still using these oral diabetes drugs. And possibly as many as ten to fifteen thousand are dying every year as a result. The sales of **Orinase**, **DBI**, and **Tolinase** keep rising each year, and doctors keep prescribing them in ever-increasing numbers. Obviously, many doctors either refused to believe the 1970 study or just did not care to **37** let the results influence their prescribing habits. Yet an international jury and National Institute of Health–sponsored follow-up review published in 1975 supported the earlier findings and concluded that these drugs are dangerous and should probably be abandoned.[17] An editorial published in the *JAMA* comes down firmly against use of oral diabetes medicine.[18] Before a doctor prescribes these drugs, the editorial suggests, "Informed consent should be obtained from all patients and should include a full description of those risks and the potential benefits." Also included in this statement is the following point: "If physicians are willing to take the time to encourage effective dietary regimens, the inconvenience to the patient will be a small price to pay for prolongation of a relatively healthy life." The American Diabetes Association has suggested that these oral diabetes drugs should only be employed in patients with mild to moderate diabetes that will *not* respond to diet, and in patients who refuse to take insulin injections. In other words, any doctor who prescribes a pill for diabetes in an older person without first trying other forms of treatment is taking an unnecessary risk and may not be helping to prolong the life of his patient. But what the hell do you do? You try to have confidence in your physician, and yet he tells you to keep on taking your medicine even though you have just read in the newspaper that it is dangerous. He gives you a snow job or some doubletalk that the whole story isn't in yet and you better follow his instructions. Yet if you went to another doctor, he might give you a completely different argument and tell you to get off the stuff. The patient is screwed no matter what. About all I can say is, Follow your own best judgment and common sense and look for a doctor who does not love to push pills.

A similar case of questionable prescribing policy involves the antibiotic **Chloromycetin** (**Chloramphenicol**). This potent drug has experienced cycles of popularity when it was administered for something as ridiculous as a cold or sore throat. Then, because medical journals would start reporting an increased incidence of fatal anemia cases directly associated with **Chloromycetin**, doctors would cut back on their prescriptions. Once the publicity and indignant editorials disappeared, doctors forgot the dangers. Back came the prescriptions. Despite the fact that **Chloromycetin** has almost no place in modern American therapy, and other safer drugs are generally preferable, it continues to be prescribed and sold.

Another area where doctors are still behind the eightball is that of the treatment of ulcers. Medical evidence to the contrary, physicians almost always insist that their ulcer patients maintain a bland diet. Way back in 1953 it was pretty clear that mild and bland food had absolutely nothing to do with the cure or improvement of an ulcer. But even today, Dr. Thomas C. Chalmers has reported that in two hospitals recently checked, thirty-five out of thirty-eight doctors prescribed this old-fashioned diet. So guys, live a little, you can even eat those hot tamales or whatever turns you on. If it doesn't make your stomach hurt, it probably won't do it any harm.

Another story about the prescribing of a meaningless drug is probably one of the greatest American medical tragedies of all times (and perhaps one of the best-kept secrets as well). Between 1946 and 1960, it was a popular medical practice to administer **Diethylstilbestrol (DES)** (a synthetic estrogen hormone) to women who were diagnosed as having "high risk" pregnancies: women who had either experienced trouble with an earlier pregnancy or suffered a miscarriage. Sometimes doctors assumed a potential problem pregnancy and prescribed **DES** "just to be on the safe side." They hoped that by prescribing **DES** they could improve the chances of a normal delivery.

Between 1966 and 1969, Dr. Arthur L. Herbst, working at the Massachusetts General Hospital, noted seven cases of an extremely rare vaginal cancer in young women between the ages of fifteen and twenty-two.[19] Dr. Herbst, an inquisitive and brilliant physician, initiated a search for the possible factors responsible for this sudden crop of rare and highly lethal cancers. What he discovered was that the mothers of these seven girls had received **Stilbestrol (DES)** during their pregnancies. The clear implication of his work was that somehow the mothers' ingestion of this pill many years ago during their pregnancies had set up the conditions that would later trigger the formation of vaginal cancer in their offspring. That is, the baby's exposure to **DES** while still in the womb resulted in **39** cancer as much as twenty-two years later. Since his first study was published in 1971, Dr. Herbst has published much more material and set up a national registry that records all new cases of this kind of cancer. In 1972 Dr. Herbst noted ninety-one additional cases of vaginal and cervical cancer in patients ranging from eight to twenty-five years of age.[20]

The dosage regimen for this synthetic estrogen hormone was highly variable and almost diabolical in its complexity. In those Stone Age years of the 1940's, it was recommended that the prospective mother begin taking 5 milligrams a day at about the sixth week of her pregnancy.[21] She was to increase this dose by 5 milligrams every two weeks until the fifteenth week. At that time she was to increase the dose by 5 milligrams *each* week until by the end of her pregnancy she would be consuming the unbelievable dose of 125 milligrams a day of **DES**. If a woman was conscientious about following her doctor's instructions, it would mean that by the time of delivery she might have received a total of well over 10,000 milligrams of **Stilbestrol**. One might feel relieved knowing that a great many women did not conform to that ridiculous dosage schedule and therefore might have protected their female children. Unfortunately, Dr. Herbst has reported that one girl developed cancer even though her mother only consumed 1.5 milligrams per day, and another girl demonstrated signs of malignancy even though her mother had only received **DES** for a total of seven days during the first trimester of the pregnancy.[22] This means that we still do not know if there is a "safe" dose of this drug which would not have resulted in the development of cancer.

Many of these young women have died from this cancer which they developed as a result of a drug which was consumed by their mothers many years ago. We have no idea how many young women are still at risk. To quote Dr. Herbst (1974), "The total number of young girls exposed to **Stilbestrol** in utero in the United States is unknown, but a reasonable estimate is hundreds of thousands or possibly more."[23] As of March 1, 1974, Dr. Herbst noted, "At present, the Registry of Clear-Cell Adenocarcinoma [cancer] of the genital tract in young females contains data on over 170 cases of vaginal and cervical carcinoma (100 of which are vaginal) from the United

States and abroad, most of which have been related to pre-natal exposure." Dr. Herbst has also noted that as many as one of three postpubertal girls whose mothers received **DES** during pregnancy developed benign, gland-like tumor cells in their genital tracts. Whether these tumors will go on to be-come malignant has not yet been determined, but the danger exists and all "at risk" young women should be examined yearly if their first tests are normal. Anything suspicious should be followed carefully every three to six months. Fortu-nately, some preliminary work carried out in the Departments of Gynecology and Pathology of Massachusetts General Hospi-tal and Harvard Medical School have indicated that applica-tion of a local hormone, progesterone, in the form of vaginal suppositories may be useful in improving or at least temporar-ily eliminating the benign tumors. This may prevent the for-mation of future malignancies.

Female children may not be the only ones at risk. Recent animal research done by Dr. John McLachlan (*Science* 190:991–992, 1975) indicates that male offspring might also suffer complications as a result of **DES** that was ingested by their mothers during pregnancy. Mice injected with this estro-gen hormone produced males that experienced abnormalities within their reproductive tracts. These changes were appar-ently responsible for the unexpectedly high incidence of sterility (60 percent) that was observed. Preliminary investiga-tion of human males indicates that inflammation of the pros-tate and other abnormalities may also exist. Although physi-cians have devoted most of their time to tracking down female problems, this new research should stimulate greater interest in all **DES** offspring.

The real crime and paradox in this whole tragic story is that there has never been adequate documentation proving that **DES** was actually beneficial in preventing miscarriages or problem pregnancies in the first place. Hard to believe, isn't it? A drug which has caused so much misery—and who knows how much more—probably never really did any good. A per-fect case of a useless drug messing up people's lives needlessly.

Unfortunately, the **DES** story is not yet over. Besides the perhaps hundreds of thousands of women (and possibly men) still at risk, **Stilbestrol** is being implanted in and fed to ani- *41*

mals, particularly cattle, in order to increase their weight. In 1954 it has been estimated that 75 percent of the cattle in America were fed this hormone. Although many countries have banned the use of this drug for this purpose (Canada often refuses to buy beef raised in the United States because of this very fact), the United States has been playing politics. It was banned from cattle feed for a few years because residues were turning up in the meat sold in supermarkets. But in January, 1974, it was once again approved for use as a feed-grain additive to cattle and sheep. While it is true that the levels of **DES** which might show up in your plate of meat at the dinner table are infinitesimal when compared to the amount women received in the late 1940s, it is ridiculous that anyone should be exposed at all, since it is a known cancer-producing drug. Its presence as a food additive is merely to add weight to cattle. That would be great if it went to protein. Sadly, all that it does is increase the fat and retained water and salt. Greed triumphs once again.

An even greater horror, if possible, was the recent approval by the FDA of the use of **DES** as a "morning-after pill." This idea, although brilliant on the surface, turns out to be a real menace. The concept of the morning-after pill is the following. For those who are absent-minded or careless (lots of women forget to take their birth control pills on the average of twice a month) or who get so involved in love-making that they cannot take time out to insert their diaphragms, medical science will provide a "morning-after pill." This is supposed to prevent pregnancy after the act, which in the case of rape could be a great benefit. At a dosage of 25 milligrams twice a day for five days, young women will be exposed to 250 milligrams in a very short period of time. This dose is higher than that capable of producing cancerous tumors in animals, and higher than the exposure level the National Cancer Institute recommends. Nevertheless, on February 10, 1975, the Food and Drug Administration gave final approval for **DES** as a morning-after pill. It is available commercially as **Diethylstilbestrol** and **Dicorvin**, but who knows what new preparations will soon become available.

This whole sad story has been described in detail, not to **42** beat you over the head or scare you unnecessarily, but to demonstrate how impossible it is to predict with absolute certainty the safety of any drug we consume. Women who took **DES** in good faith twenty-five years ago on the recommendation of their doctors in order to "save" their pregnancies, unknowingly put their daughters at risk. A woman asking her doctor about side effects would have been assured in those days that there were no complications. Yet today we know that this is a dangerous drug. It is still being prescribed as a morning-after pill and may be administered to some of the very young women who are in danger.

Drugs and Pregnancy Don't Mix

The account of **Diethylstilbestrol** is reminiscent of another medical nightmare involving the ingestion of a drug during pregnancy. The **Thalidomide** tragedy, which resulted in birth defects and terrible misery, was also brought on by the administration of a drug to pregnant women. Both examples offer us a costly lesson: any drug is a potential threat to the unborn child. Your doctor may reassure you that it is okay to consume his prescribed medication, but then I'll bet the doctors who prescribed **DES** and **Thalidomide** were convinced that it was okay to administer those two drugs. Therefore, a rule of thumb is to avoid *all* drugs during pregnancy if at all possible.

That includes easily ignored nonprescription agents like aspirin. It is well documented that the lowly aspirin tablet may be dangerous. Once it has dissolved in the mother's stomach and reached her bloodstream, it quickly passes into the circulatory system of her unborn baby. There, it could seriously affect the blood-clotting ability of the baby once it has been delivered. A couple of aspirins once in a great while for a headache during a pregnancy will not be a threat, but the frequent intake of this *drug* can be an unneeded risk.

The National Foundation–March of Dimes recently held a symposium at which they resolved that a woman should stay away from all drugs—both those which can be bought over the counter and those which require a prescription—unless *43* she was absolutely positive that she was not pregnant. There are, of course, circumstances in which, for the safety of the mother and the fetus, it is essential that a woman continue taking her medication. Nevertheless, caution during pregnancy is a must. Since the first few months of pregnancy are the most serious in terms of fetal exposure, it is during this time that women must be most wary. A woman may not even realize that she is pregnant while she is taking a drug. A case in point is the use of birth control pills. Clearly, a woman who is on the Pill is taking it because she does not wish to become pregnant. But mistakes are made, and even a lapse of a few days could result in an unwanted fertilization. Or, quite possibly, that one-in-a-thousand long shot happens and the Pill does not do the job. In any event, it is possible for a woman to continue taking her birth control pills after she has become pregnant. In fact, some fool of a medical administrator has even suggested that a coed on the Pill continue taking it for up to two months after she has missed her period. This practice could be disastrous. A report from the University of Colorado Medical Center has indicated that women who had received the estrogen-progesterone type of birth control pill during their pregnancies have borne babies with multiple birth defects. The authors conclude that until more definitive data is available, "it would be prudent to emphasize the need to document the absence of pregnancy before undertaking oral contraception."[24] Since this report, Dr. Dwight Janerich of the Institute of Birth Defects in Albany, New York, has "found that women exposed early in pregnancy to synthetic estrogen and progesten are nearly five times as likely as those not exposed to have offspring with defects of arms and legs. . . . Dr. Janerich also suggests women should wait up to three months after discontinuing oral contraceptives containing either hormone before attempting to conceive."[25] Drs. A. H. Nora and J. J. Nora have also discovered that some hormonal pregnancy tests themselves may produce multiple defects not completely different from those seen with **Thalidomide**.[26] This means that women should also avoid hormonal "withdrawal-type" pregnancy tests.

Despite all warnings, too many women continue to consume **44** drugs during pregnancy. One study has revealed that 82 percent of the pregnant women surveyed had received medicine prescribed by their physicians and 65 percent had taken some form of nonprescription drug. Dr. Eric W. Martin states "... that 92 % of pregnant women are given at least one drug by their physician."[27] No one ever expects common, often-prescribed drugs like minor tranquilizers or muscle-relaxants to be dangerous. And yet an absolutely dynamite study published in the *New England Journal of Medicine* hinted that **Librium, Librax, Libritabs,** and **Menrium** [all are **Chlordiazepoxide**], as well as **Meprobamate [Equanil, Miltown, Bamadex, Deprol, Kessobamate, Meprospan, Meprotabs, Milpath, Milprem, Miltrate, PMB,** and **Pathibamate**] could also cause birth defects.[28] The authors state, "Although our findings support the suggestion that **Meprobamate** may be teratogenic in man and point some suspicion at **Chlordiazepoxide,** they are not conclusive. On the other hand, they suggest that **Meprobamate [Equanil, Miltown]** and **Chlordiazepoxide [Librium, Librax]** may not be safe during early pregnancy. We conclude that the prescription of these drugs to women of childbearing age should be restricted to cases with strong indications, and it would be prudent to assure that the woman is taking precautions against pregnancy."

These investigators also discovered during the course of their investigation that "many women under-reported the drugs prescribed by their physicians; many did not know the names of the drugs prescribed, and many described the medicines that they were taking by color or by the way in which they used them." This whole thing just makes me want to cry. And remember, female people, just because **Valium** has not yet been studied does not mean it can be considered perfectly safe.

Once the baby is born, its mother still can't let down her vigilance. A nursing mother may easily pass on a drug from her milk to the newborn baby. Due to the scarcity of information about the injurious effects of sustained drug-administration on the newborn, it would be wise once again to stay away from all medicines. **Tetracycline, Penicillin** (it could increase the baby's susceptibility to allergy later in life), arthritis medication, and birth control pills are only some of the potentially harmful pharmaceuticals to be avoided. *Medical Letter* has gone **45** on the record stating, "A physician who prescribes a drug for a nursing mother should consider whether the benefits to the patient outweigh a possible danger to the infant."[29]

The question of contraception, whether it be vasectomy for men or IUDs and The Pill for women, remains controversial. Recent evidence raises serious doubts about the safety of the coil (IUD), especially if, as occasionally happens, the woman becomes pregnant. A sharp increase in the incidence of deaths and uterine infections among women with IUDs has led the FDA to issue a warning, and some manufacturers have even recalled their "models". The verdict on vasectomies is also far from in. In some individuals there appear to be psychological and physical after-effects to this operation. Finally, birth control pills are still a source of hot debate and investigation within the medical profession. (Female doctors often refuse to take the very same oral contraceptives that they prescribe.) For more information on contraception, tune in to Chapter 9.

Are The Benefits Worth the Risks?

Drugs do not always exert their deleterious effects in an obvious and clearly detectable manner. In some instances, the side effects only become apparent over a long period of time and may not even be associated with the drug which is being ingested.

Lupus (SLE or Systemic Lupus Erythematosus) is a serious, but often difficult to diagnose, generalized problem which can be precipitated by a variety of medicines. This illness can be slow and insidious in onset. It is difficult if not impossible to completely cure, but fortunately the drug-induced variation is often reversible once the offending medicine has been removed. So how do you recognize lupus? The symptoms are very variable, but joint ache typical of arthritis is a common feature. Fever, muscle ache, and skin rash may also accompany a generally lousy, out-of-sorts feeling. Since important organs may become involved (such as kidney, liver, and lungs), it is essential that the medication be stopped at the first suspicion of trouble.

At the risk of beating a dead horse, three other drugs must be mentioned. One, **Reserpine**, is a potent medicine for lowering blood pressure and is sold under various names including **Serpasil** and **Rau-Sed**. Blood pressure preparations which contain **Reserpine** as an ingredient are **Diupres, Hydropres, Regroton, Salutensin, Ser-Ap-Es,** and **Rauzide. Rauzide** actually contains a chemical which is similar to **Reserpine**. So what about it? A flood of studies published in 1974 in England suggested that **Reserpine** might be associated with the development of breast cancer in women.[30,31,32] The investigations, carried out in Boston, England, and Finland, all found an increased incidence of breast cancer in women taking this kind of medicine. The Boston group, Boston Collaborative Drug Surveillance Program, demonstrated that the risk of developing breast cancer was three times higher in the women exposed to **Reserpine.** This study involved the analysis of the records of 25,000 patients admitted to twenty-four hospitals in the New England area. Although many doctors have not accepted these findings, on the basis that not enough work has been done yet, it might be a good idea for women over fifty to change medications until the final chapter is in. **Reserpine** is used by as many as three million Americans.

While there is still significant controversy surrounding the association between **Reserpine** and cancer, most experts are in agreement that another drug, **Premarin**, is much more dangerous. Dr. Harry Ziel and Dr. William Finkle (from the Kaiser Permanente Medical Center in California) recently reported that women who take estrogen hormones for problems associated with menopause face a five to fourteen-fold increased risk of coming down with cancer of the uterine lining (endometrical carcinoma).[33] The longer the exposure to drugs like **Premarin**, the greater the danger. Data collected by the California Tumor Registry supports this research and reveals a frightening increase in the incidence of uterine cancer (50 to 100 percent) just during the last few years.

It is estimated that as many as 5 million women regularly take hormones to relieve symptoms of menopause. One study carried out in western Washington revealed that as many as 51 percent of women past menopause had used estrogens.[34] In 1974 **Premarin** was the fifth most frequently prescribed **47** drug in America, following just behind such old standbys as **Darvon** and **Librium**.[35]

Many medical authorities feel that hormone preparations such as **Premarin** are vastly overprescribed. While possibly decreasing symptoms such as hot flashes, nervousness, and bone softening, estrogens cannot restore youthfulness. Besides cancer, other problems associated with estrogen administration are gallstone disease and blood clotting disorders (which could lead to strokes or coronary disease). Dr. Sidney Wolfe, Director of Ralph Nader's Health Research Group, has been a vocal critic of physicians who hand out hormone prescriptions like candy. He has stated that "Use will decline if patients are fully informed of the risks and 'questionable' benefits."[36]

Another drug of dubious value is **Atromid-S (Clofibrate)**. During the last ten years it has been very popular in the medical profession to insist upon decreasing cholesterol levels in susceptible patients. Besides diet, one of the methods doctors have employed is the drug **Atromid-S**. Although relatively safe, this medicine can produce nausea, diarrhea, gas, and vomiting. It may also produce such flu-like symptoms as muscle aches and exhaustion, and anemia has been reported. Some men have even noted a decreased interest in sex. Of course all these side effects would be well worth it if life was prolonged. Recent scientific investigation, however, now brings into question the therapeutic benefits of **Atromid-S**. The Coronary Drug Project studied more than eight thousand American men for up to eight years, and found that the men who took this drug had no fewer fatal heart attacks than the men who received nothing.[37] Now before you throw out your medicine, it must be emphasized that the men studied had already suffered at least one heart attack before participating in the research. Men with high blood cholesterol levels who have never had heart trouble might benefit from this drug. That remains to be established.

Finally, taking a drug may not be the only problem we have to worry about. The cessation of medication may not always be a simple matter. **Inderal (Propranolol)**, a drug prescribed to hundreds of thousands of people for heart problems—notably angina and irregular heartbeats—is very effective and should be used when prescribed. But what you must be aware of is that it cannot be stopped suddenly. An abrupt halt to this therapy could be extremely dangerous for an angina patient.[38] A fatal heart attack is not impossible after sudden withdrawal of **Inderal.** If it becomes necessary to discontinue this form of therapy, the dose should be gradually reduced over weeks with medical supervision.

Clearly it is not possible to list all the potential drug reactions or prepare patients for unpredictable dangers. What we have seen is that drug safety and effectiveness cannot be taken for granted. Adverse reactions to drugs will put you into the hospital as fast as, if not faster than, the original illness. People who are lucky enough to survive their reaction may be left with permanent disabilities. Kidney and liver damage are not infrequent. Deafness and blindness are not impossible. Serious drug reactions may leave their marks on the nervous and digestive systems, and these disabilities may last for months, for years, or forever.

Your doctor has a responsibility to make sure that you know the side effects of the drugs he prescribes and that you understand his instructions about dosage schedules and other drug interactions. The potential risk of any given drug must be weighed against its benefits, and your physician must allow *you* to make that decision. According to the American Medical Association, "A physician must obtain the consent of his patient before he can render any form of treatment."[39] And the patient's consent must be an "informed consent." Your pharmacist also has a moral obligation to inform you of the name of the drug you are taking as well as its expiration date and proper storage procedures. You have the responsibility to care for your medicine correctly and observe your body for any new or unusual reactions. Common sense and caution are important, especially when it comes to medications which you buy without a prescription. And remember that, though a drug may appear to be perfectly safe, it is impossible to predict with any kind of assurance what the long-range effects may be, especially upon an unborn child. It is time we stop insisting on a prescription or a shot. "Doctor, can't you please give me something," is an expression that should disappear. If a drug is necessary, your doctor will prescribe it without any encouragement from you, and you should take it according to his in- *49* structions. But what are you going to do about the drugs like **DES, Tolinase, Orinase, DBI, Meltrol, Reserpine, Premarin,** or **Chloromycetin**? There is evidence that under certain circumstances the benefits of these drugs might not be worth the risks. Ultimately, it is your decision, and I hope you use your common sense and make it wisely.

References

1. Talley, Robert B., and Laventurier, Marc F. "Drug-Induced Illness." *JAMA* 229:1043, 1974.
2. Editorial: "Inform the Patient." *JAMA* 211:654, 1970.
3. Mazzulo, J. M., and Lasagna, L. " 'Take Thou' . . . But Is Your Patient Really Taking What You Prescribed?" *Drug Ther.* 2 (11): 11–15, 1972.
4. Blackwell, Barry. "Drug Therapy Patient Compliance." *New Engl. J. Med.* 289: 249–252, 1973.
5. Caranasos, George J. "Drug-Induced Illness Leading to Hospitalization." *JAMA* 228:713–717, 1974.
6. *FDC REP.* 43:5, 1970. Cited in Martin, *Hazards of Medication*, P. 123.
7. Merck Sharp & Dohme, Division of Merck & Co., Advertisement for **Indocin (Indomethacin)**. *JAMA* 230:732–734, 1974.
8. Goodman, Louis, and Gilman, Alfred. *The Pharmacological Basis of Therapeutics*, 4th ed. New York: Macmillan, 1970. P. 338.
9. Caldwell, Jacques, and Cluff, Leighton, E. "Adverse Reactions to Antimicrobial Agents." *JAMA* 230:77–80, 1974.
10. Goth, Andres. *Medical Pharmacology: Principles & Concepts*, St. Louis: Mosby, 1972. P. 551.
11. Weiss, Peter J. "Stability and Expiration Dating." Presented at the Seminar on Manufacturing Controls, Proprietary Association, Cherry Hill, N.J., October 21–22, 1971.
12. Bassen, Jonas L. *Expiration Dating.* Presented at the Fourth Annual Quality Control Seminar for the Food, Drug & Cosmetic Industries, Region II, Clifton, N.J., March 16, 1972.
13. Graham, Joseph H. *Some Aspects of the Problem of Drug Stability.* U.S. Department of Health, Education and Welfare, Public Health Service, (Federal Department of Agriculture) 72–3025, Division of Drug Chemistry, Office of Pharmacological Research & Testing, Bureau of Drugs. P. 20.

14. Shangraw, Ralph E. "Unstable Nitroglycerin Tablets." *New Engl. J. Med.* 286:950–951, 1972.
15. Stewart, D. J. "Tetracycline's Overuse among Young Children." *Br. Med. J.* 3:320–322, 1973.
16. Zuskin, Eugenija, and Bouhuys, Arend. "Acute Airway Responses to Hair-Spray Preparations." *New Engl. J. Med.* 290:660–663, 1974.
17. Report of the Committee for the assessment of Biometric Aspects of Controlled Trials of Hypogylcemic Agents. *JAMA* 231:583–608. 1975.
18. Editorial: *JAMA* 231:624–625, 1975.
19. Herbst, Arthur L., et al. "Adenocarcinoma of the Vagina." *New Engl. J. Med.* 284:878–881, 1971.
20. Herbst, Arthur L., et al. "Clear-Cell Adenocarcinoma of the Genital Tract in Young Females." *New Engl. J. Med.* 287:1259–1264, 1972.
21. Smith, A. W. "Diethylstilbestrol in the Prevention and Treatment of Complications of Pregnancy." *Am. J. of Obst. & Gyn.* 56:821–834, 1948.
22. Herbst, Arthur L., et al. "Clear-Cell Adenocarcinoma of the Vagina and Cervix in Girls: Analysis of 170 Registry Cases." *Am. J. Obstet. Gynecol.* 119:713–724, 1974.
23. Herbst, Arthur L., et al. "The Effects of Local Progesterone on Stilbestrol-Associated Vaginal Adenosis." *Am. J. of Obst. & Gyn.* 118:607–615, 1974.
24. Nora, James J., and Nora, Audre H. "Birth Defects and Oral Contraceptives." *Lancet* 1:941–942, 1973.
25. "News Front: Dangers of Synthetic Hormones." *Mod. Med.* 42:161, 1974.
26. Nora, A. H., and Nora, J. J. "Syndrome of Multiple Congenital Anomalies Associated with Teratogenic Exposure." *Arch. Environ. Health* 30:17–21, 1975.
27. Martin, Eric W., *Hazards of Medication,* Philadelphia: Lippincott, 1971.
28. Milkovich, Lucille, and van den Berg, Bea J. "Effects of Prenatal Meprobamate & Chlordiazepoxide Hydrochloride on Human Embryonic and Fetal Development." *New Engl. J. Med.* 291:1268–1271, 1974.
29. "Drugs in Breast Milk." *Medical Letter* 16:25–27, 1974.
30. Jick, Hershel, et al. "Reserpine and Breast Cancer." *Lancet* 2:669–671, 1974.
31. Armstrong, B., et al. "Retrospective Study of Association Between Use of Rauwolfia Derivatives and Breast Cancer in English Women." *Lancet* 2:672–675, 1975.

32. Heinonen, O. P. "Reserpine Use in Relation to Breast Cancer." *Lancet* 2:675–677, 1974.
33. Ziel, Harry K., and Finkle, William D. "Increased Risk of Endometrial Carcinoma Among Users of Conjugated Estrogens. *New Engl. J. Med.* 293: 1167–1170, 1975.
34. Stadel, B. V., and Weiss, N. S. "Characteristics of Menopausal Women: A Survey of King and Pierce Counties in Washington. *Am. J. Epidemiol.* 102: 209–216, 1975.
35. "The Top 200 Drugs." *Pharmacy Times* 41: 39–46, 1975.
36. "Ob-Gyn Committee Hears Data on Estrogens And Uterine Cancer, Considers Labeling Changes." *Washington Drug & Devices Letters* 7:7, Dec. 22, 1975.
37. "News from the Heart Front on Cholesterol." *Newsweek,* Feb. 3. 1975.
38. "Medical News: Sudden Halt in Propranolol Therapy Can be Dangerous." *JAMA* 125–126, 1975.
39. Simonaitis, Joseph E. "Photographs of Patients." *JAMA* 229:844, 1974.

4.

Sexy Trade Secrets and Home Remedies: What Your Doctor Does Not Know or Will Not Tell You

Once upon a time there was something called a family doctor. This entity was often known as a GP, and more likely than not he was a family friend and confidant. Besides administering an occasional medication (which he might have made up himself), he was very big on common sense and practical advice. Unfortunately, he has been replaced by a new species known as a specialist, who is long on up-to-date modern scientific techniques but a bit short on patience and friendly suggestions. Let us see if we can bring back some of those old-fashioned home remedies and perhaps add some new ones.

What is the first thing you do after you are stung by a bee or insect? Most people probably scream a little, make futile efforts to remove the stinger, or possibly make a compress of mud or baking soda and smear it on the bite. Well folks, you can forget all those ineffective old-fashioned techniques. Now we have something that really works, and it is as close as your kitchen spice rack. *Meat tenderizer* is all it takes. Yup, just a little Adolph's (or your favorite brand)—applied as soon after the sting as possible—will do the trick. According to Dr. Harry L. Arnold (and the Health Insurance Institute), one quarter of a teaspoonful of tenderizer added to about one or two teaspoonfuls of water (enough to make a paste) will stop pain in seconds when it is rubbed into the skin at the area of the sting.[1]

Well, how can a little dab of meat tenderizer eliminate the pain of insect bites almost immediately and speed rapid recovery? It turns out that meat tenderizer contains a chemical called *papain*, which is extracted from the tropical fruit of the papaya tree. Papain is an enzyme which apparently has the ability to break down the venoms and toxic chemicals which are injected into your skin and render them harmless. It makes sense when you consider the use you put to meat tenderizer in the first place. If you feel that just plain old meat tenderizer is not good enough for your lovely skin, you can go to your friendly neighborhood pharmacist and ask for a "digestive aid" which contains papain. Often, mail-order vitamin catalogues will offer natural papaya enzyme in tablet form. The Warner Chilcott Company even manufactures such a product under the brand name **Papase**. All you have to do is smash up the tablet and make a paste. An even better method is to have the stuff ready to go in an ointment. A perfect product exists under the name **Panafil Ointment** (Rystan Company, 470 Mamaroneck Avenue, White Plains, N.Y. 10605). Although it will probably require a prescription to get, having this handy tube should be worth any inconvenience it takes.

Well, what happens when a dive-bombing mosquito selects your juicy bodily fluids to extract? It has not yet been demonstrated that tenderizer will work on mosquitoes (let me know if it does). Or what will you do if your dog's fleas decide that they would like some variety in their lives and want to try you on for size? And of course there is always the plague of the summer for country folk—poison ivy. What can you do for all these diverse and terribly unpleasant types of itches? There is an incredibly simple and effective relief no farther away than your sink. According to some expert dermatologists, applications of hot water for a brief period of time can provide almost instantaneous alleviation of itching for up to three hours.[2] I know it sounds crazy, but try it; it really works. The water should be quite hot (120—130° Farenheit), because if it is not warm enough it may make the itching worse. You can either stick the affected spot under the running water for a couple of seconds or use a hot washcloth. Several applications should do the trick for several hours. Obviously, an extensive skin involvement should not be treated in this manner, nor should poison ivy which has formed blisters. Keep in mind that prolonged heat may be dangerous in certain kinds of skin problems, so just apply it briefly. The way it works is by affecting the fine nerve network in the upper layer of your skin. By "short-circuiting" or "overloading" the itching reflex, the need to scratch is abolished. Of course, the most desirable approach in dealing with pruritis (a fancy word for itching) is to remove the underlying cause. But for insect bites, mild poison ivy, and atopic dermatitis (a chronic conditon with no known cause or cure), hot-water therapy can be the safest, cheapest, and fastest technique available.

Ah, but there are those among us who would doubt the word of the Lord. Give me **Caladryl**, or **Dermidon Anti-Itch Cream**, or **Poison Ivy Cream**, they shout. Who cares about hot water? Well, listen my children and you shall hear what poison ivy lotions you should fear: all of them. According to Dr. Albert M. Kligman, a world authority on poison ivy, not one of thirty-four popular preparations was better than tap water or simple calamine lotion.[3] And catch this: a great many of these highly promoted products may produce an allergic skin reaction right over the top of your poor poison ivy. Both the antihistamine and the local anesthetic so commonly included in things like **Ivarest**, **Rhulihist**, and **Zema-Stringent** may add to your distress in the long run. But worst of all is zirconium. It will not help, but it sure can hurt. This little honey could produce little growths on the skin up to a couple of months after the application of a formula containing zirconium. Products like **Zotox**, **Ziradryl**, **Poison Ivy Spray**, and 55

RhuliSpray contain this chemical. According to *The Medicine Show*, "Consumer Union's medical consultants believe that none of these OTC [over-the-counter] combination preparations has been shown to be superior to ordinary calamine lotion."[4] And that is the word.

Well, how about avoiding itches altogether, especially those caused by insect bites? Most of us have our own favorite brand of insect repellent, which we either love or hate depending on its effectiveness at any given time. Of course there is always one guy in every group who complains that no repellent does him any good. The question is, what really does work best? According to the United States Army, **Deet** (Diethyltoluamide) heads the list. This chemical was tested along with more than nine thousand other compounds and came out on top. Another chemical which was found to be very effective and capable of inhibiting mosquito biting was dimethyl phthalate. It stands to reason, therefore, that any product which utilizes these two goodies together will be a superior repellent. **Cutter Insect Repellent** (foam or lotion) contains the winning combination. It also makes sense to buy the product with the highest concentration of active ingredient. That way you don't have to apply as much and you get more for your money. **Skram Insect Repellent** (liquid only) contains 74.5 percent **Deet**, almost as much as is employed in United States military formulations (75 percent). Other products with a good slug of **Deet** are **Mosquiton** (lotion) and **Off** (liquid). Always avoid buying insect repellents in aerosol spray cans, since the concentration of **Deet** is always reduced; besides, you have to pay extra for the convenience. Although also effective in warding off mosquitoes, ethylhexanediol was found to lose much of its protection power as the temperature zooms up.[5] It is the major ingredient in "6-12" and **Walgreen's Insect Repellent**. For the guy who claims that nothing works, you might suggest putting on his repellent less like it was expensive perfume and more like it was supposed to be put on. Liberal and frequent applications will work wonders. And remember, repellents work because the mosquitoes hate the smell. They may swarm about and even land, but the chances are good that they will not bite. Wind, as well as heat and humidity will reduce your repellent's effectiveness, no matter what the brand, and will require more persistent and concentrated applications. Very little research has been done regarding the amount of insect repellent you absorb into your body through the skin, and what toxic effects may result. It is believed that toxicity is low, but no one can predict what long-term exposure might do. There is evidence that **Deet** is absorbed more readily than most other organic chemicals, but that does not necessarily mean anything.[6] In any case, I definitely do not recommend spraying *any* insect repellent indiscriminately on young children over and over.

Now do you want to hear something wild? As far back as 1943 it was known that simple Vitamin B₁, or **Thiamine**, when administered orally could repel insects, particularly mosquitoes.[7] Recently Mexican dermatologists have reported that **Thiamine Chloride** was effective in reducing insect bites and diminishing itching when administered in doses of 200 milligrams to adults and 100 milligrams to children.[8] They found that there was an 89 percent improvement rate in an investigation involving a hundred children with dermatological problems originating from mosquitoes, fleas, and bedbugs. What is even better, they reported no adverse reactions even in doses over 300 milligrams.

Another study, reported by Dr. H. L. Meuller, noted that "Thiamine hydrochloride taken internally has been reported to be a repellent for mosquitoes and fleas. In our experience, over 70 percent of 100 insect-sensitive patients given doses of 75 to 150 milligrams of thiamine hydrochloride daily reported that insects bothered them little or not at all while taking it, but the effect wore off rapidly if the thiamine was omitted."[9] Now get this. You don't rub this stuff on, you swallow it. It is a plain old everyday vitamin. Granted, it is a darn big dose, but like Vitamin C, it is probably eliminated in the urine when it exceeds the body's requirements. Unfortunately, none of these investigations was really carried out in a well-controlled manner under rigorous scientific testing procedures. It remains to be seen whether large doses of Vitamin B₁ really can do the trick when held up to the acid test. But you are the best judge, and come the next camping trip, why not give **Thiamine** a try?

Hemorrhoids

As long as we are speaking about itching (and painful disorders), can **Preparation H** shrink hemorrhoids, reduce inflammation, and heal injured tissue, to quote a time-honored advertisement? Poor New Yorkers have been confronted (perhaps affronted would be a more appropriate word) with swollen hemorrhoid advertisements for years while standing in the subway with nothing more interesting to read than the **Preparation H** signs. Well, to end your curiosity once and for all, the *Medical Letter*, a truly magnificent medical journal, says that there is no acceptable evidence that this drug heals hemorrhoids.[10] Just in case you have been sitting on the edge of your seat all these years wondering what was in **Preparation H**, the 1973 edition of the *Handbook of Non-Prescription Drugs* reports the following: an antiseptic (phenylmercuric nitrate), two thousand units of "skin respiratory factor" obtained from "live yeast cell derivative," (who knows what that is for) along with 3 percent shark liver oil which, though it may be a source of vitamins A and D, hardly seems very useful for hemorrhoids.[11] Therefore, **Preparation H** just doesn't work. In fact, there is very little evidence to support the claims of most of the manufacturers of hemorrhoidal products. It is unlikely that astringents, anesthetics, witch hazel, cocoa butter, or shark liver oil can shrink internal or external hemorrhoids and decrease bleeding. There is not even much hope that they can decrease pain or itching. Now listen to what the American Pharmaceutical Association's *Handbook of Non-Prescription Drugs* has to say: "Unfortunately, no documentary evidence is available regarding the effectiveness of these drugs alone or in combination in relieving the symptoms of anorectal disease."[12] Furthermore, these products may not be harmless. The possibility of an allergic reaction is always present. The *Handbook* states, "The risk of contact sensitization and hypersensitivity common to nearly all the drugs used must be considered."

Why would anyone use this junk anyway? Well, people are basically cowards when it comes to "sensitive" body parts. A 6 foot 8 inch, 275-pound lumberjack who wouldn't be afraid to tackle a mountain lion refuses to go see a doctor about piles. So to avoid embarrassment he will buy something like **A and**

D **Hemorrhoidal Suppositories** and make a fool of himself trying to insert the darned things. What makes the whole thing even more ridiculous is that a suppository, once inserted, probably slips right on by the area of discomfort without providing any measurable relief.

By the way, have you ever wondered what hemorrhoids, or piles, actually are? Since so many Americans are affected with this blasted problem (Dr. Morris Fishbein has suggested that 80 percent of the people between thirty and sixty years of age suffer to one degree or another), it might be interesting to understand the disorder and why it occurs.[13] In your behind, in the area of the lower rectum there is a network of sad little veins which often become weak and swell out. These swellings often become inflamed, develop small blood clots, and bleed. The veins swell out because they are particularly sensitive to increased pressure. What can cause this increased pressure? Well, for one thing, all you huffers and pushers, straining to defecate can really jack up the pressure. Other causes are obesity, heavy coughing, chronic constipation, frequent sneezing and working conditions which require prolonged standing or straining. Sitters can suffer too. Even pregnancy is a factor in elevating blood pressure in these veins and often results in a case of hemorrhoids. Well, what can you do about them once you have them? If they are fairly small and uncomplicated, they require little, if any, treatment. An excellent idea is to avoid sitting on the john for half an hour reading or straining, nor is it wise, as the *Merck Manual* so gracefully puts it, to "resort to excessive cleansing of the anus." Patting rather than rubbing, with a soft, slightly dampened toilet tissue is recommended (a prepackaged antiseptic version is now sold commercially). Unfortunately, Americans seem to be obsessed with the idea of regularity and come hell or high water they are going to have their bowel movement at one specific time. Somehow, this is also tied up with the fear of constipation and leads to a real neurotic concern about gastric function. Avoidance of hard stools and the subsequent pain associated with their passage can be managed with a diet high in roughage (bran, celery, cabbage, or apples for example). Other foods that might have a slight laxative effect are oatmeal, whole wheat, prunes, vegetables, and fruits. Even large doses **59** of Vitamin C could reduce the firmness of a bowel movement. Mineral oil (Ugh) will also help decrease the pain of their passage. But diarrhea is not the answer either, because stools which are too loose could aggravate the condition just as easily. In order to reduce the bothersome old itch, why not try the hot water application mentioned earlier or even a hot bath? If not relieved, go see your doctor. There are some new and very efficient techniques available which do not entail surgery. Some doctors swear by an approach which involves the tying off of the distended vein with rubber bands. They claim that the results are just as successful as surgery, with less pain or complications. Whatever your move, it is always a good idea to make sure what you have really is hemorrhoids and not something more serious.

Hiccups and Other Cups

Something less momentous or painful but nevertheless bothersome is an age-old problem which probably affects everyone at least two dozen times in their lifetime: hiccups, or singultus, to use a high-falutin' medical term. Yup, at long last there is a real cure. You can forget all that nonsense about holding your breath, or drinking water, or putting your head into a paper bag, or have someone scare the bejeezus out of you. There is a new, absolutely 100 percent cure which has been published in the *New England Journal of Medicine*. In a scientific study performed by Dr. Edgar Engelman, it was found that a teaspoonful of sugar does more than just help the medicine go down. According to their research, it was found that "one teaspoonful of ordinary white granulated sugar swallowed dry resulted in immediate cessation of hiccups in 19 of 20 patients."[14] Twelve of these poor souls had had their hiccups for longer than six hours, and eight of them from twenty-four hours to six weeks. That is just a little more alarming than your average hiccup. I have found that brown sugar works for me and goes down a bit easier, but white sugar probably works best. It has been suggested that for younger patients a few drops of water with the sugar will also help it go down and is just as effective.[15] If the dry sugar does not help after two tries, you might want to take a shot at another "new" remedy, a jigger of vinegar.[16]

Actually, it is probably not the sugar itself but the small granules which do the trick. Salt would probably work just as well, but who can swallow a whole teaspoonful of salt? The way the whole thing works is probably by setting up a local irritation in your throat. Somehow the sugar particles stimulate a nerve, which then shuts off the hiccup reflex. Whatever the mechanism, just be glad that there is finally a simple, easy cure.

Does going without a bra lead to Cooper's Droop? If one listens to the brassiere industry, the worst thing a woman can do is go without support. And the medical profession appears just as concerned. According to Dr. John Wulsin, writing in the *Journal of the American Medical Association*, the Cooper's suspensory ligaments will stretch "under the influence of gravity, more so in some women than others and specially in those breasts naturally large or fat or pregnant or lactating."[17] In typical medical mumbo-jumbo, Dr. Wulsin goes on to say that "once lengthened by tension these fibrous connections . . . do not resume youthful dimensions, despite hopeful legend, no amount of exercise will restore mammary profile. . . . Proper support for the breasts in the form of a satisfactory brassiere can be expected to minimize stretching of the intrinsic mammary connective tissue." So, according to this surgeon, no bra, sagging boobs. Now do you believe that? The other side of the story needs telling. According to *my* experts, "There's nothing like a woman's breast to make a doctor put his foot in his mouth."[18] Amen! Doctors and bra companies can hardly be considered experts on droopy breasts. They may have an interest, yes, but to date there has never been a really scientifically controlled investigation to determine the Truth. My sources have the following statement to make: "Cooper's ligaments may stretch when the breasts swell during pregnancy or when a woman gains, then loses weight. Factors such as individual tissue tone, heredity and general health all determine the degree of change. It is impossible to predict whether or not one woman's breasts will sag: A large-breasted woman *61* may have strong ligaments and a small-breasted woman may have weak ligaments. In the face of confusion, go with what's comfortable and/or pleasing to the eye."[19]

Burns

Time to change gears. A never-ending source of controversy seems to revolve around the best treatment for common household burns. So many suggestions have been offered over the years that no one seems to know whether butter, adhesive tape, or baking soda is the best treatment. Well, the controversy is now over. Without doubt, the application of cold water or a cold, wet compress is the treatment of choice.[20] One investigator reported that there was a reduction in total treatment time and burn severity by two-thirds when immediate cold-water immersion was employed for 150 patients.[21] They had suffered chemical, heat, or electric burns, some of which were quite severe. All infections were eliminated. Do not however, use ice directly because that is just too cold and could actually damage the already sensitive skin (you can, however, add a couple of ice cubes to a pan of water). By sticking the burned skin under cold water or by using a compress, you can decrease the pain right away and, surprisingly enough, actually diminish the severity of the damage done to the skin and underlying tissue. You may even prevent the formation of blisters and promote healing. Effectiveness may depend upon how soon you get the burned area under cold water, so move quickly. Ten seconds may mean the difference between a nasty blister and no obvious skin reaction. It is also a good idea to keep the burned area submerged for quite some time, from thirty minutes to several hours.

Although it has become increasingly popular to apply ointments and aerosol sprays to burns, this can be a dangerous procedure. Most of these preparations contain a local anesthetic (benzocaine is one of the most common ingredients) which can of itself produce a reaction. Often after repeated application, the patient will notice the burned area getting worse due to a sensitization (allergic response) of the skin. Sometimes this can be worse than the original burn. If the tissue has been seriously injured, these ointments can be doubly dangerous, since they may be absorbed into the body. These drugs, which are relatively harmless when applied topically, can be quite toxic when they enter the blood stream (and burned skin is a poor barrier against absorption). It is probably much better to just stick with cold water.

An equally safe but way-out therapy for burns has been suggested by Dr. Robert Blomfield.[22] He claims that the application of plain old honey to burns, bedsores, cuts, and just about any other local wound will speed healing. It sounds odd, but it certainly can't hurt, and if it works it sure is worth the try. Another skin man, Dr. James Barnes, Jr., also claims success with this type of treatment, but instead of honey he recommends plain old white sugar.[23] When it is applied under an airtight dressing, it is supposed to definitely improve the healing of bedsores.

How about sprains, twists, and tears? Which is better for these injuries—heat or cold? Ask five different experts and you will probably receive five different answers. Actually, according to the *Medical Letter*, both heat and cold are beneficial but *only* in the correct order.[24] After a minor accident, like a sprained ankle, ice packs or cold water should be applied first and should be used for up to two days. At this early state heat may actually make things worse by increasing the fluid accumulation (edema) in the damaged underlying tissue. After the second day, heat can then be applied to reduce the pain, although its advantages over cold are not clear.

In the case of arthritis and bursitis, heat has long been prescribed for relief of pain and as an aid to movement. Unfortunately, like many long-used therapies which have never been scientifically studied, this practice has disputable benefits. According to a well-controlled investigation, it was determined that heat could actually aggravate the fluid accumulation and pain of joints swollen by rheumatism.[25] Ice packs, on the other hand, afforded greater relief for pain and stiffness and seemed to improve the ability to exercise. In the final analysis, of course, you are going to use the technique which works best for you, and that is as it should be.

As long as we are discussing cold, there is an obscure medi- **63** cal phenomenon called *frigid headache* which merits elaboration. This common affliction has long been the bane of ice-cream lovers everywhere. People who slurp down very cold beverages or preparations like "slush" also suffer what can be a severe headache. According to a report published in the *New England Journal of Medicine*, this reaction results from frigid stimulation of nerves running from the palate to the brain. The investigators noted, "The symptoms were appreciably ameliorated by lingual-recoil therapy." In plain English, that means you should curl your tongue back and press it against the roof of your mouth (palate). Through this warming maneuver, the pain should rapidly diminish.

Colds and Vitamin C

Well, what about real colds? What can you do when an "upper respiratory tract viral infection" (to use elegant terminology for a cold) strikes? The first thing you should do is throw out all your so-called cold remedies. Heresy? No, just plain old horse sense. They are expensive, but more important, they do not work. Sure, Americans throw away more money on prescription and over-the-counter cough and cold remedies than for any other single type of medicine or pharmaceutical product. That does not make them effective. The advertisers may beg you to "give your cold to **Contac**," but what they really want is your money. The American public throws away close to $500 million on this stuff every year. Let's find out about products like **Coricidin "D"**, **Dristan**, **Ornade**, **Nyquil**, **Sinarest**, **4-Way Cold Tablets**, and all those other actively advertised preparations.

Most cold remedies contain a whole sinkload of ingredients. Undoubtedly, there will be a decongestant, an antihistamine, a pain-reliever (probably aspirin), and then just about anything. Caffeine is often included, along with a belladonna drying agent. There is almost no medical justification for products which contain so many different compounds all rolled up into one, and there is reason to believe that there could be a negative effect.

64

Well, what about the decongestant? The most common ingredient is something called phenylephrine. Though it might work if given in a sufficient dose (more than forty milligrams), most nonprescription cold medications have less than half that amount. According to *Consumer Reports*, "the oral dose in two **Dristan** tablets is only one-fourth of the dosage found to be *ineffective* in controlled clinical testing."[26] Oral decongestants rarely do much to relieve nasal stuffiness. Even if they did, there would be a real problem because they tend to increase blood pressure. Since there are over 22 million people in this country with high blood pressure, any medicine containing a decongestant would be quite dangerous for a large segment of the population. If you do not have high blood pressure and insist upon swallowing a decongestant for your stuffy nose, Consumer Union's medical experts suggest **Propadrine** with phenylpropanolamine or **Sudafed** with pseudoephedrine.

The other common ingredient in cold tablets is an antihistamine. It should not be included. A common effect of antihistamines is to increase and thicken the mucus already in your lungs. To quote the most authoritative textbook on medical pharmacology in the world, "despite early claims and persistent popular belief, antihistamines are of little value in combating the common cold."[27] And yet almost every cold preparation available contains a healthy dose of this unnecessary drug.

Another great misconception of the American public is the concept of tiny time pills. The idea that you can take a capsule that will speed continuous relief for hours by sustained release is bunk. These "tiny time capsules" in reality cannot provide anything like continuous, reliable liberations of active medication. There are so many things which influence an individual's ability to absorb drugs that a product which attempts to do something for everybody usually end up falling far short of expectations. Food, emotional state, and gastric function all influence drug absorption. Some people may receive a very high dose of time capsule all at once, while a slow digester may not receive a sufficient dose of drug to do him any good through the whole twelve hours. Even if **Contac** was spread out evenly over the full twelve hours (as advertised), the total dose at any one time could not be adequate, since the fifty milligrams of 65 decongestant included in this preparation is only enough for three hours of relief.

But, you exclaim, "it does too work!" Yeah, I know. You have been taking **Contac** or **Brand X** for years when you get a cold, and it makes you feel better. Well, sorry folks, but it probably does not matter a whole heck of a lot what you take when you have a cold. It seems that colds are one illness that respond magnificently to placebo treatment. That's right. The old sugar pill really makes people feel better. As long as we think it works, it will. Some people at the first sign of a sniffle give up, decide they are going to die anyway, and just make themselves and everyone around them miserable for a couple of weeks. Nothing helps these guys. Other people decide that it is no big deal and just go on, head high, suffering but grinning and bearing. The third type takes every pill in sight and probably would declare chicken soup the miracle of all times if he could buy it in capsule form.

But you want to know what does work, right? Well, that leaves us with the only ingredient in all these "cold cures" that really can do something. Sure enough, the good old-fashioned pain-reliever, aspirin. Whenever you see that now-ridiculous phrase "most recommended by doctors," you know immediately that it is nothing more than that fantastic, never to be beaten tongue-twister, acetylsalicylic acid or **aspirin**. And although it cannot cure anything, **aspirin** really can make you feel better. But why pay through the nose to buy it in brand-name preparations such as **Alka-Seltzer**, **Dristan**, or **Coricidin** when it will cost you gobs more than an equally effective bottle of el cheapo plain **aspirin**? And you can forget all those expensive aspirin brand names like **Anacin** or **Bufferin**, because what makes them work is still just plain old **aspirin**. Before you purchase your discount brand, smell it first to make sure it has not started to deteriorate. Some of the cut-rate drugstores let their aspirin sit around much too long. If you get a whiff of an acidy, vinegar-like odor when you open the bottle, you know that it has been around too long. When **aspirin** starts to go, one of its breakdown products is acetic acid. Also stay away from any of the new, time-release aspirin formulations. There have been increasing medical reports of people coming down with bleeding gastritis because of these **66** drugs.[28]

Well, if **aspirin** is so good, how about aspirin-like products that contain phenacetin or acetaminophen? Phenacetin, a pain-reliever much like **aspirin** (though somewhat less effective), has the potential to cause kidney damage if consumed frequently and in large doses. Frequently means more than ten days straight, and too much would be considered more than six tablets per day. Products which contain phenacetin include **A.P.C., A.S.A. Compound, Bromo-Seltzer, Coryban-D, Empirin Compound,** and **Sinustat.** Too much of any of these pills could promote serious kidney trouble. Kidney disease may be hard to detect for a long time, but once established it is hard, if not impossible, to reverse. Acetaminophen, another tongue-twister, though about equivalent to aspirin offers a few advantages. It is less irritating to the stomach (good for ulcer victims) and can be substituted for aspirin by patients who have an allergy to salicylates. Unfortunately, it does not possess the antiinflammatory properties of aspirin and so is not very effective for arthritis patients. It does work for headache, menstrual cramps, and muscle aches. You can find it in **Excedrin, Co-Tylenol, Neo-Synephrine Compound, Tempra, Vanquish,** and **Tylenol.** Acetaminophen-type products are often recommended for people who must take a blood-thinner at the same time as a pain-reliever. **Tylenol** is one of the favorite substitutes for **aspirin** in this situation. However, a careful medical study discovered that a dose of acetaminophen equal to four two-tablet administrations of **Tylenol** could increase the patient's susceptibility to hemorrhaging after a week of daily consumption.[29] Frequent blood testing must accompany this drug combination.

There are some people who really love nose drops. If you have never tried these handy-dandy little rip-offs, then I suggest that you do not start now. If you really dig them, start dehooking yourself. Sure they work—that is the problem. Nose drops generally have a decongestant that works by constricting the tiny capillaries and blood vessels located inside your nose. So what is wrong with that? you ask. Nothing really, since it can supply momentary relief for stuffed-up sinuses. But the hooker is a doozy. Once the decongestant effect has worn off, you are subject to an "aftercongestion" effect which is often worse than the original stuffiness. Some people really 67 get into using their nose sprays. Before long the cold has disappeared, but they are still all blocked up, just from their medicine. It may take days for this "rebound" kind of congestion to disappear, even after the medication has been discontinued. If you really have a thing for your nose spray, then please be sure not to mess up your nose more than two times in any one day.

Another goody of dubious value is the aerosol for colds. This relatively new product is marketed to relieve the signs and symptoms of colds. Although none of the "active" ingredients—menthol, eucalyptol, camphor, alcohol, thymol, or diethylene glycol—have been demonstrated to alleviate the symptoms or reduce the duration of a cold, advertising can make people buy just about anything. The active chemicals probably won't do you much good, but the "inactive" contents (those which are not listed on the can) can muck you up pretty fast.

Well, how about something really powerful, like the use of antibiotics for treating a bad cold? Without a doubt this is the most ridiculous therapy a doctor could prescribe. It almost borders on witchcraft. Illnesses due to viruses (a perfect example being the common cold or the flu) will *not* respond to any form of antibiotic medication. Even most fevers of unknown origin will not benefit from these drugs, since they too are often associated with a viral infection. If and when the actual offending organism has been specifically diagnosed (and this can only be done by laboratory culture), the correct antibiotic can be prescribed.

Another common mistake doctors make is the casual prescription of antibiotics for children with sore throats. According to Dr. D. A. Stewart, "The indiscriminate use of antibiotics for pharyngitis [sore throat] of undetermined origin in children is a common but potentially dangerous practice."[30] It could mask other infections and lead to imprecise diagnosis. A laboratory test should always be run in order to rule out a strep throat.

What is the possibility of curing a cold altogether? So far, there just isn't anything that even comes close. But next to **aspirin**, there is a succulent, simple home remedy that could very well help you clear up a cold quickly and make you feel better at the same time: Yes Virginia, there is a "wonder drug" and it is **Vitamin C**. By now, Dr. Linus Pauling's well-known vitamin C approach to prevention and cure of the common cold has stirred up tremendous controversy within the medical profession. It is very hard to understand why these health professionals have reacted with such antagonism and hostility to something as simple and effective as ascorbic acid. Yet the majority of doctors and medical researchers reacted with outrage and scientific snobbism when Dr. Pauling suggested that Vitamin C could do more than protect us from scurvy. To this day there are a great many physicians who resent and reject his views despite the fact that there is solid evidence supporting him. Fortunately, they are being proved wrong with greater and greater frequency as well-controlled, scientifically valid investigations turn up positive proof of the beneficial effects of this simple, cheap, and plentiful vitamin. In fact, one group of researchers who were highly critical of Dr. Pauling and who set out to prove him wrong once and for all had to eat crow and accept the results of their own study. Dr. T. W. Anderson and others, writing in the *Canadian Medical Association Journal*, discovered, much to their surprise, that subjects taking a thousand milligrams of Vitamin C every day (and increasing that dose to four thousand milligrams at the onset of a cold) had a 9 percent reduction in frequency and 14 percent reduction in days sick.[31] They were kept at home 30 percent less time due to illness than a group which did not receive this vitamin. The number of visits to doctors and amount of antibiotics prescribed were also diminished in the ascorbic acid subjects.

In 1974, Dr. John Coulehan and others published an extremely well-done piece of research in the *New England Journal of Medicine*. These investigators discovered that although they could not prevent the incidence of colds in a Navajo Indian boarding school, they could significantly decrease the days sick due to respiratory illness by 28–34 percent at a dose of a thousand to two thousand milligrams of ascorbic acid every day.[32] These doctors also observed a definite decrease in the cough and nasal discharge associated with colds. Of equal, if not greater, consequence was their finding that Vitamin C decreased by 30% the incidence of non-cold-related illness. This **69** confirms the work of the Canadian researchers and implies that somehow ascorbic acid protected these subjects from disease in general.

A 1973 study carried out in a Dublin, Ireland, boarding school produced some interesting results regarding sex differences. These researchers uncovered the fact that the female students had more pronounced cold symptoms than the male students. However, when the girls received the rather small dose of five hundred milligrams of ascorbic acid, the severity and intensity of their cold symptoms were reduced by 50 percent.[33] Also noted was the surprising realization that the worse the cold, the greater the utilization of Vitamin C. According to these doctors, two thousand milligrams of ascorbic acid should be prophylactic for the general population since men normally have a lower Vitamin C level than women and probably require greater supplementation.

Although we do not yet have proof positive that Vitamin C will protect us from coming down with a cold, it is almost certain that it will dramatically diminish the nasty symptoms and the number of days sick associated with upper respiratory tract viral infections. Even more startling, and perhaps more significant, is the discovery that illness in general seems to be significantly reduced. If this finding stands the test of time, it would demonstrate the absolute necessity for maintaining an adequate and continuous level of Vitamin C throughout the year. It may not put hair on your bald head or increase your bust line but for maintaining good health it looks hard to beat.

If Vitamin C is essential, what kind of a dose should you be taking? Dr. Linus Pauling, in his excellent book *Vitamin C and the Common Cold*, has suggested that there is no one dosage regimen which is perfect for everyone.[34] He has estimated that "1 gram (1000 milligrams) to 2 grams per day is approximately the optimum rate of ingestion." However, five grams and possibly even as much as ten grams of ascorbic acid could be necessary when a cold has started to take hold. This leaves it up to each individual to determine the correct amount for herself or himself. Dr. Pauling suggests that if you continue to get colds of the same severity after the ingestion of Vitamin C, you probably should increase the dose.

70 One extremely important consideration for Vitamin C users

is the dosage schedule. Since ascorbic acid is a water-soluble vitamin, the body tends to eliminate any amount which is excessive. This means that if you consumed three thousand milligrams of Vitamin C at 9:00 A.M., you would probably reach a maximum blood level in about two or three hours—at about 11:00 A.M. From that point on, you would have a steadily declining level of Vitamin C and would probably lose much of the benefit of the large morning dose. For this reason, many doctors have insisted that large doses of ascorbic acid are meaningless. In answer to this argument, it was reported to the American Chemical Society by Dr. E. S. Wagner that as you increase your intake of Vitamin C, you decrease the proportion excreted.[35] That means that the higher the dose, the more vitamin your body can retain. But to really increase the effectiveness of Vitamin C, it has been suggested that you divide the dose into at least three, and better yet five or six, different doses every four hours. In this manner, your body will maintain a more constant and continuous level throughout the day. If this is too much of a drag, why not just pop a couple of tablets at every meal?

But what about side effects? You can be sure that the medical profession has spared no effort in trying to prove Vitamin C is a dangerous substance which could produce toxicity in the large doses suggested by Professor Pauling. To date there is good evidence to substantiate Dr. Pauling when he says, "Ascorbic acid is not a dangerous substance. It is described in the medical literature as 'virtually nontoxic.' " It has even been reported that some nuts have taken as much as forty to a hundred grams (100,000 milligrams) in one day and not suffered any serious damage. Quite possibly, large doses of Vitamin C could cause a slight laxative effect, which can be reduced by taking your tablets with meals. Some doctors have warned that people with a tendency to form kidney stones should be wary of large doses of Vitamin C. This is possible, since ascorbic acid can be metabolized to oxalic acid (a substance potentially capable of forming stones). But since this is a secondary pathway of metabolism, most people will not be in jeopardy. To be on the safe side, get a lab test done, or try sodium ascorbate (chewable Vitamin C) instead of regular ascorbic acid.

A rather startling report published in 1973 mentions the "suspicion that regular daily doses of ascorbic acid of 2 grams or more may reduce fertility in some individuals."[36] Dr. M. H. Briggs, a well-known British researcher, reported that seven of his female patients who had not had any problems conceiving before or after their consumption of ascorbic acid did not become pregnant while on two grams of Vitamin C per day. While this circumstantial evidence is not conclusive, the theoretical framework for this bizarre contraceptive effect is not entirely ridiculous. According to Briggs, ascorbic acid may act as a mucolytic agent (capable of dissolving, digesting, or liquifying mucus) in the lungs. He states, "the effect of high-dose vitamin C on the prevalence of colds may, therefore, be related to its mucolytic action in the respiratory tract. A similar action is likely on the mucus of the uterine cervix. The state of cervical mucus is known to be critical for human reproduction."[37] Disruption of the normal mucus channels at the cervix may be incompatible with sperm penetration. Whether or not this phenomenon truly exists is doubtful; even if it did, some·people might consider it an advantage rather than a side effect. However, if you have been having trouble making a baby and are taking large doses of Vitamin C, it might be worth cutting back just to eliminate this far-out possibility.

For women who are taking oral contraceptives, it should be noted that Vitamin C is metabolized more rapidly than in women who are not on The Pill. Thus, anyone on birth control pills could have a diminished level of ascorbic acid in her blood (perhaps as much as a 30 percent decrease). We also know that one of the most serious complications of the Pill is that it can lead to thrombophlebitis (the formation of blood clots in veins). According to Dr. Briggs, "It is possible that some of the reported side-effects of 'the Pill' may be a consequence of this vitamin lack."[38] What is wonderful is the finding that ascorbic acid may provide a "powerful protective action against thrombosis [clotting]."[39] The investigator who made that statement observed (in a well-controlled double-blind study) that women receiving birth control pills experienced less general clotting and had a real decrease in the swelling and tenderness of existing thrombophlebitis when they

72

received one gram of Vitamin C daily.[40] This could mean that any woman on birth control pills should automatically goose her daily intake of Vitamin C to around one gram in order minimize her chances of developing thrombophlebitis.

So what else is Vitamin C supposedly good for? (An excellent and comprehensive book by Irwin Stone describes in detail most of the benefits of Vitamin C. It is called the *Healing Factor Vitamin C against Disease*.) For many years it has been felt that this wonder drug can be useful in the healing process of traumatic physical injuries. Although I know of no well-controlled studies to prove this point, it is quite possible that ascorbic acid promotes wound-healing by stimulating the formation of connective tissue, which in turn improves the formation of scar tissue. Therefore, any wound, fracture, or burn might benefit from one or two grams of vitamin C.

Another interesting area of recent study has uncovered the fact that guinea pigs fed a diet deficient in Vitamin C tend to accumulate cholesterol in their livers. This situation may stimulate the formation of gallstones.[41] Although guinea pigs are not people, this tantalizing bit of medical trivia might hold hope for gallstone sufferers. Future studies in humans will tell the story.

Of all the work going on in the ascorbic-acid field, none impresses me more than that involving arteriosclerosis. The biggest worry for any American male over thirty-five years of age is the fear of a heart attack. Although doctors are still of mixed opinion regarding the role of "hardening of the arteries," it is practically unanimous that this condition is undesirable and may contribute to heart attacks. There has been lots of emphasis placed on the need to reduce cholesterol intake, which may indirectly affect the formation of arteriosclerosis. Some very tentative and poorly controlled investigations offer tantalizing evidence that Vitamin C might help reduce cholesterol levels and maybe arteriosclerosis. Off-the-wall reports published in *Lancet* have revealed that 1000 milligrams of Vitamin C decreased blood cholesterol in healthy volunteers under twenty-five years of age.[42] In another badly designed study, sixty geriatric patients took one to three grams of ascorbic acid daily for thirty months.[43] During that time none had a heart attack, although each had a 73 history of heart trouble. Of the sixty, 83 percent experienced a mild to impressive improvement in their symptoms. Sadly, none of these tempting investigations was carried out under rigorous scientific testing procedures, so we cannot be sure the reported effects are real. Let's hope someone will carry out some good research and settle the question.

Meanwhile, there is a marvelous drug which has been carefully tested and proved to be useful in helping arteriosclerosis and arterial thrombosis. **Aspirin** rears its lovely head once again. Now don't laugh. I promised succulent and specific handy home remedies. **Aspirin** may be the best of them all. In a study completed in 1974, it was determined that one single dose of three hundred milligrams of **aspirin** (one tablet's worth) could improve life expectancy by the incredible figure of 25 percent in men who had already suffered one heart attack.[44] [This was an apparently sound scientific piece of research carried out in England with the stuffy title "A Randomized Controlled Trial of Acetylsalicylic Acid in the Secondary Prevention of Mortality from Myocardial Infarction." With a title like that it's got to be good.] A more comprehensive investigation, carried out in twenty-four hospitals of the Boston Area by the Boston Collaborative Drug Surveillance Group (including 776 heart attack patients and 13,898 control patients), concluded that although aspirin may not prevent a heart attack, it "is reasonable to suggest that aspirin may offer some protection against the development of acute myocardial infarctions [heart attacks]."[45] That means that although they do not really want to commit themselves, they think **aspirin** could protect some people from developing a heart attack.

It is intriguing to note that as far back as 1953, Dr. Sidney Cobb published an article in the *New England Journal of Medicine* where he observed that "only 4% of 191 patients with prolonged rheumatoid arthritis had died from myocardial infarction, compared with 31% of deaths in the general population of the U.S.A. from this cause.[46] This may not be a statistically appropriate comparison, but it does suggest that the continuous taking of aspirin as an analgesic may have unexpectedly reduced deaths from atherosclerotic heart disease."[47]

Fascinating! These are not crackpots talking but respectable medical experts. Clearly, the whole aspirin story is not in. We still do not know whether aspirin can be helpful in treating the actual heart attack once it has occurred. Is it useful in preventing a first heart attack, or can it be valuable in protecting against "reinfarction"? Is aspirin beneficial in the treatment of all kinds of blood clots, such as in thrombophlebitis, or is it only helpful for the heart? These are important questions that need to be answered.

Coffee and Your Heart

One issue which is still up in the air and which concerns every one of us is Can Coffee-Drinking Be Dangerous to Your Health? This controversial question has brought two eminently respectable medical research organizations to loggerheads. According to the investigators for the Boston Collaborative Drug Surveillance Program of Boston University Medical Center, heavy coffee-drinking may double your risk of suffering a heart attack when compared to people who drink no coffee.[48,49] On the other hand, the Framingham Study (an ongoing investigation of coronary heart disease since 1949 initiated by the National Heart and Lung Institute) concluded that "coffee drinking, as engaged in by the general population, is not a factor in the development of atherosclerotic cardiovascular disease."[50] These two organizations claim that there are errors of interpretation and evaluations with each other's data.

According to the Boston Group, "The authors' [of the Framingham Study] final conclusion that there is no association [between coffee and heart attacks] was based primarily on their own 'negative' . . . study, and they essentially dismissed previous positive case-control studies." The Boston folks call this a "one-sided view of the available evidence." They go further and say of the Framingham investigators, "They failed to present a point-by-point critical evaluation of any of the pertinent studies, including their own, even though such an evaluation is obviously essential for an informed overall judgment. Whereas the conclusions of Dawber et al. may well be correct, the evidence and reasoning presented in their report are un- 75 convincing to us."[51] Clearly, these guys still think that coffee-drinking could be dangerous. The Framingham people don't accept the criticism and claim that their own on-going (prospective) investigations are much more reliable than the looking-back type of study (retrospective) done by the Boston researchers.

Here is what Dawber of Framingham fame has to say: "Although retrospective studies are indispensable, the risks of bias both in cases and in controls make prospective confirmation highly desirable. The fact that prospective studies do not confirm the findings by Jick et al. [of Boston] appears to us to render their conclusions moot at best."[52] So there you are. You pay your money and you take your choice. It is refreshing to learn that the biggies can argue among themselves too. Of course, that makes it pretty hard for us laymen when it comes to deciding what to do. Chances are that it would be smarter to switch to tea if you have heart trouble, just to be on the safe side. There is some very tentative evidence that habitual tea consumption could be correlated with a decrease in the amount of cholesterol in blood and possibly decreased heart trouble.[53]

Modern medicine, in its never ending quest for progress, has lost touch with its past. While folk medicine may have frequently relied upon the placebo effect to produce success, many old-fashioned techniques really do work. In his effort to seek scientific respectability, today's specialist often overlooks simple but nevertheless scientifically valid home remedies.

I have attempted to explain how meat tenderizer can relieve the pain of bee stings, how granulated sugar can do away with hiccups, how cold water can reduce the damage done by burns, and how hot water can stop itching. These are but a few of the simple yet effective inside tips that most doctors either don't know about or prefer not to mention. Many folk remedies probably do not work, but if physicians would prescribe Vitamin C and chicken soup for colds, instead of antibiotics, there might be a lot less drug-induced illness in this country.

References

1. Arnold, Harry L. "Immediate Treatment of Insect Stings." *JAMA* 220:585, 1972.
2. Sulzberger, M. B., et al. *Dermatology: Diagnosis and Treatment.* Chicago, Yearbook, 1961. P. 94.
3. Cited in *The Medicine Show.* New York: Consumers Union, 1974. Pp. 138–9.
4. Ibid., p. 138–9.
5. Maibach, Howard I. "Use of Insect Repellents for Maximum Efficacy." *Arch Dermatol.* 109:32–35, 1974.
6. Feldman, R. J., and Maibach, H. I. "Percutaneous Penetration of Some Organic Compounds in Man." *J. Invest. Dermatol.* 54:399–404, 1970.
7. Shannon, W. R. "Thiamine Chloride—An Aid in the Solution of the Mosquito Problem." *Minn Med.* 26:799–802, 1943.
8. Ruiz-Maldonado, Ramon, and Tamayo, Lourdes. "Treatment of 100 Children with Papular Urticaria with Thiamine Chloride." *Int. J. Derm.* 12:258–260, 1973.
9. Meuller, H. L., and Samter, M. *Immunological Diseases.* Boston: Little, Brown, 1965. P. 683.
10. "Preparation H." *Medical Letter* 10:104, 1968.
11. Grosicki, T. S., and Knoll, K. R. "Hemorrhoidal Preparations." In *Handbook of Non-Prescription Drugs*, 1973 ed. Washington, D.C.: American Pharmaceutical Association, 1973. Pp. 148–154.
12. Ibid.
13. Fishbein, Morris. *Modern Home Remedies and How to Use Them*, New York: Doubleday, 1966.
14. Engelman, Edgar G., et al. "Granulated Sugar as Treatment for Hiccups in Conscious Patients." *New Engl. J. Med.* 285:1489, 1971.
15. Margolis, George. "Hiccup Remedies." *New Engl. J. Med.* 286:323, 1972.
16. Schisel, Aurelia D. "Hiccup Remedies." *New Engl. J. Med.* 286:323, 1972.
17. Wulsin, John H. "Bra-Less Cooper's Droop: Mystique of the Bra-Less Mama Maligned." *JAMA* 219:625, 1972.
18. "The Playboy Advisor." *Playboy* 21:55–56 (Sept.), 1974.
19. Ibid.
20. "Heat and Cold as Analgesics." *Medical Letter* 12:3–4, 1970.
21. Shulman, A. G. "Ice Water as Primary Treatment of Burns." *JAMA* 173:1916–1919, 1960.

22. Blomfield, Robert. "Honey for Decubitus Ulcers." *JAMA* 224:905, 1973.
23. "Sugar Sweetens the Lot of Patients with Bedsores." Cited in Medical News. *JAMA* 223:122, 1973.
24. "Heat and Cold as Analgesics." Ibid.
25. Kirk, J. A., and Kersley, G. D. "Heat and Cold in the Physical Treatment of Rheumatoid Arthritis of the Knee." *Ann. Phys. Med.* 9:270, 1968.
26. "Cold Remedies: What Helps and What Doesn't." *Consumer Reports* 39:67–69, 1974.
27. Goodman, Louis, and Gilman, Alfred. *The Pharmacological Basis of Therapeutics*, 4th ed. New York, Macmillan, 1970. P. 645.
28. Hoon, James Richard. "Bleeding Gastritis Induced by Long-Term Release Aspirin." *JAMA* 229:841–842, 1974.
29. Antlity, A. M., and Mead, J. A. "Potentiation of Oral Anticoagulant Therapy by Acetaminophen." *Curr. Ther. Res.* 10:501–507, 1968.
30. Stewart, D. A., and Moghdam, H. "Diagnosis and Treatment of Throat Infections in Children." *Canad. Med. Assoc. J.* 105:69–71, 1971.
31. Anderson, T. W., et al. "Vitamin C and the Common Cold: A Double Blind Trial." *Canad. Med. Assoc. J.* 107:503–508, 1972.
32. Coulehan, John L., et al. "Vitamin C Prophylaxis in a Boarding School." *New Engl. J. Med.* 290:6–10, 1974.
33. Wilson, C. W. M., and Loh, H. S. "Common Cold and Vitamin C." *Lancet* 1:638, 1973.
34. Pauling, Linus. *Vitamin C and the Common Cold*. New York: Bantam, 1971.
35. Orloss, Sam. "Massive Dose of Vitamin C Excreted Less." in "Medicine Today" of Bergen County, N.J., Cited in *Sunday Record,* April 21, 1974.
36. Briggs, M. H. "Fertility and High Dose Vitamin C." *Lancet* 2:1083, 1973.
37. Ibid.
38. Briggs, M. H., et al. "Vitamin C Requirements and Oral Contraceptives." *Nature* 238:277, 1972.
39. Spittle, Constance R. "Vitamin C and Deep Vein Thrombosis." *Lancet* 2:199–201, 1973.
40. Spittle, Constance R. "Atherosclerosis and Vitamin C." *Lancet* 2:793, 1970.
41. Ginter, E. "Vitamin C Deficiency and Gallstone Formation." *Lancet* 2:1198–1199, 1971.
42. Spittle, Constance R. "Atherosclerosis and Vitamin C." *Lancet* 2:1280–1283, 1971.

43. Sokoloff, B., et al. "Aging, Atherosclerosis and Ascorbic Acid Metabolism." *J. Am. Geriat. Soc.* 14:1239–1260, 1966.

44. Elwood, P. C., et al. "A Randomized Controlled Trial of Acetyl-salicylic Acid in the Secondary Prevention of Mortality from Myocardial Infarction." *British Med. J.* 1:434–440, 1974.

45. Boston Collaborative Drug Surveillance Group. "Regular Aspirin Intake and Acute Myocardial Infarction." *British Med. J.* 1:440–443, 1974.

46. Cobb, Sidney, et al. "Length of Life and Cause of Death in Rheumatoid Arthritis." *New Engl. J. Med.* 249:533–536, 1953.

47. "Editorial": *British Med. J.* 1:408, 1974.

48. "Coffee Drinking and Acute Myocardial Infarction: Report from the Boston Collaborative Drug Surveillance Program." *Lancet* 2:1278–1281, 1972.

49. Jick, Hershel, et al. "Coffee and Myocardial Infarction." *New Engl. J. Med.* 289:63–67, 1973.

50. Dawber, Thomas R., et al. "Coffee and Cardiovascular Disease: Observations from the Framingham Study." *New Engl. J. Med.* 291:871–874, 1974.

51. Jick, Hershel, and Miettinen, Olli S. "Statistics of Coffee Drinking and Myocardial Infarction." *New Engl. J. Med.* 292:265, 1975.

52. Dawber, Thomas R., et al. "Statistics of Coffee Drinking and Myocardial Infarction." *New Engl. J. Med.* 292:266, 1975.

53. Herbel, Eric S., and Scala, James. "Coffee, Tea, and Coronary Heart Disease." *Lancet* 2:152–153, 1973.

5.

Over-the-Counter Medication:
Your Friendly Neighborhood Pusher, The Local Pharmacist

Are you fed up with the constant barrage of advertising beseeching you to improve your love life, give your mouth sex appeal, or stay cool, calm, and dry? Have you had it, or are you just a little bit nervous that you, too, may have bad breath or, worse, body odor? Our universal insecurities manipulated by drug industry make us think that just to be on the safe side, a little **Scope** wouldn't hurt after all, or that **Arrid Extra Dry** is the protection we really need. It is time that we stopped falling for the ad man's high-pressure pitch. Americans are throwing over three billion dollars a year away (more than fifty dollars per family) on nonprescription medications. Dandruff, warts, athlete's foot, gas, B.O., menstrual cramps, and insomnia are but a few of the problems most of us must face. They keep reminding us that we are but poor mortal humans, normal, just like everyone else. The products which advertisers convince us we can't live without in order to "cure" these common maladies must be analyzed and evaluated for the rip-offs that they are. Let's find out what works and what doesn't.

When it comes to over-the-counter (OTC), nonprescription drugs and medications, we are our own worst enemies. Here is one place where we cannot blame the doctor for our stupidity and bad reactions. And adverse reactions there are aplenty. One study entitled "Drug-Induced Illness Leading to Hospitalization" reported, "Over-the-counter drugs were implicated in 32 of the 177 (18.1%) admissions."[1] Nonprescription drugs can be just as lethal as those our physician prescribes. They may aggravate an already existing condition or, worse, mask the symptoms of an underlying disease until it is so bad corrective procedures may not be able to reverse the harm done. Let's face it, how often do you read the warning which is now mandatory on OTC drug containers? Even if you did, chances are you neither understood it nor would pay it any attention. The New York Pharmaceutical Society recently demonstrated that of 10,000 people studied, 85 percent either did not follow the advice written on the container or did not comprehend the significance.

For openers, try this one on for size. Cough syrup is a safe, simple nonprescription drug everyone has in their home. No sweat, no problems. Right? Wrong! For most people, cough medicine is uncomplicated, with no danger of adverse effects, but for the millions of diabetics of this world it could be a real problem. And it is not the so-called active ingredients that cause the difficulty. It is rather the syrup, that yummy-tasting vehicle which may be loaded with up to 85 percent sugar. A well-controlled diabetic probably will have no trouble if he consumes a moderate dose, say four teaspoonfuls per day. But the diabetic who has some difficulty keeping his blood sugar levels constant (brittle diabetics) can compound his problem with the "simple" cough medicine. The alcohol found in many cough preparations can mess him up for the same reason. Decongestants which are often found in cold remedies and hay-fever medications such as **Contac, Coricidin "D"**, or **Dristan** may increase blood pressure and heart rate. For most people the increase is minimal and not dangerous; for those with high blood pressure or heart disease, it could be lethal. Elderly patients, always susceptible to glaucoma, must be particularly cautious with cold remedies and decongestants, since the drying agents contained in these products may increase dangerously the already high pressure in the eye. By now everyone who has ever taken an antihistamine should be familiar with the admonition, "Do not drive or operate machinery while taking this medicine," and yet how many of us really pay much attention?

The first rule when taking *any* nonprescription drug is to *read the package label*, and then follow the instructions. If your sore throat lasts more than three or four days, go see your doctor and get a throat culture rather than blindly sucking throat lozenges. If there is a warning about operating machinery or driving a vehicle, don't ignore it. If you are really conscientious you might want to read some of the literature which has been published about over-the-counter medicines. The Food and Drug Administration puts out an *FDA Fact Sheet* and *FDA Consumer*.[2,3] Much of the basic material in this chapter was synthesized from facts supplied in a terrific book called *Handbook of Non-Prescription Drugs* put out by the American Pharmaceutical Association.[4] Another source book is called *The Medicine Show*.[5] Consumers Union publishes it and without a doubt it is the most comprehensive guide to nonprescription health products available. Information gathered from these sources has made compilation of this chapter possible.

The second rule when dealing with nonprescription drugs is not to be influenced by advertising. Sure, that is easier said than done, comes the reply. And it is true that we are suckers for the subtle and not-so-subtle propaganda spewed forth over the tube. The makers of antacids spent $42.5 million in 1971 to promote sales of $108.8 million (the market is now over $200 million per year). That means they spent almost half of every dollar they made convincing us to buy their stuff. **Alka-Seltzer** is the sales leader in this field. That shouldn't be surprising. They spend the most cash on advertising. I grant you, they have clever ads, and I have been tempted to try the old "one-two" on occasions. But let's see if some of these heavily promoted products are all they are cracked up to be. Hearings held in the United States Senate in 1971 uncovered the fact that of four hundred broadly representative OTC drugs, only 15 percent were effective for what they were claimed.[6] 27 percent were probably effective, and a whopping 47 percent only possibly effective.

Basically, **Alka-Seltzer** is promoted for "headache and indigestion occurring after over-indulgence in food and drink." It is supposed to neutralize acid, relieve heartburn, and end that "full feeling" associated with overeating. How well does it satisfy its claims? All things considered, **Alka-Seltzer** probably does okay, since it contains all the necessary ingredients: sodium bicarbonate, 1,904 milligrams; citric acid, 1,055 milligrams; aspirin, 324 milligrams, monocalcium phosphate, 200 milligrams. Unfortunately, this combination of a pain-killer with an antacid is of very dubious medical value. For just a headache, you do not need to pay an outrageous price for **Alka-Seltzer**, since you are paying extra for the antacid properties. If you have indigestion or upset stomach, the last thing you want is aspirin included in the tablet. That is like trying to put out a fire with gasoline. Even though dropping their fizzy tablets into a glass of water converts the aspirin to a less irritating form called sodium acetylsalicylate, it offers no benefit for heartburn. More important, anyone who has had any alcohol in his system should never, never, never consume aspirin-like products, because the stomach lining becomes exquisitely sensitive to their hemorrhage-potentiating effects. That means if you pop two **Alka-Seltzers** after a hard night on the town so the hangover will be diminished the next morning, your stomach is going to bleed.

Alka-Seltzer also has some negative properties which could be serious. For one thing, it contains an extremely high level of sodium (surpassed only by **Bromo-Seltzer**). That means that *anyone* on a salt-restricted diet (which should include anyone with high blood pressure) must stay far away from these **Seltzers**. An average dose of two tablets will include 1042 milligrams of sodium. The Food and Drug Administration strongly recommends that people on low-salt diets should not surpass 115 milligrams of sodium per day in their antacid **83**

preparations. An average adult dose of **Alka-Seltzer** is ten times that. Finally, someone who really gets carried away and consumes eight or more tablets a day (or three capfuls of **Bromo-Seltzer**) is way over the "safe level" for citric acid established by the FDA. The point is that here we have a drug which is purchased by millions of Americans because of intense advertising. It is expensive when you analyze the basic ingredients (as much as twenty times the price of USP aspirin). The combination of aspirin and antacid is irrational, and there are some important hazards, especially for people with ulcers or high blood pressure.

What's Good For Indigestion?

Even without the aspirin (there is now a product called **Alka-Seltzer Gold** without aspirin), does this product have any real advantages over other antacid medications? In order to answer that question, it would probably help if we understood something about indigestion. Indigestion is one of those terms which is supposed to cover a multitude of sins. It is something doctors really can't get a handle on, so hundreds of OTC junk medicines have appeared to fill the gap left by the medical profession. Ask someone what his indigestion is and he may respond that it is belching, heartburn, or even nausea. It could range from stomach-ache and gas pains to overstuffing. Some people even consider their chest pains to be indigestion. This is obviously dangerous in older men, since heart trouble often manifests itself as "indigestion." It is clear then that people may be treating a multitude of different and complex problems under the same heading—indigestion. An ulcer in many cases is responsible for the misdiagnosed generalization of heartburn. Therefore, repeated use of antacids may mask a serious situation. You may feel better and even think you are doing yourself some good. Sadly, like a smoldering fire, the ulcer just keeps getting worse. By the time it is diagnosed correctly, harm has been done.

84 A few guidelines may serve to help you decide when it is

important to see a doctor and when to treat yourself. Certainly an occasional attack of stomach upset is no big deal, especially if you know that it was caused by your idiotic eating habits. When the attacks start occurring more than once every two or three weeks over a period of months, however, then it is time to hightail it to a doctor. Equally, *any* severe attack that is associated with difficulty in getting your breath or vomiting is worth a trip to the medic. Let's assume that your occasional "indigestion" is more a result of an argument with the boss or "dietary overindulgence." What are the best and worst types of antacids available?

When you are feeling cheap, or when nothing else is available, you can always resort to that old-fashioned standby, sodium bicarbonate. Otherwise known and loved under the familiar name *baking soda*, this effective antacid is no farther away than the kitchen cabinet. In this powdered form it is obviously much cheaper than brand-name preparations. It is the most important neutralizing ingredient in many of the most popular antacids, including both **Seltzer**s, **Fizrin, Eno**, and **Soda Mint**, as well as a few others. There is no doubt that baking soda works, and works fast. It is strong, with the capacity to neutralize acidity effectively. Sadly, as already mentioned, its high sodium content makes it undesirable for people with high blood pressure on low-salt diets. It should *never* be used regularly even by people without a salt restriction because it may mess up your body's chemical equilibrium. It has also been known to promote kidney stones, and worsen or prolong bladder infections, if consumed too frequently. Nevertheless, for someone with a rare attack of indigestion without any complicating problems, sodium bicarbonate will do the job without straining the pocketbook.

Calcium Carbonate, a different kind of antacid, is found in **Tums** (for the tummy) and **Pepto Bismol Tablets**. It is also an ingredient in such goodies as **Amitone, Al-Caroid, Alkets, Dicarbosil, Gustalac**, and **Ratio**. As an antacid, calcium carbonate is fast-acting and also capable of neutralizing acidity. What is even more promising is that it is cheap and lasts a relatively long time. Unluckily, we have to cross this otherwise great antacid off our list of beneficial drugs. It works, but it has the nasty habit of stimulating your own sad tummy to start **85** producing acid. So the good acid-neutralizing effect of the calcium carbonate is undone by its ability to stimulate excessive acidity. You may find yourself consuming countless tablets and trapped, just like the nose-drop junkies who have to keep spraying their congested noses to relieve the stuffiness caused by the rebound effect of the drops. It also has the potential to make kidney-stone sufferers much worse with its high calcium level. So all you **Tums**-takers, just cool it.

Okay, so far we have managed to knock some chinks in the armor of **Alka-Seltzer** and **Tums**. How about that old standby **Rolaids**? These widely promoted tablets contain dihydroxy aluminum sodium carbonate (a combination of sodium bicarbonate and aluminum hydroxide). Aluminum hydroxide is a very effective, long-acting neutralizer and though its effects are slow in starting, the sodium bicarbonate makes up for that deficiency. Unfortunately, aluminum antacids have the unpleasant consequence of producing constipation. **Aludrox** and **Amphojel** are loaded exclusively with aluminum hydroxide, and chances are pretty good that anyone who downs either of these antacids frequently will be plugged up. In addition, **Rolaids** contain a high enough dose of sodium to make their use questionable for those on low-salt diets. More than two **Rolaids** tablets a day exceeds the 115 milligrams of sodium recommended for antacid preparations. According to *Consumer Reports*, "Because of the calcium content of **Tums** and the sodium bicarbonate properties of **Rolaids**, neither product is suitable for frequent, long-term use."[7]

Well gee, if we keep eliminating all the old favorites, what can we count on to work effectively without any of these unpleasant complications? Remember that aluminum is a darn good antacid with only its constipating effects to ruin an otherwise good reputation. What would happen if we combined it with another good antacid that had a tendency to produce a laxative effect? The two together might have excellent antacid properties and cancel out each other's unwanted gastric consequences. It turns out that magnesium hydroxide is that other antacid. Remember how milk of magnesia is often used for its laxative effect? Well, it is also a pretty good antacid. Put the two together and voilà, a safe, long-acting antacid with few side effects. The following preparations contain the magic combination of magnesium (either as hydroxide or trisilicate) and aluminum hydroxide: **A.M.T.**, **Creamalin**, **Di-Gel**, **Gelusil**, **Maalox**, **Magnatril**, **Magnesium-Aluminum Hydroxide Gel USP**, **Maxamag Suspension**, **Mucotin**, **Mylanta**, **Malcogel**, **Trisogel**, and **WinGel**. A few of these preparations contain simethicone (**Di-Gel** for example), which is supposed to be good for gas. There is some doubt that it is effective—or for that matter, that anything is effective—for this problem.

To sum it all up then, resist temptation! Don't let those popular brand-name products seduce you with their snappy advertising slogans. Stick to the brands that work and have minimal complications, and remember that when you take an antacid you are merely soothing the symptoms and ignoring the real cause of the problem (overeating and drinking, if infrequent, are not cause for concern). There are many serious illnesses that can produce symptoms which are often described as "heartburn," "butterflies," "nausea," or "indigestion." Gallstones, heart disease, angina, gastritis, pancreatitis, and ulcers are just a few diseases that you may be calling upset stomach. Clearly the doctor and not an antacid are the treatment of choice for these serious problems.

It is also important not to allow yourself to fall in love with your favorite brand. There are cases of people who have consumed a roll of their "harmless" antacid daily for years, treating it almost like candy. One patient developed calcium deposits in his eyes and kidneys after four years of continuous consumption.

Above and beyond increasing our awareness and resistance to slick advertising, we are going to have to become wary of many nonprescription products which may have subtle and serious toxic effects. One famous illustration was the use of hexachlorophene. This "germ-fighter" was found in everything from toothpaste, shampoo, underarm deodorant, soap, mouthwash, and "feminine hygiene" sprays to baby powder, spray for fruit and vegetables. Fortunately, it is now available only by prescription. The main reason for the ban was the discovery that newborn children who were bathed in soaps containing hexachlorophene absorbed significant quantities into their bloodstreams. In the fall of 1972 in France, a baby powder called *Bébé* that contained hexachlorophene was held **87** responsible for the outbreak of a strange neurological disease among infants. More than thirty babies died, apparently as a direct result of the use of this powder. That this tragedy occurred at all is a black mark against regulatory agencies. As far back as 1967 investigators had determined that hexachlorophene could be absorbed directly into the blood through the skin. By 1969 the FDA had made available evidence that minuscule doses of hexachlorophene could produce major brain damage when fed to rats, yet as late as 1972, it was still being used by millions of Americans (24 million women were spending $53 million per year for vaginal sprays which contained this junk). Just imagine how much of this hexachlorophene you were absorbing as you sprayed your delicate axilla (armpit) with **Gillette Right Guard.** We are, in theory, no longer exposed to this stuff, unless it is specifically prescribed by a physician as in the case of the liquid soap, **Phisohex**, which is often pushed on unsuspecting patients with acne. In fact, people with pimples are usually ripped off when they buy expensive "antiseptic" or "antibacterial" soaps. The bacteria which may contribute to complexion problems are well below the surface of the skin and could not be reached by any soap or cleaning agent even if you applied them twenty times a day. And I don't care what the disc-jockey says. The antibacterial action will be washed away during the rinse anyway.

Even "deodorant soaps" have been called into question. Their high price and dubious value (there is no clear-cut proof that they stop body odor or prevent skin infections) do not make them worth the potential risk. According to an independent panel which reported to the FDA, "All antimicrobial chemicals used in bar soaps are absorbed into the blood."[8] The study also noted that "by selectively killing nonpathogenic microorganisms, an important ecological balance is upset which allows more dangerous organisms to thrive and cause potentially serious infections . . . it is now clear that under some conditions, the vigorous use of antimicrobials on the skin can increase rather than prevent" such infections. Many of the germs on your skin are good guys and may serve a protective function. Kill these goodies, and the baddies may take over and cause trouble.

According to Dr. Harvey Blank, head of the panel and professor of dermatology at the University of Miami, "We're talking about washing your hands with a chemical that invades your blood stream every day for a lifetime. And it's going to be awfully difficult to prove that those chemicals are safe for lifetime use." There is some possibility that long-term exposure could damage the nervous system, kidneys, or liver. **Dial, Lifebuoy, Safeguard, Phase III, Irish Spring**, and **Zest** are just a few of the antibacterial deodorant soaps. And keep in mind that many of these special soaps have chemicals which may produce an exaggerated burn or irritation to skin which is exposed to the sun. So friends, just use plain old soap (like **Ivory** or **Palmolive**) and lots of water. Forget the sexy perfume or germicide preparations. Soap and water is still the best treatment for cuts, scratches, and minor abrasions. The application of potent antiseptics like iodine, alcohol, or merthiolate (including the new aerosol sprays) not only is unnecessary but could interfere with the healing process.

As I already mentioned, the new feminine hygiene sprays are now a gigantic multi-million-dollar industry. These aerosols, which are typically referred to as "intimate sprays," are in reality nothing more than genital deodorants. We have accepted the advertiser's line which makes us feel inferior if we smell like normal people. A little soap and water can take care of any supposed "hygienic" problem a whole lot more effectively than a spray and much less dangerously. When hexachlorophene was the staple ingredient in these aerosols, there were lots of adverse skin reactions. Although that hazard has been removed, the other ingredients are not without risk. The other chemicals in these preparations include perfumes, solvents, and propellents. And you guessed it, none of those things are really good for your skin. Crotch irritation is not fun, and all too many dermatologists are faced with the delicate problem of trying to undo the damage these dandy items produce. And listen guys, don't think this is just a female problem. There have been cases of men who have had skin rashes in the penile and scrotal areas after sexual intercourse with women who used this stuff. And now that they are making the stuff in distinct, "yummy" flavors, the danger does not end with a simple crotch itch. You may end up ab-

89

sorbing the gook directly into your system, and that could be a whole lot worse than just a rash. Men and women beware— feminine hygiene deodorant sprays should be written off your list once and for all. You do not have to smell like a lilac bush to be sexy!

Menstrual Products

Another great rip-off perpetrated on American women is that of the pain-relievers advertised for "her special problem." These so-called menstrual products are purported to be effective in relieving the pain and tension associated with menstruation. Now while it is true that most doctors have tried to convince women that their cramping, upset stomach, nervousness, and headache are merely figments of their imaginations, the pharmaceutical companies which exploit the phenomenon of dysmenorrhea are equally irresponsible. Clearly a great many women do suffer some degree of discomfort, either from premenstrual tension with its accompanying retention of fluids and breast tenderness, or from menstruation itself. Probably anywhere from two thirds to three fourths of the female population are susceptible. Therefore, it would be nice to know which products work and which are worthless.

Few, if any, of the many nonprescription menstrual products have been tested scientifically in a well-controlled manner. Thus, many of the pain-relievers have not been proved better than aspirin, and some of those which have been tested have not shown themselves more effective than our friendly sugar pill. In recent years some physicians have prescribed diuretics in order to reduce some of the fluid accumulation associated with the premenstrual period. Although salt restriction might be of some value during the last week of the cycle, Dr. Walter Modell, in *Drugs of Choice 1974–1975* noted that a "well-controlled study is still needed to establish diuresis as a useful therapy for premenstrual tension and to show that the removal of fluid . . . has any connections with the relief of mental distress."[9] Therefore it is doubtful that **Pre-Mens Forte** is particularly effective, since it only contains a hundred milligrams of caffeine and ammonium chloride, a short-acting diuretic. What that amounts to is a few "stimulating" trips to the bathroom. If too many pills are swallowed, the caffeine may upset your stomach and make you jittery. Another chemical, pamabrom, is also considered a water pill although it is rather weak and of doubtful efficacy. It is included in the products **Cardui**, **Pamprin**, and **Trendar**. Another brand, **Midol**, contains a chemical which is purported to be a uterine-relaxing agent, and thus able to relieve cramping. There is some doubt about this effect, but some authors feel it is a valid claim. Try it and decide for yourself. Probably much of the benefit derived from **Midol** is due to the healthy dose of aspirin which is included.

Another common ingredient found in these preparations is pyrilamine, an antihistamine. Presumably the makers of **Cardui**, **Femicin**, and **Pamprin** are cashing in on the fact that antihistamines tend to make people drowsy or slightly sedated. Even if the dose were adequate, which it isn't (these preparations contain less than half the concentration needed to do much of anything), any sedative response is at best inconstant and will probably vanish after repeated use. And in some susceptible individuals side effects could be encountered. I cannot resist taking a potshot at one "natural" or homeopathic preparation called **Humphrey's No. 11**. This incredible menstrual product contains dried black snake root, cuttlefish bone, and dried Easter flower. I leave it to you to decide its therapeutic potential.

Besides the questionable medications above, there is a whole group of analgesics which include relief of menstrual pain as one of their secondary benefits. These products include **Excedrin**, **Empirin Compound**, **Cope**, **Vanquish**, and **Nebs**, among others. They contain a witches' brew of various analgesics plus aspirin. More often than not caffeine is thrown in for good measure, even though its value is dubious. Common ingredients besides aspirin are acetaminophen or phenacetin, pain-relievers which have been demonstrated inferior to aspirin in therapeutic value.[10] What's more, phenacetin—an ingredient in **Empirin Compound**, **A.P.C.**, **Bromo-Seltzer**, **Darvon Compound-65**, **Phenaphen**, and others—has been implicated in the possible development of *91* kidney problems. Consumers Union's medical experts have advised that people should stay away from pain-relievers that contain this drug.[11] Since June, 1973, Canada has banned the sale of all preparations that have phenacetin coupled with aspirin. To sum it up, there is almost no evidence to indicate that any of these combination pain-relievers or menstrual products offer any more relief than plain old aspirin. Even the Pharmaceutical Association's *Handbook of Non-Prescription Drugs* admits that the shotgun approach (**Vanquish**, **Cope**, and **Excedrin** are perfect examples) "appears to have no clinical advantage. . . . These combinations, for the most part, are of greater economic significance to the manufacturer than increased therapeutic benefit to the patient."[12] Now that is right from the horse's mouth.

One trick for getting more power out of your plain old aspirin tablet and less troublesome stomach irritation is to crush it. Now I wonder how many doctors ever tell their patients about that. Yet as far back as 1899, in Germany, Dr. Kurt Witthauer warned that aspirin tablets "should not be swallowed whole but allowed to disintegrate first in a little sugar water flavored with two drops of lemon juice."[13] More recently, in the *JAMA* a correspondent suggests "that the tablets be thoroughly chewed and swallowed with an adequate amount of water or that they should be crushed to a fine powder and the powder taken as a suspension in orange juice."[14] I have found that dissolution works best if you add the powder to warm water or lemon juice that can be sweetened with honey to make it more palatable. Whatever you finally decide upon, stick to plain old aspirin and forget the expensive, less effective pain-relievers.

Mouthwash: Is It Good for Anything?

An area in which the advertising industry has managed to play upon our fears of social, sexual, or job failure is with the mouthwashes. In 1971 they managed to convince gullible Americans out of $240 million in their mad scramble to prevent their best friend from whispering those fatal words, "bad breath." By now we are probably forking over more than a quarter of a billion dollars every year to ward off horrible halitosis. But do those familiar names like **Listerine, Lavoris, Scope,** or **Colgate 100** really prevent bad breath?

Bad breath, like indigestion, is merely a catch-all phrase for a symptom common to many varied and different problems. A normal, healthy mouth will not have an offensive odor, though it is true almost everyone experiences a furry, scuzzy mouth upon arising. This is typical and will disappear rapidly with talking or after breakfast since it is due to the oral inactivity of sleeping, a period of time when bacteria can act freely on food particles. While it is true that your mouth is loaded with germs (a normal adult probably has around ten million bugs in every drop of saliva), that is the way it is supposed to be. While still a baby you accumulate benign forms of streptococci, staphylococci, diplococci, and spirochetes, as well as other exotic varieties of bacteria. But this flora and fauna is important in keeping everything in balance, and without some of them this equilibrium could become upset. Any disturbance of our natural germ population could leave us more sensitive to invading microorganisms. Mouthwashes do upset our normal, resident flora. More important, however, is the question, "Does the random killing of oral bacteria with gargles really prevent halitosis?" Well, in the first place there is no way you are going to kill even a fraction of the hundreds of millions of germs in your mouth and throat with a couple of gargles. Even if you killed a large fraction of the bugs, five deep breaths or one good kiss would probably replace in spades anything you might think you had accomplished. But even more important, bad breath does not result from ordinary mouth bacteria. Assuming that your halitosis is not a result of your insecure imagination, it might be due to poor dental hygiene. Brushing and flossing your teeth will do wonders. If it is not something this simple, then an infection is a likely bet. It might originate deep within the throat, or be as superficial as a canker sore. A tooth which is decaying or abscessed will also produce an unpleasant smell. Even certain conditions such as diabetes, lung, or liver disease could result in a distinctive odor. Therefore it is obvious that a mouthwash will do little to correct the underlying condition and at best will only *93* superficially and temporarily change or "freshen" the breath.

The other major cause of bad breath comes from eating those delicious meals that contain gobs of garlic and onion. I must confess that I myself have a preference for raw onion sandwiches. Will a little **Scope** do anything to calm my dragon mouth? No! The "sweet" smell of garlic does not come from any residual odor lingering in your mouth or throat. The substance in garlic that produces the familiar fragrance is absorbed from your stomach into your bloodstream. From there it circulates all through your body, reaching your lungs, where it is exhaled with each breath. You would have to stop breathing in order to really block out the odor, and that is a bit drastic. So skip the mouthwash. A stick of chewing gum or a mint will probably do more to mask the smell than all the **Listerine** in Georgia. One remote possibility is that parsley root eaten before and after consumption of garlic will quickly diminish the offensive odor. And don't fall into the trap of believing that "breath freshener mints" will in any way relieve a chronic condition. There is only one thing to do: go see a dentist or a doctor and find out what the underlying condition is that has produced the odor. An abscess or gum disease is a serious situation which should not go untreated. Bad breath may be your early warning system.

How about sore throats? Surely something as bad-tasting as **Listerine** must be good for a sore throat even if it doesn't do anything for bad breath? Wrong again. In the first place, the infection responsible for your sore throat is in such a location that a brief gargle will not amount to much. Even if you bathe the affected tissue for many minutes, you could not kill the bugs responsible. Most sore throats are due to virus infections which will respond neither to antibiotics nor to mouthwashes. For those sore throats that are due to bacteria, only an antibiotic administered in tablet form or by injection will benefit the affected area. And the only way anyone can determine whether your sore throat is viral or bacterial in origin is by a throat culture. This is very important for severe, long-lasting infections since the possibility of a strep throat (an infection caused by Group A beta hemolytic streptoccus) is dangerous and demands penicillin treatment in order to prevent rheumatic fever or heart or kidney damage. Symptomatic treatment with mouthwashes or throat lozenges would be harmful in this case in that they might delay your trip to the doctor.

There is another important consideration to make when trying to decide to gargle or not to gargle with mouthwash. The redness and swelling associated with the pain of a sore throat are defense mechanisms so your body can increase blood flow to the infected area and help overcome the defiant demons. Some gargles or lozenges may make your throat feel better by shrinking the swollen tissue temporarily. This is probably counterproductive in the long run since it is the swelling and resulting increased blood flow which is part of the curative process. Another problem with lozenges is that they often contain a local anesthetic which is supposed to relieve the pain. Benzocaine is the most common ingredient. It has the rotten ability to produce an allergic irritation. Additionally, topical absorption of the antibacterial agents frequently included in lozenges may also lead to sensitivity reactions. What this means is that though the throat lozenge may briefly make your throat feel better, in some people it is actually setting up a more serious, long-lasting irritation of which you may not be aware.

The last straw in this whole sore throat–mouthwash scandal is the fact that a great many throat infections probably result from drying of the mucous membranes. The reason we are more susceptible to colds and sore throats in the wintertime is probably related not so much to the cooler temperatures as to the lack of humidity in the air. Some doctors feel that vaporizers which provide a fine mist of water may prevent or at least diminish many throat infections. What happens if you try to prevent a sore throat from attacking by religiously gargling with a "strong" mouthwash every night and morning? Most mouthwashes when used regularly will dry up the mucous membranes, and thus either make you more susceptible to, or aggravate, an already-existing, painful inflamed throat. The problem is that a great majority of these products contain alcohol, and alcohol is a great drying agent. Some preparations with significant alcohol levels are: **Astring-O-Sol**, 70 percent; **Dalidyne**, 61 percent; **Odara**, 48 percent; **Isodine Mouthwash/Gargle Concentrate**, 35 percent; **Oral Pentacresol**, 30 percent; **Listerine**, 25 percent; **Extra-Strength Mic-** *95*

rin, 20 percent; **Scope**, 18.5 percent; **Colgate 100**, 15 percent. A few products with somewhat lower alcohol levels which presumably are less irritating are: **Cepacol**, 15 percent; **Betadine Mouthwash/Gargle**, 8.8 percent; **Lavoris,** 5 percent; **Alkalol**, 0 percent; **Proxigel**, 0 percent; and **Greenmint Mouthwash**, 0 percent (this one has got to be innocuous since it only contains chlorophyll). If you really have to gargle in order to satisfy some primeval urge, the best thing to use is what the doctors always recommend: one-half teaspoon of salt (anything stronger may be irritating) in an eight-ounce glass of water. It will moisten your sad membranes with a physiological solution, and the very act of gargling may provide some relief.

Body Odor and Underarm Deodorants

Hopefully, we have now managed to dispel some of the fears and insecurities which the advertising industry has exploited in their pursuit of ever-increasing sales for mouthwashes and gargles. Another body function which advertisers have used to their benefit is sweating. Body odor, however, is less an advertiser's creation than is bad breath. Everyone sweats to one degree or another, and thus we all smell sometimes, since it is the germs normally present on the skin attaching on and decomposing the organic material in perspiration that produces an unpleasant aroma. On the average, we put out around one-half quart of sweat a day (save that one for your next cocktail party). It is a means of maintaining body temperature and is really an important body process. Nervous tension and emotional stress can contribute a significant amount of sweat to the normal level as well and may be responsible for much of the trouble. Obviously, good hygiene (lots of soap and water) will go a long way toward keeping down both the bacterial level and the accumulation of sweat. But since we cannot keep our underarms clean and dry all the time, a deodorant is a handy thing to have around.

Most products which are marketed to combat body odor are advertised as deodorants or antiperspirants or both. The reality is that there is very little difference between the ingredients found in antiperspirants and deodorants. In fact, the great majority of products contain exactly the same active compound (aluminum hydroxychloride). In theory, a deodorant works either by adding a "pleasant" fragrance strong enough to block out the unwanted smells or by adding an ingredient which can attack the germs located on the skin and prevent them from interacting with sweat. An antiperspirant, on the other hand, acts to inhibit normal cell function by actually blocking the sweating process, probably by producing swelling of the sweat glands. So how are you going to select the type of product which will suit your needs adequately?

Since most deodorants and antiperspirants contain similar ingredients, it may be hard to find something which is right for your particular odor problem. If your perspiration is related to anxiety, you might need a very different kind of chemical from someone who sweats either very little or only after exercise. Equally, some people have sensitive skin and cannot tolerate an antibacterial preparation with its strong irritating properties. Let's eliminate the baddies right off the bat. First, studiously avoid all products sold in an aerosol form. "Oh no," I can hear you groaning, "this guy won't let up." For reasons already mentioned in Chapter 3, the propellent and other "nonactive" ingredients in these spray cans may be quite harmful to your health (not to mention what they do to the environment). Roll-ons, sticks, creams, or pads are much preferred. Second, if you notice *any* irritation from your deodorant, change brands. Remember, you are probably absorbing some of this stuff every day for a lifetime. Two potentially troublesome agents are **Hi and Dri** cream or roll-on, and **Top Brass** roll-on. They contain the antibiotic neomycin. If you use these products without difficulty, then disregard any warning, but even though this antibiotic kills germs very effectively, it also has the tendency to sensitize the skin and produce an allergic rash.

Zirconium is a chemical which has all but been eliminated from deodorant products because it may produce an inflam- **97** matory reaction leading to the development of small benign growths on the skin. Inhaled zirconium has been shown to produce lung disease in animals. The manufacturer, Procter and Gamble, has stated that their products—**Secret, Secret Antiperspirant**, and **Sure Super Dry**—are safe, but I would be a bit nervous about the zirconium which is included.

Another chemical rarely found in antiperspirants any more is benzalkonium chloride. It too has been found to cause skin irritation. More interestingly, it becomes deactivated if applied after showering or washing because of the soapy residue left on the skin. Agents which contain this chemical are: **Clear Formula** roll-on, **Dainty Dry** roll-on, and **Spray Deodorant** by Mennen. Another brand, **5 Day** pads and roll-on, contains methylbenzethonium chloride, which has the same unfortunate properties as benzalkonium chloride.

Let us assume that you have avoided all the blatantly irritating deodorant or antiperspirant products, yet still your antiperspirant causes a burning sensation or rash, especially when applied right after a shower. There is a good possibility that it contains aluminum chloride or aluminum sulfate, two formulations which become very acidic when they come in contact with water or sweat. Perhaps you have noticed the underarms of your shirts beginning to deteriorate. Same reason. A few antiperspirants which contain these chemicals are: **Arrid** roll-on, **Ever Dry** cream, **Fresh** stick, and **Super-Dry** cream.

Probably the most effective and relatively harmless chemical component of antiperspirant-deodorant products is aluminum hydroxychloride. In fact, it shows what fools we are when we believe there is a difference between leading brands. These are but a few of the many preparations which contain alunimum hydroxychloride as their one active ingredient: **Allercreme, Aquamarine, Arrid Extra Dry** (aerosol or powder), **Ban, Calm, Chantilly, Desert Flower, Dial** (roll-on or aerosol), **Hour after Hour Antiperspirant, Manpower Super Dry, Right Guard Antiperspirant**, and **Roll-On** (by Dorothy Gray). These products are often advertised as having an extra strength, super-dry ingredient that makes them special. Nonsense. They are all identical, and you should shop around for the lowest

98 price.

Warts, Dandruff, and Athlete's Foot

So much for smells! Three other unpleasant but common human problems are warts, dandruff, and athlete's foot. How can we treat these plagues without allowing them to become embarrassing hang-ups? Warts are a common problem, especially in children. They are benign and are caused by a virus despite all popular beliefs to the contrary. Since they are induced virally, they are contagious, which means a certain degree of caution is justified to avoid spreading the wart from one part of the body to another or from one individual to another. Appealing as the practice seems to be, scratching at warts should be discouraged since it could help spread them. That goes double for nibbling or chewing, an especially common practice in youngsters. Treatment of warts depends on many variables. Many times they will disappear all by themselves after a few months. If not, one of your biggest aces in the hole is the fact that children are very susceptible to suggestion. If you make up some outrageous but safe "cure," throwing in lots of hokey techniques, the chances are that the warts will disappear over the next several weeks or months. Such magical techniques could include touching the wart with ice cubes, painting it with food coloring, or exposing it briefly to heat lamp. The bigger the production, the better the chances for success. If you want something more impressive to influence your child, you can buy a product over-the-counter under the name **Ice Mint Creme.** Although it is essentially without curative powers, it does contain exotic but harmless ingredients such as peppermint oil, eucalyptus oil, thyme oil, and lanolin. If you cannot make your own warts go away with such psychological persuasion in the fine tradition of Tom Sawyer, then your neighborhood pharmacist may be able to help.

The first thing to remember is that any treatment of warts should be approached with some degree of caution. Careless technique, coupled with a caustic chemical, could result in destruction of healthy skin. People with poor circulation (especially diabetics or elderly patients) should consult their doctor before experimenting on themselves. The most innocuous and simple technique you can try for a common wart (it is occasionally successful for plantar warts on the sole of the foot, too) is a concentrated salt-water soak. One and a half level cooking tablespoonfuls of table salt dissolved in a half cup of water will provide a 30 percent solution. Soaking a couple of times a day for a few weeks may help some people. If you do not have the patience, or if this technique does not prove beneficial, salicylic acid is probably the most common, most effective, and least injurious chemical agent employed for common warts on hands and fingers. If applied carefully, it should slowly destroy the abnormal tissue without hurting the normal skin. A 10 percent solution of salicylic acid is generally strong enough and can be put on twice a day with cotton-tipped applicator. It is often available as a gooey liquid which dries in a flexible manner and must be removed and reapplied every twenty-four hours. If you cannot purchase a 10 percent solution directly from your pharmacist as a tincture or collodion liquid, there are nonprescription brand-name preparations which contain salicylic acid. **Corn Liquid,** manufactured by De Pree, contains the right concentration. Other products with salicylic acid are: **Derma-Soft, Dr. Scholl's "2" Drop Corn-Callous Remover, Mosco, Pedolatum,** and **Rexall Corn Solvent.** Unfortunately, these preparations do not list their concentration in the *Handbook of Non-Prescription Drugs* and therefore cannot be recommended.

Plantar warts often require medical supervision because improper treatment may lead to scarring and that can be a serious situation. Uncomplicated plantar warts are often treated in the following manner. First, the wart is pared or peeled down in order to remove some of the scaly, dead tissue. Next, a 10 percent formalin solution is applied carefully with a cotton-tipped applicator. Finally, a 40 percent salicylic acid plaster cut to the exact dimensions of the wart is applied and left on the foot. It should be covered with an air-tight plastic tape. The salicylic acid plaster should be removed every three or four days and replaced with a new one. If the skin becomes sore or tender, treatment can be suspended for a few days and then resumed once the pain disappears. After two or three weeks the dead tissue can be scraped away and the applications continued. After six to eight weeks the warts should

be practically gone.

A ten percent formalin solution should be available from the neighborhood pharmacy as should a 40 percent salicylic acid plaster. Dr. Scholl makes a corn plaster that might work if you can't obtain a 40% plaster directly from your pharmacist.

If none of the techniques I have suggested work, there is one other possibility. It has been suggested that hard to treat warts are due to a deficiency in the person's immune system. If the immune system were stimulated there is a good chance that the warts might disappear all by themselves. Dr. Daniel Hyman has suggested that three desiccated liver tablets taken three times a day could do the trick.[15] It might be worth a try. If you have any doubts about the correct treatment for plantar warts, it is best to visit a dermatologist so that no damage is done.

Two commercial wart-removers include glacial acetic acid along with salicylic acid. This could be dangerous, since this concentrated acid might destroy healthy skin if applied too widely (it should not be used for plantar warts without medical supervision). The least dangerous of the two is **Wart-Away**, which contains 13.13 percent salicylic acid and 1.8 percent glacial acetic acid. It is preferable to **Compound W, Wart Remover** with its 11 percent glacial acetic acid. Another possibility is **Gets-It** with only salicylic acid (13.9 percent salicylic acid). These products are effective for regular warts and, if handled cautiously, they should do the job. Any warts which are resistant to these simple techniques should be taken to a doctor. If and when that fails, you might try your neighborhood witch.

Dandruff, more elegantly known as *seborrhea sicca*, is another complaint that has been exploited by the advertising industry. Although there has been no medical reason for the rapidly rising rate of dandruff cases treated by dermatologists over the last ten years, television commercials probably contribute to people's preoccupation with this generally normal condition. No matter how healthy your scalp may be, some scaling and flakiness is to be expected and does not merit an expensive trip to the doctor or a special dandruff shampoo. A simple soap shampoo without harsh detergents will probably control any mild flaking that does occur.

When a mild case of flaking becomes a treatable case of moderate dandruff is very much a value judgment. There comes a point, however, when your itchy scalp and embarrassingly snowy shoulders push you past the point of patient acceptance. This kind of annoying dandruff is still very much a medical enigma. Although there is still some doubt about exactly what causes dandruff, most dermatologists recognize two distinct varieties. One seems to be due to excessive drying and scaling of the scalp, while the other results from an overabundant accumulation of oil on the scalp and hair follicles. If you stop to think about it, many dandruff shampoos and remedies rarely distinguish between these apparently opposite forms of dandruff. A dandruff preparation which contains ingredients effective in relieving excessive oiliness of sebaceous glands hardly seems likely to benefit someone with excessive dryness of the scalp. In fact, the chances are pretty good that what is appropriate for one condition could aggravate the other. It is therefore very important that you read any information listed on the container before purchasing a dandruff shampoo in order to determine if it is right for you.

Another possible complication of medicated shampoo preparations involves the lottle principle. (If a little is good, then a lottle must be better.) An individual who tries to control his dandruff by constantly using these potent products may find he is not achieving the promised success. He tries another and then another brand, each time with the same unrewarding consequences. Instead of shampooing once or twice a week, he might wash his hair three or even four times. There is a very good chance that after so much overtreatment, his scalp is so irritated that the scaling and flakiness is more a result of the shampoos than anything else. A mild, neutral soap shampoo will do much to help correct this problem. The moral is clear: do not have a love affair with potent antidandruff detergent shampoos to the exclusion of other more mild varieties.

A perfect example of just such a harsh product is the dandruff rinse **Dandricide**. This popular solution contains benzalkonium chloride in a concentration of 3.3 percent. Since it is highly unlikely that germs cause common dandruff, this chemical which is nothing more than a surface antiseptic offers little promise for dandruff control. Of more significance, however, is the fact that anything greater than a 1 percent concentration could prove to be quite irritating to the skin. Although the instructions listed on the container recommend adequate dilution, an overzealous dandruff victim might well decide to add more than one capful per eight-ounce glass of water (the lottle principle again). And anyone using this antiseptic full strength would really be asking for trouble. Additionally, benzalkonium chloride is completely neutralized when it comes into contact with soap or detergents found in shampoos. Therefore, products which contain this chemical, even in safe concentrations (**Monique Dandruff Control Shampoo, Double Danderine, Rinse Away**) would have their dubious effectiveness pretty much neutralized if preceded or followed by a soapy shampoo.

Three other common ingredients found in dandruff shampoos are salicylic acid, resorcinol, and sulfur. These agents are known as *keratolytics,* which means they are somewhat caustic and can loosen up most of the dandruff and scaly cells on the scalp. (Salicylic acid is used to remove corns and warts in slightly higher concentrations.) While fine for the symptomatic relief of dandruff in people with oily skin and hair, repeated use might well produce excessive dryness for others. A few shampoos with one or more of the above antiseborrheic ingredients are: **Enden Shampoo, Ionil, Meted Shampoo, Sebaveen, Sebulex,** and **Rezamid Shampoo.** They are probably effective and reasonably safe, though far from a dandruff "cure."

A chemical ingredient which has been endorsed as one of the "most effective" dandruff-controllers by the chief of the Dermatology Clinic at the Metropolitan Hospital Center in New York City and author of the chapter on Dandruff preparations in the *Handbook of Non-Prescription Drugs* is zinc pyrithione. It is found in **Breck One Dandruff Shampoo, Head and Shoulders, Selsun Blue, Zincon,** and **ZP-11.** For someone with a serious case of dandruff which remains refractory to any or all of the above-mentioned dandricides, a visit to a dermatologist would be in order. Any condition which refuses to respond could be a warning of something more serious, like psoriasis. Even if there is little reason for alarm, your doctor can prescribe an even more potent product *103* than any of those listed above. Especially effective for dandruff resulting from excessive dryness of the scalp is a prescription shampoo called **Capsebon** (cadmium sulfide), which is less irritating and less likely to produce oiliness and loss of hair than another prescription product, **Selsun Sulfide Suspension**. Whatever you finally end up using, remember that it is important to rest your hair from harsh detergent or antiseptic solutions and that a soap shampoo may be less irritating and more helpful than all of the above-mentioned highly promoted products.

As for regular old shampoos for "normal" hair, do not let yourself be seduced into believing all the sexy commercials. Many of the so-called natural ingredients are nothing more than coconut oils and water. When pinned down, the Breck Company admitted that their claims for a "natural shine" only meant "the appearance of hair which has been cleansed of dirt but which has not otherwise been affected or altered." Furthermore, the Wella Corporation has been implying that their **Wella Balsam** shampoo could be used safely "as often as you want" although they now admit that "It is possible to damage hair to such an extent that any subsequent treatment including simple combing can cause further damage such as hair breakage." Normal hair probably does not need shampooing more than twice or three times a week under regular conditions, and even that much might be excessive for some people. Even the latest fad of hair-styling blow-dryers may dry hair too much and promote breakage and splitting.

Smelly feet. Next to dandruff, bad breath, and warts, I cannot think of anything more unpleasant. This crummy condition is basically a result of excessive sweating of your tootsies. Bacteria always present on the skin react with the proteinaceous material of perspiration to produce a disgusting fragrance. Sweaty feet also lead to the development of fungal infections, most notably athlete's foot. Though hardly a disorder restricted to athletes, the factors which promote this problem occur frequently in locker rooms and make transmission more likely. Known medically as tinea pedis, this fungal infection produces symptoms of itching and peeling of the white skin in the webs of the toes. It is an extremely common condition

104

(though often no overt symptoms are noticeable) and exists in a large portion of the population.

Anything that cuts down on excess perspiration will diminish the objectionable odor of your feet and will help prevent an attack of athlete's foot. In the summer, sandals or airy shoes can be helpful. Silk or nylon stockings should be replaced with something more porous. Whenever possible, a drying powder (simple cornstarch works best) should be used to dust shoes and toes. But even with caution, it is sometimes difficult to prevent your toes from rotting. Then it is time to move up to something that works.

Pharmacies are filled with brands of junk which claim to be effective for the treatment of athlete's foot. Many are completely useless, while a substantial number may produce allergic reactions or aggravate the infection. (Of 400 patients using typical nonprescription remedies, 40 percent were found to be allergic to one or more of the chemical ingredients.)[16] Since athlete's foot often manifests itself by irritated open sores, you have to be very careful what you spray or dust in the area of sensitivity. Many drugs may be absorbed by the feet and enter general circulation, thus leading to system toxicity. A good example is the use of boric acid preparations. Although once considered perfectly harmless, it has been discovered that this weak germicide may be readily absorbed when placed in contact with abraded tissues. There have been many cases of poisoning, and one infant died after repeated dusting with boric acid powder for a case of simple diaper rash. Therefore, if your athlete's foot is severe, it would be prudent to avoid potential boron absorption by not using the following products that contain boric acid: **Maseda Foot Powder, Jim Wade Deodorant Foot Powder, Quinsana Foot Antiperspirant, Ting, Blis-To-Sol** powder, **Carfusin** liquid, and **Daliderm.**

Other doubtful products contains the combination of camphor and phenol. Although there are many other effective chemicals, phenol does have some antifungal properties. Unfortunately, it is only helpful at concentrations which might produce irritation. Put the Camphor and Phenol together and you get a product which is much more likely to harm the moist, tender skin between your toes. Athlete's foot remedies which contain both are **Campho-Phenique** and **Daliderm.**   *105*

There are many athlete's foot products which do work because they contain relatively safe and efficient ingredients. Perhaps the best chemical available for mild, long-lasting conditions is *Tolnaftate*, a topical skin solution or cream which is nonirritating and will not produce an allergic sensitivity reaction. It is available under the brand name **Tinactin**. Use the solution first and follow it up with a powder once a cure has been established. The only hang-up is that **Tinactin** is damn expensive, but at least you get your money's worth. Another very effective combination for mild athlete's foot (especially useful when palms or soles are involved) is benzoic and salicylic acids. The two together are available in many OTC preparations, but the simple **Whitfield's Ointment** or **Tincture** are the probably the cheapest and most effective. Other brand names which contain this effective combo (often with other unnecessary goodies thrown in) are: **Bismuth Violet with Salicylic and Benzoic Acid, NP 27, Nullo Foot Cream,** and **Solvex** liquid or ointment.

Another drug which is commonly employed in the treatment of athlete's foot is undecylenic acid. There is no question that it is effective, but it is also common to observe persistence or fungal reinfection even in the presence of intensive application. Probably **Desenex** is the most familiar name associated with this chemical. Have you ever noticed that even though you can control your athlete's foot with this product, it is hard to really make it disappear and stay away? Other brands with this ingredient are: **Deso-Creme** and **Deso-Talc Foot Powder, Pertinex, Podiaspray, Solvex** spray, and **Verdefam**.

If you find yourself confronted with a serious flare-up of your infection, it is past time to go to a doctor. Though the classic treatment involves hot foot soaks of one percent (or less) potassium permanganate solution, a simpler, more effective treatment has been discovered. Because severe athlete's foot is probably caused by a combination of bacteria and fungi, it is imperative that the bacteria be eliminated quickly and efficiently. *Aluminum Chloride* in a 20 or 30 percent solution appears to be an excellent treatment.[17] By applying it twice a day with a cotton-tipped applicator you should be able to dry out the skin and make the area between the toes inhospitable to the invading bacteria. Once the bacteria are no longer a threat you can resort to **Tinactin** to clear up any residual fungus infection. If even this treatment fails, hi thee to a dermatologist to make sure you are not suffering from something more serious.

> Whether 'tis nobler in the mind to suffer
> The slings and arrows of outrageous fortune,
> Or to take arms against a sea of troubles,
> And by opposing end them? To die; to sleep;
> No more; and by a sleep to say we end
> The heart-ache and the thousand natural shocks
> That flesh is heir to, 'tis a consummation
> Devoutly to be wish'd. To die, to sleep;
> To sleep: perchance to dream . . .

And there's the rub. To sleep a natural sleep is but the quest of us poor mortals. The heart-ache, and the thousand natural shocks that flesh is heir to, tend to lead us all down that road of sleeplessness at one time or another. And the pharmaceutical industry is loathe to lose such a lucrative market. So 'tis time to take arms against these rogues who tempt you again to bed. Their false promises do not work!

Insomnia is a curse which, though it strikes us all, tends to prey more on some than on others. That the drug companies prey on us to the tune of over thirty million dollars annually for their "sleep-inducers" is a double insult. Clearly the chemicals which are so commonly found in **Compoz**, **Nite Rest**, **Nytol**, **Sleep-Eze**, **Sure-Sleep**, and **Sominex**, to name a few, are mild and hardly dangerous, but it is worth noting that "all of the sedative actions produced by over-the-counter products originally were identified as side effects when the ingredients were used for other purposes."[18] That means that chemicals advertised for promoting drowsiness were originally criticized for this very same *unwanted* effect.

More important than the origin of these drugs is the question, Are they really effective in promoting sleep? Although there have been almost no really objective tests of these OTC preparations, the leading sleep researchers in this country, Drs. Joyce and Anthony Kales, have tested **Sominex** in an excellent, well-controlled study. They scientifically determined *107* what if any difference existed between two **Sominex** tablets and a placebo. In this way they were able to remove psychological preconceptions. By the way, **Sominex** contains the same ingredients as **Compoz, Devarex, Dormin, Nite Rest, Nytol, San-Man, Sedacaps, Seedate, Sleep-Eze,** and **Sure-Sleep.** Therefore, what holds true for **Sominex** should be the same for these other medications. Let's let the Kales speak for themselves: "The results of our sleep laboratory study of **Sominex** indicate that such sleep medications at the recommended dosage (2 tablets) are ineffective in relieving moderate to severe insomnia."[19] In case that wasn't plain enough, they conclude their research with this point: "Results showed that **Sominex** in its recommended dose did not produce any favorable effects in terms of inducing sleep." That heavy artillery was published in the journal, *Current Therapeutic Research* (vol 13:143–151, 1971) and was entitled "Are Over-The-Counter Sleep Medications Effective?" What is even more alarming is that, although these preparations are not effective in putting you to sleep (except by psychological inducement), they do have the nasty habit of altering normal sleep patterns. They have been shown to "decrease the amount of time spent in dreaming sleep" (known as Rapid Eye Movement, or REM, sleep). If someone increases the dose of these drugs when he or she fails to obtain favorable results, a significant suppression of REM sleep is likely to occur. A sleep researcher, Dr. Ismet Karacan, has commented on the effects of REM-sleep or dream deprivation, "Any drug which further suppresses the slow-wave sleep and/or tampers with the adjustment of REM that appears to have taken place . . . actually exacerbates the insomniac's basic sleep problem, while giving the appearance of helping."[20] What is more, once these drugs have been discontinued, the next nights' sleep may result in "an increase in both the frequency and intensity of dreaming often in the form of unpleasant dreams and nightmares."[21] This could be quite alarming for some people, especially insomniacs, and could go on for three or four nights. These medications have also been known to produce confusion, disorientation, paranoia, and frightening hallucinations when taken by susceptible individuals or in large doses

The heart of the matter is that just about all these nonprescription sleep aids are ineffective and possibly injurious. Yet people who fear possible addiction from prescription drugs continue to swallow the advertising of the drug companies. "Take **Sominex** and see." See what? How many unnecessary pills we can take? What is more, insomniacs often insist that they obtain relief from their sleeplessness. Don't confuse me with the facts, is the battle cry. The answer to this seeming paradox is really quite clear. Insomniacs often attain significant relief from the nonactive sugar pill (as long as they think it is something potent). Most probably it is the psychological anticipation of relief that enables people to experience benefit.

Given the shortcomings and potential dangers of these drugs, what is the right form of management for the treatment of sleeping problems? The Kales have noted an extraordinarily high percentage of psychological disturbances (over 85 percent) in insomniacs. Depression and anxiety were the most frequent disorders. The Kales noted, "Despite the fact that insomniac patients are frequently disturbed, they rarely seek, and are rarely referred for, psychiatric treatment. They tend to reject the possibility of psychopathology and focus instead on the somatic [physical] aspects of their problem. The prognosis [outcome] for this group would be greatly improved if they were more often referred for psychiatric evaluation and treatment despite their rejection of psychological factors."[22] Now I am just as reluctant as the next guy to seek help from a shrink. Nevertheless, the evidence overwhelmingly supports the advisability of some form of counseling for the insomniac. At the very least the family doctor should be consulted and all those nonprescription drugs thrown out in the garbage. Prescription drugs are probably safer in the long run if used judiciously. Warm milk, or other folk remedies, probably works just as well as, if not better than, the over-the-counter junk. In fact, research reported in the editorial section of the *JAMA* indicates that a natural amino acid, tryptophan, may be the ideal sleep-inducer. It apparently promotes sleep naturally "while producing remarkably little effect on sleep stages and the architecture of sleep."[23] This amino acid is normally found in many foods, and a glass or two of milk may work by actually elevating tryptophan levels in the brain. More *109* than likely, however, it will be necessary to consume a larger dose (1 to 4 grams) in tablet form. Just for kicks and until tryptophan becomes available, why not try consuming pure carbohydrate before retiring? It might do the trick. Other possibilities include herbal teas. Catnip, sage, peppermint, valerian, skullcap, woodruff, and lemon balm teas are but a few of the "sure recipes" our grandmothers used to recommend. Exercise and mental relaxation may help some people get past their insomnia.

In conclusion, it is obvious that most of the nonprescription drugs discussed in this chapter are of dubious value. Some brands do work, and those have been listed. The consumer must be constantly on guard to resist the barrage of phony advertising that the drug industry spews forth in ever-increasing amounts. There is a "rule of nature" which says that the heavier the advertising pitch, the more likely the product will be a lemon. In case you have already forgotten which products work, and which are lemons a table has been provided for quick reference. It may even help the next time you have to make a foray to the pharmacy. Good luck!

A HANDY GUIDE TO
NONPRESCRIPTION PRODUCTS

Antacids

Pretty Good	Maybe	Not Recommended
Aludrox	Ducon	Al-Caroid
A.M.T.	Gelumina	Alka-Seltzer
Creamalin	Kudrox	Alkets
Di-Gel	Rolaids	Amitone
Gelusil	Silain-Gel	Bromo-Seltzer
Maalox	Sippyplex	Calcium Carbonate &
Magnatril		Soda
Magnesium-Aluminum		Dicarbosil
Hydroxide Gel USP		Eno
Malcogel		Fizrin
Maxamag Sus-		Gustalac
pension		Pepto-Bismol
Mucotin		Tablets
Mylanta		Ratio
Trisogel		Titralac
WinGel		Tums
		Zylase

Athlete's Foot Remedies

Pretty Good	Maybe	Not Recommended
Aluminum Chloride 30%	Desenex	Blis-To-Sol
Bismuth Violet with Salicylic and Ben- zoic Acid	Deso-Creme	Campho-Phenique
	Deso-Talc Foot Pow- der	Carfusin
	Pertinex	Daliderm
Solvex	Podiaspray	Jim Wade Deodorant Foot Powder
Tinactin (very good)	Verdefam	Maseda Foot Powder
Nullo Foot Cream		Quinsana Foot Pow- der
NP 27		Ting
Whitfield's Ointment		

Dandruff Shampoos and Rinses

Pretty Good	Maybe	Not Recommended
Breck One Dandruff Shampoo	Enden Shampoo	Dandricide
Capsebon (by prescription)	Fostex	Double Danderine
	Meted Z	Drest
Head and Shoulders	Rezamid Shampoo	Monique Dandruff Control Shampoo and Rinse
Selsun Blue	Sebaveen	
Zincon	Sebulex	Pentrax
ZP-11	Sebutone	Rinse Away Liquid/Gel
		Rinse Away Rinse

Deodorants and Antiperspirants

Pretty Good*	Maybe	Not Recommended
Allercreme	Arrid	*ALL AEROSOLS*
Aquamarine	Atomist	Arrid (roll-on)
Antiperspirant Roll-On	Ban (cream)	Clear Formula
Arrid Extra Dry	Fresh (roll-on, stick)	Fresh (cream)
Ban (roll-on)	Super-Dry (roll-on)	Hi and Dri
Calm	Ultra Ban 5000	Dainty Dry
Chantilly		Secret
Cream (Max Factor)		Secret Antiperspirant
Creme Deodorant		Sure Super Dry
Desert Flower		Top Brass
Dial		
Dry Ban		
Ever Dry (roll on)		
Fresh		
Hour after Hour Antiperspirant		
Manpower Super Dry		
Right Guard Antiperspirant		
Roll-On (Dorothy Gray)		

*All these products are essentially equivalent.
Their one ingredient is aluminum hydroxychloride.
ANY PRODUCT CONTAINING *HEXACHLOROPHENE* SHOULD BE AVOIDED!

Deodorant Soaps

Pretty Good	Maybe	Not Recommended
None	None	*Bensulfoid Lotion
		Dial
		Lifebuoy
		Irish Spring
		Phase III
		*Phisohex
		Safeguard
		*Soy-Dome Medi-cated Skin Cleanser
		Zest

*These products contain *Hexachlorphene* and should be avoided!

Menstrual Products

Pretty Good	Maybe	Not Recommended **
Aspirin	Midol	A.P.C.
Codeine*	Codurex	Cope
	Pre-Mens Forte	Cardui
	Trendar	Excedrin
		Empirin Compound
		Femicin
		Pamprin
		Vanquish

*Codeine requires a doctor's prescription.

**These products cannot be recommended because they either contain phenacetin or have not been demonstrated superior to aspirin in pain-relief.

Mouthwash and Gargles

Pretty Good	Maybe	Not Recommended

Salt water (½ teasp/ glass)	Alkalol
	Betadine
	Cepacol
	Colgate 100
	Greenmint Mouth-
	   wash
	Proxigel
	Scope
		Astring-O-Sol
		Dalidyne
		Forma-Zincol Con-
		   centrate
		Glyco-Thymoline
		Isodine
		   Mouthwash/Gargle
		   Concentrate
		Listerine
		Oral Pentacresol
		Odara
		Pain-A-Lay

Sleep Medications and Aids

Pretty Good	Maybe	Not Recommended
Tryptophan Counseling Prescription products	Warm milk Folk Remedies (teas) Exercise Mental Relaxation	Compoz Devarex Dormin Nite Rest Nytol San-Man Sedacaps Seedate Sleep-Eze Somnicaps Sominex Sure-Sleep

Wart-Removers

Pretty Good	Maybe	Not Recommended
Gets-It	Compound W, Wart	**X-Ray Treatment
Wart-Away	Remover	
Corn Liquid	Derma-Soft	
Formalin 10%	Dr. Scholl'S "2" Drop	
Salicylic Acid Plas-	Corn-Callous	
ter 40%	Remover	
Magic	*Ice Mint Creme	
	Mosco	
	Pedolatum	
	Rexall Corn Solvent	
	Salt Water Soak (30	
	percent solution)	

*Ice Mint Creme works only by suggestion.
**X-Ray Treatment for removal of warts is extremely dangerous.

References

1. Caranasos, George J., et al. "Drug-Induced Illness Leading to Hospitalization." *JAMA* 228:713–717, 1974.
2. *FDA Fact Sheet.* U.S. Department of Health, Education, and Welfare, Public Health Service, Food and Drug Administration, 5600 Fishers Lane, Rockville, Md. 20852.
3. *FDA Consumer.* Superintendent of Documents, Government Printing Office, Washington, D.C. 20402.
4. *Handbook of Non-Prescription Drugs.* American Pharmaceutical Association, 2215 Constitution Avenue, N.W., Washington, D.C. 20037.
5. *The Medicine Show.* Consumers Union, Book Dept., Orangeburg, N.Y. 10962.
6. U.S. Senate, Select Committee on Small Business, Subcommittee on Monopoly. *Hearings on Affect of Promotion and Advertising of Over-The-Counter Drugs on Competition, Small Business, and the Health and Welfare of the Public* (92nd Congr., 1st Sess., 1971).
7. "Indigestion Aids: Which Should You Use?" *Consumer Reports* 38:584–588, 1973.

8. "Medical Scene: Bar Soaps Kill Too Many 'Germs,' Panel Reports." *Modern Medicine* 42:160, 1974.
9. Modell, Walter. *Drugs of Choice 1974–1975*. St. Louis: Mosby, 1974. P. 79.
10. Moertel, C. G., et al. "A Comparative Evaluation of Marketed Analgesic Drugs." *New Engl. J. Med.* 286:813–815, 1972.
11. *The Medicine Show.*
12. *Non-Prescription Drugs.*
13. Collier, H. O. J. "Aspirin." *Scientific American* 209:97–108, 1963.
14. Blaker, Martin I. "Crushed Aspirin Tablets." *JAMA* 230:1385, 1974.
15. Hyman, Daniel. "Is There a Simple Way to get Rid of Plantar Warts?" *Modern Med.* 43, Number 14:86, 1975.
16. Underwood, G. B., et al. "Overtreatment Dermatitis of the Feet." *JAMA* 130:249–256, 1946.
17. Leyden, J. L., and Kligman, A. M. "Aluminum Chloride in the Treatment of Symptomatic Athlete's Foot." *Arch. Derm.* 111:1004–1010, 1975.
18. *Non-Prescription Drugs.*
19. Kales, Anthony, and Kales, Joyce. "Are Over-the-Counter Sleep Medications Effective? All-Night EEG Studies." *Cur. Ther. Res.* 13:143–151, 1971.
20. Karacan, I. "New Approaches to the Evaluation and Treatment of Insomnia." *Psychosomatics* 12:81–88, 1971.
21. Kales and Kales, op. cit.
22. Kales, Anthony, and Kales, Joyce. "Sleep Disorders." *New Engl. J. Med.* 290:487–497, 1974.
23. Hartmann, Ernest. "L-Tryptophan: A Possible Natural Hypnotic Substance." *JAMA* 230:1680–1681, 1974.

6.

Drug Interactions
When 1 + 1 May Equal 3

"The time has come," the Walrus said,
"To talk of many things:
Of shoes–and ships–and sealing-wax–
Of cabbages–and kings–
And why the sea is boiling hot–
And whether pigs have wings."

THROUGH THE LOOKING-GLASS

Drug interactions are the Achilles heel of the medical profession. The laws of nature no longer hold true. This is a crazy world where one plus one equals three, where down may very well be up and surely pigs have wings. In fact, mixing *117* medicines is very much like playing Russian roulette. You never know when a particular combination will produce a lethal outcome. Doctors have enough trouble trying to remember the adverse effects of each individual drug. Is it any wonder that they break down trying to predict the problems of multiple prescriptions, a situation which increases the number of potential side effects astronomically? Aspirin alone interacts with twenty-four other drugs to produce unexpected and often unwanted responses. Diuretics like **Hydrodiuril** can react adversely with thirty-four other medications. Whenever you take one medicine in the presence of another, the potential exists for a serious interaction.

One aspect of modern medicine has contributed heavily to the increasing number of serious drug interactions. While in the past one family doctor was responsible for all the medicine a patient received, now we are at the mercy of a bevy of specialists. Our old GP could keep track of what he gave us, but the modern specialist often is not interested in what another specialist has prescribed. So if your doctor does not ask you what other medications you may be taking before he prescribes something, tell him anyway. And pin him down about the chances of an unwanted interaction. That way, even if he doesn't know automatically, he might be prompted to look it up. But adverse drug interactions are not only your doctor's responsibility. Diet, environmental factors, and most important, nonprescription agents may react with more potent medications your doctor has prescribed. That includes cold remedies, pain relievers, vitamins, or even antacids. Alcohol cannot be ignored, because booze can interact with 150 other drugs or chemicals in a potentially harmful way. A good rule of thumb is to try and limit all drug consumption to one thing at a time, and if you must take more than one medicine check with your doctor about complications.

The average hospital in-patient receives at the very least nine distinct drugs while he is under surveillance. There are all too many poor souls who receive over twenty different chemicals during their hospital stay. Almost half of these patients will experience a drug reaction. Unfortunately, there is very little you can do about the prescribing habits of your doctor while you are in the hospital, since you are pretty much at the mercy of the hawk-eyed nurses who insist you take every last pill. A patient may refuse any medication offered, but this requires almost super-human courage and daring. Sometimes it is damn difficult to convince them that you can do quite nicely without a sleeping pill. Remember, however, that you are the best judge of your physical and mental well-being, and if you think you are receiving an unnecessary drug or are experiencing an adverse drug reaction, squawk like hell.

What is a drug interaction anyway? In order to answer this question adequately, one must consult an expert in this field, such as Dr. Eric W. Martin. His comprehensive book on drug interactions, *Hazards of Medication*, is a bible on drug-drug reactivity.[1] (Other excellent references can be found at the end of this chapter).[2-9] In fact, a debt of gratitude is owed to Dr. Martin because much of the background material for this chapter was obtained from his book. He suggests that a drug interaction occurs whenever the expected effects of a medication are modified "in or on the body" by another chemical. Such modification often is harmful, but on occasion it can be exploited to the patient's advantage. In fact, all of us are familiar with one drug interaction that we employ quite frequently. On New Year's Eve, the last thing the host usually serves is coffee. Obviously, we are counting on the stimulant qualities of the caffeine to antagonize the sedative and reflex-slowing effects of the booze. Another common interaction employed for our benefit occurs when a sedative is added to diet pills. The stimulant which suppresses appetite has a tendency to produce nervousness. The sedative is supposed to neutralize this common side effect. **Dexamyl** is an example of such a medication. It contains a derivative of amphetamine and a barbiturate.

A chemical which modifies the actions of another drug can do so in many ways. It may potentiate the other drug and make the anticipated effect more powerful. Thus someone who takes a tranquilizer regularly could kill himself if he drinks too much because the two together will sedate him more heavily than either drug alone.

Another possibility is that one drug might decrease the beneficial effects of another medication and thereby diminish the chances for a speedy recuperation. Such a situation occurs, for example, when the common antibiotic **Tetracycline** is prescribed simultaneously with **Penicillin**. **Tetracycline** can reduce the effectiveness of **Penicillin** and thus prolong an infection. **Tetracycline** also reacts with antacids and milk products (this is one of the most common drug interactions) and by so doing inhibits proper absorption.

Another problem may result when two incompatible chemicals are consumed together. They could interact to form an unwanted third product. Even something as simple as a laxative can indirectly interfere with another drug. The speeding up of gastric motion could hinder normal absorption and thus decrease obtainable blood concentrations.

It would be impractical to list all the places in your body where two or more drugs could influence each other, but one of the most important sites is the liver. This organ is responsible for the detoxification and elimination of a great many of the foreign chemicals which we put into our bodies. Since it is so crucial in decreasing the amount of circulating drug, its size and ability to detoxify often determine whether or not we will experience a negative reaction. On the other hand, if the liver works too well, one may find that the beneficial response of a drug is prevented because the drug is eliminated far too quickly from the bloodstream. Many drugs actually do have the power to increase the size of the liver and as a result intensify its metabolic efficiency. Hormones, antihistamines, tranquilizers, pain-killers, arthritis medicines, and insecticides are but a few of the hundreds of chemicals which possess this capability. Confused? Well, let us say Mr. Dixon enters the hospital because of a painful blood clot in his leg (thrombophlebitis). During his stay he receives an anticoagulant to thin his blood. This will hopefully prevent the clot from increasing in size. Since Mr. Dixon gets quite nervous being in the hospital, he asks for and receives both a minor tranquilizer (read "muscle-relaxant") and a sleeping pill every day for his ten-day visit. Because the sedatives and sleeping pills have the tendency to stimulate the liver's ability to metabolize the anticoagulant, the doctors find it necessary to increase the dose of blood thinner. That is, because the drug is metabolized and eliminated more rapidly in the presence of the tranquilizers, it becomes necessary to elevate the dosage in order to thin the blood adequately. When Mr. Dixon goes home, he is no longer so anxious and so he stops taking the calming drugs. Soon after discontinuing these medicines, his liver returns to its normal size and function. Unfortunately, his doctors failed to mention that he would have to decrease the dosage of his anticoagulant if he stopped the sedatives. Soon the blood-thinner reaches a higher level in his blood stream and the accumulation of anticoagulant exceeds the safe limit. Mr. Dixon starts to bleed from his gums and eventually may die because of abdominal hemorrhaging or bleeding into the brain. In this instance, the initial interaction between anticoagulant and tranquilizers was anticipated. What was not taken into account was the removal of one of the drugs and the resulting influence this might have on the other. So, we cannot only be cautious about drug-drug reactivity. Postinteraction responses may be just as dangerous.

Let's get down to brass tacks. How can we or our doctor predict the potential for an adverse drug combination before we get caught in the meat-grinder? The first thing to do is write down exactly what you are taking, including all nonprescription drugs. The list may be greater than you think, as in the case of Ms. Dobrowolski. She is thirty-eight years old and has a slight problem with diabetes accompanied by moderate high blood pressure. She also has arthritis, which can be quite painful at times. Ms. Dobrowolski receives a drug called **Orinase** for her diabetes and a mild diuretic called **Hydrodiuril** for her elevated blood pressure. Her doctor has also put her on a low-salt diet in order to facilitate this drug's therapeutic efficiency. On occasion she takes a fairly strong drug, **Butazolidin**, for the pain and inflammation associated with her arthritis. Often this is accompanied by aspirin. Since Ms. Dobrowolski does not want to increase her family beyond the three children she already has, her gynecologist prescribes a birth control pill under the brand name **Ovral**. Quite often Ms. Dobrowolski experiences gas and slight indigestion, and so she keeps a roll of **Rolaids** handy; some days she puts away the whole pack. Because she is under some psychological tension, her internist has also prescribed **Valium** to calm her nerves. In the evening when her husband comes home they always have a before-dinner martini and sometimes another *121* drink later in the evening. Frequently Ms. Dobrowolski has trouble falling asleep, so she always has a bottle of **Seconal** on her night table just in case she might need some help dozing off. In the morning she wouldn't think of starting her day off without a multiple vitamin complex and a healthy dose of **Vitamin C** and **E**. Thus Ms. Dobrowolski might well consume over eight drugs on an average day. If she comes down with an infection—and she is susceptible to urinary tract infections—an antibiotic would be added to this already impressive list. Just for fun, let's see what kind of interactions our Ms. Dobrowolski might experience and what potential adverse drug reactions could occur.

The very first blooper Ms. Dobrowolski's doctor committed was to allow her to take birth control pills. They have a reputation for aggravating diabetes and in Ms. Dobrowolski's case might be the one factor which pushes her borderline blood-sugar level over the edge from a diet-controlled case to one which requires medication. Oral contraceptives also have a tendency to provoke high blood pressure and, if not responsible for her problem, might be contributing to it. Of more significance to Ms. Dobrowolski is the fact that she will not get pregnant and that confidence is worth the risk. Unfortunately, she may not be as safe as she thinks. Both her tranquilizer, **Valium,** and her sleeping pill, **Seconal,** as well as her arthritis medicine, **Butazolidin,** have the power to stimulate her liver's ability to metabolize drugs. As a result, her birth control pill is being eliminated from her body at a much faster rate than normal. There is growing concern that oral contraceptives might be inhibited or rendered ineffective in the presence of these other medications.

Even though Ms. Dobrowolski takes a vitamin pill every day, it is probably not sufficient to meet her body's requirements. Her doctor was never very interested in nutrition and never bothered to inform himself about the effects of birth control pills upon normal metabolism. As a result, he failed to warn his patient that her contraceptive pills could dramatically alter her body's need for certain vitamins. Women on the Pill are sometimes anemic because of their low blood levels of folic acid and vitamin B_{12}. Besides increasing the intake of these important nutrients, women often need extra amounts of vitamin C and vitamin B_6 (pyridoxine). According to the World Health Organization, it would be prudent for a woman on oral contraceptives to take at least 25-30 milligrams of vitamin B_6, 4 micrograms of vitamin B_{12} and 800 micrograms of folic acid. As for vitamin C, the "correct" amount has not been established. However, it would appear that 100 milligrams per day should be the absolute minimum amount ingested.

Another problem which Ms. Dobrowolski's doctors have not taken into account is the interaction between her diabetes medicine, **Orinase,** and her arthritis medicine. **Butazolidin** may block the elimination of **Orinase,** thereby pushing its antidiabetic effect too far. The result could be *Hypoglycemia*, an acute episode of low blood sugar. The **Aspirin** she consumes will also contribute to this response. In fact, the **Aspirin** she takes along with her more potent arthritis medicine is another mistake. **Aspirin** antagonizes the therapeutic properties of **Butazolidin.** Additionally, both **Aspirin** and **Butazolidin** goose each other's ability to severely irritate the stomach (1 + 1 = 3). It is quite possible that this combination has produced Ms. Dobrowolski's upset stomach and "indigestion." Which brings up another no-no. The package of **Rolaids** Ms. Doborwolski consumes when she has stomach trouble contains sodium, something she should definitely not be taking on her low-salt diet. More than two tablets of **Rolaids** per day exceeds her safe level and will decrease the absorption of her arthritis medicine. It may also decrease the effectiveness of her blood pressure medicine. Finally, the alcohol which Ms. Dobrowolski puts away not only may diminish the benefit of her diabetes treatment, but could be lethal in combination with her tranquilizers.

So here we have Ms. Dobrowolski. She is really more typical than you think. There are millions of American men and women who routinely receive even more complex medications from their physicians. Ms. Dobrowolski could have experienced thirteen unnecessary and potentially harmful drug interactions because her doctors failed to warn her that certain chemical combinations could be dangerous. Even scarier, she might not have been able to realize that many of her problems were directly related to her various drugs. Doctors are extremely reluctant to admit to themselves or their patients that *123* symptoms or discomfort could be caused by something they prescribed. It is almost always the last possibility they consider, and then often reluctantly. What commonly happens is that the side effects encountered with one drug are treated with another. Drug Number 2 may also produce an adverse reaction. So the doctor prescribes Drug number 3, which is supposed to relieve this new condition. Drug Number 3 has its own set of complications, and the process can go on and on and on. If and when your doctor becomes aware of the gravity of the situation, it may be too late to reverse or correct some of the damage.

How can we as patients protect ourselves? Well, assuming that we have made a detailed list of everything we are taking and noted any discomfort or unusual reactions, we can go to our physician and ask him to evaluate the situation. Often when confronted with a list of drugs and symptoms he will be more interested and cautious. We can become familiar with some of the minor every-day type of interactions. It might also be a good idea if we learned which dangerous kinds of drugs may result in serious illness or death when mixed in the wrong combinations. (See table on Drug Interactions.)

One environmental problem which we can do very little about involves plain old drinking water. It seems almost every other day some dangerous chemical is discovered in the water supply. No one really knows to what extent these agents alter our reactions to other drugs, but there is growing suspicion that it could be significant. A common drug we can do something about is **Vitamin C**. Now as much as I sing the praises of Dr. Linus Pauling and his ascorbic-acid approach to good health and the common cold, it must be recognized that **Vitamin C** can influence other medications, especially when consumed in large doses. One of the most common interactions is that between **Vitamin C** and aspirin. Though this combination is hardly dangerous, it is interesting to note that **Vitamin C** slows the elimination of aspirin from the body and thus prolongs and intensifies the analgesic reaction. This might be distressing for someone with indigestion or ulcer trouble. Ascorbic acid can also lengthen the duration of action of certain barbiturates. This could be hazardous under some circumstances. Although orange juice, cranberry juice, or grapefruit juice contain relatively small amounts of ascorbic acid (under a hundred milligrams per glass), they too might affect some drugs. One example is the antibiotic **Erythromycin (E-Mycin, Erythrocin, Ilosone, Ilotycin, Pediamycin)**. This drug should never be taken with fruit juice or any acid drink because much of its antibacterial action will be destroyed by the acidity. As a point of interest, some people react to the acidity in fruits and vegetables (and **Vitamin C**) by developing cold sores in their mouths. By taking an antacid before indulging, we can take advantage of this interaction (neutralization) in order to avoid this unpleasant response.

On the other hand, **Vitamin C** could interact with certain chemicals to our benefit rather than our detriment. Certain food additives, particularly nitrites and nitrates, have been recognized as having cancer-producing potential. Biochemical investigation has suggested the possibility that these nitrite additives in food may react with certain prescription drugs to produce an even more powerful cancer agent in our bodies.[10] Their studies also offer strong evidence that **Vitamin C** can react with nitrite in our stomachs and destroy it so that no dangerous interaction can occur with other drugs. As a matter of routine, it certainly would not hurt to load up on plenty of **Vitamin C**, especially before and after consumption of any hot dogs or prepared meats.

There is another far-out interaction which you might never in a million years expect, and for sure your doctor will not tell you about it because he never heard of it. However, all you licorice-lovers, beware—too much of the stuff could possibly do a number on your body that might really mess you up. If you go hog-wild and gorge yourself, headache, high blood pressure, and heart failure could result. Any drug which affects the heart or blood pressure could prove dangerous in the presence of excess licorice.[11] So much for an obscure dalliance.

Other common drugs which are frequently implicated in drug interactions are aspirin and aspirin-like pain-relievers, alcohol, antacids, antibiotics (particularly **Tetracycline**), antihistamines, asthma medications (including aerosols and tablets), barbiturates, birth control pills, blood pressure medication, blood-thinners, cold and cough preparations, hay fever *125* medicines, sleeping pills, tranquilizers, ulcer medications, and diuretics. It would be impossible to list all the specific interactions these frequently prescribed medications could produce. The majority of these potential drug-drug reactions won't even be noticed. Many of them are bothersome but rarely life-threatening. Other interactions could be disastrous. Suffice it to say that if you are taking any of the above types of medicines or receive one in the future, be sure to consult your physician before you begin taking any *other* remedy or drug.

There are some interactions which must be prevented at all costs, because they could create serious adverse reactions, if not death. Drugs which are particularly prone to lethal combinations are: **Anticoagulants** (blood-thinners), **Antidepressants, Chloramphenicol (Chloromycetin), Cortisone-type Drugs, Diabetes Medicine, Digitalis, Dilantin, Salicylates,** and **Sedatives**. This is not to say that there are not many other drugs which cannot create dangerous situations when mixed with something else. In fact, there are over sixty individual and classes of medications which could combine to produce a life-threatening emergency. Some important and potentially grave combinations are listed in Table 1.

Table 1

DRUG INTERACTIONS

ANTICOAGULANTS (BLOOD-THINNING DRUGS)

(COUMADIN, DICUMAROL, MIRADON, PANWARFIN, SINTROM)

Interact with:

Analgesic Pain-Relievers, Including Many Arthritis Preparations

ASCRIPTIN
ASPIRIN
ASPIRIN PRODUCTS
BUFFERIN
BUTAZOLIDIN
EMPIRIN COMPOUND
INDOCIN
PHENAPHEN
PONSTEL
TANDEARIL
VANQUISH
ETCETERA

This is a good way to die unexpectedly. For starters, many arthritis medications enhance the blood-thinning response of anticoagulants. Secondly, antiarthritics tend to irritate the stomach and may lead the way to an ulcer. Put these two effects together, and your chances of a fatal hemorrhage have increased substantially. Monitor your blood-clotting factors carefully and regularly if you must take painkillers.

Alcohol

BEER
HARD STUFF
WINE

This is a bag of worms. Booze can both increase or decrease the blood-thinning effects of anticoagulants. Play it safe and stay off the sauce.

127

Antibiotics

ACHROMYCIN
AUREOMYCIN
AMPICILLIN
CHLOROMYCETIN
MYSTECLIN-F
PENICILLIN
PENTIDS
PEN-VEE-K
POLYCILLIN
SUMYCIN
TETRACYCLINE
V-CILLIN-K
ETCETERA

As everyone knows by now, many antibiotics muck up our tummies. By messing around with the normal flora and fauna in our intestinal track, antibiotics decrease the amount of **Vitamin K** these little critters usually produce. Since **Vitamin K** is an essential clotting factor, the result of this interaction is increased susceptibility to bleeding and hemorrhaging when antibiotics are administered at the same time as anticoagulants.

Antidiabetics

See table listing *Diabetes Medicine*.

Cholesterol-Lowering Medication

ATROMID-S

Don't try taking these two different drugs at the same time without very careful blood testing. **Atromid** will augment blood-thinning responses to the point of serious hemorrhage. Anticoagulant dosage should probably be reduced 30-50 percent. By the way, there is some doubt that **Atromid** will help prevent a heart attack anyway.

Interact with:

See Table listing

Epilepsy Medicines
Anticonvulsant Medication.

Foods

ONIONS
VEGETABLES
(Green)

Though probably not too important, **Onions**, if consumed in large quantities, could intensify the anticoagulant effect. Green leafy vegetables could do just the opposite and antagonize the blood-thinning effect.

Thyroid Gland Supplements

CHOLOXIN
CYTOMEL
CYTOLEN
EUTHROID
PROLOID
S-P-T
SYNTHROID
TAPAZOLE
THYTROPAR
ETCETERA

Thyroid replacement therapy combined with anticoagulant medication could be disastrous if extreme caution is not followed. Careful and regular blood tests must be made. Vulnerability to hemorrhage is the problem. In all probability the dose of anticoagulant should be decreased by about 30 percent by your doctor.

The following drugs antagonize and diminish the effectiveness of anticoagulant medication. In order to maintain therapeutic blood-thinning effects, your doctor may increase the dosage of anticoagulant. Conversely, any sudden discontinuation of the following drugs could precipitate a crisis of internal hemorrhaging if anticoagulant dosage is not reduced beforehand.

AMYTAL
BARBITURATES
BIRTH CONTROL PILLS
CORTISONE-TYPE DRUGS
DORIDEN
EQUANIL
FULVICIN-U/F
GRISACTIN

GRIFULVIN V
LASIX
LIBRAX
LIBRIUM
MILTOWN
NEMBUTAL
PHENOBARBITAL
PLACIDYL
SECONAL
ETCETERA

Because anticoagulant drugs interact in such a dangerous way with so many diversified medications, care should always be exercised if another drug is prescribed simultaneously.

ANTICONVULSANT MEDICATION (FOR EPILEPSY)

(DILANTIN, EKKO, MEBROIN, PHELANTIN)

Interact with:

Anticoagulants (Blood-Thinners)

COUMADIN
DICUMAROL
PANWARFIN
SINTROM

Watch out! **Dilantin** can soup up the horsepower of your anticoagulant. You might start to bleed internally. Conversely, anticoagulants may produce toxic blood levels of **Dilantin**.

Digitalis Heart Medications

DIGITOXIN
DIGOXIN
GITALIGIN
LANOXIN
ETCETERA

Pretty tricky interaction. Initially, **Dilantin** may make **Digitalis** drugs a heck of a lot more dangerous. After prolonged anticonvulsant treatment, **Dilantin** can decrease the effectiveness of these important heart medications. Frequent blood tests are advisable.

Sulfa Antibiotics

AZO GANTRISIN
AZOTREX
BACTRIM
GANTRISIN
GANTANOL
SEPTRA
SOXOMIDE
ETCETERA

It's like this. Some sulfa antibiotics can prevent the normal elimination of epilepsy drugs. They tend to accumulate in the body and pretty soon you've got a whole series of alarming reactions.

ANTABUSE
RITALIN

These two drugs may independently produce serious side effects if prescribed on top of **Dilantin**. Nervous system toxicity and blood ailments are but a few of the possibilities.

ANTIDEPRESSANTS (TRICYCLIC)

(AVENTYL, ELAVIL, NORPRAMIN, PERTOFRANE, PRE-SAMINE, SINEQUAN, TOFRANIL, TRIAVIL, VIVACTYL)

Interact with:

ALCOHOL
Help! This is a hazardous combination. Profound sedation may occur along with a drop in body temperature. "Beware the Jabberwock, my son!"

Anticoagulants (Blood-thinners)

COUMADIN
DICUMAROL
PANWARFIN
SINTROM
Watch out for increased anticoagulant action. Internal bleeding could occur if blood is not monitored frequently.

Anticonvulsant Medication (for Epilepsy)

DILANTIN
EKKO
MEBROIN
PHELANTIN
A depressed epileptic has really got a bum deal. The antidepressants can increase a patient's susceptibility to seizures. Your doctor may have to readjust your dose of anticonvulsant medication upward.

Blood Pressure Medication (Potent)

ALDOCLOR
ALDOMET
ALDORIL
DIUPRES
ESIMIL
EUTONYL
EUTRON
HYDROPRES
ISMELIN
RAU-SED
RESERPINE
SER-AP-ES
SERPASIL
It may be very difficult to control blood pressure adequately when antidepressant medications are added to a person's regular drug regimen. Frequent blood pressure testing is indicated and possibly a change in prescriptions. Consult your doctor.

131

MAO Inhibitors (used for depression or high blood pressure)

EUTONYL
EUTRON
MARPLAN
NARDIL
PARNATE

Beware: this is an extremely serious interaction! Excitation, delirium, rapid pulse, elevated body temperature, and convulsions are but a few of the dangerous side effects of this combination.

Minor Tranquilizers (Benzodiazepines)

LIBRAX
LIBRITABS
LIBRIUM
SERAX
VALIUM

Just too damn much head medicine. Tranquilizers and antidepressants together will put you way down. Severe sedation may make concentrating difficult and driving dangerous.

(It usually takes two weeks before the beneficial effects of antidepressant medication become apparent. It also may take two weeks for the drug to disappear from a patient's system once it has been discontinued. This time-lag must be considered if additional drugs are consumed.)

ARTHRITIS MEDICATION (POTENT ANTI-INFLAMMATORY AGENTS)

(AZOLID, BUTAZOLIDIN, INDOCIN, STERAZOLIDIN, TANDEARIL)

Interact with:

Anticoagulants (Blood-Thinners)

COUMADIN
DICUMAROL
PANWARFIN
SINTROM

This interaction keeps cropping up again and again. Strong arthritis medicines have the rotten ability to dramatically increase the blood-thinning effect of anticoagulants. The result: susceptibility to internal hemorrhaging.

Aspirin and Aspirin-Containing Pain Relievers

ASCRIPTIN
BUFFERIN
EMPIRIN COM-
POUND
PHENAPHEN
VANQUISH
ETCETERA

Mixing arthritis medicine could be messy. If you can get by with aspirin, stick with it, but if you have to use something potent, don't take aspirin too. Taken together you are asking for bad stomach trouble, maybe ulcers. Additionally, aspirin can diminish the effectiveness of the more powerful stuff.

Birth Control Pills

ENOVID
NORINYL
NORLESTRIN
ORTHO-NOVUM
OVRAL
OVULEN
ETCETERA

Some strong arthritis medicines (**Indocin** is not included) like **Butazolidin** are thought to increase the metabolism of The Pill. The result could be decreased effectiveness. In order to be really safe, you might want to check with your doctor.

Diabetes Medicine (Oral)

DIABINESE
DYMELOR
ORINASE
TOLINASE

The potent arthritis medications may cause the anti-diabetic drugs to lower blood sugar excessively. This could lead to serious metabolic complications. **Indocin** does not have this action and is probably safe to use with diabetes medicines.

ASPIRIN AND ASPIRIN-CONTAINING PRODUCTS

(ASCRIPTIN, BAYER ASPIRIN, BUFFERIN, COPE, CORICIDIN, EMPIRIN
COMPOUND, EXCEDRIN, PERCODAN, PHENAPHEN, VAN-QUISH, ETCETERA)

Interact with:

Alcohol

BEER
HARD STUFF
WINE

Ouch! **Alka-Seltzer** ads to the contrary, please don't ever mix booze and aspirin! Alcohol makes your tummy supersensitive to the irritating effects of salicylates. Significant bleeding from the stomach wall has been noted after this combination.

Anticoagulants (Blood-Thinners)

COUMADIN
DICUMAROL
PANWARFIN
SINTROM

Superscary. This could be a terrible interaction. Aspirin taken in the presence of an anticoagulant could lead to massive hemorrhaging. Anticoagulant dosage *must* be reduced in the presence of these minor pain-relievers.

Anticancer Medication

METHOTREXATE

The toxic effects of anticancer drugs may be intensified by aspirin. Monitor the blood carefully.

Arthritis Medication (Potent)

AZOLID
BUTAZOLIDIN
INDOCIN
STERAZOLIDIN
CORTISONE-TYPE
  drugs
TANDEARIL

If you've got to take one of these strong anti-inflammatory arthritis medications, do not take aspirin too! Your chances of developing painful, dangerous stomach irritation will be magnified significantly. Ulcers are not uncommon after this drug-drug interaction. Aspirin can reduce the effectiveness of some of these products, and increase the effectiveness of others.

134

Diabetes Medicine (Oral)

DIABINESE
DYMELOR
ORINASE
TOLINASE

If your doctor is foolish enough to prescribe these diabetes medicines in the first place, do not make matters worse by taking aspirin too. This interaction could lead to too drastic a decrease in blood sugar (hypoglycemia). Frequent blood tests are a must.

Drugs For Gout

ANTURANE
BENEMID

Aspirin can block the beneficial effects of these drugs. Never combine them.

VITAMIN C

A large dose of Vitamin C can prolong and possibly intensify the action of aspirin. While a useful interaction in some cases, this reaction could produce salicylate side effects (headaches, dizziness) in sensitive people.

BIRTH CONTROL PILLS (ORAL CONTRACEPTIVES)

(DEMULEN, ENOVID, LOESTRIN, MICRONOR, NORINYL, NORLESTRIN, NOR-Q.D., ORACON, ORTHO-NOVUM, OVRAL, OVULEN)

Interact with:
Drugs Which Alter Metabolism

ANTIHISTAMINES
BARBITURATES
Amytal
Nembutal
Phenobarbital
Seconal
BUTAZOLIDIN
DILANTIN
EQUANIL
MILTOWN
RIFADIN
RIMACTANE
ETCETERA

"Beware the Jubjub bird, and shun The frumious Bandersnatch!"
Female people beware. Mixing your head pills with your birth control pills could lead to trouble. More and more researchers are becoming concerned about the possibility that barbiturates, etc., may speed the metabolism of oral contraceptives in the body. That could decrease their effectivenss. In order to avoid an unwanted pregnancy, it might be a good idea to consult your doctor about possible interactions.

135

Anticoagulants (Blood-Thinning Drugs)

COUMADIN
DICUMAROL
PANWARFIN
SINTROM

Remember that birth control pills promote the formation of blood clots, especially thrombophlebitis. If you must take an anticoagulant, it may be necessary to increase its dose in order to maintain an effective therapeutic regimen.

Nicotine-Containing Devices

CIGARETTES
PIPES
CHEWING TO-
BACCO

Listen ladies, why increase your already crummy chances of developing a blood clot? Smoking, etc. has an adverse effect upon blood-clotting factors. Give up the nasty habit.

Blood-Pressure-Lowering Drugs (Potent)

ESIMIL
ISMELIN

Birth control pills mess up the effectiveness of these potent drugs. It may be difficult, if not impossible, to control blood pressure adequately.

Diabetes Medication (Oral)

DIABINESE
DYMELOR
ORINASE
TOLINASE

Very bad! Oral contraceptives may make diabetes worse. You've gotta monitor blood sugar carefully with this combination and quite possibly have your doctor increase the dose of diabetes medicine.

Vitamins

ASCORBIC ACID
FOLIC ACID
VITAMIN B6
VITAMIN B12

Birth control pills can deplete the body's levels of Vitamin C, folic acid, Vitamin B6 and Vitamin B12. Low ascorbic acid levels may account for increased susceptibility to blood-clotting. Anemia can result from lowered levels of folic acid and Vitamin B12. All of these vitamins should be supplemented by women on the Pill.

CORTISONE-TYPE ANTI-INFLAMMATORY MEDICATION

(ARISTOCORT, CELESTONE, CORTEF, CORTISONE, COR-TONE, DECADRON, DELTASONE, GAMMACORTEN, HAL-DRONE, HEXADROL, HYDROCORTONE, KENACORT, MEDROL, PARACORT, PREDNISONE, STERANE, ETCET-ERA

Interact with:
Antidepressants (Tricyclic)

AVENTYL
ELAVIL
NORPRAMIN
PERTOFRANE
PRESAMINE
SINEQUAN
TOFRANIL
TRIAVIL
VIVACTYL

Glaucoma patients beware. Irreversible damage to your eyes could easily occur if you combine a cortisone-type drug with one of these antidepressants. An increase in the pressure of the eye is the problem.

Asthma Medication (Aerosol Spray)

ALUPENT
ISUPREL
DUO-MEDIHALER
NORISODRINE

Asthma patients look out! Recent experiments on animals indicate that this one could be a killer. Although often prescribed together, cortisone-type drugs and these asthma medicines might interact to produce fatal heart rhythms.

Diuretics

DIURIL
EDECRIN
ESIDRIX
HYDRODIURIL
LASIX
ORETIC
ETCETERA

The combination of a cortisone-type drug and one of these diuretics often leads to excessive elimination of potassium from the body. Special care must be taken to supplement potassium in the diet.

Surgery Under General Anesthesia

ANESTHETICS

Whoa! This could be very dangerous. No way can someone taking cortisone-type drugs undergo surgery without special precautions being taken. If the dose of **Cortisone** is not increased before surgery, a profound drop in blood pressure may result. Death is not far behind. Consult your doctor on this one.

Vaccines (Live Attenuated)

MEASLES
SMALLPOX
RABIES
YELLOW FEVER

Careful, this one could also do you in. Cortisone-type drugs lower immunological resistance to disease. If you receive a vaccination while on **Cortisone,** a fatal illness might result. Discontinue your cortisone medicines at least three days before vaccination and stay off them for a minimum of two weeks afterward.

DIABETES MEDICATION (ORAL)

(DIABINESE, DYMELOR, ORINASE, TOLINASE)

Interact with:

Anticoagulants (Blood-Thinners)

COUMADIN
DICUMAROL
PANWARFIN
SINTROM

Careful. Anticoagulants can push the effect of your diabetes medicine too far. The resulting drop in blood sugar may lead to coma. On the other hand, antidiabetics push the blood-thinning effect of anticoagulants. Unexpected hemorrhaging is possible.

MAO Inhibitors (Antidepressants and Blood Pressure Medicine)

EUTONYL
EUTRON
MARPLAN
NARDIL
PARNATE

This drug interaction is very much like the one mentioned above. Both classes of medicines lower blood-sugar levels. Together, the effect is magnified and could lead to collapse.

The Following Drugs May Counteract the Anticipated Beneficial Effects of Diabetes Medications:

ADRENALIN
(EPINEPHRINE)
ALCOHOL
ANTIHISTAMINES
BIRTH CONTROL
PILLS

CORTISONE-TYPE
DRUGS
HAY   FEVER
PREPARATIONS
THORAZINE
THYROID
MEDICINE
DIURETICS

If you must take any of the above antagonistic drugs along with your diabetes medicine, it may be necessary for your doctor to increase the dose of the antidiabetic in order to achieve a therapeutic benefit.

The Following Drugs May Intensify the Action of Diabetes Medication; Severe Hypoglycemia Can Result:

ASPIRIN
AZOLID
BUTAZOLIDIN
CHLOROMYCETIN
GANTRISIN

ISMELIN
OXALID
SULFABID
TANDEARIL
TERRAMYCIN

DIURETICS OF WEAK TO MODERATE INTENSITY

(ALDORIL, ANHYDRON, AQUATAG, AQUATENSEN, BUTIZIDE, DIUPRES, DIURIL, DIUTENSEN, ENDURON, ESIDRIX, EXNA, HYDRODIURIL, ETCETERA)

Interact with:
Alcohol

BEER
HARD STUFF
WINE

You really don't have to worry very much about this one. What happens is that booze and water pills decrease blood pressure. If you stand up too quickly after downing a few, you may find yourself flat on your back. Caution is all that's necessary.

139

Antidepressants

See Table listing *Antidepressant Medication.*

Blood-Pressure-Lowering Drugs

ALDOCLOR
ALDOMET
ALDORIL
APRESOLINE
ESIMIL
EUTONYL
EUTRON
ISMELIN
RESERPINE
SER-AP-ES
SERPASIL
ETCETERA

Hold your horses. Before you get nervous because your doctor has prescribed a diuretic along with a strong blood pressure drug, listen carefully. Often, it becomes necessary to decrease blood pressure significantly, and the combination of a water pill and one of the drugs listed may do the job. However, this combination could decrease blood pressure too far. It might be necessary to decrease the dose. Frequent blood pressure tests are a good idea.

Cortisone-type Drugs

CORTISONE
DECADRON
DELTASONE
HALDRONE
KENACORT
PREDNISONE
ETCETERA

Prudence could save you lots of grief. Both diuretics and **Cortisone** deplete the body of potassium. This could be dangerous, especially if you were taking a Digitalis-type heart drug. Eat foods high in potassium and you should be okay. Just to be safe, have your doctor order blood tests occasionally.

Diabetes Medications

DIABINESE
DYMELOR
ORINASE
TOLINASE

This interaction is a sticky wicket. Diuretics pretty much yuck up the antidiabetic response of these diabetes agents. Unfortunately, it is almost impossible to predict whether the effect will be augmented or diminished. Frequent testing is the key.

Digitalis Heart Medication

ACYLANID
DIGITALINE
DIGOXIN
DIGITOXIN
GITALIGIN
LANOXIN

Bad, bad, bad. Digitalis medication can be quite dangerous all by itself. Add a diuretic—in order to diminish fluid accumulation or reduce high blood pressure—and you could be in real trouble. As mentioned, these diuretics deplete the body's potassium. Lowered potassium levels will make the heart supersensitive to digitalis side effects. Fatal rhythm disturbances are possible.

LICORICE

Eat your heart out, licorice-lover. Too much of this delicacy (and I do mean gobs and gobs) will screw you up but good. A little now and then won't hurt. I am talking about all you piglets out there. Licorice and water pills kick too much potassium out of your body. It could be dangerous, especially if you had to take a digitalis-type drug for your heart.

MAJOR TRANQUILIZERS

(CHLORPROMAZINE, COMPAZINE, MELLARIL, STELAZINE, THORAZINE, VESPRIN, ETCETERA)

Interact with:

Drugs Which Cause Sedation

ALCOHOL
ANTIDEPRESSANTS (Tricyclic)
ANTIHISTAMINES
BARBITURATES:
   Amytal
   Nembutal
   Phenobarbital
   Seconal
DALMANE
DORIDEN
EQUANIL
LIBRAX
LIBRIUM
MILTOWN
PLACIDYL
SERAX
VALIUM
ETCETERA

So you think a tranquilizer is a tranquilizer. Wrong! Major tranquilizers are completely different animals from minor tranquilizers. They are much more potent and are generally prescribed only for severe psychological disturbances or psychosis. When a sedative or any of the listed drugs are taken in the presence of a major tranquilizer, hazardous intensification of nervous system depression may occur. A serious fall in blood pressure is also possible. A dry mouth, dilated pupils, rapid pulse, and difficulty in urinating are not uncommon side effects of this interaction in some of these drugs. Glaucoma may be provoked or intensified.

Blood Pressure Medication (Diuretics)

ALDORIL
ANHYDRON
AQUATAG
DIUPRES
DIURIL
ESIDRIX
EXNA
HYDRODIURIL
ORETIC

If at all possible, this combination should be avoided. Major tranquilizers can reduce blood pressure. Diuretics reduce blood pressure. Put 'em together and what have you got? A potentially big reduction in blood pressure that could lead to shock.

MAO INHIBITORS

This class of drugs is used to treat both psychological depression and high blood pressure. Because they depress the action of a crucial enzyme in the body, Monoamine Oxidase (MAO), they are incompatible with a variety of substances that require this enzyme. Such interactions are extremely dangerous.

ANTIDEPRESSANTS

(NARDIL, MARPLAN, PARNATE)

BLOOD PRESSURE MEDICATION

(EUTONYL, EUTRON)

Interact with:
Tyramine-Containing Food

**AVOCADOS
BANANAS (ripe)
BEER
BROAD BEANS (pods)
CAFFEINE (excess)
CANNED FIGS
CHEESE (aged)
CHICKEN LIVER
CHOCOLATE (excess)
PICKLED HERRING
WINE
YEAST EXTRACT**

Look out! This interaction could be lethal. All these foods contain **Tyramine**, which, in the presence of the above drugs, could increase your blood pressure so much that you might blow a blood vessel. Terrible headache, vomiting, and high blood pressure may let you know that there isn't much time left.

All the following drugs should be avoided at all costs. Combined with the above MAO Inhibitors, Life-threatening reactions may result.

143

ALCOHOL
ALDOCLOR
ALDOMET
ALDORIL
AMPHETAMINES
(Diet pills)
ANTIDEPRESSANTS
(tricyclic)
ANTIHISTAMINES
ATROPINE
ASTHMA
MEDICINE
BARBITURATES-
TRANQUILIZERS
BENDOPA
BLOOD PRES-
SURE MEDI-
CATIONS
COLD REMEDIES
DEMEROL

DIABETES MEDI-
CATION (oral)
DOPAR
EPHEDRINE
INDERAL
INSULIN
ISUPREL
LARODOPA
LICORICE (ex-
cess)
RESERPINE
(Serpasil, etc.)
RITALIN
ROMILAR
SURGERY WITH
ANESTHETICS
NARCOTICS

(It usually takes at least two weeks before the beneficial effects of antidepressant medications become apparent. It also may take two weeks for the drug to disappear from a patient's system once it has been discontinued. This time-lag must be considered if additional drugs are consumed.)

SEDATIVES—SLEEPING PILLS—MINOR TRANQUILIZERS

(AMYTAL, BARBITURATES, BUTISOL, DALMANE, DORIDEN, EQUANIL, LIBRAX, LIBRIUM, MILTOWN, NEMBUTAL, NOCTEC, PHENOBARBITAL, PLACIDYL, QUAALUDE, SECONAL, SERAX, TUINAL, VALIUM, VALMID, ETCETERA)

Interact with:
Alcohol (Booze)

BEER
HARD STUFF
WINE
ANTIFREEZE

No good! Sure you have done it and nothing happened. Don't press your luck. Booze and tranquilizers *do not mix*. There is an additive effect which produces deep sedation leading to a pronounced deterioration in coordination. Any task which requires attention, especially driving, must be ruled out. This drug interaction may lead to a big fall in blood pressure as well as breathing failure. If you want to live, don't mix 'em!

Antidepressant Medication

AVENTYL
ELAVIL
MARPLAN
NARDIL
NORPRAMIN
PARNATE
PERTOFRANE
SINEQUAN
TOFRANIL
TRIAVIL
VIVACTYL

This one is pretty common. Too many doctors prescribe minor tranquilizers for depression and then add a potent antidepressant on top of it. Although probably not quite as dangerous as alcohol, antidepressants also exaggerate the sedative effects of sedatives. Just be damn careful if you take these two kinds of drugs together.

Birth Control Pills

ENOVID
NORINYL
NORLESTRIN
ORTHO-NOVUM
OVRAL
OVULEN
ETCETERA

Okay, now don't panic. This is just a note of caution. There is *some* evidence suggesting that a few drugs which cause sedation (especially barbiturates) may decrease the effectiveness of oral contraceptives. Check it out with your physician.

145

Antihistamines

PRESCRIPTION
NONPRESCRIPTION
This interaction is not terribly dangerous, but the mind-dulling effect of antihistamines can exaggerate the sedative reaction to tranquilizers.

TETRACYCLINE ANTIBIOTICS

(ACHROMYCIN, ACHROSTATIN, AUREOMYCIN, CYCLOPAR, DECLOMYCIN, MYSTECLIN-F, PANMYCIN, QIDTET, RETET, ROBITET, RONDOMYCIN, SUMYCIN, TERRAMYCIN, TETRACYCLINE, TETREX, ETCETERA)

Interact with:

All Foods Containing High Concentrations of Calcium

ALMONDS
AMERICAN
  CHEESE
BUTTERMILK
CHEDDAR
  CHEESE
CHEESE (generally)
COTTAGE
  CHEESE
CREAM
CUSTARD
ICE CREAM
MILK (whole)
MILK (nonfat)
PIZZA   WITH
  CHEESE
PUDDING
VEGETABLES
  (green)
WAFFLES
YOGURT
ETCETERA

Damn! Here is a paradox which hurts. **Tetracycline** is an antibiotic which messes up our tummies. Besides giving us indigestion, it kills off lots of good bacteria. Milk products tend to diminish the stomach upset and may replace some of the good guys which have been killed. Unfortunately, these foods contain high calcium levels and will drastically cut down on the effectiveness of **Tetracycline**. Avoid eating these foods close to the time you take your antibiotic. In fact, never consume **Tetracycline** one hour prior to, during, or two hours following a meal if you want it to work.

All Antacids or Indigestion Aids

ALKA-SELTZER
AMPHOJEL
BROMO-SELTZER
DI-GEL
ENO
GELUSIL
MAALOX
PEPTO-BISMOL
PHILLIPS'MILK
  OF MAGNESIA
ROLAIDS
SODIUM BICAR-
  BONATE
TUMS
ETCETERA

Oh no! The same crummy paradox rears its ugly head. After a few days of **Tetracycline** therapy, the one thing you do need is an antacid. It is the last thing you should take. The ingredients in antacids have a great affinity for **Tetracycline.** The resulting interaction can block proper absorption of this antibiotic and inhibit effectivenss. So, as much as you may be tempted, avoid antacids if you want your **Tetracycline** to work completely.

Other Antibiotics (Penicillin)

AMPICILLIN
AMCILL
COMPOCILLIN
OMNIPEN
PATHOCIL
PENICILLIN
PENTIDS
PEN-VEE-K
POLYCILLIN
STAPHCILLIN
V-CILLIN-K
ETCETERA

If your doctor prescribes **Penicillin** at the same time he prescribes **Tetracycline**, he is incompetent. Because these two classes of antibiotics work in a completely different manner, combining them reduces therapeutic efficiency.

Although the drug interactions which have been listed and discussed are among the most frequent and important, they do not represent even a fraction of the vast numbers of deleterious and sometimes fatal reactions which occur each year. Guidelines have been established which, with your doctor's help, should enable you to avoid dangerous complications. Use the Table frequently. In fact, every time you must take a drug, consult this chapter in order to make sure there are not special foods, over-the-counter products, or other drugs which might be incompatible with it. But do not be lulled into a false *147* sense of confidence if it appears that your drug does not interact with anything. The Table hardly even scratches the surface. Always consult your doctor if you are not sure about something. And do not let your physician beat around the bush about side effects. If he does not seem to know whether two drugs will be safe together, try consulting a pharmacist. Surprisingly, many good pharmacists know more about drugs and drug interactions than your family doctor. Unfortunately, they often fall into the rut of taking pills from one bottle and putting them into another or counting their money. Nevertheless, if you are genuinely interested they may stir up some enthusaism and search for the right answers.

Ultimately, the only way you are going to improve the odds against an adverse drug interaction is to become extremely conscious of what prescription drugs, nonprescription drugs, and environmental chemicals you put in your body. Try to avoid taking more than one drug at a time. When that becomes impossible, monitor your own system's reactivity and sensitivity. At the first sign of trouble, head straight for your doctor's office. Better yet, use the phone.

References

1. Martin, Eric W. *Hazards of Medication: A Manual on Drug Interactions, Incompatibilities, Contraindications, and Adverse Effects.* Philadelphia: Lippincott, 1971.
2. Cohen, Stanley N., and Armstrong, Marsha F. *Drug Interactions: A Handbook for Clinical Use.* Baltimore: Williams & Wilkins, 1974.
3. Hansten, Philip D. *Drug Interactions: Clinical Significance of Drug-Drug Interactions and Drug Effects on Clinical Laboratory Results.* Philadelphia: Lea & Febiger, 1973.
4. Hartshorn, Edward A. *Handbook of Drug Interactions.* Hamilton, Illinois: Drug Intelligence Publications, 1973.
5. Swidler, Gerald. *Handbook of Drug Interactions.* New York: Wiley-Interscience, 1971.
6. "Interactions of Drugs." *Medical Letter* 12:93–96, 1970.
7. "Adverse Interactions of Drugs." *Medical Letter* 15:78–80, 1973.
8. Hussar, Daniel A. "Tabular Compilation of Drug Interactions." *American Journal of Pharmacy* 141:#4, 1969.

9. Visconti, James A. "An Analysis of 50 Frequent Drug Interactions." *Pharmacy Times* 38:36–41, 1972.

10. Mirvish, Sidney, et al. "Ascorbate-Nitrite Reaction: Possible Means of Blocking the Formation of Carcinogenic N-Nitroso Compounds." *Science* 177:65–67, 1972.

11. Lambert, Martin L., Jr. "Drug and Diet Interactions." *American Journal of Nursing* 75:402–406, 1975.

7.

Allergy
or
Oh, My Aching Nose

All right already, so you've got allergies and you're miserable, especially when the ragweed hay fever season and all those yucky pollens hit. You have plenty of company. There are probably over twenty million Americans with this affliction (one out of ten). Well, me too. Yeah, I've got hay fever, and it takes a fellow sufferer to really appreciate the problem. I often wonder how many allergy specialists (who are getting rich off our misery) know what it is really like to sniffle through August and September. They turn us into pin cushions with their weekly shots and we accept it all bravely. Well, strap on your seat belt and prepare for the heavy artillery. It
is about time we rattle the cage of the allergists of this coun-

try. The bottom of their bird cage hasn't been cleaned in quite some time.

So what is an allergy? For a field that has been around for so long (allergy shots were first initiated in 1911), it is almost unbelievable that the medical profession is still so embroiled in controversies over allergic disorders. Nevertheless, there are a few basic points of agreement. An allergy is really a catch-all phrase for a reaction of the body to a substance from the external environment. It is not a universal response, because one guy may react like crazy to that damn old ragweed pollen, while someone else not even know it exists. No one really knows why some people are more susceptible to these environmental pollutants and other folks completely nonreactive. House dust, cat fur, shrimp, a drug, or even cold weather can trigger an allergic reaction. It usually hits the upper respiratory tract (eyes, nose, and throat), but all too often an allergy can snake its long, nasty tentacles down into the lungs to provoke asthma. The skin is often acutely sensitive to an allergic attack, and the resulting eczema or inflammation can produce an unpleasant, ill-defined series of eruptions. The digestive tract is not immune, and even the bloodstream may react to an onslaught, especially if drug-induced.

The specialists in this field are the allergists and the immunologists. They like to tell us that the allergic reaction is a result of an earlier contact with the offending agent, known elegantly as an antigen or allergen. This substance, be it a drug like **Penicillin** or a tiny grain of pollen, stimulates the body to produce a defender known as an antibody. Each antibody is able to recognize the specific structure of the loathesome antigen whenever it is absorbed by the body and latch on to it to form a nice tight antigen-antibody complex. This interaction produces all-out war, with the resultant, all-too-familiar allergic reaction.

Perhaps a simple analogy will clarify the situation. For all you football buffs, the offensive allergen, such as ragweed pollen, can be perceived as a football sailing through the air. The eligible receiver downfield is the antibody, just waiting for the ball to get into his hands. Once the pass is completed and he grabs the ball, all hell breaks loose, with guys jumping on him trying to destroy him and the ball. Well, the same kind of *151* chaos occurs after the antibody and antigen get together. Histamine, a chemical manufactured in the body, is released from specialized cells, and everyone who has ever had an allergy knows that histamine can really do a job on your nose.

Unfortunately, this rather simple, straightforward story is far from complete. There are many cases where an individual appears to have had no prior contact with an antigen such as **Penicillin** but develops a full-blown reaction when injected for the first time. Allergic conditions such as hives, asthma, and year-round runny noses can rarely be associated with a specific initiating agent, though we know that many situations aggravate the problem. Emotional stress, excessive physical activity, or a winter cold are but a few of the elements which may precipitate an asthmatic attack.

Okay, so now you sort of know what an allergic reaction is all about. How do you recognize it? Probably for most folks that is not the problem. Runny, itchy, stuffy nose; watery eyes; sneezing; occasional headaches; and a general blah feeling that doesn't go away until the first good frost—these enable most people to recognize seasonal hay fever. Seasonal, pollen-type allergies may result from spring tree pollens, summer grass pollens, or fall weed pollens. Fungus spores may also add their pitchfork to this devil's playground.

Food allergies may be a bit more difficult to isolate, since the response may not occur immediately after ingestion of a special delicacy, or it may be hard to determine which particular food out of a whole meal is the guilty one. Some folks react to shellfish, while others may be sensitive to onions or tomatoes. More recently, it has been observed that food additives, especially the nitrates and nitrites found in prepared meats—particularly hot dogs, bacon, and salami—can trigger a hyperactive type of allergic reaction in children. Dr. Ben F. Feingold, director emeritus of the Department of Allergy, Kaiser-Permanente Medical Center, San Francisco, has gone so far as to forbid his patients all foods containing artificial flavors and colors as well as any substance containing the chemical salicylate. It is Dr. Feingold's contention that a diet low in these chemicals could suppress, if not eliminate completely, the symptoms of hyperactivity, a behavioral and learning complication which may affect as many as five million children.

Another allergen which is responsible for much suffering is something the allergists call "house dust." Actually, this is a misleading term. A tiny animal parasite, or mite, which lives in cotton bedding and furniture stuffing, mixes well with house dust and frequently produces an allergic response. Feathers and animal dander are also common antigens which can make for year-round nasal stuffiness.

Well great, with so darn many antigens to choose from, how can we isolate the ones responsible for our individual misfortunes? The allergy specialists of this country have managed to convince millions of Americans that something called a skin test is a fine diagnostic tool for isolating the particular varmint responsible. This "impressive" (at least to anyone who has ever undergone all those little injections) and expensive series of skin tests may serve to fool the poor patient into believing that he has a whole bunch of weird allergies. How is an allergy sufferer to know that he is being hoodwinked when his dignified doctor solemnly proclaims that ragweed, feathers, alternaria (a fungus), and house dust are the sources of his trouble? You see, the skin test is often a diagnostic rip-off. Your doctor conveniently fails to mention that it is a highly unreliable technique. It involves the injection of minute quantities of suspected antigen into the skin. If a red, itchy spot appears after a few minutes, the test is considered "positive."

Let's see what doctors, allergists, and immunologists say about skin testing. Two of the most famous experts in the field of allergy and immunology, Drs. P. S. Norman and L. M. Lichtenstein, have observed, "Positive skin tests to an allergen may be found in individuals who disclaim symptoms to that allergen."[1] That is a fancy way of saying that lots of people who have never experienced any symptom of allergy to a particular agent may react in a "positive" manner when tested with a skin injection. Obviously the skin test does not reflect the real world.

Dr. Emmett Holt, Jr., a pediatrician who has studied allergy shots in children, says that a person who exhibits a positive skin reaction to a test "can be classed as allergic, and often is. But does this mean that the allergen in question is responsible for allergic symptoms from which he may suffer? Originally— in the early days of allergy—this was thought to be so, and heroic efforts were made to avoid all antigens to which the *153* skin reacted. Some patients were given lists of over four hundred things to avoid. Fortunately, it soon became apparent that this extreme point of view could not be upheld. Positive skin reactions were found in many persons with no history of allergy."[2]

Still not convinced? Try this one. Way back in 1936 a study was published in the *Journal of Allergy* entitled "Intracutaneous Tests in Normal Individuals."[3] This investigation analyzed the reactivity of 150 medical personnel (nurses, medical students, and technicians) at Johns Hopkins University. Of the total, 110 had no history of allergic disorders, while 40 had reported some degree of sensitivity. When tested, 54.5 percent of the nonallergic subjects demonstrated positive skin tests and, incredibly, only 56 percent of the allergic personnel reacted to one or more extract. Obviously, this minor difference was not significant. The authors concluded, "It is well recognized that positive skin tests are not necessarily proof of allergic disease. Occasionally these tests are entirely negative when the history and clinical manifestations lead one to anticipate positive reactions, and frequently one obtains positive reactions which cannot be correlated with either the history or the clinical manifestations of allergic disease."

Okay, that statement was made back in 1936, but there has been no good research done in more recent years to contradict this observation. Whenever normal folks are tested (that is, people with no history or symptoms of allergy), they almost invariably produce close to a 50 percent incidence of false-positive skin reactivity. In study after study allergic and nonallergic subjects alike demonstrate sensitivity to grasses, house dust, ragweed, strawberries, and the kitchen sink.[4,5] Dr. Holt makes the point, "Allergic patients likewise frequently gave skin reactions to antigens that could not be blamed for their symptoms. Cases were also encountered of marked clinical sensitivity with a negative skin test." He also states, "It has seemed to me somewhat illogical to regard the skin test as significant when it confirms the history and to disregard it when it fails to do so. By so doing one is really relying only on the history."

What all this gobbledygook means is that just because your
154 allergist says you are highly allergic to something on the basis

of a skin test, it ain't necessarily so! Once the good doctor has you convinced, he has you by the short hairs. You are locked into his therapy program for months to come, if not years, and that can cost plenty. The chances are pretty good that you may be able to determine many of the things to which you are allergic all by yourself. If you start to sneeze and itch when a cat enters the room, you don't have to pay fifty bucks to find out that you've got a cat allergy. Equally, if you have been sleeping comfortably on a feather pillow for years with no nasal stuffiness when you awake, it is unlikely that you suffer from feather allergy, despite what the allergist may tell you.

There are other considerations, however, which make the skin test suspect. Dr. Lichtenstein has observed that the identical extract, injected into two different spots on your body (forearm and back, for example) may produce completely different skin reactions: one test could be negative, while the other could be clearly positive. There is no good explanation for this anomaly. A doctor who does not employ careful and rigorous injecting techniques might produce a false-positive response mechanically. The testing extract itself may often be faulty, since it is well established that the extremely weak solutions deteriorate quickly. It is also well known that commercial allergen extracts may vary widely from one batch to another in terms of potency. All in all, it is pretty clear that skin testing can be messy. Dr. Holt sums it up like this:

> What conclusion may one draw regarding the value of the skin test as revealing the specific antigen responsible for an allergic manifestation? My conclusion is that even if there is a measure of correlation between the skin test and clinical hypersensitivity, the frequency of error—of drawing a false conclusion, with troublesome consequences—is such that the usefulness of this procedure must be seriously questioned.[6]

Now all this may sound like we are belaboring the point, but the fact is that incredible numbers of people are being duped into believing that they are extremely allergic. Common sense and a good clinical history will establish the nature of the allergy almost as well as, if not better than, an expensive series of skin tests—and believe me, they can be EXPENSIVE. Some doctors have suggested that "challenge" testing is a good, *155* cheap technique for determining specific sensitivity. It involves exposure to the suspected allergen, a food for example or an animal. If there is a reaction, which then slowly disappears, one might reasonably conclude that the thing in question is responsible for at least some of the trouble. If the response can be repeated on separate occasions you are halfway home.

There is a problem with this method, however. Even momentary exposure and withdrawal of an allergen may cause a prolonged allergic reaction. In addition, one allergen may make you more susceptible to another. For example, during hay fever season a cat may make your symptoms worse, although during the rest of the year your sensitivity to cats is minimal. Or you may find that you cannot sleep in your featherdown sleeping bag at the end of the summer (during the pollen plague), even though there was absolutely no problem during June or July. This so-called priming effect may also explain why you are still suffering hay fever symptoms in late October, well after all the pollen has disappeared. By increasing your sensitivity to other allergens, the ragweed has made you more susceptible to house dust. Therefore, it may take a month or two before your reactivity has diminished and you return to normal. All this is to say that challenge testing is only successful if you can isolate individual suspects. Trying to determine whether or not a feather pillow is partly responsible for your stuffy nose would be ridiculous in the middle of hay fever season if you are already so stopped up that you can't breathe.

Once your cooperative allergist has managed to persuade you that you are sensitive to about five or ten allergies, the fun really begins. He will no doubt recommend a course of "desensitization" shots, commonly called allergy or hay fever shots. The big question is, are shots worth the financial investment and the trauma of being turned into a pin cushion for years to come? Of course your allergist thinks so, but that is only natural. Once he has you "hooked," he can rely on a steady source of income for quite some time. During this period he exerts almost no effort. His nurse will probably administer the shots on a weekly basis. The doctor's only contact with you will be to deposit your check into his bank account.

Desensitization, Hyposensitization, or allergy shots by any

other name involve the administration of small quantities of the extract of the allergen to which you may (or may not be) sensitive. By gradually increasing the concentration of the extract, the patient will theoretically be better able to tolerate contact with the evil substance. Thus, after a couple of years of weekly or monthly injections, the patient is supposed to withstand pollen, dust, feathers, or whatever the allergist has diagnosed.

So much for the principle. How does it really work? Let's return to the football analogy in order to clarify the reasoning behind desensitization. As you will remember, the football flying through the air represents the disgusting antigen, which in this case we will call ragweed pollen. Your body has manufactured a pass receiver which can recognize the particular form of the "pollen" football and will do its damndest to pull it down. Every completed pass represents a disaster for your nose because of the histamine which gets liberated. The trick is to somehow prevent these passes from being completed. It is believed that allergy shots are able to do this. One of the most popular theories suggests that by injecting ragweed pollen extract throughout the year, your body begins to manufacture another type of antibody, called a blocking antibody. This good guy might be perceived as a pass defender who gets in the way of the ball and breaks up the play in order to prevent the liberation of histamine. Over the last few years, immunologists and allergists have gone bananas trying to measure and correlate antibody levels with clinical improvement. They assumed that if shots could increase the amount of "good" blocking antibody circulating in the body, they could prove their whole approach to desensitization was a success. Unfortunately, the expert in this field, Dr. Lawrence Lichtenstein, discovered after much investigation that it was impossible to prove increased blocking antibody levels caused a direct clinical improvement.[7] He noted that "the mechanism by which symptom relief results from immunotherapy remains elusive." So we still don't know exactly *how* allergy shots work. But the really important question for us guys that suffer is not so much How but Do they work at all?

Ask any allergy specialist whether or not immunotherapy (allergy shots) is successful, and he will enthusiastically reply *157* yes. Of course, he may very well hedge his bets by claiming that not everyone experiences the same degree of benefit. But then, your allergist has a vested interest in the advantages of this form of treatment. Would you like to get the *real* story?

Desensitization by means of extract injection has been around for over sixty years. However, the solid evidence supporting the success of immunotherapy is still controversial. Let's eavesdrop on the medical profession as they discuss the issue among themselves. Dr. F. D. Lowel, past president of the American Academy of Allergy had this to say about shots:

> The rationale of injection therapy is based chiefly on concepts borrowed from immunology and on impressions that have not been validated by experiments characterized by that type of rigid control which will reasonably exclude a role for chance or bias . . . we must admit that the value of injection therapy is far from settled.[8]
> (Presidential address to the American Academy of Allergy)

Now that is very strong! I'll bet that your allergist never mentions the fact that doubt still exists. But that was only one doctor speaking. Dr. Emmett Holt, Jr., had this to say about shots:

> To the allergist their value is unquestioned. . . . The skeptics are anathema to the allergist, but somehow or other they persist. It is they who limit the acceptance of allergy, believing that the allergists have not firmly proved their case. . . . They are conscious of inaccuracies of specific allergic diagnosis and of failure of specific therapy in patients referred to the allergists, of undue restrictions of living habits that have produced no apparent benefit and of unimpressive results from specific therapy. Clinical impressions, no matter how accurate the observer, can lead one into error. All physicians are tempted to generalize from limited experience with individual cases.[9]

What Dr. Holt is trying to tell us is that one swallow never makes a summer. Doctors are just as quick to jump to conclusions as us mortals. The fact that some patients may respond favorably to allergy shots does not prove the case. Dr. Holt goes on to state:

> The value of specific diagnosis and therapy is not to be determined by the fact that these procedures have survived for half a century. Blood letting in medicine lasted for a much longer time. Nor should one be convinced by the fact

that considerable numbers of patients are certain of benefits received. When blind studies of any doubtful therapy
are carried out, there are always substantial numbers of
patients who have received placebos who are altogether
certain of the benefit they have received. Psychological factors have an extraordinary way of coloring results.[10]

When Dr. Holt refers to "blind studies," he does not mean
that the researchers go around with blindfolds. He means that
the study is designed so that personal prejudice can not influence the results of the investigation. Allergists who may sub-
consciously find it difficult to forget the economic factors involved in injection therapy must go out of their way to plan
experiments that remove psychological influence. One such
approach is to organize a project in which neither the doctor
nor the subject will know what is being administered. One set
of patients will receive true extract; the other group will receive a placebo in the form of salt-water injections or a
"nonactive" mimic of the true extract. In this manner, the
study would be scientifically valid and is called "double-blind"
in that no one will know who got what until after the probe
has been completed. In the past, the desensitization therapy
programs have notoriously lacked such controlled precautions.

One study which *was* extremely well-controlled was published in the JAMA by Dr. Vincent J. Fontana et al. This investigation was definitive in its conclusions:

A five-year study has been done on children sensitive to
ragweed in which a comparison was made between
specific hyposensitization injections and placebo injections.
Even though the allergen injections may have had some
beneficial effect on some children, the amount of benefit
was indistinguishable from differences likely to occur in
pure randomization experiments. No justification was found
for promising any greater benefit to children treated with allergens than they would obtain from placebo injections.[11]

Now that is **dynamite!** Interestingly, some of the children improved more on the inactive placebo injections than with the
true allergy extract. This just proves that the mere act of receiving an injection (no matter what it might be) can produce
a strong enough psychological reaction to induce clinical improvement. Dr. Fontana's experiment was carried out on children between the ages of six and seventeen. It lasted five *159*

PEOPLE'S PHARMACY

years, in order to analyze the cumulative effects of desensitization shots. Obviously, he found them with little merit. He also discovered that skin testing performed after three years of injections did not reflect the children's true sensitivity as determined by actual symptoms. One might erroneously assume that Dr. Fontana was out to prove allergy shots were not effective. Significantly, before the study was initiated, he "was admittedly biased in favor of the value of specific therapy."[12] Clearly, Dr. Fontana could not be accused of influencing the results.

It is only fair, however, to mention that other investigators, employing careful precautions and controlled technique, have observed clinical improvement after allergy shots. Nevertheless, one of the foremost authorities in this field, Dr. Lichtenstein concluded, after noting some benefit from hay-fever shots, "It is our opinion based on the regimens used in this and our previous studies, that immunotherapy is not now effective enough to call for widespread use and that continued, controlled studies remain necessary."[13] Dr. Lichtenstein and his associate Dr. Philip S. Norman found it necessary to clarify this statement in an explosive follow-up letter to the *Annals of Internal Medicine*:

> We can understand the confusion that might attend our statement that immunotherapy leads to a significant amelioration of symptoms but is not now effective enough to call for widespread use. The first part of this statement is an observation; the latter is our interpretation of the clinical results achieved over the last decade in *controlled clinical trials* of both children and adults. We recognize that our interpretation of the data smacks of *heresy*. Indeed, it was stated in this fashion to introduce a note of caution in using our data to support the widespread use of immunotherapy. Simply stated, immunotherapy, requiring 15 to 20 injections the first year, a yearly continuation of the process, considerable cost in money and time, and acceptance of a real risk of systemic reactions (if high doses are sought), may not be worth the *modest* amelioration of symptoms noted in simple hay fever . . . there is another reason for our cautionary note, our studies have used the simplest model of allergic disease: ragweed hay fever. They have no bearing on the treatment by immunotherapy of perennial rhinitis, 'dust' allergy, asthma, and so forth. Few controlled studies in these areas have been carried out, and those that have

been *do not show immunotherapy to be efficacious*; we feel that each of these therapies must be subject to exacting controlled studies. [Italics mine.][14]

It is absolutely unbelievable! Allergy specialists have been shooting up their patients with extracts that have little, if any, curative power. Could it be that the modern allergist has not come such a long way from the snake-oil peddler of years past?

Well, do we have any other options, or are allergy shots the only answer to our suffering? There are other possibilities, and some of them are pretty good. To begin with, the cheapest, simplest, and most effective allergy therapy involves the removal of the offending antigen. As heart-rending as it might be, this procedure may require the removal of a favorite feather pillow or a comfortable armchair. It might be a faithful pet or a special brand of cosmetics. If dust is the culprit, most cotton or kapok stuffing material should be eliminated and frequent vacuuming instituted. Synthetic material, such as foam rubber or Dacron, should be used whenever possible, and cotton mattresses should be replaced or encased in plastic. These procedures can be a real pain in the neck, and lots of folks would rather suffer than kick their favorite cat out of the house. Dusting is a super drag. Nevertheless, if you keep away from the things which cause your allergies, you will no longer have to suffer.

Unfortunately, when it comes to seasonal pollen allergies, it is a helluva lot more difficult to avoid the stuff. There are, however, a few helpful hints which may make hay fever season easier to bear. If you live in the country, it makes good sense to cut down the ragweed which grows around your home before it has a chance to pollinate. Children should be encouraged to play indoors, or as far away as possible from ripe ragweed fields. Although air conditioning does not filter out the pollen, it does allow you to close the windows in your house, thus reducing circulating pollen.

So you are doing your best to stay away from air-borne contaminants, but let's face it, there is no way to really avoid the stuff as long as you're still breathing, unless you are wealthy enough to take an ocean cruise. What's next in the way of treatment? Well, good old **Vitamin C** is useful for more than *161* combating the common cold! There is some scientific evidence that Vitamin C has some other extremely beneficial effects, including some amelioration of allergic symptoms. Remember, most allergic reactions are a direct result of the liberation of histamine from cells within your body. Anything which diminishes this response will be beneficial to hay fever sufferers. One study seems to demonstrate that vitamin C has this ability.[15] The authors report that "ascorbic acid can inhibit the airway constriction effect of histamine in healthy human subjects and in the trachea of guinea pigs." The guinea pig is an animal exquisitely sensitive to the effect of histamine and is an excellent model for tests of allergic responsiveness. The investigators discovered that 500 milligrams of ascorbic acid protected their subjects (human) for up to six hours from the nasty constricting effects of histamine. They conclude that if Vitamin C were given in doses of 250 milligrams at three-hour intervals, it might be useful in the treatment of asthma. As any asthma victim knows, the medication she or he takes often produces unpleasant consequences which would not be encountered with ascorbic acid.

Actual clinical experience with Vitamin C in the treatment of allergy has been equivocal with many contradictory reports of success and failure. Very few well-controlled, scientifically valid studies are available. Analyzing the studies which have been done (many were undertaken during the 1930s and 1940s), one conclusion may be drawn. Where negative results were obtained (that is, where Vitamin C did not seem to decrease the symptoms of hay fever), the dose was usually 500 milligrams or less per day. When the dose exceeded 500 milligrams, the results were generally much more favorable. One researcher, Dr. Simon Ruskin, reported his subjective clinical impressions back in 1945. It was his observation that some patients responded more favorably to 750 milligrams of Vitamin C than they did to desensitization therapy.[16] A further report, published in the *Annals of Allergy* in 1949, was a bit more scientific in that two groups of patients were studied.[17] One group, in Boston, received 750–1000 milligrams of ascorbic acid, while a group in New York was put on a regimen of 1,500–2,250 milligrams. Whereas 50 percent of the Boston group seemed to manifest clinical improvement, 75 percent of the New York patients demonstrated clinical improvement. The authors concluded, "The larger dose may have played a part in producing the apparently greater improvement in the larger percentage of patients. . . . The feeling of well-being, experienced by the patients taking the tablets [ascorbic acid], was striking and was commented upon by both groups independently of the effect upon pollinosis."

Unfortunately, these tantalizing investigations have never been adequately followed up with sound, well designed experiments. One relatively recent study carried out on sixty-seven allergy patients by Dr. James A. Jackson also established clinical improvement. According to the author, "Vitamin C can be very effective in the treatment of many allergies. It may be used alone or with other agents."[18] Sadly, this study was also flawed in that there were no good controls taken. We must still wait for acceptable experimentation before we can make any definitive statement once and for all. Nevertheless, there does seem to be reasonably good evidence to indicate that large doses of Vitamin C can decrease allergic symptoms, especially the runny nose and cough. Food allergies may respond even more dramatically to this form of therapy.

If you are still skeptical, there is a higher authority. Undisputed proof comes from my father-in-law, a highly critical, superscientific, totally allergic hay fever sufferer. His words: "It works." His dose: 3,000–5,000 milligrams of Vitamin C daily.

There is one other simple, nonhazardous technique for relieving the stuffy nose associated with allergy. Have you ever noticed that when you sit or lie down your allergy symptoms tend to get worse? And that when you get up or are more active, your nose seems to open up a little bit? Apparently, there is a very good scientific explanation for this phenomenon. The extra stuffiness associated with resting seems to be related to a general decrease in brain activity. When our nervous system is more at rest, our blood vessels tend to relax. Doctors call this *diminished vascular tone*. It might lead to nasal congestion. According to a renowned allergy specialist, Dr. Paul M. Seebohm, "Another way to reverse the congestive effect of rhinitis [stuffy nose] is with exercise. Richerson and Seebohm have demonstrated complete reversal of obstructive congestion *163* to be associated with a vigorous 3-minute step-type exercise."[19] Their investigation produced evidence that exercise promoted beneficial responses that exceeded those seen with potent medication. Next time you are fed up with those swollen sinuses, why not try a little exercise? It certainly is cheaper than a decongestant.

So what happens after you have tried Vitamin C and exercise, and you still aren't satisfied with the results? It is time to move on to the heavier artillery. Now before you consider allergy shots, listen to what the highly respected scientific journal, *Medical Letter*, has to say: "Desensitization for pollen allergy appears to be justified only in patients in whom oral antihistamines or topical intranasal corticosteroids have failed."[20] Very interesting. Antihistamine medication should definitely be considered before moving on to any other form of therapy. The way these drugs work is quite fascinating. Histamine, which is released from special cells in our bodies, causes most of the allergic symptoms of sneezing, sniffling, itching, and stuffiness. An antihistamine cannot prevent the liberation of this noxious biochemical, but it can impede the interaction of histamine with the rest of our body. Thus, the symptoms of allergy should be significantly reduced. An antihistamine is much like a pass defender in football. It blocks the football (histamine), thereby preventing a completed pass. But which antihistamine should you use? There are approximately twenty-five different chemical formulations and about a hundred preparations on the market. Clearly, your doctor or allergist cannot be an expert on each one. Additionally, no two people react quite the same way to a given product. That is, antihistamines are notorious for their tremendous variability in effectiveness. No one, including your doctor, can predict with assurance your response to a particular brand name. The price and side effects are also highly variable and must be taken into consideration when a prescription is written.

The most common side effect encountered with antihistamine therapy is drowsiness. As everyone should know by now, driving under the "influence" can be lethal since attention and motor coordination may be seriously hampered. That also goes for work which requires attentiveness. Fortunately, some people are more resistant to this lethargic, unpleasant, underwater-type of feeling. But for those of us who are susceptible, it becomes necessary to experiment until we have discovered the product which produces the least amount of adverse responsiveness. One drug may knock you out of commission for hours, while another might be hardly noticeable. If your physician writes you four or five different prescriptions (each one for no longer than one week), you can rotate the medication until you have discovered the one which is right for you.

Another important consideration is cost. Whenever possible, try to get your doctor to prescribe by generic or chemical name rather than brand name. One very popular antihistamine that is supposed to cause minimal drowsiness is **Chlorpheniramine Maleate** (generic name). The brand-name product is known as **Chlor-Trimeton**. It is present in many popular over-the-counter formulations (sixty-five, to be exact), including **Allerest**, **Coricidin**, and **Ornade**. Whenever possible, just stick to the pure antihistamine, since these products often contain decongestants, sleep-inducers, caffeine, and lots of other garbage. If you think you might have high blood pressure (22 million Americans do), you must stay away from anything with a decongestant, since it will aggravate your condition.

Another common antihistamine is **Benadryl** (the generic name is **Diphenhydramine**). It is potent and effective, with a low incidence of stomach upset. Unfortunately, it produces a high degree of sedation and as many as half of all patients receiving this drug experience unpleasant drowsiness. **Pyribenzamine (Tripelennamine)** may muck up your tummy, along with its tendency to induce somnolence. It is impossible to recommend a particular brand or type of antihistamine. Experiment until you find the one which is most effective and least bothersome. If you experience fatigue, dizziness, blurred vision, or lack of coordination, reduce your dose, but first cease any activity which requires careful coordination.

All right, you have tried everything together. Still that damn stuffy nose persists and you feel lousy. What's left? *Medical Letter* recommended something called "topical intranasal corticosteroids." According to Lichtenstein and Norman, they were able to achieve the same degree of symptom relief in their patients with this nose spray that they normally obtained with hay fever shots. Since very little of this cortisone-like medication is actually absorbed into the body, these specialists noted that "this is far less time-consuming, less costly, and to our minds, as safe as or safer than immunotherapy."[21] According to Dr. Paul M. Seebohm, one common product, "**Dexamethasone (Turbinaire Decadron Phosphate**) sprayed into each nostril 3 times a day is usually very effective 24 to 48 hours after starting the treatment. When symptoms are once suppressed, the improvement can be sustained with less frequent application—e.g., once or twice a day."[22] This form of therapy does require a doctor's prescription and should only be used when all the other suggestions have not met therapeutic expectations. If all these measures fail to do the job, then it is time to visit an allergy specialist and possibly consider desensitization immunotherapy.

ANAPHYLAXIS
LIFE AND DEATH ALLERGY

So far we have just been talking about "simple" allergies. Because the problem has become so commonplace these days and is almost the in thing, people have become complacent and casual about their allergic disorders. Unfortunately, there is one kind of allergic reaction which can be a matter of life or death. For an increasing number of people, insect-sting allergy can be incredibly serious. It may be hard to appreciate the severity of anaphylactic shock after thinking in terms of hay fever or poison ivy, but believe me, this is a whole different ball game. *Anaphylaxis* is a big word which represents the type of life-threatening reaction to such diverse substances as **Penicillin, Streptomycin, Insulin, Tetanus Toxin, Local Anesthetics**, and **Aspirin**, as well as insect stings. It may begin with a marked local reaction (a bee sting which really swells up and lasts) or generalized itching. This may be followed by a feeling of uneasiness accompanied by agitation, flushing, hives, tearing, coughing, sneezing, nasal congestion, throbbing of the ears, rapid pulse, and possibly heart palpitations. Some or all of these symptoms may appear within one to fifteen minutes after the contact, though occasionally they may be delayed much longer. After these initial symptoms, a spasm of the respiratory tract may appear which will make breathing very difficult. Rapid accumulation of fluid in the tissue of the neck may also seriously interfere with respiration. Thereafter, shock is a likelihood with loss of consciousness followed by death, probably due to the severe strain placed on the heart.

Obviously, this kind of serious reaction demands quick recognition and medical supervision. Even if you haven't had a serious response to an insect sting or a drug before, it is not impossible for one to develop. Although there are thirty different kinds of insects that can produce allergic symptoms, in general the reactions to yellow jackets, wasps, hornets, and bees are the worst. Very few people are aware that "More people die from allergy to insect stings than from snake bites."[23] Although you can't bet on it, the first atypical, or greater than usual, response to a sting usually produces no serious complications. Nevertheless, this experience should serve as a warning that you may be developing an allergy. Each subsequent sting or contact will produce a more serious sensitivity. If you even suspect that you are developing an allergy, you must take certain precautions, because you may have less than thirty minutes to live once the toxic venoms have been injected into your skin. Fast action will save your life. If you are close to a doctor's office or a hospital, go there immediately as an emergency patient. Unfortunately, because there are many situations where you may not be able to get there fast enough, you absolutely must be prepared to save yourself long enough for proper medical attention. In the summertime you *must* carry a kit with you at all times which contains a syringe with adrenalin. Get your doctor to teach you how to administer the injection. No matter how much you think that you could not stick yourself, you will be amazed what you can do when it comes to a life or death situation, especially if it is your child who has the allergy. You can practice with a sterile salt-water solution and a disposable one-milliliter syringe (the type called *tuberculin* will do nicely). The shot should be injected into the soft tissue of the upper arm (not in the muscle), and if you *167* use a very short needle, such as that which comes with a tuberculin syringe, you can practically insert the needle all the way. The very thought makes you cringe, right? But this type of injection is about the least painful there is, and with a little practice you will realize that the technique is not very difficult. An excellent Emergency Insect Sting Treatment kit is available from Hollister-Stier Laboratories, P.O. Box 3145, Terminal Annex, Spokane, Wash. 99220, or 550 Industrial Drive, Yeadon, Pa. 19050. This compact kit contains a syringe already loaded with two doses of adrenalin, easy-to-follow instructions, a sterilizing swab, chewable antihistamine tablets, and a tourniquet, all in a box smaller than a pack of cigarettes. The instructions are fantastically clear and, though this product (brand name **Ana-Kit**) costs a little more than six dollars, it is certainly worth the price if it could help save your life. In order to purchase the **Ana-Kit** you will have to have a doctor's prescription, but that should not be a problem if your doctor appreciates the gravity of your allergic condition. Just in case he gets nervous that you are trying to eliminate his services, quote from the package: "The **Ana-Kit** is not intended as a substitute for medical attention or hospital care but for use by the patient when medical care is not readily available." You might even want to buy two or three kits so that one will always be handy at various locations. Do *not* store your kit in the glove compartment of your car, since the heat can destroy the adrenalin. In fact, the adrenalin will eventually decompose and have to be replaced (the **Ana-Kit** has an expiration date marked on each plastic container).

Remember, self-treatment is only a stopgap, emergency measure. Have someone rush you immediately to a doctor or call an ambulance. Children who suffer from this allergy should carry an epinephrine (adrenalin) aerosol inhalator for self-administration if no adult is around. It is not as effective as an injection, but it may provide some temporary relief during a crisis.

People who are allergic to bees often receive insect desensitization shots in hope of preventing a fatal accident. This is probably a good precaution, but it does involve some risk. There is always the possibility that a skin test or the allergy shot itself could provoke anaphylactic shock. Your physician must be prepared to treat an emergency reaction. Although some physicians have reported fantastic results from allergy injections for insect stings (a recent report in *JAMA* stated, "Results of hyposensitizing injections were excellent, with 303 of 308 subsequent stings resulting in less reaction than before beginning injections"[24]), do not allow your shots to give you a false sense of security. There have been a number of treatment failures, resulting in fatalities, in patients who had been receiving these precautionary injections. According to Dr. Philip Torsney, one patient died from a sting even though he had received a desensitization shot only five days before being stung.[25] Tragically, this person died while waiting for attention in his doctor's waiting room. Another patient died within fifteen minutes after his sting even though he too had received his last hyposensitization shot within the week. These cases are presented not to scare anyone unnecessarily, but merely to illustrate the point that immunotherapy is not foolproof and must be assisted with immediate emergency procedures when the risk of anaphylaxis presents itself.

Let's recapitulate. Allergy is still very much a medical mystery. Even though there have been great advances in recent years, there are still more questions than answers. Skin testing and desensitization injections are of questionable value. There are simpler, cheaper, and safer techniques which should be initiated in the beginning. First and foremost is the removal of all materials which could be responsible for the allergic symptoms. Allergic patients are often sensitive to animals, cotton or kapok stuffing material, and feathers. Large doses of Vitamin C may help relieve some of the symptoms, and a three-minute exercise program might relieve a stuffed-up nose temporarily. Antihistamines are a particularly useful therapeutic approach, but it is necessary to shop around until you find the particular product which is most effective and least bothersome for you. People who are taking antihistamines should never drive an automobile or operate machinery because motor coordination and judgment may be impaired. A cortisone-like nasal spray may provide relatively safe and long-lasting relief if all other measures prove insufficient. Finally, allergy shots may be tried when all else fails. Allergy to certain drugs like **Penicillin** or to insect stings can result in *169* a life-threatening condition called anaphylactic shock. Each patient should have his physician prescribe an emergency insect-sting kit which contains adrenalin (epinephrine) in a pre-loaded syringe so that in the absence of medical help the person can save his own life.

References

1. Norman, P. S., Lichtenstein, L. M., and Ishizaka, K. "Diagnostic Tests in Ragweed Hay Fever." *J. Aller. Clin. Immunol*. 52:210–224, 1973.
2. Holt, Emmett, Jr. "A Nonallergist Looks at Allergy." *New Engl. J. Med*. 276:1449–1454, 1967.
3. Grow, Max H., and Herman Nathan B. "Intracutaneous Tests in Normal Individuals." *J. of Aller*. 7:108–114, 1936.
4. Fontana, V. J., et al. "Observations on the Specificity of Skin Test Incidence of Positive Skin Tests in Allergic and Nonallergic Children." *J. of Aller*. 34:348–353, 1963.
5. Rackemann, F. M., and Simon, F. A. "Techniques on Intracutaneous Tests and Results of Routine Tests in Normal Persons." *J. of Allergy* 6:184–188, 1935.
6. Holt, op. cit.
7. Lichtenstein, L. M., et al. "Single Year of Immunotherapy for Ragweed Hay Fever." *Annals of Int. Med*. 75:663–671, 1971.
8. Lowel, F. D. "American Academy of Allergy Presidential Address." *J. of Aller*. 31:185–187, 1960.
9. Holt, op. cit.
10. Ibid.
11. Fontana, Vincent J., et al. "Effectiveness of Hyposensitization Therapy in Ragweed Hay-Fever in Children." *JAMA* 195:985–992, 1966.
12. Holt, op. cit.
13. Lichtenstein et al. "Single Year."
14. Lichtenstein, L. M., and Norman, P. S. "Hay Fever Therapy." *Annals of Int. Med*. 76:667–668, 1972.
15. Zuskin, Eugenija, et al. "Inhibition of Histamine-Induced Airway Constriction by Ascorbic Acid." *J. Aller. Clin. Immunol*. 51:218–226, 1973.
16. Ruskin, S. "High Dosage Vitamin C in Allergy." *Am. J. Digestive Dis*. 12:281–313, 1945.
17. Brown, E. A., and Ruskin, S. "The Use of Cevitamic Acid in

Symptomatic and Coseasonal Treatment of Pollinosis." *Annals of Aller*. 7:65–70, 1949.

18. Jackson, James A. "Ascorbic Acid Versus Allergies." *N.Y. J. Dentistry* 42:216–218, 1972.

19. Seebohm, Paul M. Allergy, *Family Practice* ed. H. F. Conn, Saunders, 1973. Pp. 898, 902.

20. *Medical Letter* 15:55–56, 1973.

21. Lichtenstein, Lawrence M. "Hay Fever Therapy." *Annals of Int. Med*. 76:667–668, 1972.

22. Seebohm, op. cit.

23. Barr, Solomon E. "Allergy to Hymenoptera Stings." *JAMA* 228:718–720, 1974.

24. Ibid.

25. Torsney, Philip J. "Treatment Failure: Insect Desensitization." *J. Aller. Clin. Immunol*. 52:303–306, 1973.

8.

Asthma:
A Medical Quagmire

Bronchial asthma is awful. Doctors know very little about this disorder. They treat it but rarely cure it. Sometimes it goes away all by itself, but more often it doesn't. Sometimes asthma kills.

Asthma is a problem with its roots stuck in the allergy quagmire. That is not to say that everyone with asthma is going to be allergic, but more often than not, somewhere in an asthmatic patient's family there is a history of allergic problems. Its management should be directed to a competant allergist at least for evaluation, if not for treatment. With early detection and careful management, it is possible to reduce symptoms and maintain a patient in excellent condition.

Diagnosis of this disease is a relatively easy procedure. Tightness in the chest, accompanied by difficulty or distress when breathing, is often a tip-off that something is wrong. Wheezing is generally the clincher, though allergists can make sure by using fancy equipment to measure lung capacity. There are many things which can kick off an asthmatic attack, including smoke, chemical fumes, aerosol sprays, exhaustion, sudden temperature changes, allergens, and—probably most important—emotional stress. Asthma may strike at any time, but it is interesting to note that it often hits when the patient is at rest or relaxed, well after exposure to an allergic agent or a precipitating event. This can complicate the allergist's job, since he must determine the specific allergens which sensitize his patient.

Asthma appears to result from the constriction of small circular muscles which surround and control the diameter of the air passages within the lungs. The partial closing off of these small paths or tunnels creates difficulty in breathing, and the characteristic wheeze becomes audible. Anyone who hasn't experienced the scary feeling of not being able to breathe freely cannot appreciate the terrible anxiety which can build up in the asthmatic patient. It is a sensation not terribly different from that of slow suffocation.

The symptomatic treatment of asthma is geared to relaxing the spastic contractions of these muscles, promoting expectoration of the mucus which rapidly forms, and decreasing the accumulation of fluid in the lungs. Perhaps the most famous and widely used drug in the counterattack against asthma is **Ephedrine**. It has been used for at least five thousand years and dates back to ancient China. For folks with mild to moderate problems, **Ephedrine** is quite effective in relieving asthmatic symptoms. It is somewhat less successful for patients who have a chronic daily problem because when it is used continuously (more than three times a day, every day) its effectiveness is reduced considerably. Since **Ephedrine** is available generically, it is very inexpensive. Unfortunately, physicians seem to prefer to prescribe it in the more expensive brand name preparations where it is accompanied by other drugs. Such combination drugs are not only more expensive but of dubious superiority. Common brands like **Bronkotabs, Marax,** *173*

Tedral, and **Quadrinal** all contain two or three active ingredients usually accompanied by a sedative such as **Phenobarbital.**

While the safety of **Ephedrine** has long been established, a few precautions should be observed. People with high blood pressure or heart disease should be reluctant to use this medication since its direct stimulant effect upon the heart and blood vessels could be dangerous. Folks with an overactive thyroid gland (hyperthyroidism) must also be cautious. On occasion **Ephedrine** may make urination difficult, so elderly men with a tendency towards prostate trouble should steer clear too.

Another important drug that is widely used to open up the lungs of the asthmatic is **Theophylline**. This medication is practically identical in chemical structure to caffeine. Which brings up an interesting point: if you ever get caught with your pants down, that is to say, without your medication at a moment when that old familiar tightness begins to form in your chest, don't panic. A couple of cups of strong coffee may not be as good as your traditional medicine, but caffeine does have some ability to counter lung constriction. *Theophylline* is often combined with **Ephedrine** in the hopes of enhancing the relaxation effect of each drug alone. Unfortunately, recent medical research has established that such formulations do not necessarily improve effectiveness. In fact, such drug preparations seem to increase the likelihood of producing unwanted side effects. Clinical pharmacologists and asthma experts recommend that physicians prescribe either one drug or the other and avoid combination pills whenever possible. **Theophylline** is also available generically and is relatively inexpensive. Administered as an elixir, in liquid form, it is absorbed rapidly and probably better than when given as a tablet. The common side effects of stomach pain, nausea, and vomiting may also be reduced when **Theophylline** is taken as an elixir.

Another therapeutic mainstay in the treatment of asthma is the aerosol nebulizer. In some ways it is more popular for a sudden attack, since relief is experienced almost immediately. That is because the fine mist is absorbed directly into the

lungs, where the problem is. **Ephedrine** tablets may take fifteen to thirty minutes before they begin to provide assistance. Unfortunately, popularity and safety are two separate things. There is still a great cloud of controversy hanging over the use of aerosol asthma sprays. In the late 1960s it was discovered that a great many asthma patients in England and Australia had died, a surprising increase over previous decades. In England alone perhaps as many as 3,500 asthmatics died during the sixties.[1] There were numerous reports of patients who were found dead with their bronchodilator aerosols still clutched in their hands.[2] Unexpected deaths were uncovered in patients who had recently overused their spray before hospital admission. This sudden growth in asthma mortality was correlated with a particular aerosol nebulizer which was marketed in those countries and which apparently contained a large dose of **Isoproterenol**.[3] The reason this epidemic of asthma deaths apparently didn't affect the United States or Canada was that the concentration of this drug found in the North American varieties was about one-fifth the strength of that sold in England.[4] Death was attributed to the fact that these drugs can produce fatal heart rhythms in high doses.

There are two basic kinds of asthma inhalers. One contains **Isoproterenol**, a drug which produces a rapid dilation of the air passages of the lungs and an increase in the heart rate. The other type of aerosol contains **Adrenalin** or **Epinephrine** (the British call it **Adrenaline**, the Americans call it **Epinephrine**). Both aerosols work much the same way and are quite effective. **Isoproterenol** is available in this country by prescription as the brand-name products **Isuprel, Duo-Medihaler, Medihaler-Iso,** and **Norisodrine Aerohalor. Epinephrine** is obtainable both by prescription and over the counter. It is found in such products as **Bronkaid Mist, Primatene Mist, Asthmahaler, Asthma Meter, Bronko-Meter** and **Medihaler-Epi**.

Although many doctors doubted the published reports of aerosol-related asthma mortality, recent investigations have forced physicians to reexamine the question of the aerosols' safety and effectiveness. In 1974, two brands which were available without prescription as **Asthma Nefrin** and **Vapo-Nefrin** were pulled off the market by the FDA because too much medication was being squirted into patients' lungs. As a *175* result, too much epinephrine was being absorbed by the body and side effects could have been encountered. The recall of these OTC products occurred right on the heels of another FDA decision. The prescription preparation **Vapo-N-Iso Metermatic** had also been withdrawn from pharmacy shelves. Are these just isolated, coincidental situations or are the problems associated with vaporizer inhalators real?

Perhaps the greatest problem associated with bronchodilator sprays is overuse. A person who suffers from asthma gets highly anxious during an attack and will do anything to open up his breathing passages. This often means that he will keep taking puff after puff from his nebulizer even though he is not experiencing adequate relief. What happens is very similar to the nose-spray situation. According to Irvin Caplin and John Haynes, "The relief of the nasal obstruction is followed by a rebound irritation and swelling of the nasal mucosa. Medication is required more and more frequently. Cure results only when nose drops are discontinued. We feel we are dealing with the same type of mechanism in the asthmatic who used adrenergic drugs (**Epinephrine** and **Isoproterenol**). We have discontinued the use of aerosol nebulizers in the treatment of our asthmatic patients."[5] There you have it. Overuse of an asthma inhaler may well lead to a paradoxical aggravation of symptoms after a brief period of improvement. Children are particularly susceptible to overuse of this form of therapy. The nebulizer may become a crutch, producing physiological as well as psychological habituation. Dr. Caplin and Dr. Haynes stated that many of their chronic patients "were returned to relatively good health by only one change in their management—the discontinuation of aerosolized adrenergic drugs". Anyone who uses, or allows his child to use, the inhaler more than four times a day may be asking for trouble.

Apart from overuse, it has been observed that these agents may "dry" the secretions in the lungs. This can be a very dangerous situation since it leads to the production of thick mucus plugs. Once that occurs, a sustained asthma attack may result, which is tough to treat. Asthma sufferers should always be encouraged to drink lots of fluids and expectorate the gunk that accumulates in their lungs. An even more serious situation is the possibility that these drugs could react with another asthma medicine to cause potentially fatal heart irregularities. According to Dr. Giancarlo Guideri and Dr. David Lehr, **Isoproterenol (Isuprel)** may interact with the drugs of the cortisone class (**Decadron, Prednisone**, etc.). In their animal investigations, these researchers discovered that cortisone-type drugs could sensitize the heart in such a way that it would be extremely susceptible to **Isoproterenol**-induced heart stoppage.[6] It is even conceivable that the 'epidemic of sudden death' seen in England was due in part to this interaction. Until evidence has been presented which proves there is no danger, people using **Isoproterenol** inhalators should be very wary of any cortisone-type medicine.

Asthma sprays may be helpful in aborting a short asthma attack in patients who suffer from mild to moderate respiratory distress. Nevertheless, their potential for overuse, especially in children, should encourage patients to substitute another form of therapy. Oral **Ephedrine** may not be as fast, but it has been proved safe and effective. Both **Epinephrine** and **Isoproterenol** have the ability to stimulate the heart and should be avoided by people with cardiovascular disease. Finally, if the anticipated improvement does not occur after two puffs of the inhaler, overuse may be the problem, and the patient should follow Dr. Caplin's advice to discontinue use of the aerosol nebulizer completely.

Once a doctor feels that he cannot control his patient with **Ephedrine** or an aerosol product, he often brings up the heavy artillery. More often than not that means **Cortisone** derivatives. They include **Aristocort, Celestone, Decadron, Delta-Cortef, Haldrone, Meticorten**, and **Prednisone**, to name a few. These drugs are employed in the treatment of an incredible number of medical problems. They are injected into the bruised and battered knees of football players and the elbows of tennis bums in order to relieve the inflammation associated with abused joints. They are taken orally by arthritis patients to relieve pain and swelling. **Cortisone**-type drugs are used to prevent tissue rejection in organ transplant operations. They are also used for a variety of allergic illnesses. These are just a few of the many applications to which these corticosteroids are put. They cannot cure anything; at best, they may relieve the symptoms, but they rarely promote full recovery. The tantalizing relief which they afford often produces a subtle addiction both physically and psychologically. Unfortunately, continued use of these medications can produce some very serious adverse reactions.

Some of the most important consequences of long-term corticosteroid therapy are decreased resistance to infections, impaired wound-healing, increased blood pressure, weight gain, stomach ulcers, muscle weakness, skin problems, fluid retention and loss of potassium, susceptibility to fractures of bones, menstrual irregularities, psychological disturbances, impaired growth in children, and complication of diabetes management. These drugs should only rarely (and only then with great caution) be given to people who suffer from ulcers, thrombophlebitis, or any infection. The above list is only a partial inventory of potential side effects. Many patients will not experience any of these problems, but they are a constant threat.

The really big question is, Are the benefits of **Cortisone**-type drugs worth the risk for asthma patients? According to Drs. Vincent Fontana and Angelo Ferrara of the Department of Pediatric Allergy at St. Vincent's Hospital and Medical Center of New York:

> The insidious side effects that follow long-term steroid therapy are what concern us and they should be considered by all physicians. It has been our experience, and certainly the experience of others who have been left with the responsibility of "weaning" children from steroid therapy, that the most disastrous effects of cortisone treatment are not metabolic. The more important iatrogenic effects [illnesses caused by doctors] are: addiction, the postponement of proper allergic investigations and management, emotional changes, and, last but not least, the unresponsiveness of the child to all other anti-asthmatic medications after he has been on steroid therapy for a long period of time . . . a grave responsibility rests with the physician who starts a child on steroids except in life-threatening situations. After years of steroid therapy, these children become both pulmonary and emotional cripples who ultimately become the responsibility of the convalescent homes in Denver.[7]

In a report prepared by the Drug Committee of the Research Council of the American Academy of Allergy, "The
178 Side Effects of Prolonged Corticosteroid Treatments in Pa-

tients with Asthma," some startling facts were uncovered. For one thing, of the 122 patients who were studied, 76 percent were "steroid dependent." What that means is that the majority of these people would have had trouble discontinuing their use of this class of medicines. It was also noted that the side effect rate was 2.44 per patient. This heavy-duty committee concluded, "The Committee does not condone the use of any of the corticosteroids, unless a life-threatening situation is involved. Before Corticosteroid therapy is undertaken, every other means of controlling the patient should be attempted."[8]

Physicians, particularly allergists, seem to be reporting an increased incidence in asthma mortality. Severity of symptoms also seems to be on the rise. Could it be that modern asthma therapy may be working to the detriment of the patient even though his symptoms are being temporarily alleviated? Dr. Fontana seems to think so. He has stated, "The possibility that the increased and promiscuous use of therapy, whether it be steroids, nebulization, or antimicrobial may be a contributing factor to an increase in the asthma mortality rate must be questioned and precisely studied."[9] Dr. Murray Peshkin makes an even stronger case: "Long-continued use of steroids should be recognized for what it is, namely, an admission of failure by the physician to control the patient's asthma syndrome through allergy practices; so the drug is used as the lesser of two evils."[10]

That kind of statement will probably make a lot of asthma patients very nervous. But don't rush to your medicine cabinet to throw out any **Cortisone**-type drugs you may have been taking. Anyone who has been on this kind of medication for any length of time can't just stop it cold turkey. You have literally become hooked, and it will take time for your body to readjust to the absence of these drugs. Your adrenal gland secretes its own **Cortisone**. When you ingest **Cortisone** in pill form, your own body ceases to manufacture it. If you suddenly stop taking your medication, your system will be left defenseless, since **Cortisone** is an essential biochemical for dealing with many natural problems. Slow withdrawal of the drug under a doctor's supervision is imperative. Gradual reduction of the dose over weeks or even months is necessary for safety's sake.

Well heck, what is an asthma patient to do if most of the **179** medications his doctor prescribes are dangerous and of questionable value? How about good old **Vitamin C**? Oh No! I can hear you groaning already. This guy really is a fanatic. It is true that there is not too much good evidence to support the claim that ascorbic acid will improve the symptoms of asthma sufferers, but there is some. For one thing, asthmatics often have decreased levels of ascorbic acid in their bloodstream.[11] One might conclude from this observation that asthma patients might require more Vitamin C than normal folks. Dr. Zuskin et al. noted in the *Journal of Allergy and Clinical Immunology* that ascorbic acid could diminish, if not prevent completely, the symptoms of byssinosis, a lung disease which strikes textile workers who breathe fiber dust.[12] The authors also stated in the same article, "Ascorbic acid can inhibit the airway constriction effect of histamine in healthy human subjects" and might be quite useful in the treatment of asthma without producing side effects. Their suggestion is that a patient ingest 250 milligrams every three hours throughout the day. Vitamin C is clearly not a cure or even a potent remedy, but it might help relieve some of the problems for a mild case of asthma.

There is, however, a relatively new development in the management of asthma which holds some light for real scientific benefit. **Cromolyn Sodium** (brand name: **Intal** or **Aarane**) offers a fresh approach for asthma treatment. It is a powder-type medication administered through an aerosol inhalator directly into the lungs much the same way the previously mentioned nebulizers are used. All similarity ends there. It cannot in any way relieve the symptoms of an ongoing asthmatic attack. What it *can* do, however, and this may be much more important in the long run, is prevent or reduce the chances of an asthmatic attack's occurring altogether. In other words, this drug may have prophylactic value. In a well-controlled study published in *Clinical Pediatrics*, it was observed that prior administration of **Cromolyn** produced slow and progressive improvement.[13] It decreased the need for other medications (specifically, cortisone-type drugs and aerosol bronchodilators). Patients had fewer asthmatic attacks and were able to exercise more freely. A general sense of increased well-being and improved bodily vigor was also noted. It is important to be aware of the fact that this medication does not start working immediately. It may take two to four weeks or even a few months before significant improvement is noted and fair evaluation can be made. But even more important, do not become complacent. Too many parents, doctors, and children take the treatment for granted and after a few months of success begin to reduce the number of inhalations performed each day. Instead of the recommended four puffs, the drug may be used only two or three times daily. Inhalations must be performed properly, so it is imperative that parents supervise their children's use of this medication at least until the correct technique becomes a learned behavior.

No one knows exactly how **Cromolyn** works. One possibility is that it protects or stabilizes the cells which contain histamine. In so doing, these cells are much less likely to react to something stressful. If no histamine is released, it is logical to assume that few, if any, asthma symptoms will occur. Hopefully, this form of asthma therapy will be able to withstand the test of time. Early enthusiasm often pales, though at the moment there does seem to be cautious optimism regarding **Cromolyn**. It may not be a miracle cure, but it does seem to provide solid improvement for a majority of patients. Although children seem to benefit more dramatically than adults, anyone under five years of age probably cannot master the skill required to self-administer the inhaler.

Are there any side effects associated with **Cromolyn** therapy? It is of course very difficult to predict what problems may show up after long-term use, especially in children. To date, the only apparent difficulties include an occasional rash or some temporary wheezing. One group of investigators reported no drug-induced toxic or allergic effects.[14] Very little of the drug appears to be absorbed by the body, and what is absorbed can be rapidly eliminated. At the moment it seems that the small risk is worth the therapeutic benefit. A 1974 *JAMA* editorial stated that half of the children on cortisone-type steroid medication could reduce their dosage 50 percent if they were using **Cromolyn**. An astounding 80 percent of these children responded favorably to this medical approach.[15] If your doctor has not yet tried this medication, you might want to suggest a trial course.

Another promising technique in the management of asthma involves self-regulation of medicine and dose. Obviously, it is hard to determine the effectiveness of any therapeutic regimen at any given moment. Thus it is impossible to determine whether a patient is receiving an adequate dose of drug or an excessive amount. However, it is now possible for patients to measure their own lung capacity. An instrument called the Wright Peak Expiratory Flow Meter is a "relatively simple apparatus, which almost anybody above the age of 4 or 5 years can learn to use reliably."[16] Just as more and more patients are being taught to take their own blood pressure at home so that they can regulate their medication schedule, so the asthmatic may employ this technique to "avoid both excessive and insufficient drug use."

Ultimately, biofeedback may hold the real solution to the asthma patient's problems. If we can learn to control our own brain waves and heart rate and blood pressure, why not our lungs? One doctor has already suggested that by using a simple stethoscope taped to an asthmatic patient's chest, the individual can "listen to the sound of his own breath while he is being taught a simple breathing exercise combined with meditation-relaxation procedure."[17] In this manner he might be able to "develop varying degrees of voluntary control over bronchial spasms." As crude as the technique may be, it seems worth a try. Hopefully, more precise biofeedback methods will be developed in the future.

The asthma patient must be constantly vigilant in his attempts to avoid things which will aggravate his condition. Pollutants, aerosol cans, noxious odors, and chemicals must be avoided at all costs, and that includes tobacco smoke. Any parent that smokes around an asthmatic child should be horsewhipped. All allergens which sensitize the individual must be removed from his evironment. One such allergen may be **Aspirin**. It is a little-known fact that 2.3–20 percent of the adult asthma population may be sensitive to **Aspirin**.[18] This group of patients should be considered "exceptionally prone" to an adverse reaction to this drug. Although the toxic response may manifest itself soon after **Aspirin** ingestion, it is more likely to be delayed a few hours. For this reason, the asthmatic may not associate his sudden attack of wheezing with anything in particular. The asthma patient who suspects sensitivity should be very wary. It is not easy to avoid the aspirin ingredient, acetylsalicylic acid, which is present in many pain relievers and even some arthritis medicines. Many foods contain salicylates either naturally (almonds, apples, peaches, etc.) or as an additive.[19] Cake mixes, snack foods, and many candies contain this product. It is best for an asthma victim to avoid all highly artificial sweets if he even thinks he might be allergic to **Aspirin**.

Asthma is a serious lung disease which requires expert attention. The patient should be reluctant to use a bronchodilator inhaler, even though it may provide prompt relief. It could prove to be a dangerous crutch in the long run if used more than sporadically. Drugs of the **Cortisone** variety (**Aristocort, Celestone, Decadron, Prednis, Prednisone**, etc.) should be withheld until all other approaches have been tried and have failed. Bacterial infections that affect the lungs should receive prompt treatment. Patients should improve their physical fitness through specially developed exercise programs that will not adversely influence their lungs. The Committee on Rehabilitation Therapy of the American Academy of Allergy recently reported that brief exercise of from one to two minutes can actually open up constricted lungs.[20] Such sports as swimming or baseball are highly recommended but any exercise that requires vigorous activity for prolonged periods of time will likely make the asthmatic's condition worse. Desensitization injections have produced conflicting results in controlled trials but must certainly be entertained when faced with severe asthma. With childhood asthma, psychological evaluation and counseling must be considered! According to Dr. Murray Peshkin,

> Psychotherapy should occupy not the last place in the line of therapeutic measures but rather the front of the therapeutic regimen, with the idea that steroid therapy may be avoided. It is our impression that if appropriate measures to decrease anxiety and tension and increase emotional security in children with asthma were initially and persistently carried out, it then could be reasonably assumed that the incidence of intractable asthma would drop appreciably and with it the use of steroid therapy.[21]

Ultimately, the single most important factor in asthma man- **183** agement is probably the physician. It is worth the time and effort to seek out a doctor who has the patience to make a careful and complete diagnosis, who undertakes drug therapy conservatively, and who communicates frankly with his patients.

References

1. Altman, L. K. "Asthma Deaths Laid to Overdose of Drug." New York *Times*, July 23, 1972. P. 1.
2. Greenberg, M. J., and Pines, A. "Pressurized Aerosols in Asthma." *Brit. Med. J.* 1:563, 1967.
3. Halpern, S. R. Editorial: "Management of Childhood Asthma." *JAMA* 229:819, 1974.
4. Altman, op. cit.
5. Caplin, Irvin, and Haynes, J. T. "Complications of Aerosol Therapy in Asthma." *Annals of Aller.* 27:659, 1969.
6. Guideri, Giancarlo, et al. "Extraordinary Potentiation of Isoproterenol Cardiotoxicity by Corticoid Pretreatment." *Cardiovas. Res.* 8:775–786, 1974.
7. Fontana, Vincent J., and Ferrara, Angelo. "Corticosteroid Therapy in Asthma." *J. of Aller.* 41:58–59, 1968.
8. Brown, Earl B. "Reply to Corticosteroid Therapy in Asthma." *J. of Aller.* 41:60, 1968.
9. Fontana, Vincent J. "Statistics, Mortality, and Asthma." *J. of Asthma Research* 8:91–93, 1971.
10. Peshkin, Murray M. "Deaths of Institutionalized Children with Intractable Asthma." *J. of Asthma Research* 8:928, 1970.
11. Goldsmith, G. A., et al. "Vitamin C (Ascorbic Acid) Nutrition in Bronchial Asthma." *Arch of Int. Med.* 67:597–608, 1941.
12. Zuskin, E., et al. "Inhibition of Histamine-Induced Airway Constriction by Ascorbic Acid." *J. Aller. Clin Immunol.* 51:218–226, 1973.
13. Lecks, Harold I. "Clinical Experience with the Use of Cromolyn Sodium in Asthmatic Children." *Clin. Ped.* 13:420–425, 1974.
14. Smith, John Morrison, and Pizarro, Yvonne A. "Observations on the Safety of Disodium Cromoglycate in Long-Term Use in Children." *Clin. Aller.* 2:143–151, 1972.
15. Editorial: "Management of Childhood Asthma." *JAMA* 229:819–820, 1974.

16. Falliers, Constantine J. "Self-Measurement for Asthma." *JAMA* 230:537–538, 1974.
17. Abdullah, Syed. "Biofeedback for Asthmatic Patients." *New Engl. J. Med.* 291:1037, 1974.
18. Falliers, Constantine J. "Aspirin and Subtypes of Asthma: Risk Factor Analysis." *J. Aller. Clin. Immunol.* 52:141–147, 1973.
19. Noid, H. Earleen, Schylze, Tom W., and Winkelmann, Richard K. "Diet Plan for Patients with Salicylate-Induced Urticaria." *Arch. Dermatol.* 109:866–869, 1974.
20. "Asthmatic Children Benefit From Intermittent Exercise." *JAMA* 231:1017–1018, 1975.
21. Peshkin, op. cit.

9.
Contraception:
The Pill, the IUD, and Vasectomy

So you don't want to make a baby. What you *do* want is a simple, safe, and effective means of contraception. You have heard an awful lot about the side effects of birth control pills, but what is myth and what is real? Even the intrauterine device, or IUD, has come under fire in recent years. Doctors either do not know or will not tell the whole story, which means that many women are caught somewhere between a rock and a hard place. Everyone wants an uncomplicated, sure method of birth control, but at the same time they want to know the risks that may be involved. Informed consent is an established requirement for *any* form of medical treatment and certainly should hold true for prescribed contraceptives, yet we hear time after time about the paucity of information which is provided to women on the Pill or the IUD. Not all doctors do complete medical examinations or take detailed medical histories. Rarely does the patient receive relevant information regarding recent discoveries. Isn't it time you learned the facts?

How do you choose your contraceptive? First, its gotta work. If you check out the little quote on the back of your toothpaste tube (**Colgate** and **Crest**), you will find that the American Dental Association stresses three words: "When used in a *conscientiously applied program.*" Same thing holds true for your contraceptive. If you are sloppy or forgetful, whatever you use will not work as well as it should. Statistics on birth control vary notoriously from one organization to another. Nevertheless, they do provide a reasonably objective means for comparing relative effectiveness of the various forms of contraceptives available. The Office of Student Services of the University of Michigan has listed the following figures in terms of pregnancies per hundred woman-years. That is a snazzy way of saying what percentage of women may become pregnant over the course of one year using each of the following techniques:

EFFECTIVENESS OF VARIOUS CONTRACEPTIVE TECHNIQUES

CONTRACEPTIVE	PREGNANCIES PER 100 WOMAN-YEARS
The Pill	0.05
Condom *and* Foam	0.1–5.0
IUD	1.5–8.0
Condom Alone	5–20
Diaphragm	10–20
Vaginal Spermicides	15–25
Rhythm Method	15–30
Withdrawal	20–30
Nothing At All	40

187

Clearly, the Pill is by far the most reliable method of birth control. While a condom and foam used together are equally as effective as the IUD, some people object to the fuss, muss, and bother. That leaves birth control pills and intrauterine devices as the contraceptives most dependable and most widely accepted. What do we know about them?

The Pill

(Demulen, Enovid, Loestrin, Micronor, Norinyl, Norlestrin, Nor-QD, Oracon, Ortho-Novum, Ovral, Ovulen)

Oral contraceptives have been available in this country since 1960. This form of birth control represented a revolutionary breakthrough for effective family planning. Today, well over eight million American women use the Pill, because it works and because it is essentially hassle-free. Nevertheless, a cloud of controversy has followed this drug ever since it was introduced. The moral issue reared its ugly head. Nervous nellies feared that the youth of America would all become sex-crazed. The medical issue was not without its own problems. Doctors and patients alike recognized that "minor" disturbances were a price that had to be paid for the convenience of this form of birth control. Many women taking The Pill have encountered such side effects as stomach cramps, nausea, vomiting, headaches, breakthrough bleeding, breast tenderness and enlargement, irregular menstrual flow, and weight gain due to fluid accumulation (*edema*). These complaints are not considered serious, and vast numbers of women are willing to grin and bear them. What is more insidious and alarming is the fact that many more serious side effects seem to keep cropping up. The majority of these adverse reactions were not known or suspected back in 1960, or even five years ago for that matter, which raises an important question: Is it possible that there are other, even more severe complications lurking around that have not yet been discovered?

There ain't no doubt that the Pill makes the blood clot faster, so that women using oral contraceptives are more likely to come down with nasty things like thrombophlebitis and pulmonary embolism.[1-6] Thrombophlebitis is a painful irritation of a vein, usually in the leg, caused by the formation of a blood clot. You may recall that Richard Milhous Nixon suffered from this affliction. A pulmonary embolism occurs when a clot breaks loose from some other part of the body and lodges in the lungs.

As scary as these side effects may be, they do not compare with the recent discovery that women taking birth control pills are more likely to come down with a heart attack than women who use some other form of contraception. This could be due to a clot lodging in a main artery of the heart. It was not until 1975 that two British medical groups uncovered evidence demonstrating that the risk of heart attack is almost three times higher for women aged thirty to thirty-nine and more than five times higher for women over forty.[7,8] If one were to add in other risk factors, such as cigarette smoking, diabetes, high blood pressure or obesity it has been calculated that a woman could be over seventy times more susceptible to a heart attack if she was also on the Pill. Thus it is felt that oral contraceptives actually interact with other risk factors to dramatically increase the possibility of serious side effects.[9]

As a result of the work done in England, and following a recommendation put forth by their own expert advisory committee, the United States Food and Drug Administration decided to urge women over forty to use some other method of contraception. Does that mean that women under forty are safe? Not by a long shot. Just because the FDA decided to warn women over forty, it should not be assumed that everyone else is safe.

Another serious new development in the story of the Pill is its apparent potential for causing stroke. In 1973 it was first learned that women who take oral contraceptives are nine times more likely to suffer a stroke than women who do not.[10] The investigation which uncovered this information was undertaken by neurologists in 12 cities and included almost six hundred women, in ninety-one hospitals, between the ages of fifteen and forty-four—a comprehensive study. A stroke, which is usually caused by a blood clot's lodging in one of the major arteries of the brain, could lead to paralysis, speech im- *189* pairment, blindness, or death. Since it is rare for young women to develop this disastrous condition, it is surprising that young women on the Pill are more vulnerable to stroke than older women. The written word cannot begin to convey the terrible personal tragedy that results from a stroke, especially for a person with a family and a life which should be full and healthy.

A follow-up report published in 1975 confirmed the conclusions of the first study.[11] It was also discovered that a woman with moderate to severe high blood pressure also has a greatly increased chance of coming down with a stroke. Such a person, if she uses the Pill, would be twenty-five times more likely to be struck down than a person with normal blood pressure who does not use the Pill. Doctors have not yet decided for sure whether birth control pills themselves increase blood pressure, but there are enough reports floating around to indicate that it is a good possibility. One careful British study completed in 1974 observed that the rise in blood pressure could be considerable.[12] It is possible that a woman on the Pill could be hit with a double whammy. Her drug may raise her pressure, which in turn may make the already existing possibility of stroke more likely. The doctors representing the Collaborative Group for the Study of Stroke in Young Women concluded:

> ... we believe that oral contraceptives should not be used by women with any degree of high blood pressure. Our data also suggests that the use of oral contraceptives and heavy smoking interact to increase the risk of hemorrhagic stroke.... On the basis of information derived from other studies ... oral contraceptives should not be used by women with classical or complicated migraine nor by women whose headache symptoms are aggravated by the use of these medications.[11]

Twenty-three million Americans suffer from some degree of high blood pressure. Countless millions more smoke like fiends. It is fair to assume that thousands of hypertensive

190

women are literally taking their lives in their hands by using this form of contraception.

Well, exactly what are the risks? How do you convert abstract illnesses into understandable reality? Dr. Martin P. Vessey, a famous British researcher, has estimated that a young woman has only one chance in ten thousand of developing a stroke while using The Pill.[13] That sounds like pretty good odds—hardly even cause for alarm. But if you figure there are eight million users, it might be expected that anywhere from five hundred to eight hundred young women each year will develop this grave illness in the United States alone. Over a ten-year period, as many as eight thousand women could be struck down. In point of fact, there have already been thousands of law suits filed about which the public has heard virtually nothing. One report has it that "A San Jose grand jury has awarded $1,248,000 to a young California woman totally blinded by blood clots caused by birth control pills. It was the largest award on public record against a manufacturer of the pills."[14] Even if it is difficult to learn exactly how many women have experienced serious clotting disorders, there is no doubt that this is an alarming problem which has been often underestimated.

Black women may be particularly susceptible to the danger of blood clots if they use birth control pills. Women with sickle cell anemia or sickle cell trait (8–11 percent of black people in the United States have this genetic trait) are the ones at risk. There is a paradox with the less severe form of this disease. A person with sickle cell trait may remain free of any symptoms most of his or her life, but once an attack occurs it can snowball. As sickling occurs, the blood gets "thicker," and this could lead to "log-jamming" of cells in small blood vessels. This in turn cuts down on oxygen delivery and leads to increased sickling. Oral contraceptives may potentiate or even trigger such an attack. In 1967, Roy Haynes and James Dunn reported three cases of black women who developed blood clots in the lung after using birth control pills.[15] One twenty-six-year-old woman with sickle cell trait had never had any *191* clotting problems until eight months after she started using an oral contraceptive (**Enovid**). At that time she showed up in the hospital with fever, chest pain, and a cough, which proved to be symptoms of a blood clot in her left lung. After two weeks she was sent home and resumed taking her birth control pills. Two months later she was back again, this time with a clot in the right lung. When that was cured, she was again sent home but was cautioned to stay off the Pill for about ten months. Exactly eleven months later, one month after she started taking the drug again, she was hit with another serious clot in the left lung. This time she needed intensive care with blood transfusions and antibiotics. Once cured, her doctor discontinued oral contraceptives for good and inserted an IUD. She experienced no further problems.

Another investigator, Dr. Jonathan Greenwald, reported an unusual stroke in a young black woman who had sickle cell trait and was taking oral contraceptives.[16] Dr. Greenwald concluded that any black woman who considers using oral contraceptives should first have a blood test for sickle cell disease. If the laboratory findings are positive for sickle cell trait or disease, "alternative contraceptive methods must be given strong consideration."

Should we just throw our hands up in despair and give in to things like thrombophlebitis and stroke, or is there something we can do about these dreadful clotting disorders? It has already been noted that women who use the Pill have a diminished level of **Vitamin C** in their bodies. Some women have been reported to have as much as 30–50 percent less of this crucial vitamin in their bloodstream when they use oral contraceptives.[17] Quite conceivably these drugs cause ascorbic acid to be metabolized faster than it normally would be. According to one physician, "It is possible that some of the reported side-effects of the pill may be a consequence of this vitamin lack."[18] It may just be that by increasing your daily intake of Vitamin C you could reduce the chances of developing blood clots. While clearly this is only an experimental approach, there is little harm in trying ascorbid acid.

An even more exciting possibility can be proposed. Investigators have recently discovered that simple aspirin may help prevent blood clotting. The National Heart and Lung Institute has recently initiated a major study to test the theory that aspirin may avert heart attacks. If such is the case, there is good reason to believe that one or two aspirin tablets per day could reduce the incidence of clotting disorders associated with oral contraceptives.

Okay, let's face it, thrombophlebitis, pulmonary embolism, and stroke are some of the risks associated with The Pill. But just as millions gamble on the relationship between cigarette smoking and cancer, millions are willing to gamble that the Pill won't thus affect them. What about cancer, however? Do oral contraceptives increase a woman's likelihood of developing this dread disease? Reports in the press have been contradictory. Some say the Pill reduces the incidence of cancer, while others claim that it magnifies the risk. Well, what is the truth?

Unfortunately, as is the case with almost everything in medical science, there is no one Truth. Whenever you deal with a controversial issue, especially one as volatile as that of the Pill, there are bound to be conflicting research accounts. Add to that the fact that millions, perhaps hundreds of millions, of dollars are involved, and doctors are scared that they could set off a panic.

Most of the attention has been directed to the problem of breast cancer. This is certainly understandable since it is such a common and dangerous form of cancer. Unfortunately, it has taken attention away from other possible problem spots, but we will touch on them later. Many investigators have reported unequivically that oral contraceptives do not lead to an increase in the number of cases of breast cancer, and some doctors have even reported that women who use the Pill are *less* likely to come down with this disease.[19-22] While it is quite possible that birth control pills do not lead to breast cancer in the typical user, research by Dr. Maurice Black, professor of pathology at New York Medical College, seems to indicate that not everyone is safe. He discovered that women who have never borne children or who had no children before they were twenty-seven years of age were more likely to develop breast cancer if they used oral contraceptives.[23] However, women who have an early pregnancy may be less likely to come down with breast cancer if they use the Pill. At least for **193** the moment, it would seem that the danger of breast cancer is not great for most women using this method of birth control.

This should not allow us to rest easy. Birth control pills affect the whole body, not just the tissue of the breast. Something which is not widely known or publicized by the medical profession is the fact that oral contraceptives modify the tissues of a woman's reproductive tract, specifically the cervix and the lining of the uterus. There is no longer any doubt that the Pill causes an abnormal or unusual increase in the cells of these important organs. These changes are often described in the medical literature as *hyperplasia*. They are caused by both the usual estrogen-progesterone pills and the newer progestin or "mini pill" (**Micronor** and **Nor-Q.D.**) contraceptives.[24-29]

The modifications, or overgrowth, in tissue structure which these drugs seem to produce, although quite disturbing, are hard to evaluate. Most pathologists do not like what they see under the microscope, but they are careful not to make any frightening statements. Although phrases like "may be mistaken for cancer" or appears to be similar to adenocarcinoma [a cancerous growth]", keep cropping up, no one has yet reached for the panic button.

It has long been known that estrogen, the hormone which is found in most birth control pills, could lead to cancer in animals. As far back as 1957, Meissner and his associates were able to produce cancer (specifically adenocarcinoma) in the uterine tissue of rabbits.[30] Other doctors have found that certain precancerous changes and even some human cancers seemed to be caused by the hormones found in birth control pills.[31,32]

It was not until November 1975 however, that the first report of a direct association between oral contraceptives and uterine cancer appeared in the medical literature. Dr. Steven Silverberg and Dr. Edgar Makowski announced that they had discovered twenty-one cases of endometrial carcinoma (cancer of the uterine lining) in women who had been taking birth control pills.[33] Their report shook the medical profession to its foundation.

Once the smoke cleared, the Food and Drug Administration decided that it was time to review the whole situation. Most of the blame was directed at the sequential type of oral contraceptives, specifically **Oracon, Ortho-Novum SQ**, and **Norquen**. An FDA advisory committee recommended that the package labels be changed to include a strong warning that this type of pill is less effective and less safe than other oral contraceptives.

While most of the attention has been directed at the sequential type of birth control pills, it has not been established that the more frequently prescribed products known as combination oral contraceptives do not also pose a risk of cancer. Two cases of endometrial carcinoma were associated with this class of pill. With only one research report to go on, no one knows the actual potential for risk, but you can be sure that we have not heard the end of this story.

Also made public in 1975 were statistics from the California Tumor Registry. It was reported that uterine cancer had increased by a horrifying thirty-five percent among affluent white women living in the San Francisco Bay Area. Similar data is expected to be obtained from Los Angeles. The increase, particularly noticeable in women over the age of fifty, was believed to be related to the use of postmenopausal estrogens. It has become quite the fad in recent years for women past menopause to take hormone replacements. Long term evaluation of such treatment, however, appears to be lacking.

DES (Diethylstilbestrol) was one of the first synthetic estrogens developed. It is currently being used as a morning-after pill so that a woman can prevent pregnancy *after* intercourse. This drug has been held responsible for the production of cancer in the genital tracts of young women.[34,35] Although **DES** has already been discussed in detail (see Chapter 3), one additional point must be made. Although there have "only" been 170 cases of cancer reported so far, there has been an extremely high incidence of cervical tissue abnormalities found in young women who had prenatal exposure to **DES**. Dr. Arthur Herbst revealed in a 1975 report that of 133 young women examined, 84 percent manifested some degree of cervical or vaginal pathology generally in the form of "biopsy-proved erosion."[36] Are the effects of **DES** so very different from those of other oral contraceptives? A similar 84 percent incidence of cervical abnormality was discovered in *195* women taking "regular" birth control pills at a family planning clinic in Fort Belvoir, Virgina.[37] No one knows if these hormone-induced cervical changes will ever go on to become cancerous. It is the million-dollar question. Dr. Herbst has used a lot of medical mumbo jumbo to imply that **DES** induced changes could "provide the base from which these adenocarcinomas develop."[38] That is still speculation and cannot be supported by any real direct evidence. It makes me very nervous, and it probably makes a lot of doctors nervous, even though they rarely admit it.

We do not know how many years it could take for any potential cancers to become real cancers. In one case, prenatal exposure to **DES** did not provoke cancer until twenty-nine years later.[39] Dr. Herbst himself admits that it could be many years before we have a good idea of the true risk for **DES**-exposed women. That could just as easily hold true for birth control pills.

Where does this leave the woman who is taking the Pill? Is it possible to translate all this into something that people can understand? Well, even if there is no danger of developing cancer of the cervix or uterus (that is not a given), it is hardly reassuring to know that tissue abnormalities in these organs are a frequent side effect after prolonged use of oral contraceptives. That still does not answer the question, Do oral contraceptives increase a person's likelihood of developing cancer? Maybe they don't, but then again maybe we are sitting on top of a giant time bomb. Let's just say that the final word is not yet in. It would be wise to pay close attention to any and all medical reports which are sure to be published in future years.

So far, it has been established that birth control pills can cause blood-clotting disorders in the form of thrombophlebitis, pulmonary embolism, heart attack, and stroke. There have also been reports that abnormal cellular changes, which may or may not be related to later cancer development, occur in the lining of women's reproductive tracts. A new discovery must now be added to this growing list of adverse reactions. In the February 3, 1975, issue of *JAMA*, it was announced that some women who had been using the Pill had **196** been found to have liver tumors:

Concern is mounting over the possible relationship between oral contraceptives and benign primary liver tumors
that sometimes rupture with subsequent life-threatening
hemorrhage. Such patients may turn up in emergency
rooms.[40]

You would think that something as significant as a liver
tumor would have been discovered a long time ago. However,
the first report to implicate birth control pills as the causative
agent was not published until 1973. Dr. Janet Baum had observed seven cases of benign liver tumors in women on oral
contraceptives. She was very cautious in the way she presented
her information but it was impossible for her not to draw the
conclusion that the drugs were responsible.[41] Since that first
report, additional cases have been discovered.[42] According to
one doctor, "Cases are popping up all over the country and in
Europe now. But the exact incidence will not be known for
some time."[43] How interesting that until now "primary liver
tumors" in young women, like stroke, had been considered
rare! In the last two years almost as many cases have been announced as in all the medical literature since 1913.[44] Already
over fifty cases have been reported in a relatively short period
of time, and it is likely that the number will jump dramatically
as doctors begin to realize that this problem exists.

Dr. E. Truman Mays, professor of surgery at the University
of Kentucky College of Medicine, believes that many doctors
do not report cases of abdominal hemorrhaging because they
assume it is due to something "routine" like a ruptured ulcer,
ovary troubles, or a spleen misfunction. Few doctors apparently consider liver involvement in a young woman who has
internal bleeding. However, Dr. Mays stressed that "within the
last few years we have encountered many young women . . . who have had tumors in the liver—a few malignant."
Dr. Mays goes on to make a very disquieting point:

We don't know the number of women who have died with
these liver tumors undiagnosed. It is probably not as rare
as one might think. It might be called something else at
first, as I have indicated. Even I called them something
else at first. There are still many unknowns.[45]

It appears that these tumors, which do not show up in
routine liver tests, may be caused by any of the various birth
control pills on the market. It also seems that the tumors ap- *197*

pear after any length of time and are not restricted to long-term users of these drugs. One woman developed symptoms after only six months on oral contraceptives.[46]

Liver tumors are news, but it is nothing new that The Pill could damage a woman's liver. It has long been realized that oral contraceptives can cause liver enlargement and increase the level of liver enzymes. Between 10 percent and 40 percent of women using the Pill may suffer some degree of cellular malfunction. There could be a decreased flow of bile, and too many women experience jaundice.

It is a good bet that your doctor has not mentioned any of the side effects we have just listed. Has he mentioned the following problem?

> Women of childbearing age who used Oral Contraceptives appeared to be twice as likely to have gallbladder disease as women of similar age who were non-users.[47]

That observation was made after a far-reaching investigation by the Boston Collaborative Drug Surveillance Program.[48] In a follow-up study the same group of researchers found that older women (forty-five to sixty-nine years of age) who received estrogen replacement pills, like **Premarin**, also suffered an increased incidence of gallbladder disease. These women, who had taken hormones for menopausal and post-menopausal symptoms, apparently encountered a risk two and a half times as great as women who had not received these drugs. This might serve as a cautionary note to women who are anxious to jump on the hormone replacement bandwagon.

What's a woman supposed to do? The Pill works. It is nice and neat—no fuss, no bother. That such things as strokes, liver tumors, heart attacks, pulmonary embolisms, high blood pressure, uterine cancer, and gallbladder disease have only become apparent in the last few years makes one wonder if other nasty surprises are in store. An editorial published in the January 22, 1976 issue of *The New England Journal of Medicine* made the following points about birth control pills and estrogen replacement therapy:

> These facts raise serious questions concerning the *rationale* or use of such drugs. Birth control pills are to prevent conception, and estrogens are given to ease the symptoms of menopause. Neither drug is given to treat a

disease, but rather to alter normal homeostasis to produce a desired effect. . .The levels of the exogenous estrogen-progesterone preparations are higher than normally occurs in estrous cycle, and the periodic oscillations of the natural hormones are lost. In short, the pill abolishes the normal cycle, distorts metabolism and causes serious diseases in some users.

The question is how to achieve birth control. There is no doubt that the pill is effective. However, it is a double-edged sword; it prevents ovulation but produces diseases. Certainly, other methods of birth control are now available to both sexes. The whole question of the use of drugs to alter normal metabolism must be raised. Drugs have an established role in the treatment of disease. But should they be used to abolish the normal estrous cycle or to change postmenopausal physiology?[49]

No one really knows whether the adverse reactions which have been reported will affect more than a handful of the eight million users of these drugs. There are no easy answers. I personally would not use this drug if I were a woman. I advise my friends to think twice before they use oral contraceptives. But women should not be discouraged from using birth control pills. Rather, they should be informed of *all* the potentially serious side effects. Too few doctors are willing to give this kind of information to their patients. Each woman must weigh all the evidence and then decide what is right for her.

THE INTRAUTERINE DEVICE (IUD)

(Copper 7, Dalkon Shield, Lippes Loop, Saf-T-Coil)

Next to the Pill, the IUD is probably the single most effective contraceptive method available today. By the end of 1970 as many as twelve million women around the world had received one. According to the Food and Drug Administration, it is currently being used by between four and six million in the United States alone. What do we know about this form of family planning?

The intrauterine device is as old as the hills. Rumor has it that Arab nomads, not wishing to have their female camels become pregnant while crossing the deserts, would insert small stones into the uteruses of the animals in order to prevent pregnancy. Our modern plastic device is not so very different. It acts much like a wrench thrown into a gear box in order to clog the machinery. Now that may seem like a crude analogy but, amazing as it may seem, no one knows exactly how the darned things *do* work. The most frequently cited theory has it that the IUD causes a minor but persistent irritation in the uterus. This local inflammatory reaction is thought to prevent pregnancy by interfering with implantation of the fertilized egg.

There is no doubt that the intrauterine device has certain advantages. Since it is not a chemical contraceptive there is no pill-taking and no interference with the body's hormonal rhythm. Once in place, it can theoretically be ignored, thus requiring no preplay preparation as in the case of the diaphragm or foam. The FDA has given it high marks for effectiveness, rating the IUD 95 percent successful in preventing pregnancy. This form of contraception is relatively inexpensive, except for the one-shot medical visit necessary for proper placement. If a woman has one inserted after a pregnancy, it will not interfere with her production of milk, so she can nurse her child and at the same time be protected from another pregnancy; oral contraceptives on the other hand, may affect the production of milk in as many as 33 percent of all mothers who use them, and adversely affect the baby. Finally, if the IUD is removed, a woman who decides to become pregnant should be able to do so without any trouble. This is not always the case with the Pill. In fact, a number of women find it impossible to conceive after having used birth control pills. Given this sort of information, it would seem that the IUD is an ideal method of contraception.

But is it safe? Do its advantages outweigh its disadvantages? This is a tough question, but recent information and research indicate that the risks of the IUD could be much greater than anyone ever anticipated. Extrapolating from statistics provided by the ad hoc Obstetric-Gynecology Advisory Committee of the Food and Drug Administration, 15,000–50,000 women could be hospitalized each year because of IUD-induced problems.[50] In 1973 the Center for Disease Control, with help from the American Medical Association and the American Osteopathic Association, estimated that 7,900 women had been hospitalized in only six months because of IUD-related illness. That makes over 15,000 cases in that year alone.

In May, 1974, the A. H. Robins Company, makers of the **Dalkon Shield**, notified the public and the medical profession that 36 women had become pregnant while their device was in place, developed septicemia (blood poisoning), and subsequently miscarried. These spontaneous septic abortions apparently resulted because bacteria had entered the uterus. Of the 36 women who had experienced this reaction, 4 died. Since that time the death toll has risen rapidly as doctors began reporting their tragedies. Only five months later it was reported to the FDA that the **Dalkon Shield** might be held responsible for 219 infected pregnancies and 13 deaths.[51] It is estimated that perhaps as many as 2 million American women are currently using this particular IUD. As the controversy surrounding this device mounted, the FDA decided to withdraw it from the market. But then, almost immediately (December, 1974), the FDA decided to make it available again "under a tightly controlled distribution and reporting system." An effort was made to attribute most of the problems seen with the **Dalkon Shield** to the special characteristics of its tail (a plastic thread used to determine if the IUD is in place and to facilitate removal).[52] However, a committee of the Food and Drug Administration admitted that any differences which existed were unlikely to account for all the problems.

Contrary to medical and popular opinion, the **Dalkon Shield** is not the only IUD which has come under attack. As of October 25, 1974, the FDA had compiled data which implicated another IUD, the **Lippes Loop**. This agent has been associated with 17 deaths and 50 infected miscarriages, while the **Saf-T-Coil**, yet another popular product, was implicated in 4 deaths and 14 septic abortions. On December 20, 1974, the U.S. Department of Health, Education, and Welfare released a news article which stated, "The total number of recorded septic abortions associated with IUD use is 287." At least 39 **201** young woman had died, apparently because of their IUD. It seems likely that these figures will increase as more and more doctors begin adding their horror stories to the mounting list.

Why are women developing pelvic infections with an IUD in place? Why are women getting pregnant with the IUD in place? Why are women developing blood poisoning and having septic abortions with the IUD in place? Why are women dying with the IUD in place? What the hell is going on? Remember how no one *really* knows how the IUD is supposed to work? Well, maybe there is an explanation for this whole messy situation.

A few years ago, Dr. William J. Ledger, working in the Department of Obstetrics and Gynecology at the University of Michigan, was doing basic research on rabits in order to determine the antifertility mechanisms of the intrauterine device. In an unpublished study supported by a Population Council grant, Dr. Ledger discovered bacteria growing in the uteruses of rabbits which had been implanted with a large foreign body (essentially an IUD). The organisms were sensitive to penicillin and streptomycin. Dr. Ledger and his associate, Dr. Suhasini Dikshit, concluded: "a local uterine infection can play a role in the mechanism preventing implantation when a large uterine foreign body is utilized in the rabbit."[53]

Dynamite! It has always been assumed that the contraceptive effect of the IUD stemmed from some amorphous irritation or local inflammation in the wall of the uterus. Could it be that a very small, otherwise undetectable local *infection* also contributes to this birth control mechanism? Could that infection sometimes get out of hand?

If one of the ways that an IUD works is by setting up a little old infection, what would happen if you gave an antibiotic and effectively wiped out that infection? You might expect that the IUD would not work so well. When Dr. Ledger did that, he found something which surprised him quite a bit. Female rabbits given a healthy dose of antibiotics after intercourse were less protected than they normally would have been. Somehow the antibiotic was inhibiting, or actually counteracting, the contraceptive action of the bunny IUD. Dr. T. R. Wrenn also found that antibiotics could wipe out the antifertility effects of an IUD-like device in rats.[54] It seems logical to assume from these limited animal experiments that local inflammation is not the only mechanism that makes the IUD work. A limited infection within the uterus could also help prevent implantation of a fertilized egg. Take an antibiotic and you wipe out the infection. Wipe out the infection and you wipe out the contraceptive effect. Wipe out the contraceptive effect and you're pregnant.

Rats and rabbits are not people. How can we tell whether or not an infectious process is part of the mechanism by which the IUD works in humans? Well, so far we don't know, but Dr. Ledger made a startling observation with regard to this point. During the course of his rabbit study he encountered a number of women who had become pregnant with an IUD in place. The pregnancies had coincided with the administration of antibiotics given for such unrelated problems as kidney infections. Dr. Ledger himself admits that these random clinical observations were without statistical validity. Nevertheless, one can't help wondering whether or not some drugs, particularly antibiotics, could inhibit the protective action of the IUD and thus lead to an unwanted and dangerous pregnancy. Whatever it is that causes some women to become pregnant while using an intrauterine device, we know that this is an extremely hazardous situation. If the device is not removed quickly and carefully, such pregnancies could lead to life-threatening septic abortions.

As of March, 1975, it was known that forty women had died and thousands had been hospitalized because of severe uterine infections. It would be nice if the FDA and the medical profession would find out what is actually happening. In December, 1974, the Food and Drug Administration came out with the following statement:

> The ad hoc obstetric-gynecology advisory committee cannot make final recommendations concerning various IUD's because sufficient data are not yet available. Nevertheless, it is our considered opinion that the admittedly limited data suggest that certain serious hazards to IUD use may exist.[55]

It is shocking that there is still so little known. The IUD has been used since 1962 and has been inserted into millions and millions of women. We do not know whether or not antibiotics can cancel out the contraceptive action of the IUD. We do not know if any other drugs can. We do not know why women occasionally get pregnant with an IUD in place, and we do not know why they develop dangerous infections. These questions must be answered. Otherwise, women will continue to develop pelvic infections or complicated pregnancies, and some will die.

So far we have documented the really scary side effects which might be encountered with the IUD. There are a number of other, less serious, complaints which must also be considered.

For some women, introduction of the device into the uterus can be a painful and dangerous experience. A 1974 article in the *American Journal* of *Obstetrics* and *Gynecology* has indicated that the preparatory procedure and actual IUD insertion can cause dramatic changes in a woman's heart beat.[56] Of twenty-five women who were studied, more than half had slowing of the heart rate and some encountered sudden declines in blood pressure. This was associated with dangerous rhythm disturbances. For someone with heart disease, insertion of an IUD could be a hazardous procedure.

Dr. C. D. Williams of the Aspen Clinic in Colorado had this to say about IUD placement:

> In women who have not had a full-term pregnancy, I've removed two of every three devices I've inserted. There is a certain amount of pain and discomfort on insertion; the woman is very often incapacitated for twenty-four to forty-eight hours; and then there's the possibility of rejection or infection. I'd say I've had about ten percent of my cases end with infection."[57]

Dr. Williams's observations may not be typical, but it is clear that serious pelvic infections are a real problem. Writing in the *International Journal of Fertility* (1973), Ira M. Golditch and his associates stated that, "The frequently insidious onset of IUD-associated infection necessitates early recognition and prompt remedial action."[58] These physicians found that the early warning signs of infections were irregular spotting, mucus-type discharges from the vagina, and an unpleasant odor.

204 Other unpleasant possibilities associated with this form of contraception include increased menstrual flow. Periods may be irregular, sometimes accompanied by profuse bleeding which could last longer than usual. Some medical experts have recommended frequent hemoglobin testing so that anemia can be detected and iron pills added to a woman's daily vitamin intake. Break-through bleeding (between menstrual periods) has also been known to occur. Some women even experience cramps which put them out of commission for a couple of days. Occasionally, a woman goes in to have her IUD removed and the doctor can't get the darned thing out. This is a particular problem for those devices which are promoted for their high retention rate. Fortunately, there are no longer many around.

It is disquieting to learn that there have been recalls of many early IUDs. Many of these models were health hazards. The **Majzlin Spring** was one device particularly prone to problems. Because of the possibility of intestinal obstruction, the **Butterfly**, the **Birenberg Bow**, and the **Inhiband** have been eliminated from the medical market place.

It is hard to say whether the advantages of the IUD outweigh the disadvantages. Certainly it is an important method of birth control, but the adverse reactions which have been discovered in recent years lead one to conclude that it may not be the ideal form of contraception originally anticipated. Since failures do occasionally occur, any woman who becomes pregnant with an IUD in place should immediately seek expert medical attention.

Vasectomy

Why should women bear the responsibility of contraception, especially if there are so many problems associated with The Pill and the IUD? Unfortunately, much less attention has been paid to male contraception by reproductive physiologists and by drug companies. Some of the birth control pills which have been developed for men have proved unsatisfactory because **205** they reduce sexual desire and occasionally produce female characteristics, such as breast enlargement. There has been some talk that ordinary aspirin might hold some hope for reducing male fertility, but that has not been adequately investigated. To date, the only effective male techniques of birth control remain the condom or the vasectomy. Since the condom (prophylactic, rubber, sheath, skin, etc.) depends to a great extent upon the motivation of the user in order to be effective, its batting average is not as good as other forms of contraception. That is not to say that it can't be highly successful, just that many men do not use the device as carefully as they should. That leaves vasectomy as the only sure male birth control method.

Vasectomy is a simple surgical technique which can be performed in a short period of time under local anesthesia in a clinic or doctor's office. It involves the cutting and tying off of the tubes which carry sperm. The Planned Parenthood Association rates it a low-risk, highly successful approach to family planning. Theoretically, there is no hormonal disturbance and no reduction in sexual appetite. But, as is the case with the Pill and the IUD, there are still some questions which have not yet been fully answered.

One of the biggest drawbacks to widespread acceptance of sterilization is its permanence. Men are told that the operation is nonreversible and that restoration of fertility is practically impossible. Doctors in India, however, have quite a different story. They claim that a new surgical technique allows them to undo the vasectomies of a sizable number of patients. After selecting twenty patients that had favorable qualifications, one group claimed that they were able to recanalize 90 percent successfully.[59] This high rate of accomplishment may be due to the fact that only those patients with good surgical potential were accepted. Nevertheless, the doctors make the point that if vasectomies were carried out with an eye to the future, surgical restoration could be made much easier. Of course successful surgical restoration does not mean that pregnancy will result, but the chances are greatly improved.

Even if it were possible to remove the disadvantage of permanence, can vasectomy be considered a safe and simple procedure? Over the last few years, mounting evidence has caused the bright image of this operation to be tarnished. For one thing, psychological disturbances have been observed in some patients after vasectomy.[60,61] There have been complaints of insomnia, anxiety, and pain, sometimes accompanied by weight loss.[62] These symptoms may well by psychosomatic in nature, but that does not make them any less real for the sufferer. Unexplained cases of blood clotting, specifically thrombophlebitis, have also been reported.[63,64] Since symptoms may not appear for a long time after the operation, it is difficult, if not impossible, for the patient to determine whether his thrombophlebitis is related to his operation. One physician has made the following observation about thrombophlebitis and vasectomy:

> When confronted by a relatively young couple who have several children and are seeking counsel about contraception, the conscientious and conservative physician—aware of the many shortcomings and potential hazards of presently available birth-control pills and devices—understandably may be enthusiastic in recommending vasectomy. Unfortunately, our experience would suggest that such a recommendation might carry long-term risks, especially in men who are prone to thrombophlebitis.[65]

This doctor reported numerous case histories to back up his point. One thirty-six-year-old executive, who had enjoyed excellent health prior to his vasectomy, developed problems two months after the operation. Chest pains were attributed to small blood clots in the lungs which might have originated from thrombophlebitis of the left leg. Another patient, a thirty-six-year-old postman, consulted the doctor because of "a 20-pound weight loss in recent months, recurrent infections, peptic-ulcer-like symptoms, . . . severe weakness, and profuse sweats. He had undergone vasectomy two years previously."[66] The physician discovered swollen lymph nodes, inflammation of the prostate gland, and "a somewhat enlarged and tender left testicle." There is no way that a cause-and-effect relationship can be established between the vasectomy and the symptoms, but it does make you wonder.

If you stop to think about what a vasectomy really is, some interesting possibilities present themselves. This minor operation in no way stops the sperm factory. Millions and millions of the little devils keep being made every day, even after *207* surgery, and every day they keep piling up at the barricade at the end of the assembly line, where the tubes were tied off. Have you ever considered what happens to the buggers? A vasectomy is very much like pinching off the end of a garden hose. The production of water or sperm is not halted; only the flow is blocked. Given the fact that the male hose (vas deferens) is not as strong or impermeable as a garden hose, it is not surprising to learn that some of the remnants of sperm cells are absorbed into the body. Usually, sperm is ejaculated and never comes into contact with the "internal" parts of the body. How does the body react when it sees something never before encountered?

Generally, when the system absorbs something "foreign," it builds a defending molecule or antibody to seek out and destroy the invader. Thus, when you get German measles as a kid, your body makes antibodies which protect you from future encounters. Antibodies also reject foreign tissue and make organ transplants difficult. All these different kinds of reactions fall under the broad category of immunological response. Sometimes the system goes haywire. For reasons not altogether clear, the body may begin to turn against itself. It no longer can recognize friend from foe, or self from nonself. When this happens, we have something called *autoimmune disease*: the body begins to make antibodies which may attack important organs.

Autoimmune diseases have only recently been recognized as major medical problems. One such illness with a formidable name is systemic lupus erythematosus (lupus for short), and it lives up to its appellation. Internal organs are affected (almost "rejected," as if they were foreign) and a generalized wasting condition occurs. There are other autoimmune diseases. It is thought that multiple sclerosis occurs when the body begins to reject its own nervous tissue. A muscle disorder, myasthenia gravis, may also turn out to be caused by autoantibodies. Even arthritis is thought to be in some way provoked by autoimmunity.

If sperm cells, or the remnants of sperm cells, are never usually seen by the body or its immune system, what would happen if, as is the case after vasectomy, this stuff is absorbed into the body proper? The body naturally perceives the material as "foreign" and begins to make antibodies against it. One doctor has suggested that men who suffer from thrombophlebitis after vasectomy could be suffering an autoimmune response.[67] The antibodies which are produced may help dispose of the spermies unable to leave the body, but who knows what damage they might do to other parts of the anatomy.

Immunological changes are not the only possible problem which might arise after vasectomy. A different disorder has been reported in rats which had received experimental vasectomies. These rats had a reduced level of male hormone in their urine after the operation. Their testes were smaller and cysts developed within their reproductive machinery. The authors of this investigation conclude their article with the statement, "pending estensive study of the endocrine and somatic [physical] effects of vasectomy in man greater caution be observed in the use of vasectomies as a routine contraceptive procedure."[68] Once again it is clear that a highly touted method of birth control requires more research before a final stamp of approval can be given.

Needless to say, what I want is a nice, safe, simple method of birth control as much as, if not more than, the next person. I love sex, and anything that makes it easier should be supported. But questions have been raised about the safety of the Pill, the IUD, and vasectomy. No one has yet been able to prove that the dangers which have been discussed are a problem for a majority of the millions of people who rely on any of these forms of birth control. It may be that only an insignificant fraction of the total population will suffer any of the potential side effects we have discussed. For the person it happens to, the statistics don't matter. What is scary is that we just do not know. To date, neither the medical profession not the federal regulatory agencies have enough information to be able to make absolute statements one way or the other. It seems frightening to me that procedures being used by so many people require additional testing.

One thing is for sure. The old-fashioned techniques, while not being so clean and neat, can do the job if used conscientiously. And it is unlikely that they do any damage. The condom, the diaphragm, and even spermicidal foam appear to be safe and reasonably effective. Obviously, they are not as good **209** as the Pill, the IUD, or sterilization. However, if lovers combine any of the various techniques, they find their protection level greatly enhanced. The condom and foam together achieve nearly the same degree of effectiveness as the birth control pill. A diaphragm coupled with the rhythm method can also work. No one can tell someone else what is right for them. It is up to each individual or couple to decide what is the most appropriate method of birth control. But that decision should be made from awareness, not ignorance.

References

1. Royal College of General Practitioners. "Oral Contraception and Thrombotic Disease." *J. Coll. Gen. Pract.* 13:267–279, 1967.
2. Inman, W. H. W., and Vessey, M. P. "Investigation of Deaths from Pulmonary, Coronary and Cerebral Thrombosis and Embolism in Women in Child-Bearing Age." *Brit. Med. J.* 2:193–199, 1968.
3. Vessey, M. P., and Doll, R. "Investigation of Relation Between Use of Oral Contraception and Thromboembolic Disease: A Further Report." *Brit. Med. J.* 2:651–657, 1969.
4. Sartwell, P. E., et al. "Thromboembolism and Oral Contraceptives: An Epidemiological Case-Control Study." *Am. J. Epidem* 90:365–370, 1969.
5. Markush, R. E., and Seigel, D. G. "Oral Contraceptives and Mortality Trends from Thromboembolism in the United States." *Amer. J. Public Health* 59:418–434, 1969.
6. Anderson, T. W. "Oral Contraceptives and Female Mortality Trends." *Canad. Med. Assoc. J.* 102:1156–1160, 1970.
7. Mann, J. I., and Inman, W. H. "Oral Contraceptives and Death From Myocardial Infarction." *Br. Med. J.* 2:245–258, 1975.
8. Mann, J. I., et al. "Myocardial Infarction in Young Women With Special Reference to Oral Contraceptive Practice." *Br. Med. J.* 2:241–245, 1975.
9. Shapiro, Samuel. "Oral Contraceptives and Myocardial Infarction." *New Engl. J. Med.* 293:195–196, 1975.
10. Collaborative Group for the Study of Stroke in Young Women. "Oral Contraception and Increased Risk of Cerebral Ischemia or Thrombosis." *New Engl. J. Med.* 288:871–878, 1973.
11. Collaborative Group for the Study of Stroke in Young Women.

Oral Contraceptives and Stroke in Young Women. *JAMA* 231:718–722, 1975.

12. Weir, R. J., et al. "Blood Pressure in Women Taking Oral Contraceptives." *Br. Med. J.* 1:535–539, 1974.

13. Vessey, M. P. "Oral Contraceptives and Stroke." *New Engl. J. Med.* 289:218, 1973.

14. Crawford, Anne. "Settlements Kept Secret in Pill Suits." *The Record* 80:1–2, 1974.

15. Haynes, Roy L., and Dunn, James M. "Oral Contraceptives, Thrombosis, and Sickle Cell Hemoglobinopathies." *JAMA* 200:994–996, 1967.

16. Greenwald, Jonathan G. "Stroke in a Woman with Sickle Cell Trait Taking Oral Contraceptives." *Connect. Med.* 35:231–232, 1971.

17. Harris, A. B., et al. "Reduced Ascorbic-Acid Excretion and Oral Contraceptives." *Lancet* 2:201–202, 1973.

18. Briggs, Michael, and Briggs, Maxine. "Vitamin C Requirement and Oral Contraceptives." *Nature* 238:277, 1972.

19. Vessey, M. P., et al. "Oral Contraceptives and Breast Neoplasia." *Br. Med. J.* 3:719–724, 1972.

20. McBride, W. G., et al. "Comparative Study of Adverse Effects of Oral Contraceptives." *Med. J. Austra.* 2:246–250, 1974.

21. Gray, Laman H. "Effects of Estrogenic Therapy on the Breast." *Southern Med. J.* 64:835–838, 1971.

22. Taylor, H. B. "Oral Contraceptives and Pathologic Changes in the Breast." *Cancer* 28:1388, 1971.

23. Black, Maurice M., and Leis, Henry P. "Mammary Carcinogenesis." *N.Y. State J. Med.* 1601–1605, June 15, 1972.

24. Taylor, Herbert B., et al. "Atypical Endocervical Hyperplasia in Women Taking Oral Contraceptives." *JAMA* 202:637–640, 1967.

25. Gall, Stanley A., et al. "The Morphologic Effects of Oral Contraceptive Agents on the Cervix." *JAMA* 207:2243–2247, 1969.

26. Ryan, G. M., Jr., et al. "Histology of the Uterus and Ovaries After Long-Term Cyclic Norethynodrel Therapy." *Amer. J. Obstet. Gynec.* 90:715–725, 1964.

27. Candy, and Abell, Murray R. "Progestogen-Induced Adenomatous Hyperplasia of the Uterine Cervix." *JAMA* 203:323–326, 1968.

28. Mingeot, R., and Fievez, C. L. "Endocervical Changes with the Use of Synthetic Steroids." *Obstet. Gynec.* 44:53–59, 1974.

29. Maqueo, M., et al. "Morphology of the Cervix in Women Treated with Synthetic Progestins." *Amer. J. Obstet. Gynec.* 96:944–998, 1966.

30. Meissner, W. A., et al. "Endometrial Hyperplasia, Endometrial Carcinoma, and Endometriosis Produced Experimentally by Estrogen." *Cancer* 10:500, 1957.
31. Kistner, R. W. "Histologic Effects of Progestins on Hyperplasia and Carcinoma in Situ of the Endometrium." *Cancer* 2:946, 1959.
32. Gusberg, S. B., and Kaplan, A. C. "Precursors of Corpus Cancer: IV. Adenomatous Hyperplasia as Stage 0 Carcinoma of the Endometrium." *Am. J. Obstet. Gynecol.* 87:662, 1963.
33. Silverberg, Steven G., and Makowski, Edgar L. "Endometrial Carcinoma in Young Women Taking Oral Contraceptive Agents." *J. Obstet. Gynec.* 46:503–506, 1975.
34. Herbst, A. L., et al. "Adenocarcinoma of the Vagina: Association of Maternal Stilbestrol Therapy with Tumor Appearance in Young Women." *New Engl. J. Med.* 284:878–881, 1971.
35. Greenwald, P., et al. "Vaginal Cancer after Maternal Treatment With Synthetic Estrogens." *New Engl. J. Med.* 285:390–392, 1971.
36. Herbst, Arthur L., et al. "Prenatal Exposure to Stilbestrol." *New Engl. J. Med.* 292:334–339, 1975.
37. Gall et al., op. cit.
38. Herbst et al., "Prenatal Exposure."
39. Herbst, Arthur L., et al. "Clear-Cell Adenocarcinoma of the Vagina and Cervix in Girls: Analysis of 170 Registry Cases." *Am. J. Obstet. Gynecol.* 119:713–724, 1974.
40. "Medical News: A Few Women Taking the Pill Found to Have Benign Liver Tumors." *JAMA* 231:451–452, 1975.
41. Baum, Janet K., et al. "Possible Association Between Benign Hepatomas and Oral Contraceptives." *Lancet* 2:926–929, 1973.
42. O'Sullivan, J. P., and Wilding, R. P. "Liver Hamartomas in Patients on Oral Contraceptives." *Br. Med. J.* 3:3–4, 1974.
43. "Medical News", op. cit.
44. Baum, op. cit.
45. "Medical News", op. cit.
46. Editorial: "Liver Tumours and the Pill." *Br. Med. J.* 3:51–52, 1974.
47. Ingelfinger, F. J. Editorial: "Gallstones and Estrogens." *New Engl. J. Med.* 290:51–52, 1974.
48. Boston Collaborative Drug Surveillance Programme. Oral Contraceptives and Venous Thromboembolic Disease, Surgically Confirmed Gallbladder Disease, and Breast Tumours. *Lancet* 1:1399–1404, 1973.
49. Small, Donald M. "Hormone Use to Change Normal Physiology—Is the Risk Worth it?" *New Engl. J. Med.* 294:219–221, 1976.

50. Ad Hoc Obstetric-Gynecology Advisory Committee. "Report of Safety and Efficacy of the Dalkon Shield and Other IUD's." October 29–30, 1974.
51. Ibid.
52. Tatum, Howard J., et al. "The Dalkon Shield Controversy." *JAMA* 231:711–717, 1975.
53. Dikshit, Suhasini, and Ledger, William J. "A Role of Antibiotics in the Contraceptive Effectiveness of an Intrauterine Foreign Body in the Rabbit." Unpublished report.
54. Wrenn, T. R., Weyant, J. R., and Bitman, J. *Abstracts, Society For the Study of Repro.* 3:23, 1970.
55. Ad Hoc Committee, op. cit.
56. Sherrod, Dale, B., and Nicholl, Willard. "Electrocardiographic Changes during Intrauterine Contraceptive Devices Insertion." *Am. J. Obstet. Gynecol.* 119:1044–1051, 1974.
57. Epstein, Helen. "IUD: The Bloody Truth." *Viva* 2:45 Apr., 1975.
58. Golditch, Ira M., et al. "Serious Pelvic Infection Associated with Intrauterine Contraceptive Device." *Int. J. Fertil.* 18:156–160, 1973.
59. Pardanani, D. S., et al. "Surgical Restoration of Vas Continuity after Further Clinical Evaluation of a New Operation Technique." *Fertil. Steril.* 25:319–324, 1974.
60. Johnson, M. H. *Amer. J. Psychiat.* 121:482, 1964.
61. Ziegler, F. J., et al. *Psychosom. Med.* 28:56, 1966.
62. Wig, N. N., and Singh, S. "Psychosomatic Symptoms Following Male Sterilization." *Indian J. Med. Res.* 60:1386–1392, 1972.
63. Roberts, H. J. "Thrombophlebitis after Vasectomy." *New Engl. J. Med.* 284:1330, 1971.
64. Alt, W. J. "Thrombophlebitis and Pulmonary Emboli Following Vasectomies." *Mich. Med.* 72:769–770, 1973.
65. Roberts, H. J. "Delayed Thrombophlebitis and Systemic Complications after Vasectomy: Possible Role of Diabetogenic Hyperinsulinism." *J. Amer. Geriatric Soc.* 16:267–279, 1968.
66. Ibid.
67. Ibid.
68. Sackler, Arthur M., et al. "Gonadal Effects of Vasectomy and Vasoligation." *Science* 179:293–295, 1973.

10.

Drugs from Pregnancy through Childhood, or Medicine Could Be Hazardous to Your Child's Health

Kids really have a bum deal. Their parents and teachers won't leave them alone, but the drug companies virtually ignore them. The problem revolves around the drugs which the doctor has in his little black bag. According to the Food and Drug Administration, "Overall, about three-quarters of the thousands of drugs that are available today for adults are not approved for the treatment of children."[1] Dr. Alan K. Done, professor of pediatrics and pharmacology at Wayne State University in Detroit, has stated that drug companies have neglected childhood drugs because of the expense of testing the medication and establishing their safety.[2] The problem is a bit

stickier than that. No one wants to take the responsibility for using children in experiments, even if they are sick and would require medication anyway. Drug manufacturers are particularly careful to avoid this quagmire. They conveniently cover their asses by putting a disclaimer on most drug labels which goes something like "safety and dosage have not been established for pediatric use." Such a statement is a cop-out because it absolves the drug company of all blame, yet leaves the conscientious doctor hanging in limbo.

On the surface it might appear that this is a very simple matter. Any drug which has not been proved safe just should not be used. Unfortunately, things are much more complicated. A great many of the untested drugs could be valuable tools in the fight against childhood diseases.

In order to understand the depth of the dilemma, let's take a look at the hypothetical case history of little Johnny Jones. This nine-year-old has been suffering from a severe ear infection for five weeks. None of the antibiotics that his pediatrician has prescribed have helped. Over the last few days the infection has become much worse. Johnny is now suffering intense pain and has developed dizzy spells and has trouble walking because the infection has affected the center of balance within his ear. The doctor knows that the antibiotic **"XYZ-Mycin"** will kill the invading bacteria because a culture has demonstrated that this is the only effective drug for Johnny's infection. The medication has been used for over six years in adults with excellent results and few adverse reactions, but it is still untested in children. What should the doctor do? If he withholds the drug, the situation could rapidly deteriorate even further. However, the drug might be harmful for children. What would you do if you had to make this decision? This nasty predicament occurs all too frequently in medical practice.

Because physicians must fight illnesses in children where no approved drugs are available, they often pretend that the child is just a small adult and prescribe by the seat of their pants. For years it has been assumed that you could take the adult dosage for any given drug and by applying a fancy formula calculate an equivalent children's dose. (In order to learn the various tricks used to compute drug dosages for children, turn to Table 1 at the end of the chapter). While it is true that *215* some drug doses can be safely figured with a formula, we now know that this practice can be damn dangerous. Kids are not just miniature adults. Their internal organs are not fully developed and they often react differently to drugs than adults. A prime example is the drug **Amphetamine**. Aptly nicknamed "speed," this drug acts as a stimulant in adults. For this reason it is used to prolong stamina, even after fatigue has set in. However, if you give this drug to a child, the chances are that you will calm him down because it acts as a sedative upon the developing nervous system.

Apart from the fact that drugs often affect children differently from adults, it is also well known that drugs may be more dangerous for children. While aspirin can be ingested in large quantities by an adult, a child may well develop a life-threatening toxic reaction after a dose considered small for adults. The common antidiarrheal agent **Lomotil** (*Diphenoxylate*) is safe and effective for adults but can be hazardous to children. Relatively small doses may produce serious side effects. Even some frequently prescribed broad-spectrum antibiotics like **Chloramphenicol, Novobiocin, Streptomycin,** and **Sulfas** can be dangerous if administered to youngsters.

Drugs and the Unborn

The problem of drugs and kids is not restricted to the lack of adequately tested medications. While the fetus is still in the mother's womb, it is all too often being exposed to dangerous drugs. Recent medical investigations confirm the fact that most pregnant women end up taking an excess number of drugs. Frequently they are prescribed by the woman's physician. One would think that after the **Thalidomide** tragedy, women and doctors would have learned a lesson. Unfortunately, that does not seem to be the case. A study published in the *British Medical Journal* revealed that of 1,369 women, 97 percent took at least one medication during the course of their pregnancy.[3] Dr. John Forfar of the University of Edinburgh found in his investigation of 911 women that 82 percent had received medicine prescribed by their doctors and that 65 percent had taken over-the-counter drugs. He also learned that 85 percent of the women used alcohol during the pregnancies and 57 percent smoked.[4] In a study of middle- and upper-class Houston women, it was discovered that they used an average of ten different drugs during pregnancy, with antibiotics and antacids heading the list. One woman took twenty-five aspirin tablets every day throughout her pregnancy; when questioned she replied, "If I'd known aspirin was a drug, I wouldn't have taken it."[5]

That is often the crux of the problem. Most people overlook many of the chemicals that they commonly consume. Antacids, alcohol, nicotine, aspirin, tranquilizers, vitamins, and laxatives can all affect the unborn baby. Even if a woman is extra-careful about self-prescribed products, she is often at the mercy of her doctor. If an obstetrician or pediatrician tells a pregnant woman to take an antibiotic or a blood pressure drug, she automatically assumes that doctor knows best. Such an assumption may not always be valid. Even worse is the fact that the fetus is most susceptible to birth defects during the first few weeks of pregnancy. A woman could be taking a hazardous drug even before she realizes that she is pregnant. For all of these reasons, Dr. Kurt Hirschhorn of Mount Sinai Medical Center in New York emphatically told a meeting of the National Foundation–March of Dimes that no woman in her child-bearing years should take any drug that is not essential to preserve her health unless she is absolutely positive she is not pregnant.[5]

If doctors will not take extra precautions to prevent pregnant women from receiving dangerous prescription products, then women themselves will have to take on the responsibility for protecting their unborn children from the potential dangers of drug-induced birth defects. Unless the withholding of a particular drug would endanger the mother or baby, no woman should receive any medication during the nine month gestation period. Antinausea preparations such as **Bonine**, **Antivert**, and **Marezine** should no longer be taken for morning sickness since malformations have been observed in the offspring of animals exposed to these drugs during pregnancy.[6,7,8] Even the old-favorite tranquilizers like **Librium**, *217*

Librax, **Equanil**, and **Miltown** can no longer be taken with complete assurance. One group of investigators has observed that while their study was not conclusive, "meprobamate [**Equanil, Miltown**, etc.] and chlordiazepoxide [**Librium, Librax**, etc.] may not be safe during early pregnancy."[9] Other researchers have determined that there is no danger to the unborn baby,[10] but until the debate is over it might be prudent to avoid these medicines unless they are absolutely necessary.

If you would like to know what drugs may be hazardous to the unborn baby, turn to Table 2. While some of the adverse reactions noted are not serious, others may be extremely dangerous. Just because a drug is not included on the list does not guarantee that it is safe for the fetus. Equally, consumption of one of the medications during pregnancy does not mean that it will be bad for your baby. The statistical probability is often extremely low that any damage will occur. The list is provided to alert women and doctors to drugs which are potentially dangerous and should be avoided, if possible, during pregnancy. Medical references document all known or suspected adverse reactions, and you should consult them when in doubt.

Drugs and the Nursing Mother

The newborn baby is not safe from dangerous side effects after delivery. Many drugs can be transmitted from a lactating mother to her baby through breast milk. Picture the following situation. A woman bears her fourth child and decides that she does not want any more kids. After two or three months she begins taking birth control pills on the recommendation of her gynecologist. She never bothers to ask her pediatrician whether her oral contraceptive might be dangerous to her nursing baby. Yet one of the American Medical Association's consultants, Dr. Spellacy, has this to say: "It is neither wise nor advisable to prescribe oral contraceptives to nursing mothers."[11] This is just one example, but it is equally true for many other commonly prescribed medications and even lots of nonprescription drugs. Table 3 provides a list of drugs which may be hazardous to nursing infants. Unless specifically advised otherwise, it might be prudent for a new mother to bottle feed her baby if she must use any of the listed drugs.

Babies may also be susceptible to the hazards of special antibacterial bathing soaps or dusting powders. There is no longer any doubt that hexachlorophene can be absorbed directly through the skin and poses a definite threat of brain damage. A committee of the American Academy of Pediatrics has gone so far as to recommend no bathing of newborns. The only cleansing this committee condones, and then only after the infant's temperature is normal, is gentle rinsing of the head, face, and diaper area. These expert pediatricians suggest that cotton and sterile water be used, or at most a gentle, nonmedicated soap that is "carefully and thoroughly rinsed off."[12]

Once a newborn baby has managed to survive all the pitfalls and dangers of the first few months of life, you would think that the worst would be over. Such is not the case. The infant is very vulnerable to drugs and even worse, the administration of drugs. Because it is virtually impossible to get a young child to swallow a pill, doctors often resort to injections to get medicine into kids. One of the favorite shots is something called an IM, or intramuscular, injection. This involves the placement of drug between the layers of muscle. Because muscle tissue is liberally supplied with small capillaries, the medicine reaches the blood stream very quickly and reliably. Unfortunately, extra caution must be used for this kind of shot since the possibility of hitting a nerve or blood vessel is always present. "Drop foot" is a kind of limp caused by nerve damage resulting from improperly administered medicine. Children, especially infants, should *never* receive an injection in the buttocks. In the first few years of life a child's bottom just does not have enough muscle to protect the sciatic nerve from possible destruction. In the past, deformities or limps were often attributed to polio while in reality an improper buttock injection was responsible. The proper place for an intramuscular shot is the triceps muscle of the arm or the outer surface of the thigh muscle, where it is much safer and less painful. Writing about long-acting **Penicillin** preparations, one doctor **219** has gone so far as to state that "all such preparations should be injected into the midlateral aspect of the thigh in both adults and children."[13] And yet I will bet that most adults and a great many young people regularly get stuck in the butt. Although most pediatricians no longer give intramuscular injections into the buttocks, many general practitioners do.

More important than how drugs are administered, however, is the problem of *what* is administered. At the risk of beating a dead horse, I cannot resist discussing the abuse of **Tetracycline** once more. This broad-spectrum antibiotic is prescribed more than any other antibacterial agent. It is handed out under many names, so it is hard for a patient to know exactly what he is receiving and also because **Tetracycline** is always more expensive when sold as a brand name product. Some of the most popular brands are **Achromycin, Aureomycin, Azotrex, Kesso-Tetra, Achrostatin V, Cyclopar, Mysteclin-F, Panmycin, Robitet, Sumycin,** and **Tetracyn.** Every doctor is taught that this antibiotic has the capacity to produce permanent and disfiguring discoloration (mottling) of teeth in children; nevertheless, it is prescribed and administered frequently. In a study of 505 youngsters ranging in age from three to five years, "It was found that 70% of the children had been given the antibiotic during their first three years of life, each having received on average 2.4 courses. This represented an increase of 12% in tetracycline usage in children of this age as compared with a similar series five years ago."[14] The medical irresponsibility that this report seems to have uncovered is indefensible.

Ampicillin is another broad-spectrum antibiotic which is prescribed almost as frequently as **Tetracycline.** It is available both generically and in name-brand preparations such as **Amcill, Alpen, Omnipen, Penbritin, Polycillin, Principen,** and **Totacillin.** A recent article in *JAMA* has the following to say about pediatric use: "Certain practices, such as the administration . . . of ampicillin to children less than 10 years of age is particularly hazardous, and their use for prophylaxis or for any situation lacking a clear indication is to be condemned."[15]

Another drug, **Aminophylline,** is used extensively in the treatment of bronchial asthma. It is often included in such preparations as **Amesec, Aminodur, Mudrane, Rectalad-**

Aminophylline, and **Somophyllin**. It too can be dangerous for young children and should be only administered with extreme caution. Reactions such as high fever, delirium, convulsions, and coma have been reported.

But doctors are not the only people to blame. Well-meaning parents are also guilty of administering incorrect or dangerous medicines to their children. A study conducted by Georgetown University in 1975 revealed that as many as 20 percent of kids under two received potentially dangerous nonprescription drugs. Something as simple as **aspirin** can be quite hazardous to a young person if it is administered in anything but a child's dose. So shape up, Mom and Dad, you should be as cautious about giving drugs to your kids as you are about taking drugs yourselves.

Bed–Wetting: Are Drugs Justified?

Bed-wetting, yecch! Lots of kids suffer this common problem, but that does not make it any easier to bear. As many as 10–15 percent of all five-year-olds encounter the embarrassment of enuresis (the doctor's sanitized word for bed-wetting), and that is one heck of a lot of soggy sheets. Because parents quickly throw up their hands in disgust and charge off to their family doctor seeking action, physicians have taken the easy way out and started prescribing a drug called **Imipramine**. A cloud of controversy has risen over the use of this potent medication, which is sold under the brand names **Tofranil** and **Presamine**. Originally, **Imipramine** was used as an antidepressant drug for adults who experienced severe and sometimes suicidal bouts of psychological depression. In 1968 it was noted that people treated with the drug experienced difficulty in urination.[16] Not long after that, some bright clinician hit upon the idea of employing **Tofranil** for the treatment of enuresis. Initial reports were enthusiastic. At last a clean, neat, and best of all, simple cure for bed-wetting was announced to the world. Other heavy-duty antidepressant drugs like **Elavil** (*Amitriptyline*) and **Aventyl** (*Nortriptyline*) were tried **221** and also received good reviews. But what about the side effects?

Although serious adverse reactions are not frequently reported, some investigators have observed, "unfortunately psychological effects on children are relatively common. Between one in five and one in ten of the children treated with imipramine are said to have become nervous and irritable and to have had difficulty sleeping. Other adverse effects include restlessness, tearfulness, dizziness, nausea, and difficulty with concentration on schoolwork."[17] Other relatively common responses are constipation, weight loss, and anxiety. Parents should be extremely cautious about keeping these medicines out of reach of children, because in recent years there have been a number of accidental poisonings leading to fatalities. Despite any assurances your pediatrician may give you, no one yet knows what the long-term effects of **Imipramine** may be upon growth and development.

Before parents start administering **Tofranil** to their kids, there are a few important facts they should know. First, it should definitely not be given to any child less than six years of age because serious adverse effects could result.[18] Second, this potent medicine should not be used if the problem is relatively infrequent or if the bed-wetting seems to be associated with a temporary crisis like a death in the family or a parental separation. Reassurance and encouragement will go a long way in helping to resolve occasional bed-wetting due to emotional stress. Finally, and most important, these antidepressant drugs have a lousy cure record: when the drug is discontinued, the chances are pretty good that the kid will start wetting his bed once again.[19,20]

One of the real tragedies of **Imipramine** therapy is that it allows the doctor to ignore the cause of the problem, whether it be physical or psychological. A few doctors have decried the fact that some children are placed on drug programs for years while an actual disease process is overlooked.[21] Although "simple" bedwetting is infrequently caused by urinary-tract infections, small bladder capacity, or any other physical abnormality, all children should have a complete physical examination and urinalysis before heavy-duty drug treatment is initiated.

Well what are the alternatives to **Imipramine?** Even patient parents can hardly be expected to grin and bear it. As hard as it may be, the first rule is: Do not lose your cool! Punishment will not only not help matters but will probably make things worse. Experts in the field are convinced that much bed-wetting results from emotional stress, such as the arrival of a new baby, difficulty in school, or parental disharmony. With luck, enuresis of this type will disappear all by itself when the psychological environment improves. Parents can speed the process along by offering encouragement and prizes for dry nights. The child should have the responsibility for keeping a chart of dry and wet nights and should receive lots of praise, accompanied with gold stars and a special treat, for each success. The kid should also have the responsibility for changing wet sheets and seeing that they are placed in an appropriate place for washing. In this way the idea is transmitted without punishment that the child is responsible for his actions. It may also be of some benefit to cut down on fluid intake well before bedtime and have Mom or Dad wake up the kid at various intervals throughout the night.

If these hints are not helpful and patience starts to wear thin, it may be time to bring on the heavy artillery. Of all of the techniques available, conditioning is probably the most reliable and long-lasting in terms of success. Conditioning involves the use of a battery-operated apparatus which sounds an alarm when a small amount of urine touches two electrodes and closes a circuit. If placed under the kid's sheet, it will wake him up at the first sign of wetting. The device is sold for twenty to thirty-five dollars under various hokey names such as "Wee Alarm" and "Wee-Alert." In order to work effectively, the child should be encouraged not to wear pajama bottoms. Lots of reassurance should be provided in the beginning, because kids can be frightened by the mystery or complexity of the thing. Each child should be taught how to set the alarm himself and what is expected—that whenever the buzzer goes off he or she is expected to get up and go to the bathroom and then reset the alarm. Mom and Dad should be prepared to wake the kid up at the sound of the ring during the first few weeks of treatment until the child gets the hang of things. If the conditioning process is continued for about a **223** month after a cure is established, the chances of relapse will be significantly reduced.

According to one expert from the American Medical Association's Department of Drugs, "The results of conditioning treatment are impressive when they are compared with the use of antidepressant drugs [**Tofranil**, for example]. With adequate preparation of the family and persistent support on the part of the physician 60% or more of the children will be dry when followed up a year after treatment. The drawback of this treatment is the time and effort required of the family and the physician, a number of families will not persevere."[22] I find it tragic that parents and doctors could risk the hazards and uncertain success of drug therapy for the safety and superiority of conditioning just because of a lack of patience.

Hyperactive Children: Drugs Or Diet?

If you think that the problem of bed-wetting is a sticky wicket, then wait until you hear about the controversy surrounding hyperkinesis. This medical term has been loosely employed to describe a whole series of "learning disorders" in schoolchildren. Some medical authorities have estimated that as many as 3–10 percent of all kids suffer from this problem.[23] According to pediatrician Dr. Ben Feingold, a pediatrician and allergy specialist at the Kaiser-Permanente Medical Center in San Francisco, over five million children in the United States alone may be suffering this disorder.

What is hyperkinesis, or—as the snobs prefer to call it—"minimal brain dysfunction"? Part of the problem is that no one really does have a good definition which may be why so many kids get classified as hyperkinetic. A whole range of symptoms has been described: inability to concentrate, impulsivity, distractibility, physical activity, and impatience are but a few. As should be obvious to any parent, however, almost all children will manifest some of these "symptoms" at one time or another. Since there is no special test or neurological examination which can positively diagnose hyperkinesis, personal prejudice may be as important as medical expertise in drawing the diagnostic line. Often the child's teacher is the one who does the initial evaluating, and that can leave the door open to abuse. A poor teacher may push for the diagnosis "minimal brain dysfunction" because it allows the child to be categorized and takes attention away from a lousy teaching technique. An obnoxious kid, or one who is bored and frustrated, may prove to be a discipline problem but that is no reason to categorize him or her as hyperkinetic.

There is no doubt, however, that true hyperkinesis does exist. Some kids have such a short attention span that it becomes a real learning disability even though they may have a normal or above-average IQ. These children just can't sit still for more than a few minutes at a time. In fact, they could be dubbed perpetual motion machines. Wide swings in mood may be accompanied by impulsive and disruptive behavior that frequently lead to temper tantrums. Needless to say, such conduct can destroy classroom discipline and make home life unbearable for parents, as well as for other brothers and sisters.

In recent years, in some parts of the country, it has become popular to treat this problem with powerful drugs which act upon the central nervous system. In 1974 one medical expert estimated that at least 300,000 children in elementary schools in the United States were on stimulant medications.[24] In some communities there was an increase of more than 60 percent in the use of these drugs between 1971 and 1973. From all indications it would appear that the trend is definitely in the direction of greater reliance upon pharmacological treatment.

Paradoxically, drugs such as **Amphetamine**, which are used to keep adults awake and alert or to suppress appetite, will actually calm down a hyperactive child. For this reason **Benzedrine**, **Dexedrine**, **Ritalin**, and **Cylert**, as well as other excitatory medications, are frequently prescribed. Some doctors and teachers have enthusiastically supported the use of these stimulants for the treatment of minimal brain dysfunction. While it is true that many children with true hyperkinesis show dramatic improvement after such drugs are administered, some health professionals fear that these medications may end up being overprescribed. Dr. Carl Kline, an expert in **225** the field of learning disabilities from the University of British Columbia, has this to say: "It is my belief that if these drugs were outlawed, children would not be at all deprived of essential medication, but that doctors would be forced to make more accurate diagnoses and seek better means of handling the hyperactive behavior of a certain small percentage of their little patients."[25] Other doctors have emphasized the need to evaluate the youngster completely before jumping on the drug bandwagon.

Although few teachers or school health personnel like to face it, some doctors are beginning to discuss the possibility that long-term administration of stimulant drugs may lead to some unwanted side effects. Reduced growth is the primary subject of concern, but other adverse reactions have also been reported.[26,27] Even avid supporters of **Amphetamine**-type drugs have come down hard on the side of careful and continuous monitoring of drug effects. It has been recommended that any child receiving these drugs for long periods of time have the medication periodically withdrawn so that an evaluation of progress can be made.[28]

Until recently, the most important question concerning **Ritalin** or **Amphetamine** administration has not been asked. Do these drugs make a difference in the long-term outcome of minimal brain dysfunction? A comprehensive examination of this subject carried out at the Montreal Children's Hospital discovered a startling fact. At the end of five years, hyperkinetic children who had received drugs (either **Ritalin** or **Chloropromazine**) did not differ significantly from children who had not received medication.[29] Although it appeared that hyperactive kids treated with **Ritalin** were initially more manageable, the degree of improvement and emotional adjustment was essentially identical at the end of five years to that seen in a group of kids who had received no medication at all.

Before parents throw their hands up in despair, they might want to consider another approach to the treatment of hyperkinesis. Dr. Feingold has come up with a revolutionary new treatment for this disorder. Dr. Feingold believes that diet may have a lot to do with the problem in the first place. Artificial flavors and colors could be responsible for many of the cases of hyperkinesis. It is this doctor's contention that such symptoms as inability to concentrate, restlessness, and hyperactivity may actually be due to an allergic reaction caused by the synthetic food additives found in so much of the junk kids eat today. Even foods made specifically for youngsters (like certain breakfast cereals) often contain excess amounts of artificial chemical ingredients. Dr. Feingold maintains that about 50 percent of his youthful patients return to normal once they are placed on a diet devoid of all artificial flavors and colors, and that usually within one month they can be taken off **Amphetamine** stimulants or powerful tranquilizers.[30]

Most health professionals, as well as federal regulatory agencies, have resisted the idea that diet could influence children's behavior. Dr. Feingold has reported that the Food and Drug Administration has been "like a brick wall, giving me no support, only discouragement, as though they were representatives of the food industry, rather than a government agency."[31] Nevertheless, Dr. Feingold persevered, and by 1975 the FDA, in a dramatic shift, admitted that there might be something to his approach. Investigators at other medical centers have also found some tentative evidence to support Dr. Feingold's findings.

The K-P (Kaiser-Permanente) diet involves the elimination of all food that contains artificial flavors or colors. Candy bars, hot dogs, powdered drink mixes, ready-to-eat cereals, soft drinks, bakery goods (except plain), luncheon meats, and "yummy" toothpastes are but a few of the foods loaded with synthetic junk. You can be almost certain that any processed food will contain some amount of artificial flavor or color. All medicines and vitamins that contain artificial flavoring or coloring are banned, and all drugs with aspirin must be eliminated because the possibility exists that it too can be harmful. Some fruits and vegetables are also banned in Dr. Feingold's diet. Apples, apricots, cherries, cucumbers, currants, grapes, oranges, peaches, prunes, raspberries, and strawberries all contain the natural chemical salicylate, which may also promote allergic hyperactivity. It is possible, however, to reintroduce foods with natural salicylates after four to six weeks, one item at a time, if there is no adverse reaction.

Whether or not hyperactivity is in part due to food allergy, **227** no one knows for sure. Preliminary evidence is tantalizing. Some doctors even believe that milk, corn, and chocolate can cause allergic reactions which can contribute to the problem. Extensive testing under controlled scientific conditions remains to be done. Even without a final verdict, however, it is certainly worth trying Dr. Feingold's diet before resorting to potent drug therapy.

Poisoning

Medicine can be a valuable tool in the fight against childhood illness. It can also be dangerous when used casually or without proper precautions. Parents should be particularly careful about leaving drugs around the house. Over three million children under the age of five suffer from accidental drug poisoning every year. Aspirin alone probably accounts for over one million of those cases. Kid-proof containers can be difficult to get open, but they are worth the extra effort if they help prevent accidents. Even with special bottles, children manage to get into drugs that are dangerous. Parents should always be prepared for any emergency.

Treatment of poisoning involves certain basic principles. If the poison that has been swallowed is not corrosive or irritating and if the patient is still conscious, vomiting should be induced immediately. If a finger down the throat does not do the trick, an emetic (a chemical that causes vomiting) should be used. Every family should have **Ipecac Syrup** handy in the medicine cabinet at all times. One half to one teaspoonful should induce vomiting within fifteen to twenty minutes in a child less than one year old, especially if it is followed by one to two glasses of water. Everyone else can tolerate one to three teaspoonfuls of **Ipecac**. If after twenty minutes vomiting has not occurred, a second dose may be administered, but no more after that. Additional doses can be toxic. Once vomiting has been successfully induced, it is time to try and absorb any residual poison left in the stomach. This is best accomplished with **Activated Charcoal** which is effective for just about all poisons except cyanide. Mix one or two large tablespoons of powder in an eight ounce glass of water until you have a nice, soupy glop. (If already in liquid form, one ounce of a 25 percent solution is a proper dose.) Administer the dose frequently until medical attention is obtained.

If the child has swallowed anything corrosive such as acid, alkali (lye), gasoline, kerosene, strychnine, cleaning fluid, turpentine, or any other petroleum product, vomiting can be extremely hazardous. In such cases, demulcents such as milk, egg white, aluminum hydroxide gel, gelatin solution, flour and water, or oil may be of some value by diluting the corrosive concentration. Immediate hospitalization is necessary.

It would be wise for any family with children to always have **Ipecac Syrup** and **Activated Charcoal** on hand at all times. Both can be purchased without a prescription from your pharmacist. Commerical kits for first-aid emergency use are available. I strongly recommend the *Poison Antidote Kit* which is made by Bowman Pharmaceuticals, 110 Schroyer Avenue, S.W., Canton, Ohio 44702. Their kit, which sells for a reasonable price (about $6.50), contains both necessary ingredients coupled with clear instructions for use. The best answer, however, is to avoid accidental poisoning altogether by taking the precaution to keep medicines out of reach of curious hands.

Kids are people too. Unfortunately, they are at the mercy of parents, doctors, and drug companies that are not responsive to their special problems. Although little is known about the way in which medications affect children, hardly anything is being done to correct the situation. While drug treatment can be of value, or even crucial, for many childhood illnesses, the casual use of potent chemicals for disorders that might respond to other techniques is to be condemned.

References

1. Thompson, Richard C. "Evaluating Drugs for Use in Children." *FDA Consumer* 9(2):14–18, 1975.
2. Kotulak, Ronald. "Medicine OK For Children? No One Knows." Chicago *Tribune* Service, March, 1975.

229

3. Nelson, M. M., and Forfar, J. O. "Associations Between Drugs Administered During Pregnancy and Congenital Abnormalities of the Fetus." *Brit. Med. J.* 1:523–527, 1971.

4. Marx, Jean L. "Drugs During Pregnancy: Do They Affect the Unborn Child?" *Science* 180:174–175, 1973.

5. Brody, Jane E. "Most Pregnant Women Found Taking Excess Drugs." New York *Times*, March 18, 1973.

6. "Drugs in Pregnancy." *Medical Letter* 14:94–96, 1972.

7. Huff, Barbara B., ed. *Physician's Desk Reference*. Oradell, N.J.: Medical Economics Company, 1974.

8. "Morning Sickness." *Medical Letter* 16:47, 1974.

9. Milkovich, Lucille, and Van den Berg, Bea J. "Effects of Prenatal Meprobamate and Chlordiazepoxide Hydrochloride on Human Embryonic Development." *New Engl. J. Med.* 291:1268–1271, 1974.

10. Harty, Stuart C., et al. "Antenatal Exposure to Meprobamate and Chlordiazepoxide in Relation to Malformations, Mental Development, and Childhood Mortality." *New Engl. J. Med.* 292:726–728, 1975.

11. Spellacy, W. N. "Oral Contraceptives Contraindicated for Nursing Mother." *JAMA* 221:1415, 1972.

12. "News Front: Don't Bathe the Newborn, Cautions AAP Committee." *Mod. Med.* 43(4):21, 1975.

13. Darby, Charles P., et al. "Ischemia Following an Intragluteal Injection of Benzathine-Procaine G Mixture in a 1-Year-Old Boy." *Clin. Pediatr.* 12:485–7, 1973.

14. Stewart, D. J. "Prevalence of Tetracyclines in Children's Teeth—Study II: A Resurvey After Five Years. *Brit. Med. J.* 3:320–322, 1973.

15. Caldwell, Jacques R., and Cluff, Leighton E. "Adverse Reactions to Antimicrobial Agents." *JAMA* 230:77–80, 1974.

16. Dinello, F. A., and Champelli, J. "The Use of Imipramine in the Treatment of Enuresis. A Review of the Literature," *Canad. Psychiatr. Assoc. J.* 13:237–241, 1968.

17. Stewart, Mark A. "Treatment of Bedwetting." *JAMA* 232:281–283, 1975.

18. "Imipramine for Enuresis." *Medical Letter* 16:22–24, 1974.

19. Shaffer, D., et al. "Control of Enuresis with Imipramine." *Arch. Dis. Child.* 43:665–671, 1968.

20. Forsythe, W., and Merrett, J. D. "A Controlled Trial of Imipramine (Tofranil) and Nortriptyline (Allegron) in the Treatment of Enuresis." *Br. J. Clin. Pract.* 23:210–215, 1969.

21. Ginsburg, Arthur. "Enuresis: Treatment with Imipramine." *JAMA* 228:289–290, 1970.

22. Stewart, Mark, op. cit.
23. Sleator, Esther K., et al. "Hyperactive Children: A Continuous Long-Term Placebo-Controlled Follow-Up." *JAMA* 229:316–317, 1974.
24. Kroger, John M., and Safer, Daniel J. "Type and Prevalence of Medication Used in the Treatment of Hyperactive Children." *New Engl. J. Med.* 291:1118–1120, 1974.
25. Kline, Carl L. "Prevalence and Management of Hyperactive Children." *New Engl. J. Med.* 292:536, 1975.
26. Safer, D. J., et al. "Depression of Growth in Hyperactive Children on Stimulant Drugs." *New Engl. J. Med.* 287:217–220, 1972.
27. Safer, D. J., and Allern, R. P. "Factors Influencing The Suppressant Effect of Two Stimulant Drugs on the Growth of Hyperactive Children." *Pediatrics* 51:660–667, 1973.
28. Sleator et al., op. cit.
29. Weiss, G., et al. "Effect of Long-Term Treatment of Hyperactive Children with Methylphenidate." *Can. Med. Assoc. J.* 112:159–165, 1975.
30. Franks, Lucinda. "F.D.A., In Shift, Tests Pediatrician's Diet for Hyperactive Children." New York *Times*, February 9, 1975.
31. Ibid.

TABLE 1
Calculation of Dosages for Children

Not all dosages for children can be calculated by applying a simple formula to an adult dose. Some drugs can be very toxic to kids, even at a reduced level. The following reference guide is provided merely as an aid and should not be relied upon for all medications, especially not for those that could be hazardous.

A. *Clark's Rule*: Take the weight of the child in pounds and divide by 150. The answer will represent the fraction of the adult dose.

$$\frac{Weight\ of\ the\ child\ in\ pounds}{150} \times \text{Adult dose} = \text{Child's dose}$$

Example: Johnny weighs 50 pounds.

$$\frac{50}{150} = 1/3 \text{ of the adult dose}$$

B. *Young's Rule*: Take the age of the child and divide this by the age plus 12. The answer should be in fraction form and will represent the part of the adult dose recommended for a child.

$$\frac{Age\ of\ the\ child}{Age + 12} \times \text{Adult's dose} = \text{Child's dose}$$

Example: Johnny is aged 4.

$$\frac{4}{4 + 12} = 1/4 \text{ of the adult dose}$$

C. *Cowling's Rule*: Take the age of the child at his or her next birthday and divide by 24.

$$\frac{Age\ at\ next\ birthday}{24} \times \text{Adult dose} = \text{Child's dose}$$

Example: Johnny will be 4.

$$\frac{4}{24} = 1/6 \text{ of the adult dose}$$

TABLE 2
DRUGS THAT MAY BE PARTICULARLY DANGEROUS TO A FETUS*

ACHROMYCIN (TET-RACYCLINE) ....May lead to permanent discoloration or staining of developing teeth; possible disturbance of bone growth.[1,2,3]

ALDACTAZIDE ....Blood disorders are a possibility in the newborn.[1,4,5]

ALVA-TRANQUIL (contains BROMIDE)..............Can produce skin eruptions in the newborn.[6]

ANDROID (METHYLTES-TOSTERONE)..........Masculinization of female fetus; abnormal bone growth; irregular sexual development.[2,7,8]

ANTICOAGULANTS (blood thinners) ....When used close to delivery, fetal death may occur due to intrauterine hemorrhaging.[2,9,10]

ANTICONVULSANTS (DI-LANTIN, etc.) ....Cleft lip; cleft palate; other abnormalities. If withholding anticonvulsants would be injurious to the mother, folic acid may counteract these malformations.[2,11,12,13]

ANTIVERT (MECLIZINE)....Malformations reported in animal studies; further investigation is necessary.[2,4,14]

ARALEN (CHLOROQUINE) .May lead to increased risk to fetus; safety has not been established.[4,10,15]

ASPIRIN (SALICYLATES) ..May make newborn more susceptible to bleeding; could increase gestation, prolong labor, and complicate delivery.[16,17,18,19,20]

ATABRINE (QUINACRINE) .Possibly injurious to fetus during the treatment of intestinal parasites in mother.[21]

AZOGANTANOL (sulfa drug)..................Can produce kernicterus, a form of jaundice in the newborn often associated with brain damage; animal studies have indicated that other abnormalities are possible.[2,4,9,10,22]

AZOGANTRISIN (sulfa drug)..................Can produce kernicterus, a form of jaundice in the newborn often associated with brain damage; animal studies have indicated that other abnormalities are possible.[2,4,9,10,22]

BACTRIM (sulfa drug) .....Can produce kernicterus, a form of jaundice in the newborn often associated with brain damage; animal studies have indicated that other abnormalities are possible.[2,4,9,10,22]

*Not all children exposed before birth to drugs on this list will develop birth defects. For some of these drugs the statistical probability of complications is low.

Just because a drug is not included in this list does not guarantee its safety for the unborn child. Always consult your doctor.

BAMADEX (DEXTROAM-PHETAMINE) ....Heart defects and blood vessel malformations.[23,24,25,26]

BARBITURATES (most brands) ....Large doses may lead to weakened breathing in newborn after delivery.[1,2,9]

BIRTH CONTROL PILLS (all brands) ....New and controversial; malformations of arms and legs; defects of internal organ systems.[27,28,29]

BLOOD TONICS (IODIDES) .Without special precautions, goiter may occur in the fetus.[1]

BONINE (MECLIZINE) ......Malformations reported in animal studies; further investigation necessary.[2,4,14]

BUTAZOLIDIN (PHENYL-BUTAZONE) ....May produce goiter in newborn.[1]

CALCIDRINE SYRUP ......Should not be used for prolonged periods during pregnancy.[1,4]

CHLOROMYCETIN (CHLORAMPHENICOL) ..May cause "gray baby syndrome"; dangerously toxic and may cause death to unborn child.[30,31]

CHLORPROMAZINE (THORAZINE) ....Fetal jaundice; nervous system disorders.[4]

COLCHICINE ....Possibly injurious to fetus.[32,33]

CORTISONE ....Controversial; Possibility of cleft palate.[1,8,34]

COUMADIN (WARFARIN) ..When used close to delivery, fetal death may occur due to intrauterine hemorrhaging.[2,9,10]

CYTOXAN (CYCLOPHOS-PHAMIDE) ....Deformities and abortions.[35]

DELTA-CORTEF (PRED-NISOLONE) ....Controversial, possibly increased risk to fetus.[3,4,36]

DEMULEN (birth control pill) New and controversial; malformations of arms and legs; defects of internal organ systems.[27,28,29]

DEXAMYL (DEXTROAM-PHETAMINE) ....Heart defects and blood vessel malformations.[23,24,25,26]

DEXEDRINE (DEXTROAM-PHETAMINE) ....Heart defects and blood vessel malformations.[23,24,25,26]

*Not all children exposed before birth to drugs on this list will develop birth defects. For some of these drugs the statistical probability of complications is low.

234 Just because a drug is not included in this list does not guarantee its safety for the unborn child. Always consult your doctor.

DIABINESE (CHLOR-PROPAMIDE) .... May cause low blood sugar in newborn.[53]

DICUMAROL (BISHYD-ROXYCOUMARIN) ...... When used close to delivery, fetal death may occur due to intrauterine hemorrhaging.[2,9,10]

DIETHYLSTILBESTROL (DES) .... Could cause vaginal cancer and tissue abnormalities in female offspring.[37,38,39]

DIET PILLS (DEXTROAM-PHETAMINE) .... Heart defects and blood vessel malformations.[23,24,25,26]

DILANTIN (DIPHENYLHY-DANTOIN) .... Cleft lip; cleft palate; other abnormalities; if withholding anticonvulsants would be injurious to the mother, folic acid may counteract these malformations.[2,11,12,13]

DIUPRES (water pill) .... Blood disorders are a possibility in the newborn.[1,4,5]

DIURIL (water pill) .... Blood disorders are a possibility in the newborn.[1,4,5]

DIUTENSEN (water pill) ... Blood disorders are a possibility in the newborn.[1,4,5]

DUPHASTON (PROGES-TERONE) .... Possible masculinization of female fetus.[7,28,40]

DYAZIDE (water pill) .... Blood disorders are a possibility in the newborn.[1,4,5]

ELIXOPHYLLIN-KI .... May cause goiter in the unborn child, which can lead to additional complications.[1,41]

ENDURON (water pill) ..... Blood disorders are a possibility in the newborn.[1,4,5]

ENOVID (birth control pill) . New and controversial; malformations of arms and legs; defects of internal organ systems.[27,28,29]

ESIDRIX (water pill) .... Blood disorders are a possibility in the newborn as well as jaundice.[1,4,5]

ESKALITH (LITHIUM CAR-BONATE) .... Could produce fetal goiter and other unwanted side effects.[1,4]

ESKATROL (DEXTROAM-PHETAMINE) .... Heart defects and blood vessel malformations.[23,24,25,26]

FEDRAZIL (CHLORCY-CLIZINE) Potentially injurious to the unborn child.[2,4]

---

*Not all children exposed before birth to drugs on this list will develop birth defects. For some of these drugs the statistical probability of complications is low.

Just because a drug is not included in this list does not guarantee its safety for the unborn child. Always consult your doctor.

235

GANTANOL (sulfa drug) ... Can produce kernicterus, a form of jaundice in the newborn often associated with brain damage; animal studies have indicated that other abnormalities are possible.[2,4,9,10,22]

GANTRISIN (sulfa drug) .... Can produce kernicterus, a form of jaundice in the newborn often associated with brain damage; animal studies have indicated that other abnormalities are possible.[2,4,9,10,22]

GLUTEST (TESTOS-TERONE) .... Masculinization of female fetus; abnormal bone growth; irregular sexual development.[2,7,8]

HALDOL (HALOPERIDOL) . Controversial: Investigations in animals suggest possible malformations: further study is required.[44,45,46]

HEROIN .... Addiction in unborn babies leading to withdrawal after birth; weakened breathing after delivery.[2,35]

HORMONE PREGNANCY TESTS .... This withdrawal-type pregnancy test may lead to malformations (controversial).[27,42,43]

HYDRODIURIL (water pill) .. Blood disorders are a possibility in the newborn as well as jaundice.[1,4,5]

HYDROPRES (water pill) ... Blood disorders are a possibility in the newborn as well as jaundice.[1,4,5]

INDOCIN (INDOMETHACIN) Not recommended during pregnancy.[47]

IODIDES (expectorants) .... May lead to goiter in the unborn child.[1,41]

LASIX (FUROSEMIDE) ..... Animal studies indicate malformations.[48,49]

LITHANE (LITHIUM CAR-BONATE) .... Could produce fetal goiter and other unwanted side effects.[1,4]

LITHIUM CARBONATE ..... Could produce fetal goiter and other unwanted side effects.[1,4]

LOESTRIN (birth control pill) New and controversial; malformations of arms and legs; defects of internal organ systems.[27,28,29]

MAREZINE (CYCLIZINE) .. Malformations reported in animal studies; further investigation is necessary.[2,4,14]

MEBROIN (DIPHENYLHY-DANTOIN) .... Cleft lip, cleft palate; other abnormalities; if withholding anticonvulsants would be injurious to the mother, folic acid may counteract these malformations.[2,11,12,13]

---

*Not all children exposed before birth to drugs on this list will develop birth defects. For some of these drugs the statistical probability of complications is low.

Just because a drug is not included in this list does not guarantee its safety for the unborn child. Always consult your doctor.

**METANDREN (METHYL-
TESTOSTERONE)** . . . . Masculinization of female fetus; abnormal bone growth; irregular sexual development.[7,8]

METHADONE . . . . Prolonged withdrawal symptoms in newborn.[50]

METHOTREXATE . . . . Abortions, malformations, cleft palate.[1,51]

MICRONOR (birth control pill) . . . . New and controversial; malformations of arms and legs; defects of internal organ systems; possible masculinization of female fetus.[7,28,40]

MIGRAL (CYCLIZINE) . . . . . . Malformations reported in animal studies; further investigation is necessary.[2,4,14]

MIRADON (ANISINDIONE) . . Increased risk to fetus.[4]

MUDRANE (IODIDE) . . . . . . Can cause goiter in the unborn child.[1,41]

MYLERAN (BUSULFAN) . . . Cleft palate, malformations, irregular sexual development.[35]

MYSOLINE (PRIMIDONE) . . . Tendency to hemorrhage in the newborn. Mothers should receive **Vitamin K** for one month prior to delivery to prevent this occurrence.[4,12]

**MYSTECLIN-F (TETRACY-
CLINE)** . . . . Permanent discoloration of developing teeth.[1,2,3]

**NERVINE (contains
bromide)** . . . . Can produce skin eruptions in babies.[6]

NICOTINE (smoking) . . . . Potentially detrimental; smaller birth weight of baby; possible premature delivery; higher risk of death to fetus.[52]

**NOCTEC (CHLORAL HY-
DRATE)** . . . . In large dose may be injurious to the fetus.[1]

NORINYL (birth control pill) New and controversial; malformations of arms and legs; defects of internal organ systems.[27,28,29]

**NORLESTRIN (birth control
pill)** . . . . New and controversial; malformations of arms and legs; defects of internal organ systems.[27,28,29]

NOR-Q.D. (birth control pill) New and controversial; malformations of arms and legs; defects of internal organ systems. Possible masculinization of female fetus.[7,27,28,29,40]

ORACON (birth control pill) New and controversial; malformations of arms and legs; defects of internal organ systems.[27,28,29]

*Not all children exposed before birth to drugs on this list will develop birth defects. For some of these drugs the statistical probability of complications is low.

Just because a drug is not included in this list does not guarantee its safety for the unborn child. Always consult your doctor.

ORETON (TESTOSTERONE) Masculinization of female fetus; abnormal bone growth; irregular sexual development.[7,8]

ORINASE (TOLBUTAMIDE) . Not recommended for use during pregnancy because it leads to prolonged low blood sugar in newborn.[1]

ORTHO-NOVUM (birth control pill) .... New and controversial; malformations of arms and legs; defects of internal organ systems.[27,28,29]

OVRAL (birth control pill) .. New and controversial; malformations of arms and legs; defects of internal organ systems.[27,28,29]

OVULEN (birth control pill) . New and controversial; malformations of arms and legs; defects of internal organ systems.[27,28,29]

PANMYCIN (TETRACYCLINE) .... Permanent staining of developing teeth.[1,2,3]

PANWARFIN (WARFARIN) . When used close to delivery, fetal death may occur due to intrauterine hemorrhaging.[2,4,9]

PARADIONE (PARAMETHADIONE) ... Possibility of malformations.[4,12]

PHENOBARBITAL .... In large doses this barbiturate could cause breathing difficulties in the new-born; animal studies indicate possible feminization of male behavior.[2,10,54]

PLACIDYL (ETHCHLORVYNOL) .... Not recommended in early pregnancy.[4,55]

POTASSIUM IODIDE .... May cause goiter in the unborn child, which can lead to additional complications.[1,41]

PREDNISONE .... Controversial: safety not established; may affect adrenal glands.[34,36]

PRELUDIN (PHENMETRAZINE) .... Malformations have been reported in animal studies. Further investigation is required.[1,4,8]

PRESAMINE (IMIPRAMINE) Inconclusive and controversial; safety during pregnancy has not been established.[56,57]

QUADRINAL (IODIDE) ..... May cause goiter in the unborn child, which can lead to additional complications.[1,41]

QUINAMM (QUININE) ...... Should not be used during pregnancy; may lead to deafness or blood disorders in the newborn.[4,58]

*Not all children exposed before birth to drugs on this list will develop birth defects. For some of these drugs the statistical probability of complications is low.

Just because a drug is not included in this list does not guarantee its safety for the unborn child. Always consult your doctor.

QUINETTE (contains DES) . Could cause vaginal cancer in female offspring.[4,37,38]

QUININE .... May lead to deafness or blood disorders in the newborn.[1,58]

RADIOACTIVE IODINE ..... May lead to goiter, hypothyroidism, or cretinism in the newborn.[2,59]

RAUDIXIN (RAUWOLFIA) .. Can cause nasal congestion leading to breathing problems in the newborn; decreased appetite may be an additional complication.[2,4]

RAUZIDE (RAUWOLFIA) ... Blood disorders are a possibility in the newborn as well as jaundice; can cause nasal congestion leading to breathing difficulties.[1,2,3,4]

REGROTON (RESERPINE) . Blood disorders are a possibility in the newborn as well as jaundice; can cause nasal congestion leading to breathing difficulties; decreased appetite may be an additional complication.[1,2,4,5]

RESERPINE .... Increased lung secretions and nasal congestion leading to generalized breathing difficulties; lack of appetite may be another side effect.[2,4]

ROBITET (TETRACYCLINE) Permanent staining of developing teeth.[1,2,3]

SALUTENSIN (RESERPINE) Blood disorders are a possibility in the newborn as well as jaundice; can cause nasal congestion leading to breathing difficulties; decreased appetite may be an additional complication.[1,2,4,5]

SER-AP-ES (RESERPINE) .. Blood disorders are a possibility in the newborn as well as jaundice; can cause nasal congestion leading to breathing difficulties; decreased appetite may be an additional complication.[1,2,4,5]

SERPASIL (RESERPINE) ... Increased lung secretions and nasal congestion leading to generalized breathing difficulties; lack of appetite may be another side effect.[2,4]

SK SOXAZOLE (sulfa drug) Can produce kernicterus, a form of jaundice in the newborn often associated with brain damage; cleft palate and other abnormalities have been reported in animal studies.[2,4,10,22]

STREPTOMYCIN .... Can cause deafness in the newborn child.[1,2]

*Not all children exposed before birth to drugs on this list will develop birth defects. For some of these drugs the statistical probability of complications is low.
Just because a drug is not included in this list does not guarantee its safety for the unborn child. Always consult your doctor.

THE PEOPLE'S PHARMACY

SULFA DRUGS . . . . Can produce kernicterus, a form of jaundice in the newborn often associated with brain damage; cleft palate and other abnormalities have been reported in animal studies.[2,9,10,22]

SUMYCIN (TETRACYCLINE) Permanent discoloration of developing teeth.[1,2,3]

TAPAZOLE (METHIMAZOLE) . . . . Administration of this drug during pregnancy is complicated. Without special precautions it may cause goiter, hypothyroidism, or cretinism.[1,4]

TETRACYCLINE . . . . Permanent discoloration and staining of developing teeth; possible bone growth disturbances.[1,2,3]

TETREX (TETRACYCLINE) . Permanent discoloration of developing teeth.[1,2,3]

THORAZINE (CHLORPROMAZINE) . . . . Can cause fetal jaundice and nervous system disorders.[1,4]

TOFRANIL (IMIPRAMINE) . . Inconclusive and controversial; safety during pregnancy has not been established.[56,57]

TOLINASE (TOLAZAMIDE) . Contraindicated during pregnancy.[4]

TRIDIONE (TRIMETHADIONE) . . . . . . Possibility of malformations.[4,12]

VACCINATIONS . . . . Many vaccinations, including rubella and smallpox, should be done long before pregnancy.[10,60]

VIBRAMYCIN (TETRACYCLINE) . . . . Permanent staining of developing teeth.[1,2,3]

VITAMIN A (in excess) . . . . . Possibly injurious to eyes; may cause cleft palate.[1,61,62]

VITAMIN C (in excess) . . . . . Doses greater than one thousand milligrams per day may possibly cause scurvy in the newborn when **Vitamin C** levels drop after delivery.[2,62,63]

VITAMIN D (in excess) . . . . . May cause dangerously high levels of calcium.[58,62]

VITAMIN K (in excess) . . . . . Can produce kernicterus, a form of jaundice in the newborn which may be associated with brain damage.[2,64]

*Not all children exposed before birth to drugs on this list will develop birth defects. For some of these drugs the statistical probability of complications is low.
Just because a drug is not included in this list does not guarantee its safety for the unborn child. Always consult your doctor

240

TABLE 3

DRUGS TAKEN BY LACTATING MOTHERS THAT MAY ADVERSELY AFFECT NURS-ING BABIES*

Aldoclor (Chlorothiazide)
Alva-Tranquil (Bromide)
Anticancer Drugs
Aristocort (Cortisone-type)
Atropine
Azo-Gantanol (Sulfa Drug)
Azo-Gantrisin (Sulfa Drug)
Azotrex (Sulfa Drug)
Azulfidine (Sulfa)
Bactrim (Sulfa Drug)
Bamadex (Dextroamphetamine)
Barbiturates
Bentyl w/Phenobarbital
Benzedrine (Amphetamine)
Betapar (Cortisone-Type)
Blood Tonics (Iodides)
Bromides
Butiserpazide (Reserpine)
Cafergot (Ergotamine)
Celestone (Cortisone-Type)
Chardonna (Phenobarbital)
Chloromycetin (Chloramphenicol)
Cortisone
Coumadin (Warfarin)
Decadron (Cortisone-Type)
Delta-Cortef (Cortisone-Type)
Delta-Dome (Cortisone-Type)
Deltasone (Cortisone-Type)
Demulen (Birth Control Pill)
Deronil (Cortisone-Type)
Dexamyl (Dextroamphetamine)
Dexedrine (Dextroamphetamine)

Dicumarol (Bishydroxycoumarin)
Diupres (Reserpine)
Diuril (Chlorothiazide)
Diutensen-R (Reserpine)
Ekko (Diphenylhydantoin)
Enovid (Birth Control Pill)
Ergomar (Ergotamine)
Ergotamine
Eskabarb (Phenobarbital)
Eskatrol (Dextroamphetamine)
Exna-R (Reserpine)
Gantanol (Sulfa Drug)
Gantrisin (Sulfa Drug)
Gynergen (Ergotamine)
Heroin
Hexachlorobenzene
Hydergine (Ergotamine)
Hydromox-R (Reserpine)
Hydropres (Reserpine)
Iodides-Iodine
Kenacort (Cortisone-Type)
Laxatives
Lipo Gantrisin (Sulfa Drug)
Loestrin (Birth Control Pill)
Mebroin (Diphenylhydantoin)
Metatensin (Reserpine)
Meticortelone (Cortisone-Type)
Meticorten (Cortisone-Type)
Micronor (Birth Control Pill)
Migral (Ergotamine)
Miradon (Anisindione)
Modane (Danthron)

*Not all babies exposed to drugs on this list will develop adverse reactions. For some of these drugs the probability of complication is low.

Just because a drug is not included in this list does not guarantee its safety for the nursing infant. Always consult your doctor.

Selected references: 1, 4, 65, 66, 67, 68, 69

Mudrane (Iodide)
Naquival (Reserpine)
NegGram (Nalidixic Acid)
Nicotine (Smoking)
Norinyl (Birth Control Pill)
Norlestrin (Birth Control Pill)
Nor-Q.D. (Birth Control Pill)
Obotan (Dextroamphetamine)
Oracon (Birth Control Pill)
Orasone (Cortisone-Type)
Ortho-Novum (Birth Control Pill)
Ovulen (Birth Control Pill)
Pamine PB (Phenobarbital)
Panwarfin (Warfarin)
Phelantin (Diphenylhydantoin)
Phenobarbital
Potassium Iodide
Prednisone (Cortisone-Type)
Pro-Banthine (Propantheline)
Proklar-M (Sulfa Drug)
Prydon (Atropine)
Quadrinal (Phenobarbital)
Quinamm (Quinine)
Quinine
Radioactive Iodine

Raudixin (Rauwolfia)
Rau-Sed (Reserpine)
Rauwiloid (Rauwolfia)
Rauzide (Rauwolfia)
Regroton (Reserpine)
Renese-R (Reserpine)
Reserpine
Salutensin (Reserpine)
Septra (Sulfa Drug)
Ser-Ap-Es (Reserpine)
Serpasil (Reserpine)
Sidonna (Atropine)
Sintrom (Acenocoumarol)
SK Soxazole (Sulfa Drug)
Sonilyn (Sulfa Drug)
Sosol (Sulfa Drug)
Sterazolidin (Cortisone-Type)
Sulla (Sulfa Drug)
Sulfa Drugs
Tapazole (Methimazole)
Terfonyl (Sulfa Drug)
Tetracycline (?)
Thiosulfil (Sulfa Drug)
Trac Tabs (Atropine)
Urobiotic-250 (Sulfa Drug)

Table References

1. Martin, Eric W. *Hazards of Medication*. Philadelphia: Lippincott Company, 1971. P. 275.
2. "Drugs in Pregnancy." *Medical Letter* 14:94–96, 1972.
3. Cohlan, S. Q. "Fetal and Neonatal Hazards From Drugs Administered during Pregnancy." *N.Y. State J. Med.* 64:493–499, 1964.
4. Huff, Barbara B., ed. *Physician's Desk Reference*. Oradell, N.J.: Medical Economics, 1974.
5. Rodriguez, S. V., et al. "Neonatal Thrombocytopenia Associated With Ante-Partum Administration of Thiazide Drugs." *New Engl. J. Med.* 270:881–884, 1964.
6. Sapeika, B. A. "The Passage of Drugs across the Placenta." *S. Afric. Med. J.* 34:49–55, 1960.
7. Marx, Jean L. "Drugs During Pregnancy: Do They Affect the Newborn Child?" *Science* 180:174–175, 1973.

8. Grumback, M. M., and Ducharne, J. R. "The Effects of Androgens on Fetal Sexual Development." *Fert. Steril.* 11:157–180, 1960.
9. Silverman, Milton, and Lee, Philip R. *Pills, Profits, And Politics.* Los Angeles: University of California Press, 1974. P. 268.
10. Apgar, V., et al. "Should You Give Her That Drug during Pregnancy?" *Patient Care* 3:84–92, 1969.
11. Speidel, B. D., and Meadow, S. R. "Maternal Epilepsy and Abnormalities of the Fetus." *Lancet* 2:839–843, 1972.
12. Zellweger, Hans. "Anticonvulsants during Pregnancy: A Danger To the Developing Fetus?" *Clin. Ped.* 13:338–346, 1974.
13. Annegers, J. F., et al. "Do Anticonvulsants Have Teratogenic Effect?" *Arch. Neurol.* 31:364–373, 1974.
14. "Morning Sickness." *Medical Letter* 16:47, 1974.
15. "Chloroquine (Aralen) and Fetal Injury." *Medical Letter* 7:9–10, 1965.
16. Lewis, Richard B., et al. "Influence of Acetylsalicylic Acid, An Inhibitor of Prostaglandid Synthesis, on the Duration of Human Gestation and Labor." *Lancet* 2:1159–1161, 1973.
17. Waltman, Richard, and Tricomi, Vincent. "Aspirin and Pregnancy." *New Engl. J. Med.* 291:53, 1974.
18. Richards, J. D. "Congenital Malformations and Environmental Influences in Pregnancy." *Brit. J. Prev. Soc. Med.* 22:218–225, 1969.
19. Collins, E., and Turner, G. "Salicylates and Pregnancy." *Lancet* 2:1494, 1973.
20. Bleyer, W. A., and Breckinridge, R. T. "The Effects of Prenatal Aspirin on Newborn Hemostasis." *JAMA* 213:2049–2053, 1970.
21. Atabrine package insert (brochure).
22. Weinstein, L., and Dalton, D. "Host Determinants of Response to Antimicrobial Agents." *New Engl. J. Med.* 279:526–528, 1968.
23. Gilbert, Enid F., and Khoury, George H. "Dextroamphetamine and Congenital Cardiac Malformations." *J. Pediatr.* 76:638, 1970.
24. Nora, J. J., et al. "Dextroamphetamine Teratogenicity Malformations in Mice Induced by Dexamphetamine Sulfate." *Lancet* 2:1021, 1965.
25. Nora, J. J., et al. "Homologies for Congenital Heart Diseases: Murine Models Influenced by Dextroamphetamine." *Teratology* 1:413–416, 1968.
26. Nora, J. J., et al. "Maternal Exposure to Potential Teratogens." *JAMA* 202:1065, 1967.
27. Nora, A. H., and Nora J. J. "Syndrome of Multiple Congenital Anomalies Associated with Teratogenic Exposure." *Arch. Environ. Health.* 30:17–21, 1975.

28. Janerich, D. T., et al. "Oral Contraceptives and Congenital Limb Reduction Defects." *New Engl. J. Med.* 291:697–700, 1974.
29. Nora, James J., and Nora, Audrey H. "Birth Defects and Oral Contraceptives." *Lancet* 1:941–942, 1973.
30. Sutherland, J. M. "Fatal Cardiovascular Collapse of Infants Receiving Large Amounts of Chloramphenicol." *Am. J. Dis. Child.* 92:761–767, 1959.
31. Goodman, Louis S., and Gilman, Alfred. *The Pharmacological Basis of Therapeutics*, 4th ed. London: Macmillan, 1970.
32. Diamond, Liebe S. "Treatment of Hyperuricemia and Gout." *New Engl. J. Med.* 286:267, 1972.
33. Goldfinger, Stephen E. "Treatment of Gout." *New Engl. J. Med.* 285:1303–1306, 1971.
34. Villee, Dorothy B. "What Risk to Fetus From Maternal Steroid Therapy?" *JAMA* 230:1202–1203, 1974.
35. Apgar, V. "Drugs in Pregnancy." *JAMA* 190:840–841, 1964.
36. Warrell, D. W., and Taylor, R. "Outcome for the Fetus of Mothers Receiving Prednisolone During Pregnancy." *Lancet* 1:117–118, 1968.
37. Herbst, Arthur L., et al. "Adenocarcinoma of the Vagina." *New Engl. J. Med.* 284:878–881, 1971.
38. Herbst, Arthur L., et al. "Clear-Cell Adenocarcinoma of the Genital Tract in Young Females." *New Engl. J. Med.* 287:1259–1264, 1972.
39. Herbst, Arthur L., et al. "Prenatal Exposure to Stilbestrol A Prospective Comparison of Exposed Female Offspring with Unexposed Controls." *New Engl. J. Med.* 292:334–339, 1975.
40. Hussey, Hugh H. Editorial: "Teratogenic Effects of Progestogen/Estrogen." *JAMA* 230:1019–1020, 1974.
41. Galina, M. P., et al. "Iodides During Pregnancy, Apparent Cause of Neonatal Death." *New Engl. J. Med.* 267:1124–1127, 1962.
42. Janerich, Dwight T., et al. "Problems of Oral Contraceptives Given during Pregnancy." *New Engl. J. Med.* 292:112–113, 1975.
43. Kaufman, Robert T. "Birth Defects and Oral Contraceptives." *Lancet* 1:1396, 1973.
44. Kopelman, Arthur E., et al. "Limb Malformations Following Maternal Use of Haloperidol." *JAMA* 231:62–64, 1975.
45. Archer, John P. "Another Possible Teratogen?" *JAMA* 231:69, 1975.
46. Vichi, F. "Neuroleptic Drugs in Experimental Teratogenesis." In Bertelli, A., ed. *Teratology*. Amsterdam: Excerpta Medica, 1969. Pp. 87–101.

47. Indocin package insert (brochure).
48. Lasix package Insert (brochure).
49. Mitchell, J. R., et al. "Hepatic Necrosis Caused by Furosemide." *Nature* 251:508–510, 1974.
50. Rajegowda, A. K., et al. "Methadone Withdrawal in Newborn Infants." *J. Pediatr.* 81:532, 1972.
51. Stuart, D. M. "Teratogenicity and Terotogenic Drugs." *Pharm. Index* 8, 1966.
52. Kullander, Stig, and Bengt, Kallen. "A Prospective Study of Smoking and Pregnancy." *Acta Obstet. Gynaec. Scand.* 50:83–94, 1971.
53. Zucker, P., and Simon, G. "Prolonged Symptomatic Neonatal Hypoglycemia Associated with Maternal Chlorpropamide Therapy." *Pediat.* 42:824, 1968.
54. Brody, Jane E. "Most Pregnant Woman Found Taking Excess Drugs." From "Symposium on Drugs and the Unborn Child" (March 15–16, 1973). New York *Times*, March 18, 1973.
55. Wolfe, Sidney, and Hoffman, Connie. Health Research Group's Report to FDA Commissioner, Alexander M. Schmidt, 1973.
56. Juhana, Idanpaan-Heikkila. "Possible Teratogenicity of Imipramine/Chloropyramine." *Lancet* 2:282–283, 1973.
57. McBride, W. G. "Limb Deformities Associated with Iminodibenzyl Hydrochloride." *Med. J. of Australia* 1:492, 1972.
58. Lenz, W. "Malformations Caused by Drugs in Pregnancy." *Am. J. Dis. Child.* 112:99–106, 1966.
59. Adamson, K., and Joelson, I. "The Effects of Pharmacological Agents upon the Fetus and the Newborn." *Am. J. Obstet. Gynec.* 96:437–460, 1966.
60. "Pregnancy and Other Contraindications to Smallpox Vaccination." *Medical Letter* 7:37–38, 1965.
61. Cohlan, S. Q. "Congenital Anomalies in Rats Induced by Excessive Intake of Vitamin A during Pregnancy." *Pediatrics* 13:556–567, 1964.
62. "Nutrition in Pregnancy." *Medical Letter* 15:67–68, 1973.
63. Cochrane, W. A. "Overnutrition in Prenatal and Neonatal Life: A Problem?" *Canad. Med. Assoc. J.* 93:893, 1965.
64. Lucey, J. F., and Dolan, R. C. "Hyperbilirubinemia of Newborn Infants Associated With Parenteral Administration of Vitamin K Analogues to Mother." *Pediatrics* 23:553–560, 1959.
65. Vorherr, Helmuth. *The Breast Morphology, Physiology, and Lactation.* New York: Academic Press, 1974.
66. Vorherr, Helmuth. "Drug Excretion in Breast Milk." *Postgrad.*

245

      Med. 56:97–104, 1974.
67. "Potential Effects on Nursing Infants of Drugs Taken in Excessive Amounts by Lactating Mothers." *Mod. Med.* 43:167, 1975.
68. "Drugs in Breast Milk." *Medical Letter* 16:25–27, 1974.
69. Spellacy, W. N. "Oral Contraceptives Contraindicated for Nursing Mother." *JAMA* 221:1415, 1972.

11.

Preventing High Blood Pressure and Heart Attack with and without Drugs

Next to cancer, nothing strikes fear into people's minds quite so fast as a diagnosis of heart disease. And well it may. In the United States of America, Public Health Enemy Number 1 is heart disease and other cardiovascular problems. Over one million people die from heart attacks and strokes each year. That is not to mention the 22 million who suffer from high blood pressure. It has been guesstimated by reliable medical authorities that as many as 20 percent of all adults in North America suffer from blood pressure above the normal range. If you think about that for a moment, it means that one out of every five of your friends probably has hypertension (the medical term for high blood pressure), and quite possibly you 247 do too. But by now you probably do not need to be reminded of the problem. The barrage of scary publicity put out by the AMA and the American Heart Association most likely has you uptight enough already. The question is, what do we know about heart trouble and high blood pressure and what should you do about them once you've got them?

The fact of the matter is that nobody knows from nothing when it comes to diseases of the cardiovascular system. Although your doctor may pretend that he is on top of the situation, the truth is more like the blind leading the blind. That goes for high blood pressure, heart attack, arteriosclerosis, thrombophlebitis, heart rate irregularities, etc. Hard to believe, isn't it? Just ask your physician what causes any of the above problems and see what he says. He will either tell you straight out that we don't really know very much, or he will cook up such a complicated story that it would confuse your average park ranger. Even though hundreds and hundreds of millions of dollars have been poured down the research tubes, we are still a long way from solving the riddles of heart disease.

Unfortunately, the medical profession is like a dinosaur. It takes a long time for messages to get from the brain to the tail and even longer to slow the beast down once it has got started. I have already belabored the point that doctors are slow to discard outmoded medical techniques (blood-letting lasted for centuries, and many doctors still insist that ulcer patients should follow a bland diet even though there is no sound scientific evidence to support this regimen). Despite the fact that your physician is still pretty much in the dark when it comes to the heart, chances are good that he has you on some high-powered medications or a restrictive diet. Take cholesterol, for example—a dastardly demon if ever there was one. Lots of doctors decry this evil substance and love to put their patients on medication or a low-cholesterol diet in order to reduce it. Yet eliminating cholesterol per se won't do you a damn bit of good. The case against dietary cholesterol is built upon some very circumstantial evidence, and the value of drug therapy is downright dubious. This is not to say that diet should be ignored. In fact, the right kind of diet can be extremely important. Nevertheless, a low-cholesterol diet is worthless in and of itself if it is not accompanied by some other important practices.

Cholesterol is not the only villain in the heart-disease story. There are lots of sacred cows floating around the medical profession. Sugar has been implicated, as has lack of exercise, coffee-consumption, pollution, cigarette-smoking, soft water, sluggish thyroid gland (see the book *Heart Attack Rareness In Thyroid-Treated Patients* by Broda Barnes, M.D.), and psychological stress. Emotion and prejudice seem to play as great a role as hard scientific evidence in determining which of the contradictory theories your doctor will accept or reject. It is unlikely that any one of these "enemies" is solely responsible, but a good case can be made for a combination of factors. This chapter contains straight talk. I am going to explain the stuff that doctors don't tell you about, especially when it comes to the drugs they prescribe for high blood pressure, high cholesterol, and heart disease. We are going to destroy some myths and explore some revolutionary new ideas.

High Blood Pressure

Let's start with high blood pressure to get the ball rolling. So what *is* blood pressure anyway? At the risk of getting too simplistic, try thinking of the cardiovascular system as a pump and a set of pipes. The pressure in the system at any given moment depends upon the power of the pump and the diameter of the pipes. The force created by the thrust of the blood pushing against the walls of the pipes or arteries creates your blood pressure. Since your heart acts much like an on-off pump in that it contracts and relaxes on the average seventy-two times per minute, the pressure varies between a high and low point. The peak pressure at the moment of contraction is called the *systolic pressure*. When the heart relaxes between beats the pressure drops to its lowest level, or *diastolic pressure*. Normally, a young adult has a blood pressure of about 120/80. This means that when the heart contracts, during systole, the pressure reaches 120 millimeters of mercury; when it relaxes, **249** during *diastole,* the pressure drops to 80 millimeters of mercury. Don't let the metric units freak you out. Just think of it as a measure of pressure not unlike the pounds per square inch which measure tire pressure.

Since the old pumper does not normally vary very much in the amount of force or power it exerts with each contraction, what really regulates the pressure is the diameter of the pipes. Just as you can regulate the pressure in your garden hose by adjusting the size of the nozzle, so too your body can regulate your blood pressure by varying the diameter of the blood vessels. Not only does blood pressure vary between high and low points during contraction and relaxation, it varies depending upon lots of environmental conditions. The arteries change their diameter dramatically depending upon your activity. When you are sleeping, they increase their diameter and the blood pressure drops. During excitement, such as love-making, the diameter narrows and pressure shoots up. Thus, a normal person could start the day off in bed with a pressure of 110/75 and end up with a pressure of 150/90 during an argument with the boss.

Although some variation in blood pressure is normal and even necessary for proper physiological function, some folks maintain a level that is almost always greater than it should be. That is called hypertension. High blood pressure can strike anyone. Sure, older folks are more susceptible, but youth is no guarantee that you are safe. In fact, it is the young hypertensive patient who suffers the most. People who are overweight are good candidates for raised pressure, and for some inexplicable reason, black people are more vulnerable to this disease than whites. A study carried out in the metropolitan Washington, D.C., area in 1975 uncovered the startling fact that as many as "one half of the black adult outpatients attending clinics might be expected to have elevated blood pressures."[1]

What all this means is that no one is immune. Well, so what? What's a little high blood pressure among friends anyway? While it is true that a little high blood pressure may not be too serious for older folks (some medical authorities have been tempted to speculate that it can be a natural or even necessary part of the ageing process), hypertension cannot be shrugged off easily. The heart of the problem is that like cancer, high blood pressure can go relatively undetected for long periods of time without producing any overt symptoms. Many people who go for ten or fifteen years with elevated pressure don't notice any specific problems. During that time, however, insidious damage can be done to the body.

Hypertension forces the heart to work harder in order to circulate the blood adequately around your system. The heart may become weakened over this period of time and lose some of its pumping power. Congestive heart failure is more common in folks with high blood pressure. The blood vessels also suffer from the constant battering that they receive from blood cruising along at higher-than-normal pressure. Deposits of fat somehow accumulate in the walls of arteries, leading to arteriosclerosis, otherwise known as hardening of the arteries. Researchers believe that arteriosclerosis increases the chances of coming down with a heart attack. The accumulation of fat and cholesterol in arteries is not restricted to the vessels in the heart. This "hardening" process may occur simultaneously in the brain and increase a person's likelihood of coming down with a stroke (people with hypertension are three to five times as prone to strokes as people with normal pressure). Other organs are not immune from the ravages of high blood pressure; the kidney and even the eye can be damaged.

By now it should be obvious that elevated blood pressure is not something to ignore. On the other hand, it is not something to get all panicky over. A lot depends upon the degree of hypertension, the age when it becomes apparent and, most important, what is done to correct the situation. In years gone by, all too many doctors ignored or downplayed the significance of high blood pressure. Treatment was often initiated only reluctantly. Nowadays doctors are better informed, but they may overreact by resorting to powerful medications before carefully evaluating their patient or considering the drugs' potential for serious side effects.

The very first thing that you have to learn is how to take your own blood pressure. The detection of hypertension is too important to be left up to your doctor, and that goes for its presence as well as its absence. For all kinds of reasons, a blood pressure determination in a doctor's office may not re- *251* flect the true state of your cardiovascular system. The very act of entering a doctor's office can raise your pressure over the "normal" limits. I know that I get pretty anxious when I visit my doctor, and that in itself can send the pressure up. Lots of studies have demonstrated that home determinations are usually lower than "official" office measurements.[2] All too many physicians are ready and willing to begin treatment on the basis of just one or two elevated readings. How unfortunate it would be if unnecessary therapy were started due to anxiety artificially induced by a trip to the doctor. It is also true, however, that sometimes a patient, by doing it at home, may pick up a case of high blood pressure that a doctor has missed.

There is an easy way for you to determine whether or not you have high blood pressure: learn how to take it yourself. For one thing, you can do it in the peace and quiet of your own house, an atmosphere more reflective of your regular blood pressure anyway. Second, and even more important, you will be able to record your pressure frequently over a long period of time in order to chart fluctuation. Since it is not the occasional increase in pressure but rather the sustained elevation that is of concern, who but you yourself is best equipped to monitor blood pressure frequently?

Unfortunately, very few doctors are willing to take the time or effort to teach the patient self-monitoring techniques. Other medics object to patient involvement on "philosophical grounds," as witness the following exchange between three doctors during a medical symposium on high blood pressure:

> DR. PAGE: Do you think that home blood pressures are worth doing?
> DR. DUSTAN: Yes, but the usefulness of the entire population is limited because home readings require from the patient a continued commitment to help maintain his health and not all patients can do this. It requires of the physician continuing interest even though the patient's problem seems to be solved by treatment, and not all physicians are capable of this.
> DR. PAGE: Roughly how many people among your practice do you think are capable of taking their own pressures?
> DR. DUSTAN: All of them, and all of them do.
> DR. WILKINS: I do not agree. Only a minority of my patients take their own blood pressures. Why? Maybe this is

philosophical, but I believe the emotional burden of disease should not be borne by the patient but by the physician, the family, or other supporting elements. In some patients, the emotional stimulus of taking one's own blood pressure may have adverse influences. He becomes anxious about the reading, about the procedure . . .

DR. DUSTAN: One's attitude toward home reading, I think, depends to a considerable degree on how much experience one has had with them. As far as an emotional burden is concerned, somewhere along the way the patient has to realize it is *his* illness, and he is only being asked to assist in obtaining the information the doctor needs to treat him better.[3]

I must say that I am on Dr. Dustan's team as far as this argument is concerned. It is time doctors started to realize that patients are usually intelligent human beings, capable of participating in their own treatment programs. Home determinations not only enable the patient and doctor to establish the presence or absence of high blood pressure, but allow for excellent analysis of the success or failure of medical therapy. A blood pressure monitoring device should be as much a part of everyone's home as a thermometer. The pressure of your blood is just as important as the pressure in the tires of your car. Do not neglect either one.

In order to measure your blood pressure properly, you will need a stethoscope and a sphygmomanometer. Don't let this complicated-sounding word put you off. It is merely a simple medical instrument consisting of an inflatable arm cuff and a pressure gauge. When the cuff is blown up with a little rubber air bulb, it cuts off the circulation in your arm. In so doing, it prevents blood from being pumped to your lower arm and fingers. As air from the valve in the bulb is slowly released, the pressure in the cuff begins to drop. As the pressure between the cuff and your vessels equalizes, blood will once again be able to flow. By placing a stethoscope over the artery in the crook of your arm you will be able to hear the first sound of blood being pumped. (The brachial artery is located by feeling for a pulse just above the elbow on the inside of the arm about one inch above the fold formed when the arm is bent). The first audible sound you hear represents the systolic, or peak, blood pressure. If you continue to slowly let air out and lower the pressure in the temporary tourniquet, you will **253** be able to hear the pulse beat regularly as it is recorded through the stethoscope. When the muffled sound of blood cruising through the artery begins to disappear or is no longer heard, the diastolic pressure has been reached and should be recorded. As mentioned earlier, the "normal" young adult reading should be around 120/80 (120 represents that point on the gauge where the first—systolic—sound is heard, and 80 represents the place at which the sound disappears, or the diastolic pressure). Your doctor should be more than willing to spend the few minutes necessary to teach you the proper technique for recording your own home blood pressure. The only drawback to this method of taking blood pressure is that it usually requires the assistance of someone else.

What kind of blood pressure measuring device should you purchase? There are lots on the market. Some are outrageously expensive, some are complicated, and some are downright worthless. The October, 1974, issue of *Consumer Reports* has an excellent article on "Do-It-Yourself Blood Pressure Devices." Order this back issue or go to your nearest public library and make a xeroxed copy of this terrific review. Not only does it explain blood pressure, providing extremely clear instructions for home determinations, it also recommends which brands to consider buying.

It would be impossible to summarize the important points made by the people from Consumers Union. Suffice it to say that in order to take an accurate blood pressure, you can take either of two routes. For between thirty-five and fifty dollars you can purchase a perfectly acceptable mercury sphygmomanometer, and for less than ten dollars a fine stethoscope. The other possibility is to lay out a bundle for a sophisticated "automatic" measuring device. *Consumer Reports* poohpoohs the automatic variety, which can run between a hundred and two hundred dollars. While it is true that the old-fashioned mercury meter is certainly reliable and much cheaper, the "electronic" models can be operated by one person. It is virtually impossible for anyone to take an accurate blood pressure reading alone without someone else around to lend a hand. The other advantage of the automatic blood pressure equipment is that it eliminates the need to listen for the first and last sound of the pulse through the stethoscope, a procedure which can be a little tricky for the inexperienced. Nevertheless, I tend to agree with Consumers Union. The extra price may not be worth the extra convenience. Also worth considering is the fact that the mercury sphygmomanometer may maintain accuracy better than some of the automatic equipment. An aneroid, gauge-type meter can be affected by many environmental conditions and often becomes unreliable.

According to *Consumer Reports*, the best buy for the money is the *HI/LO Baumanometer* 0661-0620. I would concur completely. It is manufactured by the highly reputable W. A. Baum Company, Copiague, N.Y. 11726 which has been making quality blood pressure measuring equipment for physicians for fifty years. The unit (including stethoscope) runs about forty-three dollars. Very thorough, easy-to-understand instructions are supplied with this apparatus. If, for whatever reason, the glass tube that holds the mercury should break, Baum will replace it free of charge. Unfortunately, I am not entirely satisfied with the old-fashioned bell-shaped stethoscope supplied with the equipment. Unless it is placed exactly over the brachial artery, it may be difficult to hear the sounds. Once you get the hang of it, however, it works quite nicely. If you have trouble, consider buying a diaphragm-type stethoscope. Other mercury sphygmomanometers that are rated acceptable by Consumers Union are the Sears and Montgomery Wards models, available for about thirty-five dollars without stethoscope.

If you are alone, without anyone to assist you in taking your own blood pressure, or if the standard sphygmomanometer is just too tricky for you to get a handle on, then you might want to invest in an automatic model. An excellent apparatus is one called *SphygmoStat*, available from Technical Resources, 14 Green Street, Waltham, Mass. 02154. The B100 model costs about $100 and is well worth the investment. It is easy to use and has a unique cuff that allows a single individual to slip it firmly around his arm without the stress and strain encountered with most other instruments.

One blood pressure monitor that I cannot recommend is the *BPI Blood Pressure Indicator* Model 2200 made by Parke-Davis. Although it sells for about $165 there is some question about its accuracy. The model that I tested all too frequently produced serious errors, particularly in people with high blood pressure.

Whatever device you finally purchase, you should take it to your family physician for instructions on proper use and to see if the values that you obtain correspond to those that your doctor gets using his own equipment.

Okay, you have a blood pressure monitoring device and you know how to use it. Now what? Well, the first thing to do is record your pressure regularly on a daily basis (it should become a habit just like brushing your teeth, once in the morning and once before retiring) and keep a chart so that you can show your doctor how you are doing. He or she will be able to use this information in order to determine whether or not it is necessary to begin treatment and then whether or not your therapeutic program is successful.

When do you have hypertension? How high is too high? In the old days doctors usually did not start to worry unless the pressure reached 160/95. More recently, some have suggested that therapy should be initiated a little sooner. In point of fact, there is a great controversy within the medical community as to when a patient should be considered hypertensive and treatment started. Usually it is the diastolic pressure that concerns doctors the most since it more accurately reflects the state of the arteries and the disease process.

A diastolic pressure below 90 is perfectly normal. If you are over forty and have a diastolic pressure of 90 or less, you should consider yourself lucky because you must be doing something very right. A diastolic pressure between 90 and 100 is no reason for undue concern. It *is* reason to keep an eye out and monitor the pressure frequently, especially if you are under forty-five. Check with your physician to see if he wants to consider the possibility of treatment. Once diastolic pressure gets between 100 and 110, you can be considered a moderate hypertensive, and treatment should be proposed. If diastolic pressure gets much over 115, the problem is very serious and requires careful medical attention.

It would appear from what I have just said that the question of high blood pressure is a simple matter. If the pressure goes over the "normal" limit, it should be treated. Unfortunately, it is not nearly so straightforward. Hypertension is probably not one simple disease. There are many factors that should be considered before drug therapy is begun. First and foremost is whether or not the blood pressure is consistently high. One reading, or even a couple of readings, over the "safe" level is no call to treatment unless it is so high as to be considered serious. It is sustained high blood pressure that requires attention. Secondly, the age of the patient and the degree of hypertension must be taken into account. Finally, a lot depends on where your doctor's head is at.

A recent report entitled "Natural History of Hypertension, A Case for Selective Non-Treatment" offers some interesting insights into the diagnosis and treatment of high blood pressure. According to the author, Dr. John Fry, "Current opinion suggests that high blood-pressure leads to increased morbidity [sickness] and mortality, and that control of even moderate or mild hypertension results in improvement compared with no treatment. However, these opinions may be unrepresentative in that they have tended to be based on selected populations and exclusive age-groups."[4] Coming from a member of the medical profession these days, that is a heretical statement, because the trend has been toward encouraging treatment. What Dr. Fry discovered was that the age at which hypertension was first observed becomes a critical factor in terms of the outcome of the disease. For people who are over the age of sixty when high blood pressure is first detected, mild elevations do not seem to pose an increased risk of illness or death, according to Dr. Fry. Young or middle-aged persons, on the other hand, are much more likely to develop serious complications or even kick the bucket if they develop hypertension and do not treat it. Dr. Fry concluded that selective nontreatment may be perfectly acceptable for patients in whom mild high blood pressure is not detected until after the age of sixty. Vigorous medical intervention is recommended, however, for people—especially men—who develop hypertension at a younger age.

A few years back another set of investigators uncovered the fact that older women seemed to resist senility somewhat better if they had mild high blood pressure. Whether this can be confirmed or not, selective nontreatment might be advisable for some segments of the population. Yet other physicians in-

257

sist that treatment is absolutely essential for everyone who demonstrates any signs of increased pressure, even if it is mild (90–99 diastolic). They too appear to be able to back up their position. You would do best to leave the decision to your doctor and hope that he is keeping up with the controversy.

Once blood pressure creeps over the "normal" limits and stays there in a young or middle-aged person, almost everyone would agree that it is time to do something. More often than not, doctors immediately stick their hypertensive patients on some form of drug therapy. Getting blood pressure down with drugs may not always be the best way to start off. Although doctors rarely pursue them, there are other initial alternatives to pharmacological treatment.

Numero uno in a program of blood pressure control should be weight reduction. Overweight is a contributing factor in the elevation of blood pressure. Of course, losing weight is always easier said than done. I have been trying to lose my spare tire for about three years now and my lack of success just proves that I talk a better game than I practice. Blood Pressure Law Number 1 still is: Lose excess weight.

Restriction of salt intake is the second most important part of any program of blood pressure control. One superficial study actually discovered that people with high blood pressure seem to have a "salt hunger" that drives them to consume four times the amount of salt and fluids that "normal" people do.[5] In fact, the need to oversalt food may serve as a prediagnostic warning that a person may be suffering from high blood pressure. Although it is virtually impossible to eliminate salt from the diet completely, because it is in so many prepared foods, the hypertensive can learn to resist adding extra salt to his or her food. So, Blood Pressure Law Number 2 is: Fight the urge to reach for the salt shaker.

Even more important than salt restriction or overweight is physical activity. While increase in blood pressure seems to be an inevitable concomitant of ageing in highly developed societies such as ours, many "primitive" cultures do not demonstrate this kind of maladaptation.[6] Primitive peoples are almost always more active than we are, and high blood pressure seems to be a disease they can avoid. A comprehensive investigation carried out a few years back in the United States also seems to confirm the observation that habitual physical activity may militate against high blood pressure.[7] After assessing the physical activity and general health of about seventeen hundred men in Tecumseh, Michigan, researchers concluded that the more active the men, the lower their blood pressure, both systolic and diastolic. Interestingly, the difference in pressure between active and inactive men occurred regardless of age.

Exercise and physical conditioning should definitely be a crucial part of any program designed to lower blood pressure. Numerous scientific investigations have determined that after a period of medically supervised physical training, blood pressure can drop dramatically.[8,9] In one study, hypertensive patients were able to reduce their systolic blood pressure thirteen points on the average after a conditioning period.[10] Now, don't rush out to start jogging a mile every day. The quickest way to a heart attack is unsupervised and overdone physical activity. Medical supervision is a must, and your doctor should be more than willing to recommend a safe program of exercise after he has done a complete medical checkup in order to determine your capabilities.

The best exercise program is one that schedules regular activity. At least three sessions should be planned each week. Thirty minutes to one hour should be sufficient to provide adequate conditioning. After a brief period of warm-up calisthenics, get into a total body exercise such as bicycling, jogging (moderate), or swimming. Don't be a dummy and start exercising in hot weather or after a meal. That is a quick way to end up flat on your back. It is also wise to avoid a superhot shower right after your workout, since that can put a strain on the cardiovascular system. Just cool off for a few minutes and then take a moderately warm shower. Some doctors recommend that modest activity should be interspersed with brief periods of strenuous exercise. The point of this phase of the program is to jack up the heart rate to about 70 percent of its maximum capability. If chest pains develop at any point, it is reason to reduce the degree of exertion and have your doctor reevaluate the exercise program, but it is not reason to discontinue. If you are not in good shape to begin with, *do not* start out your physical training as if you were trying to make up *259* for lost time. A gradually intensified program is the most beneficial and safest method to good health.

Before high-powered drugs are employed to reduce high blood pressure, a program of exercise and weight control should be tried. Any half-intelligent human being should value her or his life enough to make this kind of effort for a healthy heart and cardiovascular system. Therefore Blood Pressure Law Number 3 is: Exercise.

Perhaps the most promising and provocative new approach to the control of blood pressure involves biofeedback and techniques of mental relaxation. Although still in its infancy, the science of biofeedback offers an exciting new method for the management of many disease processes. By providing continuous visual or auditory information about the state of the internal physiology, a person is able to learn how to control things like heart rate, brain waves, or blood pressure, processes that were once considered involuntary bodily functions beyond conscious human control. Preliminary investigation seems to indicate that an individual may be capable of reversing many maladaptive disease syndromes such as hypertension through biofeedback. Coupled with a program of mental relaxation, significant reduction in elevated blood pressure may be possible. One medical investigation carried out in England combining a yoga relaxation technique and a "relaxometer" biofeedback apparatus produced amazing results. Of the twenty hypertensive patients studied, sixteen demonstrated dramatic improvement. "Their average systolic pressure fell from 160 to 134 mm. Hg. [mercury] and their average diastolic pressure fell from 102 to 86 mm. Hg."[11] Not only did these people drop into normal blood pressure ranges, but many were able to reduce or eliminate completely their use of blood pressure medications. A follow-up study published in 1975 indicated that improvement was sustained over the course of more than a year.[12]

Most doctors scorn such "unscientific" techniques as yoga, meditation, or biofeedback. No course in these areas is taught in medical school, and doctors understand little about them. However, Dr. Herbert Benson, an associate professor of medicine at Harvard University and director of the Hypertension Section at Beth Israel Hospital in Boston, has produced solid scientific evidence that blood pressure can be controlled through mental processes.

Originally, Dr. Benson concentrated his efforts on animals, training monkeys by systematic rewards and punishments to regulate their own pressure either upward or downward. This work was extended to people through biofeedback technology, and similar results were obtained. During the course of his work, Dr. Benson considered applying techniques of mental relaxation to see if comparable reductions were achievable. Students who were into transcendental meditation had approached Benson and offered to participate in his study. In a recent interview Dr. Benson confided, "At first I didn't want to get involved with them. The whole thing seemed a bit far out, and somewhat peripheral to the traditional study of medicine. But they were persistent, and so finally I did agree to study them."[13]

Fortunately, because Dr. Benson was open-minded, he discovered something quite exciting. Although blood pressure did not drop during the meditation period, other important physiological processes did vary. "What we found," said Benson, "was that during the meditation itself there were distinct changes. The essence of these changes could be, I think, summarized by saying that the whole body's metabolism slows down. And it slows down to a degree that would be seen otherwise only after several hours of sleep. In this case, however, the changes occur within a few minutes of starting what I now like to call the 'relaxation response.' "[14]

It was not long after this startling discovery that Dr. Benson applied the techniques of transcendental meditation to a group of hypertensive patients. By recording their blood pressure weeks before they learned how to meditate, he was able to establish baseline blood pressure levels. He then followed their blood pressure for months after they learned the mental relaxation technique. Here are Dr. Benson's words: "What we found was that, yes, there were decreases that took place in the blood pressure; but these had nothing to do with the meditation session per se. The blood pressure was simply lower across the board. There had been a carry-over from the meditation, which could be measured at any point during the day. The decrease wasn't, by the way, curative; pressure was simply somewhat lowered. And the fall was very clearly related to meditation. Because in cases where the person, for one reason or another, stopped the practice, his or her blood pressure began climbing again—and was usually right back where it had initially been within the space of three weeks."[15] Dr. Benson has published his findings in *The American Journal of Physiology, Psychomatic Medicine, Scientific American*, and other reputable medical journals. He can hardly be considered a crackpot.

Although transcendental meditation or TM as it has come to be called, appears to be an effective method of mental relaxation, it probably has no advantages over any other meditative techniques, whether they be zen or yoga or what-have-you. Dr. Benson has in fact developed his own noncultic, "nonreligious" program of mental relaxation. His procedure goes as follows:

(1) In a quiet environment sit in a comfortable position.
(2) Deeply relax all your muscles, beginning at your feet and progressing up to your face—feet, calves, thighs, lower torso, chest, shoulders, neck, head. Allow them to remain deeply relaxed.
(3) Breathe through your nose. Become aware of your breathing. As you breathe out, say the word 'one' silently to yourself. Thus: breathe in . . . breathe out, with 'one'. In-. . . out, with 'one' . . .
(4) Continue this practice for 10 to 20 minutes. You may open your eyes to check the time, but do not use an alarm. When you finish, sit quietly for several minutes, at first with your eyes closed and later with eyes open.[16]

This form of simple mental relaxation is probably excellent. It should be practiced twice a day, in the morning and the evening, with your eyes closed. Try not to do it too close to mealtime (preferably before eating or at least two hours after a meal). If you find that distracting thoughts keep barging in, try to ignore them by maintaining the breathing pattern accompanied by the silent *one*.

Unfortunately, as noted earlier, the medical profession is slow to accept revolutionary new approaches when they have been conditioned to believe in the tried-and-true value of drug therapy. As a pharmacologist, I should be on their side, but as a person concerned about our overmedicated society I always prefer to seek alternatives to drugs whenever possible. Biofeedback monitoring equipment may not be widely available yet, but in the future it is bound to be manufactured at reasonable cost. Mental relaxation techniques will probably be helpful whether they be transcendental meditation, yoga, zen, or Dr. Benson's simple breathing exercise. By measuring your own blood pressure, you will be able to determine how you are doing.

Okay, now you have cut down your salt intake, lost your spare tire, and got into a regular pattern of exercise and a mental relaxation trip, but your blood pressure is still too high. (Or, you are a lazy no-good average kind of person who can't be bothered.) Then it is time to get that blood pressure down with drugs.

Drugs *can* make a difference. They can save your life! Just because I advocate starting out with other forms of therapy, do not get the idea that I am against using drugs. If you cannot control your blood pressure with any of the previously mentioned methods, it is absolutely imperative that you get the pressure down with medication. A decrease in moderate to severe high blood pressure will reduce serious illness and prolong life.[17,18,19] The sooner therapy is initiated, the better are the chances of preventing a heart attack or a stroke.

The goal of hypertensive therapy should be to achieve the best results possible. That should not, however, be done at the expense of the well-being of the patient. All too often doctors feel compelled to seek textbook solutions to the problems of hypertension. They raise drug dosages or move up to more potent medication in their never-ceasing quest for normalization. This may lead to adverse reactions that are not well tolerated by the patient. Since most people will have to take their medicine for the rest of their lives, serious side effects may prove so discouraging that the patients opt to eliminate drugs altogether. This can be a terrible mistake. Recent investigation indicates that even if blood pressure cannot be brought down to perfectly normal levels, modest improvement will afford protection against serious cardiovascular complications.[20] If you are not comfortable with your drug regimen, discuss the problems with your physician. He or she may be able to change your program.

There is no ideal drug for the treatment of hypertension. Each agent is capable of producing side effects. Since people vary in their responses to hypertensive medication, the only truly effective treatment is that which is individualized for each and every patient. It is not enough for your doctor to stick you on some drug, tell you to take it twice a day, and then make another appointment for three months in the future. There has to be constant monitoring of blood pressure levels (this is where home determinations come in handy) and excellent communication between doctor and patient. There are no shortcuts to successful therapy.

Any doctor worth his salt will start off his hypertensive patients on water pills (diuretics). This form of drug therapy is often quite effective for mild to moderate high blood pressure, and side effects are usually minimal. After a week or so, blood pressure should drop between ten and fifteen points, which is about all that can be expected for this introductory stage of treatment. Some of the safest and most effective drugs belong to the class of thiazide diuretics. The most common are:

Anhydron	(Cyclothiazide)
Aquatag	(Benzthiazide)
Diuril	(Chlorothiazide)
Enduron	(Methyclothiazide)
Esidrix	(Hydrochlorothiazide)
Exna	(Benzthiazide)
Hydrodiuril	(Hydrochlorothiazide)
Metahydrin	(Trichlormethiazide)
Naqua	(Trichlormethiazide)
Naturetin	(Bendroflumethiazide)
Oretic	(Hydrochlorothiazide)
Renese	(Polythiazide)

According to the *Medical Letter*, one of the few objective, nonprofit publications concerned with the evaluation of prescription drugs, there are few differences between these various diuretics. Therefore, it would be to your advantage to have your physician prescribe the cheapest generic product available, given the fact that you may be taking this kind of medication for a very long time. For example, **Hydrodiuril, Esidrix**, and **Oretic** are all available generically as *Hydrochlorothiazide* for less than half the brand-name price.

Controlled studies have shown that more potent diuretics such as **Lasix** *(Furosemide)* or **Edecrin** *(Ethacrynic Acid)* do not lower pressure any better than thiazide-type water pills. In fact, there is good reason to believe that **Lasix** is less effective.[21] It is, however, much more expensive than most of the milder diuretics. Since the more powerful diuretics, such as **Lasix** and **Edecrin**, may produce more side effects, their use in the treatment of hypertension seems questionable except in special circumstances (**Lasix** is safer for patients with kidney disease).

Although uncommon, occasionally there may be some problems associated with the use of the milder thiazide diuretics. Some patients develop skin rashes, especially after exposure to the sun. Weakness and anemia have been occasionally reported. Dryness of the mouth and sometimes an unpleasant aftertaste may be part of the price the hypertensive must pay to get his blood pressure down. None of these side effects are particularly dangerous, though any unusual reaction should always be reported to your physician.

Although not specifically a side effect, one of the more important problems encountered with these diuretic drugs is the fact that they can foul up a routine urinalysis. Many patients taking these agents are falsely diagnosed as diabetic because sugar shows up in their urine.[22] A doctor who is not aware of the fact that water pills can screw up the standard glucose-tolerance test may make an incorrect diagnosis of diabetes and initiate unnecessary treatment.

The most frequent and troublesome side effect associated with diuretic treatment involves changes in blood chemistry. That makes it virtually impossible to detect without laboratory analysis. Therefore, each patient should have a blood test done before therapy is started. Each month thereafter an evaluation of the patient's blood chemistry should be made until the doctor is satisfied that there are no complications.[23] At regular intervals during the year, additional lab tests should be required.

Potassium depletion is the most troublesome problem of **265** diuretic therapy. Most patients will run into it unless they make a special effort to make sure their diet is high in foods containing this mineral. Unfortunately, most doctors do not know which foods to recommend (due to a serious lack of training in nutrition), and so they often resort to prescribing potassium chloride supplements in the form of pills, syrup, or salt substitutes. These preparations are less satisfactory than proper diet unless the patient also happens to be on digitalis-type medication, which requires an extra amount of potassium. The problem with potassium supplements is that they are poorly tolerated. Stomach irritation, abdominal cramps, nausea, diarrhea, ulcers, and a terrible taste are some of the more frequent complications. A recent evaluation of the use of these special preparations cautions against routine use and suggests that overzealous prescribing of potassium by physicians should be questioned.[24] Instead of resorting to supplements, doctors should be recommending a diet high in potassium-containing foods. The following list should prove invaluable for the patient on water pills because it lists not only relative concentrations of potassium but caloric content as well.

HIGH-POTASSIUM FOODS (per three-ounce portion)

	Calories	Potassium (mg/100 gm)
Almonds	598	773
Apricots (dried)	332	1260
Apples (dried)	353	730
Avocados	167	604
Beef (hamburger, lean)	219	558
Cocoa powder (plain)	300	1500
Cress (garden)	32	606
Dates	274	648
Figs	274	640
Flounder	202	587
Halibut (broiled)	171	525
Horseradish (raw)	87	564
Lichees (dried)	277	1100

Molasses (light)	252	917
Molasses (blackstrap)	213	2927
Peaches (dried)	262	950
Peanuts (roasted)	582	701
Peanut butter	581	670
Pecans	687	603
Potato (baked, with skin)	93	503
Prunes	255	694
Raisins	289	763
Rye wafers, whole grain	344	600
Sesame seeds	563	725
Soybean flours	350	1750
Squash (butternut)	68	609
Sunflower seeds	560	920
Wheat germ	363	827
Yeast (brewer's)	283	1894
Yeast (torula)	277	2046

(Source: Composition of Foods, Agriculture Handbook œ8, Agricultural Research Service, U.S. Department of Agriculture, Washington, D.C.)

Two diuretics do not deplete potassium levels as much as those previously mentioned. These so-called potassium-sparing medications include **Dyrenium** (*Triamterene*) and **Aldactone** (*Spironolactone*). Because their effect upon blood chemistry, especially potassium, is minimal, it would appear that these agents offer a real advantage over most other diuretics. Indeed, their sales over the last few years have been quite impressive. One medical authority on hypertension, however, has expressed strong doubt that these drugs lower blood pressure as effectively as the potassium-wasting diuretics.[25] To get around this drawback, the manufacturer of **Aldactone** combined their drug with a potassium-wasting agent, *Hydrochlorothiazide,* and gave the resulting product the name **Aldactazide** (*Spironolactone* and *Hydrochlorothiazide*). The combination of these two diuretics in one pill would appear ideal, since effective blood-pressure lowering ability was added to potassium preservation. Judging from its sales figures over the last five years this formulation has been a big winner for the drug company, especially since it sports a fancy price tag.

But what about safety? In June, 1975, the Food and Drug **267**

Administration's Cardiovascular Advisory Committee reviewed the safety of both **Aldactone** and **Aldactazide**. The issue of toxicity arose after the drug company that produced the products (G. D. Searle) announced the findings of a seventy-eight-week rat toxicity study in which it was discovered that extremely high doses of the drugs could induce benign tumors.[26] Whether this poses a problem has yet to be determined, but some restrictions in labeling and use appear justified (Personal communication from FDA representative). Safety aside, even though **Aldactone** and **Aldactazide** do eliminate the need to worry about potassium supplements, one medical expert feels that "this advantage is usually not great enough to justify the additional expense for most patients."[27]

Once a doctor has evaluated the progress of his hypertensive patient, he or she may decide that a diuretic is not sufficient to do the job. At this point it is not uncommon for a physician to either add an additional drug or prescribe a product that already has a fixed combination of antihypertensive medications (experts usually recommend the former course). One frequently employed second-line agent is **Reserpine**. This drug is sold either generically, as **Reserpine**, or as a brand-name product called **Serpasil** or **Rau-Sed**. It is also available as a primary ingredient in many blood pressure preparations.

Fixed-Combination Formulations Containing Reserpine

Butiserpazide	**Raudixin**
Diupres	**Rauwiloid**
Diutensen-R	**Rauzide**
Exna-R	**Regroton**
Hydromox R	**Salutensin**
Hydropres	**Ser-Ap-Es**
Metatensin	**Serpasil-Apresoline**
Naquival	**Serpasil-Esidrix**

Until 1974 **Reserpine** was considered a relatively safe and effective preparation for the treatment of blood pressure that refused to go down with just a diuretic. However, in 1974 three important medical investigations were published that linked the drug to the development of breast cancer in women. The studies had been carried out independently in Boston,[28] England,[29] and Finland,[30] and all found an increased incidence of cancer in women taking this kind of medicine. The Boston group (Boston Collaborative Drug Surveillance Program) demonstrated that the risk of developing breast cancer was three times higher in women exposed to **Reserpine**. This study involved the analysis of the records of 25,000 patients admitted to twenty-four hospitals in the New England area.[31]

Even with this evidence, many doctors feel that not enough work has been done to merit restriction of this drug. Therefor it is still prescribed in large quantities. However, even if the question of cancer had not arisen, there is still some doubt that **Reserpine** should be considered a primary agent for the treatment of high blood pressure.

Reserpine produces a high incidence of unpleasant side effects. Drowsiness, diarrhea, nausea, sedation, fatigue, stomach ulceration, slow heartbeat, nasal congestion, muscular rigidity, nightmares, and psychological depression (sometimes severe enough to lead to thoughts of suicide) are but a few of the more common adverse reactions sometimes encountered. A gain in weight is not unusual, due to accumulation of fluids and an increased appetite. Although medics rarely mention it, impotence or decreased libido has occasionally been known to occur. A review article published in *The New England Journal of Medicine* noted the following: "The high frequency of depressive reactions that may be insidious and easily rationalized or passed unnoticed both by the patient and his physician make rauwolfia alkaloids (Reserpine) less desirable than oral diuretics for long-term treatment of hypertension."[32] Another medical authority on high blood pressure has written this about **Reserpine**-type drugs: "They are relatively weak antipressor [blood pressure–lowering] agents and because of the high incidence of adverse effects evoked by their administration, I rarely prescribe them for oral use."[33] Given the fact that **Re-** *269*

serpine offers few advantages over other second-line agents, it would appear that its use is not justified except in special situations.

One drug which can be considered a mainstay in the medical management of most degrees of hypertension is **Aldomet** (*Methyldopa*). When combined with a diuretic, as in the case of **Aldoclor** (*Methyldopa* and *Chlorthiazide*) and **Aldoril** (*Methyldopa* and *Hydrochlorothiazide*), its effectiveness is increased, and it can be beneficial for folks with moderate to severe hypertension. In patients with some kidney damage, **Aldomet** can be particularly useful, since it does not damage this vital organ, something some other drugs may do. Side effects associated with **Aldomet** are infrequent. Drowsiness may show up early in treatment, but it usually disappears after a few days or weeks (if you are always sleepy after taking this drug, your doctor may have to reduce the dose). Occasionally constipation and cramps have occurred, as well as drying out of the mouth. Disturbances in concentrating ability have been reported, as have skin eruptions, nasal congestion, depression, reduction of sexual desire, and drug fever. Fortunately these problems are not common and usually do not pose difficulty for the great majority of hypertensive patients.

If a combination of **Aldomet** and a diuretic do not seem to control blood pressure adequately, most doctors will add either **Apresoline** (*Hydralazine*) or **Ismelin** (*Guanethidine*) to the drug regimen. Although both drugs are quite effective, they do have a rather high incidence of annoying side effects. **Apresoline** is often associated with nausea, diarrhea, headache, loss of appetite, and heart palpitations. Less frequently, the drug may produce fluid retention, nasal congestion, unpleasant taste, dry mouth, anxiety, aggravation of angina, and psychological disturbances. If drug fever or a generalized, arthritis-like achey feeling develops, the drug should be discontinued immediately. Although rarely indicated as the sole drug for the treatment of high blood pressure, **Apresoline** can be beneficial in combination with other agents for the control of severe hypertension.

Ismelin is usually reserved for the management of severe high blood pressure. It has the tendency to produce quite a few unwanted adverse reactions. Besides making the patient dizzy every time he or she stands up quickly (especially in the morning), **Ismelin** commonly causes weakness, severe diarrhea, slow heartbeat, nasal congestion, aggravation of asthma, loss of sexual potency, and inhibition of ejaculation in males. As unpleasant as these reactions may be, it could be necessary to put up with them in order to reduce dangerously high levels of blood pressure. Remember, your life is at stake. Sometimes the dose can be reduced when this drug is combined with other medications, such as a diuretic or **Aldomet**.

Whatever drug your doctor selects for the treatment of your high blood pressure, continuous monitoring of blood pressure is mandatory. Most doctors start their patients off on water pills and then add other medications one at a time after careful evaluation of progress. (Either **Aldomet** [*Methyldopa*] or **Apresoline** [*Hydralazine*] are usually prescribed). Treatment should be tailored to each patient on an individual basis and the dose should be adjusted frequently in order to correspond to changing medical conditions. Weight reduction, salt restriction, and exercise may in themselves be capable of reducing blood pressure and are always worth trying before drugs are prescribed. Biofeedback and mental relaxation techniques may be the hope for the future and are certainly worth investigating.

Heart Attack

So much has been written about heart attacks that they hardly seem worth discussing, and yet there are so many misconceptions, controversies, and downright contradictions floating around that it would be criminal if some attempt was not made to set the record straight. The first question that must be answered is: What the devil is a heart attack anyway? A heart attack occurs when a blood clot lodges in one of the major arteries that feed the heart itself with blood. As the circulation to the heart is reduced, damage occurs and part of the heart "dies." Life-threatening complications set in, and the *271* greatest fear is that the heart will start beating irregularly or perhaps even stop altogether.

What causes a heart attack? That is the million-dollar question. Although there are lots of theories, no one can say for sure what causes a blood clot to break loose and gum up the works. The best bet is that atherosclerosis gunks up the arteries, and that promotes clotting. What actually starts the whole process remains a mystery, but we do know that there are certain risk factors that can predispose an individual to a heart attack.

Heredity, high blood pressure, overweight, cigarette-smoking, psychological stress, physical inactivity, Vitamin D, improper diet, high cholesterol, sluggish thyroid gland, soft water, excess coffee-consumption, and pollution have all been implicated in one way or another as contributing factors toward heart attack. As already mentioned, probably no one thing causes a heart attack, but rather a combination of many of the above elements can increase your chances significantly.

How can you tell if you are eligible for a coronary? There is no simple test that reveals susceptibility. Obviously untreated high blood pressure is important. If you carry around a spare tire, if you sit on your butt all day, if you smoke like a fiend, and if you are under a lot of tension, your life insurance salesman is not going to be very happy. Physicians like to run expensive electrocardiogram (EKG) tests to measure the state of the heart. Unfortunately, a single office EKG is a poor predictor of heart capability. It is impossible to tell from this simple test whether or not the arteries are clogged up or whether an individual is eligible for a heart attack. However, an exercise electrocardiogram, or stress test, is a valuable tool in the diagnosis of heart disease. By recording heart activity during exercise, often on a treadmill, it is possible for a trained clinician to detect many coronary abnormalities well ahead of time.[34] According to an article sponsored by the American Heart Association and published in *JAMA*, "Exercise testing should be performed routinely in all men who reach 35 years of age, especially in those with coronary risk factors, in order to maximize the benefits of early preventive and therapeutic interventions. The exercise test should be repeated at least every five years in those over 35, and yearly in those who demonstrate an ischemic response [reduced blood flow]."[35]

It is unfortunate that few internists or cardiologists are equipped to run an exercise electrocardiogram in their offices. They should, however, insist that their patients have such a treadmill test done at the nearest clinic or hospital. If your doctor does not suggest it, then you should request it. Such a stress test should always be done before a patient embarks on an ambitious physical fitness program, in order to determine true capabilities.

Another test that is much simpler is only as far away as your nearest mirror. Four doctors from the Division of Cardiology at the Mount Sinai School of Medicine in New York discovered that patients with coronary artery disease frequently showed up with a "diagonal ear-lobe crease."[36] What was that again? You read right. Ear-lobe crease. For reasons that are not entirely clear (genetic? physiological?), people with clogged arteries seem to have a greater chance of having a diagonal fold, crease, or wrinkle in one or both of their ear-lobes. This is to say not that everyone with a crease is a candidate for a coronary, just that it could serve as an early warning sign of coronary artery disease and might merit further study, specifically with an exercise electrocardiogram.

Even if your electrocardiogram is perfectly normal and you do not have this weird ear-lobe thing, you are still not immune from arteriosclerosis, heart disease, or a heart attack. What can you do to prevent a mucked-up heart? Scientific studies over the past few years suggest strongly that regular physical activity can provide protection against coronary heart disease. Not only does vigorous activity seem to prevent formation of arteriosclerosis, reduce high blood pressure, lessen symptoms of angina, and increase the efficiency of the heart, it would appear that the chances of coming down with a heart attack are dramatically diminished![37,38,39,40]

One of the most comprehensive investigations into the question of physical activity and coronary heart mortality was carried out among longshoremen in the San Francisco Bay area from 1951 to 1972.[41] A total of 6,351 workers were studied in order to determine whether the type of work a man did could influence the health of his heart. It was discovered that those **273** longshoremen, whose jobs require vigorous physical exercise had a lower rate of heart attacks than other longshoremen who were less active (light or sedentary type of work). The authors concluded that heavy, energy-expending work can serve as a protective mechanism against the development of coronary artery disease.

Not everyone has the "luxury" of a physically demanding job. Since most of us have occupations that do not require the kind of protective exertion that longshoremen get, does that mean we are condemned to die from a heart attack? Absolutely not! Recreational physical exercise may not be as regular or sustained as on-the-job activity, but it can serve a protective function and increase longevity, even for people who already have coronary artery disease and angina.[42,43,44] But short bursts of exercise at lunchtime or occasional sports activity are not enough to do the job. A round of golf on weekends or a leisurely set of mixed doubles hardly gets the heart beating. What you need is a regular program of physical exercise that is planned and supervised by a physician. Before starting out it is always a good idea to have a stress test done in order to evaluate the condition of those arteries. Start out nice and easy and slowly work up to a rigorous workout. Each session should begin with a brief period of calisthenics (five to ten minutes) followed by thirty to sixty minutes of regular exercise. Take another five to ten minutes to cool down and relax. This kind of activity should be scheduled at least three times a week. Jogging, bicycle-riding, swimming, tennis, or even a brisk walk can all be effective forms of exercise. Group exercise sessions may be more practical, and if you can get into such a program, so much the better. Avoid isometric exercise, such as weight-lifting, since it may cause dangerous increases in blood pressure. Once you have started an exercise program, you should plan on maintaining it for the rest of your life, since stopping may be worse than not starting at all.

Lack of exercise is not the only important factor that can predispose an individual to a coronary. Until recently, psychological stress and personality type had been pretty much ignored in the search for evil demons. However, during the last few years some heart experts have begun to look more towards the state of mind of an individual than they do towards physical factors. Drs. Meyer Friedman and Ray Roseman, who have become famous as a result of their book, *Type A Behavior and Your Heart*, contend that a particular kind of behavior pattern or personality type can contribute to heart disease just as much as smoking, poor diet, overweight, or high cholesterol.[45]

What is a Type A personality? According to the originators of the theory, a Type A person is highly competitive and aggressive, totally involved in her or his job, and constantly striving for achievement. This kind of behavior is characterized by haste, impatience, restlessness, hyperalertness, hard-driving conscientiousness, and forceful expression. A Type A person will have "hurry sickness"—he or she never seems to have enough time to do all the things that he feels must be accomplished each day. He is constantly racing the clock. This kind of person finds it terribly difficult to wait in line (as at a movie or a restaurant), gets very impatient if he must follow behind slow-moving traffic, tends to move and eat more rapidly than others, and will almost always feel guilty about relaxing or "goofing off."

According to Drs. Friedman and Roseman, the Type A personality is seven times as likely to have heart disease as the rest of the population. Unfortunately, the Type A pattern may not be easy to change. For one thing, our society generally rewards the hard-driving, conscientious individual. It is also hard to get a Type A person to admit a personality flaw. This kind of guy may agree that he has a few bad habits, but until it happens, he is convinced that he will not get sick or suffer with a heart attack. It is always the other guy, never the Type A that has problems. Finally, the person with this kind of behavior pattern may have difficulty eliminating the behavior because the very act of changing may make him anxious.

Changing life-styles is not easy for anyone, but it is probably more difficult and yet more important for the Type A than for anyone else. Behavior-modification training may offer benefits, but it is often hard to get this kind of person into such a program. Mental relaxation techniques such as yoga or meditation can also be helpful, but once again, they require a commitment to change. A Type A person must want to live and therefore sincerely wish to change. He will have to learn **275** how to get over the "hurry sickness" and how to eliminate activities rather than add new ones. It is possible to arrive late for appointments without feeling guilty. Most of us Type B's do it all the time. You can too! The first step to changing behavior and hopefully prolonging life could be to go out and buy the book *Type A Behavior and Your Heart*. It's never too late to change.

Unfortunately, many doctors do not believe their patients can learn to change their habits. Little encouragement is provided to exercise or reduce tension. More often than not, physicians would rather hand out a restrictive diet or prescribe pills.

Doctors hate cholesterol. They are convinced that it is a primary cause of coronary heart disease, and they have managed to scare millions of Americans into eliminating eggs from their morning breakfasts. When they fail to bring down blood cholesterol in this manner, physicians frequently resort to drug therapy. But cholesterol is an essential biochemical necessary for the development of new cells and tissue. Just because it has received a bad press does not make it any less important. It is manufactured by your own body (bet you didn't know that), and without it you would be in bad shape. Cholesterol has many indispensible physiological functions, one of which is to increase the solubility of absorbed fats (from foods) and assist in the transport of these fats from your stomach to storage depots in other parts of your body. The cholesterol that you eat in your food is not nearly as responsible for raising your blood cholesterol as is that made by your own body in response to the fat consumed in meat and other foods. Therefore, if you merely eliminated cholesterol from your diet without cutting down significantly on saturated fats, you would do little to lower your serum cholesterol.

Even more important is the question whether diet will actually prevent heart attacks. Solid scientific evidence supporting this view is downright puny. Here is what one physician had to say about a colleague's theories on the evils of cholesterol:

> He relates the risk of developing coronary heart-disease (C.H.D.) to plasma-cholesterol and finds it greater in men with a high cholesterol. From this observation he deduces that the risk can be reduced by lowering the plasma-

cholesterol. This is as illogical as observing that the incidence is greater in men who are bald and deducing that they would benefit from wearing a wig. If he wishes to show that lowering the serum-cholesterol is beneficial then he must contrast the risk of C.H.D. between a group of men with a high cholesterol who have had it lowered and a group with a high cholesterol which is allowed to remain high.[46]

One study recently completed attempted to answer the question whether cholesterol-lowering drugs could prolong life in patients who had already suffered one or more heart attacks. The two most important drugs studied were **Atromid-S** (*Clofibrate*) and *Niacin* (*Vitamin B₃*). As a rule, doctors prescribe these two drugs to heart-attack patients and patients who demonstrate high blood cholesterol levels as a matter of course with the hopes of reducing coronary mortality. The study into the effectiveness of **Atromid-S** and *Niacin* was undertaken by the Coronary Drug Project Research Group, a nationwide collaborative effort sponsored by the National Heart and Lung Institute. Over 8,300 patients were evaluated for at least five years, with the majority followed up for a longer period of time. This was no fly-by-night operation. It was carefully planned and executed. Final results were published in January, 1975 in *The Journal of The American Medical Association*.

What was discovered was that both **Atromid-S** and *Niacin* were indeed capable of reducing blood cholesterol and triglycerides. That had been anticipated. But what about the really big question—did this reduction of "fat" in blood in any way prolong life? The answer was amazing for its lack of ambiguity: "The percentage of deaths in the Clofibrate and placebo groups were nearly the same: 25.5% for the Clofibrate and 25.4% for placebo. On the basis of the total follow-up experience ranging from 5 to 8½ years per patient, the percentage of deaths in the Niacin group was somewhat, but statistically insignificantly, lower than in the placebo group; 24.4% for Niacin vs 25.4% for placebo." The conclusions of the project were truly fantastic:

> On balance, there is no evidence from the coronary drug project to lead to a recommendation for the use of Clofibrate as a therapeutic agent in men with coronary heart dis-

ease. . . . There is no evidence from the coronary drug project that the use of Niacin will prolong life in persons with CHD (coronary heart disease).[47]

Not only did this extensive investigation show that the drugs did not do a thing to prolong life, but it discovered there were some serious side effects associated with their use. For patients on **Atromid-S**, there was a definite increase in thromboembolism ("The percentage of patients prescribed anticoagulants during the first five years of follow-up was 37% higher in the Clofibrate group than in the placebo group"). Other frequent adverse reactions were heartbeat irregularities, decreased libido, breast tenderness, excess incidence of angina pectoris, poor circulation, and a dramatic increase in the incidence of gallstone-formation. Niacin was also associated with side effects, including skin problems (flushing, itching, and rash), stomach upset, changes in blood chemistry, and heartbeat irregularities.

Although this study did not purport to establish the effectiveness of these drugs in preventing a *first* heart attack, it seems quite clear that neither **Atromid-S** nor *Niacin* will do a thing to prolong life for people who have already suffered a coronary. Whether or not pharmaceutical agents can prevent the development of coronary heart disease by lowering serum cholesterol and triglycerides remains to be demonstrated. Even the makers of **Atromid-S** have been forced to admit that the value of their medication has not yet been proved. The official package insert states quite clearly, *"It has not been established whether the drug-induced lowering of serum cholesterol or lipid levels has a detrimental, beneficial, or no effect on the morbidity [sickness] or mortality due to atherosclerosis or coronary heart disease. Several years will be required before current investigations will yield an answer to this question."*[48] (Italics mine) Given the incidence of side effects and the unknown value of these medications, it hardly seems justified to recommend their use.

If you or your doctor really think you have to lower your serum cholesterol levels, then diet is certainly the first place to start. Saturated fats should be reduced as much as possible. It must be admitted, however, that there is still little evidence to prove diet can help prevent death from coronary artery disease. Nevertheless, it cannot hurt and may be well worth the effort. If it aids in reducing excess pounds, then for sure it has succeeded.

Even with a healthy diet, you may find yourself worrying about cholesterol, arteriosclerosis, and heart attack, but you may not want to get sucked into taking a heavy-duty drug like **Atromid-S**. Why not consider plain old aspirin? That may not be as silly as it sounds. In 1974 a comprehensive British research project discovered that a single aspirin tablet taken daily could improve life expectancy by 25 percent in men who had already suffered one heart attack.[49] That is truly incredible. The Boston Collaborative Drug Surveillance Group undertook an even larger investigation comparing 776 patients hospitalized for heart attack with almost 14,000 patients who had been hospitalized with other disorders. It was found that people who took aspirin regularly had a significantly lower incidence of fatal heart attacks.[50]

There is sound theoretical evidence to support the theory that aspirin could help prevent heart attacks. It is well known that acetylsalicylic acid (aspirin) can reduce clotting factors in blood, specifically platelet aggregation. Because the thing that causes a heart attack is a blood clot, it is only logical to concentrate on this stage of the problem. While doctors have concentrated on earlier steps, such as serum cholesterol and arteriosclerosis, it would appear to me that the problem worth studying is blood clotting, and aspirin may be the solution.

It is interesting to note that as far back as 1953 evidence appeared to indicate that aspirin could be beneficial.[51] Dr. Sidney Cobb "found that only 4 percent of 191 patients with prolonged rheumatoid arthritis had died from myocardial infarction (heart attack), compared with the 31 percent of deaths in the general population of the U.S.A. from this cause. This may not be a statistically appropriate comparison, but it does suggest that the continuous taking of aspirin as an analgesic may have unexpectedly reduced deaths from atherosclerotic heart disease."[52] A more recent look at rheumatoid arthritis seems to confirm the observation that patients with this disease have considerably less sickness and death due to heart attacks even though they have just as much coronary arteriosclerosis as everyone else.[53] This just adds more support to the theory that aspirin may prevent the last and most important step in the development of a heart attack: blood clots. Maybe arthritis victims have something to cheer about after all.

On the basis of preliminary evidence, even before the British and Boston studies were published, one heart specialist saw fit to write the following commentary in *Lancet*:

> I suggest that men over the age of twenty and women over the age of forty should take one aspirin tablet (0.325 g.) a day on a chronic, long term basis in the hope that this will lessen the severety of arterial thrombosis and atherosclerosis. Exceptions to this would be people with bleeding disorders, aspirin allergy, uncontrolled hypertension, and those with a history of bleeding lesions of the gastrointestinal tract [ulcers] or other organ system. . . . The treatment I advise may turn out to be completely ineffective but the financial cost will have been slight. However, to me the rationale for this regimen seems sound, the risks small, and the possible benefits enormous.[54]

Dr. Lee Wood made that statement in 1972, before the British and Boston studies had even been completed. Nothing in the intervening years has contradicted him. On the contrary, evidence has accumulated to support his point of view.

If you decide to follow Dr. Wood's advice, remember that aspirin should always be swallowed with a full eight-ounce glass of water. Better still, crush your aspirin and then dissolve it in a glass of orange juice or a honey-lemon mixture. If that is too much trouble, then you can always take a mouthful of milk, add an aspirin tablet, and chew thoroughly, washing away the unpleasant taste with another couple of swallows. In this way you will get better absorption and less stomach irritation.

Well dear reader, that is about all I have to say about high blood pressure and heart attacks. Keep in mind the following points and you will improve your chances quite significantly:

Exercise may be good—overweight may be bad bad bad.
Controlled blood pressure may be good—high blood pressure may be bad.
Diet May be good—atherosclerosis may be bad.
Biofeedback may be good—psychological stress may be bad.
Aspirin may be good—smoking may be bad.
Vitamin C may be good—Vitamin D may be bad.

Tea may be good—coffee may be bad.
Hard water may be good—soft water may be bad.
Active thyroid gland may be good—sluggish thyroid may be bad.
Mental relaxation may be good—Type A behavior pattern may be bad.

References

1. Mroczek, William J., et al. "Detection of Hypertension Blood Pressure Determination in Outpatient Clinics of Medical School-Affiliated Training Programs." *JAMA* 231:1264–1266, 1975.
2. "Symposium on Hypertension: The Treatment of Essential and Malignant Hypertension." *Mod. Med.* 40 (6):75–113, 1972.
3. Ibid.
4. Fry, John. "Natural History of Hypertension A Case for Selective Non-Treatment." *Lancet* 2:431–433, 1974.
5. Schecter, "Salt Hunger Marks Hypertensive Patient." *JAMA* 225:1311, 1973.
6. Epstein, F. H., and Eckhoff, R. D. "The Epidemiology of High Blood Pressure—Geographic Distributions and Etiologic Factors." In *The Epidemiology of Hypertensions*. J. Stamler and R. Stamler, eds. New York: Grune & Stratton, 1967. Pp. 155–166.
7. Choquette, Gaston, and Ferguson, Ronald J. "Blood Pressure Reduction in Borderline Hypertensives Following Physical Training." *Can. Med. Assoc. J.* 108:699–703, 1973.
8. Montoyle, Henry J., et al. "Habitual Physical Activity and Blood Pressure." *Medicine and Science in Sports* 4 (4):175–181, 1972.
9. Boyer, J. L., and Kasch, F. W. "Exercise Therapy in Hypertensive Men." *JAMA* 211:1668, 1970.
10. Bonanno, J. A., and Lies, J. F. "Effects of Physical Training on Coronary Risk Factors." *Am. J. Cardiol.* 33:760, 1974.
11. Patel, C. H. "Yoga and Bio-Feedback in the Management of Hypertension." *Lancet* 2:1053–1055, 1973.
12. Patel, C. H. "12-Month Follow-Up of Yoga and Bio-Feedback in Management of Hypertension." *Lancet* 1:62–63, 1975.
13. Scarf, Maggie. "Tuning Down with TM." *N.Y. Times Mag.* Feb. 9, 1975. P. 27.
14. Ibid.

15. Ibid.
16. Ibid.
17. "Effects of Treatment on Morbidity in Hypertension: Results in Patients with Diastolic Blood Pressures Averaging 115 Through 129 mm Hg., Veterans Administration Cooperative Study Group on Antihypertensive Agents." *JAMA* 202:1028–1034, 1967.
18. "Effects of Treatment on Morbidity in Hypertension: II. Results in Patients with Diastolic Blood Pressure Averaging 90 through 114 mm Hg, Veterans Administration Cooperative Study Group on Antihypertensive Agents." *JAMA* 213:1143–1152, 1970.
19. Freis, E. D. "The Clinical Spectrum of Essential Hypertension." *Arch. Intern. Med.* 133:982, 1974.
20. Taguchi, J., and Freis, E. D. "Partial Reduction of Blood Pressure and Prevention of Complications in Hypertension." *New Engl. J. Med.* 291:329–331, 1974.
21. Anderson, J., et al. "A Comparison of the Effects of Hydrochlorothiazide and of Frusemide in the Treatment of Hypertensive Patients." *Quart. J. Med.* 40:541, 1971.
22. Melson, Harry. "Diabetic? Be Sure—Doctor Says Many under Care Don't Have Disease." *Los Angeles Times*, March 3, 1975.
23. Gifford, Ray. W. "Drugs for Arterial Hypertension." In *Drugs of Choice 1974–1975*, Walter Modell, ed. St. Louis: Mosby, 1974. P. 364.
24. Wilkinson, P. R. "Total Body and Serum Potassium During Prolonged Thiazide Therapy for Essential Hypertension." *Lancet* 1:759–762, 1975.
25. Gifford, op. cit.
26. Lublin, Joann S. "Outlook for 2 Searle Hypertension Drugs Clouded Further by Broker Report, Letter." *The Wall Street Journal*, June 9, 1975. P. 8.
27 Gifford, op. cit.
28. Boston Collaborative Drug Surveillance Program. "Reserpine and Breast Cancer." *Lancet* 2:669–671, 1974.
29. Armstrong, B., et al. "Retrospective Study of Association between Use of Rauwolfia Derivatives and Breast Cancer in English Women." *Lancet* 2:672–677, 1974.
30. Heinonen, O. P. "Reserpine Use in Relation to Breast Cancer." *Lancet* 2:675–677, 1974.
31. Boston Collaborative Drug Surveillance Program, op. cit.
32. Page, Lot B., and Sidd, James J. "Medical Management of Primary Hypertension II." *New Engl. J. Med.* 287:1018–1022, 1972.
33. Gifford, op. cit.

34. "Forum: How Helpful Are Resting ECG's?" *Mod. Med.* 43(11):56–59, 1975.

35. DeBusk, Robert. "The Value of Exercise Stress Testing." *JAMA* 232:956–958, 1975.

36. Lichstein, Edgar, et al. "Diagonal Ear-Lobe Crease: Prevalence and Implications as a Coronary Risk Factor." *New Engl. J. Med.* 290:615–616, 1974.

37. Kannel, W. B. "Habitual Level of Physical Activities and Risk of Coronary Heart Disease." *Can. Med. Assoc. J.* 96:821, 1967.

38. Brown, J. et al. "Nutritional and Epidemiologic Factors Related to Heart Disease." *World Rev. Nutr. Diet.* 12:1, 1970.

39. Fox, S. M. "Exercise Testing and Exercise Training in Coronary Heart Disease." In *Relationship of Activity habits to Coronary Heart Disease.* Naughton, J. P., and Hellerstein, H. T., eds. NY: Academic Press, 1973. P. 3.

40. Tavel, Norton E. How Much Exercise for Your Cardiac Patient? *Mod. Med.* 43(11):48–51, 1975.

41. Paffenbarger, Ralph S., Jr., and Hale, Wayne E. Work Activity and Coronary Heart Mortality. *New Engl. J. Med.* 292:545–550, 1975.

42. Gottheimer, V. "Long-Range Strenuous Sports Training for Cardiac Rehabilitation." *Am. J. Cardiol.* 22:426, 1968.

43. Rechnitzer, P. A., et al. "Longterm Follow-up Study of Survival and Recurrence Rates Following Myocardial Infarction in Exercising and Control Subjects." *Circulation* 45:853, 1972.

44. Hellerstein, H. K. "The Effects of Physical Activity: Patients and Normal Coronary Prone Subjects." *Minn. Med.* 52:1335, 1969.

45. Roseman, Ray H., et al. "Coronary Heart Disease in the Western Collaborative Group Study." *JAMA* 233:872–877, 1975.

46. Bignall, J. C. "Coronary Heart Disease and Blood Cholesterol." *Lancet* 1:1034, 1975.

47. Coronary Drug Project Research Group. "Clofibrate and Niacin in Coronary Heart Disease." *JAMA* 231:360–381, 1975.

48. Atromid-S Advertisement. *JAMA* 231:1336, 1975.

49. Elwood, P. C. "A Randomized Controlled Trial of Acetylsalicylic Acid in the Secondary Prevention of Mortality from Myocardial Infarction." *Brit. Med. J.* 1:436–440, 1974.

50. Boston Collaborative Drug Surveillance Group. "Regular Aspirin Intake and Acute Myocardial Infarction." *Br. Med. J.* 1:440–443, 1974.

51. Cobb, Sidney, et al. "Length of Life and Cause of Death in Rheumatoid Arthritis." *New Engl. J. Med.* 249:533–536, 1953.

52. Editorial: Aspirin and Atherosclerosis. *Br. Med. J.* 1:408, 1974.
53. Davis, R. D., and Engelman, E. G. "Incidence of Myocardial Infarction in Patients with Rheumatoid Arthritis." *Arthritis Rheum.* 17:527–533, 1974.
54. Wood, Lee. "Treatment of Atherosclerosis and Thrombosis with Aspirin." *Lancet* 2:532–533, 1972.

12.

How to Save Money on Prescription Drugs

You want to save money on expensive drugs. So what else is new? But are you really serious? It may not be as easy as you think. Everyone likes to bitch and moan about the high cost of living, but when it comes down to the nitty-gritty, only a few folks are willing to take the time or effort to really do anything. This is especially true when it comes to prescription drugs, because people treat medicine as if it were sacred. Attitudes must change so that people can view their medication just like any other consumer product. I am going to give you lots of ammunition for the war on excessive drug-costs, but you are going to have to be willing to use it if you expect these pearls to do any good. Judging from past behavior, your **285** doctor and your pharmacist will probably resist feeble attempts to reduce prescription drug costs. Nevertheless, there is a way to beat the game and come away with significant savings on many medications if you are determined and start out well prepared.

Most doctors, intentionally or not, are working against your pocketbook by prescribing the most expensive drugs available, even though perfectly acceptable cheaper alternatives are often obtainable. And how much do you want to bet that your pharmacist is not trying very hard to save you money either? If you are willing to take on these bastions of the medical establishment, read on. By the time you finish this chapter you are going to know more than your physician about prices and how to save some big bucks in the murky world of prescription drugs.

The first thing that the consumer (a patient is really nothing other than a health consumer) must learn is how to read a prescription. People's Law Number 1: Know Your Medicine. If your doctor will not tell you exactly what medication he has prescribed, then it is up to you to figure it out for yourself. Although the pharmacist and the physician have long had a secret code (usually composed of Latin abbreviations), it is an easy nut to crack, especially with regard to the information required for saving money. Basically, all you need to know is the name of the drug, the form (tablets, capsules, elixir, etc.), the potency (100 milligrams, or whatever) and the amount you are to receive (40 tablets, 100 capsules, etc.). Check out the handy-dandy example and see if you can get the hang of it.

Unfortunately, most doctors specialize in writing illegibly. They may also resort to such abbreviations as *disp., cap.* (easily figured out to mean *dispense, capsule*), or less comprehensible jargon such as *Sig.: 5 gtt., t.i.d., p.c.* The pharmacist translates this to mean "*label the prescription: 5 drops, three times a day, after meals.*" Fortunately, it is not necessary for you to be able to understand this last bit of nonsense since it is not relevant to the cost of the drug, and the pharmacist will write it out in English on the label anyway.

Okay, now you know how to find out what medication you are supposed to take, but in the quagmire of prescription

John Doe, M.D.
777 Medical Rip-Off Center
Anywhere, U.S.A.
Telephone: HElp 7-1234

Name John Q. Public   Date Mayday 1976
Address Brokeville   Age 30

R̥

Ampicillin Capsules, 250 mg.
Dispense 100 capsules
Label: Take one capsule three times a day

John Doe, M.D.

drugs there can be an awful lot in a name. By now most people have heard the word *generic* batted around and are aware that it has something to do with reduced prices. Unfortunately, it has not helped many patients save money. That is because generic prescribing is misunderstood and rarely exploited to full advantage.

Whenever a pharmaceutical manufacturing company develops a new drug in their medicinal chemistry laboratories, it receives a number. For months and often years it is known merely by this numerical name. Once it reaches the clinical testing phase, however, it acquires an official name. This label is often called the *generic*, established, or nonproprietary name and is usually created by a quasi-official organization under the direction of the American Medical Association and the American Pharmaceutical Association, among others. Once the medication has passed all of the hurdles of screening and clinical testing and is ready to hit the medical market place, it receives a nice, shiny brand name which is usually easy to pronounce, catchy, and a snap to remember. This easily promoted brand name (also known as the *trade* or proprietary name) is quite different from the official generic title, which is often hard to spell, difficult to remember, and practically impossible to pronounce.

Let's take a look at a few examples. **Tylenol** is a pain-killer 287 almost equal to aspirin in terms of potency. Doctors prescribe it frequently even though it is available over-the-counter without a prescription. Although almost everyone knows about **Tylenol**, because it is easy to pronounce and remember, few people know the generic name, *Acetaminophen*. Another generic name that few folks recognize is *Chlordiazepoxide*. Yet the brand name for this product is practically a household word as **Librium**. This antianxiety medication is one of the most frequently prescribed drugs in our country today. **Dilantin** is the trade name for an anticonvulsant medication called *Diphenylhydantoin Sodium*. **Darvon** is an overrated pain-killer that has been highly promoted. Millions of dollars' worth is sold every year. Try on its generic name *Propoxyphene Hydrochloride* for size and it is hard not to stumble. Or how about the tongue-twister *Pentaerythritol Tetranitrate*, which is a drug used for the treatment of angina pectoris? Clearly the brand name **Peritrate** is much easier to deal with. It should be clear by now that the generic name can be tough to get a handle on, which unfortunately is one of the reasons why doctors get into the habit of prescribing the simpler brand-name forms.

Once a pharmaceutical company has developed a new drug, they receive a patent and are granted exclusive rights to manufacture and distribute that medication for seventeen years. That means that no other pharmaceutical company can make or sell that product, either by brand name or by generic name, until the patent expires and the drug enters the public domain. This seems reasonable in the sense that a drug company must spend millions and millions of dollars to create and test new drugs, most of which will not pass all the rigid testing procedures set up by the federal regulatory agencies. The result is that lots of money is lost on research and development. For the ones that make it, however, the sledding is all downhill. If the drug catches on, gobs of money will pour into the company's coffers every year and no one will be able to compete until the seventeen-year time period is up. Even after a product enters the public domain, the original manufacturer stands to keep his hold on most of the lucrative profits, in ways to be discussed later on.

When the drug patent expires, so does exclusivity. Any other firm that wishes can begin manufacturing the same

medication. Although it is often marketed and sold under the
original nonproprietary generic name, the new manufacturers
can give the drug their own brand names. Thus you could
buy the popular pain-killer **Darvon Compound** by its brand
name which is sold by Eli Lilly & Company, the original manufacturer, or you could purchase it under the generic name
Propoxyphene Hydrochloride from any of twenty-five other companies. This drug is also sold by Lederle Laboratories as
Dolene and by Ulmer Pharmacal Company as **Progesic
Compound.**

Although many of the drugs that are prescribed today are
available generically, the majority are relatively new and still
retain their seventeen-year patents. This means that they cannot be manufactured or sold by other drug companies under
the generic label or another brand name. Thus **Valium**, the
most frequently prescribed drug in this country, cannot be
sold under its generic name, *Diazepam*, until after 1985, when
its patent expires. **Librium**, on the other hand will soon be
available as the generic equivalent *Chlordiazepoxide Hydrochloride*
because it enters the public domain during 1976.

Taking into consideration all of the above information,
People's Law Number 2 is: Know What Drugs Are Available
Generically. The following list of popular brand name products is only a partial list of drugs that could just as easily be
prescribed by generic name.

Table 1
Popular Brand-Name Drugs that are Available Generically

Brand Name	Generic Name	Function
Achromycin V	Tetracycline	Antibiotic
Antivert	Meclizine	Nausea, vertigo
Aristocort	Triamcinolone	Antiinflammatory
Azo Gantrisin	Sulfisoxazole w/ Phenazopyridine	Antibacterial
Benadryl	Diphenhydramine	Antihistamine
Butisol Sodium	Butabarbital Sodium	Sedative
Chlor-Trimeton	Chlorpheniramine Maleate	Antihistamine

Darvon	Propoxyphene HCl	Pain Killer
Decadron	Dexamethasone	Antiinflammatory
Dilantin	Diphenylhydantoin	Epilepsy therapy
Doriden	Glutethimide	Sedative
E-Mycin	Erythromycin	Antibiotic
Equanil	Meprobamate	Antianxiety
Erythrocin	Erythromycin	Antibiotic
Esidrix	Hydrochlorothiazide	Diuretic
Fiorinal	Butalbital Compound	Pain-killer, cough
Gantrisin	Sulfisoxazole	Antibacterial
Hydrodiuril	Hydrochlorothiazide	Diuretic
Hydropres	Hydrochlorothiazide w/ Reserpine	Blood pressure
Ilosone	Erythromycin	Antibiotic
Isordil	Isosorbide Dinitrate	Angina pectoris
Lanoxin	Digoxin	Heart failure, etc.
Librium*	Chlordiazepoxide	Antianxiety
Macrodantin	Nitrofurantoin	Antibacterial
Miltown	Meprobamate	Antianxiety
Nembutal	Pentobarbital	Sedative
Omnipen	Ampicillin	Antibiotic
Orinase	Tolbutamide	Diabetes Treatment
Pavabid	Papaverine HCl	Poor Circulation
Pediamycin	Erythromycin	Antibiotic
Pentids	Penicillin G	Antibiotic
Pen-Vee-K	Penicillin VK	Antibiotic
Phenergan	Promethazine	Antihistamine/nausea
Polycillin	Ampicillin	Antibiotic
Premarin	Estrogens, Conjugated	Hormone Therapy
Principen	Ampicillin	Antibiotic
Seconal	Secobarbital	Sedative
Ser-Ap-Es	Hydralazine, Hydrochlorothiazide, Reserpine	Blood Pressure
Serpasil	Reserpine	Blood pressure
Sudafed	Pseudoephedrine HCl	Decongestant
Synthroid	Thyroxine	Hypothyroidism
Tedral	Theophylline, Ephedrine, Phenobarbital	Bronchial Asthma
Teldrin	Chlorpheniramine Maleate	Antihistamine
Tenuate	Diethylpropion HCl	Weight Reduction
Terramycin	Oxytetracycline	Antibiotic
Thorazine	Chlorpromazine	Major Tranquilizer
Tylenol W/WO Codeine	Acetaminophen w/wo Codeine	Pain-killer
V-Cillin K	Penicillin VK	Antibiotic

*LIBRIUM enters the public domain in Feb. 1976

Table 1 was just meant to whet your whistle. If you want a much more complete guide, turn to the index (Tables 2 and 3) at the end of the chapter.

Well, so what. All we have managed to do in a long winded way is explain the difference between a generic name and a brand name. How does that affect you, the consumer? For openers, it can make one hell of a difference in the price you pay for your prescription drugs. There are over seventy companies that supply the broad-spectrum antibiotic *Tetracycline*, which has been in the public domain for a long time. About fifty suppliers make generic-named products available, while about twenty pharmaceutical houses provide brand-name preparations. Of the brand-name *Tetracyclines,* some of the most familiar are **Achromycin V, Sumycin, Panmycin, Robitet**, and **Tetracyn**.

An extraordinary investigation carried out by the Council on Economic Priorities (CEP) revealed some mind-boggling facts about the differences in these antibiotic prices. In 1974, the price to the pharmacist for one thousand 250-milligram capsules of *Tetracycline Hydrochloride* varied from $4.12 to $50.00.[1] Needless to say, the brand-name products were invariably the most expensive and the generic the least expensive. In 1975 the most expensive brand-name *Tetracycline* was something called **Tet-Cy** supplied by Metro Medications. Its published price to the pharmacist was $58.50 for one thousand capsules. This was about seven times as high as the price of $8.40 for the same amount supplied as generic *Tetracycline* sold by H. L. Moore Drug Exchange.[2]

Probably no one would make a fuss about the tremendous differences between brand-name drug prices and generic-name drug prices if the usual competitive system were working. One would assume that all else being relatively equal, you would receive the cheapest available form of the drug when you went to get your prescription filled. No way. According to *Consumer Reports*, the patient consistently gets stuck with the most expensive drugs available. More prescriptions are written for **Achromycin V** than any other *Tetracycline*, even though it is one of the most expensive.[3] H. L. Moore Drug Exchange, which sells the cheapest *Tetracycline*, has insignificant sales.

Oxytetracycline is another frequently prescribed antibiotic. It 291 is a kissing cousin of simple *Tetracycline*. There are twenty-one suppliers of this drug, seven of which provide only brand-name preparations. The other fourteen supply generic equivalents. The 1975 published prices for one hundred 250-milligram capsules ran from $1.95 (supplied generically by H. L. Moore) to $20.57 for the brand-name product called **Terramycin,** supplied by Pfizer Laboratories.[4] Guess which product had the greatest sales? Right again; **Terramycin** was by far the biggest seller. In fact, **Terramycin** controls approximately 99 percent of the whole *Oxytetracycline* market, even though it costs more than ten times the price of the cheapest generic equivalent.[5]

These are not isolated events. According to *Consumer Reports*, "The story is similar for *ampicillin* and *erythromycin*. The most expensive *ampicillin*, **Polycillin**, sold by Bristol Laboratories, controls the largest share of the market, 24 percent." *Consumer Reports* also noted, "Abbott Laboratories' **Erythrocin**, the highest-priced *erythromycin* product, controls 60 per cent of the market. Sherry's erythromycin, marketed to pharmacists for less than half **Erythrocin**'s price, does not have significant sales. Squibb's **Pentids**, the most expensive *penicillin G*, has 78 per cent of the sales of *penicillin G*. Parke, Davis, & Co.'s **Chloromycetin,** the most expensive *chloramphenicol*, has 99 per cent of the sales of *chloramphenicol*."[6] I could go on and on giving examples, but why throw a drowning man an anchor. By now it should be clear that the big drug companies eat their cake and have it too.

Well, why? How is it possible that the most expensive brand name products consistently outsell their generic equivalents by such a phenomenal margin? Why isn't competition working? The answer is simple. The friendly family physician is the reason. He or she is the one who writes your prescription, and he or she is the one who specifies time in and time out the most expensive brand-name products. That raises another why. If the kindly doctor is out for your best interests, why is he or she always prescribing the costliest drugs available if something else will do?

For one thing, it is easy to get used to the brand-name pharmaceuticals. Remember that for seventeen years your doctor only has access to the proprietary products, so prescribing them becomes a habit. Second, the big pharmaceutical companies spend millions and millions of dollars advertising the hell out of their brand-name goodies. Almost all major medical journals are loaded to the gills with fancy ads (in my opinion, many of which appeal to an infant's mentality). On top of that, company representatives, or detail men, call regularly at doctors' offices to give pep talks about their line of products and to hand out lots of freebie samples. However none of these approaches should really make any difference to a conscientious doctor if he has his patient's best interests at heart. There must be some other, more reasonable, explanation.

The argument which your doctor will almost always resort to when defending his practice of prescribing expensive brands is that they are superior in quality to the el cheapo generic varieties. Since no one wants a prescription for lousy medicine, this approach usually shuts a patient up pretty fast. By the time the doctor is finished, you will probably apologize for mentioning the subject and end up meekly retreating with your tail between your legs. But does his argument hold water?

Now just so you know which side of the fence I am on I am going to make the story crystal clear. If your doctor hands you this tired line, he is fooling you in the worst way. The inequality of drugs routine is usually just plain untrue. Although there have been some exceptions, there is very little solid evidence that demonstrates generic drugs to be inferior. But don't take my word for it; listen to what the experts have to say.

Let's start with antibiotics, because they are prescribed with great regularity. That is where your doctor is on the thinnest ice if he tries to convince you that expensive brand-name drugs are more reliable than generic equivalents. For one thing, the Food and Drug Administration tests and certifies each batch of antibiotic for all pharmaceutical manufacturers before any product can be released for market. But even more important than that is the fact that very few companies actually manufacture antibiotics. A relatively few major firms produce the bulk of the products and then sell them to lots of other pharmaceutical suppliers for distribution.

293

While over seventy companies supply *Tetracycline* as either a generic product or a name-brand preparation, it was discovered by the CEP that "only four firms manufacture the bulk ingredient within the United States according to the U.S. Tariff Commission. No more than ten firms manufacture the final dosage form."[7]

That, ladies and gentlemen, is dynamite! Although it is darn near impossible to find out who supplies what to whom, the Council on Economic Priorities did come up with some tantalizing bits of information. Here is what they found:

> CEP found that it is a widespread practice for one firm to manufacture a product and sell that product to different firms, which in turn sell at different prices under different brand names. For example, taking into account only the major firms, we find that Milan Laboratories manufactures final dose form *Erythromycin* for Smith Kline, Pfizer, Parke-Davis, Squibb, and Wyeth, each of which sells the *Erythromycin* under its own name. Bristol Laboratories manufactures *Ampicillin* for itself as well as for Smith Kline, Robins, Parke-Davis, and Wyeth. Beecham sells *Ampicillin* to Pfizer, Lederle and Ayerst. Not only do each of these firms sell each of these products at different prices, but small generic houses purchase final dose form antibiotics from the same manufactures. Milan *Erythromycin* is sold through Sherry for $5.70 and through Squibb for $11.83 (Average Wholesale Price) as **Ethril**. Since it is safe to assume that these products are not therapeutically different, different sales figures are due to imagined differences in quality and difference in price, which are the residual effect of the patent system and/or the effectiveness of established sales forces and promotional networks.[8]

As exasperating as it is to learn that numerous pharmaceutical suppliers charge different prices for the same product, it is even more disturbing to hear that the same company often charges wildly variable prices for their own identical product. For example, ICN Pharmaceuticals buys *Ampicillin* from Bristol Laboratories. According to the Council on Economic Priorities, ICN Pharmaceuticals sells one hundred 250-milligram capsules as a generic product for $7.50. ICN also sells the same *Ampicillin* under the brand name **Acillin** for $14.80. Larger, more "respectable" firms are just as guilty of this practice.

What does all this mean to the consumer? How can we

translate wholesale prices to the pharmacist into something meaningful? *Consumer Reports* took the information provided by CEP and extended it to the level of a patient's pocketbook so that the average guy could see how this whole process is working against him. If your doctor prescribed one hundred 250-milligram tablets of *Erythromycin* as Parke Davis's brand name product **Erypar**, it is possible that you would have to pay as much as $31.74. If, on the other hand, it was prescribed generically as simple *Erythromycin*, and if the doctor specified that he wanted Sherry to be the supplier, you would only pay $11.40, thereby saving almost $20.00. Since Milan Laboratories manufactured both products originally, they are identical in every way except price. Guess which product was prescribed most frequently by your doctor? Right again. Parke Davis's **Erypar** had big sales in 1973, while Sherry's were insignificant. And yet here is a clear-cut case where the brand-name product could not be superior to the nonproprietary generic.

In summing up the results of their extensive investigation into the equivalence of generic and brand name antibiotics, the Council on Economic Priorities stated, "On the basis of the data submitted and the information gathered CEP felt safe in assuming that price comparisons were legitimate, that therapeutic differences between like antibiotics have been exaggerated and have not been sufficiently explored . . ." Also included in the study was the observation, "as far as the therapeutic superiority argument is concerned, based on our evaluation of currently available data, there is no evidence that the branded firms have a record superior to that of generic suppliers."[9]

Carrying the inquiry even further, *Consumer Reports* has quoted a former director of FDA's Bureau of Drugs, Dr. Henry Simmons, as saying, "Based on many years of experience with this program we are confident that there is no significant difference between so-called generic and brand name antibiotic products on the American market."[10]

By now you should be exasperated and indignant. Your doctor insists that he prescribes expensive antibiotics because they are of superior quality, and yet you now know that many antibiotics are produced by the same manufacturers and **295** merely priced according to the "reputation" of the supplier even when they are identical. The doctor's argument won't wash, at least not for most of the important antibiotics.

Okay, so now you have convinced your doctor that he should prescribe antibiotics by generic name, but he still insists that all other medications in the public domain should be prescribed by brand name in order to be safe. Here is some ammunition you might want to fire in his direction. In 1967 a Task Force on Prescription Drugs was formed to look into this very question. It fell under the supervision of the Department of Health, Education, and Welfare and had some very impressive medical authorities on its investigatory committee. After an exhaustive twenty-month review of all the evidence, the following statement was made: "We have reached the conclusion that—except in rare instances—drugs which are chemically equivalent, and which meet all official standards, can be expected to produce essentially the same biological or clinical effects."[11] In 1969 Dr. John Adriani, chairman of the American Medical Association's Council on Drugs, had this to say about the frequent assumption that generics are inferior: "The paucity of convincing and well-documented data of clinical significance causes one to suspect that the situation has been grossly exaggerated."[12]

Even with all this weighty evidence, most doctors resisted the concept that nonproprietary drugs could be equivalent to proprietary ones. To settle the question once and for all, a congressional investigation was initiated by the Office of Technology Assessment. It was headed by the dean of the Yale University School of Medicine, Dr. Robert Berliner. *Consumer Reports* summarized its findings, which were published in July, 1974: "The OTA panel concluded that the great proportion of chemically equivalent products—85 to 90 percent, according to Dr. Berliner's estimate—presents no problems of therapeutic equivalency and could be used interchangeably. 'Most drugs ought to be prescribed generically,' Dr. Berliner told Consumers Union."[13]

Low-cost generic drugs have been used successfully in Veterans Administration hospitals, public service hospitals, American military operations, state welfare programs, and many foreign drug programs. They should be good enough for the family doctor.

All right, you have checked the tables at the end of this chapter and discovered which prescription drugs are available generically. You have managed to convince your doctor that he should save you some money by prescribing them instead of expensive, branded products. You have your shiny generic prescription clutched in your sweaty fist and now you are off to your neighborhood pharmacist. Success at last, right? Wrong! You are not even halfway home. The highest hurdle of all is waiting just around the corner.

Your druggist is in business to make money, not to save you any bread on your prescription drug costs. A recent article in *JAMA* sums up the problem nicely: "Generic prescribing will not lead to the lowest-cost equivalent therapy. Even if products are generically equivalent and prescribed generically, there is no guarantee that the prescription will be filled with the lowest-priced generic equivalent or even, for that matter, with an average priced one. In fact, the term generic prescribing as commonly used is a misnomer based on a misconception."[14] This means that the final link in the chain, the pharmacist, can ruin the whole thing. A prescription written in generic form merely leaves the choice up to the pharmacist as to what product to select.

Your pharmacist can and often does fill prescriptions written generically with expensive brand-name products. Since he will write only the generic name on the label, you have no way of knowing this. Here is a hypothetical example. Mr. John B. Public (B. for Broke) charges into his neighborhood pharmacy with a generic prescription for *Penicillin G*. While the pharmacist could fill it with Ulmer Pharmacal Company's brand, which he purchased for approximately $1.45 for a hundred tablets (400,000 International Units), he could just as easily fill it with Squibb's popular brand-name product **Pentids 400**, which cost him $10.04 from his drug wholesaler.[15] (Source: *Drug Topics Red Book*, 1975). After the usual mark-up, Mr. Public could end up paying an extra $15.00 or $20.00 for the Squibb branded *Penicillin G*, even though the doctor wrote a generic prescription.

There is another problem. Some generic drugs cost more than the brand-name equivalents (just the reverse of the usual situation), and if a pharmacist chooses to stock this variety, you are up the creek. One example worth mentioning involves **297**

Tetracycline. In 1975 Tracy Pharmacal Company supplied one thousand 250-milligram capsules of this antibiotic generically to drug stores for about $37.50. That was significantly more than Pfizer's brand-name **Tetracyn** which had a 1975 list price of $29.95 per thousand capsules.[16] Since there are almost always a large number of generic suppliers, the final price depends upon which company your druggist buys from. The following table demonstrates what this is all about:

GENERIC PENICILLIN V AND VK
100 Tablets each 250 milligrams

GENERIC SUPPLIER	TYPE	PRICE
H. L. MOORE DRUG EXCHANGE	V	1.95
WEST-WARD, INC.	V	2.60
COMER PHARMACEUTICALS	V	2.75
COLUMBIA MEDICAL CO.	V	2.95
GENEVA GENERICS	VK	2.95
PHARMECON, INC.	V	3.00
SHERATON LABS	V	3.00
ZENITH LABORATORIES	V	3.25
TOWNE, PAULSEN, & CO.	VK	3.50
ULMER PHARMACAL CO.	VK	4.75
ROBINSON LABORATORY	V	4.97
ARCUM PHARM. CORP.	V	5.00
RAWAY PHARMACAL CO.	V	6.55
BARRE DRUG CO.	V	7.25
HUDSON PHARM. CORP.	VK	7.70

SOURCE: 1975 *Drug Topics Red Book* (of Wholesale Prices)

A quick glance at the table will show that there is a tremendous difference between H. L. Moore's *Penicillin V* at $1.95 and Barre Drug Company's *Penicillin V* for $7.25, even though both products are generic *Penicillin*. Your druggist can select whichever generic product he desires or, if he is so inclined, can fill your prescription with Lilly's **V-Cillin** at over $8.50 per hundred tablets.

Alright already. Enough figures. What can the poor patient do? The answer is simple. People's Law Number 3: *Have your doctor specify the manufacturer with the lowest price*. This is nothing new. In fact, the most prestigious pharmacology textbook in the world long ago suggested to doctors, "In writing prescription orders it is *best to use the nonproprietary name followed by the name of the manufacturer in parentheses*. This not only eliminates the necessity for memorizing multiple drug names but also assures the physician that the product of a particular manufacturer will be dispensed."[17] Unfortunately, doctors are rarely willing to take the time to find out which generic manufacturers supply the cheapest brands, even though it would only take a few minutes. Another problem is that the pharmacist can squirm out of this trap by claiming that he does not stock that particular company's drugs. Therefore, People's Law Number 4 is: *Have your physician specify the cheapest generic drug that is stocked*. This may not be the perfect answer, but at least it improves your chances.

Even if the doctor specifies the cheapest generic drug available and even if your pharmacist carries that drug, there is nothing to say that your pharmacist can't mark up the price. In fact, it is common for pharmacists to increase their prices on cheap generic drugs more than they do for expensive brand names. The Council on Economic Priorities discovered, "When the price of medication to the drug store is low, the amount of money added on to pay for the pharmacist's services is large enough to obscure the price differences that exist between firms." This means that the consumer gets screwed again. While generic prescribing is always a good idea when it is possible, it does not guarantee that the pharmacist will pass his savings on to you, the consumer.

What in hell is going on? Here I promise to save you money and all I have managed to do is show you how hard it can be. All right, enough beating around the bush, there is a way to save some big bucks and it is really quite simple. It comes down to the old practice of comparison shopping. You can only save money when you shop around. Since you always check prices before buying household appliances and groceries, why not for your medications? And let me tell you, drug prices vary considerably more than most other consumer **299** goods. Usually the cost of a particular toaster does not vary more than 20–30 percent within a given community. The price of a given drug can vary as much as 500 or 600 percent, depending upon which pharmacy you buy it in. In the fantastic book *Pills, Profits, and Politics* by Milton Silverman and Philip R. Lee, the following situation was noted:

> In a large midwestern city, another survey disclosed that the identical prescription—one for fifty tablets of Miltown, 400 mg—cost from $4.25 to $4.50 in five stores owned by one chain, from $3.82 to $4.57 in four stores owned by a second chain, and from $3.95 to $6.50 in fourteen independent pharmacies. In these same stores, when the prescription was written generically, the cost to the patient ranged from $2.38 to $6.35. One pharmacy charged $6.35 for the Miltown prescription and the identical price for the prescription that was filled with a low-cost generic product. Another pharmacy charged $4.50 for the Miltown prescription and $5.50 for the prescription that ordered a generic but was filled with Miltown.[18]

These anecdotes represent merely the tip of the iceberg. **Miltown** is a relatively inexpensive drug used for relieving anxiety. Can you imagine what kind of variability exists for some of the really expensive pharmaceutical products? Just to give you an idea of what can go on, I am including a table prepared by the Consumers Federation of America. This list of comparative prices was gathered from a survey of 147 pharmacies in 81 communities in 17 states and the District of Columbia in July and August, 1972. It shows how the same drug purchased in exactly the same amount in different pharmacies can fluctuate inexplicably.

Amazing, isn't it? Lots of folks say, "The heck with it. A couple of bucks is not worth shopping around for." But as is apparent from this table, the difference can be a lot more than a couple of bucks. If one pharmacy charges $2.50 for one hundred tablets of generic *Tetracycline* and another gets away with $20.00 for the same product, that is one hell of a difference. Even taking into consideration different generic sources, that kind of difference is unjustified. When it comes to something exactly identical such as the brand-name cold remedy **Tuss-Ornade Spansules**, there is absolutely no excuse for a difference in price of $15.00.

COMPARATIVE RETAIL PRICES OF SELECTED PRESCRIPTION DRUGS

Product	High	Low	Median	Ratio of High to Low Price
Penicillin G: 100 400,000-U	$15.00	$1.50	$4.75	10.0
Tetracycline: 100 250-mg	20.00	2.50	4.75	8.0
Thyroid: 100 1-gr	3.90	0.63	1.25	6.2
Achromycin V: 100 250-mg	17.94	3.47	6.50	5.2
Tuss-Ornade Spansules: 100	20.00	5.00	12.85	4.0
Insulin Squibb U-80 10cc—all types	2.98	0.88	1.89	3.4
Actifed: 100	10.00	2.99	5.95	3.3
Equanil: 100 400-mg	13.15	4.60	7.90	2.8
Flagyl: 100 250-mg	25.00	9.20	17.00	2.7
Premarin: 100 1.25-mg	15.89	6.09	7.75	2.6
Sumycin: 100 250-mg	10.00	4.05	6.00	2.5
Pentids: 100 400,000-U	15.95	6.50	11.59	2.4
Benadryl Kapseals: 100 50-mg	6.35	2.77	4.00	2.3
Valium: 100 5-mg	15.00	6.75	9.38	2.2
Diuril: 100 500-mg	11.25	5.09	6.95	2.2

SOURCE: Derived from *Prescription Drug Pricing: An Almost Total Absence of Competition* (Washington, D.C.: Consumers Federation of America), September, 1972. As cited in: *Pills, Profits, and Politics.*

How is it possible to explain the wild variability that this table demonstrates? Clearly, different pharmacies have different operating expenses. The overhead for a small independent store is much greater proportionally than for a huge discount chain. Nevertheless, these considerations do not tell the whole story. Drs. Silverman and Lee point up the incongruities in *Pills, Profits, and Politics*: "It is difficult to explain how the price for the same prescription dispensed by the same pharmacy may vary on different days of the week and even at different times of the same day. Even more distressing was the discovery in a University of Kansas Medical Center survey that the price for the identical prescription in low-income black neighborhoods was substantially higher to poorly dressed black patients than to well-dressed whites."[19]

Many people have to take medications for long periods of time. If you are on a blood pressure medication, for example, *301* you may end up taking your medicine for years and years. If you have to take your drug three times a day and if you could save only $.10 per tablet by buying the drug generically at a pharmacy that charges fair prices, you could save $108.00 per year. That ain't bad!

In general, discount drug stores or chain stores charge significantly less for prescription drugs than neighborhood independent pharmacies. Many times a modest increase in price is justified and worth paying. I love Mom-and-Pop drugstores because they usually have a personal touch that can't be measured in dollars. Large chains are often nothing more than prescription factories. Many times the pharmacists in these huge stores are so busy filling prescriptions that they don't have time to answer your questions. Your neighborhood druggist, on the other hand, is usually a patient fellow who will explain any problems or side effects associated with your medicine. He probably knows you and can keep an eye on your special pharmaceutical problems. If your doctor makes a mistake, and it does happen, the local pharmacist may be more apt to catch it than the large, impersonal chain that doesn't know you from a hole in the wall. If these special considerations exist and if they are important to you, then forget what I have said about saving money. If, however, you are interested in keeping drug costs down, shop around. Call up three or four stores to find out exactly what they charge for the same prescription. Most chain drugstores now post their price lists. Use this information. Since some pharmacists are rip-off artists and will take every penny that they can get, you—the consumer—must learn how to fight back.

At the end of this book is a price list that includes frequently prescribed prescription durgs. It was obtained from Osco Drug, Inc., one of the biggest drugstore chains in the country and represents 1976 prices. The Osco Drug store chain has been a leader in providing comparative price information for its customers. (A complete guide to drug costs can be obtained by requesting the *Prescription Price Booklet* from Osco Drug, Inc., Oakbrook, Illinois 60521). Although there will be some slight change in price over the next few years, this guide should serve as a handy index to comparative

prices. By consulting the listing for your particular prescription you can, at a glance, obtain a rough idea of what the drug should cost. Keep in mind that these prices were gathered from chain stores and will therefore be somewhat lower than independent pharmacies. Nevertheless, if your drugstore is charging wildly different prices from these ball park figures, then you know that you are getting taken.

Bringing It All Back Home

If you really want to save money on your prescription drug costs, here is a quick summary of how to do it.

1) Find out exactly what medicine your doctor is prescribing for you, the potency, and the amount.
2) Learn how to read and understand a prescription if your doctor won't tell you what you need to know.
3) Check Tables 2 and 3 at the back of this chapter in order to find out if your drug is available generically. (In fact, you might want to give your physician a copy of this page so that he will know which drugs can be prescribed generically.)
4) Ask your doctor to prescribe generic drugs instead of expensive brand-name products whenever feasible. If possible, get him to specify the particular pharmaceutical supplier which sells the cheapest product that is stocked by the local pharmacies.
5) Have your doctor prescribe enough medication to last you a reasonable length of time. (The larger the prescription, the less the cost per pill.)
6) Check the guide provided at the end of this book in order to get a rough idea of what a reasonable price for your prescription should be.
7) COMPARISON-SHOP. Call the pharmacies in your area and find out what they charge for your particular prescription.

These suggestions may sound like an awful lot of trouble just to save a couple of bucks, but as we have already pointed out, sometimes the savings can be significant. Even more important, however, is the fact that there is more working here than just money. If you let your doctor and your pharmacist get away with their old tricks, you will just perpetuate the problem. There is a principle involved and you should stand up for it. Generic drugs are good drugs. They are a lot *303* cheaper and should be prescribed more frequently. Pharmacies have a responsibility to charge fair prices. If they don't, you have the responsibility to shop comparatively until they do. Ultimately the whole problem of variable drugstore costs could be eliminated if we followed in the footsteps of Ontario, Canada. There, pharmacists are only allowed to charge a fixed "dispensing fee" no matter what medication is used to fill a prescription. In this way there is no incentive to select expensive brands or mark up cheap generic products. Until that day comes, however, it is up to you to shop around and do the job yourself.

References

1. Brooke, Paul A. *Resistant Prices A Study of Competitive Strains in the Antibiotic Markets*. New York: Council on Economic Priorities, 1975.
2. *Drug Topics Red Book 1975*. Oradell, N.J.: Medical Economics Company, 1975.
3. "How to Pay Less for Prescription Drugs." *Consumer Reports* 40:48–53, 1975.
4. *Drug Topics*.
5. "How to Pay Less."
6. Ibid.
7. Brooke, op. cit.
8. Ibid.
9. Ibid.
10. "How to Pay Less."
11. *Competitive Problems in the Drug Industry*, Part 9, p. 3718. Testimony of Dr. Philip R. Lee, Assistant Secretary, Office of Health and Scientific Affairs, U.S. Department of Health, Education, and Welfare.
12. Adriani, John. Statement in U.S. Senate. *Competitive Problems* 12:5128, 1969.
13. "How to Pay Less."
14. Kemp, Bernard A., and Moyer, Paul R. "Equivalent Therapy At Lower Cost." *JAMA* 228:1009–1014, 1974.
15. *Drug Topics*.
16. Ibid.

17. Goodman, Louis S., and Gilman, Alfred. *The Pharmacological Basis of Therapeutics*, 4th ed. London: Macmillan, 1970. P. 1702.
18. Silverman, Milton, and Lee, Philip R. *Pills, Profits, and Politics*. Berkeley: University of California Press, 1974.
19. Ibid.

Table 2
Brand-Name Drugs That Can Be Prescribed and Purchased Generically

Brand Name	Generic Name
Achromycin V	Tetracycline HCl
Alpen	Ampicillin
Amcill	Ampicillin
Aminodur	Aminophylline
Amphojel	Aluminum Hydroxide Gel
Amytal	Amobarbital
Android	Methyltestosterone
Antivert	Meclizine
Antora	Pentaerythritol Tetranitrate
Apamide	Acetaminophen
Aristocort	Triamcinolone
Artane	Trihexyphenidyl HCl
Apresoline	Hydralazine
Aquachloral Supprettes	Chloral Hydrate
Aquatag	Benzthiazide
Aralen Phosphate	Chloroquine Phosphate
Armour Thyroid	Thyroid
Azo Gantrisin	Sulfisoxazole w/Phenazopyridine
Azo-Stat	Phenazopyridine
Bacarate	Phendimetrazine Tartrate
Benadryl	Diphenhydramine
Bendopa	Levodopa
Benemid	Probenecid
Bentyl	Dicyclomine HCl
Benzedrine Sulfate	Amphetamine Sulfate
Betapar	Prednisone
Betapen-VK	Penicillin VK
Bicol	Bisacodyl
Bonine	Meclizine HCl
Bontril PDM	Phendimetrazine Tartrate
Bristacycline	Tetracycline
Bristamycin	Erythromycin
Bronkolixir	Theophylline, Ephedrine, Phenobarbital
Bu-Lax	Dioctyl Sodium Sulfosuccinate
Butibel	Butabarbital Sodium w/Belladonna
Buticaps	Butabarbital Sodium
Butisol Sodium	Butabarbital Sodium
Cafergot	Ergotamine w/Caffeine
Capital	Acetaminophen

306

Brand Name	Generic Name
Cerespan	Papaverine
Cetacort	Hydrocortisone
Chloromycetin	Chloramphenicol
Chlor-PZ	Chlorpromazine
Chlor-Trimeton	Chlorpheniramine Maleate
Choloxin	Thyroxine
Colace	Dioctyl Sodium Sulfosuccinate
ColBENEMID	Probenecid w/Colchicine
Comfolax	Dioctyl Sodium Sulfosuccinate
Compocillin-VK	Penicillin VK
Coricidin	Chlorpheniramine Maleate, Aspirin, Caffeine
Cort-Dome	Hydrocortisone
Cortef	Hydrocortisone
Cyantin	Nitrofurantoin
Cyclopar	Tetracycline HCl
Cyclospasmol	Cyclandelate
Cytomel	Liothyronine
Darvon	Propoxyphene HCl
Decadron	Dexamethasone
Demerol-HCl	Meperidine HCl
Dilantin	Diphenylhydantoin
Dimetane	Brompheniramine Maleate
Delta-Cortef	Prednisolone
Delta-Dome	Prednisone
Deltasone	Prednisone
Dermacort	Hydrocortisone
Deronil	Dexamethasone
Dexedrine	Dextroamphetamine Sulfate
D-Feda Gyrocaps	Pseudoephedrine HCl
Dicorvin	Diethylstilbestrol
Diodoquin	Diiodohydroxyquin
Dolene	Propoxyphene HCl
Domeboro	Aluminum Sulfate
Dopar	Levodopa
Doriden	Glutethimide
Doxinate	Dioctyl Sodium Sulfosuccinate
Dramamine	Dimenhydrinate
Dulcolax	Bisacodyl
Duotrate	Pentaerythritol Tetranitrate
Dyspas	Dicyclomine HCl
Ekko	Diphenylhydantoin
Elixophyllin	Theophylline
E-Mycin	Erythromycin
Equanil	Meprobamate
Erypar	Erythromycin

307

Brand Name	Generic Name
Erythrocin	Erythromycin
Esidrix	Hydrochlorothiazide
Eskabarb	Phenobarbital
Eskalith	Lithium Carbonate
Ethril	Erythromycin
Euthroid	Thyroxine
Exna	Benzthiazide
Fastin	Phentermine
Felsules	Chloral Hydrate
Feosol	Ferrous Sulfate
Fero-Gradumet	Ferrous Sulfate
Fer-In-Sol	Ferrous Sulfate
Fiorinal	Butalbital Compound
Formtone-HC	Hydrocortisone w/Iodochlorhydroxyquin
Fulvicin-U/F	Griseofulvin
Furadantin	Nitrofurantoin
Gammacorten	Dexamethasone
Gantanol*	Sulfamethoxazole*
Gantrisin	Sulfisoxazole
G-Recillin	Penicillin G
Grifulvin V	Griseofulvin
Grisactin	Griseofulvin
Hexadrol	Dexamethasone
Histaspan	Chlorpheniramine Maleate
Hydrodiuril	Hydrochlorothiazide
Hydropres	Hydrochlorothiazide w/Reserpine
Hytone	Hydrocortisone
Ilosone	Erythromycin
Ilotycin	Erythromycin
Ionamin	Phentermine
Isordil	Isosorbide Dinitrate
Kaon	Potassium Gluconate
Kenacort	Triamcinolone
Kessobamate	Meprobamate
Kessodanten	Diphenylhydantoin
Kessodrate	Chloral Hydrate
Kesso-Mycin	Erythromycin
Kesso-Pen	Penicillin G
Kesso-Pen-VK	Penicillin VK
Kesso-Tetra	Tetracycline
Kudrox	Magnesia and Alumina
Lanoxin	Digoxin
Larodopa	Levodopa
Ledercillin VK	Penicillin VK
Letter	Thyroxine
Libritabs**	Chlordiazepoxide**

Brand Name	Generic Name
Librium**	Chlordiazepoxide
Lithane	Lithium Carbonate
Lithonate	Lithium Carbonate
Luminal	Phenobarbital
Maalox	Magnesia and Alumina
Macrodantin	Nitrofurantoin
Mandelamine	Methenamine Mandelate
Melfiat	Phendimetrazine Tartrate
Meprotabs	Meprobamate
Metahydrin	Trichlormethiazide
Metandren	Methyltestosterone
Meticortelone	Prednisolone
Meticorten	Prednisone
Miltown	Meprobamate
Mol-Iron	Ferrous Sulfate
Mylanta	Magnesia and Alumina
Naqua	Trichlormethiazide
Nebralin	Pentobarbital
Nebs	Acetaminophen
Nembutal	Pentobarbital
Neo-Corovas Tymcaps	Pentaerythritol Tetranitrate
Neosporin	Bacitracin, Neomycin, Polymyxin
Neo-Synephrine	Phenylephrine HCl
Nico-400	Nicotinic Acid (Niacin)
Nicobid	Nicotinic Acid (Niacin)
Nicocap	Nicotinic Acid (Niacin)
Nilprin 7½	Acetaminophen
Nitro-Bid	Nitroglycerin
Nitroglyn	Nitroglycerin
Nitrong	Nitroglycerin
Nitro-SA	Nitroglycerin
Nitrospan	Nitroglycerin
Nitrostat	Nitroglycerin
Noctec	Chloral Hydrate
Omnipen	Ampicillin
Orasone	Prednisone
Oretic	Hydrochlorothiazide
Oreton Methyl	Methyltestosterone
Orinase	Tolbutamide
Oxy-Kesso-Tetra	Oxytetracycline
Panmycin	Tetracycline
Pavabid	Papaverine HCl
Pediamycin	Erythromycin
Pen A	Ampicillin
Penapar VK	Penicillin VK
Penbritin	Ampicillin

309

Brand Name	Generic Name
Pensyn	Ampicillin
Pentids	Penicillin G
Pentritol	Pentaerythritol Tetranitrate
Pen-Vee K	Penicillin VK
Peri-Colace	Dioctyl Sodium Sulfosuccinate w/Casanthranol
Peritrate	Pentaerythritol Tetranitrate
Pfizer-E	Erythromycin
Pfizer Pen	Penicillin G
Pfizerpen VK	Penicillin VK
Phenergan	Promethazine
Pil-Digis	Digitalis
Pipanol	Trihexyphenidyl HCl
Plegine	Phendimetrazine
Polycillin	Ampicillin
Premarin	Estrogens, Conjugated
Principen	Ampicillin
Priscoline	Tolazoline
Pro-Banthine	Propantheline Bromide
Probital	Propantheline
Progesic	Propoxyphene HCl
Proloid	Thyroglobulin
Pyribenzamine	Tripelennamine HCl
Pyridium	Phenazopyridine
QIDamp	Ampicillin
QIDmycin	Erythromycin
QIDpen G	Penicillin G
QIDpen VK	Penicillin VK
QIDtet	Tetracycline
Quadrinal	Theophylline, Ephedrine, Phenobarbital
Quibron	Theophylline
Quinette	Diethylstilbestrol
Quinidex	Quinidine Sulfate
Quinora	Quinidine Sulfate
Raudixin	Rauwolfia Serpentina
Rau-Sed	Reserpine
Remsed	Promethazine
Retet	Tetracycline
Rexamycin	Tetracycline
Robicillin VK	Penicillin VK
Robimycin	Erythromycin
Robitet	Tetracycline
Seco-8	Secobarbital
Seconal	Secobarbital
Ser-Ap-Es	Hydralazine, Hydrochlorothiazide, Reserpine
Serpasil	Reserpine

Brand Name	Generic Name
Serpasil-Esidrix	Hydrochlorothiazide, Reserpine
SK-Ampicillin	Ampicillin
SK-APAP	Acetaminophen
SK-Bamate	Meprobabmate
SK-65 Capsules	Propoxyphene HCl
SK-Erythromycin	Erythromycin
SK-Penicillin VK	Penicillin VK
SK-Petn	Pentaerythritol Tetranitrate
SK-Soxazole	Sulfisoxazole
SK-Tetracycline	Tetracycline
Somophyllin	Aminophylline
Sorbitrate	Isosorbide Dinitrate
Sosol	Sulfisoxazole
Soxomide	Sulfisoxazole
S-P-T	Thyroid
Statobex	Phendimetrazine Tartrate
Stental	Phenobarbital
Sudafed	Pseudoephedrine HCl
Sumycin	Tetracycline
Supen	Ampicillin
Sustaverine	Papaverine HCl
Synthroid	Thyroxine
Tanorex	Phendimetrazine Tartrate
Tedral	Theophylline, Ephedrine, Phenobarbital
Teldrin	Chlorpheniramine Maleate
Tempra	Acetaminophen
Tenuate	Diethylpropion HCl
Terramycin	Oxytetracycline
Tet-Cy	Tetracycline
Tetrachel	Tetracycline
Tetracyn	Tetracycline
Tetrex	Tetracycline
Theobid	Theophylline
Thorazine	Chlorpromazine
Totacillin	Ampicillin
Trantoin	Nitrofurantoin
Tremin	Trihexyphenidyl HCl
Tuinal	Secobarbital and Amobarbital
Tylenol	Acetaminophen
Tylenol w/Codeine	Acetaminophen w/Codeine
Uri-Tet	Oxytetracycline
Uticillin VK	Penicillin VK
V-Cillin K	Penicillin VK
Vasospan	Papaverine HCl
Veetids	Penicillin VK
Vioform-Hydrocortisone	Hydrocortisone w/Iodochlorhydroxyquin
WinGel	Magnesia and Alumina

*Gantanol (*Sulfamethoxazole*) enters the public domain in 1976.
**Librium & Libritabs (*Chlordiazepoxide*) enter the public domain in 1976.

TABLE 3
Generic Drugs in the Public Domain*

Acetaminophen
Aluminum Hydroxide Gel
Aluminum Sulfate
Aminophylline
Amobarbital
Amphetamine Sulfate
Ampicillin
Bacitracin, Neomycin, Polymyx-
in
Benzthiazide
Bisacodyl
Brompheniramine Maleate
Butabarbital Sodium
Butabarbital Sodium
 w/Belladonna
Butalbital Compound
Chloral Hydrate
Chloramphenicol
Chlordiazepoxide (1976)
Chloroquine Phosphate
Chlorpheniramine Maleate
Chlorpromazine
Codeine Sulfate
Cyclandelate
Dexamethasone
Dextroamphetamine Sulfate
Dicyclomine HCL
Diethylproprion HCL
Diethylstilbestrol
Digitalis
Digoxin
Diiodohydroxyquin
Dimenhydrinate
Dioctyl Sodium Sulfosuccinate
Dioctyl Sodium Sulfosuccinate
 w/Casanthranol
Diphenhydramine
Diphenylhydantoin
Ergotamine w/Caffeine
Erythromycin
Ferrous Sulfate
Glutethimide
Griseofulvin
Hydralazine HCL

Hydrochlorothiazide
Hydrochlorothiazide
 w/Reserpine
Hydrocortisone
Hydrocortisone
 w/Iodochlorhydroxyquin
Isosorbide Dinitrate
Levodopa
Liothyronine
Lithium Carbonate
Magnesia and Alumina
Meclizine
Meperidine HCL
Meprobamate
Methenamine Mandelate
Methyltestosterone
Nicotinic Acid
Nitrofurantoin
Nitroglycerin
Oxytetracycline
Papaverine HCL
Paregoric
Penicillin G
Penicillin V & VK
Pentaerythritol Tetranitrate
Pentobarbital
Phenazopyridine
Phendimetrazine Tartrate
Phenobarbital
Phentermine
Phenylephrine HCL
Potassium Gluconate
Prednisolone
Prednisone
Probenecid
Probenecid w/Colchicine
Promethazine
Propantheline Bromide
Propoxyphene HCL
Pseudoephedrine HCL
Psudoephedrine HCL w/
 Chlorpheniramine Maleate
Quinidine Sulfate
Rauwolfia Serpentina

Reserpine
Reserpine
  w/Hydrochlorothiazide
Phenazopyridine
Secobarbital
Secobarbital and Amobarbital
Sulfamethizole
Sulfamethoxazole (1976)
Sulfisoxazole
Sulfisoxazole
  w%Phenazopyridine

Tetracycline HCL
Theophylline
Theophylline, Ephedrine
Phenobarbital
Thyroglobulin
Thyroxine
Tolazoline HCL
Tolbutamide
Triamcinolone
Trichlormethiazide
Trihexyphenidyl HCL
Tripelennamine HCL

*Whenever feasible, these drugs should be prescribed instead of more costly brand-name equivalents.

13.

Self-Treatment: Traveling in Afghanistan, or What to Do When the Doctor Won't Come

This chapter is for anthropologists, adventurers, travelers, reporters, back-to-the-landers, Arctic explorers, and hermits. In fact, it is for anyone who does not have access to medical treatment and needs some basic medications in order to take care of himself or herself. The information which is provided should *not* serve as a substitute for adequate medical supervision. It can, however, serve as a guide for someone who finds himself isolated from modern medical assistance either by chance or by design. It may also provide vital suggestions when the doctor says, "take two aspirin and call me in the morning." For the traveler, this chapter could help

alleviate some of the suffering associated with traveler's diseases such as "turista" otnerwise known as "Montezuma's Revenge," "Delhi Belly," or more simply, "the G.I.'s." And for those who can't find traditional medical services, there are recommendations for stocking your own little black bag.

Once upon a time Americans were self-reliant. They knew how to care for themselves. Today, we are pretty much helpless. We need someone to fix our car, do our hair, raise our food, install our plumbing, repair our appliances, and take care of us when we are sick. In the good old days, not only did we do much of the fixin' ourselves, there was usually someone in the family who did the healin' too. Great-grandmother probably had a remedy for lots of common ailments. Very few folks would rush off to the doc unless they thought they had something serious. Today, we run to the doctor for just about everything. It has been said that a majority of the illnesses in our modern society are psychosomatic in nature. At the very least, we worry and overtreat a great many minor ailments. Too many of us are ready to zoom off to the physician with a headache, a "bad" blister, or a tummyache. If the thermometer indicates a fever (even if it is under 2°), it seems like a major medical emergency. By the way, there is nothing that says a minor fever should be reduced. In fact, there is some reason to believe that a slight fever could be advantageous in fighting infection and that this benefit is lost if the fever is brought down with drugs.[1]

For most of the common, everyday things that go wrong, it is hardly necessary to make a doctor's appointment. Quite often the price is outrageous and they don't do anything special anyway. It is too bad that we don't train more paramedics or "barefoot doctors" who could care for most of our simple ills both quickly and cheaply.

Before we learn how to treat ourselves, let's find out how doctors treat us. In this way we can learn what kinds of drugs we might want to have on hand. If we look at the physician's hit parade of prescription products, we find that our doctor's favorite medications do not cure anything anyway. For the most part, today's medic is treating the symptoms rather than the causes of illness. By looking at the most frequently prescribed medicines, we are provided a peek behind the sterile gauze curtain of medical practice.

Without any doubt, your doctor's most popular drug is **Valium**. This tranquilizer is prescribed as if it were candy. **Valium** is used to treat everything from stomach-aches and sinusitis to pulled muscles and hemorrhoids. It can do nothing more than soothe our psyches. Doctors like to pass this drug off as a muscle-relaxant even though it is probably no more capable of relaxing our muscles than a couple of stiff drinks. They are afraid that if they tell the patient that **Valium** is a tranquilizer he will be insulted by the implication that the trouble is in his head or that the doctor cannot really cure the problem.

The Number 2 drug on the hit parade is usually **Librium** (also sold under the name **Librax**). A close cousin of **Valium**, this drug is also a tranquilizer or, as it is euphemistically called, an antianxiety medication. Both of these drugs are capable of calming you down, but there is some doubt that they are any better at it than a simple barbiturate that costs half the price. Their action upon the body is very similar.

Darvon is almost always your doctor's third most popular drug. It is touted as a potent pain-killer. That is a bunch of bull! Scientific tests have found that **Darvon** is no more effective (and probably less so) than plain aspirin for reducing pain.[2] Doctors also love to prescribe **Empirin Compound with Codeine** and **Phenaphen with Codeine**. There is no doubt that these products work and work well, but that is because they contain aspirin, codeine, and phenacetin.

Besides pain-killers and sedatives, cold and cough remedies are extremely popular with physicians. **Dimetapp**, **Ornade**, and **Actifed** are just a few of the combinations commonly prescribed. They contain numerous drugs, including antihistamines, decongestants, and drying agents. The medical experts for Consumers Union have condemned this shotgun pharmaceutical approach to the common cold.

Arthritis preparations like **Indocin** and **Butazolidin** are also old favorites, as is the anti-inflammatory agent **Prednisone**. Not one of the mentioned medications can cure anything. It is certainly true that they can make life more bearable, and I am all for relieving suffering, but it is equally true that they often serve to mask the symptoms while allowing the underlying problem to progress. For an overworked doctor, it is easier to prescribe **Valium** than it is to spend the time to locate the cause of the trouble. Couldn't we treat ourselves just as successfully?

So you'd rather do it yourself. You want to play doctor. My first recommendation is, don't. Whenever possible let the body heal itself. If doctors were a little more reluctant to prescribe potent drugs, there would be a lot fewer doctor-induced illnesses. Patience, common sense, and chicken soup often work just as well as expensive pharmaceutical preparations. Proper prevention is even better.

There comes a time when patience does not work. All the tender loving care and chicken soup in the world may not help your suffering when you start to really itch, or come down with nausea, or find yourself running to the bathroom with diarrhea. You are going to need some simple medicines to help you get by. This chapter will help you use the remedies correctly. Many of the drugs which will be recommended will serve more than one function, thereby saving space and money. Many will be available over-the-counter but some will require a prescription. If you have an understanding doctor, he should be happy to help you prepare your own black bag, especially if you explain that you will be on a trip that could put you out of reach of medical assistance.

Stocking the Medicine Cabinet
or
Preparing Your Own Black Bag

If I were allowed to take only one drug with me to a desert island, I would pick **Codeine**. Although it is true that this medication cannot cure in the true sense of the word, it can relieve quite a few common and distressing medical problems. **Codeine** is an excellent pain-killer. Mild to moderate pain of almost any variety will be greatly reduced, whether it is caused by a toothache, a headache, or menstrual cramps. If you take **Codeine** and aspirin together, you can really zap pain because of a "supraadditive" effect. What that means is that the com- *317* bination of the two is greater than a simple addition of each one (1+1=3). In order to achieve this pain-killing power, you need about thirty milligrams of **Codeine** and about six hundred milligrams (two tablets) of aspirin. This combination is much, much more effective than simple **Darvon** for relieving troublesome pain, and much cheaper.

Codeine can also alleviate the annoyance of diarrhea. Turista is a drag whether you get it in Mexico, Russia, or Joe's Greasy Spoon. A Kaolin/pectin suspension may do something for a minor case of the runs, but let me assure you, it will not do much for a full-blown attack. **Lomotil** is a synthetic narcotic (by prescription only) which also works very well, but it is not recommended for your children (they should be given something safe like **Kaopectate** or **Paregoric**). The usual dose of **Lomotil** is two tablets four times a day, but that large a dose may not be necessary for everyone. The least amount necessary is a good rule to follow. A dose of fifteen milligrams of **Codeine** every four to six hours will do the same job and cost a lot less. Some doctors recommend ten to fifteen drops of **Tincture of Opium** repeated every one to two hours in an acute emergency.

Something else that **Codeine** can handle is a bad cough. In fact, **Codeine** is the standard to which all other cough preparations are usually compared. For a mild hack, a piece of hard candy, lots of fluids, and a steam or mist inhalation should do the trick. Cough medicine should be avoided if possible, because a mild cough may actually serve a protective function by ridding the lungs of mucus. Most coughs are self-limiting anyway, since they only last a few days. If you have a really nasty, painful cough you want relief, **Codeine** is your drug. It will be just as effective whether you take it as a tablet or in an elixir. A dose of fifteen to thirty milligrams should do nicely. If the cough is very bad and does not go away after a few days, it is time to see a doctor.

There we have it. Three of the most commonly treated medical disorders—pain, diarrhea, and coughs—can be handled well with **Codeine**. It also has a slight sedative action which can calm you down when there isn't anything else around. The calming action might even help put you to sleep if you suffer from temporary insomnia and don't have a sleeping pill.

If **Codeine** is such a great drug, why isn't it used or prescribed more often? Unfortunately, most states now require a prescription before they will allow a pharmacy to dispense **Codeine**. Doctors are often reluctant to prescribe this drug in its pure state, even though they hand out prescriptions for products which contain it almost every day. Some of the favorites are: **Actifed-C, Ambenyl Expectorant, Empirin Compound w/Codeine, Novahistine-DH, Phenaphen w/Codeine, Phenergan Expectorant w/Codeine,** and **Tylenol w/Codeine.** While it is true that there is a light abuse potential, the reality of the situation is that pure **Codeine** is almost never "habit-forming" in the small doses which are used for cough-suppression or diarrhea relief. Drug companies have made millions playing on the fears of people and doctors by claiming that their non-habit-forming preparations are somehow safer than the older and much cheaper **Codeine**.

If you cannot purchase **Codeine** without a prescription, you will have to rely upon your physician, Ten tablets of a 30-milligram potency will get you through most short-term medical emergencies and could hardly be "abused." For diarrhea or cough, you can divide each tablet in half and achieve therapeutic benefit. Because this drug has multiple actions (it can alleviate problems each of which would normally require a different medication), it is ideal for a trip or medicine cabinet. However, your doctor may resist prescribing this cheap and efficient medicine on the grounds that he knows what is best. In that case, make sure that he prescribes some **Lomotil** so you can be prepared for potential traveler's diarrhea and something like **Capital w/Codeine** for pain. This product only contains 30 milligrams of **Codeine** and 325 milligrams of acetaminophen, an aspirin-like analgesic which is less likely to irritate the stomach. **Tylenol w/Codeine** will do exactly the same thing. Obviously, these drugs can be abused just as easily as plain **Codeine** if a person really sets his mind to it. They should only be used for short-term medical emergencies.

Drugs for the Digestive Tract

Diarrhea

For the traveler, diarrhea is probably the most common and most unwanted companion on any trip. **Codeine** or **Lomotil** may be the wanderer's best friend, but these drugs only slow down intestinal spasms; they cannot do anything about the cause of the problem. What is responsible for the traveler's diarrhea in the first place? Surprising as it may seem, doctors are still debating the causes of the "Aztec two-step" or "the Katmandu Crud." It used to be thought that a one-celled organism, the amoeba, was responsible. While it is true that this parasite can send you dashing to the bathroom, amebiasis probably only accounts for a small proportion of the trouble. More recently, blame has fallen on another bug. It was discovered that the parasite *Giardia lamblia* was present in the stool specimens of many tourists who suffered from the common symptoms of abdominal cramps, diarrhea, nausea, fatigue, and loss of appetite. Some investigators, however, think that turista is not caused by a parasite at all but by either a bacterium called *E coli* or by a virus which cannot be isolated or treated.

All four of these potential villains can be transmitted by bad water or food, so it would be smart to watch what you eat or drink. In countries where refrigeration is not the best, or food-handlers not so careful, plain old food poisoning could do you in. Tainted food can produce vomiting, cramps, and diarrhea which may be difficult to differentiate from that caused by the other baddies. The only way to determine the true source of the problem is to have a laboratory analyze a few stool samples.

No matter what causes travelers' diarrhea, it is a very unpleasant experience that can ruin a vacation. Most folks want relief and they want it fast. It is hardly reassuring to be told that the problem will usually disappear all by itself after a few days and that the most appropriate treatment is rest, lots of fluids such as fruit juices, ginger ale, or cola (with added salt to replace what has been lost), and a light diet. Some doctors even believe that the "runs" offer a useful purpose. Drs.

Michael Merson and Eugene Gangarosa writing in *JAMA* suggest that, "Diarrhea appears to be nature's attempt to clear the intestine of noxious and harmful agents; it is a protective mechanism that prevents the multiplication, localization, and invasion of pathogens in the intestine."[3] If the knowledge that mild diarrhea is actually beneficial under certain circumstances is not reassuring, then you can always resort to antidiarrhea drugs like **Lomotil**, **Codeine**, **Paregoric** or **Tincture of Opium**.

In days gone by, it was very common for people to take drugs prophylactically, hoping to stave off diarrhea in the first place. Antibiotics or sulfa drugs may slightly reduce the incidence of travelers' diarrhea but they are not without side effects. By changing the normal bacterial population in the gut they may actually make a person more susceptible to some intestinal infections. Travelers and Peace Corps Volunteers consumed vast quantities of a drug called **Entero-Vioform** (generic name: **Iodochlorhydroxyquin**). It is still sold over the counter in many foreign countries for any kind of stomach disorder. Recently, this drug has come under close scrutiny. Not only has its effectiveness been strongly questioned but its safety as well. Heavy use of this medication has been linked with nerve and eye damage that may not be reversible. Countries like Japan, Australia, Sweden, and the United States have either restricted its use or banned it altogether. Sadly, many other countries, especially in Latin America, still actively push it on a nonprescription basis. Since it is sold under so many brand names, it may be hard to avoid. A few examples are: **Amebil**, **Amoenol**, **Bactol**, **Barquinol**, **Chinoform**, **Cliquinol**, **Entero-Vioform**, **Enteroquinol**, **Enterozol**, **Entero-Septol**, **Hi-Enterol**, **Iodo-Enterol**, **Mexaformo**, **Nioform**, **Romotin**, and **Vioform**.

A close cousin of **Entero-Vioform** is **Diodoquin** (**Diiodohydroxyquin**). All too often it is prescribed in this country for nonspecific diarrhea in young children. Abroad, it is widely promoted for the treatment of amebic dysentery. **Diodoquin** is a common ingredient in many of the diarrhea drugs which can be purchased for turista. Doctors now feel that it too may cause damage to the eye if given to patients (especially children) for extended periods of time. Because of the risks as- *321* sociated with this drug and with **Entero-Vioform**, they should not be used indiscriminately or prophylactically. If possible, avoid buying any over-the-counter products with which you are not familiar when visiting a foreign country.

Anthropologists and adventurers may not appreciate these words of caution. People who live in a foreign country for any length of time may require a drug to stop the dreadful stomach cramps which may occur. A bad case of amebic dysentery or giardiasis requires a cure. **Diodoquin** will knock out amoebas if taken at a dose of 650 milligrams (one tablet) three times a day for three weeks. This dose is probably safe for an adult if the treatment is not repeated often. An even better drug to take on a long trip or adventure abroad is something called **Flagyl** (generic name: **Metronidazole**). This medicine will kill amoebas dead if taken in a dose of 750 milligrams three times a day for five to ten days. Its advantage over **Diodoquin** is that it will kill the parasite both within the stomach and without, particularly in the liver, where the amoeba can do the most damage. It will also zap *Giardia*, but at the reduced dose of only 250 milligrams three times a day for five to ten days. **Flagyl** can temporarily give your mouth a very unpleasant, metallic taste, but that is a problem which is easier to live with than debilitating diarrhea. You absolutely cannot drink any booze while on this medication (that goes for wine and beer, too) because the combination will make you very sick.

Flagyl should never be used prophylactically because it is a powerful drug that should be reserved only for serious illness. Recent warnings published by Ralph Nader's Health Research Group indicate that this drug may have tumor producing potential that does not warrant its routine use, especially in the case of mild vaginitis. **Flagyl** should also be shunned by pregnant women since its potential for producing birth defects has not been adequately tested.

We now know how to cure a case of the G.I.s if it is caused by amoebas or *Giardias*. It would be a lot better if we could avoid traveler's diarrhea altogether. "Don't drink the water" is an age-old warning that still holds true. But it goes further than that. People often become fanatic about not drinking the water, but before going to bed they brush their teeth with water. That could be all it takes. A bottled beverage which is consumed in a glass with ice cubes could do you in just as easily. The carbonated drink is safe, but the ice could be the culprit. Water can always be purified by boiling or by adding two to four drops of 4 percent chlorine bleach, or five to ten drops of 2 percent tincture of iodine for each quart of water. Let it sit between fifteen and thirty minutes to make sure all the baddies get killed. Stay away from raw fruits and vegetables unless you peel them, and avoid uncooked foods. Be cautious, but don't become so paranoid that it ruins your trip.

Nausea and Vomiting

Nausea and vomiting are usually one-shot affairs. If you are going to lose your lunch, there is not much you can do about it, especially if the cause is dietary indiscretion or too much vino. There are times, however, when you want something to stop vomiting, particularly if it is caused by motion sickness. No traveler should venture out without the old classic, **Dramamine (Dimenhydrinate)**. It works well and can be obtained without a prescription in almost every corner of the world. Because it is an antihistamine, it has a tendency to cause sedation and drowsiness. Another antihistamine, **Phenergan (Promethazine)** is my prescription recommendation for motion sickness, vomiting, and some allergic disorders, including nonspecific itching. It is one of the most effective antinausea drugs available, and its strong sedative properties can be put to advantage as a substitute sleeping pill. In order to prevent vomiting you will probably need a dose of twenty-five milligrams twice a day. As with any antihistamine, you should not drive or operate machinery while taking this drug.

Poisoning:
How and When to Induce Vomiting

There are times when it is desirable to induce vomiting. For a family with children it is absolutely mandatory to have an emergency poison control kit handy at all times. You can never predict when your kids are going to sneak into the medicine cabinet and consume something dangerous. Aspirin **323** may be lethal in young children. So what kind of stuff should you have ready in case of a crisis?

Well, for one thing, forget that old "universal antidote." The tannic acid in the solution can be toxic to the liver. Basically, when someone has swallowed something they should not have, there are two courses of action to be followed. First, if the agent swallowed is not corrosive, get the person to throw up before too much has been absorbed. Second, follow that up with something that will absorb the leftovers without letting them pass into the blood stream.

Do *not* allow your child to throw up if he or she has swallowed acids, strong alkali (like lye), petroleum distillates (such as gasoline, kerosene, cleaning fluid, fuel oil, or turpentine), or strychnine. Regurgitation of a caustic liquid will only expose all that burned tissue to irritation one more time and could risk rupture of the stomach or esophagus. The thing to do in this case is try to dilute the stuff with either milk or water.

If the poison is a drug or something which is not caustic, and the patient is conscious, the best and fastest way to get the darned stuff out is with a finger down the throat. If you cannot get the kid to gag and vomit with this approach, then you will need something more potent. **Ipecac Syrup** can be purchased without a prescription from your pharmacist. Have it on hand at all times. For kids less than one year old, one half to one teaspoonful is the correct dose. For children older than one year and for adults, three teaspoonfuls should be adequate. If you have not induced vomiting in twenty minutes you can try a second dose, but no more.

After vomiting has been accomplished, give activated charcoal to soak up whatever poison was not eliminated. The optimum dose is one ounce of a 25 percent suspension. You can mix the powder yourself until you have a nice soupy glop. It too can be purchased from your pharmacist. Remember, these are only stopgap measures. You should rush your child immediately to the emergency room of the nearest hospital or contact the nearest poison control center.

Prevention is always the best policy. It would be a good idea to buy drugs only in kidproof containers and keep them well out of reach. Flavored aspirin accounts for too damn many of **324** the 500,000 accidental poisonings each year to justify their use. Educate children about the dangers of poisoning and then remove temptation.

Antacids and Ulcers

No medicine chest or black bag would be complete without an antacid. Dietary indiscretion is a fact of life for all too many Americans, so we might just as well be prepared. Any product which contains magnesium and aluminum hydroxide will be effective and safe (see page 84 for specific products). It would be wise to avoid products which contain calcium carbonate because of "rebound hyperacidity." Antacids with a high sodium content like **Alka-Seltzer** should be shunned by people on low-salt diets. If used infrequently, sodium bicarbonate (baking soda) will do in a pinch, but only for folks not suffering high blood pressure.

Ulcers require medical attention. If you are going on a vacation, however, you might want to take along something to protect yourself in case of an acute attack. For a mild ulcer, the cornerstone of therapy is still antacids. Any kind which has aluminum and magnesium in a liquid suspension is acceptable. **Maalox** and **Mylanta** are old favorites which will be effective if taken one hour after meals and at bedtime. A flare-up may require more frequent consumption. It could also help to eat small, high-protein meals repeatedly throughout the day. By the way, don't worry about food. To quote a medical manual: "There is no evidence that specific diets are beneficial in the treatment of peptic ulcer."[4] The patient is her or his own best judge when it comes to what he can tolerate and what he cannot. Anything which reduces psychological stress is also advantageous. It is absolutely imperative that an ulcer victim avoid drugs which could aggravate his condition. Some of the worst are medications which aid arthritis sufferers, like ASPIRIN, **Cortisone** (and its derivatives), **Butazolidin**, and **Indocin**. Blood pressure medicines that contain **Reserpine** (**Diutensen, Ser-Ap-Es, Serpasil**, etc.) should also be eschewed.

Diverticular Disease and Your Colon

Many stomach diseases of our modern western civilization apparently stem from our dietary habits. Respectable medical *325* authorities in England have pointed their fingers at a lack of dietary fiber to account for such diverse problems as diverticular disease, appendicitis, and even cancer of the colon.[5] There is no doubt that diverticulosis is on the rise in western nations. Countries like the United States and England have a high incidence of colon disorders, while other nations (usually those which are underdeveloped) have a very low incidence.

Paradoxically, doctors in this country have long treated most colon disturbances with a low-residue, low-fiber diet. According to Dr. Neil Painter et al., "Thus diverticular disease is caused by the low-residue diet that has been recommended for its treatment for nearly 50 years despite the lack of any convincing evidence of its beneficial effect. By contrast . . . in 70 patients with diverticular disease the addition of fibre in the form of unprocessed bran alleviated or abolished the symptoms of the condition."[6]

Fiber does not add much nutritionally (and for this reason has often been neglected or removed from our diets), but it does help maintain normal intestinal function. A diet which is high in unrefined foods (including fresh fruit, vegetables, whole-grain bread, and flour) and bran is cheap and apparently effective in preventing signs of diverticular disease. It may also help prevent appendicitis, tumors of the colon and rectum and, better yet, hemorrhoids. Hemorrhoids are often caused by constipation and straining. Soft, easy bowel movements could alleviate this problem. It is sad that American physicians spend almost no time in medical school studying nutrition or its effects upon disease processes. According to the British researchers, current United States medical practices only contribute to the problems of diverticular disease.

Laxatives

Americans are hung up on stomach function. Regularity has become a fetish that is worshipped almost like a deity. Incredible as it may seem, there are more than seven hundred different nonprescription laxatives sold in this country. It is worth $300 million each year for the drug industry. The Food and Drug Administration released a report in March, 1975, that said one of every four ingredients used in laxatives is either worthless or unsafe. According to the FDA, "There is widespread misuse of self-prescribed laxatives. Prolonged laxative use can in some instances seriously impair normal bowel function." So watch out for advertisements which claim laxatives contain "natural ingredients." There is nothing natural about laxatives.

It is rare that a diet high in bran or roughage will not solve the problem. Large doses of Vitamin C may also have a slight laxative action. But if you really want something more powerful than **All-Bran**, there are a few things that can be recommended. Mineral oil is an old standby that will work best on an empty stomach or when taken at bedtime. It should not be used in conjunction with other laxatives. Don't get hooked on it, since prolonged use will screw up your absorption of vitamins A, D, and E.

Consumers Union recommends mild, bulk-producing laxatives, if mineral oil does not turn you on. You could try **Cellothyl**, **Dialose**, **Disoplex**, or **Serutan**, all of which contain methylcellulose. Other relatively innocuous products contain something called *psyllium,* available in **Effersyllium**, **Metamucil**, **Mucilose**, **Plova**, **Regulin**, and **Syllamalt**. Stay away from products like **Ex-Lax, Feen-a-Mint, Fletcher's Castoria, Laxaid, Correctol, Phenolax, Senokot,** etc. They can hurt your intestinal machinery by stimulating gastric motility above and beyond the call of duty.

Drugs for Your Skin

Cuts and Scratches

The idea that if it hurts, it must be good for you, has long been the mainstay of home remedies. The louder a kid hollers, the better it is. We have developed a ritual of pouring potent antiseptics that hurt like hell over our wounds and scratches. Killing germs is somehow associated with healing wounds. That is nonsense. Once again we have been convinced *327* by companies that promote products like **Mercurochrome.** Minor cuts require absolutely no special attention. They should be washed carefully with plenty of mild soap and water, and that is all. Remove any dirt that may have penetrated the wound but resist pouring special "degerming" junk on the tender skin.

Now I know that it is hard to resist temptation. If dear old Mom painted your scratches with **Merthiolate, Medi-Quik,** or **Unguentine,** you are going to want to do the same thing for your kid. If you can't fight the urge, then at least use something which is harmless and reasonably effective. Plain old alcohol is one of the best germ-fighters we have. Do not pour the stuff directly over abraded tissue, because it will only make the kid scream bloody murder and do nothing for the healing process. Gently wipe the skin *around* the wound and then cover it with a bandage. If that is too simple, you could purchase some tincture of iodine. It is one of the oldest (first used in 1839) and most effective antiseptics available. It kills everything, including bacteria, fungi, and viruses. It also has a low tissue toxicity, so it can be applied around a scratch with little fear. If you take it on your trips, you can use it to purify water which may be suspect (iodine will even kill amoebas better than chlorine). Add three drops to one quart of water, and it will be safe to drink in fifteen minutes.

But what happens when the skin does become infected? Again, the conservative approach is preferable. Hot water soaks or compresses will increase blood flow to the area and enable your own body to do the rest. A wet-oozy skin infection is also best treated by soaks or compresses. Dermatologists have long acknowledged that "wet-to-wet" treatment will paradoxically dry out the skin lesion.

Try to resist using a topical antibiotic cream. These agents have a tendency to produce an allergic sensitization of the skin which could aggravate an underlying infection. If you must use something, then it is best to use an antibiotic which has a low potential for allergic reactivity. **Achromycin Ointment** or **Terramycin Topical Ointment** (both are **Tetracycline** derivatives) are relatively harmless and can be purchased without a prescription. Since these antibiotics probably won't do you much harm, you can use them with a clear conscience, but don't expect them to do very much good, either. For a serious skin infection, see your doctor. He will prescribe an oral antibiotic that will be specific for the kind of infection which you have.

What To Do for Sunburn

No vacation would be complete without one good case of sunburn. Dermatologists have been shouting their heads off for years about the horrors of too much sun. While it is true that wrinkling, spotting, and ageing are a few of the dangers of excessive exposure, people want a tan. Most folks are even willing to risk the threat of skin cancer in order to soak up the rays. Since most of us are only going to expose ourselves for a few short weeks out of the year anyway, what the heck. As long as we use an effective suntan lotion and don't stay out too long at any one time, the dermatologists shouldn't get too upset.

There is an incredible amount of ineffectual rubbish sitting on your pharmacist's shelves. Of all the junk that you can buy to prevent sunburn, there is only one really effective preparation. By unanimous agreement, the medical profession has endorsed **PABA** (**Para-Aminobenzoic Acid**). It is available in **Pre-Sun**, **Pabanol**, and **Parafilm**. Of the three, **Pre-Sun** is probably the best buy for the money. These products may be more expensive than some of the other junk available ($2.50 to $3.00 per four ounces), but they are worth it since they actually can prevent sunburn. If your skin is particularly sensitive to the sun it may be necessary to apply the lotion ahead of time (thirty to forty minutes). Be smart—increase your tan slowly each day rather than all at once. The dermatologists are right, you know. Too much sun is dangerous.

What do you do when you forget the **PABA** and a painful burn results? First, do not use any of the numerous pharmaceutical preparations available. Things like **Americaine, Kip First Aid Spray, Medicone Dressing Cream, Morusan, Noxzema Sunburn Spray, Solarcaine, Unburn,** and **Unguentine Spray** all contain the local anesthetic benzocaine. These ingredients may temporarily provide some slight relief (probably psychological more than anything else), but in the long *329* run they may actually irritate your skin and thereby add to your woe. Probably the best approach is to take four aspirin tablets every three hours. Even the American Pharmaceutical Association's *Handbook of Non-Prescription Drugs* admits that plain aspirin could be better than any topical remedy on the market.[7] In order to protect your stomach from such a large dose of aspirin, it would be wise to crush the aspirin and take it with a large glass of water. If that is too much of a drag, you can place the aspirin tablets in your mouth, take a large mouthful of milk and, while the milk is still in your mouth, chew the tablets thoroughly. By washing down your aspirin with milk, the unpleasant taste is minimized and there is less gastric irritation. If the pain is unbearable, a cool (not ice-cold) tub of water, followed by a paste of baking soda and corn starch, will provide some relief. One tablespoon of each added to a small amount of cool water will make a paste that can be applied as a wet dressing.

There are some medications which will sensitize your skin to the sun. They could help you develop a very severe and painful burn which **PABA** cannot prevent. If you are taking, or ever take, any of the following drugs, you had best stay in the shade:

Anhydron   **Gantanol**
Azo Gantrisin   **Gantrisin**
Chlorpromazine   **Hydrodiuril**
Compazine   **NegGram**
Declomycin   **Orinase**
Diabinese   **Phenergan**
Diuril   **Stelazine**
Dyazide   **Temaril**
Fulvicin   **Thorazine**

During the summer it is also a good idea to stay away from deodorant soaps, because they too contain ingredients which may allow the sun to produce an exaggerated burn. Some of the brands to watch out for are **Lifebuoy**, **Irish Spring**, **Safeguard**, and **Zest**.

Insect Bites and Itching

Nothing can ruin a camping trip faster than a bad itch. An ounce of prevention is worth two birds in the bush any day. **Cutter Insect Repellent** (foam or lotion) is an excellent preparation. So is **Skram Insect Repellent** (liquid only). No medical kit should be without one of them. Even better, why not stock up on some **Thiamine**? **Vitamin B₁**, when taken orally, may prevent mosquitoes from sucking up your precious bodily fluids. It apparently creates a smell at the level of your skin which the mosquitoes hate. The dose for an adult is two hundred to three hundred milligrams per day (one hundred to two hundred milligrams for children). Because it is a water-soluble vitamin, like Vitamin C, it would be smart to stagger the dose throughout the day so it is not excreted all at once.

Oops! You forgot the insect repellent and the mosquitoes were especially hungry. Or maybe that romp in the hay turned out to be a roll in the poison ivy. Whether your itching is caused by chiggers, prickly heat, or insect bites, hot water may be the fastest, cheapest, and most effective treatment around. The advantages of hot water for minor itching have already been discussed in detail (see Chapter 4). Momentary application of water 120–130° Fahrenheit (slightly painful, but not so hot it will burn) should eliminate a minor itch for up to four hours. A hot bath or hot water compress could even help relieve the itching of hemorrhoids.

When itching gets out of control and becomes generalized over your entire body, it is time for something special. Add one cup of **Aveeno Oatmeal** to a tub of luke warm water and soak for ten to twenty minutes. Be careful—the bath tub could become very slippery. Put a towel at the bottom to prevent a broken neck. If you do not have a colloidal oatmeal preparation handy, you can always use kitchen cornstarch (a fancy medical brand is called **Linit**). Just add one cup of cornstarch powder to four cups of water and mix it up thoroughly. Then put the glop in a tub of water and mix it around completely. A twenty-to-thirty-minute lukewarm soak is good for almost any generalized inflammatory skin condi- *331* tion. It will help relieve rashes, itching, crotch irritation, or an allergic reaction.

After you are done drying yourself off (gentle patting is preferable), you may want to gook up your skin with a topical preparation. *Do not* use any of the highly promoted local anesthetic sprays since they may aggravate your condition. You can make up a **Burow's Solution** of aluminum acetate. Dissolve one **Domeboro** tablet (available in pharmacies without a prescription) in a pint of water and mix it up well. Loosely bandage the insect bite, poison ivy, or inflammatory spot. Pour the mixture over the bandage little by little every fifteen or twenty minutes in order to keep the dressing wet. If your patience allows, maintain the procedure for at least four hours. This solution is not only useful for its antiinflammatory, mildly astringent, and mildly antiseptic action: it can also be employed for an external ear infection. One tablet of **Domeboro** dissolved in a quart of water (1:40 **Burow's Solution**) makes an excellent preparation. Place a wick of cotton or gauze in the ear and instill a few drops of this liquid every two hours to keep it wet. Change the wick every day in order to bring out any gunk which may have collected.

Another topical preparation (one which is applied externally to the skin) good for itching is plain **Calamine** lotion. Even gulping down a few aspirin tablets could be of some value. However, if you want some heavy artillery to fix up your suffering skin, you should have a **Cortisone** cream handy.

Cortisone can relieve a great many skin problems, including dermatitis, eczema, itching, allergy, hemorrhoidal discomfort, vulvar irritation, crotch rot, rash, or general inflammation. Some doctors swear by topical **Cortisone** preparations for everything. It is not a panacea, but it may offer relief in an emergency. Three common brands are **Carmol HC**, **Cetacort Lotion**, and **Hytone Cream**. A prescription is required. They all contain **Hydrocortisone** and can be applied three or four times per day. They have a low potential for creating allergic sensitivity, but if an irritation develops, discontinue their use promptly. Pregnant women should probably avoid this stuff or only apply it to small, localized areas. **Cortisone** is not curative, but it certainly can save the day if your skin needs soothing relief.

Ouch! Insect stings can really hurt. To be prepared, always have meat-tenderizer in your kit. Make a water paste and immediately apply it to the affected spot (for a detailed description see Chapter 4). Better yet, get your doctor to prescribe **Panafil Ointment**. This is a ready-to-use mixture of papain, the enzyme found in the papaya fruit. It is the same ingredient as in meat-tenderizer. This snazzy ointment can be applied to wounds which become infected or do not heal rapidly enough. **Panafil** is made by the Rystan Company, Little Falls, N.J. 07424.

If you are allergic to insect bites, particularly bee stings, it is more than an ouching matter. Because this could be a life-or-death situation, you must carry an emergency kit with you at all times during the summer months. Although desensitization shots may be helpful, they are usually carried out with something called whole-insect-body extract. It is not nearly as effective as pure venom extract.[8] Because preparation of the whole-body extract may destroy the venom, it is not surprising to learn that there have been fatalities even after allergy desensitization shots. For this reason it would be wise to have your physician prescribe a kit. An excellent emergency insect sting treatment kit called **Ana-Kit** is available from Hollister-Stier Laboratories, Box 3145 T.A., Spokane, Wash. 99220. For a detailed description of the contents of this compact kit, see Chapter 7.

Fungus Infections:
Athlete's Foot and Crotch Rot (Jock Itch)

Brace yourself sports fan, when it comes to athlete's foot I've got the inside story hot off the press. First off, there are two kinds of athlete's foot: a mild, relatively benign form, and a potent, hard to handle form. If all you have is a little dry scaling between a couple of toes you are in luck, because that will hardly cause you any grief. If you want to cure this condition, then buy **Tinactin**, you will be fixed up in no time. Forget the **Desenex**, and **Daliderm**, the **Quinsana Foot Powder** or what ever else you've been using and lay out the extra bucks for something that works really well.

If, on the other hand, you have itchy, white, soggy, yucky 333 smelling gunk between your toes, then you've got something that requires more than **Tinactin**. First off, ignore what you've been hearing all these years about it being a simple fungus infection. According to two heavy-duty dermatologists, Drs. James Leyden and Albert Kligman, this kind of athlete's foot is probably caused by a combination of nasty bacteria *and* fungi, which means that it won't respond favorably if you just treat it with a fungicide.[9]

What do you do if you have the potent form of athlete's foot? The first thing you have got to do is get rid of the bacteria because they are causing most of the damage. How did they get there in the first place? If you think about it for a minute you will probably realize that your athlete's foot gets worse during the summer. That is because feet sweat more during hot weather. Moisture, whether it be caused by exercise, tight shoes, or anxiety enables all kinds of gross organisms to start growing between your toes. To get rid of the bacteria you have to get rid of the moisture. The simplest thing to do would be to wear sandals all summer, but that could be impractical for some folks. An even better trick would be to apply some sort of medication that would kill the bacteria and simultaneously dry up all the moisture in the tissue between your toes. Drs. Leydon and Kligman believe that they have discovered the ideal agent. It is **Aluminum Chloride** in a 20 to 30 percent solution. This common chemical has been used for years as an underarm deodorant or antiperspirant. It is even better in the treatment of athlete's foot. By drying the skin it makes the area between your toes inhospitable to the invading bacteria while at the same time directly killing the buggers. **Aluminum Chloride** should be applied twice a day until the whiteness, wetness, itchiness, and yucky smell have disappeared. Never apply it after a shower or when feet are wet since it will burn and sting. There is one other word of caution. If you have any open, irritated sores between your toes, you had better avoid this potent agent since it could aggravate the irritation. In this case you'd better resort to something called **Castellani Paint**.

Any good pharmacist should be able to make you a thirty percent **Aluminum Chloride** solution that you can apply twice a day with a *Q-tip*. It is a nonprescription product. If, however, your pharmacist never heard of such a thing and appears unwilling to go to any trouble to obtain it, you can get your doctor to prescribe something called **Drysol**. It is nothing but **Aluminum Chloride** (20%) in an 80% alcohol solution. It is used as an antiperspirant for folks who sweat a lot. For some dumb reason it is only available by prescription. Since the alcohol evaporates so quickly, you may have to apply **Drysol** more than twice a day to achieve satisfactory results.

Once the bacteria are gone, you can resort to using the fungicide, **Tinactin**, in order to get rid of any fungi still hanging around. During hot, humid weather it would be wise to also continue using **Aluminum Chloride** once a day as a prophylactic measure in order to prevent flare-ups.

Jockstrap Itch

Although "crotch rot" is often an unpleasant consequence of sports activities, it certainly is not restricted to athletes. Tight clothing and obesity will favor the growth of organisms in the groin, especially during the summer months. A starch or colloidal oatmeal bath can be soothing. Light clothing which prevents chafing will also go a long way toward solving the problem. Anything which soaks up sweat, like talcum powder or **Zeasorb Powder**, will help prevent the condition from starting in the first place.

If the irritation is very unpleasant, it may be useful to apply a potassium permanganate compress. Dissolve one tablet (three hundred milligrams) in three quarts of water in order to make a 1:10,000 solution. A compress of this concentration will be antibacterial, astringent, and antifungal. Watch out, though—any crystals which are not completely dissolved could burn the skin. This stuff will also stain like crazy. Fingernails can be cleaned with a 3 percent hydrogen peroxide solution. When the skin has been completely dried, it may be beneficial to apply a **Cortisone** cream like **Hytone** to the affected area.

Acne and What To Do About It

Dermatology has been in the dark ages for years, especially when it comes to the problem of pimples. Little valid scientific work has been done, and myths still abound. Everything from *335* too much masturbation (or too little) to bad diet has been implicated in the search for a cause to those nasty little red blotches. Teenagers are still led to believe that vigorous scrubbing may help clean up their problem. Where doctors feared to tread, the drug companies cared to enter. In 1970, $35 million was spent on over 150 nonprescription acne preparations, most of which do absolutely nothing to clear up pimples. Disc jockeys have laid down a line of hype that would fool a walrus. As a result, acne sufferers have spent enormous amounts on products like **PropaPH, Pro-Blem, Sebacide, Stri-Dex Medicated Pads, Tackle, Teenac, Therapads**, and **Ting**. The contents and concentrations of most of the nonprescription products are so weak that they work, if at all, more on the brain than on the skin. When tested scientifically, there are only a few over-the-counter brands that do anything at all.

What can a kid with acne do? First let's eliminate the *don'ts. Don't wash your face excessively*! It is easy to become fanatical and start scrubbing away six or more times a day. Two or three times is adequate. Pimples are rarely caused by dirt. *Don't* worry about diet. If you don't think your complexion gets worse, you can drink all the milk you want and eat nuts, chocolate, or whatever. *Don't* get carried away with cosmetics, including special acne cosmetics. They can jam things up and make those zits worse. *Don't* go to a dermatologist who uses X-ray treatment; it could be dangerous. *Don't* waste your money on all the junk products floating around.

Despite the hip talk and heavy duty sell techniques, there are only a few nonprescription acne aids that can do some good. They all contain the chemical benzoyl peroxide. They are **Benoxyl, Loroxide, Oxy-5, PanOxyl, Persadox**, and **Vanoxide.** These babies are all pretty much equivalent, so pick the cheapest one. They work by drying and peeling the skin. There may even be some redness and irritation, but that is to be expected if it is mild. Start the first few days with one light application to a small portion of one side of your face. Never, ever apply these agents after washing your face, while it is still wet. Always wait a good while until the skin is completely dry. If the scaling, redness, and inflammation is not too uncomfortable or embarrassing, you can extend the application to half of the face. If well tolerated, the applications can lightly cover the whole face and even be increased to more than once a day (two or three times is the maximum). The object is to dry out the old pimples and prevent the new ones from forming. Take care not to get the gunk anywhere near eyes or sensitive tissue around the corners of the mouth or nose. Lots of folks stop the treatment when their skin dries out. That is foolish, since it is the therapeutic objective in the first place.

So much for the nonprescription stuff. There is something much better for acne, but it requires a prescription. The magic bullet is called **Tretinoin.** and it is available under the brand names **Retin-A or Aberel.** Without any doubt, this is the best pimple product in the world today. It should serve as an anchor for any successful acne treatment, whether the problem is mild, moderate, or severe. Unfortunately, **Retin-A** or **Aberel** can only be purchased with a prescription, which is a damn shame given the fact that they work better than anything else.

Very few dermatologists or regular doctors prescribe **Tretinoin** for their patients because either they don't know about it, they don't know how it is supposed to be used, or their experience is unsatisfactory due to their lousy technique. Successful therapy requires patience, concern, commitment, and good patient-doctor communication. Very few doctors seem willing to take the time necessary to achieve the desired results. Pay attention to what I have to say and you will know more about how to really clear up acne problems than most doctors. I have obtained most of my information once again from Drs. Albert Kligman and James Leyden. If you want to read their work yourself I highly recommend the article "Acne Vulgaris A Treatable Disease" published in the journal *Postgraduate Medicine* (vol. 55, pages 99 to 105, February, 1974).[10]

Tretinoin works by producing peeling and drying of the skin. Pimples which already exist are sloughed off. Any pimples which are developing but have not yet appeared will be brought to the surface and extruded. The trick to successful treatment with **Tretinoin** requires that the acne sufferer follow a few simple procedures. The first important step is to discontinue the use of any other skin preparations for pimples. Throw out the **Tackle**, **PropaPH**, or whatever, and let your *337*

THE PEOPLE'S PHARMACY

face recuperate for a day or two. At the same time cut out frequent face washing, especially with strong, antibacterial soaps. Stick with mild soap like *Ivory* and then restrict yourself to only washing twice a day. Now you can start to apply **Retin-A**. It is best to begin with the cream—0.05 percent strength (it is also available in a stronger 0.1% cream and a liquid form). Never, never put the medication on your face after washing. If the skin is wet it will penetrate much faster and cause problems. Always start treatment cautiously. Do not smear the stuff all over the face. Instead apply a little bit to one cheek the first night. A little burning or stinging may occur, but that is nothing to worry about. After a day or two, the cheek which is receiving the applications should turn a little red. If the reaction is too strong, the applications should only be made once every other day, instead of once each night. After a while the face will toughen up so that it is possible to use the cream once a day in order to maintain moderate redness and peeling. By the way, be very careful about going out in the sun while using **Tretinoin**. The chances of coming down with a severe sunburn are greatly enhanced due to a sensitizing action. Always use an effective suntan lotion that contains PABA (Para-aminobenzoic acid) such as **PreSun**.

The toughest thing about using **Tretinoin** is that it requires the patience of a saint. Do not expect immediate improvement. In fact, you should expect your skin condition to get worse. Not only do redness, peeling, and burning reach a peak after three or four weeks, but pimples which were developing below the skin's surface will be forced up to the surface where they will become painfully visible. This is why most doctors and patients give up on **Retin-A**. But it is just this aggravation of the problem that will ultimately produce the pot of gold at the end of the suffering. It may take two or even three months for real progress to be noted. There is no doubt, however, that for the great majority of folks afflicted with pimples, the short-term suffering is well worth the long-term improvement. Once your skin has cleared up do not stop using **Tretinoin**. It may have to be used for a couple of years until all signs of acne have disappeared.

For folks who have a really bad case of zits, **Tretinoin** may not be strong enough to do the job all by itself. Dr. Kligman

338

has found that adding an oral antibiotic such as **Tetracycline** will enhance the beneficial action of the topical skin cream. Unfortunately, long-term **Tetracycline** administration often produces side effects. In women, vaginitis (an infection of the vagina) is not uncommon, especially if the person is also using birth control pills. Stomach upset is also a likely outcome with some diarrhea and gas. For these reasons, **Tetracycline** as well as its derivative (**Declomycin**) should never be used for a mild case of acne, or even a moderate case unless **Tretinoin** has been used first. In the future, antibiotic ointments that can be applied to the skin may eliminate the problems associated with oral **Tetracycline**. Dr. Kligman has obtained excellent results with **Tretinoin** and topical **Erythromycin**. Unfortunately, these antibiotic creams are not yet being manufactured.

After all the years of suffering it is nice to know that medical science has at last come up with a technique for treating acne. It may not be a cure, but it sure is an improvement over all the garbage that has been promoted for so long. The only difficult part of the whole therapy is getting your doctor to prescribe **Tretinoin** in the first place. Once you have passed that roadblock the rest should be relatively easy.

There is one word of caution about nonprescription pimple products which cannot be left unmentioned. Black people cannot use preparations which contain the ingredient *resorcinol*. This chemical can cause discoloration and really mess up the skin. The following drugs and cosmetic aids are only a partial list of products which contain resorcinol:

Acne	**Contrablem**
Acne Aid	**Komed**
Acne-Dome	**Microsyn**
Acnomel	**Phisoac**
Acnycin	**Resulin**
Bensulfoid	**Rezamid**
Cenac	**Tackle**
Clearasil	

Headache, Migraine

Nothing can spoil a trip or vacation faster than a headache. In fact, nothing can spoil anything faster than a headache. Headaches may be provoked by lots of things, including infections, high blood pressure, nasal congestion, tumors, fatigue, and too much booze. Your everyday, garden-variety headache, however, probably does not belong in any of these categories. Doctors love to pin the blame on tension and psychological stress. They are probably right. Unfortunately, stress is part of our way of life. Until average people are able to change their life-styles, headaches will probably be something they have to put up with.

Numero uno for the treatment of the common headache is still aspirin. Although most commercials for pain-relief never admit it, the ingredient "most often prescribed by doctors" is nothing but good old acetylsalicylic acid. If you want something more potent, you could combine aspirin with codeine. Most minor attacks should respond nicely to this formula. **Empirin Compound w/Codeine** is your doctor's favorite prescription product containing this combination. It also contains caffeine and phenacetin. If not used frequently, this is a perfectly adequate preparation, but when consumed regularly, it is possible the phenacetin could do damage to your kidneys.

If you have a sensitive stomach which can't handle solid *Aspirin* tablets, you can always try the old milk in the mouth trick. Take a mouthful of milk and hold it while popping in two aspirin tablets. Chew the mess up well and swallow, washing down any left-over aspirin with another couple of slurps of milk. The milk kills the nasty flavor of chewed-up aspirin. Another version of the same game is called crush and mush. It requires smashing up the aspirin and trying to dissolve it in some liquid (orange juice or honey and lemon) before putting it in your mouth. If neither of these approaches turn you on then you could resort to a buffered preparation. A small teaspoonful of baking soda taken with two aspirin tablets will theoretically promote rapid absorption of the aspirin and reduce stomach irritation. Unfortunately, the buffering action of baking soda probably speeds the elimination of the pain killer from the body and thereby reduces its effectiveness. A couple of Vitamin C tablets will counter this negative action and give your aspirin greater efficiency. If none of the above suggestions proves successful, you can always substitute the drug **Acetaminophen** for aspirin. It may not be quite as effective, but it won't irritate the stomach nearly as much as aspirin. It is available under many brand names including the now famous **Tylenol**. Whenever possible ask the pharmacist for the cheaper generic product which is sold as just plain **Acetaminophen**.

Headaches caused by nasal congestion may respond to a topical decongestant like **Neo-Synephrine**. Be careful, however; frequent use may lead to rebound congestion and drug-induced headaches. **Sudafed** and **Propadrine** are oral decongestants which may be of some value for folks who do not suffer from high blood pressure. It is worthwhile to keep in mind the fact that very few long-lasting headaches which seem to arise in the facial area are actually due to nasal congestion or sinusitis. It is only the relatively short, rapid-onset nasal headache accompanied by congestion and discharge that will respond to a decongestant.

Killer headaches of the migraine variety are terrible. There is no doubt that the emotional state will affect the onset and frequency of attacks. They may start out with depression, loss of appetite, visual disturbances, disorientation, and irritability. Once the pain really hits, the other symptoms may vanish. If you are one of the unlucky ones, though, everything will merge into one gigantic blur of agony. Nausea is a common occurence, extremities may feel cold, and light may hurt the eyes. All in all, this is nothing less than a living hell.

There is no single therapeutic approach to migraine. Susceptible individuals may develop migraines after ingesting certain foods. Only trial and error can establish the guilty agents. Common offenders are cured meats such as bacon, salami, hot dogs or ham. Citrus fruits have been implicated in some individuals, as have foods cooked with monosodium glutamate. Anyone suspecting some foods are the culprit should try eliminating them. Strong cheese (particularly cheddar), legumes (such as soy bean products, peas, lentils, licorice, or peanuts) chicken livers, chocolate, cola drinks, red wines, pickled herring, and canned figs are frequently at fault. Strong *341* odors have been known to precipitate an attack so care should be taken to avoid smoke, chemicals, paint or even potent perfumes. Determining which environmental factors might be responsible for a severe headache can be extremely difficult, but it is one avenue worth pursuing before moving on to other approaches.

Some people may respond well to psychological counseling. Others may find that peaceful meditation will work wonders. Unfortunately, environmental conditions do not always allow such luxury. For the future, biofeedback promises advantages which no other therapy can match. It can teach us how to consciously relax muscle tone and relieve tension. There are relatively few doctors or health professionals who are equipped to utilize this new technology. When we do learn how to control our bodies, it may be possible to eliminate the need for pharmacological treatment.

Aspirin and codeine may help stave off a mild migraine assault. They will do very little for a severe onslaught. There is only one drug that will work. It is a potent medication and it should not be used in a casual manner as if it were just another drug for headaches. **Ergotamine** (sold under the brand names **Cafergot, Ergomar, Gynergen**, and **Migral**) was originally obtained from a fungus which grows on molding grain, particularly rye. It was discovered as far back as 600 B.C. During the Middle Ages, people were thought to be possessed by St. Anthony's Fire or the Holy Fire because they danced around in a bizarre fashion. In reality, these "epidemics" were caused by burning sensations in the arms and legs produced by the consumption of contaminated grain which contained **Ergotamine**. Because this drug has the tendency to constrict blood vessels and reduce blood flow to the extremities, a stinging and burning feeling is experienced. It was not until 1926 that this drug was first found to be useful for the treatment of migraine. Today, it is still the agent of choice.

Ergotamine can relieve the torment of migraine only if it is used correctly and carefully. It can be a dangerous drug if the warnings are not heeded. At the very first sign of an attack it is imperative that the migraine-sufferer start taking his medicine. Only by acting promptly is it possible to obtain real relief. Once the headache has a chance to get a foothold, **Ergotamine** will be much less effective. Here is a case where stoicism does not pay. Toxic dosage levels may have to be employed if a person does not act quickly. Only the smallest amount of drug necessary to achieve relief should be used. If at all possible, the patient should lie down in a dark room for at least two hours after taking the drug so that it can exert maximum benefit.

If your doctor prescribes **Cafergot**, you should take one tablet at the very first sign of migraine. This can, if necessary, be followed by one tablet every half hour up to a maximum of six tablets. No more than ten tablets of **Cafergot** may be safely consumed during any given week even if there is more than one attack during that time.

Sometimes the nausea associated with a migraine attack makes it hard to swallow any pills. If you hate rectal suppositories, you might ask your medic for **Ergomar**. This **Ergotamine** drug can be placed under the tongue and dissolved slowly. The maximum dose is three tablets in one day and only five for any given week.

None of the drugs which contain **Ergotamine** can be used by pregnant women. They must also be avoided by people with bad circulation, arteriosclerosis, heart disease, angina, thrombophlebitis, kidney or liver disease, or high blood pressure.

Because these potent medications can be helpful in alleviating the incredible suffering of migraine, patients tend to abuse them. Instead of taking a few tablets over the course of an attack, they start increasing the dose until they have surpassed the safety limit. This can have grave consequences. For one thing, overuse (more than ten tablets of **Cafergot** per week) can paradoxically produce headache, nausea, vomiting, and diarrhea. Thus, a vicious circle is established. The patient takes **Ergotamine** for a terrible headache and nausea. If the drug does not provide adequate relief, he increases the dose until soon the drug itself is causing the problem. Not realizing this, the patient takes more drugs and again compounds the situation. Other symptoms of overuse are weakness, itching, and muscle pain. The feet and legs may feel cold and become numb. If use of the drug is not halted, the impaired circula-

343

tion could lead to gangrene. If used promptly and in moderate doses, **Ergotamine** can be an effective, safe drug for treating killer headaches. Used injudiciously, the drug can be dangerous.

Nose Trouble (Colds and Allergy)

No matter where you are, a cold is a bummer, but it is especially crummy on a trip or a vacation. Resist the urge to buy and use all kinds of nonprescription cold remedies. Products like **Contac** or **Dristan** contain barely enough active ingredients to wash behind the ears and their usefulness is highly doubtful. For the 22 million Americans with high blood pressure, the decongestants found in many of these "shotgun" preparations could be dangerous. If you feel that a decongestant is in order, then buy it separately as **Sudafed** or **Propadrine,** rather than in combination with other medicines. Better yet, stick with **Vitamin C** and aspirin, but remember they can interact. Don't take them at the same time since they influence each other's excretion rate. By taking one about two hours after the other and alternating throughout the day you will achieve maximum benefit.

Summer travelers may find that their allergies will disappear in foreign lands. That is because the pollens we have in the USA are not common to other parts of the world. Count your blessings. If you find that your allergies have followed you, then try large doses of **Vitamin C** and add a simple antihistamine that has the least reputation for causing sedation. Your best bet would be **Chlor-Trimeton** (generic name: **Chlorpheniramine**).

If you find yourself in a remote part of the world without a pharmacy, you can always fall back on one of the pills you brought along for motion sickness. **Phenergan** can be used to fight allergies and itching, but it may put you to sleep. One tablet every four to six hours will handle most problems. As already pointed out, it can double as a sleeping pill if you didn't bring one along.

Urinary Tract Infections

Anyone who has ever experienced the pain and discomfort of a kidney or bladder infection does not have to be told how unpleasant it can be. For those fortunate enough to remain uninitiated, cystitis can have you running to the bathroom almost every few minutes and the suffering can be intense. It is a more common problem than most people think. Millions and millions of women are affected each year. Birth control pills may dramatically increase susceptibility to infection, but the symptoms may not be as apparent. If cystitis strikes on a trip, especially in a foreign country, it can be particularly trying. First, it can really cramp your style, and second, it may be difficult to explain the trouble to a doctor who does not speak your language.

So what are you going to do? Go to your doctor. The burning and itching while urinating usually makes a person want to stop drinking all fluids just to avoid the encounter. That is the worst thing you can do. If you consume massive amounts of liquids it may be possible to head the infection off before it gets hold. Two to three quarts of water per day is essential. By combining large doses of **Vitamin C** (one thousand to two thousand milligrams every four hours) with lots of liquids, your chances of beating it are greatly enhanced.[11]

Ascorbic acid in high concentrations can kill bacteria within the kidneys. For a woman who develops a kidney infection during the first three months of pregnancy, **Vitamin C** is often the preferred drug since it is probably the least toxic to the baby.

If lots of water and ascorbic acid do not rapidly relieve the problem, it is time to take more drastic action. First, proof must be obtained that the symptoms are really being caused by a urinary tract infection. Other nasties could conceivably produce similar signs and symptoms. In years past, the only way for a woman to determine what caused her suffering would be to make an appointment with a doctor who then would order a urine culture. By the time a laboratory took the urine specimen, did the analysis, and sent the record to the physician, quite a few days could have passed. Meanwhile, the infection often remained untreated. On a vacation this delay ***345***

THE PEOPLE'S PHARMACY

could be disastrous, especially if the person was traveling around on one of those "if it's Wednesday it must be Rome" trips. Fortunately, medical science has now provided women with a marvelous new diagnostic technique for determining urinary tract infections that is cheap, fast, and easy to use.

The new test is called **Microstix** and it is made by the Ames Division of Miles Laboratories, Elkhart, Indiana 46514. It should be available without a prescription. The procedure merely requires that a woman collect a small amount of urine in any receptacle in the privacy of her own home and then test it with a small plastic strip. If one part of the strip turns pink in 30 seconds, the woman can be almost certain that she is suffering from a urinary tract infection. In order to determine the actual bacteria causing the infection she would still have to take the strip to her doctor or hospital laboratory in order to have the strip analyzed by incubation.

Unquestionably, most doctors will scream bloody murder if they hear that their female patients are learning how to detect infections by doing a simple test in their own homes. Nevertheless, one of the country's medical experts on urinary tract infections, Dr. Calvin Kunin, has recently published some fascinating observations in *JAMA*:

> In our view, the demonstrated reliability of dipping the strip by untrained subjects and the logistic advantages of self-testing offer great promise for use as a screening test for urinary tract infections in the general population, and for use in office practice. . . . We are particularly attracted by the ability of the patient to perform either test in the privacy of her home and the advantage of using a first-morning specimen, when the bacterial count is expected to be highest. . . . These features, combined with clear evidence that untrained subjects can reliably read the test, strongly suggest that it may be the single most useful method currently available for screening large populations for urinary tract infections at lowest cost.[12]

Okay, you have determined that you have an infection; now what? Well, you will need a drug that can kill the bugs that have invaded the plumbing. Ideally, a number of different medications should be tested against your particular urine culture in order to establish the best drug. It is quite common, however, to initiate treatment before the lab results are in.

346

Doctors frequently prescribe a sulfa drug called **Gantrisin** (**Sulfisoxazole**). It is effective against a number of different bacteria, it is inexpensive, and it is safer than many of the newer "high-powered" antibiotics. Even after drug therapy is begun, urine should be tested with **Microstix** test strips every morning to make sure the drug is killing the bacteria. If improvement is not detected after the first few days, it could reasonably be assumed that the drug is not doing its job. **Gantrisin** can be purchased (with a prescription) in five-hundred-milligram tablets (0.5 grams). The initial dose is usually four tablets, (2 grams) followed by two tablets every four hours. Treatment is usually continued from seven to fourteen days. Substantial fluid intake is always a good idea.

There are some things that few doctors mention about **Gantrisin**. First, do not ever take Vitamin C at the same time you are on **Gantrisin**. Although it is safe by itself, this drug (or any sulfa drug) could damage the kidneys if the urine becomes acidic, a common occurrence when consuming large amounts of ascorbic acid. Second, stay out of the direct sun. This drug can sensitize your skin and help produce an exaggerated sunburn.

Other relatively inexpensive drugs that are used to treat urinary tract infections are the antibiotics **Ampicillin** and **Tetracycline**. Chronic and recurrent infections usually require more potent antibiotics, some of which can produce serious side effects. An old-fashioned medication which is frequently forgotten by physicians is **Mandelamine**. It is not an antibiotic and it has a low potential for toxicity. It is useful for long-term suppression of infections and works best when the urine is acidic. Large doses of Vitamin C (4,000 milligrams to 12,000 milligrams per day) can increase its effectiveness dramatically. The correct dose of **Mandelamine** is four grams daily taken in one-gram doses after each meal and at bedtime.

Urinary tract infections can be a real pain in the ass, but with proper diagnosis and treatment they can be handled. Women should encourage their doctors to provide them with the self-diagnostic test strip called **Microstix**. Anyone using the birth control pill should test her urine at regular intervals because undetected infections are much more common in this group of women. Drug therapy should be undertaken with an *347* eye towards selecting inexpensive medications that are not likely to produce side effects.

Recommended Reference Material

These drugs and therapeutic procedures will serve for many of the most common problems an individual or family may encounter at home or on a short trip. If you want to sink your teeth into something more formidable, some excellent books are available. Unfortunately, most of them have been written for the health professional and can be hard to wade through. It is not necessary to understand every word in order to glean the most important points. One example is provided by the *Merck Manual* on the treatment of hemorrhoids:

> Some hemorrhoids which are uncomplicated or cause only slight bleeding at long intervals do not require any treatment beyond efforts to correct the underlying cause. In the early stages, altering the defecating pattern may sometimes reduce the size of internal hemorrhoids and eliminate protrusion and bleeding. The patient should be instructed not to attempt defecation unless there is a real urge, and not to spend more time at stool than is necessary for evacuation without straining. Administration of mineral oil will help soften the stool and prevent the pain and straining caused by passage of large, hard stools. The patient should avoid trauma when cleaning the anal area after bowel movements by patting rather than rubbing the area with soft, slightly dampened toilet tissue. Excessive cleansing of the anus, intrarectal administration of medications, and digital manipulation of the anal area should be discouraged. Chronic factors (e.g. obesity, prostatism, chronic cough, cirrhosis of the liver) must be evaluated and corrected if possible. Internal hemorrhoids appearing during pregnancy usually disappear after delivery.[13]

Although this passage was written in stuffy medical terms, it is reasonably easy to understand, complete, and honest in its approach. By stating that "intrarectal administration of medications . . . should be discouraged," it is clear that the author is putting down products like **Preparation H** and **Vaseline Brand**

Hemorr-Aid, without coming right out and saying so. You will find that you are better able to understand medical problems than you might have expected.

There are a few basic books any home should have regarding health and sickness. A list of titles, publishers, and addresses is provided at the end of this chapter. Before purchasing anything else, it would be advisable to have a paperback medical dictionary. For less than two dollars it is possible to buy Dr. Robert Rothenberg's *The New American Medical Dictionary and Health Manual*. Do not let yourself get hung up looking for each word that you do not understand. Only use the dictionary to fill the gaps which can make medical books incomprehensible.

The book that I would take with me to a desert island is *The Merck Manual of Diagnosis and Therapy*, edited by David N. Holvey. The twelfth edition, published in 1972, cost only eight dollars. This book is compact and extremely well indexed, and provides information on 99 percent of most people's medical problems. There are tables of normal laboratory standards and ready reference guides to drugs and therapies. Frequent use will not destroy the binding and the dictionary-like indexing system will allow fast location of most things. It is written for health professionals, so be prepared to wade through some big words that may float right over your head.

Dr. Walter Modell has been editing the book called *Drugs of Choice* for a long time. A new edition appears every two years. It is one of the most understandable medical texts available. Although aimed at physicians, it is written in a comprehensible manner and is organized so beautifully that most laymen will be able to use it effectively. It lists the best drugs for almost every illness around and includes some of the most common side effects that could be encountered. The only drawback to this fine book is its price. The 1974–1975 edition costs a whopping $23.75. As I said, it is aimed at doctors.

If you are particularly concerned about the problems of drug side effects and interactions, you cannot be without *Hazards of Medication: A Manual on Drug Interactions, Incompatibilities, Contraindications and Adverse Effects*. It is written by Eric W. Martin and, although it is reasonably easy to understand, its value is contained in the table of drug interactions, *349* more than four hundred pages long. The table will tell you at a glance what other drugs or chemicals could interact with anything you might be currently taking. It too is geared to the physician and carries an outrageous price tag of $27.50.

No home medicine chest would be complete without a copy of *The Medicine Show*. It is cheap ($3.50) and is unbiased, since it is published by the editors of *Consumer Reports*. It is written for the consumer so there will be no problem understanding the medical terminology. Because it specializes in nonprescription drugs, it will not cover any complex medical treatment.

Another book which is relatively inexpensive and filled with valuable information is the *Handbook of Non-Prescription Drugs*. Edited by George B. Griffenhagen and Linda L. Hawkins, this fine work is published by the American Pharmaceutical Association, 2215 Constitution Avenue, N.W., Washington, D.C. 20037. The information contained in this book may be impossible to find anywhere else, especially on the drugs we buy. For example, have you ever wanted to know what is in stuff like **Anacin, Preparation H, Clearasil, Listerine, Ex-Lax, Nytol**, and **Arrid Extra Dry**? This book will provide the answers. The 1973 edition cost $7.50 and is available directly from the publisher.

None of these books is perfect. For the money, *The Medicine Show* and *The Merck Manual* are the best buys and between them you can learn lots about both prescription and nonprescription drugs. Next in line would have to be *Drugs of Choice*. If you are serious about your health, you should have some of these books in your home. If you do not trust your doctor or just want to check up on something he recommended, these books will enable you to do so.

There is a table of drugs and reference material provided at the end of this chapter. It is not necessary to stock your medicine cabinet with every drug which is recommended. This formulary is only meant to serve as a guide in helping you to build up a supply of medications which could assist you in treating common, everyday medical problems. All drugs must be considered dangerous and should not be abused or left in a place which is accessible to children. Because medications do deteriorate, it would be helpful if your pharmacist would type the expiration date of each drug on the label before he gives it to you. In this way you will be able to discard and replace anything which might decompose. Whenever possible, be patient and let the body heal itself. If in doubt, always consult your doctor.

Stocking Your Medicine Cabinet: A Practical Guide to Medications

OTC = Over-The-Counter
R_x = Prescription Only

ACNE   OTC

1. **BENZOYL PEROXIDE**
Available in the following nonprescription products:
BENOXYL, LOROXIDE, OXY-5, PERSADOX, VAN-OXIDE

Apply sparingly to one side of the face only for the first few days. If it does not cause too much irritation and redness, extend application to the whole face and slowly increase the number of daily applications to a maximum of two or three times a day. Do not get this stuff anywhere near your eyes, mouth, nose, or neck. These lotions work by drying the skin, but if the skin becomes excessively dry, they should be discontinued temporarily.

2. **TRETINOIN** (Vitamin A acid; Retinoic Acid) R_x
Available in the following prescription products: **ABEREL** or **RETIN-A**

This topical prescription product is the most effective acne aid available for mild to severe skin problems. Treatment should begin with the weakest form, the 0.05 percent cream. Applications must be started even more cautiously than benzoyl peroxide treatment, because it produces extreme redness and peeling in some people.

During the first two to five weeks, RETIN-A paradoxically makes acne worse, but this is followed by dramatic improvement which is long-lasting. Combined with a topical antibiotic, such as ERYTHROMYCIN RETIN-A gives excellent therapeutic results.[14]

ALLERGY   OTC

1. **VITAMIN C**: tablets
Usual dose for allergy: 2,000 to 5,000 milligrams per day, divided into smaller doses taken throughout the day. Buy ascorbic acid in small quantities and store it in the refrigerator to preserve potency.   If taken with aspirin, **VITAMIN C** will be less effective because it will be eliminated from the body at a faster than usual rate.

Physical examination

A basic examination involves a general inspection of body surface, shape, and movement, and measurement of pulse rate, respiration rate, temperature, and blood pressure. By touching and pressing, trained fingers can learn much about organs near the surface. The stethoscope permits listening to meaningful sounds produced in the lungs and heart. And all body openings—eyes, ears, nose, mouth and throat, and often the lower bowel—are checked.

For women, a search is made for indications of breast cancer and masses or tender areas in the abdomen which may indicate tumors; the Pap test—a microscopic examination of cells in secretions from the cervix or opening of the uterus—is becoming routine.

Laboratory tests

A urine sample may be tested for indications of such conditions as kidney disease, bladder infections, and diabetes. Blood tests may determine the amount of various chemicals in the blood, the shape and number of red and white cells, and the hemoglobin content. Certain tests can detect an infection or irregularity in the body not readily found by other means. Finally, a chest x-ray is practically routine.

timely *tips*

... on health and safety

Be a medical watchdog

A watchdog can protect your home from ruin and your family from harm. But he can't protect your most valuable possession—good health.

Keep a watch on good health with a periodic examination, which your physician will suit to your individual needs. If you are over 35 years of age, you'll need a checkup each year. Persons over 50 may need one even more frequently. The examination usually includes a health history, a physical examination, and some laboratory and x-ray studies.

Health history

Questions about your use of alcohol and medications, sleep habits, and your work may give the physician clues to your health. Questions about past illnesses or injuries, illnesses in the family, and the causes of death of relatives often give meaning to conditions found during examination.

2. **CHLOR-TRIMETON**(*Chlorpheniramine*): four-milligram   **OTC**
tablets

Usual adult dose: one tablet three or four times a day.
(one-half tablet may work for some people). Children's
dose: under twelve years old, one-half tablet, three or four
times a day.

This antihistamine is less likely to cause drowsiness than
other antihistamines, but you should not drive or operate
machinery after taking it. It can be used for sneezing, runny
nose caused by allergy, itching, hives, and other skin allergies.

Nonprescription compounds containing *Chlorpheniramine* include **ALLEREST TABLETS, COLREX
COMPOUND, C3, CORICIDIN**, and **TETRAMINE T.R.**   **OTC**

3. **PHENERGAN**(*Promethazine*): 12.5- or 25-milligram tablets   **Rx**
Usual dose: one 25-milligram tablet before bed is best;
12.5 milligrams with meals and before bed if needed. The
smallest dose which works is preferred.

PHENERGAN causes drowsiness in most people,
which makes it less useful as an allergy treatment. It is
effective for itchy skin allergies as well as stuffy nose.
Never try to drive or do anything requiring mental alertness
after taking **PHENERGAN**.

This drug is more useful for motion sickness, nausea,
and vomiting than it is for treating allergies because of the
sedative properties.

CAUTION: Do not take **PHENERGAN** with: alcohol,
barbiturates, or strong pain-killers.

There are many other antihistamines. If the two which
are recommended do not work effectively, or if they produce excessive sedation, get your physician to prescribe
various other types in order to determine the most suitable
brand for your particular constitution.

ATHLETE'S FOOT AND CROTCH ROT

1. **TINACTIN** (Tolnaftate): cream, solution or powder   **OTC**
This is the most effective preparation there is for treating
mild athlete's foot and most other skin fungus infections.
Because this medication is potent, it should be applied
sparingly: two or three drops of solution suffice for the foot,
including between-the-toe places. Application twice a day
for two or three weeks should cure most infections. Powder

353

can be used with the solution or after healing to help keep those moist areas from getting infected again. Dust **TINACTIN POWDER** on one or two times a day as a preventive measure.

If the athlete's foot is still going strong after four weeks of treatment, it may not be athlete's foot. See a doctor.

CAUTION: Keep out of eyes!

2. **ALUMINUM CHLORIDE**: 30% solution OTC

If your pharmacist cannot make up this product, it can be purchased with a prescription under the brand name **DRYSOL**. It should only be applied to dry skin, never after a bath or shower. **ALUMINUM CHLORIDE** will eliminate moderate to severe athlete's foot and should be used twice a day. In the case of open, irritated sores, **CASTELLANI PAINT** should be substituted.

Once the worst part of the infections has been cleared up you can start using **TINACTIN** in order to clear up any residual fungus infection.

3. **POTASSIUM PERMANGANATE**: three hundred-milligram tablets (0.3 Gm.) OTC

Dissolve one tablet in three quarts of lukewarm or cool water to make a 1:10,000 concentrated solution. This beautiful purple liquid has astringent, germicidal, and anti-fungal action. It should be used as a wet compress. Undissolved crystals can burn the skin, and the solution should be made up fresh each time it is used—don't use leftovers.

A wet dressing of **POTASSIUM PERMANGANATE** 1:10,000 can be useful for many skin infections or inflammations, including poison ivy. It also will purify drinking water. It stains, but fingernails will come clean with a 3 percent hydrogen peroxide solution.

4. **ZEASORB MEDICATED POWDER** OTC

This superabsorbent powder can be used to dust sweaty feet or body areas. It will help prevent conditions which promote fungal growth.

BEE STINGS AND BEE-STING ALLERGIES

1. **MEAT TENDERIZER** (any brand with Papain) OTC

One-quarter teaspoon of tenderizer added to one to two teaspoons of water will make a paste which should be applied immediately to the sting. This should relieve the pain and reduce the inflammation.

Do not rely on this treatment if you are allergic to bee stings.

2. **PANAFIL OINTMENT, PAPASE** tablets   R_x

Both of these prescription products contain papain as a major ingredient. **PANAFIL** is in a ready-to-use ointment form, while **PAPASE** tablets should be crushed and made into a wet paste. Both of these preparations should work as well as, if not better than, plain meat tenderizer in alleviating stings. **PANAFIL** can also be used for infected cuts or wounds which do not heal rapidly.

3. **ANA-KIT EMERGENCY INSECT STING TREATMENT KIT**   R_x

If you are allergic to bee stings, you should not venture out without this excellent compact kit. It contains all of the necessary equipment for emergency treatment of serious allergic reactions, including a preloaded syringe containing adrenalin and easily understood precise instructions for its use.

Available with a prescription from Hollister-Stier Laboratories, Box 3145 T.A., Spokane, Wash., 99220.

BURNS

1. COLD WATER

All burns, including chemical, electrical, and thermal, respond magnificently to ice-cold water immersion or ice-cold moist towels. The faster the application the more complete the relief of pain and speed of recovery. Water should be kept between 41° and 55° Fahrenheit by adding a few ice cubes to a pan of tap water.

To be effective, cold treatment must be maintained until it is no longer painful to remove the affected part from the water. This may take anywhere from thirty minutes to five hours. Although this treatment requires patience, it will dramatically eliminate pain and will prevent damage and promote healing.[15]

After cold treatment, some doctors recommend application of honey to the burn, covered by a dry gauze bandage.

CONSTIPATION

1. Proper diet, high in roughage with plenty of fresh fruits, vegetables, and whole grains, will help to avoid this problem. Two teaspoons of unprocessed bran can be taken with milk, water, or juice daily to increase roughage in the diet.

Large doses of *Vitamin C* (1-3 Gm./day) may also help.

2. **MINERAL OIL**: liquid   OTC *355*

Usual dose: 1 or 2 tablespoons. Mineral oil should be taken only at bedtime, *never* at mealtime, because it interferes with vitamin absorption. Mineral oil is not recommended for pregnant women and babies.

DO NOT TAKE mineral oil with other laxatives.

3. Mild, bulk-producing laxatives: **OTC**
   Nonprescription products containing methylcellulose:
   CELLOTHYL, DIALOSE, DISOPLEX, SERUTAN
   Nonprescription products containing psyllium:
   EFFERSYLLIUM, METAMUCIL, MUCILOSE, PLOVA, REGULIN, SYLLAMALT
   Follow the instructions on the package. Try not to get into a laxative habit.

COUGH

1. Coughs that are productive—bringing up mucus—should be treated conservatively by sucking on hard candy, drinking lots of fluids, and inhaling steam or mist. This type of cough will usually go away by itself.

2. **CODEINE**: fifteen-milligram tablets, thirty-milligram tablets **Rx**
   Usual adult dose: fifteen-milligram tablets or half a thirty-milligram tablet every four to six hours. This treatment should be reserved for unproductive coughs.
   Follow the precautions for **CODEINE** listed under the heading *Pain*. If a nasty cough persists more than a few days, see a doctor.

3. **DEXTROMETHORPHAN**-containing cough remedies: **OTC**
   ROBITUSSIN-DM, ROBITUSSIN COUGH CALMERS, ROMILAR COUGH DISCS, SILENCE IS GOLDEN SYRUP and **LOZENGES, ST. JOSEPH COUGH SYRUP FOR CHILDREN.**
   Although these non-narcotic cough remedies offer no greater advantage than **CODEINE**, they can be purchased without a prescription. The products which are listed have been selected because they contain the least amount of "extras" along with the cough-suppressant Dextromethorphan.

CUTS AND SCRATCHES

1. Wash carefully with soap and water.

2. If necessary, **ALCOHOL** or **TINCTURE OF IODINE** may be applied around the edges of the wound.

3. Skin infections or infected scratches should be treated by soaking in hot water.

4. **PURE NATURAL HONEY** can be applied under a dry dressing every two or three days. It is reported to be a valuable cleansing and healing agent.[16]

5. **ACHROMYCIN OINTMENT** (*Tetracycline*): one half- and one-ounce tubes ·OTC
   TERRAMYCIN TOPICAL OINTMENT (*Oxytetracycline*) OTC
   These ointments can be spread on the skin for antibiotic action. It is unlikely they will speed recovery, but they may be psychologically rewarding.

DIARRHEA

1. **CODEINE**: fifteen-milligram tablets; thirty-milligram tablets Rx
   Usual dose: one fifteen-milligram tablet or half a thirty-milligram tablet every four to six hours. Maximum daily dose: sixty to seventy-five milligrams. **CODEINE** should not be used casually, as it can be habit-forming, though this is extremely uncommon if used infrequently.
   CAUTION: do not take **CODEINE** with alcohol, barbiturates, or tranquilizers.

2. **LOMOTIL** (*Diphenoxylate*) 2.5-milligram tablets Rx
   Usual adult dose: 2 tablets four times a day. A smaller dose may work just as well.
   LOMOTIL is not safe for children, people with liver trouble, and people with glaucoma. **LOMOTIL** should not be used casually because it can be habit-forming, though this is extremely uncommon if used infrequently.
   CAUTION: do not take **LOMOTIL** with alcohol, barbiturates, or tranquilizers.

3. **TINCTURE OF OPIUM**: liquid solution Rx
   Usual dose: ten drops three or four times daily. Dose can be adjusted for individual needs. Observe the same precautions as for **CODEINE**.

4. **KAOPECTATE**: liquid suspension OTC
   Usual adult dose: four to eight tablespoons as needed. Children's dose: four tablespoons if older than twelve; six-twelve years: two to four tablespoons; three-six years: one to two tablespoons.

357

DIARRHEA CAUSED BY AMOEBAS (E. hisolitica)   Rx

1. **DIODOQUIN** (*Diiodohydroxyquin*): 650-milligram tablets
   Usual adult dose: one tablet three times a day for three weeks. This drug should not be used too frequently for amoebic dysentery. Prolonged use in adults may cause eye damage. Children are more susceptible to this danger.
   This drug will only cure amoebas in the intestines. If there are amoebas in the liver, another drug must be used, such as **ARALEN** (see Malaria).
   Caution must be exercised by the patient who has thyroid disease.

2. **FLAGYL**(*Metronidazole*): 250-milligram tablets   Rx
   Usual adult dose for Amebiasis: 750 milligrams (three tablets) three times a day for five to ten days.
   Usual adult dose for giardiasis: 250 milligrams (one tablet) three times a day for five to ten days.
   Usual adult dose for vaginitis caused by trichomonas: 250 milligrams (one tablet) three times a day for ten days, but see warning on page 000.
   FLAGYL will cure amoebas in the intestines and the liver. It should not be taken by pregnant women or anyone who has had a blood disease. If **FLAGYL** gives you a bad headache or makes you dizzy, you should stop taking it immediately.
   CAUTION: do not take **FLAGYL** with alcohol.

INSECT BITES AND ITCHING

1. **CUTTER INSECT REPELLENT** (Deet +): foam or lotion   OTC
   SKRAM (Deet): liquid   OTC
   These two insect repellents are among the most effective available. Apply liberally if the bugs are hungry.

2. **THIAMINE HYDROCHLORIDE** (Vitamin B$_1$): tablets   OTC
   Taking 150 milligrams to 300 milligrams of this vitamin daily will keep mosquitos and fleas from biting.
   Children's dose: 75–150 milligrams per day.[17]

3. **HOT WATER**
   This is the fastest and most effective relief for minor itching. The water should be between 120° and 130° Fahrenheit (uncomfortably hot, but not hot enough to burn). Application for a few seconds should provide several hours' relief.

4. **AVEENO OATMEAL**   **OTC**

Generalized itching over the entire body may be treated by soaking for ten to twenty minutes in a tub of lukewarm water to which one cup of colloidal oatmeal has been added.
CAUTION: Tub may become slippery. Place a bathtowel in the bottom of the tub to prevent slipping and sliding.

5. **CORNSTARCH** (Kitchen or **LINIT** brand)   **OTC**

One cup powder dissolved in four cups cool water added to a tub of lukewarm water will provide similar relief to the oatmeal bath.

6. **BURROWS SOLUTION (DOMEBORO)**: tablets   **OTC**

One tablet dissolved in a pint of water will make a solution which can be applied as a wet dressing to insect bites, poison ivy, or inflamed areas. The dressing should be kept moist for up to four hours.

7. **CALAMINE LOTION**   **OTC**

Apply as needed for relief of itching.

8. **CARMOL HC, CETACORT LOTION, HYTONE CREAM**   **Rx**

All of these topical creams contain Hydrocortisone. They may be applied three to four times per day and will provide relief for the following skin problems:

Itching	Eczema
Allergy	Hemorrhoids
Dermatitis	Crotch Rot
Rash	General Inflammation

LEG CRAMPS AND FATIGUE

1. **VITAMIN E**   **OTC**

It has been reported in the medical literature that a daily dose of four hundred to eight hundred International Units can reduce the discomfort of nighttime leg cramps or "restless legs." There has even been the suggestion that exercise cramps and poor leg circulation will benefit from this dose of **VITAMIN E**.[18]

2. **QUINAMM**(*Quinine & Aminophylline*) tablets   **Rx**

Usual adult dose: 1 tablet before bedtime. If necessary this dose can be increased to one tablet after supper and one tablet upon retiring.

This drug may be useful in alleviating the symptoms of nighttime leg muscle cramps (including those related to diabetes, arthritis, thrombophlebitis, arteriosclerosis, vericose veins).

CAUTION: do not take **QUINAMM** if you are pregnant or of child-bearing potential. If you are allergic to *Quinine* or have the enzyme deficiency glucose-6-phosphate dehydrogenase, you must also avoid this medication.

If the drug produces stomach cramps, take it with a small snack. If you notice ringing in the ears, skin rash, visual disturbances, or deafness discontinue the drug immediately.

MALARIA   Rx

1. **ARALEN**(*Chloroquine*): five-hundred-milligram tablets
    Usual adult dose for an acute attack of malaria: Initially, two tablets followed by one additional tablet six-eight hours later. Then take one tablet each day for the next two days. A total of five tablets should be taken over the course of three days and should provide symptomatic relief for sudden flare-ups.

    Malaria attacks can be suppressed by taking one **ARALEN** tablet once a week on the same day.

    ARALEN will kill any amoebas which have escaped from your tummy and sneaked into your liver. The usual adult dose is two tablets per day for two days, followed by one tablet daily for two to three weeks. It should be accompanied by another drug which will kill the parasite in your intestinal tract (DIODOQUIN).

    CAUTION: This drug should not be used by pregnant women or anyone with psoriasis, liver damage, or eye trouble. Keep out of reach of children! Discontinue this medicine immediately if you experience visual disturbances.

2. **ATABRINE**(*Quinacrine*): one hundred milligram tablets   Rx
    Usual adult dose and children over eight years: two tablets every six hours for five doses followed by one tablet three times a day for six days.

    Children between four and eight years old: two tablets after meals the first day, followed by one tablet twice a day for six days.

    Children one to four years old: one pill after meals the first day followed by one pill every day for six days.

    ATABRINE should always be taken with a full glass of water after meals.

    This drug is also effective in killing the intestinal parasite *Giardia lamblia*, often implicated in producing traveler's diarrhea. Usual adult dose: one pill three times a day for one week. It may also be of value in the treatment of amoebic dysentery and tapeworm under a doctor's supervision.

CAUTION: *not safe* for pregnant women, patients with psoriasis, or people with severe psychological disturbances. Patients over sixty should be especially careful as should anyone with liver disease or alcoholism.

MIGRAINE   Rx

1. ASPIRIN and CODEINE
Usual adult dose: ten grains of **ASPIRIN** plus thirty milligrams of **CODEINE** every four hours.

Preparations with this combination are too numerous to list. They will be of use in mild attacks: see *Pain* for a description of dose and precautions.

2. ERGOTAMINE: tablets or suppositories   Rx
Available in:
CAFERGOT, ERGOMAR, GYNERGEN, MIGRAL
Usual adult dose: depends upon individual medication. **ERGOTAMINE** must be used early, at the very first signs of an attack. Otherwise, its effectiveness is reduced. The smallest amount of drug necessary to achieve relief should be used. The quantity of **ERGOTAMINE** which can be used safely in one week is strictly limited, and this limit must not be exceeded. Excessive doses produce paradoxical headache, nausea, and other symptoms of migraine. If used carefully **ERGOTAMINE** is the most effective drug for severe migraine.

CAUTION: *do not take* **ERGOTAMINE** if you are pregnant or if you have poor circulation, arteriosclerosis, heart disease, angina, thrombophlebitis, high blood pressure, or kidney or liver disease.

DO NOT TAKE **ERGOTAMINE** with decongestants, asthma medications (ephedrine, epinephrine, or isoroterenol), or the antibiotic TAO.

NAUSEA AND VOMITING (Motion Sickness)   OTC

1 **DRAMAMINE** (*Dimenhydrinate*): fifty-milligram tablets
Usual adult dose for motion sickness: one tablet taken thirty minutes to one hour before departure.

Children's dose: one-half tablet taken up to three times daily. The effect should last four hours.

361

Young children should not take this medicine except with a physician's approval.

Drowsiness may be severe when taking this drug. Never undertake any activity which requires attention or coordination. The sedative action of this drug can be put to good advantage as a sleeping pill.

If possible, do not take **DRAMAMINE** concomitantly with the following antibiotics: *Kanamycin, Neomycin, Ristocetin, Streptomycin,* and *Vancomycin.* Damage to the ear is possible.

2. **PHENERGAN**(*Promethazine*): twenty-five-milligram tablets   **Rx**

   Usual adult dose: one tablet (twenty-five milligrams) taken one-half to one hour before departure. If necessary, the dose can be repeated eight hours later.

   Usual children's dose: one-half tablet. This drug can be used effectively as a sedative to promote sleep both for children or adults. Twenty-five milligrams should be an adequate dose for this purpose. See additional uses for **PHENERGAN** under *Allergy.*

   CAUTION: PHENERGAN is an antihistamine drug and can cause dulling of the senses. Never undertake any activity which requires mental alertness.

   Do not take **PHENERGAN** with alcohol, barbiturates, tranquilizers, or strong pain-killers.

NAUSEA AND VOMITING OF PREGNANCY (Morning Sickness)

1. AVOID ALL DRUGS! Unless vomiting is serious, no medication should be taken, because of potential danger to the fetus. Consumption of toast or a cracker before arising in the morning may help. Eat small meals high in carbohydrates frequently throughout the day, interspersed with good fluid intake.

2. **CAUTION**: The following drugs are often prescribed for nausea and vomiting or headache. They have been shown to produce birth defects in animals. Do not take any of the following if you are pregnant or could become pregnant: **ANTIVERT, BONINE, MAREZINE, MIGRAL.**

PAIN (Headaches, Toothaches, Menstrual Cramps, . . .)

1. **ASPIRIN**: five-grain tablets (325 milligrams)   **OTC**

   Usual adult dose for mild pain: one or two tablets repeated every three to four hours. Aspirin is absorbed better and is less irritating to the stomach if it is crushed and "dissolved" or chewed with a mouthful of milk. Always take Aspirin with a full glass of liquid. A pinch of baking soda at the same time will also counteract irritation if you are susceptible to this problem.

Vitamin C taken at the same time will make the Aspirin work harder and longer and could be advantageous if you want a bigger punch for pain.

CAUTION: do not take **ASPIRIN** with alcohol, anticoagulants, antidepressants, arthritis medicines, or oral diabetes medicine.

2. **CODEINE**: various doses; thirty-milligram tablets preferred R_x

Usual adult dose: one tablet every 4 hours. Combined with two Aspirin tablets, Codeine is a powerful pain-killer which is superior to anything else on the market, especially **DARVON**.

Codeine should not be used casually, as it can be habit-forming, though this problem has been somewhat exaggerated.

CAUTION: do not take **CODEINE** with alcohol, barbiturates, or tranquilizers.

3. **CAPITAL WITH CODEINE** R_x
TYLENOL WITH CODEINE
tablets in various doses

Usual adult dose: one or two tablets every four hours. These preparations contain **Acetaminophen** instead of aspirin. They can be used by people who are sensitive to aspirin or who for other reasons cannot take salicylates.

POISONING

1. **IPECAC SYRUP** (IPECHAR): Liquid **OTC**

Usual dose: three teaspoonfuls

Usual dose for children under one year of age: one-half to one teaspoonful. This medicine will usually induce vomiting within fifteen to twenty minutes. A second dose may be administered after twenty minutes if the first try was unsuccessful, but no more after that. Additional doses may be toxic.

CAUTION: do not induce vomiting if the poison which was swallowed is corrosive: acid, alkali (lye), gasoline, kerosene, cleaning fluid, turpentine, or any other petroleum product. If the patient is unconscious, vomiting is extremely dangerous.

If you do not have an emetic, (a drug which induces vomiting) stick your finger in the person's throat in order to produce vomiting.

2. **ACTIVATED CHARCOAL** (powder or liquid)   **OTC**
   Usual dose: one large tablespoon of powder in a glass of
   water well mixed to form a soupy glop. If in liquid form: one
   ounce of a 25 percent suspension.
   Activated charcoal should follow vomiting in order to
   soak up any poison which is left in the stomach. Repeat the
   dose frequently.

3. **POISON ANTIDOTE KIT**: (Charcoal and Ipecac)   **OTC**
   This excellent kit contains everything you need in case of
   an emergency in a handy, ready-to-use form. It is available
   from the Division of Bowman Pharmaceuticals, Inc., Canton, Ohio 44702.

4. In the case of corrosive or irritating poisons it is best to
   dilute the poison before rushing the patient to the
   emergency room of the nearest hospital. Demulcents such
   as milk, egg white, gelatin solution, aluminum hydroxide
   gel, flour and water, or oil may be of some benefit. Do not
   induce vomiting!

SUNBURN   **OTC**

1. **PABA(Para-Aminobenzoic Acid)**: suntan lotion
   Available in: **PRE-SUN**, **PABANOL**, and **PARAFILM**.
   These products are the most effective for preventing
   sunburn when used in a "conscientiously applied program"
   of limited exposure.
   If you have very sensitive skin, you should apply the
   lotion half an hour before sunbathing.

2. Now that you look like a boiled shrimp, you need something
   for the pain: four aspirin every three hours (chewed with
   milk or taken with an antacid to ward off stomach irritation).

3. A cool (not cold) soak in the tub may be followed with a
   gooey paste of baking soda and cornstarch (1 tablespoon
   of each in 2 quarts of cool water) will give some relief.

4. A cortisone cream may be of some value in relieving the
   pain. Some relatively safe prescription products which can
   be recommended are:
   CARMOL HC, CETACORT LOTION, HYTONE CREAM.   **Rx**

ULCERS AND ANTACIDS

1. **ALUMINUM** and **MAGNESIUM HYDROXIDE**: liquid or   **OTC**
   tablets

Almost any of the numerous antacid preparations available that contain the above combination will be effective. A liquid suspension probably works better than a solid tablet (relief will be faster and more complete).

For mild ulcers, take one hour after meals and at bedtime. More frequent consumption may be advisable during a severe flare-up.

Antacid brands which have proved to be effective are: **ALUDROX, MAALOX, MAGNESIUM-ALUMINUM HYDROXIDE GEL**, and **MYLANTA**.

CAUTION: People with ulcers should avoid the following drugs: Aspirin, cortisone drugs, Arthritis medicines like **BUTAZOLIDIN** or **INDOCIN**, and **RESERPINE** (found in the blood pressure drugs **DIUTENSEN, SER-AP-ES,** and **SERPASIL**).

URINARY TRACT INFECTIONS (Cystitis)

1. At the first signs of Cystitis, drinking great quantities of fluid and taking Vitamin C in 500 mg. to 1000 mg. doses frequently throughout the day may help stave off an infection or lessen its severity.

2. **SULFISOXAZOLE**: Found in the following brand name drugs: **Rx**
GANTRISIN, AZO GANTRISIN, SK-SOXAZOLE, SOSOL, SOXOMIDE
This sulfa drug is one of the safest; effective against most organisms causing urinary tract infections.

Usual adult dose of **GANTRISIN**: four (five hundred milligrans) tablets initially followed by two tablets every four hours for seven days. Drink lots of liquids while taking **Sulfisoxazole** to prevent kidney damage.

CAUTION: do not take **SULFISOXAZOLE** with **VITAMIN C**. An acid urine is very dangerous. If you are pregnant, or allergic to sulfa drugs these drugs are dangerous and should not be taken. If you develop fever and sore throat, and become pale or jaundiced, you should get medical attention. The drug may be messing up your blood.

DO NOT take **Sulfisoxazole** with alcohol, anticoagulants, **DILANTIN, MANDELAMINE,** or oral diabetes medicines.

3. **MANDELAMINE(Methenamine)**: one or one-half Gram tablets   **Rx**
Usual adult dose: one Gram tablet or two five-hundred-milligram tablets after each meal and at bedtime.

365

Acid urine is necessary for **MANDELAMINE** to be effective. Large doses of **Vitamine C** (four to twelve Grams daily) are recommended. **MANDELAMINE** is more beneficial than **GANTRISIN** for chronically recurring urinary in-.ections, although it is less effective for an acute attack.

MANDELAMINE can be taken safely for prolonged periods of time.

CAUTION: do not take **MANDELAMINE** if you have kidney disease. Do not take **MANDELAMINE** with bicarbonate of soda, gelatin, or sulfa drugs, including **GANTRISIN**.

Recommended Medical Reference Books for Home Use

1. **The Merck Manual of Diagnosis and Therapy**
   Editor, David N. Holvey
   Merck & Company., Inc.
   Rahway, N.J. 07605
   (ISBN 0-911910-01-8)
   Approximate Price $8.00

2. **The Medicine Show: Consumers Union's Practical Guide to Some Everyday Health Problems and Health Products**
   By the Editors of Consumer Reports
   Consumers Union
   Orangeburg, N.Y. 10962
   Price $3.50

3. **Drugs of Choice**
   By Walter Modell, M.D.
   C. V. Mosby Co.
   11836 Westline Industrial Drive
   St. Louis, Mo. 63141
   (ISBN 0-8016-3439-3)
   Approximate Price $24.00

4. **Handbook of Non-Prescription Drugs**
   Edited by George B. Griffenhagen
   and Linda L. Hawkins
   American Pharmaceutical Association
   2215 Constitution Avenue, N.W.
   Washington, D.C. 20037
   Approximate Price $7.50

5. **The New American Medical Dictionary
and Health Manual**
By Robert E. Rothenberg, MD.
New American Library
P.O. Box 999
Bergenfield, N.J. 07621
(451-J6284)
Price $1.95

6. **HAZARDS OF MEDICATION: A MANUAL ON
DRUG INTERACTIONS, INCOMPATIBILITIES,
CONTRAINDICATIONS AND ADVERSE EFFECTS**
By Eric W. Martin, PH.D.
J. B. Lippincott
E. Washington Sq.
Philadelphia, Pa. 19105
(ISBN 0-397-50288-5)
Approximate Price $27.50

7. **THE NEW HANDBOOK OF PRESCRIPTION DRUGS**
By Richard Burack, M.D.
Ballantine Books, Inc.
201 East 50th Street
New York, N.Y. 10022
(SBN 345-23840-0-150)
Approximate price $1.50

References

1. Kluger, Matthew J., Ringler, Daniel H., and Anver, Miriam R. "Fever and Survival." *Science* 188:166–168, 1975.
2. Moertel, C. G., et al. "A Comparative Evaluation of Marketed Analgesic Drugs." *New Engl. J. Med.* 286:813–815, 1972.
3. Merson, M. H., and Gangarosa, E. J. "Travelers Diarrhea." *JAMA* 234:200–201, 1975.
4. Holvey, David N., ed. *The Merck Manual of Diagnosis and Therapy*, 12th ed., Rahway, N.J., Merck, 1972. Pp. 689–690.
5. Burkitt, D. P., et al. "Dietary Fiber and Disease." *JAMA* 229:1068–1074, 1974.
6. Painter, N. S., et al. "Unprocessed Bran in Treatment of Diverticular Disease of the Colon." *Brit. Med. J.* 2:137–140, 1972.

7. Hall, Nathan A. "Burn and Sunburn Remedies." In *Handbook of Non-Prescription Drugs*. Washington, D.C.; American Pharmaceutical Association, 1973. Pp. 144–145.

8. Busse, William B., et al. "Immunotherapy in Bee-Sting Anaphylaxis." *JAMA* 231:1154–1156, 1975.

9. Leyden, J. L., and Kligman, A. M. "Aluminum Chloride in the Treatment of Symptomatic Athlete's Foot." *Arch. Dermatol.* 111:1004–1010, 1975.

10. Kligman, Albert M., et al. "Acne Vulgaris A Treatable Disease." *Postgrad. Med.* 55:99–105, 1974.

11. Stone, Irwin. *The Healing Factor "Vitamin C" Against Disease*. New York: Grosset and Dunlap, 1974. Pp. 138.

12. Kunin, Calvin M., and DeGroot, Jane E. "Self-Screening for Significant Bacteriuria." *JAMA* 231:1349–1353, 1975.

13. Holvey, David N., *op. cit.*, p. 750.

14. Mills, Otto H., Kligman, Albert M., and Stewart, Rebecca. "The Clinical Effectiveness of Topical Erythromycin in Acne Vulgaris." *Cutis* 15:93–96, 1975.

15. Shulman, Alex G. "Ice Water as Primary Treatment of Burns." *JAMA* 173:1916–1919, 1960.

16. Blomfield, Robert. "Honey for Decubitus Ulcers." *JAMA* 224:905, 1973.

17. Meuller, H. L. "Insect Allergy." in *Immunologic Diseases*, Samter, M., Ed. Boston: Little, Brown, 1965. P. 683.

18. Ayres, Samuel Jr., and Mihan, Richard. "Vitamin E Supplements and Fatigue." *New Engl. J. Med.* 290:580, 1974.

Afterword

Writing this book has been a gas. It's been fun tweaking the noses of the medical profession and drug companies, and I hope I have written something of value for you, the health consumer. Now I would like some feedback. Please write and tell me whether or not you liked this book and whether or not it was helpful. If you have some recommendations for improvement, send them along, because some day I may rewrite the mother and I sure would hate to make the same dumb mistakes twice in a row. If you have some of your own handy-dandy home remedies or cures, send them along. I promise to check them out and include them in my next publication (and you will get the credit). Finally, if you have any questions about the material covered in this book, I will try to write to you personally.

Address all cards and letters to:

Joe Graedon
c/o St. Martin's Press
175 Fifth Avenue
New York, N.Y. 10010

14.

A GUIDE TO CHAIN STORE PRICES OF FREQUENTLY PRESCRIBED DRUGS*

BRAND NAME	GENERIC NAME	STRENGTH	QUANTITY			
			12	24	50	100
ACHROMYCIN-V 250MG	Tetracycline HCl	250mg	.89	1.57	3.05	5.7
ACHROMYCIN-V 500MG	Tetracycline HCl	500mg	1.78	2.88	6.05	10.5
ACTIFED TABLETS	Triprolidine HCl	2.5mg	.89	1.57	3.05	5.7
	Pseudoephedrine HCl	60mg				

*Information listed was supplied by OSCO DRUG, INC. and was based on 1976 costs to th consumer. These prices are representative of many national chain store drug retail values. This tab can be used as a comparison for approximating fair prices for your own prescription products. Mc drug prices change very little from year to year.

BRAND NAME	GENERIC NAME	STRENGTH	QUANTITY			
			12	24	50	100
ACTIFED-C EXPECTORANT	Triprolidine HCl	2mg	2oz.	4oz.	8oz.	16oz.
	Pseudoephedrine HCl	30mg	1.89	2.84	4.43	7.90
	Codeine Phosphate	10mg				
	Glycerol Guaiacolate	100mg				
AFRIN SPRAY	Oxymetazoline HCl	0.5mg		15cc		
	Glycerin	3.8mg		1.69		
	Sorbital	40mg				
ALDACTAZIDE	Spironolactone	25mg	1.75	3.30	6.65	12.90
	Hydrochlorothiazide	25mg				
ALDACTONE	Spironolactone	25mg	1.76	3.31	6.68	12.96
ALDOMET	Methyldopa	250mg	1.08	1.95	3.85	7.30
ALDORIL	Hydrochlorothiazide	15mg	2.10	3.26	5.63	9.90
	Methyldopa	250mg				
AMBENYL EXPECTORANT	Bromodiphenhydramine	3.75mg	2oz.	4.0z.	8oz.	16oz.
	Diphenhydramine HCl	8.75mg	1.88	2.82	4.39	7.82
	Codeine Sulfate	10mg				
	Ammonium Chloride	80mg				
	Potassium Guaiacol.	80mg				
AMCILL	Ampicillin Trihydrate	250mg	2.88	4.71	8.33	15.11
AMINOPHYLLINE	AMINOPHYLLINE	100mg	1.09	1.27	1.93	2.91
AMPICILLIN 250MG	AMPICILLIN	250mg	1.40	2.60	5.20	10.00
AMPICILLIN 500MG	AMPICILLIN	500mg	2.60	5.00	10.20	20.00
ANTIVERT-12.5	Meclizine	12.5mg	.91	1.63	3.18	5.95
ANTIVERT-25	Meclizine	25mg	2.39	3.53	6.28	11.01
APRESOLINE	Hydralazine	10mg	1.27	1.89	2.90	4.75
ARISTOCORT TABLETS	Triamcinolone	1mg	1.71	2.47	3.78	6.61
ARISTOCORT TABLETS	Triamcinolone	2mg	2.47	3.68	6.61	11.66
ARISTOCORT TABLETS	Triamcinolone	4mg	3.50	6.06	10.91	19.46

371

BRAND NAME	GENERIC NAME	STRENGTH	12	24	50	100
ARTANE TABLETS	Trihexyphenidyl HCl	2mg	1.11	1.33	2.05	3.14
ATARAX TABLETS	Hydroxyzine HCl	10mg	1.93	2.90	4.88	8.41
ATARAX TABLETS	Hydroxyzine HCl	25mg	2.49	3.73	6.69	11.83
ATARAX TABLETS	Hydroxyzine HCl	50mg	2.74	4.22	7.73	13.91
ATROMID-S	Clofibrate	500mg	.97	1.94	4.05	8.10
AZO GANTANOL	Sulfamethoxazole	0.5Gm	2.62	4.00	7.26	12.96
	Phenazopyridine HCl	100mg				
AZO GANTRISIN	Sulfasoxazole	0.5GM	.92	1.64	3.20	6.00
	Phenazopyridine HCl	50mg				
BENADRYL CAPSULES	Diphenhydramine HCl	50mg	.89	1.27	2.43	4.46
BENDECTIN	Doxylamine Succinate	10mg	2.71	4.17	7.63	13.70
	Pyridoxine HCl	10mg				
	Dicyclomine HCl	10mg				
BENTYL TABLETS	Dicyclomine HCl	20mg	1.94	2.93	4.95	8.55
BRISTACYCLINE 250MG	Tetracycline	250mg	1.66	2.38	3.60	6.24
BRONKOTABS	Theophylline	100mg	1.67	2.39	3.63	6.30
	Ephedrine Sulfate	24mg				
	Glyceryl Guaiacolate	100mg				
	Phenobarbital	8mg				
BUTAZOLIDIN ALKA	Phenylbutazone	100mg	1.39	2.58	5.15	9.90
	Aluminum Hydroxide	100mg				
	Magnesium Trisilicate	150mg				
BUTISOL SODIUM	Sodium Butabarbital	30mg	1.20	1.75	2.59	3.93
CAFERGOT	Ergotamine Tartrate	1mg	2.84	4.43	8.16	14.77
	Caffeine	100mg				
CHLORTRIMETON TABLETS	Chlorpheniramine	8mg	1.71	2.47	3.78	6.61
CHLORTRIMETON TABLETS	Chlorpheniramine	12mg	1.93	2.91	4.91	8.47

BRAND NAME	GENERIC NAME	STRENGTH	12	24	50	100
CLEOCIN						
CAPSULES 150MG	Clindamycin HC1	*150*mg	4.39	7.83	14.60	26.84
COMBID	Isopropamide Iodide	5mg	2.24	4.28	8.70	17.00
	Prochlorperazine	*10*mg				
COMPAZINE TABLETS 5MG	Prochlorperazine	5mg	2.15	3.35	6.13	10.70
COMPOCILLIN-VK	Potassium Phenoxy-	*250*mg	2.42	3.60	6.43	11.30
TABLETS 250MG	Methyl Penicillin					
COUMADIN 5MG	Warfarin Sodium	5mg	.89	1.40	2.70	5.00
COUMADIN 10MG	Warfarin Sodium	*10*mg	2.04	3.14	5.38	9.40
CYTOMEL 25MCG	Liothyronine Sodium	25mcg	1.22	1.80	2.70	4.15
DALMANE	Flurazepam HCl	*30*mg	2.01	3.08	5.25	9.14
CAPSULES 30MG	Flurazepam HC1	*30*mg	1.96	2.97	5.04	8.72
DARVON COMPOUND-65	Propoxyphene HCl	*65*mg	1.12	2.05	4.05	7.70
	Phenacetin	*162*mg				
	Aspirin	*227*mg				
	Caffeine	*32.4*mg				
DARVON-N	Propoxyphene Napsylate	*100*mg	2.06	3.16	5.43	9.50
DARVON-N with ASA	Propoxyphene Napsylate	*100*mg	2.07	3.18	5.47	9.59
	Aspirin	325mg				
DBI-TD CAPSULES 50MG	Phenformin HCl	50mg	1.65	3.09	6.23	12.05
DECADRON						
TABLETS 0.5MG	Dexamethasone	0.5mg	2.57	3.89	7.03	12.51
DECLOMYCIN	Demeclocycline HCl	*150*mg	4.07	7.19	13.27	24.19
DEMULEN-21	Ethynodiol Diacetate	*1*mg	**21**			
	Ethinyl Estradiol	50mcg	2.29			
DIABINESE	Chlorpropamide	250mg	1.44	2.67	5.35	10.30
DIGOXIN	**DIGOXIN**	0.25mg	.89	.89	.89	1.00
DILANTIN	Diphenylhydantoin	*100*mg	.89	.89	1.30	2.20
DIMETANE TABLETS 4MG	Brompheniramine	4mg	1.22	1.80	2.70	4.15

373

THE PEOPLE'S PHARMACY

BRAND NAME	GENERIC NAME	STRENGTH	12	24	50	100
DIMETAPP ELIXIR	Brompheniramine	4mg/5cc	2oz.	4oz.	8oz.	16oz.
	Phenylephrine HCl	5mg/5cc	.89	1.60	3.20	6.40
	Phenylpropanolamine	5mg/5cc				
DIMETAPP EXTENTABS	Brompheniramine	12mg	1.41	2.63	5.16	10.11
	Phenylephrine HCl	15mg				
	Phenylpropanolamine	15mg	1.38	2.56	5.12	9.83
DIUPRES TABLETS 250MG	Chlorothiazide	250mg				
	Reserpine	0.125mg	.99	1.77	3.48	6.55
DIURIL	Chlorothiazide	500mg	.89	1.58	3.07	5.73
DONNATAL ELIXIR	Atropine Sulfate	0.0194mg	2oz.	4oz.	8oz.	16oz.
	Hyoscyamine HBr	0.1037mg	.89	1.09	2.18	4.36
	Hyoscine HBr	0.0065mg				
	Phenobarbital	16.2mg				
DONNATAL TABLETS	Atropine Sulfate	0.0194mg	.89	.89	1.24	2.07
	Hyoscyamine HBr	0.1037mg				
	Hyoscine HBr	0.0065mg				
	Phenobarbital	16.2mg				
DORIDEN	Glutethimide	0.5Gm	2.08	3.22	5.54	9.73
DRIXORAL	Dexbrompheniramine	6mg				
	D-Isoephedrine Sulfate	120mg	2.48	3.71	6.65	11.75
DYAZIDE	Hydrochlorothiazide	25mg				
	Triamterene	50mg	1.31	2.42	4.83	9.25
E-MYCIN	Erythromycin	250mg	2.91	4.77	8.44	15.33
ELAVIL TABLETS 25MG	Amitriptyline HCl	25mg	1.36	2.52	5.03	9.65
ELIXOPHYLLIN ELIXIR	Theophylline	80mg/15cc	2oz.	4oz.	8oz.	16oz.
	Alcohol	20%	1.36	2.07	3.18	5.31
EMPIRIN COMPOUND 3	Aspirin	3½gr	2.03	3.11	5.33	9.30
	Phenacetin	2½gr.				
	Caffeine	½gr.				
	Codeine	½gr.				

374

BRAND NAME	GENERIC NAME	STRENGTH	QUANTITY			
			12	24	50	100
EQUAGESIC	Meprobamate	*150*mg	2.13	3.31	6.04	10.53
	Aspirin	*250*mg				
	Ethoheptazine Citrate	*75*mg				
EQUANIL TABLETS 400MG	Meprobamate	*400*mg	1.87	2.79	4.45	7.95
ERYTHROCIN FILMTABS	Erythromycin Stearate	*250*mg	2.40	4.80	9.45	17.34
ERYTHROMYCIN	ERYTHROMYCIN	*250*mg	2.40	3.55	6.33	11.10
ESIDRIX TABLETS 25MG	Hydrochlorothiazide	*25*mg	1.36	2.06	3.25	5.45
ETRAFON (2-25)	Perphenazine	*2*mg	2.60	3.95	7.15	12.75
	Amitriptyline HCl	*25*mg				
EUTHROID TABLETS 1	Liotrix	*1*gr.	1.24	1.83	2.78	4.30
EUTHROID TABLETS 3	Liotrix	*3*gr.	1.39	2.13	3.50	6.05
EXNA	Benzthiazide	*50*mg	1.94	2.93	4.95	8.55
FIORINAL TABLETS	Butalbital	*50*mg	1.38	2.11	3.46	5.97
	Aspirin	*200*mg				
	Phenacetin	*130*mg				
	Caffeine	*40*mg				
FLAGYL ORAL TABLETS	Metronidazole	*250*mg	2.68	5.16	10.53	20.65
FULVICIN-UF 500MG	Griseofulvin	*500*mg	4.17	7.39	13.68	25.00
GANTANOL TABLETS	Sulfamethoxazole	*0.5*Gm	1.18	2.16	4.28	8.15
GANTRISIN TABLETS	Sulfisoxazole	*0.5*Gm.	.89	1.17	2.22	4.03
GRIFULVIN V 500MG	Griseofulvin	*500*mg	4.35	7.76	14.45	26.55
GRISACTIN						
TABLETS 500MG	Griseofulvin	*500*mg	4.17	7.39	13.69	25.03
GYNERGEN	Ergotamine Tartrate	*1*mg	2.66	4.07	7.41	13.27
HALDOL TABLETS 1MG	Haloperidol	*1*mg	2.55	3.85	6.94	12.33
HYDERGINE	Ergot Alkaloids	*0.5*mg	2.43	3.61	6.45	11.35
HYDRODIURIL 50MG	Hydrochlorothiazide	*50*mg	.89	1.57	3.05	5.70

375

THE PEOPLE'S PHARMACY

BRAND NAME	GENERIC NAME	STRENGTH	12	24	50	100
HYDROPRES	Reserpine	.125mg	.95	1.69	3.31	6.22
TABLETS 25MG	Hydrochlorothiazide	25mg				
HYGROTON						
TABLETS 50MG	Chlorthalidone	50mg	1.23	2.25	4.48	8.55
ILOSONE						
PULVULES 250MG	Erythromycin Estolate	250mg	3.52	6.94	12.75	23.14
INDERAL	Propranolol HCl	10mg	1.30	1.95	3.08	5.00
INDOCIN CAPSULES 25MG	Indomethacin	25mg	1.28	2.37	4.72	9.03
ISMELIN TABLETS 10MG	Guanethidine Sulfate	10mg	2.45	3.65	6.53	11.50
ISORDIL ORAL TABLETS	Isosorbide Dinitrate	5mg	1.38	2.10	3.34	5.62
KEFLEX PULVULES 250MG	Cephalexin Monohydrate	250mg	5.31	9.27	17.61	32.87
LANOXIN TABLETS 0.25MG	Digoxin	0.25mg	.89	.89	.89	1.00
LASIX	Furosemide	40mg	1.37	2.54	5.07	9.73
LIBRAX	Clidinium Br	2.5mg	1.20	2.19	4.35	8.30
	Chlordiazepoxide HCl	5mg				
LIBRITABS 5MG	Chlordiazepoxide	5mg	1.80	2.65	4.16	7.37
LIBRITABS 10MG	Chlordiazepoxide	10mg	2.05	3.16	5.42	9.48
LIBRITABS 25MG	Chlordiazepoxide	25mg	2.73	4.21	7.70	13.84
LIBRIUM 5MG	Chlordiazepoxide	5mg	.89	1.53	2.98	5.55
LIBRIUM 10MG	Chlordiazepoxide	10mg	1.02	1.85	3.63	6.86
LIBRIUM 25MG	Chlordiazepoxide	25mg	2.73	4.21	7.70	13.84
LINCOCIN	Lincomycin	250mg	3.23	5.40	9.77	17.98
LITHANE	Lithium Carbonate	300mg	1.21	1.77	2.65	4.04
LOESTRIN 1/20	Norethindrone Acetate	1.5mg	20			
	Ethinyl Estradiol	20mcg	2.19			
LOMOTIL TABLETS	Diphenoxylate HCl	2.5mg	1.20	2.39	4.99	9.97
LUMINAL 32MG	Phenonbarbital	32mg	.99	1.08	1.29	1.92
MACRODANTIN 50MG	Nitrofurantoin	50mg	2.97	4.89	8.70	15.85

BRAND NAME	GENERIC NAME	STRENGTH	12	24	50	100
MANDELAMINE						
TABLETS 1GM	Methenamine Mandelate	1.0Gm	1.95	2.96	5.00	8.65
MARAX TABLETS	Ephedrine Sulfate	25mg	1.81	2.67	4.21	7.46
	Theophylline	130mg				
	Hydroxyzine HCl	10mg				
MEDROL TABLETS 4MG	Methylprednisolone	4mg	3.52	6.08	10.96	19.57
MELLARIL TABLETS 50MG	Thioridazine	50mg	2.60	3.94	7.14	12.73
MEPROBAMATE 400MG	MEPROBAMATE	400mg	.89	.89	1.50	2.99
MEPROSPAN CAPSULES	Meprobamate	400mg	2.79	4.33	7.95	14.35
MEPROTABS	Meprobamate	400mg	1.93	2.91	4.90	8.45
MILTOWN TABLETS 400MG	Meprobamate	400mg	1.93	2.91	4.90	8.45
MINOCIN	Minocycline HCl	100mg	6.71	11.86	22.17	41.99
MYCOLOG						

			1mg/Gm	15Gm	30Gm
CREAM/OINTMENT	Triamcinolone				
	Neomycin Sulfate	2.5mg/GM	4.34	7.84	
	Gramicidin	0.25mg/GM			
	Nystatin 100,000	units/Gm			

			15	30
MYCOSTATIN VAGINAL	Nystatin 100,000	Units		
TABLETS			3.55	5.45

BRAND NAME	GENERIC NAME	STRENGTH	12	24	50	100
MYSTECLIN F CAPSULES	Tetracycline HCl	250mg	3.85	6.75	12.34	22.33
	Amphotericin B	50mg				
NALDECON TABLETS	Chlorpheniramine	5mg	2.53	3.82	6.88	12.21
	Phenylpropanolamine	40mg				
	Phenylephrine	10mg				
	Phenyltoloxamine	15mg				
NAQUA TABLETS 2MG	Trichlormethiazide	2mg	1.34	2.03	3.18	5.31
NATURETIN TABLETS 5MG	Bendroflumethiazide	5.0mg	2.14	3.33	6.07	10.59
NEGGRAM	Nalidixic Acid	500mg	3.79	6.63	12.10	21.85
CAPLETS 500MG						

THE PEOPLE'S PHARMACY

BRAND NAME	GENERIC NAME	STRENGTH	12	24	50	100
NICOTINIC ACID	NICOTINIC ACID	100mg	1.00	1.09	1.31	1.96
NITROBID CAPSULES	Nitroglycerin	2.5mg	2.01	3.08	5.25	9.14
NITROGLYCERIN	(Sublin)	1/100gr				1.10
NITROGLYCERIN	NITROGLYCERIN	1/400gr				1.10
NITROGLYN TABLETS	Nitroglycerin	1/10gr				12.19
NITROGLYN TABLETS	Nitroglycerin	1/50gr				9.70
NITROSPAN CAPSULES	Nitroglycerin	2.5mg				9.53
NOCTEC						
CAPSULES 500MG	Chloral Hydrate	500mg	1.68	2.41	3.67	6.38
NOLUDAR						
CAPSULES 300MG	Methyprylon	300mg	2.06	3.18	5.46	9.56
NOR-QD	Norethindrone	0.35mg	1 month			
			2.69			
NORGESIC	Orphenadrine Citrate	25mg	2.45	3.65	6.54	11.53
	Aspirin	225mg				
	Phenacetin	160mg				
	Caffeine	30mg				
NORINYL 1/80	Norethindrone	1mg	21	28		
	Mestranol	80mcg	2.09	2.09		
NORLESTRIN						
TABLETS 1MG	Norethindrone Acetate	1mg	21	28		
	Ethinyl Estradiol	50mcg	1.99	1.99		
NORLESTRIN 2.5MG	Norethindrone Acetate	2.5mg	21	28		
	Ethinyl Estradiol	50mcg	1.99	1.99		
NORPRAMIN						
TABLETS 50MG	Desipramine HCl	50mg	3.30	5.55	10.48	18.60

378

BRAND NAME	GENERIC NAME	STRENGTH	QUANTITY			
			12	24	50	100
NOVAHISTINE-DH LIQUID	Chlorpheniramine	2mg	2oz.	4oz.	8oz.	16oz.
	Codeine Phosphate	10mg	1.95	2.94	4.83	8.32
	Phenylephrine HCl	10mg				
	Chloroform	13.5mg				
NOVAHISTINE	Chlorpheniramine	2mg	4oz.			
EXPECTORANT	Codeine Phosphate	10mg	3.10			
	Phenylephrine HCl	10mg				
	Glyceryl Guiacolate	100mg				
	Chloroform	13.5mg				
OMNI-TUSS LIQUID	Phenyltoloxamine	5mg	2oz.	4oz.	8oz.	16oz.
	Chlorpheniramine	3mg	3.09	5.13	8.90	16.25
	Ephedrine	25mg				
	Guaiacol Carbonate	25mg				
	Codeine	10mg				
OMNIPEN CAPSULES	Ampicillin	250mg	2.50	3.75	6.74	11.92
OMNIPEN CAPSULES	Ampicillin	500mg	3.69	6.44	11.70	21.04
ORACON	Ethinyl Estradiol	100mcg	21	28		
	Dimethisterone	25mg	1.99	1.99		
ORETIC TABLETS 50MG	Hydrochlorothiazide	50mg	1.73	2.51	3.88	6.80
ORINASE	Tolbutamide	500mg	1.16	2.12	4.20	8.00
ORNADE SPANSULES	Chlorpheniramine	8mg	1.65	3.09	6.23	12.06
	Phenylpropanolamine	50mg				
	Isopropamide Iodide	2.5mg	1.52	2.84	5.70	11.00
ORTHO-NOVUM 1/50	Norethindrone	1mg	21			
	Mestranol	50mcg	2.09			
ORTHO NOVUM 1/80	Mestranol	80mcg	21			
	Norethindrone	1mg	2.09			

379

BRAND NAME	GENERIC NAME	STRENGTH	12	24	50	100
OVRAL	Norgestrol	0.5mg	21	28		
	Ethinyl Estradiol	50mcg	2.19	2.19		
OVULEN	Ethynodiol Diacetate	1mg	20	21		
	Mestranol	100mcg	2.29	2.29		
PANMYCIN	Tetracycline HCl	250mg	1.31	1.98	3.07	5.09
PAPASE TABLETS	Proteolytic Enzymes 10,000	Units	2.64	4.03	7.33	13.10
PARAFON FORTE	Chlorzoxazone	250mg	2.42	3.59	6.42	11.28
	Acetaminophen	300mg				
PAVABID	Papaverine HCl	150mg	1.46	2.72	5.45	10.50
PEDIAMYCIN CHEWABLE	Erythromycin	200mg	3.61	6.27	11.35	20.35
PEDIAMYCIN SUSPENSION	Erythromycin	200mg	60cc	90cc	150cc	
			3.66	4.39	6.74	
PENBRITIN CAPSULES	Ampicillin Trihydrate	250mg	2.88	4.71	8.33	15.11
PENBRITIN CAPSULES	Ampicillin Trihydrate	500mg	4.44	7.93	14.81	27.27
PENICILLIN G POTASSIUM	PENICILLIN G POTASSIUM	200 U	.89	.89	1.50	2.99
PENICILLIN G POTASSIUM	PENICILLIN G POTASSIUM	400 U	.89	.89	1.50	2.99
PENTIDS "200"	Penicillin G Potassium	200 U	.89	1.73	3.60	7.20
PENTIDS "400"	Penicillin G Potassium	400 U	1.26	2.52	5.25	10.50
PENTIDS "800"	Penicillin G Potassium	800 U	2.87	4.69	8.29	15.03
PEN-VEE K TABLETS 125MG	Penicillin Potassium Phenoxymethyl	125mg	1.86	2.76	4.40	7.84
PEEN-VEE K TABLETS 250MG	Penicillin Potassium Phenoxymethyl	250mg	2.42	3.59	6.40	11.25
PEN-VEE K TABLETS 500MG	Penicillin Potassium Phenoxymethyl	500mg	3.67	6.39	11.61	20.87
PERIACTIN TABLETS	Cyproheptadine HCl	4mg	1.95	2.95	4.99	8.62
PERITRATE TABLETS 10MG	Pentaerythritol	10mg	.89	1.17	2.22	4.0

BRAND NAME	GENERIC NAME	STRENGTH	12	24	50	100
PERITRATE SA	Pentaerythritol	*80*mg	1.38	2.56	5.12	9.83
PERTOFRANE 50MG	Desipramine HCl	*50*mg	3.29	5.54	10.45	18.54
PFIZERPEN 200,000 UNITS	Penicillin G Potassium	*200* U	.89	.89	1.65	3.29
PFIZERPEN 400,000 UNITS	Penicillin G Potassium	*400* U	.89	.90	1.88	3.75
PHENAPHEN						
w/CODEINE #3	Phenacetin	*195*mg	2.10	3.25	5.60	9.85
	Aspirin	*162*mg				
	Penobarbital	*16.2*mg				
	Codeine Phosphate	*32*mg				
	Hyoscyamine Sulfate	*0.03*mg				
PHENERGAN						
12.5 TABLETS	Promethazine	*12.5*mg	1.37	2.10	3.33	5.60
PHENERGAN						
25MG TABLETS	Promethazine	*25*mg	1.99	3.02	5.14	8.92

BRAND NAME	GENERIC NAME	STRENGTH	2oz.	4oz.	8oz.	16oz.
PHENERGAN						
EXPECTORANT	Promethazine HC1	*5*mg				
	Ipecac	*0.17*min	.89	1.42	2.83	5.66
	Potassium Guaiacol.	*44*mg				
	Chloroform	*0.25*min				
	Citric Acid	*60*mg				
	Sodium Citrate	*197*mg				
PHENERGAN						
EXPECTORANT	Codeine Phosphate	*10*mg				
WITH CODEINE	Promethazine HCl	*5*mg	.89	1.59	3.18	6.36
	Ipecac	*0.17*min				
	Potassium Guaiacol.	*44*mg				
	Chloroform	*0.25*min				
	Citric Acid	*60*mg				
	Sodium Citrate	*197*mg				

BRAND NAME	GENERIC NAME	STRENGTH	12	24	50	100
PHENOBARBITAL	PHENOBARBITAL	*30*mg	.89	.89	.89	.89
PHENOBARBITAL	PHENOBARBITAL	*100*mg	.89	.89	.89	.89

381

BRAND NAME	GENERIC NAME	STRENGTH	12	24	50	100
PLACIDYL						
CAPSULES 500 MG	Ethchlorvynol	500mg	2.03	3.12	5.34	9.32
POLARAMINE TABLETS	Dexchlorpheniramine	2mg	1.22	1.80	2.70	4.15
POLYCILLIN CAPSULES	Ampicillin Trihydrate	250mg	2.50	5.01	10.44	20.87
PREDNIS	Prednisolone	5mg	1.27	1.88	2.88	4.71
PREDNISOLONE	PREDNISOLONE	5mg	1.33	2.01	3.14	5.23
PREDNISONE	PREDNISONE	5mg	.89	.89	1.00	1.59
PREMARIN	Conjugated Estrogens	1.25mg	1.03	1.86	3.65	6.90
TABLETS 1.25MG						
PRESAMINE 25MG	Imipramine HCl	25mg	2.40	3.56	6.35	11.14
PRINCIPEN CAPSULES	Ampicillin Trihydrate	250mg	2.87	4.69	8.29	15.02
PRO-BANTHINE	Propantheline Bromide	15mg	.96	1.72	3.38	6.35
PROLOID TABLETS 60MG	Thyroglobulin	60mg	.89	.89	.95	1.49
PROVERA TABLETS 2.5MG	Medroxyprogesterone	2.5mg	2.13	3.32	6.05	10.55
PYRIBENZAMINE TABLETS	Tripelennamine HCl	25mg	1.16	1.67	2.43	3.60
PYRIDIUM 100MG	Phenazopyridine HCl	100mg	1.93	2.91	4.90	8.45
QUADRINAL TABLETS	Ephedrine HCl	24mg	1.89	2.82	4.72	8.08
	Theophylline Calcium	130mg				
	Phenobarbital	24mg				
	Potassium Iodide	320mg				
QUINAMM	Quinine Sulfate	260mg	2.84	4.43	8.15	14.75
	Aminophylline	195mg				
RAUDIXIN	Rauwolfia	100mg	2.02	3.10	5.29	9.23
RAUZIDE	Bendroflumethiazide	4mg	2.47	3.69	6.62	11.68
	Rauwolfia	50mg				
REGROTON	Chlorthalidone	50mg	2.77	4.29	7.86	14.17
	Reserpine	0.25mg				
RESERPINE	RESERPINE	0.25mg	.89	.89	.89	.99

BRAND NAME	GENERIC NAME	STRENGTH	QUANTITY			
			12	24	50	100
RITALIN	Methylphenidate HCl	10mg	2.02	3.09	5.28	9.20
ROBAXIN	Methocarbamol	500mg	2.09	3.23	5.58	9.80
ROBITET CAPSULES	Tetracycline HCl	250mg	1.29	1.93	2.98	4.90
RONDOMYCIN CAPSULES	Methacycline HCl	150mg	3.75	6.56	11.95	21.55
SALUTENSIN	Hydroflumethiazide	50mg	2.81	4.37	8.03	14.51
	Reserpine	0.125mg				
SANSERT	Methysergide	2mg	3.75	6.56	11.95	21.55
SELSUN SUSPENSION	Selenium Sulfide	2½%	4oz.			
			3.50			
SERAX CAPSULES 10MG	Oxazepam	10mg	1.78	2.61	4.08	7.20
SER-AP-ES	Hydrochlorothiazide	15mg	1.24	2.29	4.55	8.70
	Hydralazine HCl	25mg				
	Reserpine	0.1mg				
SERPASIL	Reserpine	0.25mg	.89	1.25	2.39	4.38
TABLETS 0.25MG						
SINEQUAN	Doxepin	25mg	2.90	4.75	8.40	15.25
CAPSULES 25MG						
SORBITRATE SUBLINGUAL	Isosorbide Dinitrate	5mg	1.39	2.43	3.50	6.05
STELAZINE TABLETS 2MG	Trifluoperazine	2mg	1.47	2.74	5.49	10.58
STERANE	Prednisolone	5mg	1.39	2.14	3.51	6.07
STERAZOLIDIN	Phenylbutazone	50mg	2.44	3.63	6.49	11.43
	Prednisone	1.25mg				
	Aluminum Hydroxide Gel	100mg				
	Magnesium Trisilicate	150mg				
SUMYCIN	Tetracycline	250mg	.89	1.52	2.95	5.50
SYNALAR						
CREAM/OINTMENT	Flucinolone Acetonide	0.025%	15GM	60GM		
			3.73	8.25		

383

| BRAND NAME | GENERIC NAME | STRENGTH | QUANTITY ||||
			12	24	50	100
SYNTHROID						
TABLETS 0.1MG	Sodium Levothyroxine	*0.1*mg	1.12	1.34	2.08	3.20
TALWIN	Pentazocine HCl	*50*mg	2.62	3.99	7.24	12.83
TANDEARIL	Oxyphenbutazone	*100*mg	1.55	2.90	5.83	11.25
TAO CAPSULES	Troleandomycin	*250*mg	4.71	8.07	15.09	27.83
TEDRAL SA TABLETS	Theophylline Anhydrous	*180*mg	2.53	3.81	6.88	12.20
	Ephedrine HCl	*48*mg				
	Phenobarbital	*25*mg				
TEDRAL-25	Theophylline	*130*mg	1.78	2.61	4.08	7.20
	Ephedrine HCl	*24*mg				
	Butabarbital	*25*mg				
TELDRIN	Chlorpheniramine	*8*mg	1.87	2.79	4.45	7.95
TENUATE DOSPAN	Diethylpropion HCl	*75*mg	3.35	5.96	10.70	19.05
TERRAMYCIN CAPSULES	Oxytetracycline HCl	*250*mg	3.73	6.51	11.86	21.36
TETRACYCLINE	**TETRACYCLINE HCL**	*250*mg	.89	.89	1.61	2.82
TETRACYN CAPSULES	Tetracycline HCl	*250*mg	1.27	1.89	2.90	4.75
TETREX CAPSULES	Tetracycline Phosphate	*250*mg	3.91	6.87	12.60	22.84
THORAZINE						
TABLETS 10MG	Chlorpromazine	*10*mg	1.28	1.92	2.95	4.85
THORAZINE	Chlorpromazine	*25*mg	1.36	2.06	3.25	5.45
TABLETS 25MG						
THYROID	**THYROID**	*1* grain	.89	.89	.89	1.10
THYROLAR	Liotrix	*1*gr	1.24	1.82	2.78	4.30
TIGAN CAPSULES	Trimethobenzamide HCl	*100*mg	2.03	3.12	5.34	9.32
TOFRANIL TABLETS 25MG	Imipramine HCl	*25*mg	2.52	3.78	6.81	12.07
TOLINASE						
TABLETS 100MG	Tolazamide	*100*mg	1.77	2.59	4.03	7.11

BRAND NAME	GENERIC NAME	STRENGTH	QUANTITY			
			12	24 ·	50	100
TOLINASE TABLETS 250MG	Tolazamide	250mg	2.63	4.02	7.30	13.06
TRANXENE 7.5MG	Chlorazepate	7.5mg	2.11	3.27	5.65	9.95
TRIAVIL TABLETS 2/25	Perphenazine	2mg	2.68	4.11	7.49	13.42
	Amitriptyline HCl					
TRILAFON TABLETS 4MG	Perphenazine	4mg	2.01	3.07	5.23	9.11
TUSS-ORNADE	Chlorpheniramine	8mg	1.88	3.57	7.22	14.04
SPANSULES	Caramiphen Edisylate	20mg				
	Phenylpropanolamine	50mg				
	Isopropamide Iodide	2.5mg				
TYLENOL	Acetaminophen	300mg	2.10	3.26	5.63	9.90
W/CODEINE 30MG	Codeine Phosphate	30mg				
UNIPEN CAPSULES	Sodium Nafcillin	250mg	5.01	8.68	16.37	30.39
VALISONE CREAM	Betamethasone	1.2mg/GM	5GM 2.42	15GM 3.74	45GM 6.50	
VALIUM TABLETS 2MG	Diazepam	2mg	1.00	1.81	3.55	6.70
VALIUM TABLETS 5MG	Diazepam	5mg	1.28	2.36	4.70	8.99
VALIUM TABLETS 10MG	Diazepam	10mg	1.91	3.62	7.32	14.24
VASODILAN 10MG	Isoxsuprine HCl	10mg	2.04	3.14	5.38	9.40
V-CILLIN-K TABS. 250MG	Penicillin Potassium	250mg	1.38	2.76	5.75	11.50
	Phenoxymethyl					
V-CILLIN-K TABS. 500MG	Penicillin Potassium	500mg	3.52	6.09	10.99	19.62
	Phenoxymethyl					
VIBRAMYCIN CAPS. 50MG	Doxycycline	50mg	6.29	11.04	20.45	38.55
VIOFORM-HC CREAM 0.5%	Iodochlorhydroxyquin	3%	15GM	30GM		
	Hydrocortisone	0.5%	3.20	4.80		

385

THE PEOPLE'S PHARMACY

BRAND NAME	GENERIC NAME	STRENGTH	12	24	50	100
VISTARIL CAPSULES 25MG	Hydroxyzine Pamoate	25mg	2.49	3.73	6.69	11.83
VIVACTIL TABLETS 10MG	Protriptyline HCl	10mg	2.60	3.96	7.18	12.80
ZORANE 1/20	Norethindrone Acetate	1mg	28			
	Ethinyl Estradiol	20mcg	2.19			
ZYLORPRIM TABLETS 100MG	Allopurinol	100mg	1.04	2.09	4.35	8.69

386

Index

Progesterone, 235; see also Birth control
  pills
Proklar-M, 242
Proloid, 129, 310
Promethazine, 290, 310, 323, 353, 362
Propadrine, 65, 341, 344
Propantheline, 242, 310
Propantheline Bromide, 310, 312
Propa PH, 336, 337
Propoxyphene HCl, 288, 289, 290, 307,
  310, 311, 312
Propranolol, see Inderal
Prostate, 174
Proxigel, 96, 114
Prydon, 242
Pseudoephedrine, 65
Pseudoephedrine HCl, 290, 307, 311,
  312
Psyllium, 327, 356
Pulmonary edema, 27
Pyribenzamine, 165, 310
Pyridium, 310
Pyrilamine, 91
Pyrosis, see Heartburn

Qid-Amp, 310
QIDmycin, 310
QIDpen G, 310
QIDpen VK, 310
Qidtet, 146, 310
Quaalude, 145
Quadrinal, 174, 238, 242, 310
Quibron, 310
Quinacrine, 233, 360–361
Quinamm, 238, 359–360
Quinette, 239, 310
Quinidex, 310
Quinidine sulfate, 310, 312
Quinine, 8, 359–360
  pregnancy and, 238, 239, 242
Quinora, 310
Quinsana Foot Powder, 105, 111, 333

Rabies, 138
Rapid eye movement, 108
Rash, 9; see also Allergy and Itching
Ratio, 85, 111
Raudixin, 268, 310
  pregnancy and, 239, 242
Rau-Sed, 131, 268, 310
  pregnancy and, 242
Rauwiloid, 268
  pregnancy and, 242

Rauwolfia,
  pregnancy and, 239, 242
Rauwolfia Serpentina, 310, 312
Rauzide, 268
  pregnancy and, 239, 242
Rectalad-Aminophylline, 220–221
Regroton, 268
  pregnancy and, 239, 242
Regulin, 327, 356
Remsed, 310
Renese, 242, 264
Reserpine, 46–47, 49, 268–270, 290,
  310, 312
  drug interactions and, 131, 140, 144
  pregnancy and, 239, 241, 242
  ulcers and, 325
Resorcinol, 103, 339
Resulin, 339
Retet, 146, 311
Retin-A, 337, 338, 352
Rexall Corn Solvent, 100, 115
Rexamycin, 310
Rezamid, 339
Rezamid Shampoo, 103, 112
Rheumatoid arthritis, 23, 25, 63, 74; see
  also Arthritis
Rhulihist, 55
RhuliSpray, 55
Right Guard, 36, 98, 112
Rinse Away, 103, 112
Ritalin, 130, 144, 225–226
Robicillin VK, 310
Robimycin, 310
Robitet, 146, 220, 239, 291, 310
Robitussin Cough Calmers, 356
Robitussin-DM, 356
Rolaids, 34, 86, 111, 121, 123, 147
Romilar, 144
Romilar Cough Discs, 356
Romotin, 321
Rondomycin, 146

Safeguard, 89, 113, 330
Saf-T-Coil, 199, 201; see also Intrauter-
  ine Device
St. Joseph Cough Syrup for Children,
  356
Salicylates, 100, 101, 103, 106, 115, 126,
  183, 233; see also Aspirin
Salt, 61
Salt Water Soak, 115
Salutensin, 239, 242, 268
San-Man, 15, 108, 114